Cindy Lee Johnson

Denis Johnson is the author of seven works of fiction,
three collections of poetry, and one book of reportage.
He is the recipient of a Lannan Fellowship and a Whiting
Writers' Award, among many other honors for his work.

ALSO BY DENIS JOHNSON

Seek: Reports from the Edges of America & Beyond

The Name of the World

Already Dead: A California Gothic

Jesus' Son

Resuscitation of a Hanged Man

The Stars at Noon

Fiskadoro

Angels

POETRY

*The Throne of the Third Heaven of the Nations Millennium
General Assembly: Poems, Collected and New*

The Veil

The Incognito Lounge

ADDITIONAL PRAISE FOR TREE OF SMOKE

"*Tree of Smoke* is a Vietnam war novel almost without peer, in which 'the abyss is alive. . . .' [Johnson] has written the best work of his career, an existential tour de force."
— *The Plain Dealer* (Cleveland)

"A brutal beauty of a book . . . the visceral, poetic writing is unmistakable, and unforgettable." — *Elle*

"Damn impressive, a layered, rich, sweaty accomplishment of massive proportions, a novel whose first three pages are nothing short of perfect . . . A mammoth portrait of humanity in conflict."
— *Entertainment Weekly*

"Johnson is a fine stylist of the world of soulful disaster."
— NPR's *All Things Considered*

"*Tree of Smoke* is a brilliant pillar of fire. . . . Haunting, tragic, and humane." — *Men's Vogue*

"A heartbreaking portrait of war." — *Outside*

"There is so much going on in *Tree of Smoke,* and so many levels of symbolism, that it is hard to do the story justice here. . . . Johnson brings his talents as a poet to bear, especially when describing the jungles and cities of Asia."
— *San Francisco Chronicle* (cover review)

"With its humane depiction of the most private battles within battles, *Tree of Smoke* ought to take its place among the great American novels of any war." — *The New York Sun*

"*Tree of Smoke* is a masterpiece."   —Chris Offutt

"Johnson is a gifted writer with a knack for erudite and colorful dialogue, and his sense of time and place is visceral and evocative. With this worthy addition to Vietnam literature, he confidently joins the ranks of Tim O'Brien, Larry Heinemann, and Michael Herr."   —*Booklist* (starred review)

"Ugly and fascinating with many shattering scenes . . . gripping."
                    —*Library Journal* (starred review)

"A tense, seductive hall of mirrors that will transport readers to the edge of mortality and reality . . . *Tree of Smoke* captures the full spectrum of war."   —*Paste*

"[An] epic, wrenching new novel . . . [Johnson is] immensely talented [and] delivers a beautifully layered, insightful, and visceral montage of stories."   —*The Seattle Times*

"*Tree of Smoke* is vintage Johnson, combining the grim, gritty realism of *Angels*, the everyday hallucinatory absurdity of *Jesus' Son*, and the post-apocalypse invention of *Fiskadoro*. . . . Johnson can mold language to theme like a sculptor sculpting clay."   —*The Oregonian*

"This vivid conjuring of an ill-advised foreign war informs the present as much as the past."   —*GQ*

"What buoys Johnson's writing and lends it a poetic cast are its odd angles and unusual vantages, along with his gift . . . for striking metaphor. . . . When the action in *Tree of Smoke* drifts into odd, even bizarre corners, Johnson's originality shines forth."
                    —*Bookforum*

"A redefinition of the issues done in a poetic style that captures the beauty of the landscape of Southeast Asia, as well as the moral confusion of the Westerners trapped in the war's spell . . . As a piece of pure writing it is one of the year's best in fiction."

—*Pittsburgh Post-Gazette*

"*Tree of Smoke* should be considered the literary bible of the Vietnam War—and perhaps the bible of war itself."

—*LA Weekly*

"Johnson's writing is sublime: His urgent, visceral prose conveys the humanity at the heart of even the most messed-up situations, often redeeming that humanity in the process."   —*The Tennessean*

"*Tree of Smoke* is a great read, an amazing achievement."

—*The San Diego Union-Tribune*

"*Tree of Smoke* is an irreplaceable addition to the teeming literature on the 'Asian War.'"   —*Fanzine*

"[Johnson] reminds us that some war stories are too big for celluloid. . . . Magisterial . . . Johnson's prose propels the narrative forward without neglecting existential undertow or spiritual malaise."   —*Playboy*

"Daring . . . formal inventiveness."   —*Salon.com*

"His command of language is simultaneously masterful and effortless, his observations are consistently and overwhelmingly honest, and he has an uncanny ability to infuse even the most horrific moments with an overwhelming sense of humanity."

—*Austin American-Statesman*

"[*Tree of Smoke*]'s dark sense of wartime humility is coupled with evocative, poetic language. . . . Masterful and unforgettable."

—*The Washington Times*

DENIS JOHNSON

TREE OF SMOKE

PICADOR

FARRAR, STRAUS AND GIROUX

NEW YORK

Portions of this book originally appeared in slightly different form
in *McSweeney's* and *The New Yorker*.

Grateful acknowledgment is made for permission to reprint the following
material: "The Widow's Lament in Springtime," by William Carlos Williams,
from *Collected Poems: 1909–1939, Volume I,* copyright © 1938 by New
Directions Publishing Corp. Reprinted by permission of New Directions
Publishing Corp. British rights from Carcanet Press Limited.

ISBN-13: 978-0-312-42774-0
ISBN-10: 0-312-42774-3

Designed by Jonathan D. Lippincott

First published in the United States by Farrar, Straus and Giroux

First Picador Edition: September 2008

10 9 8 7 6 5 4 3 2 1

ACKNOWLEDGMENTS

It is a pleasure to thank the people and organizations whose encouragement and kind assistance made this writing possible:

The Lannan, Whiting, and Guggenheim Foundations; the Rockefeller Foundation's Bellagio Center; Texas State University–San Marcos's Department of English; Bob Cornfield, Robert Jones, and Will Blythe; Rob Hollister; Ida Miller, Nick Hoover, Margaret, Michael, and French Fry; William F. X. Band III; and beautiful Cindy Lee.

For details of the early military career of the character Colonel Sands, the author is indebted to the memoir *Warriors Who Ride the Wind*, by William F. X. Band (Castle Books Inc., 1993).

Again for H.P. and Those Who

1963

Last night at 3:00 a.m. President Kennedy had been killed. Seaman Houston and the other two recruits slept while the first reports traveled around the world. There was one small nightspot on the island, a dilapidated club with big revolving fans in the ceiling and one bar and one pinball game; the two marines who ran the club had come by to wake them up and tell them what had happened to the President. The two marines sat with the three sailors on the bunks in the Quonset hut for transient enlisted men, watching the air conditioner drip water into a coffee can and drinking beer. The Armed Forces Network from Subic Bay stayed on through the night, broadcasting bulletins about the unfathomable murder.

Now it was late in the morning, and Seaman Apprentice William Houston, Jr., began feeling sober again as he stalked the jungle of Grande Island carrying a borrowed .22-caliber rifle. There were supposed to be some wild boars roaming this island military resort, which was all he had seen so far of the Philippines. He didn't know how he felt about this country. He just wanted to do some hunting in the jungle. There were supposed to be some wild boars around here.

He stepped carefully, thinking about snakes and trying to be quiet because he wanted to hear any boars before they charged him. He was aware that he was terrifically on edge. From all around came the ten thousand sounds of the jungle, as well as the cries of gulls and the far-off surf, and if he stopped dead and listened a minute, he could hear also the pulse snickering in the heat of his flesh, and the creak of sweat in his ears. If he stayed motionless only another couple of seconds, the bugs found him and whined around his head.

He propped the rifle against a stunted banana plant and removed his headband and wrung it out and wiped his face and stood there awhile, waving away the mosquitoes with the cloth and itching his crotch absent-mindedly. Nearby, a seagull seemed to be carrying on an argument with itself, a series of protesting squeaks interrupted by contradictory lower-pitched cries that sounded like, *Huh! Huh! Huh!* And something moving from one tree to another caught Seaman Houston's eye.

He kept his vision on the spot where he'd seen it among the branches of a rubber tree, putting his hand out for the rifle without altering the direction of his gaze. It moved again. Now he saw that it was some sort of monkey, not much bigger than a Chihuahua dog. Not precisely a wild boar, but it presented itself as something to be looked at, clinging by its left hand and both feet to the tree's trunk and digging at the thin rind with an air of tiny, exasperated haste. Seaman Houston took the monkey's meager back under the rifle's sight. He raised the barrel a few degrees and took the monkey's head into the sight. Without really thinking about anything at all, he squeezed the trigger.

The monkey flattened itself out against the tree, spreading its arms and legs enthusiastically, and then, reaching around with both hands as if trying to scratch its back, it tumbled down to the ground. Seaman Houston was terrified to witness its convulsions there. It hoisted itself, pushing off the ground with one arm, and sat back against the tree trunk with its legs spread out before it, like somebody resting from a difficult job of labor.

Seaman Houston took himself a few steps nearer, and, from the distance of only a few yards, he saw that the monkey's fur was very shiny and held a henna tint in the shadows and a blond tint in the light, as the leaves moved above it. It looked from side to side, its breath coming in great rapid gulps, its belly expanding tremendously with every breath like a balloon. The shot had been low, exiting from the abdomen.

Seaman Houston felt his own stomach tear itself in two. "Jesus Christ!" he shouted at the monkey, as if it might do something about its embarrassing and hateful condition. He thought his head would explode, if the forenoon kept burning into the jungle all around him and the gulls kept screaming and the monkey kept regarding its surroundings carefully, moving its head and black eyes from side to side like someone following the progress of some kind of conversation, some kind of debate, some kind of struggle that the jungle—the morning—the moment—was having with itself. Seaman Houston walked over to the monkey and laid the rifle down beside it and lifted the animal up in his two hands, holding its buttocks in one and cradling its head with the other. With fascination, then with revulsion, he realized that the monkey was crying. Its breath came out in sobs, and tears welled out of its eyes when it blinked. It looked here and there, appearing no more interested in him than in anything else it might be seeing. "Hey," Houston said, but the monkey didn't seem to hear.

As he held the animal in his hands, its heart stopped beating. He gave it a shake, but he knew it was useless. He felt as if everything was all his fault, and with no one around to know about it, he let himself cry like a child. He was eighteen years old.

When he got back to the club down near the water, Houston saw that a school of violet-tinted jellyfish had washed up on the gray beach, hundreds of them, each about the size of a person's hand, translucent and shriveling under the sun. The island's small harbor lay empty. No boats ever came here other than the ferry from the naval base across Subic Bay.

Only a few yards off, a couple of bamboo cabins fronted the strip of sand beneath palatial trees dribbling small purple blooms onto their roofs. From inside one of the cabins came the cries of a couple making love, a whore, Seaman Houston assumed, and some sailor. Houston squatted in the shade and listened until he heard them giggling no more, breathing no more, and a lizard in the cabin's eaves began to call—a brief annunciatory warble and then a series of harsh, staccato chuckles—*gek-ko; gek-ko; gek-ko . . .*

After a while the man came out, a crew-cut man in his forties with a white towel hitched under his belly and a cigarette clamped between his front teeth, and stood there splayfooted, holding the towel together at his hip with one hand, staring at some close but invisible thing, and swaying. An officer, probably. He took his cigarette between his thumb and finger and drew on it and let out a fog around his face. "Another mission accomplished."

The neighboring cabin's front door opened and a Filipina, naked, hand over her groin, said, "He don't like to do it."

The officer shouted, "Hey, Lucky."

A small Asian man came to the door, fully dressed in military fatigues.

"You didn't give her a jolly old time?"

The man said, "It could be bad luck."

"Karma," the officer said.

"It could be," the little fellow said.

To Houston the officer said, "You looking for a beer?"

Houston had meant to be off. Now he realized that he'd forgotten to leave and that the man was talking to him. With his free hand the man tossed his smoke and snaked aside the drape of the towel. To Houston he said—as he loosed almost straight downward a stream that foamed on the earth, destroying his cigarette butt—"You see something worth looking at, you let me know."

Feeling a fool, Houston went into the club. Inside, two young Filipinas in bright flowered dresses were playing pinball and talking so fast, while the large fans whirled above them, that Seaman Houston felt his equilibrium give. Sam, one of the marines, stood behind the bar. "Shut up, shut up," he said. He lifted his hand, in which he happened to be holding a spatula.

"What'd I say?" Houston asked.

"Excuse." Sam tilted his head toward the radio, concentrating on its sound like a blind man. "They caught the guy."

"They said that before breakfast. We knew that."

"There's more about him."

"Okay," Houston said.

He drank some ice water and listened to the radio, but he suf-fered such a headache right now he couldn't make out any of the words.

After a while the officer came in wearing a gigantic Hawaiian-print shirt, accompanied by the young Asian.

"Colonel, they caught him," Sam told the officer. "His name is Oswald."

The colonel said, "What kind of name is that?"—apparently as outraged by the killer's name as by his atrocity.

"Fucking sonofabitch," Sam said.

"The sonofabitch," said the colonel. "I hope they shoot his balls off. I hope they shoot him up the ass." Wiping at his tears without embarrassment he said, "Is Oswald his first name or his last name?"

Houston told himself that first he'd seen this officer pissing on the ground, and now he was watching him cry.

To the young Asian, Sam said, "Sir, we're hospitable as hell. But generally Philippine military aren't served here."

"Lucky's from Vietnam," the colonel said.

"Vietnam. You lost?"

"No, not lost," the man said.

"This guy," the colonel said, "is already a jet pilot. He's a South Viet Nam Air Force captain."

Sam asked the young captain, "Well, is it a war over there, or what? War?—budda-budda-budda." He made his two hands into a submachine gun, jerking them in unison. "Yes? No?"

The captain turned from the American, formed the phrases in his mind, practiced them, turned back, and said, "I don't know it's war. A lot people are dead."

"That'll do," the colonel agreed. "That counts."

"What you doing here?"

"I'm here for helicopters training," the captain said.

"You don't look hardly old enough for a tricycle," Sam said. "How old are you?"

"Twenty-two years."

"I'm getting this little Slope his beer. You like San Miguel? You mind that I called you a Slope? It's a bad habit."

"Call him Lucky," the colonel said. "The man's buying, Lucky. What's your poison?"

The boy frowned and deliberated inside himself mysteriously and said, "I like Lucky Lager."

"And what kind of cigarettes you smoke?" the colonel asked.

"I like the Lucky Strike," he said, and everybody laughed.

Suddenly Sam looked at young Seaman Houston as if just recognizing him and said, "Where's my rifle?"

For a heartbeat Houston had no idea what he might be talking about. Then he said, "Shit."

"Where is it?" Sam didn't seem terribly interested — just curious.

"Shit," Seaman Houston said. "I'll get it."

He had to go back into the jungle. It was just as hot, and just as damp. All the same animals were making the same noises, and the situation was just as terrible, he was far from the places of his memory, and the navy still had him for two more years, and the President, the President of his country, was still dead — but the monkey was gone. Sam's rifle lay in the brush just as he'd left it, and the monkey was nowhere. Something had carried it off.

He had expected to be made to see it again; so he was relieved to be walking back to the club without having to look at what he'd done. Yet he understood, without much alarm or unease, that he wouldn't be spared this sight forever.

Seaman Houston was promoted once, and then demoted. He glimpsed some of Southeast Asia's great capitals, walked through muggy nights in which streetside lanterns shook in the stale breezes, but he never landed long enough to lose his sea legs, only long enough to get confused, to see the faces flickering and hear the suffering laughter. When his tour was up he enlisted for another, enchanted above all by the power to create his destiny just by signing his name.

Houston had two younger brothers. The nearest to him in age,

James, enlisted in the infantry and was sent to Vietnam, and one
night just before the finish of his second tour in the navy, Houston
took a train from the naval base in Yokosuka, Japan, to the city of
Yokohama, where he and James had arranged to meet at the
Peanut Bar. It was 1967, more than three years after the murder of
John F. Kennedy.

In the train car Houston felt gigantic, looking over the heads
of pitch-black hair. The little Japanese passengers stared at him
without mirth, without pity, without shame, until he felt as if his
throat were being twisted. He got off, and kept himself on a
straight path through the late drizzle by following wet streetcar
tracks to the Peanut Bar. He looked forward to saying something
in English.

The Peanut Bar was large and crowded with sailors and with
scrubbed-looking boy merchant marines, and the voices were
thick in his head, the smoke thick in his lungs.

He found James near the stage and went over to him, holding
his hand out for a shake. "I'm leaving Yokosuka, man! I'm back on
a ship!" was the first thing he said.

The band drowned out his greeting—a quartet of Japanese
Beatles imitators in blinding white outfits, with fringe. James, in
civvies, sat at a little table staring at them, unaware of anything but
this spectacle, and Bill fired a peanut at his open mouth.

James indicated the performers. "That's gotta be ridiculous."
He had to shout to make himself even faintly audible.

"What can I say? This ain't Phoenix."

"Almost as ridiculous as you in a sailor suit."

"They let me out two years ago, and I re-upped. I don't
know—I just did it."

"Were you loaded?"

"I was pretty loaded, yeah."

Bill Houston was amazed to find his brother no longer a little
boy. James wore a flattop haircut that made his jaw look wide and
strong, and he sat up straight, no fidgeting around. Even in civilian dress he looked like a soldier.

They ordered beer by the pitcher and agreed that except for a few strange things, like the Peanut Bar, they both liked Japan — though James had spent, so far, six hours in the country between flights, and in the morning would board another plane for Vietnam — or at any rate, they both approved of the Japanese. "I'm here to tell you," Bill said when the band went on break and their voices could be heard, "these Japs have got it all plumb, level, and square. Meanwhile, in the tropics, man, nothing but shit. Everybody's brain is boiled fat mush."

"That's what they tell me. I guess I'll find out."

"What about the fighting?"

"What about it?"

"What do they say?"

"Mostly they say you're just shooting at trees, and the trees are shooting back."

"But really. Is it pretty bad?"

"I guess I'll find out."

"Are you scared?"

"During training, I seen a guy shoot another guy by accident."

"Yeah?"

"In the ass, if you can believe it. It was just an accident."

Bill Houston said, "I saw a guy murder a guy in Honolulu."

"What, in a fight?"

"Well, this sonofabitch owed this other sonofabitch money."

"What was it, in a bar?"

"No. Not in a bar. The guy went around back of his apartment building and called him to the window. We were walking past the place and he says, 'Hang on, I gotta talk to this guy about a debt.' They talked one minute and then the guy I was with — he shot the other one. Put his gun right against the window screen, man, and pop, one time, like that. Forty-five automatic. The guy kind of fell back inside his apartment."

"You gotta be kidding."

"No. I ain't kidding."

"Are you serious? You were there?"

"We were just walking around. I had no idea he was gonna kill someone."

"What'd you do?"

"Just about filled my britches with poop. He turns around and sticks his gun under his shirt and, 'Hey, let's get some brew.' Like the incident is erased."

"What was your comment about all this?"

"It kind of felt like I didn't want to mention it."

"I know—like, shit, what do you say?"

"You can bet I was wondering what he thought about me as a witness. That's why I missed the sailing. He was on our rig. If I'd shipped out with him, I'd've gone eight weeks without closing both eyes."

The brothers drank from their mugs simultaneously and then sought, each in his own mind, for something to talk about. "When that guy got shot in the ass," James said, "he went into shock immediately."

"Shit. How old are you?"

"Me?"

"Yeah."

"Almost eighteen," James said.

"The army let you enlist when you're only seventeen?"

"Nope. I done lied."

"Are you scared?"

"Yeah. Not every minute."

"Not every minute?"

"I haven't seen any fighting. I want to see it, the real deal, the real shit. I just want to."

"Crazy little fucker."

The band resumed with a number by the Kinks called "You Really Got Me":

> *You really got me—*
> *You really got me—*
> *You really got me—*

Before very much longer the two brothers got into an argument with each other over nothing, and Bill Houston spilled a pitcher of beer right into the lap of somebody at the next table—a Japanese girl, who hunched her shoulders and looked sad and humiliated. She sat with a girlfriend and also two American men, two youngsters who didn't know how to react.

The beer dribbled off the table's edge while James fumbled to right the empty pitcher, saying, "It gets like this sometimes. It just does."

The young girl made no move at all to adjust herself. She stared at her lap.

"What's wrong with us," James asked his brother, "are we fucked up or something? Every time we get together, something bad happens."

"I know."

"Something fucked-up."

"Fucked-up, shitty, I know. Because we're family."

"We're blood."

"None of that shit don't matter to me no more."

"It must matter some," James insisted, "or else why'd you haul yourself all this way to meet me in Yokohama?"

"Yeah," Bill said, "in the Peanut Bar."

"The Peanut Bar!"

"And why'd I miss my ship?"

James said, "You missed your ship?"

"I should've been on her at four this afternoon."

"You missed it?"

"She might still be there. But I expect they're out of the harbor by now."

Bill Houston felt his eyes flood with tears, choked with sudden emotion at his life and this place with everybody driving on the left.

James said, "I never liked you."

"I know. Me too."

"Me too."

"I always thought you were a little-dick sonofabitch," Bill said.

"I always hated you," his brother said.

"God, I'm sorry," Bill Houston said to the Japanese girl. He dragged some money from his wallet and tossed it onto the wet table, a hundred yen or a thousand yen, he couldn't see which.

"It's my last year in the navy," he explained to the girl. He would have thrown down more, but his wallet was empty. "I came across this ocean and died. They might as well bring back my bones. I'm all different."

The afternoon of that November day in 1963, the day after John F. Kennedy's assassination, Captain Nguyen Minh, the young Viet Nam Air Force pilot, dove with a mask and snorkel just off the shore of Grande Island. This was a newfound passion. The experience came close to what the birds of the air must enjoy, drifting above a landscape, propelled by the action of their own limbs, actually flying, as opposed to piloting a machine. The webbed fins strapped to his feet gave him a lot of thrust as he scooted above a vast school of parrot fish feeding on a reef, the multitude of their small beaks pattering against the coral like a shower of rain. American Navy men enjoyed scuba and skin-diving and had torn up all the coral and made the fish very timid so that the entire school disappeared in a blink when he swam near.

Minh wasn't much of a swimmer, and without others around he could let himself feel as afraid as he actually was.

He'd passed all the previous night with the prostitute the colonel had paid for. The girl had slept on the floor and he in the bed. He hadn't wanted her. He wasn't sure about these Filipino people.

Then today, toward the end of the morning, they'd gone into the club to learn that the President of the United States, President John Fitzgerald Kennedy, had been murdered. The two Filipinas

were still with them, and each girl took one of the colonel's substantial arms and held on as if keeping him moored to the earth
while he brought his surprise and grief under control. They sat at
a table all morning and listened to the news reports. "For God's
sake," the colonel said. "For God's sake." By afternoon the colonel
had cheered up and the beer was going down and down. Minh
tried not to drink very much, but he wanted to be polite, and he
got very dizzy. The girls disappeared, they came back, the fan went
around in the ceiling. A very young naval recruit joined them and
somebody asked Minh if a war was actually being waged somewhere in Vietnam.

That night the colonel wanted to switch girls, and Minh determined that he would follow through as he had last night, just to
make the colonel happy and to show him that he was sincerely
grateful. This second girl was the one he preferred, in any case.
She was prettier to his eyes and spoke better English. But the girl
asked to have the air conditioner on. He wanted it off. He couldn't
hear things with the air conditioner going. He liked the windows
open. He liked the sound of insects batting against the screens.
They didn't have such screens in his family's house on the
Mekong Delta, or even in his uncle's home in Saigon.

"What do you want?" the girl said. She was very contemptuous
of him.

"I don't know," he said. "Take off your clothes."

They took off their clothes and lay side by side on the double
bed in the dark, and did nothing else. He could hear an American
sailor a few doors down talking to one of his friends loudly, perhaps telling a story. Minh couldn't understand a word of it,
though he considered his own English pretty fair.

"The colonel has a big one." The girl was fondling his penis.
"Is he your friend?"

Minh said, "I don't know."

"You don't know is he your friend? Why are you with him?"

"I don't know."

"When did you know him the first time?"

"Just one or two weeks."

"Who is he?" she said.

Minh said, "I don't know." To stop her touching his groin, he clasped her to him.

"You just want body-body?" she said.

"What does it mean?" he said.

"Just body-body," she said. She got up and shut the window. She felt the air conditioner with the palm of her hand, but didn't touch its dials. "Gimme a cigarette," she said.

"No. I don't have any cigarette," he said.

She threw her dress on over her head, slipped her feet into her sandals. She wore no underclothes. "Gimme a coupla quarters," she said.

"What does it mean?" he said.

"What does it mean?" she said. "What does it mean? Gimme a coupla quarters. Gimme a coupla quarters."

"Is it money?" he said. "How much is it?"

"Gimme a coupla quarters," she said. "I wanna see if he gonna sell me some cigarette. I wanna coupla pack cigarette—a pack for me, and one pack for my cousin. Two pack."

"The colonel can do it," he said.

"One Weenston. One Lucky Strike."

"Excuse me. It's chilly tonight," he said. He got up and put his clothes on.

He stepped out front. From behind him he heard the small sounds of the young woman inside dealing with her purse, setting it on a table. She clapped and rubbed her hands and a puff of perfume drifted past him from the open window and he inhaled it. His ears rang, and tears clouded his sight. He cleared a thickness from his throat, hung his head, spat down between his feet. He missed his homeland.

When he'd first joined the air force and then been transferred to Da Nang and into officers' training, only seventeen, he'd cried every night in his bed for several weeks. He'd been flying fighter jets for nearly three years now, since he was nineteen years old.

Two months ago he'd turned twenty-two, and he could expect to continue flying missions until the one that killed him.

Later he sat on the porch in a canvas chair, leaning forward, forearms on his knees, smoking—he actually did possess a pack of Luckies—when the colonel returned from the club with his arms around both the girls. Minh's escort had a pack in her hand and waved it happily.

"So you explored the briny deeps today."

Minh wasn't sure what he meant. He said, "Yes."

"Ever been down there in any of those tunnels?" the colonel asked.

"What is it?—tunnels."

"Tunnels," the colonel said. "Tunnels all under Vietnam. You been down inside those things?"

"Not yet. I don't think so."

"Nor have I, son," the colonel said. "I wonder what's down there."

"I don't know."

"Nobody does," the colonel said.

"The cadres use the tunnels," Minh said. "The Vietminh."

Now the colonel seemed to grieve for his President again, because he said, "This world spits out a beautiful man like he was poison."

Minh had noticed you could talk to the colonel for a long time without recognizing he was drunk.

He'd met the colonel only a few mornings back, out front of the helicopter maintenance yard at the Subic base, and they'd sought each other out continually ever since. The colonel had not been introduced to him—the colonel had introduced himself—and didn't appear to be linked to him in any official way. They were housed together with dozens of other transient officers in a barracks in a compound originally constructed and then quickly abandoned, according to the colonel, by the American Central Intelligence Agency.

Minh knew the colonel was one to stick with. Minh had a custom of picking out situations, people, as good luck, bad luck. He drank Lucky Lager, he smoked Lucky Strikes. The colonel called him "Lucky."

"John F. Kennedy was a beautiful man," the colonel said. "That's what killed him."

1964

Nguyen Hao arrived safely at the New Star Temple on his Japanese Honda 30 motorbike, in dress pants and a box-cut shirt, wearing sunglasses, the pomade melting in his hair. It was his sad errand to serve as his family's only representative at the funeral service for his wife's nephew. Hao's wife was down with chills. The boy's parents were deceased, and the boy's only brother was flying missions for the air force.

Hao looked back to where he'd dropped off a friend from his youth named Trung Than, whom everybody had always called the Monk and who'd gone north when the country had been partitioned. Hao hadn't seen the Monk for a decade, not until this afternoon, and now he was gone: he'd hopped backward off the bike, removed his sandals, and padded off barefoot down the path.

Hao made sure to take the motorbike slowly over anything looking like a puddle, and when he reached the rice paddies he walked the machine most carefully along the dikes. He had to keep his clothes clean; he'd be overnighting here, probably in the schoolroom adjacent to the temple. The village wasn't far from Saigon, and in better times he might have motored back in the dusk, but the critical areas had expanded such that nowadays after three in the afternoon the back roads over to Route Twenty-two would be hazardous.

He set his straw bedroll on the earthen floor just inside the schoolroom's doorway, so as to be able to find his bed later in the night.

No life showed itself among the string of huts other than foraging chickens and stationary old women visible in the doorways. He pulled aside the wooden lid of the concrete well and lowered the bucket and drew himself a drink and a wash from out of the dark. The well was deep, drilled by a machine. The water came clear and cool into his hand and onto his face.

No sound from the temple. The master probably napped. Hao rolled his motorbike into the interior—rough lumber, with a roof of ceramic shingles and a dirt floor, about fifteen by fifteen meters, not much bigger in area than the downstairs of Hao's own house in Saigon. Rather than disturb the master, he turned and went out even before his eyes adjusted to the dimness, but already the must of the floor and the aroma of joss sticks had wakened his boyhood, when he'd served here at the temple for a couple of years. He felt something tugging at him from that era, a thread connected to a sadness which was generally inert and which quickly forgot itself. So much of this had been laid over by the rest of his life.

Also he felt a confused sadness over his nephew's preposterous death. Inconceivable. On first hearing of it Hao had assumed the boy had perished in an accidental fire. But in fact he'd burned himself alive—as had two or three elder monks in recent times. But those others had killed themselves spectacularly in the Saigon streets in order to cry out against chaos. And they were old men. Thu was only twenty, and he'd set himself afire out in the bush beyond the village in a solitary ceremony. Incomprehensible, crazy.

When Master woke he came out not in his robe, but dressed for the fields. Hao stood up and bowed his head, and the master bowed very deeply, a small man with a large rib cage and stick-limbs, his head covered with stubble—it occurred to Hao that Thu had probably been the one who'd shaved him. Poor dead Thu. "I was going to take up a hoe this afternoon," the master said. "I'm glad you've stopped me."

They sat on the porch and made a start at polite conversation, moving into the doorway while a loud rain came over. The master apparently chose to let the chatter of this downpour serve the purposes of small talk, because when it was over he spoke immediately of the death of Thu, saying it mystified him. "But it brings you back to see us. Every fist grips its gift."

"The atmosphere of the temple is very strong," Hao said.

"You always seemed uncertain here."

"But I'm doing what you suggested. I've made my doubt into my calling."

"That's not quite the way to phrase it."

"Those were the words you used."

"No. I said you must allow your doubt to become your calling, you must permit it. I don't suggest that you make it so, only that you let it be so. Let your doubt be your calling. Then your doubt will be invisible. You'll inhabit it like an atmosphere."

The master offered a bit of champooy, which Hao declined. He put the spicy dried fruit in his own mouth and sucked on it vigorously, frowning. "A certain American is coming to the service."

"I know him," Hao said. "Colonel Sands."

The master said nothing, and Hao felt forced to go on: "The colonel knows my nephew Minh. They met in the Philippines."

"He told me so."

"Have you met him personally?"

"He's come several times," the master said. "He cultivated an acquaintance with Thu. I think he's a kind man. Or at least a careful man."

"He's interested in the practice. He wants to study the breath."

"His breath smells of the meat of cattle and cigars and liquor. And what about you? Have you continued with the breath?"

Hao didn't answer.

"Have you continued your practice?"

"No."

The master spat out the pit of his champooy. A skeletal puppy darted from under the porch and gobbled it quickly, trembling, and then dematerialized. "In their dreams," the old man said, "dogs travel back and forth between this world and the other world. In their dreams they visit the before-life, and they visit the afterlife."

Hao said, "The Americans are going to become somewhat active here, somewhat destructive."

"How do you know?" The question was very indiscreet, yet

even in the face of Hao's silence he persisted: "Did this American tell you?"

"Thu's brother told me."

"Minh?"

"Our air force will participate."

"Will young Minh bomb his own country?"

"Minh doesn't fly a bomber."

"But will the air force destroy us?"

"Minh told me to get you out of here. I can't tell you more than that, because it's all I know." Because to traffic in information any more specific than that terrified him. Would have terrified anyone. Should have terrified the master.

Hao raised another matter: "I just saw the Monk. He showed up at my house and asked me for money. Then I took him here on the back of the motorbike."

The master only studied him with his eyes.

Yes, he'd known the master must have heard from Trung. "How long since you've seen him?"

"Not long," the master admitted.

"How long has he been back?"

"Who can say? And you? How long since you've seen him?"

"Many years. He has a northern accent now." Hao stopped himself from saying more, stared at his feet.

"It disturbed you to see him."

"He came to my house. He wanted money for the cause."

"For the Vietminh? They don't take taxes in the city."

"If he asked, they must have told him to ask. It's extortion. Then he insisted I take him here on the motorbike."

The master said, "He knows he's safe. He knows you won't name him to his enemies."

"Maybe I should. If the Vietminh have their way, that means the destruction of my family business."

"And of our temple, probably. But these outsiders are destroying the entire country."

"I can't give money to Communists."

"Maybe I can get word to Trung that you have no money. That you've spent it for something."

"For what?"

"Something that puts you beyond reproach."

"Tell him, please."

"I'll just say you've done all you can."

"I'm indebted."

Hao could feel tomorrow morning's mist beginning to shape itself almost immediately as the sun fell behind the nearest hill to the west, called Good Luck Mountain. The fortunes of the mountain had altered, however. The construction arm of the American military was making an encampment up there, most people guessed a permanent landing zone for helicopters. News had reached his ears that they planned to distribute mixtures alongside Route One and Route Twenty-two to kill the vegetation there. Depriving ambushers of cover was a good idea, he thought. But this was the loveliest country on the earth. Sorrow and war lay all over it, true, but the sickness of sorrow had never before penetrated the land itself. He didn't like to see it poisoned.

On account of this American colonel's possible arrival they delayed the memorial until past four in the afternoon, but the colonel didn't come, and the risk of ambush would keep him off the roads now, and they went ahead without him. They held the service in the temple. Eight of the villagers attended, seven old men and someone's grandchild all sitting in candlelight around the temple's centerpiece without a corpse to look at, only a small crowd of bric-a-brac, mostly wooden Buddhas painted gold. A scintillating battery-run decoration of the type found in GI taverns topped the whole display: a disc on which changing bands of light revolved clockwise. The master was more than audible. He spoke as if he were teaching. As if nobody ever learned anything. "We Vietnamese have two philosophies to sustain us. The Confucian tells us how to behave when fate grants us peace and order. The Buddhist trains us to accept our fate even when it brings us blood and chaos."

The Americans arrived by last light in an open jeep. Either

they had no fear of the roads, or they'd bivouacked with the American military construction group above, on Good Luck Mountain. The brawny colonel, in civilian dress as always, had the wheel, driving with a rifle jutting up between his knees, smoking a cigar, accompanied by a U.S. infantryman and also by a Vietnamese woman in a white blouse and gray skirt whom he introduced as Mrs. Van, an employee of the United States Information Service.

They'd brought a projector and a collapsible screen and intended to show a one-hour film to the people of the village.

Colonel Sands bowed to the master, and then they shook hands vigorously, in the American way. "Mr. Hao, we're going to set up the projector in the main room, if that's all right. Will you please tell him that?"

Hao translated and told the colonel that the master saw no obstacle. The young soldier arranged the machine, the cords, and four folding canvas chairs—"for the elders," the colonel said—as well as a small generator which he set going a few meters beyond the temple's wooden walls and which filled the valley with its racket and scented the whole region with its exhaust. Hao explained that he and the master had to visit a sick villager but might come to see part of the film later on. The colonel said he understood, but Hao wasn't sure he did. And as dusk arrived, and then the darkness, and as it grew evident that nobody at all would come, Colonel Sands asked to have the show played just for himself. The movie machine, powered by the noisy generator, filled the temple with flickering illumination and a hollow booming voice and strident music. The film, *Years of Lightning, Day of Thunder*, recounted the brief, tragic, heroic span of President John F. Kennedy's life. The American soldier and Mrs. Van also watched. Mrs. Van had come along to translate the narrative for the audience, but of course there was no need. The colonel had said it would go on for fifty-five minutes, and five minutes short of that, under cover of the darkness, Hao and the master crept in to join the Americans, the master sitting on his pillow at the head of the room, behind the portable screen, where he couldn't see anything, actually, and Hao in a chair beside the young soldier. Mrs. Van, sitting behind the colonel, glanced at Hao but seemed to decide he could translate for himself. In fact he couldn't. To fathom English speech he usually needed faces and gestures. And anyway the colonel was already talking more loudly than the recording, seated with his arms crossed over his fists, addressing himself in bitter tones to the shining spectacle as the music swelled and the view closed in on the eternal flame marking John F. Kennedy's grave, a squat torch which the Americans intended to keep alight forever. "The eternal flame," the colonel said. "Eternal? If you can kill the man, you can sure as hell kill his flame. The thing is this: We're all dead in the long run. In the end we're dirt. Let's face it, our whole civilization is a layer of sediment. In the end some mongrel barbarian wakes up in the morning and stands with one foot on a rock and the other on the kicked-over vessel of Kennedy's eternal flame. And that vessel is cold and dead, and that sonofabitch doesn't even know he's standing on it. He's just taking a piss in the morning. When I get up in the morning and step behind the tent to break wind and void my bladder, whose grave am I pissing on? — Mr. Hao, is my English too fast? Am I getting across?"

Hao made out the colonel's intent, and, Yes, he wanted to agree, it's all simply water coursing into larger and then still larger seas, and only what we do in this moment can save us . . . His vocabulary allowed him to say, "It's true. I think so. Yes."

Both men were distracted now by a small rat or frog hopping boldly into the room through the front door. The colonel astonished Hao by reacting to this intrusion violently, flinging himself bodily at the small man and knocking him backward, chair and all, so that the back of Hao's head struck the packed dirt floor and a pain burst over his sight like an explosion of freezing needles. His vision cleared as the object, for that is what it was, and not some rodent, stopped only a meter from his face, and he understood that it was probably a grenade; it was his death. Something clapped down over the grenade. The soldier had covered it with his helmet and now lowered himself, not rapidly, but with some reluctance, and covered the helmet with his body, staring at first at the dirt of the floor and then looking toward Hao's face, only inches away, so that his eyes were readable as he curled himself around his terror. Long seconds passed in a voluminous silence.

The silence held. More long seconds. The soldier's face did not change, and he didn't breathe, but his soul came back into his eyes and he stared at Hao with some comprehension.

Hao became aware that the colonel lay across his chest, had thrown himself there just as the soldier had thrown himself over the helmet. He became aware of pain in his calves, his head, of the big American colonel's weight. Hao sucked hard at the atmosphere, he was suffocating. The soldier himself exhaled the air he'd been harboring, and Hao felt the soldier's breath bathe his face. At last the colonel placed his palms on the floor either side of Hao's shoulders and heaved himself to his knees, and Hao was able to fill his lungs.

The colonel stood up like a very old man and bent to grip the soldier's arm. "Nothing happening, son." The soldier was deaf. "Get up. Get up, son. Come on, now, son. Get up." The youngster, finding life in his body, overcame some of his shock and rolled himself over. Quickly the colonel tossed the helmet aside, scooped up the hand grenade, pitched it underhanded toward the doorway, but it struck the wall and made it only as far as the threshold, and he said, "Damn it all." He approached it, bent and took a firm hold of it, and strode out the door and to the well. He moved the lid aside and tossed the device into the depths. Then he walked back to the building and turned off his generator.

The others followed him out, perhaps inadvisedly. Mrs. Van tended to the soldier, talking rapid English, brushing at his shirt and trousers energetically, almost hysterically, as if batting at flames. When she was done she started on Hao, swiping at the back of his shirt. "These are bad people," she said in English. "This is what happens with these horrible people."

The master came out of the temple. From his place behind the screen he'd witnessed almost nothing. When Hao told him about the grenade, he took two long steps backward away from the lip of the well.

The colonel said, "Look, I'm sorry. The well was the quickest place to come to mind."

Hao translated the colonel's apology and then the master's reply: "I believe it's safe."

"If that grenade goes off, it's gonna muddy up your water."

The master said, "Later it will become calm again."

"That thing must be deep. And is it concrete?"

Hao said, "Concrete construction."

"It's top-notch."

"Top-notch?"

"It's very well made."

"Yes. It was placed by the Swiss Red Cross."

"When was this?"

"I don't know when."

The colonel said, "They heard that noisy goddamn generator, didn't they?"

By way of an answer, Hao pursed his lips.

Hao stood by politely while the visitors reloaded their gear and radioed the encampment on Good Luck Mountain.

"We'll scoot on up the hill," the colonel said.

"Good. There it's more secure," Hao agreed.

In minutes a patrol of three jeeps arrived, and many soldiers, and the convoy roared away into the night.

Hao crept into the schoolroom and felt along the wall for a nail. He undressed and hung up his shirt and trousers, swept his straw mat with his hands, unrolled two yards of linen to cover him against the mosquitoes. The master heard him from the other side of the wall, in the temple, and called goodnight. Hao replied softly and lay back in his shorts and undershirt in the pitch-dark.

This colonel—Hao had never encountered him in a uniform. It seemed fitting. Somehow he thought of all Americans as civilians, although in his entire life he'd seen only government Americans and military Americans, and a few missionaries. Just the same, he thought of Americans as cowboys. The young soldier's courage astounded him. Maybe it was good they'd come to Vietnam.

But even through the wall he could feel the master's anger at himself for dealing with the colonel. The American was attractive, fascinating, but the Americans were, in the end, just another horde of puppet-masters. The curtain falls on the French, the curtain rises, now the American puppet-drama. But the time of slaves and puppets was over. A thousand years under China, then the French domination—all of it finished. Now comes freedom.

Hao spoke softly to Master. He wished him lucky dreams. He himself couldn't sleep. His bowels smoldered with fear. What if another grenade rolled toward him out of the night? Listening for his murderers, he became aware of the oppressive life of the jungle, of the collective roar of insects, as big as any city's at noon. A curse lay over everything. His wife was sick, his nephew was dead, the wars would never stop. He found his sandals with his feet and went out to the well and drank from the can in the dark and recollected himself. Nothing could hurt him. He'd lived, he'd known love, he'd been shown much kindness. Lucky life!

After rolling the device into the temple, Trung turned and ran behind the row of huts as quietly as he could and entered the trail. Only a few meters along, he slowed down, listening. Voices, movement. But no blast.

A minute; two minutes. If the noise had come he might not have heard it for the booming of his blood.

He stood in the narrow thoroughfare with his arms wrapped around his middle, grief wringing itself out of him. He hadn't expected the fools to be sitting there next to the American. He hadn't wept in years.

If I'd actually killed them, I might weep less.

This outpouring was good. The old women said, Scatter your tears, they're good for the crops. He'd cried for lots of reasons in his youth. Not much since then.

He moved on down the path. In Saigon they'd given him only the one grenade. Well.

He'd been told to wait for the American civilian who brought the film projector. A specific target. He hadn't asked why then they hadn't sent a good shot, with a rifle. He guessed the American's death was meant to seem incidental.

He had to take to the creek briefly to get around a hamlet where lived some noisy dogs. Heading downstream he reached the house of the region's head cadre. The occupants slept. In the tiny garden behind it he squatted with his rump against a tree trunk, draped his head with a rag, and put his face down onto his knees. He rested for two hours.

He didn't know why he'd asked his old friend Hao for funds. He hadn't been instructed to initiate any contact. He didn't think he should examine his motives.

Immediately after the roosters' second crow, he woke the cadre and reported his failure. He was issued a Chinese Type 56 rifle and two banana clips, each holding thirty rounds, and told to go back to the encampment of ragtag boys by the Van Co Dong River, a "lost command" of Hoa-hao guerrillas. They'd declared themselves ready to submit to relocation and indoctrination.

"Has there been any trouble?" he asked the cadre.

"No one has harmed them. You won't encounter any tensions."

"All right. Keep the gun. But let me have a flashlight."

The river ran high. Trung had to make his way to a ford well above the encampment, cross over, and hike back downstream, some five or six kilometers overall.

He hooted as he came to an outpost, a lean-to of banana leaves and bamboo, but no one answered.

The path led to a black scarred region close by the river, formerly a market square. The people here had been driven out by a plague, and later a practitioner had ordered the buildings burned in a superstitious ceremony. A small barn nearby still stood upright and now served as a barracks.

The youngsters had grouped out back of the structure to bury one of their comrades. A two-week bout of malaria, they explained, had ended in his extinction. They'd stripped him of his clothes. They sprinkled grains of rice into his open mouth, lowered the naked youth into a grave about four feet deep without any kind of casket, and covered him with damp, yellowish clots of earth.

Trung stood by watching, waving the flies away from his face. The boys gathered around the mound in silence for about a minute. Finally one spoke up. "It's bad," he said. "There goes one more."

They were all young, many still in their teens. Their group had never been part of the Vietminh. They were ignorant mountain people from Ba Den who didn't know how to bury their dead.

When they'd finished he stood with them out back of their barracks to address them, but he could only repeat what others had already said.

"We can get you medicine against malaria. It's possible we can relocate you north, to a collective farm we call a kolkhoz, where you'll live in peace and order. But if you want to go on fighting, we can put you to better use.

"We are centralized. We have an iron structure. We are closed into a single fist that disappears up a sleeve when it has to. Our will is unshakable. Our will is our weapon. The greatest colonialist armies can't stand against it. We drove out the French, and we'll drive out the Americans, and we'll slaughter and bury their puppets. Do they claim victories? Let them. The invaders are fighting the ocean. No matter how many waves they beat down, the ocean of our resolve is always there.

"Do you want to be free? Personal liberation is national liberation. The men who led you in the beginning understood this, they learned it with the Hoa-hao, and they took you this far. Now you must come with us and go through to the end—which is the beginning we have all hoped for, the first day of our national freedom."

It had been long enough since he'd stopped attending classes that he didn't know anymore what he was saying.

Trung had been sent here because of the time he'd spent serving at the New Star Temple in the nearby village. It was assumed he probably knew these people. A slight mix-up. As little children, orphan boys, they'd been recruited—kidnapped—far upriver by Hoa-hao guerrillas, originally from the Mekong Delta, who'd been driven into the hills by the Vietminh. The boys' leaders had abandoned the young recruits, or been killed. Meanwhile the village of their ancestors had vanished, dispersed by the fighting. Over a period of years the boys had worked their way farther and farther down the Van Co Dong, finding no welcome anywhere and finally stopping along this stretch well-known in the region for its particularly virulent strain of malaria, called "piss-blood." Nobody bothered them while one by one they died.

Trung explained that his own people came from Ben Tre, but he'd spent years and years in the North. Right now, until reunification, the heart of Vietnam lay in the North. "After reunification, all of Vietnam will be our home. Millions of square kilometers of Vietnam with no partition, no relocation, no disruption of the national fabric. We will lie down at night in peace and wake up to another day of peace. And those of us who die on the way, like your friend, will find peace in the grave."

Look at you, he thought, from your births to your deaths only exile, wandering, war.

"What will it be like on the kolkhoz farm?"

"Do you want work? There you'll have work and freedom."

"But we've been on our own a long time. We're already free."

"On the farm it's a different kind of freedom."

Yes, yes, yes, nothing but crap, what a monstrosity, he cursed himself for participating. Die here, die there, he wanted to say.

Just stay away from the kolkhoz. "It's time to take you to a group forming to head north. There's a camp near Bau Don. It's a long hike. We can make it in a day if we start very early tomorrow."

"We've already talked about it," one of the men told him. "There's nothing else we can do. We'll go north. But tonight the moon is empty. We can't travel tomorrow. Right after the empty moon, it's bad luck to start a journey. We just lost another one, thanks to bad luck."

"The malaria doesn't come from bad luck or spiteful gods. It's caused by living creatures too small to see, as venomous as a snake, but smaller than a speck of dust. We call these creatures microbes.

"Young brothers, let this sink into your ears. We all die. Do you want to die at the hands of a microbe? The ultimate victory will be composed of many defeats. Do you want to be defeated by a microbe? The sooner we go, the better."

They only looked at him as if they couldn't understand him. Probably many of them couldn't, coming from so far upriver, a region of different dialects. "We'll think about it," the man said.

While they talked among themselves, Trung stood aside and looked away. The same man came and touched his arm. "We'll go tomorrow."

"If that's your decision," Trung said, "then good."

The whole group had stayed up all the previous night with their sick comrade. Everyone was tired. There was nothing to do, so they dispatched a few sentries and the rest hung around the barracks. Trung sat down against the wall. He noticed flattened cigarette packs covering leaks all over the thatched ceiling. Several gaunt cats skulked around eating bits of garbage from the floor.

One of the guerrillas, a one-eyed youngster, brought in an armload of green coconuts. He pointed to his chest. "My Mosa," he told Trung in some sort of mountain tongue. "My *name*," another corrected him. "My name Mosa," he said, turning his head sideways to center Trung in his one functioning eye. He smiled: his teeth, in the way of these mountain tribes, had been filed down

flat. With a machete half as large as his own leg he scalped the
tops of the coconuts. They drank the milk and scraped at the
floppy translucent meat with shards from the shell.

The men offered him a cot and even gave him a small pillow.
They arranged themselves in a bivouac tableau: Outside a man
stood sentry; inside five men played cards while one kibitzed and
another snored nearby. Trung tried to nap, but he couldn't sleep.
He imagined they spent many days like this. The wind died off
outside. He could hear the swollen river rubbing along the banks.
The day grew dark. The sentries abandoned their outposts upriver
and came in for the evening meal. Altogether there didn't seem to
be more than fifteen of these quiet, emaciated men strung along
this part of the Van Co Dong, protecting themselves from all who
might come, they didn't care who, and they didn't seem to realize
no one was coming.

They kept the cook-fire smoldering all night to drive away the
mosquitoes. Trung slept with his bandanna over his nose and
mouth. The others didn't seem to mind the fumes.

The rain came long after dark. The men started stowing their
gear in leak-free spots, and they all rearranged themselves, repeating, "Move it! Move it!" They lay back in their new positions
while the rain strung itself down all around them through the
roof. Nobody talked because of the watery noise. By the light of
candles Trung saw their faces staring out at nothing. But their spirits rose. There was singing and laughter. They were good boys.
They were only doing whatever came along to be done. As the
rain got harder, they stuck more flattened cigarette packs here and
there in the ceiling.

At midnight four dogs snuck in. Trung was the only one awake.
He aimed his flashlight around as they prowled silently. When its
beam hit them, they bolted out the open doorway. The light cut
through the cook-smoke and played over the men and boys sleeping
in groups of two or three. They lay side by side, their arms draped
around one another, or touching in a casual, familial way.

At dawn he crept outside, sat cross-legged on the damp ground, and cleared his mind by focusing on the progress of the breath in and out of his nostrils, as during his boyhood he'd done every morning and evening at the New Star. And he'd been doing it again now, daily, for nearly a year, and had no notion why. The practice was making a lousy Communist of him. In fact he was no longer persuaded that blood and revolution made useful tools for altering the concepts in a person's mind. Who said it?—probably Confucius—"I can't beat a sculpture from a stone with a sledgehammer; I can't free the soul of a man by violence." Peace was here, peace was now. Peace promised in any other time or place was a lie.

The four dogs last night—they'd been the Four Noble Truths, dogging his lies into the darkness.

—Losing track. He returned his awareness to the movement of his breath.

Again he wondered why he'd asked Hao for money.

Hao's face when he saw me: like the puppy I played with too roughly. The little thing came to fear me. I loved it. Ah, no—

—Sooner or later the mind grasps at a thought and follows it into the labyrinth, one thought branching into another. Then the labyrinth caves in on itself and you find yourself outside. You were never inside—it was a dream.

He returned his attention to the breath.

Morning—a mist hiding the river and a cloud caught on the peaks beyond. He heard the boys stirring within, waking to the earth's richest triumph, another day outside the grave. Groggy-eyed, everyone shuffled forth, blankets wrapped around them, to pee. "Young men, while you live," he told them, "find out how to wake up from this nightmare." They looked at him with sleepy faces.

1965

As had become the weekly routine, on Monday night William "Skip" Sands of the U.S. Central Intelligence Agency tested his energies by accompanying a patrol of the combined Philippine Army and Philippine Constabulary in a fruitless search for invisible people among dark mountain places. This time his friend Major Aguinaldo couldn't come along, and nobody else had any idea what to do with the American. They drove the rutted roads all night wordlessly, noisily, in a convoy of three jeeps, looking for any sign of Huk guerrillas, as was the routine, and seeing none, as was the routine, and just before dawn Sands came back to the staff house to find the lights dead and the air conditioners silent. For the third time this week the local power had failed. He opened his bedroom to the jungle and sweltered in his bedclothes.

Four hours later the window unit came to life, and he woke quickly and completely in sheets damp from sweat. He'd overslept, had probably missed breakfast and would have to omit his morning calisthenics. He showered quickly, dressed himself in khaki pants and a native box-cut shirt, a gauzy dress item called a barong tagalog, a gift from his Filipino friend Major Aguinaldo.

Downstairs he found a place set for him at the otherwise bare mahogany dining table. The ice had melted in his water glass. Beside it lay the morning's newspapers, which were actually yesterday's, delivered in a courier pouch from Manila. The houseboy Sebastian came out of the kitchen and said, "Good morning, Skeep. The barber is coming."

"When?"

"He's coming now."

"Where is he?"

"He's in the kitchen. You want breakfast first? You want egg?"

"Just coffee, please."

"You want bacon and egg?"

"Can you stand it if I just have coffee?"

"What kind of egg? Over easy."

"Bring it on, bring it on."

He sat at the table before a wide window that looked onto the insane spectacle of a two-hole golf course surrounded by overripe jungle. This tiny resort—a residence, servants' quarters, a shed, and a workshop—had been built to serve vacationing staff of the Del Monte Corporation. Sands hadn't yet met anybody from Del Monte and by now no longer expected to. Only two other men appeared to be staying here, one an English specialist on mosquitoes and the other a German whom Sands suspected of being a more sinister kind of specialist, perhaps a sniper.

Bacon and eggs for breakfast. Tiny eggs. The bacon was always tasty. Rice, no potatoes. A soft bread roll, no toast. Filipinos moved around the place in white uniforms, with mops and cloths, keeping the grime and mildew at bay. A young man wearing only black boxer shorts skated past the archway to the main room on the downturned halves of a coconut husk, polishing the wooden floor.

Sands read the front page of *The Manila Times*. A gangster named Boy Golden had been slain in the living room of his apartment. Sands studied the photo of Boy Golden's corpse, in a bathrobe, limbs flung crazily and the tongue lolling from between the jaws.

The barber appeared, an old man toting a wooden box, and Skip said, "Let's go out back." They stepped through French doors onto the patio.

The day was clear and looked harmless. Still he feared the sky. Rain six weeks straight, from the moment of his arrival in Manila in mid-June, and then one day it just shuts off. This was his first trip beyond the borders of America. He'd never resided outside of Kansas until he'd taken himself and a red-orange suitcase on the bus to Bloomington, Indiana, for the university; but several times as a child and once again in his teens he'd visited Boston to stay with his father's side of the family, boarding almost a whole summer the last time among a gauntlet of relations, an Irish horde of big cops and veteran soldiers like mastiff guard dogs, and their worried poodle wives. They'd overwhelmed him with their unselfconscious vulgarity and loud gregariousness, embraced him, loved him, uncovered themselves as the family he'd never found among his mother's midwestern group, who treated one another like acquaintances. He had scant memory of his father, a casualty of Pearl Harbor. His Boston Irish uncles had shown Skip who to become, had marked out the shape he'd fill someday as a grown man. He didn't think he was filling it. It only set off how small he was.

Now from these Filipinos he felt the same warmth and welcome, from these charming miniature Irishmen. He'd just begun his eighth week in the Philippines. He liked the people, he hated the climate. It was the start of his fifth year serving the United States as a member of its Central Intelligence Agency. He considered both the Agency and his country to be glorious.

"I just want you to cut the sides," he told the old man. Under the influence of the late President Kennedy he'd begun to let his crew cut grow out, and also just recently—under the influence, maybe, of the region's Spanish vestiges—he'd started a mustache.

As the old man clipped at his head Sands consulted a second oracle, the Manila *Enquirer*: the biggest front-page article announced itself as the first of a series devoted to reports by Filipino pilgrims of startling miracles, including asthma cures, a wooden cross that turned to gold, a stone cross that moved, a plaster icon who wept, another icon who bled.

The barber held an eight-by-five-inch mirror before his face. It was good he didn't have to show this head around the capital. The mustache existed only as a hope and the hair had reached a middle state, too long to go unnoticed, too short to be controlled. How many years had he kept his crew cut?—eight, nine—since the morning of his interview with the Agency recruiters who'd come to the campus in Bloomington. Both men had worn business suits

and crew cuts, as he'd observed the previous afternoon, spying on
their arrival at the faculty guest residence—the arrival of the crew-
cut recruiters from Central Intelligence. He'd liked the word
Central.

He felt, here, a day's drive from Manila on terrible roads, central to nothing. Reading superstitious newspapers. Staring at the
vines on the stucco walls, the streaks of mildew on the walls, the
lizards on the walls, the pimples of mud on the walls.

From his perch here on the patio Sands detected tension in
the air, some sort of suppressed quarrel among the workers—he
didn't like to think of them as "servants"—of the house. It pricked
his curiosity. But having been raised in the American heartland he
was dedicated to steering clear of personal controversy, to ignoring
scowls, honoring evasiveness, fending off voices raised in other
rooms.

Sebastian came out onto the patio looking quite nervous and
said, "Somebody here to see you."

"Who is it?"

"They will say. Let me not say."

But twenty minutes went by, and nobody came out to see him.

Sands finished his haircut, went into the cool parlor room with
its polished wooden floor. Empty. And nobody in the dining area
other than Sebastian, setting the table for lunch. "Was somebody
here to see me?"

"Somebody? No . . . I think nobody."

"Didn't you say I had a visitor?"

"Nobody, sir."

"Great, thanks, keep me guessing."

He took himself to a rattan chair on the patio. Here he could
either read the news or watch the English entomologist, a man
named Anders Pitchfork, chip a golf ball with a three-iron back
and forth between the two full-sized greens of the very undersized
golf course. Its two or so acres of lawn were minutely tended and
biologically uniform, circled by high chain-link with which the
surrounding plant life grappled darkly and inexorably. Pitchfork, a

graying Londoner in Bermuda shorts and a yellow Banlon shirt, an expert on anopheles mosquitoes, spent his mornings here on the course until the sun cleared the building's roof and drove him away to do his job, which was to eradicate malaria.

Sands could see, down the colonnade, the German visitor taking breakfast in his pajamas on the private patio outside his room. The German had come to this region to kill someone—Sands believed this having spoken to him only twice. The section chief had accompanied him from Manila and, though the chief's visit had been ostensibly about squaring Sands away, he'd spent all his time with the German and had instructed Sands to "stay available and leave him alone."

As for Pitchfork, the malaria man with the unforgettable name—just gathering information. Possibly running agents, of sorts, in the villages.

Sands liked to guess everybody's occupation. People came and went on murky errands. In Britain this place might have been called a "safe house." In the U.S., however, in Virginia, Sands had been trained to consider no house safe. To find no island anywhere in the sea. The colonel, his closest trainer, had made sure each of his recruits memorized "The Lee Shore" from Melville's *Moby-Dick*:

> But as in landlessness alone resides the highest truth, shoreless, indefinite as God—so, better is it to perish in that howling infinite, than be ingloriously dashed upon the lee, even if that were safety! For worm-like, then, oh! who would craven crawl to land!

Pitchfork placed his ball on a tee, selected a big-headed wood from the golf bag lying by the green, and drove one over the fence and deep into the vegetation.

Meanwhile, according to the *Enquirer*, pirates had seized an oil tanker in the Sulu Sea, killing two crewmen. In Cebu City, a mayoral candidate and one of his supporters had been shot full of holes by the candidate's own brother. The killer supported his brother's opponent—their father. And the governor of Camiguin Province had been shot down by, the paper said, "an amok," who also killed two others "after becoming berserk."

And now the German practiced against a rubber tree with a blowgun: of other than primitive manufacture, Sands guessed, as it broke down neatly into three sections. Assembled, it ran better than five feet in length, and the darts looked seven or eight inches long—white, tapered; like overlong golf tees, as a matter of fact. The German sent them deftly into his target's hide, pausing often to mop at his face with a hankie.

Skip had an appointment down in the village with his friend, Philippine Army Major Eddie Aguinaldo.

Skip and the German assassin, who may not have been an assassin, or even a German, rode together halfway down the mountain to the market. They took the air-conditioned staff car, gazing out the closed windows of the backseat at the thatched homes of warped, rough-cut lumber, at tethered goats, wandering chickens, staggering dogs. As they passed the grannies who squatted on the dusty stoops, spitting red betel nut, squads of tiny children detached themselves from the old crones and ran alongside the car.

"What is that? They're saying something."

"'Chez,'" Sands told the German.

"What is that? Did you say 'chez'? It means? What does it mean?"

"Their parents used to ask the GIs for matches. 'Matches! Matches!' Now they just shout, 'Chez, chez, chez.' They don't know what it means. There aren't any GIs around anymore, and if they want a match they say 'posporo.'"

But the old women grappled after the children angrily, in a way he hadn't seen before. "What is the matter with these people?" he asked the German.

"They need a better diet. The protein is too little."

"Do you sense it? Something's up."

"It's too little fish high up in the mountain. The protein is too little."

"Ernest," Skip said, leaning forward and talking to the driver, "is something going on in the village today?"

"Maybe something, I don't know," Ernest said. "I can ask around for you." He came from Manila, and his English was excellent.

Major Eduardo Aguinaldo, in crisp fatigues, waited in the rear seat of a black Mercedes outside the Monte Mayon, a restaurant run by an Italian and his Filipino family. Pavese, the Italian, served whatever people would buy, which wasn't much. For visitors Pavese made a quite delicious spaghetti Bolognese with a lot of goat's liver in it. The major welcomed the German and insisted he call him "Eddie" and insisted he join them for lunch.

To Skip's surprise, the German accepted. Their guest ate robustly, voluptuously. He wasn't fat, but food seemed his passion. Skip hadn't seen him so happy. He was a bearish, bearded character with thick brown rims for his glasses and skin that burned rather than tanned, and big soft lips that got wet when he talked.

"Let's get some of Pavese's espresso, because it's full of life," Aguinaldo said. "Skip was up all night. He's tired."

"Never! I'm never tired."

"Were my men good to you?"

"Most respectful. Thanks."

"But you didn't locate any Huks."

"Not unless they were hiding by the road and we never saw them."

"What about the PC boys?"

"The PC?" These were the Philippine Constabulary. "The PC were fine. They kept pretty much to themselves."

"They don't care for the army's assistance. I won't say I can blame them. It's not a war. These Huks are only renegades. They've been reduced to the status of bandits."

"Correct." But these excursions amounted to Sands's only strategy for gaining points and landing a reassignment to Manila or, even better, to Saigon. Above all, these jungle patrols relieved him of the uneasy feeling that he'd undergone rigorous training, swung by ropes along the faces of cliffs, parachuted into thunderclouds, sweated while following recipes for highly explosive materials, clambered over barbed wire, traversed rushing streams in the dark of night, been interrogated for hours while tied to a chair, all in order to become a clerk, nothing more than a clerk. To compile. To sort. To accomplish what any spinster librarian could accomplish. "And what did you do last night?" he asked Eddie.

"Myself? I turned in early and read James Bond."

"You're kidding."

"Perhaps we'll go on patrol this evening. Will you come?" Aguinaldo asked the German. "It can be quite exhilarating."

The German was confused. "What is the purpose?" he asked Sands.

"Our friend won't be coming," Sands told Eddie.

"I'm going farther down," the German explained.

"Farther down?"

"To the train."

"Oh. The station. Going to Manila," Aguinaldo said. "A pity. Our little patrols can be bracing experiences."—As if they came often under fire. Nothing of the kind had ever happened, as far as Skip knew. Eddie was boyish, but he liked to seem menacing.

Three weeks ago, in Manila, Sands had seen Eddie playing Henry Higgins in a production of *My Fair Lady*, and he couldn't erase from his mind the picture of his friend the major overly rouged and powdered and strutting the boards in a smoking jacket; pausing; turning to a beautiful Filipino actress and saying, "Liza, where the devil are my slippers?" The audience of Filipino businessmen and their families had been swept to its feet, roaring. Sands too had been impressed.

"What is that thing you're practicing with?" Sands asked the German.

"You mean the sumpit. Yes."

"A blowgun?"

"Yes. From the Moro tribe."

"Sumpit is a Tagalog word?"

"I think it's very generally used," Eddie said.

"It's a word used everywhere in these islands," the German agreed.

"And what's it made of?"

"The construction, you mean?"

"Yes."

"Magnesium."

"Magnesium. For goodness' sake."

"Quite sturdy. Quite weightless."

"Who forged it for you?"

He'd asked just to make conversation, but was shocked to see a look pass between Eddie and the assassin. "Some private people in Manila," the German said, and Sands let the topic die.

Following the meal they all three took espresso coffee in tiny cups. Before coming to this remote village, Sands had never tasted it.

"What's going on today, Eddie?"

"I don't know what you mean."

"Is it some sort of—I don't know—some sort of sad anniversary? Like the day of some great leader's death? Why does everybody seem so morose?"

"You mean tense."

"Yeah. Tensely morose."

"I believe they've been spooked, Skip. There's a vampire about. A kind of vampire called aswang."

The German said, "Vampire? You mean Dracula?"

"The aswang can turn into any person, assume any shape. You see instantly the trouble—it means anybody can be a vampire. When a rumor like this starts, it floods a village like cold poison. One night last week—last Wednesday, around eight o'clock—I saw a throng outside the market, beating an old woman and crying, 'Aswang! Aswang!' "

"Beating her? An old woman?" Skip said. "Beating her with what?"

"With anything that came to hand. I couldn't quite see. It was dark. It seemed to me she escaped around the corner. But later a storekeeper told me she changed into a parrot and flew away. The parrot bit a little baby, and the baby died in two hours. The priest cannot do anything. Even a priest is helpless."

"These people are like demented children," the German said.

After they'd eaten and their companion had continued in the staff car down the mountain toward the railway line for Manila, Skip said, "Do you know that guy?"

"No," Eddie said. "Do you really think he's German?"

"I think he's foreign. And strange."

"He met with the colonel, and now he's leaving."

"The colonel—when?"

"It's significant that he hasn't introduced himself."

"Have you asked him his name?"

"No. What does he call himself?"

"I haven't asked."

"He never talked of paying. I'll pay." Eddie conferred with a plump Filipina whom Skip believed to be Mrs. Pavese, and came back saying, "Let me get fruit for tomorrow's breakfast."

Sands said, "I understand the mango and banana are good this time of year. All the tropical fruit."

"Is that a joke?"

"Yes, it is." They entered the market with its low patchwork tarpaulin roof and its atmosphere of rank butchery and vegetable putrefaction. Unbelievably deformed and crippled beggars scrambled after them, dragging themselves along the hard earthen floor. Little children approached too, but the beggars, on wheeled carts, or on leg stumps socked with coconut shells, or scar-faced and blind and toothless, lashed out at the children with canes or the butt ends of severed limbs and hissed and cursed. Aguinaldo drew his sidearm and pointed it at the roiling little pack and they reared backward in one body and gave up. He dickered briskly with an old lady selling papayas, and they got back into the street.

Eddie took Sands in his Mercedes back to the Del Monte House. Nothing had, as yet, transpired between them. Sands held back from asking if their meeting had a point. Eddie went inside with him, but not before he'd opened the car's trunk and taken out a heavy oblong package of brown paper tied with string. "I have something for you. A going-away gift." At his urging they sat again in the backseat—upholstered in leather and covered with a white bedsheet going gray.

Eddie held the package on his knees and unwrapped an M1 carbine of the paratrooper's type, with a folding metal stock. Its barrel's wooden foregrip had been refinished and etched with an intricate design. He handed over the weapon to Skip.

Sands turned it in his hands. Eddie moved a penlight over the engraving. "This is remarkable, Eddie. It's fantastic work. I'm so grateful."

"The sling is leather."

"Yes. I can see that."

"It's quite good."

"I'm honored and grateful." Sands meant it sincerely.

"A couple of boys at the National Bureau of Investigation had a go at it. They're wonderful gunsmiths."

"Remarkable. But you call it a going-away gift. Who's going away?"

"Then you've received no order as of yet?"

"No. Nothing. What is it?"

"Nothing." The major smiled his affected Henry Higgins smile. "But perhaps you'll get an assignment."

"Don't put me in the bush, Eddie, don't put me in the rain! Don't put me in a dripping tent!"

"Have I said anything? I'm as ignorant as you are. Have you spoken about it with the colonel?"

"I haven't seen him for weeks. He's in Washington."

"He's here."

"You mean in Manila?"

"Here, in San Marcos. In fact, I'm sure he's in the house."

"In the house? For God's sake. No. It's a gag."

"I understand he's your family."

"It's a gag, right?"

"Not unless he's the one making such a gag. I spoke to him by telephone this morning. He said he was calling from this house."

"Huh. Huh." Sands felt stupid to be making only syllables, but he was past words.

"You know him quite well?"

"As well as—huh. I don't know. He trained me."

"That means you don't know him. It means he knows you."

"Right, right."

"Is it true the colonel is actually your relative? He's your uncle or something?"

"Is that the rumor?"

"Perhaps I'm prying."

"Yes, he's my uncle. My father's brother."

"Fascinating."

"Sorry, Eddie. I don't like to admit it."

"But he's a great man."

"It's not that. I don't like to trade on his name."

"You should be proud of your family, Skip. Always be proud of your family."

Sands went inside to make sure it was a mistake, but it was completely true. The colonel, his uncle, sat in the parlor having cocktails with Anders Pitchfork.

"I see you're dressed for the evening," the colonel said, referring to Skip's barong, standing and offering his hand, which was strong and slightly wet and chilled from holding his drink. The colonel himself wore one of his Hawaiian-patterned shirts. He was both barrel-chested and potbellied, also bowlegged, also sunburned. He didn't stand much taller than the Filipino major but seemed mountainous. He wore a silver flattop haircut on a head like an anvil. He was at the moment drunk and held upright by the power of his own history: football for Knute Rockne at Notre Dame, missions for the Flying Tigers in Burma, antiguerrilla operations here in this jungle with Edward Lansdale, and, more lately, in South Vietnam. In Burma in '41 he'd spent months as a POW, and escaped. And he'd fought the Malay Tigers, and the Pathet Lao; he'd faced enemies on many Asian fronts. Skip loved him, but he was unhappy to see him.

"Eddie," the colonel said, taking the major's hand in both his own, moving the left hand up and gripping him above his elbow, massaging the biceps, "let's get drunk."

"Too early!"

"Too early? Darn — and too late for me to change course!"

"Too early! Just tea, please," Eddie told the houseboy, and Skip asked for the same.

The colonel looked with curiosity at the package under Skip's arm. "Fish for dinner?"

"Show him!" Eddie said, and Skip laid the M1 on the brass coffee table, nested in its open wrapping.

The colonel sat down and held the rifle across his knees just as Skip had done in the car moments ago, reading its intricate engravings with his fingers. "Fantastic work." He smiled. But he looked at no one when he smiled. He reached beside him to the floor and handed Skip a brown paper grocery bag. "Trade you."

"No, thanks," Skip said.

"What's in the sack?" Eddie asked.

"Courier pack from the ambassador," the colonel said.

"Ah! Mysterious!"

As ever, the colonel drank from two glasses at once. He waved his empty chaser at the houseboy.

"Sebastian, are you all out of Bushmills?"

"Bushmills Irish whiskey coming up!" the young man said.

Pitchfork said, "The servants seem to know you."

"I'm not a frequent visitor."

"I think they're in awe of you."

"Maybe I'm a big tipper." The colonel rose and went to the bucket on the sideboard to scoop ice into his glass with his fingers and stood looking out at the grounds with the air of somebody about to share a thought. They waited, but instead he sipped his drink.

Pitchfork said, "Colonel, are you a golfer?"

Eddie laughed. "If you tempt our colonel out there, he'll decimate the landscape."

"I stay out of the tropical sun," the colonel said. He stared lovingly at the rear end of a maidservant as she set out the tea service on the low brass table. When the others all held something in their hands, he raised his glass: "To the last Huk. May he soon fill his grave."

"The last Huk!" the others cried.

The colonel drank deeply, gasped, and said, "May the enemy be worthy of us."

Pitchfork said, "Hear, hear!"

Skip carried the paper sack and the beautiful gun to his quarters and laid both on his bed, relieved to take a minute alone. The maid had opened the room to the day. Skip cranked shut the louvered windows and turned on his air conditioner.

He poured out the contents of the sack onto the bed: one dozen eight-ounce jars of rubber cement. Such was the stuff of his existence.

The colonel's entire card catalog system, over nineteen thousand entries ordered from the oldest to the latest, rested on four collapsible tables shoved against the wall either side of Skip's bathroom door, over nineteen thousand three-by-five cards in a dozen narrow wooden drawers fashioned, the colonel had told him, in the physical plant facilities at the government's Seafront compound in Manila. On the floor beneath the tables waited seven thirty-pound boxes of blank cards and two boxes full of thousands of eight-by-eleven photocopies, the same nineteen-thousand-card system in duplicate, four cards to a page. Skip's main job, his basic task at this phase of his life, his purpose here in this big bedroom

beside the tiny golf course, was to create a second catalog
arranged by categories the colonel had devised, and then cross-
reference the two. Sands had no secretary, no help—this was the
colonel's private intelligence library, his cache, his hidey-hole. He
claimed to have accomplished all the photocopying by himself,
claimed Skip was the only other person to have touched these
mysteries.

The large guillotine-like paper cutter and the long, long ranks
of the jars of glue. And the dozen card drawers, sturdy three-foot-
long troughs like those in libraries, each with four digits stenciled
across its face—

2242

—the colonel's lucky number: February 2, 1942, the date of his
escape from the hands of the Japanese.

He heard the colonel telling a story. His roar carried through
the house while the others laughed. Sands felt in his uncle's presence a shameful and girlish despair. How would he evolve into
anyone as clear, as emphatic, as Colonel Francis Sands? Quite
early on he'd recognized himself as weak and impressionable and
had determined to find good heroes. John F. Kennedy had been
one. Lincoln, Socrates, Marcus Aurelius . . . The colonel's smile
as he'd examined the gun—had the colonel known beforehand
Skip was to receive this weapon? Sometimes the colonel had a
way of smiling—irritating to Skip—a knowing play of his lips.

Long before he'd followed his uncle into intelligence—in fact,
before the existence of the CIA—as a child, Skip had made of
Francis Sands a personal legend. Francis lifted weights, he boxed,
played football. A flier, a warrior, a spy.

In Bloomington that day nine years ago, the recruiter had
asked, "Why do you want to join the Agency?"

"Because my uncle says he wants me as a colleague."

The recruiter didn't blink. As if he'd expected the response.
"And who's your uncle?"

"Francis Sands."

Now the man blinked. "Not the colonel?"

"Yes. In the war he was a colonel."

The second man said, "Once a colonel, always a colonel."

He'd been a freshman then, eighteen years old. This move to Indiana University had been his first relocation since 1942, when, following his father's death on the *Arizona* at Pearl Harbor, his newly widowed mother had brought him from San Diego, California, back to the plains of her beginnings, to Clements, Kansas, to spend the rest of his childhood with her in the quiet house, in the sadness that didn't know what it was. She'd brought him home to Clements in early February, in precisely the month that her brother-in-law Francis Xavier, the captured Flying Tiger, made his escape over the side of a Japanese prisoner-of-war ship and into the China Sea.

On graduation Skip had accepted employment with the CIA, but even before training was returned to school to get a master's in comparative literature at George Washington University, where he helped Nationalist Chinese exiles with their translations of essays, stories, and verse from the Communist mainland. The handful of journals publishing such pieces were funded almost entirely by the CIA. He got a monthly stipend from the World Literature Foundation, a CIA front.

At the mention of his uncle that day in 1955, both recruiters had smiled, and Skip smiled too, but only because they smiled. The second man said, "If you're interested in a career with us, I think we can accommodate you."

They'd certainly done so. And here before him stretched that career: nineteen thousand notes from interviews, almost none of them comprehensible to him—

Duval, Jacques (?), owner 4 fishing boats (helios, souvenir, devinette, renard). [*Da Nang Gulf*], wife [*Tran* Lu (Luu??)] inf st boats poss criminal/intel use. Make no profit fishing. CXR

—the last three letters designating the interrogator who'd made the entry. Skip had taken to adding notes of his own, quotations from his heroes—"Ask not what your country can do for you . . ."—on cards marked JFK, LINC, SOC, the thickest batch from the *Meditations* of Marcus Aurelius, messages the old Roman emperor, besieged and lonely at the edges of his empire, had written to himself in the second century after Christ:

> Nothing can be good for a man unless it helps to make him just, self-disciplined, courageous, and independent; and nothing bad unless it has the contrary effect. MAM

As Skip approached the dining room, Pitchfork seemed to be hollering, "Hear, hear!"

They'd already been served a course of fish and rice. Skip took his place before an empty plate at the colonel's left elbow, and the houseboy brought him his portion. They ate by the dim light from candelabras. When the power failed it hardly changed the atmosphere. The hum of air conditioners ceased in the wings, the fan in the parlor ceiling stopped its muttering and revolving.

Meanwhile, the colonel held forth, his fork mostly in the air, one hand gripping his tumbler as if pinning it to the table. He spoke in a Boston Irish accent overlaid by years on air force bases in Texas and Georgia. "Lansdale's one true goal is to know the people, to learn from them. His efforts amount to art."

"Hear, hear!" cried Pitchfork. "Completely irrelevant, but hear, hear!"

"Edward Lansdale is an exemplary human being," the colonel said. "I say it without blushing."

"And what has Lansdale got to do with the aswang or any of our other legends?" Eddie said.

"Let me say it again, and maybe you'll hear me this time," the colonel said. "Edward Lansdale's overriding fascination is with the people themselves, with their songs, their stories, their legends.

Whatever comes out of that fascination in the way of *intelligence*—
do you get it?—it's all by-product. God, that fish was skinny. Sebastian, where's my little fish? Where did it go? Hey—are you giving
him my fish?" The houseboy Sebastian at that very moment was
offering Skip a second go at the platter of bangos. Skip knew this to
be the colonel's favorite. Had even the cook been warned of this
visit? "Okay, I've landed a whale," the colonel said, taking another
helping. "I'll postpone telling you my story about the aswang."

Sebastian, unbidden, forked yet a third fish onto the colonel's
plate and headed for the kitchen, laughing to himself. Back there
the staff talked loudly, happily. Around the colonel and his kidding, Filipinos grew giddy. His obvious affection for them had a
way of driving them nuts. Eddie too. He'd unbuttoned his tunic
and switched from ice water to Chardonnay. Skip could see the
evening ending with phonograph records littering the polished
floor and everybody doing the Limbo Rock, falling on their asses.
Suddenly Eddie said, "I knew Ed Lansdale! I worked with him
extensively!"

Had he? Eddie? Skip didn't see how this could be true.

"Anders," Skip asked Pitchfork, "what is the scientific name of
this fish?"

"The bangos? It's called milkfish. It spawns upriver, but lives in
the sea. Chanos salmoneus."

Eddie said, "Pitchfork speaks several languages."

The bangos were tasty, troutlike, not at all fishy. AID had
helped put in a hatchery at the bottom of the mountain. The colonel ate steadily and carefully, stripping the morsels of flesh from
the tiny bones with his fork and washing them down with several
whiskeys during the meal. His habits hadn't changed: after five
each evening he drank voluminously and without apology. The
family's not-quite-articulated assumption was that the Irish drank,
but drinking before five was undisciplined and decadent, and
patrician. "Tell us about the aswang. Give us a tall tale," he said to
Eddie.

"Well, all right," Eddie agreed, once again assuming, Skip believed, some of the character of his Henry Higgins, "let's see; once upon a time, which is how these things begin, there lived a brother and sister with their mother, who was in fact a widow following the death of the father in a tragic accident of some kind, I'm sorry I don't remember what kind, but I'm sure it was heroic. I'm sorry you didn't give me a warning to consult with my grandmother! But in any case I'll try to remember the tale. Two young children, a brother and sister, and now I apologize once more, because it was a pair of orphans, both their parents had been killed, and it was not after all their mother, but their mother's old aunt who was caring for them in a hut some distance from one of our villages in Luzon. Perhaps our own village of San Marcos, I'm certainly not ruling that out. The boy was strong and brave, the young girl was beautiful and kind. The great-aunt was—well, you can predict, I'm sure—she liked to torment the two fine children with too many tasks, too much harsh language, and blows with a broom to get them to hurry up. The brother and sister obeyed her without complaining, because in fact they were quite dutiful.

"The village had been happy a long time, but lately a curse had fallen, and a bloodthirsty aswang fed on the lambs, also upon the young goats, and worst of all it fed on the little children, and especially on the young girls like the sister. Sometimes the aswang was seen as an old woman, sometimes in the form of a gigantic boar with savage tusks, sometimes even as a lovely young child to lure the little ones into the shadows and suck their innocent blood. The people of the region were terrified, they failed to smile anymore, they stayed in the houses at night near their candles, they never went to the forest, to the jungle, to gather the avocados or any beneficial plants, or to hunt for meat. They gathered in the chapel of the village each afternoon to pray for the death of the aswang, but nothing helped, and, even, they were sometimes suddenly taken in a bloody murder while walking home from these prayers.

"Well, in the manner of these things, a saint appeared to the brother and sister, Saint Gabriel in the rags of a wanderer one day coming along in the jungle. He met the children at the well when they came to get some water, and he gave the boy a bow and a sack of arrows—what do you call that sack?"

"A quiver," Pitchfork said.

"A quiver of arrows. That's rather a beautiful phrase. He gave the lad a quiver of arrows and a very strong bow and charged him to stay all night in the granary at the bottom of the path, because there he would slay the aswang. Many cats gathered in the granary at night, one of whom was in fact the aswang, who assumed this form in order to camouflage. 'But, sir, how will I know the aswang, because you haven't given me arrows to shoot every cat?' And Saint Gabriel said, 'The aswang will not play with its rat when it catches one, it only tears the rat in pieces instantly and revels in its blood. When you see a cat do that, you must shoot him right away, because that one is the aswang. Of course, if you fail, I don't have to inform you you're going to feel yourself being torn apart by the fangs of the aswang, and it will drink your blood as you die.'

"'I am not afraid,' the boy said, 'because I know you are Saint Gabriel in a disguise. I am not afraid, and with the help of the saints, I won't fail.'

"When the boy returned to his home with these arrows and such, the aunt of his dead and departed mother was refusing to let him go out. She said he must sleep in his bed every night. She attacked him with her broom and confiscated his weapons and hid them in the thatch of the hut. But for the first time, the boy disobeyed his guardian and stole them back that night, and crept away to the granary with one candle, and waited in the shadows of the place, and I will assure you they were very eerie shadows! And silhouettes of rats scurrying among the shadows. And silhouettes of cats creeping everywhere, about three dozen. Which one would be the aswang? Let me just tell you that a pair of fangs glowed red in the night, the hiss of an aswang was heard, then the cry, and as a horrible visage leapt at his throat, the boy loosed an arrow and heard a thump when the creature fell back, and then a strangled moaning came, and then he heard the claws scraping as the wounded fiend dragged itself to protection somewhere. Surveying the scene, the young hero found the severed leg of a giant cat with deadly claws, the left foreleg, and his arrow was lodged through and through it.

"The young hero returned home, and his ugly old guardian scolded him. His sister was also awake. Great-Aunt served them tea and some rice. 'Where did you go, brother?' 'I fought the aswang, sister, and I think I wounded it.' And sister said, 'Beloved Aunt, you too were absent in the night. Where were you?'

"'I?' said the beloved aunt. 'No, I was here with you all night.' But she served the tea quickly, and made her excuses to go lie down.

"Later that day the two children found the old woman hanging by her neck from the tree outside. Beneath her the blood pooled, dripping from the place where she was missing her left arm. Earlier, as she poured the tea, she had kept from them beneath her robe the sight of her severed arm, dripping her life's blood, the poisonous blood of the aswang.

"It's an old story," Eddie said. "I've heard it many times. But the people believe it will happen, and now they believe it happened here, yesterday, this week. My God," he said, pouring himself more Chardonnay, shaking the bottle upside down over his glass while his small audience applauded, "have I sat here talking and drinking an entire bottle?"

The colonel was already turning the screw in another cork. "You've got Irish in you, fella." He raised a toast: "Today is the birthday of Commodore Anders Pitchfork. Salud!"

"Commodore?" Eddie said. "You're joking!"

"I'm joking about the rank. But not about the birthday. Pitchfork: Can you remember where you were on your birthday twenty-four years ago?"

Pitchfork said, "Exactly twenty-four years ago I was swinging under a parachute on a very dark night, dropping into China. I didn't even know the name of the province. And who was flying that plane I'd just jumped out of? Who was it gave me a half dozen candy bars and kicked me out into the sky? And headed back to a comfy bunk!"

"And who never made it because the bastards shot me down? And who was it you gave a hard-boiled egg in a POW camp twenty days later?"

Pitchfork pointed at the colonel. "Not because I'm generous. Because it was the poor feller's birthday."

Eddie's mouth was open. "You survived the Jap camp?"

The colonel shoved his chair back and wiped at his face with his napkin. He perspired, he blinked. "Having been a dishonored guest of the Japanese . . . how to put it . . . I know what it means to be a prisoner. Let me rephrase that—let me rephrase that—give me a minute and let me rephrase that . . ." He stared dully from under, at Skip in particular, while Skip developed the uncomfortable notion that the colonel had forgotten himself and would now deliriously change the subject.

"The Japanese," Sands prompted him, lacking the strength not to.

The colonel sat shoved away from his dinner, his knees splayed, his right hand gripping his drink and set on his thigh, his back absolutely straight, and the sweat charging down his crimson face. This is a great man, Sands announced to himself. Distinctly but silently he said it: A person of tortured greatness. At such a moment he couldn't help dramatizing because it was all too wonderful.

"They were short on cigars," the colonel said. His rigid forbearing demeanor inspired awe, but not necessarily confidence. He was drunk, after all. And so sweaty they might have been viewing him through broken glass. But a warrior.

Sands found himself speaking inwardly again: Wherever this journey takes us, I will follow.

Pitchfork said, "In that war, I knew precisely who to hate. We were the guerrillas. We were the Huks. And that's who we need to be to beat the bastards in Vietnam. Lansdale proves it, if you ask me. We need to be the guerrillas."

"I'll tell you who I think we need to be," the colonel said. "I'll tell you what Ed Lansdale's learned to become: aswang. That's what Ed Lansdale is. Aswang. Yes. I'm going to take two breaths, get sober, and tell you." He did draw a breath, but cut it short to tell Pitchfork, "No, no—don't go hollering hear, hear."

Eddie shouted. "Hear, hear!"

"All right, this is my aswang story: In the hills there above Angeles, up there above Clark Air Base, Lansdale had the Filipino commandos he worked with kidnap two Huk guerrillas right off one of their patrols, took the two boys at the tail end of the group. Strangled them, strung them up by the legs, drained the blood out of each one"—the colonel put two fingers to his own neck— "through two punctures in the jugular. Left the corpses on the path for the comrades to find the next day. Which they did . . . And the day after that, the Huks cleared out of there entirely."

"Hear, hear!" said Pitchfork.

"Now. Just let's consider for a minute," the colonel suggested. "Didn't these Huks live in the shadow of death anyhow? Lansdale and his strike force were killing them off in small engagements at the rate of half a dozen per month, let's say. If the threat of their daily pursuers couldn't impress them, what was it about the death of these two boys that ran them out of Angeles?"

"Well, it's superstitious fear. Fear of the unknown," Eddie said.

"Unknown what? I say we look at it in terms we can utilize," the colonel said. "I say they found themselves engaged at the level of myth. War is ninety percent myth anyway, isn't it? In order to prosecute our own wars we raise them to the level of human sacrifice, don't we, and we constantly invoke our God. It's got to be about something bigger than dying, or we'd all turn deserter. I think we need to be much more conscious of that. I think we need to be invoking the other fellow's gods too. And his devils, his aswang. He's more scared of his gods and his devils and his aswang than he'll ever be of us."

"I think that's your cue to say, 'Hear, hear!'" Eddie said to Pitchfork. But Pitchfork only finished his wine.

"Colonel, did you just come from Saigon?" Eddie asked.

"Nope. Mindanao. I was down in Davao City. And Zamboanga. And over by this place Damulog, little jungle town— you've been there, haven't you?"

"A couple of times, yes. To Mindanao."

"Damulog?"

"No. It doesn't sound familiar."

"I'm surprised to hear that," the colonel said.

Eddie said, "Why would you be surprised?"

"When it comes to certain aspects of Mindanao, I was told you were the man to talk to."

Eddie said, "I'm sorry, I can't help you."

The colonel swiped at Skip's face with his napkin—"What's this?"

Eddie said, "Ah! The first to mention the mustache! Yes, he's turning himself into Wyatt Earp." Eddie himself sported one, the young Filipino's kind, widely spaced black hairs sketching where a mustache might go were one possible.

"A man with a mustache has to have some special talent," the colonel said, "a special skill, something to exonerate his vanity. Archery, card tricks, what—"

"Palindromes," said Anders Pitchfork.

Sebastian appeared, with an announcement: "Ice cream for dessert. We must eat it all, or it's melting without any power."

"We?" The colonel said.

"Perhaps if you don't finish, we will have to finish in the kitchen."

"No dessert for me. I'm feeding my vices," the colonel said.

"Oh, for goodness' sake!" Eddie said. "For a minute I forgot what is a palindrome. Palindromes! Yes!"

The lights came on, the air conditioners labored to life here and there in the building. "Eat that ice cream anyway," the colonel told Sebastian.

Following dinner they adjourned to the patio for brandy and cigars and listened to the electronic bug-destroyer and talked about the thing they'd avoided talking about all through dinner, the thing everybody talked about eventually, every day.

"My God, I tell you," Eddie said, "in Manila we got the news around three in the morning. By dawn everybody knew. Not even by radio, but from heart to heart. Filipinos poured into the streets of Manila and wept."

The colonel said, "Our *President*. The President of the United *States*. It's bad stuff. It's just bad stuff."

"They wept as for a great saint."

"He was a beautiful man," the colonel said. "That's why we killed him."

"We?"

"The dividing line between light and dark goes through the center of every heart. Every soul. There isn't one of us who isn't guilty of his death."

"This is sounding—" Skip didn't want to say it. Religious. But he said it. "This is sounding religious."

The colonel said, "I'm religious about my cigars. Otherwise . . . religion? No. It's more than religion. It's the goddamn truth. Whatever's good, whatever's beautiful, we pounce, and whap! See those poor critters?" He pointed at the wires of the bug-killing device, where insects crashed and flared briefly. "The Buddhists would never waste electricity like that. Do you know what 'karma' is?"

"Now you're getting religious again."

"By God, I am. I'm saying it's all inside us, the whole war. It *is* religion, isn't it?"

"What war are you talking about? The Cold War?"

"This isn't a Cold War, Skip. It's World War Three." The colonel paused to shape his cigar's ember on the bottom of his shoe. Eddie and Pitchfork said nothing, only stared at the darkness—drunk, or

exhausted by the colonel's intensity, Skip couldn't guess which—
while the colonel, predictably, had surfaced clear-eyed from the
cloud he'd seemed lost in earlier. But Skip was family; he had to
show himself equal to this. To what? To scaling that social Mount
Everest: an evening of dinner and drinks with Colonel Francis X.
Sands. In preparation for the ascent, he took himself to the sideboard.

"Where are you going?"

"I'm just pouring myself a brandy. If it's World War Three, I'd
better have some of the good stuff."

"We're in a worldwide war, have been for close to twenty years.
I don't think Korea sufficiently demonstrated that for us, or anyway our vision wasn't equal to the evidence. But since the Hun-
garian uprising, we've been willing to grapple with the realities of
it. It's a covert World War Three. It's Armageddon by proxy. It's a
contest between good and evil, and its true ground is the heart of
every human. I'm going to transgress outside the line a little bit
now. I'm going to tell you, Skip: sometimes I wonder if it isn't the
goddamn Alamo. This is a fallen world. Every time we turn
around there's somebody else going Red."

"But it's not just a contest between good and evil," Skip said.
"It's between nuts and not nuts. All we have to do is hang on until
Communism collapses under the weight of its own economic silli-
ness. The weight of its own insanity."

"The Commies may be out of their minds," the colonel said,
"but they aren't irrational. They believe in central command and
in the unthinkable sacrifice. I'm afraid," the colonel said, and
swallowed from his snifter; the hesitation made it seem the end of
his statement: that he was afraid . . . He cleared his throat and
said, "I'm afraid it makes the Communists uncontainable."

This kind of talk embarrassed Sands. It had no credit with
him. He'd found joy and seen the truth here in a jungle where the
sacrifices had bled away the false faith and the center of command
had rotted, where Communism had died. They'd wiped out the

Huks here on Luzon, and eventually they'd wipe out every one of them, all the Communists on earth. "Remember the missiles in Cuba? Kennedy stood up to them. The United States of America stood up to the Soviets and backed them down."

"At the Bay of Pigs he turned tail and left a lot of good men dying in the dirt—No, no, no, don't get me wrong, Skip. I'm a Kennedy man, and I'm a patriot. I believe in liberty and justice for all. I'm not sophisticated enough to be ashamed of that. But that doesn't mean I look at my country through some kind of rosy fog. I'm in Intelligence. I'm after the truth."

Pitchfork spoke from the dark: "I knew a lot of good Chinese in Burma. We laid down our lives for each other. Some of those same folks are now good Communists. I look forward to seeing them shot."

"Anders, are you sober?"

"Slightly."

"God," Skip said, "I wish he hadn't died! How did it happen? Where do we go from here? And when do we get through one day where we don't say these things over and over?"

"I don't know if you know it, Skip, but there's an element on the Hill thinks we did this. Us. Our bunch. In particular, the good friends of Cuba have come under scrutiny, the folks who ran the Bay of Pigs. Then we have the investigation, the commission, Earl Warren and Russell and the others—Dulles was on it, working to keep any suspicion away. Worked very hard at it. Made us look guilty as hell."

Eddie lurched upright. His face was a shadow, but he seemed unwell. "I can't think of one single palindrome," he announced. "I'll take my leave."

"You're feeling all right?"

"I need to drive the roads with some air in my lungs."

"Give him air," the colonel said.

"I'll walk you to the car"—but Skip felt the colonel's hand on his arm.

"Not at all," Eddie said, and soon they heard his Mercedes start up on the other side of the house.

Silence. Night. Not silence—the dark screeching insect conflagration of the jungle.

"Well," the colonel said, "I didn't think I'd get anything out of old Eddie. I don't know what they're up to. And why does he say he worked extensively with Ed Lansdale? He wasn't out of short-pants around Lansdale's time. In '52 he must've been a tiny babe."

"Oh, well," Sands said, thinking that when passion stirred Major Eddie's heart, he tended to speak in a kind of poetry—you wouldn't do it justice to call it lying.

"How have you been keeping yourself busy?"

"Riding around at night with Aguinaldo. And familiarizing myself with the card catalog, as instructed. In the horrible manner instructed. Clipping and gluing."

"All right. Very good, sir. Any questions?"

"Yeah: Why do the files make no reference to this region what-soever?"

"Because they weren't compiled here. Obviously they're from Saigon. And its environs. And a bunch from Mindanao, which I inherited. Yes, I am the section officer for Mindanao, which has no section. Anything you need?"

"I'm stacking the duplicates back in the boxes after I get them down to size. I'll need more of those drawers."

The colonel grabbed the seat of his chair between his legs and drew himself close to Skip. "Just use the cardboard boxes, okay? We're going to ship them out soon." Again he seemed taken by drink, his gaze was vague, and probably, if it could be seen, his nose was red, a reaction to liquor featured by all the men on his side of the family; but he was brisk and certain in his speech. "Other questions?"

"Who is this German? If that's what he is."

"The German? He's Eddie's man."

"Eddie's man? We had lunch with him today and Eddie didn't seem to know him at all."

"Well, if he's not Eddie's man I don't know whose man he could possibly be. But he ain't mine."

"Eddie said you'd met with him."

"Eddie Aguinaldo," the colonel said, "is the Filipino equivalent of a goddamn liar. Any other questions?"

"Yeah: Anders, what are these little dabs of mud on the walls?"

"Beg pardon?"

"These little pocks of mud? Do they have something to do with insects? Aren't you an entomologist?"

Pitchfork, waking from his nap, took a meditative taste of his brandy. "I'm more about mosquitoes in particular."

"The deadlier pests," the colonel said.

"I'm rather more about draining swamps," Pitchfork said.

"Anders has been giving me a very good report on you. Positively bragging on you," the colonel said.

"He's a good lad. He's got the right kind of curiosity," Pitchfork said.

"Have any of our bunch in Manila contacted you?"

"No. Unless you call Pitchfork basically living here a form of contact."

"Pitchfork isn't with our bunch."

"Then what is he?"

"I'm a poisoner," Pitchfork said.

"Anders is actually and honorably employed by the Del Monte Corporation. They contribute plenty to malaria eradication."

"I'm all about DDT and swamp recovery. But I don't know what sort of organism might make the little mud dabs."

Colonel Francis Sands tipped back his head and poured half a snifter down his spout, blinked against the dark, coughed, and said, "Your own dad—my own brother—lost his life in that sleazy Jap run on Pearl Harbor. And who were our allies in that war?"

"The Soviets."

"And who's the enemy tonight?"

Skip knew the script: "The Soviets. And who's our ally? The sleazy Japs."

"And who," said Pitchfork, "was I fighting in the Malay jungle in '51 and '52? The same Chinese guerrillas who helped us with the Burma business in '40 and '41."

The colonel said, "We've got to keep hold of our ideals while steering them though the maze. I should say through the obstacle course. An obstacle course of hard-as-hell realities."

Skip said, "Hear, hear!" He disliked it when his uncle dramatized the obvious.

"Survival is the foundation of triumph," Pitchfork said.

"Who's on first?" the colonel asked.

"But in the end," Pitchfork said, "it's either liberty or death."

The colonel raised his empty glass to Pitchfork. "At Forty Kilo, Anders manned a little crystal radio set for seven months. To this day he won't tell me where he kept it hid. There were at least a dozen little Jap sonsabitches in that camp did nothing but think how to locate that contraption day and night." Forty Kilo had been the Burmese railroad outpost where their work gang had been interned by the Japanese in 1941. "We used coconut shells for rice bowls," he said. "Everybody had his own coconut shell." He reached out and clutched his nephew's wrist.

"Uh-oh," said Skip, "am I losing you?"

The colonel stared. "Uh."

He leapt to bring his uncle back: "Colonel, the file catalog goes back to Saigon at some point, am I right?"

The colonel peered at him in the dark, moving slightly, making many tiny adjustments in his posture, as if balancing his head on his neck. Apparently as a kind of focal exercise he examined his cigar stub, trying it at various distances, and seemed to rally, and sat up straighter.

Sands said, "I've been working on my French. Get me assigned to Vietnam."

"How's your Vietnamese?"

"I'd need to brush up."

"You don't know a single word."

"I'll learn. Send me to the language school in California."

"Nobody wants Saigon."

"I do. Set me up in an office over there. I'll look after your card files. Appoint me your curator."

"Talk to my ass; my head aches."

"I'll make every little datum accessible and retrievable—you'll just comb through with these two fingers and zip-zip, sir, whatever you want pops up at you."

"Are you so in love with the files? Have you fallen under the spell of rubber cement?"

"We're going to beat them. I want to be there for that."

"Nobody wants to go to Saigon. You want Taiwan."

"Colonel, with the very deepest respect, sir, what you implied before is completely mistaken. We're going to beat them."

"I didn't mean we don't beat them, Skip. I meant we don't beat them automatically."

"I realize that. I expect them to be worthy of us."

"Aaaah—despite all my best efforts, you're one of these new boys. You're a different breed."

"Send me to Vietnam."

"Taiwan. Where the living's good and you meet all the people on their way up. Or Manila. Manila is number two, I'd say."

"My French is improving. I'm reading well, always did. Send me to the language school and I'll land in Saigon talking like a native."

"Come on. Saigon's a revolving door, everybody's in and out."

"I need rubber bands. Big long thick ones. I want to batch your cards by regions until you get me some more drawers. And more card tables. Give me a room and two clerks in Saigon. I'll write you an encyclopedia."

The colonel chuckled, low, wheezing—sarcastic, histrionic—but Skip knew it for a happy sign. "All right, Will. I'll send you to the school, we'll work that out. But first I need you to go on assignment for me. Mindanao. I've got an individual down there I want more on. Would you mind poking around Mindanao a little bit?"

Sands vanquished a rush of fear and said emphatically, "I'm your man, sir."

"Get in there. Have intercourse with snakes. Eat human flesh. Learn everything."

"That's pretty broad."

"There's a man named Carignan down there, a priest, he's been there for decades and decades. Father Thomas Carignan. You'll find him in the files. Familiarize yourself with the stuff on this guy named Carignan. American citizen off in the boonies there, a padre. He's receiving arms or such."

"What does that mean?"

"Well, I don't know what it means. That's the phraseology. Receiving guns. I've got nothing elaborated."

"And then what?"

"Off you go. See the man. Looks like we're gonna finalize the file."

"Finalize?"

"We're laying the ground for it. Those are the orders."

" 'Finalize' seems . . ." He couldn't quite finish.

"Seems?"

"This sounds to be about more than files."

"It'll be months before any decisions. Meanwhile, we want things in place. If it's a go, that's not us. You are there only to report to me. You'll transmit the report through the VOA station there on Mindanao."

"And then I'm your cataloger in Vietnam?"

"Vietnam. Better ship your M1 home to Mama. We don't issue that ammo anymore."

"Shit. I think I'll have another brandy."

The colonel held out his glass while Skip poured. "A toast— but not to Vietnam. To Alaska. Yowza!"

Anders and Skip raised their drinks.

"This is a happy coincidence. Because I wanted to give you a little task, and I think if your conduct in the field is as exemplary

as I'd predict for you, then I'll have every reason to get you reas-
signed."

"Are you playing me? Have you been playing me all night?"

"All night?"

"No. Not all night. Since—"

"Since when, Skip?" He drew on his cigar so his fat face
bloomed orange in the darkness.

"You're a vaudevillian."

"Playing you?"

"Since I was twelve."

The colonel said, "I went to Alaska once, you know. I toured
the Alaska-Canada road they built there during the war. Fantastic.
Not the road, the landscape. The mighty road was just this insignificant little scratch across that landscape. You've never seen a world
like that. It belongs to the God who was God before the Bible . . .
God before he woke up and saw himself . . . God who was his own
nightmare. There is no forgiveness there. You make one tiny mistake and that landscape grinds you into a bloody smudge, and I do
mean right now, sir." He looked red-eyed around himself, as if he
only halfway recognized his environment. Sands willed himself
not to be too disconcerted. "I met a lady who'd lived there for quite
some years—later, that is, just last Christmas is when I had the
pleasure. An elderly woman now, she spent her youth and most of
middle age near the Yukon River. I got to talking about Alaska, and
she had only one comment. She said: 'It is godforsaken.'

"You poor, overly polite sonsabitches. I read your silence as
respect. I appreciate it too. Would you like me to get to the point?

"The lady's remark set me thinking. We'd both had the same
experience of the place: Here was something more than just an
alien environment. We'd both sensed the administration of an
alien God.

"Only a few days before that, couple of days before at the most,
really, I'd been reading in my New Testament. My little girl gave it
to me. I've got it right now in my kit." The colonel half rose, sat

back down. "But I'll spare you. The point is—aha! yes! the bastard
has a point and isn't too damn drunk to bring it home—this is the
point, Will." Nobody else ever called him Will. "St. Paul says
there is one God, he confirms that, but he says, 'There is one God,
and many administrations.' I understand that to mean you can
wander out of one universe and into another just by pointing your
feet and forward march. I mean you can come to a land where the
fate of human beings is completely different from what you understood it to be. And this utterly different universe is administered
through the earth itself. Up through the dirt, goddamn it.

"So what's the point? The point is Vietnam. The point is Vietnam. The point is Vietnam."

In late September Sands took the train from the town at the bottom of the mountain into Manila. It was hot. He sat by an open
window. Vendors came aboard at stops with sliced mango and
pineapple, with cigarettes and gum for sale as singles, from open
packs. A small boy tried to sell him a one-inch-square snapshot of
what it took him a long time to understand was a woman's naked
groin, very close up.

As instructed, he would neither appear at the embassy nor contact anybody in Manila concerning his assignment. He might have
looked up the major, but he'd been specifically cautioned to steer
clear of Eduardo Aguinaldo. But the officer's club at the Seafront
compound hadn't been forbidden him, and they served the best
pork chops he'd ever tasted. At the station in Manila he barged rapidly through the horde of beggars and hustlers, right hand clutching his wallet in his pants pocket, and rode to the compound on
Dewey Boulevard in a taxi that smelled strongly of gasoline.

At the air-conditioned Seafront club he could look out the
southern window at the sun descending into Manila Bay or across
the room out the northern window at the swimming pool. Two
solid-looking men, probably marine guards from the embassy,
practiced trick dives from the board, somersaults, back flips. A

black-haired American woman in a tawny, leopard-spotted two-piece shocked him. It was practically a French bikini. She spoke to her teenage son, who sat on a deck chair's extension staring at his feet. She wasn't young, but she was fabulous. All the other women at the pool wore full one-piece suits. Skip was afraid of women. The pork chops came, succulent, moist. He didn't know enough about cooking even to guess at the trick for coming up with pork chops like this.

Leaving, he bought a flat pack of Benson & Hedges cigarettes from the display at the cashier's counter, though he didn't smoke. He liked to give them away.

He waited for a cab just outside the club, stood in the late light looking over the wide grounds, the jacarandas and acacias, the spike-topped wall, and, at the compound's entrance, the American flag. At the sight of the flag he tasted tears in his throat. In the Stars and Stripes all the passions of his life coalesced to produce the ache with which he loved the United States of America—with which he loved the dirty, plain, honest faces of GIs in the photographs of World War Two, with which he loved the sheets of rain rippling across the green playing field toward the end of the school year, with which he cherished the sense-memories of the summers of his childhood, the many Kansas summers, running the bases, falling harmlessly onto the grass, his head beating with heat, the stunned streets of breezeless afternoons, the thick, palpable shade of colossal elms, the muttering of radios beyond the windowsills, the whirring of redwing blackbirds, the sadness of the grown-ups at their incomprehensible pursuits, the voices carrying over the yards in the dusks that fell later and later, the trains moving through town into the sky. His love for his country, his homeland, was a love for the United States of America in the summertime.

The flag rolled in the salty breeze, and beyond it the sun soon sank. He'd never seen in nature anything as explosively crimson as these sunsets on Manila Bay. The dying light charged the water and low clouds with a terrifying vitality. A shabby taxi stopped in front of him, two carefully nondescript young men of the Foreign Service got out of its backseat, and the anonymous young man from the Intelligence Service took their place.

Carignan woke after a sweaty dream that felt like a nightmare, left him shaking, but what of the dream should frighten? Dream, or visit: a figure, a monk with a pale region where his face should have been, telling him, "Your body is the twig that ignites the passion between your love of Jesus and the grace of God." He'd drifted so far from English that certain of the phrases felt erased even as he turned them over in his mind and tried them with his lips—passion, ignite. Years since he'd so much as whispered words like that. And it surprised him that he should dream about grace or Jesus Christ because it had been many years too since he'd let such things trouble him.

The loneliness of my own life—Judas's solitary journey home.

He rose from his bed in the corner of the mildewed church, walked to the pale brown river with an ingot of pale brown soap. Two little boys stared at him as they fished with hand lines from the broad back of a carabao, the local domesticated water buffalo. A second such beast nearby wallowed deep in a mud hole beside the bank, only its nostrils visible, and some of its horn. Wearing his zoris and underclothes, shoving the soap beneath his garments, Carignan bathed briskly, lest the leeches take hold.

By the time he'd returned and changed into clean undershorts, put on khakis and a T-shirt, affixed his collar, Pilar had some tea going.

The priest sat on a stump beside a wobbly table under a palm tree and smoked the day's first cigarette and sipped from a china cup. He told Pilar, "I'll go to see the Damulog mayor today. Mayor Luis."

"All the way to Damulog?"

"No. We'll both go to Basig, and we'll meet."

"Today?"

"He says today."

"Who told you?"

"The Basig datu."

"All right. I'll take everything to my sister's and do the washing there."

"No services until Sunday morning." He only had to tell Pilar, and everyone would know.

"All right."

"We'll meet with three other datus. It's because of the missionary—do you remember the one who disappeared?"

"Damulog missionary."

"They think he's been found."

"Hurt?"

"Dead. If he's the one."

Pilar crossed herself. She was middle-aged, a widow, with many relatives, both Muslim and Catholic, and took good care of him.

He said, "Please bring my tennis shoes."

A gray day, but he wore his straw hat as he hiked the ten kilometers down the red earthen road to Basig. The wind came up, the stalks shook and shuddered, also the palms, also the houses. An infestation of tiny black beetles numerous as raindrops roamed the gusts and sailed past. Children playing on the paths whooped when they saw him and ran away. In Basig he made for the market square, speculating as always that life would improve if he lived it here in a town. But the town was Muslim, and they wouldn't have a church in it.

Before he reached the market the Basig datu and the two datus from Tanday, a village in the hills—men nearly sixty, all three of them, in ragged jeans or khakis, in conical hats like his own, one bearing a long spear—joined him on either side, and now in the safety of town the children cried softly from the shade of thatched awnings, "Pa-dair, Pa-dair"—Father, Father . . . The four men marched together into the café to kill time before the arrival of Mayor Luis. Carignan had rice with a dish of goat's meat, and instant coffee. The others had rice and squid.

Carignan bought a pack of Union cigarettes and got one going, and if these Muslims didn't like it, too bad. But they asked him for some, and they all four sat smoking.

Mayor Luis had sent word last week that the people in possession of the corpse and its effects had been told, already, what identifying features to look for. The datus had said they'd return as far as Basig with the verdict—was this the missing American missionary?—on Tuesday. Carignan believed today was already Thursday. It didn't matter.

The jeepney from Carmen arrived covered with passengers and shed them like a gigantic husk. The mayor from Damulog would be on it.

People walked by the café's door and past the windows and looked in, but nobody entered. A toothless drunken old man sat alone at another table and mumbled a song to himself. Quite different music came from out back, where a few kids squatted around a U.S. Army crank radio. The clearest station came from Cotabato. Months-old American pop tunes. They went for the hot beat or the sad ballads.

Petite and potbellied Mayor Luis of Damulog came into the café smiling, clapping his hands, behaving like his own entourage. He joined them and surveyed the scene, such as it was.

"Did you ask them?" he said in English.

"No."

Speaking Cebuano, Luis said to Saliling, the oldest, the man with the spear: "The people who found the dead man at the Pulangi River."

"Yes."

"We told them to look for the shoes. We sent a drawing. And the label of the shirt. We sent a drawing."

Saliling said, "They have only bones. And the ring from the finger."

"On his left hand? A gold ring?"

"They didn't say."

"This hand. The left hand."

"No. They didn't say."

"Did they look at the teeth? He has metal placed in his teeth. Did you tell them?" He jabbed his finger at his own mouth and asked Carignan, "Do you have? Can you show them?"

Carignan opened wide and jutted a view of his molars at the three datus, who seemed to enjoy this display.

"Did they find metal in the teeth?" the mayor asked.

Saliling said, "We will look for these kind of teeth. But there is a problem in our barangay we want to talk about."

"I am not the datu of your barangay. You are the datu. This is your position, not my position."

"Our schoolhouse needs repairs. The roof keeps out the sun, but not the rain."

"He wants money," the mayor said to Carignan in English.

"I can speak Cebuano," Carignan said.

"I know. I just like to talk when these Muslims can't understand. I am a Christian, sir. Seven Day. I am Seven Day. But we are all one family against these Muslims."

"This lost missionary is Seventh-Day too, isn't he?"

"Yes. It's very sad for the town of Damulog."

"Give the man fifty pesos."

"Do you think I have fifty pesos? I'm not rich!"

"Tell him you'll pay it later."

Luis said to Saliling, "How much to repair the school?"

"Two hundred."

"I can give twenty. Not now. Next week."

"The boards are expensive. At least one hundred fifty for the boards."

"I have boards in Damulog. If you need boards, I can give you boards."

"Some boards and some funds."

"Twenty-five in funds."

Saliling spoke with the others. Luis looked to Carignan, but the priest shook his head. He didn't recognize the dialect.

"Ten boards of at least ten feet," Saliling said in Cebuano. "The thick ones."

"Yes."

"How much will you give in funds?"

"Forty is the limit. I'm not pretending."

"Fifty."

"All right. Fifty pesos in funds, and ten thick boards. Next week."

The datus went into conference. The missus of the café arrived, a hunched, worried woman bringing two bread rolls for the priest, also a metal spoon, though he'd already eaten his meal with his fingers like the others. On the belief that white men liked bread, not rice, she always headed for the market for rolls when he appeared in town.

Saliling said, "It's fine if you wait for one week. Right now we have to travel back to Tanday, and then over the hills to the Pulangi River."

"They haven't gone yet to the river!" Luis said in English.

"I understand."

"These Muslim people are slow. They enjoy wasting our time."

The missionary had been missing since before the rainy season. This news of a corpse had come over a month ago.

The datu Saliling said, "We'll meet here in two weeks. Or we'll come to Damulog. We will bring an answer, and you will bring the lumber and the funds."

"Not two weeks—one week, please! Mrs. Jones is waiting. Poor Mrs. Jones!"

The men spoke in the other dialect among themselves. "No," the datu said, "it can't be done in a week. It's far and the people of the Pulangi River aren't trustworthy. They aren't Muslims. They aren't Christians. They have other gods."

Carignan felt bad for Mrs. Jones, the missionary's wife. He had a thought: "Maybe we can go along, and arrange to bring back the body to Damulog."

Luis said, "I'm willing to travel with you as far as Tanday, if we both go. As for crossing the Pulangi River—no. I don't want to die. I want to live long."

"All right."

"Will you go with them, Father?"

"Yes."

"By yourself?"

"If I'm with them, I'm not by myself."

They agreed: the datus would find Luis in Damulog in two weeks. Luis ordered a San Miguel. "I like the Catholic restaurants," he told his companions. "In our Seven Day we get no beer. It's not healthy." The missus urged on them some tidbits, meat from a large jar. Townspeople clustered either side of the café's doorway, staring with open mouths.

"I can get avocado," the missus told Carignan. "Come for lunch and I'll make you the avocado milkshake."

He had a bite of carabao meat tenderized in spices, incredibly gamy. He nodded his appreciation, and now they were bringing out a whole plate of it for him. It wasn't bad. But the aftertaste was too much like a carabao's smell. Voices from the throng at the door—"Pa-dair, Pa-dair, Pa-dair."

Judas went out and hanged himself.

"I will say a prayer for everyone," the priest called to them.

Saliling got to his feet and charged at the intruders. He stomped his bare foot, shook his spear. The group backed away a few paces.

The missus began striking the old drunk at the next table with her limp hand, yelling unintelligibly. He seemed oblivious.

"Hah, your followers want to confess," Luis said.

Judas threw himself from a high place and his belly broke on the stones. He wondered if these people, merely surviving, knew anything of guilt. The gnarled mahogany creatures hobbling here

to confess themselves. He left with the others, the datus shoving
the villagers aside. "I am going to pray. Everyone must pray. Pray
to the saints in Heaven."

He would go with the two datus to their barangay, called Tanday.
There was no jeep to Tanday and, after a point, no road. They
would walk. Carignan understood only that the people holding
the missionary's remains lived by the Pulangi River. How long a
journey to find them, he couldn't guess. The datus said twenty-
five kilometers, but it was silly of him to ask, because how could
they know? Out of courtesy they offered an estimate: two days'
hiking. The datus insisted they leave right away in order to make
Tanday by nightfall.

They walked together until noon, as far as Maginda. There the
datus accomplished the kindness of borrowing for him a horse, no
bigger than a pony, with a wooden saddle on its back. Preceded by
the three old men, the meager animal lurched beneath Carignan's weight for a few kilometers, to the bottom of the hill below
the barangay of Tanday, and then he had to get off and climb the
path behind it as the dark came down over the endless folds of the
low mountains.

The pathway up the hill was wide and in that respect easy,
hacked clear by the villagers, but it was steep, and he was winded.
He'd grown too old for adventures—how old? Sixty, almost. He
couldn't remember exactly. Halfway along they heard a low whistle, and a fourth escort joined them. "Good evening, Pa-dair," he
said in English. "I will accompany you." The young man identified himself as Robertson, a nephew of Saliling. Robertson's face
was invisible in the evening glow.

Thoughts of Judas, images, the monk, the dream, had come
back to him throughout the day. The monk in the dream with the
silver cloud for a face. Maybe he could find someone to interpret
it for him.

They made the crest and went to the schoolhouse for the
night. The men brought him a supper of sticky white rice and a

green plant they called hwai-an, and soon, because the night was black, there was nothing to do but turn in. He lay on his side on the wooden floor like the others, without a mat or cover. He couldn't sleep. The air smelled different from that of his bedroom by the stinking river near Basig, the schoolroom was stuffy, the huge leaves of banana plants crowded the windows, and even the lizards clucking in the eaves sounded foreign. Near midnight it started raining steadily, harder and harder, until the storm made as if to shatter the metal roof, drowning them first with sound, threatening to drown them very soon with water. The drops drove themselves through the seams of the corrugated sheets, and Carignan pulled two desks together and crawled underneath for protection. Villagers with even leakier roofs crept into the pitch-dark schoolroom until they must have made nearly two dozen. When the downpour quit, he could hear it roaring down off the hillside for hours.

He woke at dawn having scarcely slept and stepped out to relieve his bladder against the side of the schoolhouse. After the night of rain it was cool, without a breath of wind. At this hour the land seemed to lie open, ready to give up its secret.

What offering would I lay at the foot of the cross of the thief?

He passed gas, and some children peeking at him from around the corner pursed their lips and imitated the sound and laughed.

What consolation at the foot of his death?

Without preliminaries or farewells the three datus came out and resumed the journey. They carried nothing, so he carried nothing. Although they went barefoot, he wore his Keds.

They navigated a slick path downward to a long ridge and stumped along it toward another mountain. One edge of the world turned red and the sun came rolling over on them, burning away the vapors below and seeming to fashion from the mist itself a grander and more complicated vista full of hills and ravines and winking creeks and vegetation tinted not just the innumerable values of green, but also silver, black, purple. They stopped at a barangay of several huts on the adjoining hill and had native coffee and each a bowl of rice. Saliling spoke with the headman in the Bisayan dialect, and Carignan heard them discussing some gunfire they'd heard across the valley just this morning. "He has warned us of some fighting ahead," Robertson said, and Carignan said, "I heard him say it." They began hiking again.

They came down the other side of the mountain onto a wide, level trail beaten smooth by carabao hooves. Gradually the way narrowed until Carignan had to draw his arms to his chest in order to keep from being savaged by thorns on either side. Saliling led the march, the tip of his spear scraping the leaves overhead and knocking last night's rain into Carignan's face. The others crouched behind the priest. Suddenly Saliling left the trail and lunged into a sea of elephant grass through which, somewhere in the region of their feet, traveled a six-inch-wide path. Now they had the sun bearing down from overhead and yet, beneath their progress, a thick red mud that seemed alive, clinging to Carignan's shoes, building up on the soles, clambering up over the sides, engulfing him up to the ankles. In their bare feet the others ambled over it easily, while Carignan struggled along among them with his tennis shoes encased in red cakes as heavy as concrete. He took off his Keds lest they be stolen by the stuff, and joined them by the laces and dangled them from his fist.

As they left the mesa and descended toward a creek deep in a ravine, Carignan despairing of yet another descent, yet another climb, there came a faint crackling from somewhere behind the next peak, and they fell under the shadow of a mass of smoke in the sky ahead of them, a black column rising straight upward in the windless day. There shall be blood and fire and palm trees of smoke—from Joel, wasn't it? Incredible how the English came back. And the scripture too, back from the darkness. Joel, yes, the second chapter, usually translated "pillars of smoke," but the original Hebrew said "palm trees of smoke."

As they crossed the creek at the pit of the ravine Carignan tried to clean his shoes. The mud didn't dissolve in water, he had to scrape and rub at it with his fingers. The water looked clear. He wondered if it was potable. Somewhere along its length every creek in the region had a clan or village irrigating from it, sewage going in, animals bathing. He had a desperate thirst, his whole being pounded with it, but the men didn't drink, so he didn't drink. He pulled his wet shoes onto his bare feet. Now they made directly toward the black monolith of fumes.

They crested the rise and picked along down a path both muddy and rocky toward a barangay of several huts, all burning, nearly gone, down to their boards, and the boards still black and smoking. Saliling cupped his hand beside his mouth and hooted. An answer came. Around the side of an abutment they found an old man dressed in a burlap G-string. Carignan sat on a patch of coarse grass and waved the smoke away from his eyes while Saliling and his nephew spoke to the villager. "He say the Tad-tad came to destroy," Robertson told the priest. "But everybody escaped. He is too old to escape. They shot him in the hand, and he is hiding." The Tad-tad were a Christian sect. Their name meant "chop-chop."

Of the inhabitants here nobody was left now but this old man with a bullet hole in his hand, which he'd wrapped in a poultice of leaves and flies' eggs. "Even if they have a bad wound, they never cut off their limbs in this clan," Robertson explained. "It isn't necessary, their wounds never infect, because they allow the eggs to hatch and eat of the rot of their flesh."

"Ah. Aha," Carignan said.

"It is a good way. But sometimes it makes him sick, and he dies."

The old man seemed immensely so, with a shrunken monkey's face and leathery flesh that drooped from his bones at the joints. Toward the back of his mouth he had two or three teeth which he used, at this moment, to gnaw at a mango with intense concentration. He answered Saliling's questions gruffly, but when he was done with the fruit he tossed away the pit and showed Carignan his anting-anting, a bracelet of hollow seeds around his waist. Its magic, he explained, guaranteed him a peaceful death. Therefore his bullet wound meant nothing.

The old man spoke a Cebuano-Bisayan dialect Carignan could make out pretty well, though young Robertson translated: "He just needs to drink some blood from the monkey, and he'll be new again."

"Take me to the river with you," the old man said. "I want to drink some mud."

"Now he wants to go with us," Robertson said.

"Yes. I understand."

"This clan says the mud gives life. He wants the river."

"I know what he says," the priest insisted.

The old man pointed eastward over a hill and spoke of a storyland, a legendary place.

"He says that over that mountain is the place called Agamaniyog."

"The children tell these stories," Carignan said.

Still pointing east, the old man said, "Agamaniyog. It is the land of coconuts."

Carignan said, "Agamaniyog is for children."

"Then don't go there," the old man said.

They began again, wading down the middle of the creek through the tight valley and then up the facing mountainside, clutching at shocks of weed to pull themselves upward, Carignan afflicted every step of the way by the goads of the Accuser: I am evil in the sovereignty of my will, and incompletely repentant. But a little, a little repentant. But very incompletely. I have failed in the spirit of my sonship. He stifled the devil's voice, which was his own, and trained his hearing on the outer sounds, the shivering of wet leaves in the wind, guffaws of parrots, the dishonest glibness of small monkeys in the bush. The plants closed over them. The path was only a figment now in Saliling's mind. Carignan blundered after, kept upright by the fear that if he went down he'd be lost in the vegetation. His clothes were sopped, even his pockets were full of his sweat. The path widened again, and they came onto a ridge overlooking the world. The going was easier now. In less than two hours they stood above the Arakan Valley, some five kilometers wide, and the olive-drab Pulangi River running through it. Gigantic acacia trees shaped like mushrooms, ten stories high and their crowns a hundred feet across, hid the riverside from view. Saliling hadn't once spoken to him, but he turned now and said in Cebuano, "Look back—you see where we came. It's twenty kilometers to there." Carignan looked west: the gray-green jungle washed in a rosy light, crumbling into the cauldron of the sunset.

They were another hour hiking down into what was left of the barangay of Tatug. Last year's flooding had pasted down the grasses and toppled the houses from their low stilts, but the people still lived here. Carignan, so drained he couldn't raise his hands to get his hat off, sat down on a mound he was vaguely aware must be that of a grave. Other graves surrounded him, not quite yet grown over by the relentless clawing grass and ground vines. Something had massacred a dozen of these people, more, twenty, twenty-five—a plague, a flood, marauders. He found strength to take his hat off. He heard children laughing, he heard a woman weeping. "Come, get out of here, you must not sit here," Robertson said. Saliling had him by the arm. Robertson said, "See, we have a box." He held in his hands a box made of grub-eaten, salvaged boards. "These are the bones of your countryman."

In pursuit of his first official operation as an intelligence officer, Sands arrived at the Manila domestic airport at 4:15 a.m. on a Saturday to take a DC-3 to Cagayen de Oro, the northernmost city on the island of Mindanao, and added himself to the throng at the sellers' windows, scores of people half asleep, their hankies draped over their necks, fanning themselves slowly with wilted journals, milling gently but resolutely forward into the blunt faces of the clerks. Then they disappeared before actually getting on the

plane. Skip's name came fortieth on the wall's chalk-written waiting list, but the first thirty-nine travelers didn't show, and he was
the first to board the DC-3, which carried a total of five passengers
over the iridescent jungles and the black sea and landed without
mishap on a bumpy strip of red ground. These DC-3s, he understood, could fly with a wing shot off—he'd heard tales from the
colonel.

Sands found a cab to the De Oro market, omitted breakfast,
and boarded a passenger bus heading south across the island. He
carried an inexpensive camera, an Imperial Mark XII in pastel
green missing its flash attachment, but he spent most of his time
looking at the ripe, spongy landscape. They made good speed,
slowing nearly to a halt to let passengers on and off, but never
quite stopping. In every hamlet vendors ran alongside selling
sliced mango and pineapple wrapped in paper, and Coca-Cola in
wobbling plastic baggies knotted shut and pierced with a drinking
straw, and this was his fare until the journey broke for the night in
Malaybalay, a city in the central mountains.

Throughout this passage waves of homesickness broke over
him, not for the States, not for Kansas, or for Washington, but for
the house in the mountains on Luzon, with its air-conditioned
bedrooms and its Campbell's soup and Skippy peanut butter from
the embassy's Seafront commissary. These tiny bouts of panic he
welcomed as signs of a deepening immersion in his environment.
A notion the colonel had advanced intrigued him: one God, but
different administrations. His fears dragged him also to the far end
of this assignment—who would read his report on Father Thomas
Carignan, how would his report impress them?

Malaybalay, though poor and constructed mostly of plywood
and galvanize, was populous and full of noise and movement. Next
to the Catholic church square he found a hotel and a room with a
Muslim-style private bath—a stall enclosing both a toilet hole and
a cold-water faucet with three feet of rubber hose attached. This
exotic system plunged him into a spiritual nausea. He'd expected
on assignments of this kind to experience isolation and terror; but

not merely at the sight of the plumbing. He lay on the bed gasping while the strength boiled out of his blood. The narrow room's windows were too high to see out of. The air of this world seemed to carry no oxygen, only the bleating of children and the racket of the streets. He made his way downstairs with his camera and sat on a stone bench in the square, getting a shoeshine. The shine boy, he couldn't have been more than seven or eight, worked up a sweat, great drops beaded his upper lip, and he banged his brush on the box decisively to signal his customer should switch his feet. Sands snapped his picture. The boy had poise and pretended not to notice. This would do it, this would steady him, this child's face. He paid plenty, went into the church—no walls, just a great dome over banks of pews—and waited for the Saturday evening liturgy. A few others joined him. Dusk came. Bats flitted around the square outside. The Latin soothed him. During the homily the youthful priest spoke Bisayan, but Skip recognized many English terms— "demonic possession"—"exorcisms"—"fallen angels"—"spiritual investigation"—"psychological investigation." When the congregation rose to take Communion, he left them to it and stepped back into the devastatingly foreign city.

By stopping passersby until he found an English-speaker, he learned of a Western-style restaurant and soon sat down at La Pasteria, an Italian place getting perhaps part of its menu out of cans, but offering also fresh tossed salad and antipasta with radishes and fresh celery, even olives. White tablecloths, candles in Chianti bottles, and a phonograph on which the staff spun seventy-eight rpm Dixieland recordings.

The wooden shutters lay open to an evening mountain breeze as cool as could be had at this latitude. Beside one of the windows, alone, sat a woman Sands was convinced must be British or American, young but somehow not youthful, businesslike, something like a spinster librarian or a pastor's maiden sister. But throughout the meal, whenever he glanced at her, she stared back with a disorienting candor.

As the waiter cleared her place, she rose and walked directly to

Skip's table. She carried her coffee cup and set it down next to his. She held out her hand. "We've been staring at each other all night. We might as well be introduced. I'm Kathy Jones."

She shook his hand, and held it. Not in mere friendship. Her eyes locked on his, her gaze almost tearful, hot with need. Sands was speechless. He'd never known what to do about women. Her false smile, melting with desperation, shocked his heart with pity. She was ill, or drunk, maybe both.

"Oh, for God's sake," she said, and turned away with a small laugh or sob. Leaving her coffee on his table, she went out quickly.

Sands shook inside, and he couldn't eat. Nevertheless he ordered dessert. When it came—cannoli—the waiter lingered beside him in a grisly state of self-consciousness and finally succeeded in saying, "The lady did not pay today. Will you be the one to pay?" and Skip paid.

The next afternoon, stepping from the bus onto the unpaved main street of the village of Damulog, he was greeted by a small plump man who apparently made a habit of inspecting new arrivals and who introduced himself as Emeterio D. Luis, Damulog's mayor. Luis took him over to the only hotel, owned by a man named Freddy Castro, along the way pointing out the important places in Damulog, the market, the restaurant, the cockfights building, the dry-goods store.

Damulog lay at the end of the concrete road, end of the bus route, end of the power lines. Though electricity reached there, the town had no sewers and, as far as Sands could learn, no indoor plumbing, certainly not at Mr. Castro's hotel, which was constructed of sturdy wood but where, that afternoon, the rain worked not only through the roof but through two intervening stories to drip from the ceiling of his ground-floor room. Keeping his bed and belongings dry needed some thoughtful arrangement. At dusk both the mayor and Mr. Castro, a young man with good English, took him to one of the town's five springs, where Sands, in his checkered undershorts and yellow zoris, before an audience of women and openmouthed children, bathed in clear water flowing from a pipe in a hillside.

"Have your bath, have your bath, you are safe," the mayor promised him. "We have no crocodiles here. We have no malaria. We have no marauders. I believe we are seeing some organized activity from the Muslim groups in the south, but in Cotabato only. We are not in Cotabato. This is Damulog. Welcome to Damulog."

When Skip's back was turned, the children called out to him. The island of Mindanao had seen no U.S. military; therefore nobody called him Joe. The children called him "Pa-dair, Pa-dair . . ." Father . . . Mistook him for a priest.

Those were strange dreams last night, Lord . . .

She sat on a bench in the market piecing together last night's terrors, waiting for the 6:00 a.m. departure, waiting for coffee while nearby two half-awake women opened their stall for commerce. I stood at the seat of Judgment, but what before that, what, I had my purse, I stepped into a shop to buy a pencil, but the shop was a stage in a big black stadium at the end of the world, and now I was dead and had to account for my sins. And I couldn't. And the darkness was my eternal death.

Whose voice had whispered in the dream? But the lady was prepared now to sell her some coffee, pouring hot water from a thermos into the plastic cup over a spoonful of powdered Nescafé. The lady turned on her transistor radio—DXOK from Cotabato City, pop tunes followed by a 6:00 a.m. break for five Hail Marys.

The bus waited, but the driver hadn't come. Whether they left on schedule hardly interested her. She wore no watch, hadn't owned one for years.

And who's this? Not thirty feet away, seating himself at another stall and getting himself a sugar roll, was the man before whom she'd acted like an idiot at the restaurant, at La Pasteria.

Idiot, idiot! But last night at the sight of him she'd felt such an ache, such thirst. In his Philippine-made apparel, brown slacks, brown sandals, white box-cut sport shirt, in the dusk of candle-light, with his shaggy head and mustache, he'd looked so much like Timothy the young arrival, Timothy the bringer of good news and bright fellowship. And she'd thrown herself at this American as blindly as she would have done at Timothy if Timothy had come back to her out of the blank question into which he'd dematerialized.

No dawn yet. Strange weather on this mountain, the sunlight fell on you like an anvil, but it was cool in the shade, after nightfall almost chilly. She hunched in her parka sweater, her face invisible in the shade of its hood, and observed the American from thirty feet away. For that first instant last night, Timothy, I thought he was you and my blood leapt to my head and fingers and I could hardly see, and here, drinking Coca-Cola at six in the morning with his arm hooked through the strap of his cotton satchel, Timothy, he still looks just like you. Now another man arrived, probably the bus driver, and sat down next to the American and ordered coffee. Way up in the tin eaves, frail fluorescent lights attended by a glory of winged bugs . . . Sleepy stall women wrapped in light blankets beside wooden cases opened up to display boiled eggs, cigarettes, candy, sugar rolls. Timothy, are you alive? The woman at the stall beside me is weaving tiny boxes for party favors out of coconut leaves. Another woman goes by bent over a short broom, just a sheaf of straw, sweeping . . . May I always remember the truth I feel right now . . . Timothy, we live, we die.

The driver opened his bus and the American boarded behind him. Impossible to get on that bus, to be seen. She'd take a later one. She turned her back and asked for an egg and a roll and more Nescafé, and then gathered her things and walked. She carried her things in a brown paper bag with string handles.

She sat on a bench in Rizal Plaza and watched half a dozen women and children spreading the rice harvest on the basketball court, walking through it with rakes to turn the grains. She had nowhere else to go. Better to gamble on the less dependable afternoon schedule than to stay another night. The city had no Seventh-Day church, and so she'd lodged at a rooming house, where the fact of a woman traveling alone had created a tense solicitousness that felt to her like hatred. Everybody trying to be polite. That's why she'd gone to La Pasteria, though she could hardly afford it—thus for going there in the first place she'd had an excuse, but none for opening herself to the stranger.

Had he really looked so much like Timothy? From her paper luggage she fished a pack of photos, the sole reason for this trip. Last week amid the miscellany of Timothy's belongings she'd found a roll of film, and had traveled all this way to reach a man with a darkroom. Most of the frames had come out, twenty or so photos, three showing Timothy, two only peripherally—Timothy with a group of engineers from Manila, looking at the site for a future water plant, Mayor Luis dashing into the foreground like a large, happy rodent; Timothy close but blurred, apparently instructing the novice photographer—and one of Timothy with his arm around the shoulders of Kathy herself, posing with a Filipino wedding party in front of a pink stucco church. The rest were shots he'd meant to send to the newlyweds: Cotabato City; Kathy recognized the pink church. She'd stayed at his side on what he called "a junket," nearly a hundred kilometers over washed-out roadways with dozens of other passengers in a jeepney designed for eight people. At the church in Cotabato they'd received him as a god, petitioned him with their cares, burdened him with small offerings, beseeched him to attend the wedding of strangers, allowed him to record the occasion with his German-made camera.

Besides these photos her paper sack held yesterday's change of clothes and a small pillow she put between herself and the wooden bench on the bus she rode down off the mountain that afternoon. The road fell gradually, looking straight into the distance, the view ahead lovely and vast, eleven hundred blends of green under slowly massing black and gray thunderheads. The air howled through the open windows, smelling at first of pine, next of the fermenting lowlands. The bus drove through a downpour and arrived in Damulog still dripping at 4:00 p.m.

No Mayor Luis at the bus stop today. He must be off wagering. She heard the men roaring at the cockfights in the building across the square. She'd watched once, from a distance, lingering outside in the street. The birds wore razors strapped to their spurs and cut each other to pieces within seconds.

She and Timothy lived not far from the square in a three-bedroom house with screened windows and a tight roof, sharing it with their servant Corazon and also, usually, two or three of Cory's nieces, not always the same ones. She found the house empty. On Sabbaths and Sundays the girls went home to barangay Kinipet.

After the piney scent and relative cool of the mountain city, she could smell her home again, the damp wood and sour linen. The house was dark. She pulled the overhead chain in the kitchen—the power worked. Roaches ran for the corners. Cory had left her some rice in a covered bowl. The ants were at it. What a desperate, horrible place this was without Timothy.

She tossed the food, bowl and all, in the dirt by the margin of the property and left, three minutes after returning to her home.

She ate supper at the Sunshine Eatery and got trapped there by the day's second rainstorm. The town's electricity failed, and she waited out the weather in the candle-lit place talking with a man named Romy, here from Manila with a survey team, and with Boy Sedosa, who wore the uniform of a constabulary patrolman. Romy drank from a pint of Old Castle Liquor and Sedosa from a pint of Tanduay rum. Thelma, the patroness of the People's Sunshine Eatery, sat on a high stool behind the counter across the room listening to a transistor radio.

The American who looked like Timothy came in dripping wet, carrying what looked like a camera looped to his wrist, and hesitated just inside the door. The talk stopped. He sat at the next table and asked for coffee. If he recognized her, he was too polite to say so.

Ah, she might have known. Damulog was the end of the bus line and the only stop offering lodging.

He placed his camera on the table. They all watched him drink his coffee while the rain continued steadily.

A gang of young drunks took over the café, horsing around and knocking over tables and chairs. By candlelight they made fright-ening, violent silhouettes. Thelma clapped her hands and laughed as if they were her own boys. They left, and she went about right-ing the furniture. Patrolman Sedosa stirred himself to direct the beam of his flashlight out after them into the rain. Then a crazy lady came inside to beg. She and Thelma embraced like kin, which they may well have been.

Patrolman Sedosa, though keeping his chin and shoulders straight, sank toward the candle flame. He stared at the American at the next table until the American was forced to take notice. "I would like to request your name."

"My name is William Sands."

"I see. William Sands." Sedosa's face belonged in the movies—dead drunk eyes among fat, greasy features. His nose was sharp, Arabic. He didn't blink. "Not touching in any way on your per-sonality," Sedosa said, "but can you show me some papers permit-ting you to travel in our province?"

"I don't have any ID with me at all," the American said, "I've only got one pocket." He wore a white T-shirt and what appeared to be bathing trunks.

"I see." Sedosa stared at him as if forgetting him.

"I'm a friend of Mayor Luis," Sands said. "He officially approved my visit."

"Are you working for the United States Army, perhaps?"

"I'm with the Del Monte Corporation."

"I see. That's good. I am just checking."

"I understand."

"Just ask for Boy Sedosa when you need my assistance," the patrolman said.

"Okay. And please call me Skip."

"Skeep!" Sedosa said.

And Romy from the survey team said, "Ah! Skeep!"

And Thelma, on her stool behind her jars of food, clapped her hands and cried, "Hello, Skeep!"

"Here's to Skip," Kathy said.

Did he realize? He'd offered his nickname. Trouble would never touch him again in this town.

He raised his glass to them all.

"I see you're carrying a camera around in the rain," she said.

"I'm not making much sense tonight," he admitted.

"Do you take it with you every minute?"

"Nope. I try not to get attached. If you're not careful, it can turn into your eye, the only dream you see through."

"Did you say 'dream'?"

"Pardon?"

"Did you say it turns into the only dream you see through?"

"Did I? I meant 'eye.' Your camera turns into your eye."

"A strange slip there, sir. Did you dream about being a photographer when you were young?"

"No, I didn't, ma'am. Did you dream about being Sigmund Freud?"

"Have you got a grudge against Sigmund Freud?"

"Freud is half of what's wrong with this century."

"Really? What's the other half?"

"Karl Marx."

It made her laugh, though she disagreed. "Probably the first time either one was ever mentioned in this town," she said.

Romy, the surveyor, grappled across the intervening space for the American's hand and shook it. "Will you please give us the honor of your company?" He pulled until the American moved his chair and joined them. "Can you please enjoy a coffee with us? Or something even more enjoyable?"

"Sure. Who wants a cigarette? They're a little damp."

"That's quite all right," Patrolman Sedosa said, and accepted one and held it near the candle's flame to get it dry. "Ah! Benson & Hedges! It's a good one!"

Seeing the American again now, even closer this time, she felt nothing stir in her. She wished something would. The town ran with mud and reeked of every kind of dung and infestation. Now that she'd seen this place without Timothy, she didn't want it with him or without him.

The men discussed bantamweight Filipino boxers she'd never heard of. Tiny moths scattered themselves on the tabletop, around the candle stuck upright in a gallon jug formerly containing Tamis Anghang Banana Catsup, whatever that was. The men discussed politicians who didn't interest her. They discussed basketball, something of a national passion. When she got tired of it she walked home through a light drizzle, in the pitch-dark blackout, stepping in puddles and lucky to keep her feet on the road, even luckier to find the house.

She set down her shoes inside the door, made her way to the bedroom. She groped for the flashlight on the nightstand and undressed by its dim illumination. On the nightstand also lay Timothy's book, she'd found it among his things, the dreadful essays of John Calvin and his doctrine of predestination, promising a Hell full of souls made expressly to be damned, she didn't know what to do with it, kept it near her, couldn't help returning to its spiritual pornography like a dog to its vomit. She found a match, lit a coil of insecticidal incense in a dish, crawled under the mosquito net, drew the sheet to her chin . . . Certain persons positively and absolutely chosen to salvation, others as absolutely appointed to destruction . . . Lying there in the stink of her life with her hair still wet from rain. She didn't touch the book.

She woke in a glaring light: the ceiling lamp. Apparently the power lines had been dealt with. Still black outside, and the rain had ceased. She took her sandals into the kitchen, tossed them at the sink to drive away the cockroaches, turned on the light, poured a glass of cold water from the refrigerator—gas-powered—and sat at the table looking at the photographs. Going for the film had been something to occupy her while she waited for somebody to bring her the ring, the band, which may or may not have been gold, from the finger of a corpse washed up along the Pulangi River. The river people hadn't sent the ring. Rather than disturb the bones or this sole ornament, they'd gone looking for Westerners who might claim some kinship with these relics. After weeks of deliberation among themselves they'd bartered for an insignificant consideration, just fifty pesos.

She was looking through his eyes at this wedding party.

They'd been warned they'd be photographed, had prepared themselves. Some of the little girls were dolled up with lipstick and powder, their black hair made brilliant with pomade.

His eyes had seen, his mind had processed exactly this moment on the broken steps of the pink church. In the right-hand background a sign—"TREADSETTERS / a new horizon in the world of retreading"—and effigies of Saint Michael floating above a crowd of celebrants, with the blades of his swords swaddled in tinfoil. It was Michaelmas. Muslims, Catholics, everyone danced the praises of the warrior-saint. As Timothy fiddled with the flash attachment the groom's family began to exclaim and laugh, and when the flash popped they denuded themselves of all human restraint, screeching and trying to hide behind one another in a bashful panic.

She took from their box in the refrigerator one of Timothy's Filipino cigars, sat down with it, held it, lit a match from the dish on the table, took several brief draws before dousing it in the sink, and sat down again at the table surrounded by the reek of him, though her head swam. She tracked any glint of memory into the void. Cigars, photographs, things he'd touched, remarks that floated back, she collected them all compulsively, as some kind of evidence.

She got back into bed without turning off the light overhead.

Immediately she opened the book of the works of Calvin, the book Timothy had found and read and wouldn't stop reading. It shocked her that there should exist a phraseology for these defilements, ideas she'd assumed to have been visited on herself alone, doubts uniquely sinful, never expressed—and Timothy must have felt the same, because he'd never spoken to her about them or about the book. In the margins he'd penciled checkmarks next to certain passages. She shut her eyes and read them with her fingers . . .

"Although, therefore, those things which are evil, in so far as they are evil, are not good, yet it is good that there should be evil things."

"And if God foreknew that they would be evil, evil they will be, in whatever goodness they may now appear to shine."

"Are we children? Will we hide from the truth that God by His eternal goodwill appointed those whom He pleased unto salvation, rejecting all the rest?"

This fluttering heart, the thrill of the abyss, the inescapable truth of my foreordained damnation.

She fell asleep with the light on, holding these terrifying affirmations against her breast.

The next morning came sunny and almost cool, the sky full of beautiful traveling clouds, everything so different from last night's cauldron of ooze. Cory came in with bread and three tiny eggs from the market and made breakfast, after which Kathy met with eight nurse's aids whom she'd trained and who now ran stations in the outlying barangays, at the moment only four stations, and six last quarter, and next quarter who knew, one or six or ten, the funding came and went.

The meeting was joined by a woman from the Upliftment Development Foundation, Mrs. Edith Villanueva, who took notes unnecessarily. Kathy's eight aids, all women, all young, all married, all of them mothers many times over, and none of them very often free of their barangays, made a party of the occasion. They had rice and sugar fried in coconut oil and wrapped in banana

leaf, rice wrapped in coconut leaf, and regular rice. "It's all rice,"
Mrs. Villanueva said somewhat apologetically.

The ladies were all very fond of her husband, had all the news
about his disappearance, spoke of him respectfully, in such a
manner as to imply he was neither dead nor alive. They called
him Timmy.

And then, lunch concluded, it was time for Mayor Emeterio
D. Luis, who held a central and elevated position by virtue of having learned everything about everyone in Damulog, who would
have been the mayor even if no such municipal office had presented itself for his occupancy. Kathy brought him the leftover
dainties arranged on a mahogany tray and draped with a silk scarf.
Although Damulog housed a post office and city hall in a three-
room cinderblock structure by the market, the mayor stayed out of
it, preferring the small parlor of his home, which got shade and a
breeze. He put Kathy in a wicker chair beside his desk, called out
loudly for ice water, and asked her about polio immunization.
She'd known him for two years. Still he took a few minutes to
address her as if she'd just landed as an emissary. "Can we bring
the polio vaccine to the outlying stations? We have problems in
the countryside. Not everyone can march along the roads with so
many children all the way to Damulog. These are the poor of the
poorest. And sometimes also there can be robbers on the road. We
don't want to be victimized by these lawless elements. These are
the poor of the poorest." Kathy had heard him use the phrase several times lately. He invariably turned the words around. Yes:
Emeterio D. Luis, the *D*, according to an engraved granite paper-
weight on his desk, standing for "Deus."

Elections were far off, but already, he told her, his opponent
for the office of mayor had slandered him, called him a coward, a
man with "white eggs." In his eyes, beneath the pains of office,
glowed a general happiness. His sister, who taught at Southern
Mindanao University, was singing tribal folk songs through a
small PA amplifier on the patio, and he listened with satisfaction,

his hands folded beside a vase of foam-rubber blossoms on top of his desk.

He talked to her about the American, Skip Sands, just as he must have spoken to Skip Sands about her. And of course he was aware she'd encountered the American in the Sunshine Eatery.

"I asked Skeep Sands if he knew the American colonel, and yes, they have a very interesting connection . . . Are you going to ask me what connection?"

"I wouldn't want to gossip."

"Gossip is un-Christian!" he said. "Unless you are talking to the mayor."

Kathy uncovered the desserts and he studied the tray like a chessboard, his hand hovering. "So many visitors!"

Kathy said, "I think you conjure them up."

"I conjure them up! Yes! I have conjured the American colonel, and the Philippine Army major, and I have conjured that other man, I think he was Swiss, what do you think he was?"

"I didn't meet him. Or the Filipino. Just the colonel."

"And I have conjured the survey team of engineers. Mrs. Luis," he asked his portly wife as she entered from the kitchen, sliding across the linoleum floor in her straw-soled zoris, "what do you think? Do you think I am a conjurer?"

"I think you have a very loud voice!"

"Kathy believes I can conjure things," he called as she continued toward the rear of the house. "Kathy," he said, "I want the survey team to do some work for me. I think you can help me to persuade them."

"I don't hold much sway with them, Emeterio."

"I have conjured them up! They must work for me!"

"Well, you'll have to do your own talking there."

"Kathy. The American called Skeep, do you know what he told me? The colonel is his relative. The colonel is his uncle, to be exact."

Kathy said, "Well!" He'd made a strong general impression,

but she couldn't remember—conjure—the colonel's face in order
to make any comparison.

"When I asked Skeep about the Filipino officer and the other
man, he pretended he doesn't know them."

"Why would he know them?"

"These people all know each other, Kathy. They are on a clandestine government mission."

"Well, everyone's under cover." She herself appeared here
under the auspices of the International Children's Relief Effort,
an organization without religious affiliation, whereas in fact she'd
come as the wife of her husband: a worker in the vineyards of
Jesus Christ.

The mayor threw his sandal at a dog that wandered in, a perfect shot, dead on the rear, and it screeched like a bird and leapt
out the door.

"It's completely outside of our ideas to gamble," he suddenly
reflected. "Gambling is against the Seven Day ideas. I'm trying to
put it behind me."

"I bet you succeed."

"Thank you. Oh—'I bet'! Yes! Ha ha! 'I bet'!" He quickly
sobered. "But you see, I go to the cockfights. It's my obligation. I
want to connect to the passions of the people."

"I'll bet you do."

Fifteen minutes had passed, and now a young woman—servant,
neighbor, or relative—set down two glasses of ice water on the desk.
Mayor Luis dabbed at the sweat on his forehead with the back of his
hand. He sighed. "Your husband Timmy." The Filipinos all referred
to her husband, for the first time in his life, as Timmy. "We will wait
for word about the remains. It's taking a little longer. I hold out
hope, Kathy, because it's possible that suddenly we might hear from
some criminal elements of people who have taken him alive. We
are victimized by so many lawless elements and kidnappers, but this
time it can be said that they give us hope." He sipped his water while
a completely candid silence enclosed him: No. No hope.

At two in the afternoon, after classes let out and while the town dozed, she opened the doors of her Damulog health station, which operated in one of the cinderblock schoolhouse's four classrooms. Upliftment Development's Edith Villanueva was on hand to observe as young mothers brought in their infants to be immunized. A couple of dozen lined up, girls as young as twelve and thirteen—and looking only nine or ten—gripped the limbs of their babes ruthlessly for the shots, and received each a can of evaporated milk, which yielded, for them, the real meaning of the visit.

Meanwhile, the American Skip Sands sat out front on the concrete porch, looking at a book; in checkered short-pants and a white T-shirt, and rubber zoris on his feet. Apparently undisturbed by the screams.

As they left, Kathy introduced Edith to the American. He started to get up, but Edith sat beside him, smoothing her skirt. "What's the book?" Edith asked. "A secret code?"

"Nope."

"What. Greek?"

"Marcus Aurelius."

"You can read it?"

"*To Himself*. Generally translated *Meditations*."

"A linguist. You are a linguist?"

"It's just for practice. I have an English translation at the hotel."

"Castro's? God, I wouldn't stay there," Edith said. "I'm taking the four o'clock bus out of here."

"Mr. Castro's roof has holes in it, but the next hotel is far, far away."

"All alone?" Edith was a married woman, and middle-aged, or she'd never have been flirting with him.

He smiled, and Kathy suddenly wanted to kick him in the side—wake him up—in the softness below the ribs. To disturb the good humor in his bright American face.

"Can I see?" Kathy said. His book was very cheap and plain,

printed by the Catholic University Press. She handed it back. "Are you a Catholic?"

"Midwestern Irish Catholic. That's a mixed-up mixture, we like to say."

"Kansas, you said, right?"

"Clements, Kansas. How about you?"

"Winnipeg, Manitoba. Or the country outside there. On the same latitude as Kansas."

"Longitude."

"Okay. We're right due north of you."

"But different countries," Edith said.

"Different worlds," Kathy said. Here they were, two weary wives, both crowding him. "Come along, then," she said, and pulled him up by his hand.

They began walking toward Kathy's street. "So you are from the midwestern United States?" Edith said.

"Yes, right, Kansas."

Kathy said, "So is my husband. Springfield, Illinois."

"Ah."

"He's missing at the moment."

"I know, I heard. The mayor told me."

Edith said, "The mayor told you—who else!"

"Emeterio tells everyone everything," Kathy said. "That's how he finds things out. The more he talks, the more people tell him. Were you waiting to see me?"

"Well, in fact, I was," he admitted, "but I've waited too long. I've gotta run."

"Run!" Edith said. "That's not at all a very Filipino thing to do."

After he'd left them, Edith said, "He didn't realize I was still with you. He wanted to see you alone."

Around four that afternoon, as they waited for Edith's bus out of town, the two women spied the American strolling among the market stalls in his Bermuda shorts, on his sunburned legs, with a hairy brown coconut in his hand. "I'm looking for someone to whack this open for me," he said.

The market square took up a full city block ringed with thatched kiosks, its interior beaten bare. They walked its borders seeking someone to deal with the visitor's coconut. The bus arrived, chaos descended, the passengers hoisted their sacks and herded their children and swung their flapping, upside-down chickens by the talons. "The driver has a bolo, I'm sure," Edith said. But Skip found a bolo-wielding vendor who topped the coconut expertly, raised it as if to drink, and offered it back to the American. Skip held it out—"Anybody thirsty?" Both women laughed. He tried the milk. Edith said, "For goodness' sake, dump that out, man. It's going to turn your stomach." Skip emptied it onto the ground and let the vendor crack the fruit into quarters.

Edith had some words with the driver and then came back to them. "I made him wash the headlights. They don't wash the headlights. It gets dark and they drive as if they had a blindfold because of so much mud." She began her goodbyes to Kathy, and her thanks, and took a long time winding up her visit. She offered her hand to Skip Sands, and he held her fingertips awkwardly. "Thank you so much," Edith said. "I think you'll be an inspiration to Damulog." There was something arch and improper in her tone.

Edith carried a gigantic multicolored straw bag with a hemp clasp. She went off swinging it, walking flat-footed in her sandals, her butt rolling like a carabao's in her silk skirt. Good. Gone. All afternoon Kathy had felt in her neck and shoulders a tenseness, a readiness to shrug off the weight of this woman's company. Each day's end stole the light from her heart, then came the night's sorrowing madness, waking, weeping, thinking, reading about Hell.

On the other hand the American, spreading out his white hankie for her on a mildewed bench, seemed pointless, stupid, soothing. He said, "Voulez-vous parler Français?"

"I'm sorry?—Oh, no, we don't do that in Manitoba. We're not those kind of Canadians. Are you really some kind of linguist?"

"Just as a hobby. I'm pretty sure a real linguist could do a whole life's work down here. As far as I can find out, nobody's tried to study the Mindanao dialects in any kind of organized way."

He picked up a slab of his coconut. The ants had found it. He blew them off and pried a chunk from it with the blade of a dark blue Boy Scouts of America pocketknife.

"Your work is tough," he said.

"Oh, yeah," she said. "I misjudged the nature of the whole proposition."

"Did you?"

"The depth of it, yes, and the seriousness."

She wanted to cry out to him to take stock of himself.

"Well, I just meant you have to deal with a lot of people."

"Once you get among the heathen, it all changes. It changes a lot. It gets a lot clearer, a lot more vivid, it gets vividly clear. Oh, well," she said, "it's the kind of thing that gets confused when you talk about it."

"I guess it would be."

"Then let's not talk about it. Do you mind if I write down a few thoughts sometime and pass them along to you? On paper?"

He said, "Sure."

"And what about you? How is your work going?"

"It's more of a holiday."

"What's Del Monte's interest here? I wouldn't think these Maguindanao plains would grow many pineapples. Too much flooding."

"I'm on vacation. I'm just touring."

"So you arrive without any explanation at all. Just a lost ambassador."

"Well, yes, I'd see it as maybe an ambassadorial kind of opportunity, if fine folks like you weren't already doing a much better job of representing us."

"Representing us who, Mr. Sands?"

"The United States, Mrs. Jones."

"I'm Canadian. I represent the Gospel."

"Well, so does the United States."

"Have you read a book called *The Ugly American*?"

He said, "Why would I want to read a book like that?"

She stared at him.

"Aah, okay, I've read *The Ugly American*," he said. "I think it's nonsense. Self-flagellation is getting to be the vogue. I don't buy it."

"And *The Quiet American*?"

"I've read *The Quiet American*, too."—And that one, she noticed, he didn't label nonsense.

She said, "We Westerners have many blessings. A freer will. We're free from certain . . ." She stalled in her thoughts.

"We have rights. Liberty. Democracy."

"That's not what I mean. I don't know how to say it. There are questions about free will." She trembled to ask him now if he'd perhaps read John Calvin . . . No. Even the question was an abyss.

"Are you feeling okay?"

"Mr. Sands," she said, "do you know Christ?"

"I'm Catholic."

"Yes. But do you know Christ?"

"Well," he said, "not in the way I think you mean."

"Neither do I."

To this he said nothing.

"I thought I knew Christ," she said, "but I was entirely mistaken."

She noticed he sat very still when he had nothing to say.

"We're not all crazy here, you know," she said.—Another one he had no reply for. "I'm sorry," she said.

He cleared his throat carefully. "You could go home, couldn't you?"

"Oh, no. I couldn't do that." She could sense him fearing to ask why. "Just because then I'd never get anything straightened out."

This American created a silence hard to resist. She had to fill it: "You know, it's not unusual, it's not weird, it's not unheard of, to go on in the middle of tragedy. Look at where we are! The sun keeps rising and setting. Each day kicks more room in your heart—what would be the word . . . the love is relentless, relentlessly pushing, it keeps pushing and kicking like a child inside you. All right, then! That's enough out of me!" What a fool I am! she almost shouted.

The setting sun lowered from the clouds and struck up at them in such a way that suddenly the entire town throbbed with a scarlet light. The American didn't comment on it. He said, "And what happens when all this is, is, is—concluded?"

"There, congratulations, you found a word."

"Sorry."

"You mean if Timothy's dead?"

"If, well—yes. Sorry."

"We don't know what happened to him. He got on the bus for Malaybalay, and we're still waiting for him to come back. He seemed ill, he promised he'd see a doctor at the sanitarium there before he kept any other appointments. As far as we know, nobody at the sanitarium saw him. We're not sure he arrived in Malaybalay at all. We've been to every town between here and there—nothing, nothing, no news."

"And I guess it's been a little while."

"Seventeen weeks," she said. "Everything's been done."

"Everything?"

"We've contacted everybody, all the authorities, the embassy, and our families, of course. We've all made a thousand calls, everyone's gone crazy a thousand times. His father came over in July and posted a reward."

"A reward. Is he pretty well off?"

"No, not at all."

"Oh."

"There's been a development, though. Some remains have been found."

True to his midwestern origins, the American reacted to this remark by saying, "Ah," and, "Uh-huh."

"So right now we're waiting for word about the corpse's effects."

"Mayor Luis told me."

"And if it's Timothy? I'll stay for a while, and then find a new post, which is what we planned on anyway. Or, if Timothy comes back to surprise us all—which he might do, you don't know Timothy—and if he does, we'll probably just go on with the plan. He's due for a change. Wanted a change, a new challenge. Meaning the same old problems in a brand-new location. And I'm a nurse, they'll take me wherever they can get me. Thailand, or Laos, or Vietnam."

"North Vietnam, or South?"

She said: "We do have people in the North."

"The Seventh-Day Adventists?"

"The ICRE—International Children's Relief Effort."

"Right, the ICRE." And suddenly he launched out passionately, "Listen, these folks around here will never have much better than what they've got. But their children might. Free enterprise means innovation, education, prosperity, all the corny stuff. And free enterprise is bound to spread, that's its nature. Their great-grandkids will have it better than we do in the States."

"Well," she said, taken aback, "those are nice thoughts, those are hopeful words. But 'these folks' can't eat words. They need some rice in their bellies, and I mean tonight."

"Under Communism their kids might eat better tonight. But their grandkids will starve to death in a world that's all one big prison."

"And how did we get on this topic, anyway?"

"Did you know the ICRE is considered a Communist front?"

"No. Is that true?" In fact she hadn't heard, and didn't much care.

"The U.S. Embassy in Saigon considers them Third Force."

"Well, Mr. Sands, I'm not a fifth column, or a third force. I don't even know what a third force is."

"It's neither Communist nor anti-Communist. But more helpful to the Communists."

"And do you folks at Del Monte spend a lot of time at the U.S. Embassy in Saigon?"

"We get bulletins from all over."

"The ICRE is a tiny outfit. We get along on grants from a dozen charitable foundations. We have an office in Minneapolis and about forty nurses in the field in I don't know how many countries. Fifteen or sixteen countries, I believe. Mr. Sands, you seem upset."

He said, "Do I? You must have been pretty upset yourself the other night."

"When?"

"In Malaybalay."

"Malaybalay?"

"Oh, come on—in the Italian place? When the mayor mentioned Kathy Jones the Seventh-Day Adventist, the name was the same. But I sure didn't think it was you."

"Why is that?"

"That night you didn't seem like any Seventh-Day Adventist."

The American seemed to be waiting in his colorful Bermuda shorts for some word from her, though plainly there wasn't any use. "The mayor and his family have been very good to me."

"Well, I mean—come on."

"We don't always tell the whole story about ourselves, do we? For instance, the mayor thinks you're not who you say you are at all. He says you're on a secret mission."

"I'm not from Del Monte, you mean? I'm a spy for Dole Pineapple?"

"Your uncle said he was from AID."

"Did you get much chance to talk to him?"

"He's a colorful old rogue."

"I guess you did. Who was he with?"

"Nobody."

"Oh. But the mayor mentioned a couple of others. A German, maybe."

"They came around much more recently."

"The other two? When were they here? Do you remember?"

"I left Friday. So they were here Thursday."

"You're saying last Thursday. Four days ago."

"One two three four, yes, four days. Is that bad?"

"No, no, no. I just wish I hadn't missed them. Who was the German with?"

"Let me see. A Filipino. From the military."

"Aha, Major Aguinaldo."

"I didn't actually see him."

"He's a friend of ours. But I'm not sure about the German guy. Was he German? I'm not sure I know him. The mayor said he had a beard."

"A Swiss, the mayor said."

"With a beard?"

"I didn't see him."

"But you saw the colonel."

"We don't see many beards around here. That must prickle. So does that mustache, I bet you."

He faced her in silence, as if in defiant expectation of her examination of him—no hat, sweat dripping from his drenched scalp, also from his drooping mustache . . . Now he allowed himself to look around, to take in the vermilion glow surrounding them just as it faded. "Wow," he said.

"My grandmother called this the gloaming."

"Sometimes it just knocks you out."

"In five minutes the skeeters will be swarming and we'll be eaten alive."

"The gloaming. Sounds Gaelic."

"There it goes. It was almost like liquid."

"Makes you feel more certain of Heaven."

"I'm not sure Heaven is really all that much to be desired," she said.

She'd assumed this would shock him, but he said, "I think I kind of know what you mean."

She said, "Do you travel with the Word?"

"The word?—Oh."

"Do you have a Bible with you—I mean at the hotel?"

"No."

"Well, we can certainly arrange to place one in your hands."

"Well—all righty."

"The Catholics don't quite cling to the Word the way the rest of us do, do they?"

"I don't know. I don't know how the rest of you do."

"Mr. Sands, how did I get on your bad side?"

"I'm very sorry," he said. "That's not the situation at all. I'm just not being very polite, and I should be ashamed."

The apology touched her. She sought to frame some gracious acceptance.

Sands said, "Who's this coming with Mayor Luis? The guy's toting a spear."

She spied the mayor and two others walking down the thoroughfare of packed mud and shallow puddles, the mayor in his white sport shirt like a muumuu over his vast belly, one of the men with him pointing a long spear toward the clouds, the other one smoking a cigarette, and instantly she knew.

"Oh, my gosh," she said, and cried, "Mayor Luis! Mayor!"

She stood up, and so did Skip Sands. In her left hand she held his white handkerchief, on which she'd been sitting. The men turned and headed toward them. "She is here, she is here," the mayor said. They seemed to bring the dusk on as they came. The end of the cigarette flared in the dark. "Kathy," the mayor said, "it's very sad."

She couldn't remember, at this moment, whether she'd ever really harbored any hope.

Mayor Luis seemed to be speaking to Skip: "I'm very sad to be the one. But unfortunately I am still the mayor."

The mayor held out the ring, and in order to take it in her fingers, she dropped the American's white handkerchief.

"Kathy, we are all very sad tonight."

"I can't see if it's inscribed."

"The inscription is there. I have such sadness bringing you this evidence."

"So that's it, then."

"Yes," Luis said.

She held Timothy's ring in her hand. "Now what? What do I do with this?" She put it on her right index finger.

"I'll let you folks go on," Skip said.

"No, don't go." She had hold of his hand.

"It's truly a tragedy," he said.

"Come, Kathy," the mayor said. "Skip will pay his sympathies later."

The mayor's younger companion tossed his cigarette into a puddle. "We have accomplished a long journey for you."

Now they had to be paid. Who paid? "Am I the one who gives you the fifty pesos?" she said. Nobody answered. "And do you have, did you bring, isn't there more?" She turned to the old man with the spear, but his face was blank, he had no English.

"Yes. We have Timmy's physical remains at my house," the mayor said. "My wife is beside them, keeping a silent vigil until I bring you. Yes, Kathy, our Timmy is deceased. It's time to mourn."

Sands walked by Mrs. Jones's house three or four times before he saw a light on inside. By then it was past eleven at night, but here people took long siestas and stayed up till all hours.

He mounted the steps and came under her porch light, a neon ring speckled with tiny insects. Through the window he saw her standing in the middle of her parlor looking lost. From her hand dangled a bottle by its neck.

Apparently she was able to see him, too. "Would you like a cigar?" she said.

"What?" he said.

"Would you like a cigar?"

A perfectly simple question he couldn't answer.

"I'm having a sip or two tonight."

He had to step back as she pushed the door open and came to sit on the porch railing. She wasn't steady, and he expected her to fall off into the dark.

"I want you to taste this."

"What is it?"

"It's brandy."

"I don't care for the hard stuff."

"It's rice brandy."

"Rice?"

"It's rice brandy. It's . . . rice brandy."

"Are you feeling—" He stopped. What a stupid way to begin. Her husband was dead.

"No."

"No?"

"I'm not."

"You're—"

"I'm not feeling."

"Mrs. Jones," he said.

"No, don't go," she said. "I asked you don't go before, and you just left. Listen, don't worry, I knew all along he wouldn't make it. That's why I grabbed your hand that time in the restaurant. I knew it was hopeless. It's hopeless, so why don't we all just—go to bed."

"Jesus," he said.

"I don't mean right now. Yes, I mean right now. Shut up, Kathy. You're drunk."

"You'd better get something in your stomach."

"I have some pork, if it hasn't turned."

"You'd better have a meal, don't you think?"

"And rolls."

"Rolls would probably—" He stopped. He'd meant to say they might absorb some of the brandy, but it was hot, his neck was painfully sunburned, and what was the point of discussing the absorbent qualities of various foods?

"What is it, young man?"

56196534578926789896789

"I'm living without air-conditioning."

She eyed him closely. She appeared more crazy than drunk.

She said, "I'm sorry to hear about your husband."

"What?"

Her blouse was half unbuttoned, split slightly almost to her navel. Surprising tiny blue flowers patterned her bra. Sweat dripped down her belly. He himself had a hurtful irritating skin rash from his armpits to his nipples. He wanted ice against his flesh. He wished it would snow.

Mrs. Jones said, "If you come in and have some brandy, I'll eat some food. It's air-conditioned."

The air conditioner was in the bedroom, and they went to bed and made some kind of love. Throughout, he felt awkward. No. Ugly. He got her hands off him immediately afterward, dressed, and walked back to the hotel with the remorse blackening his brain, gumming it up like dirty grease. A new widow, and on the very day she got the news . . . She, on the other hand, had afterward seemed unashamed, and not so drunk. She'd only seemed angry at her husband for being dead.

He walked by her house the next night but saw no light inside. He tried knocking and got no answer. Any louder and he'd wake the neighbors. He left.

The dry season hadn't come yet, but it didn't rain. Immediately after each sunset a lid of clouds pressed the heat down on Damulog and crushed the blossoms and forced its way inside everybody's head. Slowly the whole town sipped rum. Romy, the young survey engineer, started a fistfight with some Muslims in the Sunshine Eatery and they beat him up out in the square, but nobody even left the tables to watch.

On Saturday night striped wasps and small dragonflies coated the fluorescent tube in the Eatery. Mating energetically, they dropped down onto the plates. One gang after another alighted on this community, crawled all over the illumination, and then was seen no more. Mayor Luis hunted up Sands in the café. His Sabbath over, he looked for company.

"I am going to save you from the same thing every night," Luis told him, and took him for dinner to his wood and brick home with its strange linoleum floor. They ate spicy pork adobo and they drank painit, a native coffee. And Old Castle Liquor—not Scotch, not Bourbon, just Liquor. With Romy keeping to the hotel, hiding his bruises from the public, Skip had only the mayor for laughs. What of Kathy Jones? "She left to Manila on Tuesday morning," the mayor said. "She is going to accompany her husband's remains to the airport."

The news struck him a blow. "She's left for good?"

"She will meet her father-in-law, and he will take the remains to the United States."

"She's not going back with him?"

"In fact she is only going to put her husband's bones on the plane, then she's coming back to Damulog. She will not proceed all the way to the United States because of her dedication."

Next day he went with Mayor Luis and a load of four-inch iron pipe in a multicolored right-hand-drive Isuzu cargo truck to the site of the future waterworks, where a large concrete filtering station stood in a big field. It was plain to see the pipe-laying project was barely off the starting line. Mayor Luis also envisioned a stadium here someday. He paced off the perimeters of guesthouses and ball fields and a swimming pool in the midst of this empty plain of elephant grass, gesturing with his small hands.

The rain held off through the third straight night. Driven from their sweltering homes, people lay out on the basketball court, the only concrete surface in Damulog, looking up at the closed, flat, black heavens, hardly conversing, waiting for dawn.

Each night Sands roamed the town and walked several times past the house of Mrs. Jones, but never saw a light until the fourth night of his wandering.

She answered his knock, but she didn't ask him in. She looked terrible.

"You're home."

"Go away," she said.

"I'm leaving town tomorrow."

"Good. Don't come back."

"I could arrange to come back in a while," he said, "maybe in a couple weeks."

"I can't stop you."

"Can I come in and talk to you?"

"Beat it."

He turned on his heel and headed off.

"All right, all right, all right," she called. "Come here."

Late Monday morning a jeepney turned up in the square and waited there with the hood raised and a couple of men bent over the engine, another man's legs sticking out from under, and the driver sitting up front pumping the brake, exclaiming.

Sands was the first aboard. He'd hopped these things for short rides in Manila but never traversed any mountains, as he would today. These elongated jeeps looked capable of seating about a dozen people, front and back, but actually carried as many as could be loaded aboard without breaking the axles, and they traveled over any surface, always painted many garish colors and adorned with pennants and chromed trophies and whizzbang doodads of the kind appealing to teenage speedsters, and, emblazoned over the front windshield of every one, always, its title and its claim: *Commando*; *World Champion*; et cetera. This one called itself *Still Alive*.

While the repairs went on, Sands waited on the bench in the vehicle's passenger section, staring down at floorboards speckled with rice grains, jammed in with many travelers and several folks just looking for a shady place. After two hours, the problem fixed and the vehicle laden with at least twenty voyagers and their kits and sacks, it seemed to Sands the moment had come. But bodies were still being added. He counted at least thirty-two, including eleven pairs of legs draping down from the roof, and two babies,

one sleeping, one bawling. He heard baby chicks, too. The travelers had crushed themselves together closely enough to stare at the
tiny red flecks of heat damage on the surfaces of one another's eyeballs, to extend their tongues, if they felt like it, and taste the sweat
on each other's cheeks . . . His last count, before the thing began
moving, budging forward by some supernatural force, drifting
hugely out of town, like a greasy, sweaty, iceberg—of what use
brakes against such inexorableness?—stood at forty-one passengers, twenty-five in back with him, three up front, one dozen on
top. And the driver. And others climbing on at the last second, and
still more chasing after and grappling themselves aboard the roof,
until they'd built enough speed to leave the last few stragglers
laughing and waving farewell. Sands faced an old man like a
monkey, a woman like a lizard, and a little girl with the feet of a
hundred-year-old crone. Not far out of town they lurched into
a low-ceilinged forest of banana plants that muted and filtered the
roaring noon, passed tiny, dazed villages of oak-frame huts, drove,
at one point, directly through a campfire of burning bamboo in
the middle of the shattered road. Then the jeep climbed mountain switchbacks, swaying and moaning. Then a flat tire. Almost
everyone jumped off, and Sands had a chance to gather them all
together for a photo. Forty-seven people bunched themselves
around the conveyance, shrieking with fascination while he
tripped the shutter.

At three that afternoon he disembarked in Carmen: an asphalt
main street, several two-story stucco buildings, the grandest civilization he'd experienced since Malaybalay a week ago. He found
a room for the night, lay down for a nap, and didn't wake till well
past two in the morning. The town slumbered, all but the dogs,
and the sinners . . . At this solitary hour Sands repented his lust for
Kathy Jones. In his mind he fell at the foot of the Cross and
begged Jesus to pour down his cleansing blood. Mrs. Jones was
solid, made for middle age but not yet there. She had a round
face, plump cheeks, a corona of thick curly hair almost like lamb's
wool, very soft and kind brown eyes, and hands very soft but also

strong. While she talked her tongue touched her small, very even front teeth. She was intriguing, pleasant, attractive, but not nerve-wrackingly so. His soul crawled back and forth between Jesus and Mrs. Jones until he heard the roosters screaming.

Skip had his maps. He'd pored over them daily, hungrily, joyfully, loosed from his body, free as a hawk. The colonel had told him where to find the priest, Carignan; there was nothing on his Mindanao map indicating a place called Nasaday on any river called the Rio Grande. On his map of the province of North Cotabato, however, the urban churches of the diocese were pinpointed, and first thing in the morning he walked to Formation House, the resortish headquarters on the edge of Carmen. He was told that Father Haddag rested. He came out within twenty minutes, a wiry old Filipino with Communion wine on his breath. Together they looked at the map. The priest made a small mark with a pencil. "I think the church is there, or there," he said. "It's my reasonable guess." In a fantastic display of generosity, he loaned Skip a 50cc Honda motorcycle, and Skip accomplished a twenty-mile trip in a bit more than two hours, perhaps a thirty-mile trip, if he factored in the continual diagonal maneuvering thanks to the potholes. And the church waited there on its pencil mark, a lopsided concrete block with olive canvas stretched over its roof, or serving in place of a roof. Skip had passed through several hamlets on the way from Carmen, but this structure stood in awkward solitude a half mile from the nearest, on a stretch of river apparently eating the ground from beneath it.

Father Carignan, of French-Canadian descent, white-headed, leathery, with a tentative bearing and cloudy eyes, had lived here so long—for thirty-three years, in fact, through the Japanese occupation, Muslim uprisings, famous typhoons, and sudden calamitous changes in the river's course, speaking Cebuano and ministering to these sun-baked native Catholics—that he hardly had a grip on the English language anymore. Asking about Skip's origins, he inquired who his descendants were, meaning his ancestors.

Carignan made him properly welcome, had tea brought out to a table in the shade, sat across from him with his zoris slipped off and his feet together under the chair and his knees flung apart. He wore faded denim trousers and a T-shirt browned by river water. He breathed through his mouth, smoked Union cigarettes, pronounced them "Onion." When not smoking he clutched his thighs and rocked slightly in his seat, his gaze sliding down and sideways like a mental patient's. He made some effort to engage himself; when Sands spoke he faced his guest with an expression—unintentional, Sands was sure—of veiled shock, of friendly disbelief, as if Sands had come here minus his pants. He didn't appear remotely capable of running guns.

"Do they ever call you Sandy?"

"Do they ever! But my friends call me Skip."

"Skip," the priest repeated, saying "Skeep" as would a Filipino.

"I understand you helped with finding the lost missionary. Getting the remains, I mean."

"Yes. Yes, that's so, isn't it?"

"Down by the Pulangi River?"

"Yes. On the way back, coming up the hill, I fainted."

"But isn't this the Pulangi right here? That's what it says on my map."

"It's a division, how do we call it, I can't remember—a branch, you know. This part is the Rio Grande."

"A fork."

"To get to the Pulangi branch we had to hike many miles. Many miles. At night I dream I'm still hiking! Is your tea all right for you?"

"Very good, thanks."

"The water's all right. We have enough for drinking, but not for bathing. The tank made a leak." He was talking about the badly cracked concrete cistern a few yards away.

"Are there quite a few Catholics in your parish?"

"Oh, yes. Yes. Catholics. I've baptized hundreds, confirmed

hundreds. I don't know where they go afterward. I never see most of them."

"They don't come to Mass?"

"They come here in times of trouble. To them I'm not really a priest of God. They like to use witches to help them. I'm more like that."

"Ah."

"They'll come tomorrow. A few. Because it's Saint Dionysia's feast day. They believe she has power."

"Aha."

"And you."

"Me?"

"Are you a Catholic?"

"My mother wasn't a Catholic. My dad was."

"Well—the father isn't usually very religious."

"My dad died in the war. I made lots of visits to his Irish relatives in Boston. They were pretty rabidly Catholic."

"But you're confirmed?"

"Right, I had my confirmation in Boston."

"Did you say Boston? I grew up in Bridgewater. Near there."

"Yes." They were now having most of this conversation for the second time.

The priest told him, "After I left home, my mother and father moved to Boston. I talked to my mother on the telephone in 1948. I called from the new important hotel in Davao. New at that time. Still important, maybe, eh? She said she was praying for me always. Hearing her voice made her sound more far away than ever. When I got back to the parish here, it was like starting all over again on the first day. I felt far from home again."

Four tiny children, naked but for undershirts, stood at the corner of the building, staring. When Sands smiled, they screamed and ran away.

Carignan said, "I met the other man. He visited us, too."

"I'm not sure who you mean."

"The colonel, Colonel Sands."

"Oh, of course, the colonel," Skip agreed.

"But he wasn't wearing a uniform. I think the uniforms must be too hot. So I don't know what branch of the military."

"He's retired."

"He is also Sands."

"Yes. He's my uncle."

"Your uncle. I see. Are you also a colonel?"

"No, I'm not with the military."

"I see. Are you with the Peace Corps?"

"No. I'm with Del Monte. I think I mentioned that."

"Some of the people are very excited about the Peace Corps. Everybody wants a visitor if possible."

"I'm sorry to say I don't know much about it."

"And the two others yesterday. The Filipino soldier, and the other one."

"Yesterday?"

Carignan knit his eyebrows together and said, "Wasn't it yesterday?"

"Let me get the sequence of events in order," Sands said. "When did the colonel come?"

"Oh, some weeks ago. Around the feast of Saint Anthony."

"And the other two were here *yesterday*?"

"I didn't see them. Pilar told me. I went downriver to deliver the last rites—a very old woman there. Pilar said a Filipino and a white. Not a Joe. A foreigner. They had a palm-boat."

"I see, a palm-boat," Sands said, feeling the shores erode beneath his feet.

"Boston, is it," Carignan said.

"Yeah, Boston," Skip said.

"Del Monte, did you say?"

"Yes, I did. But these two visitors—how strange, huh?"

"I believe they're still on the river. I'll ask Pilar. She has all the news from the river people."

"Pilar is the housekeeper? The lady who served us the tea?"

"Is it okay? We don't have milk," the priest reminded him, as he had when they'd sat down.

"Jesus," Skip said.

The priest seemed to sense Skip's disarray. He was solicitous. "We all have a spiritual trial to go through. When I was a little boy I was very hateful toward the Jews because I said they were the crucifiers. I was very contemptuous of Judas too, because of his betrayal."

"I see," Sands said, and saw nothing.

Carignan seemed to struggle. The words stuck in his throat. He touched his mouth with his fingers. "Well, it's very much for each person to experience alone," he said, and whatever truth he meant to get at, his eyes were the visible scars of it.

"May I snap your picture?"

The priest suddenly looked studious and foreboding, his hands clasped together before his chest. Skip focused and tripped the shutter, and Carignan relaxed. He said, "You are something of a pilgrim, eh? Yes. Me too. I went on a very long hike to the Pulangi River."

"We can pray for each other," Skip said.

"I don't pray."

"You don't?"

"No, no, no. I don't pray."

The Joe liked tea. Insisted on getting it himself. Talking a great deal with Pilar about the other visitors.

Why these people kept coming was a mystery.

The Joe had seemed to enjoy riding his motorbike, bucking over the ruts into the yard, his belt strung through the handle of his cloth satchel and the satchel swinging at his side.

In the Joe's absence the children materialized around the machine, openmouthed, touching it with their fingertips.

"Here he comes!" Carignan shouted in English, and the children scattered.

Why was his English coming back to him these last few weeks? Because he'd been thinking of the American missionary? The bones in a box, saying nothing, but in every language? Maybe because he'd opened a hole in his mind when he'd first spoken to the American visitor, the colonel, the first American in years. In decades.

This colonel had come twice. He'd come alone and had behaved respectfully. He was good, and the locals responded to him with enthusiasm. But good or bad, a strong man causes trouble.

With a sense how it all must look to the visitor's eyes, Carignan regarded the red muddy path to the riverbank, the cracked cistern, the tarped roof, the mildew crawling the walls. The Joe was probably using the concrete chamber, the "facilities" downstairs—dark, grimy, separated only by a low wall from the kitchen, in which Pilar now cooked rice and sang a song. If she wanted, she could step over and stare into his face as he crouched over the hole. The Joe would want toilet paper. There was a roll of the stuff in the facilities, but it had been soaked and dried out by the weather and really couldn't be used.

Pilar stopped singing in the kitchen and came out with another tray. Sliced mango and pineapple.

"Pilar, I told you: if the American comes again, tell him I'm not here."

"It's not the same one."

"I don't like so many Americans."

"He's Catholic."

"So was the colonel."

"Don't you like the Catholic? You are Catholic. I am Catholic."

"You're being silly again."

"No. You are silly."

She resented him for failing to take advantage of her. And he understood. Who would mind if he did? It's just that he was very ashamed of any kind of touching.

She said, "That old man is coming up the road to see you. I saw him just now from the kitchen. Don't give him any food. He always comes back."

"Where's the American?"

She said in English: "Bathroom."

The old man waited until Pilar went inside before he appeared around the corner of the church, walking sideways out of a kind of deference, dressed only in khaki shorts with the legs turned up to his crotch and the waist cinched around his belly with a rope. Carignan beckoned, and the old man came and sat. Like all of them he was shrunken and almost meatless, an animated mummy. He had the flat, weary features of a very wise Eskimo. He smiled a lot. He had hardly any teeth.

"Bless me, Padair, for I have sin," he said in English without apparent comprehension, "bless me and I ask you forgiveness."

"Te obsolvo. Have some pineapple."

The old man scooped up several pieces in his hands and said, "Maraming salamat po," thanking him in Tagalog, the dialect of Luzon. The old man's preliminaries generally seemed to require statements in a variety of tongues.

"I had a visitor in my dreams last month," he revealed to the old man. "I think he brought me a message."

The old man said nothing, only concentrated on his food, his face as oblivious as a dog's.

The American guest came back from the kitchen but brought no tea. This pilgrim Joe had a jaunty gait, his limbs moving freely around the great hot furnace in his middle, the fire of suffering he didn't seem to know about.

As the Joe approached, the old man vacated the chair and squatted flat-footed beside them.

"I'm asking him about a dream I had. He can find out its message," Carignan told the American.

"Hallo, Padair," the old man said.

"He calls you Father," said Carignan.

As the old man finished his fruit and licked his fingers, he said in Cebuano, "Why do you say your dream has a message?"

Carignan said, "It was a strong dream."

"Did you wake up?"

"Yes."

"Did you go back to sleep?"

"I stayed awake all night."

"Then you had a strong dream."

"A monk, a holy man, came to see me."

"You are a holy man."

"He wore a hood. His face was a silver cloud."

"A man?"

"Yes."

"From your family?"

"No."

"Did you see his face?"

"No."

"Did you see his hands?"

"No."

"Did he show you his feet?"

"No."

The old man began speaking to Skip Sands very earnestly and a little too loudly.

"Yes. How do you do," Sands said.

The old man gripped the American's wrist. He spoke. Paused. The priest translated: "He says that in sleep, when you sleep, the spirit leaves your body. And the shepherd or herdsman of the spirits takes them up and"—he consulted with the teller—"the herdsman of the spirits chases the spirits, herds them, like sheep, down to the shore, to the seaside."

The man spoke, the priest queried him, the man tugged at the American's arm, and Carignan pieced together the tale: Herded to the shore, the spirits sink into the sea, and down there they find the world of dreams. A yellow snake guards the border to the sea of dreams. Anyone who tries to go back and forth between the two worlds will be suffocated in its coils and will die in his sleep. Carignan couldn't find the English to get it across. "He's telling a complicated story. He's a little crazy, I think."

"This world holds no memory of the before-life, and the after-life holds no memory of our sorrows. So be happy that death is coming."

Saying this, the old man rose and departed.

"Wait. Wait. What is the prophecy of my dream?"

"Didn't you hear me?" the old man said.

Father Carignan insisted on spending the night in a hammock in the church while Sands slept with the Blessed Host in Carignan's room, that is, the Host sat sleepless on the priest's dresser, and Sands tried to sleep on his bed of wooden slats and straw mat under a gauzy net. A monk's cell, perfectly appropriate to his pilgrimage. He lay in the dark. A mosquito whined outside the netting. He made a mental note to ask Carignan about something the colonel had cited from the Bible—something about there being one God but many administrations. The idea appealed to a government man. A cosmological bureaucracy . . . Now worry flooded him. The colonel, Eddie Aguinaldo, the German. They'd traveled here, and no one had told him. It wouldn't do if the colonel withheld things. It prodded at a spot of doubt he harbored, doubt in the colonel's competence, his judgment, the power of his perception. The colonel was a little crazy. But who wasn't? The problem was that the colonel might not trust his nephew's talents, might have sent him on a phony errand. He woke at one point from a dream of biblical force, a prophetic dream, assured that the island of Mindanao held no interest for the United States, that this Catholic priest couldn't possibly be running guns to Muslims, that life had called him—Skip Sands the Quiet American, the Ugly American—to this place only to enlarge his understanding in aid of his future work. Because here there lay no present work. Not one particular of the dream remained. Only this certainty.

Carignan explained to the Joe that maybe some people would come to the morning liturgy because today they celebrated a saint close to their hearts, Dionysia.

The Joe had never heard of Saint Dionysia. Nobody had. "Yes, she's very powerful here. Based on her miracles along the river she'd be canonized a saint, if she wasn't already a saint. She was martyred in the fifth century in North Africa. A stirring martyrdom."

In a homily decades before, in all innocence, Carignan had made a graphic presentation of Dionysia's last agonies to an uncharacteristically large gathering of celebrants, and now up and down the river she enjoyed a legendary status, and the people attributed to her many healings and claimed many sightings and visitations, many signs and messages. "So I try to remind people when her feast day comes. But it's not always easy for the river people to find out what the date is. They don't have calendars."

Only a few folks came to the service. Beforehand the priest baptized a newborn on the riverbank, dribbling the muddy water over its forehead. "We don't have holy water as such," he explained to the Joe. "So the bishop made a decree that all the river is holy. That's what I tell them."

Wrapped in a scarf, the child was limp, eyes shut, mouth open, blowing bubbles of phlegm. The mother was only a child herself.

The Joe said, "This baby looks very sick."

"You'd be surprised which ones die and which ones live," he told the Joe. "It's always a surprise."

They assembled for the evening Mass. He saw it all anew through the visitor's eyes: the small gray room, the warped wooden benches, the moldy earthen floor, and the congregation, an ignorant handful, ten, eleven—fourteen celebrants, the Joe included. A few old women, a few old men, some dark-eyed runny-nosed infants. The babies didn't bawl. Once in a while one or another of them hacked or made a croaking sound. The old women bleated the responses, the old men muttered evasively.

The visitor, sitting on the bench among them in his khaki pants, his dirty white T-shirt, shone forth as if he were the last American, sincere, friendly, a close listener, but at the very center of his eyes a terrified loneliness.

What were today's readings? He'd lost the book again, the schedule of liturgy. He hadn't actually consulted it for years, just read what he wanted, whatever verses the Book opened to. "Here's something." He read in English: *"If there be therefore any consolation in Christ, if any comfort of love, if any fellowship of the Spirit, if any bowels and mercies . . ."* He tried to explain in the local dialect what he thought might be meant by "bowels and mercies," and ended by saying, "I'm not sure what it means. Maybe how we feel toward our families."

He sought Matthew 27:5—*And he cast down the pieces of silver in the temple, and departed, and went and hanged himself.*

And now the homily. "In English today." He gave no reason why. Maybe it went without saying that the Joe's presence suggested this courtesy. Not that any of them would understand his thoughts in any language. Superstitious vampire-worshippers. But he himself had once seen the aswang flying with a child's bloody limb between her jaws.

"I've told them I'm going to do the homily in English. I don't really have anything prepared. We speak of our reading today, about Judas Iscariot the traitor: *And he cast down the pieces of silver in the temple, and departed, and went and hanged himself.*

"He goes back to the temple, to the ones who paid him to betray his Master. He wants to give back their dirty silver but they won't take it. Ever think why? Why they turn down perfectly good money? Why is that? 'And he cast down the pieces of silver in the temple, and departed, and went out and hanged himself.'

"I've made my last confession. Who's the person in the Bible most like me—who am I most like? Judas. Judas the betrayer—that's me. What else is there to confess? Nobody paid me to betray Jesus, but what does it matter, eh? I could never pay them back. They would never take back their dirty money."

In over thirty years he hadn't spoken at such length in his
native language. He let it run on, the English coming out of his
head as out of a loudspeaker. "My grandmother used to use that
expression, 'bowels and mercies.' I never asked her about what it
meant.

"I remember how I rejected my grandmother. I loved her very
much, I was her favorite, but then, when I came to my early teens,
twelve, thirteen, she came to live with us, and I was very unkind to
her. She was just some old woman, and I was very unkind.

"I don't like to remember that. The memory is very bitter. My
grandmother loved me, and I treated her with disrespect. I felt no
love for anyone.

"Here, of course, where the people are so poor, so sick, you
can't love them. It would pull you under. You would go under.
Everyone here knows how to love, but love them back—it's quick-
sand. I'm not the Christ. No man is the Christ.

"Other times we're the thief on the cross, the one who got crucified next to Jesus, the thief who turned to Jesus and said, 'Remember me when you get to your Kingdom.' And Jesus had mercy and
said, 'This day you shall be with me in Paradise.' I really think we
have to be one or the other. We're either the betrayer, or we're the
thief.

"I look around me and I think: How did I get here to Nasaday?
How did I get here? This is just a corner in the maze. Island in the
swamp. Judas jumped down a hole and God knows, God knows if
he's ever coming up, huh? It's entirely up to God. Who are we?
We're Judas sometimes. But Judas . . . Judas went out and hanged
himself.

"These thirty years, and more, that I've spent living with bar-
barians, living with their powerful gods and goddesses, taking
inside me the traditions, you know, which aren't fairy tales, they're
real, they're real once you take them inside you, and taking inside
my mind all the pictures of their tales and living in the adventures
of the ancestors, and the years I've spent meeting face-to-face with
their dangerous demons and saints, saints who have the names of

the Catholic saints, but only to disguise themselves . . . How many times I almost got completely lost forever, how many times I almost wandered into the part of the maze where you can never come back . . . but always comes the touch of the Holy Spirit at the last moment, before the gods and goddesses destroyed me, always at the last moment I received the reminder of who I am, and why I came here. Only a glimpse, you know, only a reminder of who I really am. And then back down into the tunnel."

The Mass said, the celebrants departed, Carignan stripped to his undershorts and zoris and went down to the river to bathe.

The sound of a motorized palm-boat, quite rare on this river, made him stop and watch. The craft passed through his view, slowing, the motor throttling down to an idle, the two men aboard peering toward the shore, coming close. Carignan waved. They passed from sight, hidden by the low sago palms growing along the bank.

He waded in up to his waist and bathed.

What a silly sermon. Because of the English, his old vexation had come awake, struggling upright and flailing in its dirty bandages—his soul and his soul's diseases.

How did I get here?—Judas pops up in the maze.

He stepped from the river with his head down but not watching his feet, preoccupied, troubled by the unkindnesses he'd done in his adolescence, none of them at all serious, but they terrified him now because they'd been perpetrated with a kind of amorality which, had it continued, would have made him very dangerous to the world.

He turned and saw among the sago fronds a most curious sight: a Western man in Western garb holding a long tube to his lips. Something like a bamboo reed. As Carignan examined this sight and prepared to make some sort of greeting, the man's cheeks collapsed and something stung the padre in the flesh over his Adam's apple and seemed to lodge there. He reached up to brush it away. His tongue and lips began to tingle, his eyes burned, and within

seconds the sensation was that of having no head at all, and then
of losing touch with his hands and feet, and abruptly he didn't
know where any part of him was, every part of him seemed to go
away. He did not feel himself collapsing toward the water, and by
the time he landed in it he was dead.

Having relieved himself beside a bush near the river, Sands
came along the path below the church and met two very little boys
riding alongside an irrigation ditch on the back of a carabao. They
smiled with shyness and doubt. "Padair. Padair . . ."

Maybe they thought he was Carignan—maybe they thought
there existed in all the universe only a single priest who took many
forms.

He tossed the kids some gum. One missed the toss and scrambled down off the wide platform of the animal's back to pluck it
from the grass at the ditch's edge. "Padair. Padair."

"I'm not your father," Sands said.

In the sunset light he watched a palm-boat race downriver
through a magical rainbow-colored mist churned up by a quite
powerful propeller, two figures on board. There was nothing about
the boatmen, so far out in the river and veiled by spray, that under
any other circumstances would have made him say, "It's Eddie
Aguinaldo and the German," nothing strong enough to rate them
a mention, say, in his report. But those two had been lurking, and
now they loomed. He was about to turn and race back to the
church for his binoculars, but here was the priest, he suddenly
noticed, swimming just offshore, and facedown. Who swims like
that? The drowned. Sands waded out in pursuit. He plunged into
a hole, and the water closed over his head. He surfaced, saw
Carignan floating, turning, heading downstream. Sands began to
swim after him, changed his mind, swam to shore and ran along
the path beside the water until he'd gotten downstream of Carig-

nan, kicked off his sandals, waded out into the deeper water, and launched out again, trying to intercept the drifting priest. He'd misjudged. Loose-limbed, cadaverlike—perhaps dead—the priest slipped rapidly away at a tangent, downstream and out toward the middle of the quarter-mile-wide water.

Again Sands gave up swimming, turned back, clambered ashore, and headed, now barefoot, down the path. He veered off toward a house, saw a banca-boat overturned on the grass beside it, hollered, no one home, tried to get it right-side up, failed, tried to drag it toward the path. A man stopped him, a muscular young man, barefoot, bare-chested, baffled, wearing red short-pants. He quickly caught the moment's urgency and grabbed a paddle leaning against the house. Each man took a side and they jerked the boat along to the shore, boarded precariously, and struck out after the corpse, the Filipino paddling and the American pointing, their small craft steadily gaining on the murdered man as he traveled toward Kingdom Come.

The next day Sands returned the Honda motorbike to the diocese and reported the death by drowning of Father Thomas Carignan. Father Haddag was saddened by the loss, and surprised to hear about it so soon. "Sometimes news takes weeks to come from the river people," he said.

This errand took all afternoon. Afterward Sands booked a room in Carmen and had chicken-on-a-stick and a bowl of rice with three men from the Department of Agriculture whom he simply ran into on the highway through town, all of them wandering up and down it looking for a restaurant. They settled for one of the roadside stands where a man barbecued gaunt legs and thighs over coconut-shell charcoals, dousing them with a mix of soy sauce, spices, and Coca-Cola. Starving dogs watched them eat. David Alverol, the chief among the three Agriculture workers, wanted to knock around town with this American, but Sands was dead tired. The other two kept their poise, while David Alverol seemed so

excited to have met the American that the American really feared
for David's sanity. He kept repeating himself, performing the
introductions several times, his face shining with sweat and also
from an inner illumination. He suggested every two minutes that
the American come to his home "for a dialogue." "You're very
jolly," he told the American. "My type of guy. Can't you come
with us for one more thirty minutes?" David got more and more
insistent, to the embarrassment of his two companions, beseech-
ing the American drunkenly with tears in his eyes as the American
got out of their government jeep in front of his small hotel—
"Please, sir, please, one half an hour only, sir, sir, I beg you, yes,
please . . ." Sands made an appointment to see them tomorrow,
warning them his schedule might prevent him from keeping it.
They parted that way, Sands and the two others understanding
he'd never be seen again, and David Alverol expecting to meet
him first thing in the morning.

Sands hadn't told Father Haddag of the eight-inch sumpit dart jutting from the neck of Carignan's corpse.

   In his room in Carmen he lay awake thinking about the German killer. What before had seemed in the German effeminate
now seemed poetic—his eyeglasses, his thick lips, the pale skin.
He trafficked intimately with death, he knew things. Sands had
thought him pompous and irritable. Now he seemed the carrier of
a transcendental burden.

Just as he got back to Damulog, little red ants hit town. They
walked all over his table at the Sunshine Eatery, all over his bed at
Castro's hotel.

   He might have continued to Davao City on the island's southern end and caught a plane for Manila. He went back to Damulog
instead. He might have spent a night there at the longest, waiting
for a bus. Instead he stayed three weeks while he composed a
report containing nothing of substance, based entirely on hearsay
from the Mayor Emeterio D. Luis, and drawing no inference as to

the nature of the priest's contacts or the responsibility for his death.

Sands was, in effect, AWOL. He buried his dereliction in his pointless labors and practiced a soldierly detachment from his bitterness. And spent his nights with Mrs. Jones.

1966

Bill Houston's Honolulu shore leave commenced with the forenoon watch, too early for a man with money to spend: on top of everything, the navy wished to deny him any nightlife. He took a shuttle bus from the naval station and across the open fields of the air force base and then through town to Waikiki Beach, wandered dejected among the big hotels, sat on the sand in his Levi's and wild Hawaiian shirt and his very clean shoes—white bucks with red rubber soles—ate grilled pork on a wooden skewer at a kiosk, took a city bus to Richards Street, booked a bed at the Armed Services YMCA, and started drinking in the waterfront bars at one in the afternoon.

He tried an air-conditioned place favored by young officers, where he sat at a table by himself smoking Lucky Strikes and drinking Lucky Lager. It made him feel lucky. When he'd collected enough change he called home on the mainland, chatted with his brother James.

That just made him more depressed. His brother James was stupid. His brother James was going to end up in the military like himself.

He strolled the waterfront with the beer thudding inside his head, a lonely feeling pulling at his heart. By 3:00 p.m. the pavement of Honolulu had baked so hot it sucked at his rubber shoe soles as he walked.

He hid inside the Big Surf Club trading beers with two men slightly older than himself, one of them a man named Kinney who'd recently joined the crew on Houston's ship—the USNS *Bonners Ferry*, a T2 tanker manned mostly by civilians, of whom Kinney was one. But he hadn't just waltzed on board for a tropical cruise. He'd spent time in the navy, lived on ship after ship, and had no real home ashore. Kinney had attached himself to a barefoot beach bum who seemed hopped up on something. The bum bought the table two pitchers in a row and eventually revealed he'd served with the Third Marines in Vietnam before landing back home on an early discharge. "Yeah, baby," the bum said. "I got the medical."

"Why?"

"Why? Because I'm mentally disabled."

"You seem all right."

"You seem all right if you buy us a beer," Kinney said.

"No problem. I'm on disability. Two forty-two a month. I can drink a serious amount of Hamm's, man, if I sleep on the beach like a Moke and eat what the Mokes eat."

"What do the Mokes eat? Who are the Mokes?"

"Around here you got the Mokes and the Howlies. We are the Howlies. The Mokes are the native fuckers. What do they eat? They eat cheap. Then there's a whole lot of Japs and Chinks, you probably noticed. They're in the Gook category. You know why Gook food stinks so bad? Because they fry it up with rat turds and roaches and whatever else gets in with the rice. They don't care. You ask them what the fuck stinks around here and they don't even know what you're talking about. Yeah, I've seen some things," the bum went on. "Over there the Gooks wear these funny straw hats, you probably seen those—they're pointy? Girls riding on a bicycle, you grab their hat when you go by and you just about yank their head off, because they're tied with a string. Yank her right off the bike, man, and she goes down fucked up in the mud. This one time I saw one where she was all bent like this, man. Her neck was snapped. She was dead."

Bill Houston was completely confused. "What? Where?"

"Where? In South Vietnam, man, in Bien Hoa. Right in the middle of town, practically."

"That's fucked up, man."

"Yeah? And it's fucked up when one of them honeys tosses a grenade in your lap because you let her get up beside you on the road, man. They know the rules. They know they should keep their distance. The ones who don't keep their distance, they probably have a grenade."

Houston and Kinney kept quiet. They had nothing comparable to talk about. The guy drank his beer. A moment almost like sleep came over them. Still nobody had spoken, but the bum said as if answering something, "That ain't nothing. I've seen some things."

"Let's see some beer," Kinney said. "Ain't it your round?"

The bum didn't seem to remember who'd bought what. He kept the pitchers coming.

James Houston came home from the last day of his third year in high school. Got off the bus raising his middle finger at the driver and whooping.

His mother had caught a ride out to work and left the truck in the driveway, as he'd asked. His little brother Burris stood in the drive with a finger in one of his ears, peering down the barrel of a cap pistol while he pulled the trigger repeatedly.

"Watch your eyes, Burris. I've heard of a kid got a spark in his eye and he had to go to the hospital."

"What are caps made of?"

"Gunpowder."

"WHAT? GUNpowder?"

The telephone rang inside.

"I'm not allowed to answer," Burris said.

"Did they turn the phone back on?"

"I don't know."

"Well, it's ringing, ain't it?"

"Shut up."

"Now it done quit, you fool."

"I wouldn't answer anyhow. It sounds like bugs talking in there. Not people."

"You're a funny feller," James said, and went inside, where it was hot and smelled a little like garbage. His mother refused to turn on the evaporative cooler unless the temperature got into the hundreds.

He carried a number of papers from school, homework, report card, year-end bulletins. He shoved them in the trash can under the sink.

The phone rang again: his brother, Bill Junior.

"Is it hot in Phoenix?"

"It's almost a hundred, yeah."

"It's hot here too. It's *sweaty*."

"Where you calling from?"

"Honolulu, Hawaii. Hour ago I was standing on Waikiki Beach."

"Honolulu?"

"Yep."

"Do you see any hula girls?"

"I see a bunch of whores is all. But I bet they'll do the hula."

"I bet they will too!"

"What do you know about it?"

"Me? I don't know," James said. "I was just saying."

"Goddamn, I wish I was back in good old Arizona."

"Well, I'm not the one who reenlisted."

"You can put me on a nice clean desert anytime you want to. It's honest heat there, ain't it? It's dry and burning. This here's mushy, is what it is. Hey, kid, imagine this, did you ever lift the lid on a kettle full of boiling sewage? That's what it's like stepping out on the street in this place."

"So," James said, "what-all else is going on?"

"How old are you, anyway?"

"I'll be seventeen here pretty quick."

"What are you gonna do?"

"What am I gonna do? I don't know."

"Are you done with school?"

"I don't know."

"What do you mean you don't know? Did you graduate?"

"I'd have to go one more year to graduate."

"Ain't nothing else to do besides graduate, is there?"

"Not where I can see. Or I was thinking about the army, maybe."

"Why not the navy?"

"Too many sailors in the navy, pard."

"You're a wiseass, pard. Better join the army, pard. Because you'd just get your ass kicked daily in my branch of the service."

James was at a loss. He didn't actually know this guy.

The operator interrupted, and Bill had to deposit more coins. James said, "Are you in a bar, or what?"

"Yeah, a bar. I'm in a bar in Honolulu, Hawaii."

"Well, I guess that's . . ." He didn't know what it was.

"Yeah. I been in the Philippines, Hong Kong, Honolulu—let me see, where else, I don't know—and the tropics ain't no tropical paradise, I'm saying. It's full of rot—bugs, sweat, stink, and I don't know what-all else. And most of the beautiful tropical fruit you see, it's rotten. It's mashed on the street."

James said, "Well . . . I'm glad you called."

"Yeah," Bill said.

"Okay."

"Okay," Bill said. "Hey, tell Mom I called, okay? And tell her I said hi."

"Okay."

"Okay . . . Tell her I love her."

"Okay. So long."

"Hey. Hey. James."

"Yeah?"

"You still there?"

"I'm still here."

"Go in the Marines, man."

"Aah, them are overrated."

"The Marines get a sword."

"The Marines are really the navy," James said, "part of the navy."

"Yeah . . . well . . ."

"Well . . ."

"Only the officers get a sword, anyway," Bill Junior said.

"Yeah . . ."

"Well, I gotta go get laid," Bill said.

"Get some!"

"What do you know about it?" his brother said, laughing as he hung up.

James searched the kitchen drawers and found half a pack of his mother's Salems. Before he got out the door the phone rang—Bill Junior.

"Is it you again?"

"Last time I looked, yeah."

"What's up?"

"Say hi to South Mountain for me."

"We don't see South Mountain no more. We see the Papago Buttes."

"On the east side?"

"We're on East McDowell."

"East McDowell?"

"Ain't that the shits?"

"You're out in the desert!"

"Mom's working on a horse ranch."

"I'll be goddamned."

"She knows about horses from when she was a little girl."

"Watch out the gila monster don't bite you."

"There ain't any shade, but it's nice. We're right up near the Pima Reservation."

"And you're in school."

"I been at Palo Verde for a while, since about October, maybe."

"Palo Verde?"

"Yeah."

"Palo Verde?"

"Yeah."

"When we lived over on South Central, our school used to

play Palo Verde in basketball or something, or football. What was the name of our school that time?"

"I went to the elementary. Carson Elementary."

"I'll be goddamned. I can't remember the name of my own high school I went to."

"Ain't that the shits?"

"Do you ever get to Florence?"

"Nope."

"Do you ever see Dad?"

"Nope," James said. "He ain't my dad, is why."

"Well, you stay out of trouble. Learn by his example."

"I don't follow none of his examples. I don't even look at his examples."

"Well," Bill Junior said, "anyway . . ."

"Anyway. Yeah. Are you really on Waikiki Beach?"

"Not really. Not right now."

"We're right about at Fifty-second and McDowell. They have a zoo over here."

"A what?"

"Yeah, a little zoo."

"Hey, tell Mom something—when is she gonna be home?"

"Later. A couple hours."

"Maybe I'll call her. I want to tell her about something. There's two guys on my ship from Oklahoma, so anyway, you know what they both said? Said I sound like Oklahoma. I said, 'Well, sir, I've never been—but my people are.' Tell Mom that, okay?"

"I'll do that."

"Tell her she started me in Oklahoma, and I come out like I'm from there."

"Okay."

"Okay!—that's short for Oklahoma!"

"I'll be goddamned," James said.

"Yeah. Ain't that the shits?"

"Okay."

"Okay. So long."

They hung up.

Drunk as a lord, James thought. Probably an alkie like his father.

Burris marched in with his cap gun in one hand and a Popsicle in the other, wearing his short-pants and nothing else, looking like a little stick man. "I think I got a spark in my eye."

James said, "I gotta get going."

"Does it look like I got a spark in my eye?"

"No. Shut up, you peculiar little feller."

"Can I ride in the back of the truck?"

"Not unless you want to get bumped out and killed."

He showered and changed, and just as he was going out, the phone rang. His brother again.

"Hey . . . James."

"Yeah."

"Hey . . . James."

"Yeah."

"Hey. Hey. Hey . . ."

James hung up and left the house.

James picked up Charlotte, and then Rollo, and then a girl Rollo liked named Stevie—short for Stephanie—Dale, and they drove out toward the McDowell Mountains looking for a party they'd heard about, a wild unchaperoned outdoor affair, supposedly, off the road and out in the desert away from anything; but if such a gathering actually went on, it was lost in a maze of dry washes, and they steered back to the highway and sat in the back of the pickup drinking beer. "Couldn't you get it no colder?" James asked.

"I stole it from the icebox in the barn," Rollo said.

"Can't even find a party on graduation night," James said.

"This isn't graduation night," Charlotte said.

"What is it, then?"

"It's the last day of school. I'm not graduating. Are you graduating?"

"Warm beer," James said.

"I'll never graduate," Charlotte said. "I don't care."

Rollo said, "Yeah, who gives a flying fuck," and they all laughed at his vulgarity, and he said, "We're country kids."

"No, we ain't," James said.

"Your mother works on a horse ranch. My dad messes with irrigation. And there's a great big barn behind my house, pardner."

"It's nicer out here," Stevie Dale said. "No cops."

"That's true," James said, "ain't nobody to bother you."

"Just mind the snakes."

"Mind this snake," Rollo said, and the girls whooped and laughed.

It was a disappointment to James that when the two girls laughed, Charlotte had to be the one who forced beer out her nose. Stevie was younger, just a freshman, but she seemed simpler and not so nervous. Stevie kept her posture straight, and she smoked in a sexy way. What was he doing with Charlotte? Actually he liked Stevie.

He dropped Rollo off, and then he drove Charlotte home. Stevie kind of ended up still in the truck. He made sure of letting Charlotte off first.

He kissed Charlotte goodbye as they stood out front of her house. She locked her arms behind his neck and clung to him, her lips slack and wet. James held her without much strength, with his left arm only, and let his right arm hang. Charlotte's older brother, out of work, came and stared from the doorway. "Shut the door or turn off the damn cooler, you fool," her mother called from within.

In the truck James asked Stevie, "You need to go home?"

"Not exactly," she said, "not really."

"You want to drive around?"

"Sure. That might be nice."

They ended up right back where they'd been with the others an hour before, looking out at the low mountains, listening to the radio.

"What's your plans for the summer?" Stevie said.

"I'm waiting on a sign."

"That means you don't have any," she said.

"Any what?"

"Any plans."

"I don't know if I should aim for just a summer job, or find something real and permanent—just not go back to school."

"You mean drop out?"

"I was thinking I'd get in the service like my dad."

She made no response to this idea. She placed her fingertip on the dashboard and rubbed it back and forth.

James had run out of conversation. His neck felt so taut he doubted he could even turn his head. Not one word to say occurred to him.

He wished she'd say something about Charlotte. All she said was, "What are you so sulky about?"

"Shit."

"What."

"I think I've gotta break up with Charlotte. I really have to."

"Yeah . . . I'd say she probably feels it coming."

"Really? She does?"

"You're just not lit up around her, James, not at all."

"You can tell, huh?"

"You've got a cloud raining down all around you."

"What about right now this minute?"

"What."

"Ain't raining down on me right this minute, is it?"

"No." She was smiling, she was the sun. "Are you really going into the service?"

"Yep. The army or the Marines. I guess you're gonna let me kiss you now, ain't you?"

She laughed. "You're funny."

He kissed her a long time and then she said, "That's what I like about you. You're funny when you're happy. And you're good-looking—that's one thing too," and they spent a while kissing, until a commercial came on the radio, and he spent some time with the dial.

"Hmmm," she said.

"What is it, Stevie?"

"I'm trying to think, does this man kiss like the army, or like the Marines? Hmmmm," she said while kissing him. She broke away. "Maybe the U.S. Air Force."

He kissed her and very gently touched her arms, her cheeks, her neck. He knew better than to put his hands where he wanted to. "I've got one warm beer left," he said.

"Go ahead. I'm not thirsty."

He sat against the driver's door, and she against hers. He was glad the sun was setting so he didn't have to worry what he looked like. Sometimes he wasn't sure the expression on his face made any sense.

Now he had to burp. He just went ahead and did it loudly and said, "Greetings from the interior."

Stevie said, "Your dad's in prison, isn't he?"

"Where'd you get *that* one?"

"Is he?"

"No, that's more my stepdad," James said. "Just some guy, really. He's my mother's fault, not mine."

"And your real dad's in the service, huh?"

James draped his arms over the wheel and rested his chin on them, staring out . . . So now she suddenly thought they should tell their worst secrets to each other.

He got out and went behind some scrub and took a leak. The sun had dropped behind Camelback Mountain southwest of them. The sky was still pure blue above and then at the horizon tinted some other color, a rosy yellow that went away when you looked at it.

Beside her again in the truck he said, "Well, I just made up my mind: I'm joining the army infantry."

"Really? The infantry, huh?"

"Yep."

"Then what? Specialize in something?"

"I'm going to get over there to Vietnam."

"And then what?"

"I'm going to fuck up a whole lot of people."

"God," she said. "You're not with the guys here, you know. I'm a female."

"Sorry about that, chief."

She put her hand on the back of his neck and touched his hair tenderly with her fingers. To stop her doing it, he sat up straight.

"That's an awful thing to say, James."

"What."

"What you said."

"It just came out. I didn't mean it, I don't think."

"Then don't say it."

"Shit. Do you think I'm that evil?"

"Everybody's got a mean side. Just don't feed it till it grows."

They kissed some more.

"Well, anyhow," he said, "what do you feel like doing at the moment?"

"What . . . I don't know. Do we have gas?"

"Yep." It thrilled him she'd said "we."

"Let's drive around and see what's going on."

"Let's take the long way." That meant he'd make a serious pass at her.

"Okay." That meant she wouldn't mind.

James stood out front of the house in the dark as his mother came home from work in Tom Mooney's convertible Chevy, staring out of the passenger side with her mouth lagging open, her face hidden by a ragged straw hat, a bandanna protecting her neck. Mooney waved to James, and James dropped his cigarette butt to the earth and stomped it out and waved. By then the Chevy had gone.

She went on inside without a word for her son, this silence both unusual and welcome.

It lasted until he followed her into the kitchen. "If you don't think that ranch has about wore me out, just come feel the muscle a-quivering on this arm. If I heat a can of soup, you better eat it.

Don't make me fuss and then just sit there dreaming your dreams."
She turned on the kitchen light and stood under it looking small
and spent. "I've got baloney and I've got tomaters. Do you want
a sandwich? Sit down, and I'll make us soup and sandwiches.
Where's Burris?"

"Who?"

"He'll be around. He's always hungry. I lost weight while I carried him to term. I started out one-nineteen, and in my ninth
month I was down to one-eleven. He fed on me from the inside."
Wiping at her face, she smeared it with dirt from her hand.

"Mom. Wash up before you cook."

"Oh, Lord," she said. "I'm just so tired I forget I'm alive. Open
the can for me, hon."

They ate peanut butter and jelly and Campbell's soup.

"I'll cut up this tomater."

"I just ate. I don't want it."

"You've got to have vegetables."

"There's vegetables in the soup. That's why it's 'Vegetable
Soup.'"

"Don't run away. I mean to talk to you. When is your school
done for the summer?"

"It finished up today."

"Come to work at the ranch, then."

"I don't know about that."

"What don't you know? Do you know a dollar when you don't
see one? Because I don't see one."

"I was thinking about the military. Maybe the army."

"When? Now?"

"I'm seventeen."

"Seventeen and crazy."

"Bill Junior was seventeen. You signed for him."

"It didn't hurt him, I suppose."

"He called today."

"He called? What did he say?"

"Nothing. He's in Honolulu."

"I've never seen a dime from him. Not that I'd ever ask it."

"If I get in the army, I'll send you some."

"Once or twice he sent some money. Not regular. He hasn't lately. And I can't ask him because my pride strangles me."

"I'll send some every payday. I swear," James said.

"You decide that on your own."

"Does that mean you'd sign for me?"

She didn't answer.

He picked up a fork and started eating sliced tomato. "You send me the envelope every month, I'll send you some money back inside it."

"Did you talk to the recruiters yet?"

"I will."

"When?"

"I will."

"Will when?"

"Monday."

"If you have the papers Monday night, and you can show me some good reasons for the service, I might sign. But if you're just dreaming, then Tuesday you better wake up and get over to the ranch with me. I've got the phone back on, but the rent is waiting on the Lord to move. Where's Burris?"

"He'll come when he's hungry."

"He's always hungry," she said, and began to say all over again the same things she'd just told him, because she was unable not to say them.

His mother was unable to be quiet. She read the Bible all the time. She was too old to be his mother, too worn out and stupid to be his mother.

Bill Houston thoroughly enjoyed beer, but there came a point where it started to stick in his throat. This tavern must face west, because the burning sun poured through the open door.

No air-conditioning, but he was used to that in the places he drank in. It was a dive, all right.

He returned from the toilet, and Kinney was still interrogating the beach bum: "What did you do? Tell me exactly what you did."

"Nothing. Fuck it."

Bill Houston sat down and said, "I got nothing against you boys. Got a little brother wants to go in the Marines."

The ex-marine was drunk. "That ain't nothing. I've seen some things."

"He's talking like he did something to some woman over there," Kinney said.

"Where?" Houston said.

"Vietnam, goddamn it," Kinney said. "Aren't you listening?"

"I've seen some things," the boy said. "What it was, they held this woman down and this one guy cut her pussy out. That stuff happens there all the time."

"Jesus God. No shit?"

"I did some of it too."

"You *did* it?"

"I was there."

Houston said, "You really" — He couldn't quite repeat it — "you really did that?"

Kinney said, "You cut up some bitch's cunt?"

"I was right there when it happened. Right nearby, right in the same — almost in the same village."

"It was your guys? Your outfit? Somebody in your platoon?"

"Not ours. It was some Korean guys, a Korean outfit. Those fuckers are senseless."

"Now shut the fuck up," Kinney said, "and tell us what the fuck you did."

"There's a lot of bad business that goes on," the man said.

"You're bullshit. The U.S. Marines would never put up with that. You're so bullshit."

The guy held up both hands like an arrestee. "Hey, wow, man — what's all the excitement about?"

"Just tell me you cut up a living woman, and I'll admit you're not bullshit."

The bartender shouted, "You! I told you before! You want beef? You want scrap?"—a big fat Hawaiian with no shirt on.

"This is a Moke right here," their companion said as the bartender threw down his rag and came over.

"I told you to get out of here."

"That was yesterday."

"I told you to get out of here with that talk. That means I don't want to see you yesterday, today, and tomorrow."

"Hey, I got a beer here."

"Take it with you, I don't care."

Kinney stood up. "Let's get the fuck out of this shit-hole Moke joint." He put his hand up under his shirt at the level of his belt.

"You pull a gun in here you gonna do time, if I don't kill you."

"I get mad easy on a hot day."

"Get out, you three."

"You making me mad?"

The young bum laughed insanely and hopped backward toward the door, dangling his arms like a monkey's.

Houston hurried for the exit too, saying, "Come on, come on, come on!" He was pretty sure he'd actually seen a gun butt in the waist of Kinney's jeans.

"See—that's a Moke, right there," the bum said. "They act all rough and tough. You get an advantage on them, and right away they cry like little babies."

They each bought a jug of Mad Dog 20/20 from a grocer who demanded they buy three loaves of Wonder Bread along with the wine, but it was still a bargain. They ate a little of the bread and tossed the rest to a couple of dogs. Soon they walked, drunk, surrounded by a pack of hungry strays, toward a glaring white strip of beach and the black sea and blue froth crashing on the sand.

A man stopped his car, a white, official-looking Ford Galaxie, and rolled down his window. He was an admiral in uniform. "Are you fellas enjoying the hell out of yourselves?"

"Yes, sir!" Kinney said, saluting by putting his middle finger to his eyebrow.

"I hope like hell you are," the admiral said. "Because hard times are coming for assholes like you." He rolled up his window and drove away.

The rest of the afternoon they spent drinking on the beach. Kinney sat against the trunk of a palm tree. The bum lay flat on his back with his Mad Dog balanced on his chest.

Houston took off his shoes and socks to feel the sand mounding under his arches. He felt his heart expanding. At this moment he understood the phrase "tropical paradise."

He told his two comrades, "What I'm saying, I mean, about these Mokes. I think they're related to the Indians that live down around my home. And not just them Indians, but also Indians that are from India, and every other kind of person you can think of who's like that, who's got something Oriental going on, and that's why I think, really, there ain't that many different kinds of people on this earth. And that's why I'm against war . . ." He waved his Mad Dog around. "And that's why I'm a pacifist." It was wonderful to stand on the beach before this audience and gesture with a half gallon of wine and talk utter shit.

However, Kinney did disturbing things. With a dreamy look on his face he tipped his bottle above his shiny black dress shoes and watched the wine dribble onto the toes. He tossed several pinches of sand in the bum's direction, speckling the bum's chest, his face, his mouth. The bum brushed it away and pretended not to realize where it was coming from.

Kinney suggested taking the party to a friend's house. "I want you to meet this guy," he told the bum, "and then we're gonna fix your bullshit."

"Fine with me, asshole," the bum said.

Kinney held up his thumb and forefinger pressed together. "I'd like to get you in a space about that big," he said.

They headed across the beach to find the house of Kinney's

friend. Houston was in agony, dealing with bare feet on the hot sand, and now on the black asphalt.

"Where are your shoes, you moron?"

Houston carried his white socks in the pockets of his Levi's, but his shoes were gone.

He stopped to purchase a seventeen-cent pair of zoris at a store. They had a sale on Thunderbird, but Kinney said his friend owed him money and promised to take them on the town later on.

Houston had loved those ivory-white bucks. To keep them white he'd powdered them with talc. And now? Abandoned to the tide.

"Is this a military base?" he asked. They were in some kind of development of cheap little pink and blue dwellings.

"These are bungalows," the bum said.

"Hey," Houston said to their companion. "What is your name, man?"

"I'll never tell," the bum said.

"He's totally full of bullshit," Kinney said.

Maybe these bungalows seemed a bit slummy, but not compared to what Houston had seen in Southeast Asia. A mist of white sand covered the asphalt walkways, and as the three of them strode among the coconut palms he heard the surf thunder in the distance. He'd passed through Honolulu several times, and he liked it a lot. It simmered and stank as much as any other tropical place, but it was part of the United States, and things were in good repair.

Kinney checked the numbers above the doorways. "This is my buddy's house. Let's go around back."

Houston said, "Why don't we just ring the doorbell?"

"I don't want to ring the doorbell. Do you want to ring the doorbell?"

"Well, no, man. He ain't my friend."

They followed Kinney around the building.

At one of the back windows, where a light shone, Kinney stood on tiptoe and peered inside, then he pressed himself against the trunk of a palm tree beside the wall and said to the beach bum, "Do me a favor, tap on the screen."

"Why should I?"

"I intend to surprise this guy."

"What for?"

"Just do it, will you? This guy owes me money, and I want to surprise him about it."

The bum scratched his fingernails along the window screen. The light went off within. A man's face hovered in the window frame, barely visible behind the screen. "What's the story, mister?"

Kinney said, "Greg."

"Who's that?"

"It's me."

"Oh, hey, man—Kinney."

"Yeah, that's right, it's me. You got the two-sixty?"

"I didn't see you there, man."

"You got my two-sixty?"

"You just back on the island? Where you been?"

"I want my two-sixty."

"Shit, man. I have a phone. Why didn't you call?"

"I wrote you we'd be pulling in the first week in June. What do you think this is? It's the first week in June. And I want my money."

"Shit, man. I don't have all of it."

"How much you got, Greg?"

"Shit, man. I can probably get some of it."

Kinney said, "You are a lying piece of genuine shit."

From his waistband he pulled a blue .45 automatic and aimed it at the man, and the man dropped like a puppet with its strings cut and disappeared. Right at that time Houston heard an explosion. He tried to understand where this noise had come from, to find some explanation for it other than that Kinney had just shot this man in the chest.

"Come on, come *on*," Kinney said.

There was a hole through the window screen.

"Houston!"

"What?"

"We're done. We're going."

"We are?"

Houston couldn't feel his own feet. He moved along as if on wheels. They passed houses, parked vehicles, buildings. Now traffic surrounded them. They'd come a long way in what seemed like three or four seconds. He was out of breath and sopped with sweat.

The crazy bum said, "That's pretty nifty, man. I think you won *that* conversation."

"I don't forgive my debtors. I don't forgive those who have trespassed against me."

"I gotta go."

"Yeah, I bet you gotta go, you stupid fuck."

"Where are we?" Houston said.

The bum was moving at a tangent now, off the sidewalk, into the street.

"Hey. I don't like your face," Kinney said as the guy left. "You crazy treacherous coward."

"What?" the guy said. "Listen, don't fuck with me."

"Don't fuck with you?"

"I think that's my bus," the guy said, and sprinted across the street right through squealing traffic and got behind the cover of a bus.

Kinney shouted, "Hey! Marine! Fuck you! Yeah! Semper Fi!"

Houston doubled up and vomited all over a mailbox.

Kinney didn't look right. A greasy film covered his eyes. He said, "Let's get a drink. Have you ever had a depth charger? Shot of bourbon in a mug of beer?"

"Yeah."

"I could use a bellyful of them bastards."

"Yeah, yeah," Houston said.

They found a place with air-conditioning, and Kinney got the two of them set up with beers and shots in a booth in the darkness at the back and began preparing depth chargers.

"This'll put some torque in your pork. Ever had one of these?"

"Sure, you drop a shot in a beer."

"Ever had one?"

"Well, I just know how you make one," Houston said.

Without any sense of the intervening hours, Houston awakened
sweaty and all bitten up by mosquitoes and sand fleas, a sagging
mattress swallowing him alive, a headache pounding against his
skull. He could hear the surf pounding also. His first fully conscious thought was that he'd seen one man shoot another man,
just like that.

He seemed to be quartered in some kind of open-air bedroom.
He made his way to the faucet in the corner, where he drank
deeply of the sweet water and peed, first removing from the sink a
wet bedsheet with a large black-rimmed hole burned in its middle. He found his watch, wallet, pants, and shirt, but he'd lost his
shoes on the beach, he now remembered, and he was pretty sure
he'd left his kit bag at the Y. His seventeen-cent zoris seemed to
have walked away on their own.

His wallet held a five and two ones. He collected ninety cents
in coins scattered on the bamboo floor. He stepped out to get his
bearings.

His head swam. The water he'd gorged on was making him
drunk all over again.

The sign said KING KANE HOTEL, and it said SAILORS WELCOME.

He kept an eye out for Kinney, but he didn't see anyone at all,
not a living soul. It was like a desert island. Palms, the bright beach,
the dark ocean. He headed away from the beach, toward town.

He didn't return to the *Bonners Ferry*. He had no intention of
getting anywhere near her berth, or anywhere else he might run
into Kinney, the last person he wanted to see. He missed the sailing and spent two weeks ashore without liberty, sleeping on the
beach and eating once per day at a Baptist mission on the waterfront, until he was confident Kinney was closer to Hong Kong
than to Honolulu; then he turned himself in to the Shore Patrol
for a week's recuperation in the brig.

His rate was rolled back to E-3 and he was a seaman again,

which meant he automatically lost his Boilerman rating. This was
the second demotion of his career. The first had resulted from
"repeated minor infractions" during his tour at Subic Bay Naval
Base—after he'd taken to the warrens of vice outside its gates.

Houston spent the following eighteen months assigned to
grunt work and garbage detail on the base in Yokosuka, Japan,
mostly with rowdy black men, low-aptitude morons, and worthless
bust-outs like himself. More often than he liked, he remembered
the admiral in Honolulu who'd lowered the window of his white
Ford Galaxie and promised, "Hard times are coming."

Because he now had a girlfriend who let him go all the way,
James forgot about the army for a while. Once or twice a week he
put an air mattress and a sleeping bag in the back of his mother's
pickup and snuck Stevie Dale out of her unconscious household
and made love to her in the predawn desert chill. Twice, sometimes three times in a night. He kept a tally. Between July 10 and
October 20, at least fifty times. But not as many as sixty.

Stevie didn't seem moved to participate. All she did was lie there.
He wanted to ask her, "Don't you like it?" He wanted to ask,
"Couldn't you move a little bit?" But in the atmosphere of disappointment and doubt that fell down around him after their lovemak-
ing, he was unable to communicate with her at all, other than to
pretend to listen while she talked. She talked about school, about
subjects, teachers, cheerleaders—of whom she was one, just an alternate, but she expected to join the main squad next year—nonstop in
his ear. Her gladness was a fist stuffing him deeper into the toilet.

He had more on his mind than his love life. He worried about
his mother. She didn't make much money at the ranch. She
exhausted herself. She'd grown thinner, knobbier. She spent the
first half of every Sunday at the Faith Tabernacle, and every Saturday afternoon she drove a hundred miles to the prison in Florence
to see her common-law husband. James had never accompanied

her on these pilgrimages, and Burris, now almost ten, refused to serve as escort—just ran away into the neighborhood of shacks and trailers and drifting dust when the poor old woman started getting herself ready on Saturday and Sunday mornings.

James didn't know how he felt about Stevie, but he knew his mother broke his heart. Whenever he mentioned enlisting in the service, she seemed willing to sign the papers, but if he left her now, how would it all turn out for her? She had nothing in this world but her two hands and her crazy love for Jesus, who seemed, for his part, never to have heard of her. James suspected she was just faking herself out, flinging herself at the Bible and its promises like a bug at a window. Having just about reached a decision in his mind to quit school and see the army recruiters, he stalled for many weeks, standing at the top of the high dive. Or on the edge of the nest. "Mom," he said, "every eagle has to fly." "Go ahead on, then," she said.

The army turned him down. They wouldn't take minors. "The Marines will take you when you're seventeen, but the army won't," he told his mother.

"Can't you wait a half a year?"

"More like three-fourths of a year."

"That's a lot of growing and learning you could do in school, for your education. Then you could graduate and be ready for your service, ready all the way through."

"I got to go."

"Go in the Marines, then."

"I don't want the Marines."

"Why not?"

"They're too stuck up."

"Then why are we talking about the Marines?"

"'Cause the army won't take me till I'm eighteen."

"Not even if I sign?"

"Not even if anybody signs. I need a birth certificate."

"I have your birth certificate. It says '1949.' Couldn't you just as easy change it to '1948'? Just close up the tail on the nine to where it looks like a eight."

On the last Friday in October, James went back to the army recruiter with a lying birth certificate and came home with instructions to report for muster on Monday.

The first two weeks of his basic training at Fort Jackson in South Carolina were the longest he'd experienced. Each day seemed a life entire in itself, lived in uncertainty, abasement, confusion, fatigue. These gave way to an overriding state of terror as the notions of killing and being killed began to fill his thoughts. He felt all right in the field, in the ranks, on the course with the others, yelling like monsters, bayoneting straw men. Off alone he could hardly see straight, thanks to this *fear*. Only exhaustion saved him. Being driven past his physical limits put a glass wall between him and all of this—he couldn't quite hear, couldn't quite remember what he'd just been looking at, what he'd just been shown. He waited only for sleep. He dreamed hysterically throughout, but slept for as long as they let him.

They assigned him to Vietnam. He knew it meant he was dead. He hadn't applied, hadn't even asked how you apply, they'd just handed him his fate. Four days out of basic, here he carried his lunch toward a table in the enlisted mess, the steamy odor of reconstituted mashed potatoes rising toward his face, and his legs felt like rubber as he stepped toward a future scattered with booby traps and land mines: they'd be on patrol and he'd be too far ahead of the others in a line of guys in the jungle, he'd be in *front* and he'd step on something that would just rip the veins right out of him, splash him around like paint—before the noise hit his ears, his ears would be shredded—you just, probably, hear the tiniest beginning of a little hiss. There was no sense sitting here, spooning up his lunch off a partitioned tray. He should be saving his life, getting out of this mess hall, disappearing maybe in some big town where they had dirty movies that never close.

Two of the guys came over and started talking about dying in battle.

"Are you trying to get me spooked worse than I am already?" James said, trying to sound humorous.

"The odds are you won't get killed."

"Shut up."

"Really, there's not that many battles or anything."

"Did you see that guy over there?" James said, and they had: three tables away sat a very small black man in dress greens, a first sergeant. He didn't look big enough to join the army, but on his chest he wore many ribbons, including the blue one with five white stars signifying the Congressional Medal of Honor.

Whenever they saw a soldier with decorations, James and the others made a point of passing close to get a look. That was it, wasn't it?—to be drinking a cup of coffee with this person inside of you hardened and blackened by heroic deeds, and kids walking by with a weak feeling in their stomachs, trying not to stare. But in order to enjoy it, you had to get home alive.

When the others left, James returned to the line for another helping. People complained about the food, and therefore James complained too; but actually he liked it.

The black man with the blue ribbon on his chest beckoned him to his table.

James didn't know what to do but go on over.

"Come on, sit down," the sergeant said. "You got that look."

"Yeah? What look?"

"Just sit down," the sergeant said. "I ain't that black."

James joined him.

"I says you got that look."

"Yeah?"

"The look says I wanted to drive a tank or work on helicopter engines, but instead they sending me to the jungle and get shot at."

James said nothing, lest he weep about it.

"Your sarge told me, Conrad, Conroy."

"Sergeant, yeah," James said, extremely nervous. "Sergeant Connell."

"Why didn't you think of something to volunteer for, to get you out of it?"

Now James feared he'd laugh. "Because I'm stupid."

"You're going to the Twenty-fifth, right? Which brigade?"

"The Three."

"I'm from the Twenty-fifth."

"Yeah? No shit?"

"Not the Three, though. The Fourth."

"But the Three—are they, are they—you know—fighting?"

"Some units are. Unfortunately, yes."

James felt if he could only say, Sarge, I don't want to fight, he would surely save himself.

"You worried about getting killed?"

"Sort of, you know, I mean—*yeah*."

"Nothing to worry about. By the time The Thing eats you, you all emptied up, you ain't thinking. Nothing but jazz happening."

James couldn't quite take comfort from this statement.

"Yep." The small black man hunched forward, touching the fingertips of each hand together rapidly. "Come here. Listen," he said. James leaned toward him, half afraid the man might grab him by the ear or something. "In a combat zone, you don't want to be a pin on a map. Sooner or later the enemy's going to hammer on that pin with a superior force. You want to have some mobility options, don't you? You want some decision-sharing, don't you? That means you want to volunteer for a Recon outfit. That's a voluntary thing. You volunteer for that. After that, you never, never volunteer for nothing, nothing, nothing, not even to jump in bed with a red-hot female, not even James Bond's girlfriend. That's rule number one, is don't volunteer. And rule number two is that when in the foreign land, you don't violate the women, you don't hurt the livestock, and if possible not the property, except for burning the hooches, that goes with the job."

"That's a Medal of Honor you got there."

"Yes, it is. So you listen to what I say."

"All right. Okay."

"I might be black as coal, but I'm your brother. You know why?"

"I don't guess I do."

"Because you're going over to the Twenty-fifth as a replacement, ain't you?"

"Yes, sir."

"Don't sir me, I ain't your sir. You going to the Twenty-fifth, right?"

"Right."

"Okay. And you know what? I came from the Twenty-fifth. Not the Third Brigade, the Fourth. But anyway, *I* could be the one you're replacing. So I giving you the dope."

"Okay. Thanks."

"No, you don't thank me, I thank you. You know why? It's me you could be replacing."

"You're welcome," James said.

"Now: what I just said, you take all this under your advisement."

"Will do."

James enjoyed the way they talked in the infantry, and he tried to talk that way too. Mobility options. Pin on a map. Superior force. Under advisement. These were the same phrases a recon sergeant had used while delivering a talk to their barracks just two weeks earlier. Now the phrases rang true, they made sense. One fact stood out clear: if you had to be a grunt, you might as well be recon.

After more than a year in the States, in California—two months at the Defense Language Institute in Carmel, and nearly twelve months at the Naval Postgraduate School in Monterey—Skip Sands returned to Southeast Asia and, somewhere between Honolulu and Wake Island, flying miles above the Pacific on a 707, came into the shadow of the mystery that would devour him.

After the 707 to Tokyo he went by prop plane to Manila, by train to the bottom of the mountain north of there, by car once again to the staff house in San Marcos, ready for a confrontation

with Eddie Aguinaldo, and also happy at the prospect of the
major's pointless sweaty jungle night patrols, only to find that the
patrols had been discontinued and Eddie Aguinaldo was nowhere
around. The Huks had been declared extinct. Anders Pitchfork
was long gone. For company Sands had only the household crew
and occasional vacationing staff from Manila, usually overworked
couriers who slept a lot. He waited nearly a month for one of them
to bring word from the colonel.

Word arrived in a courier pouch, on a photo postcard of the
Washington Monument. A yellow seal pasted to a corner warned,
KEEP OFFICIAL BUSINESS UNDER WRAPS / COUNSEL CORRESPONDENTS
TO USE ENVELOPES / THANK YOU / YOUR AMERICAN POST OFFICE.

> Merry Christmas somewhat early. Pack your files, the whole
> show. Head to Manila. See the Section. I'm in Langley
> bouncing a desk off the walls. Saw Boston last week.
> Your Aunt and Cousins send warmest wishes. See you in
> Saigon. Unc FX.

But the files were already packed, or so he assumed. His first
day back he'd found, in the closet he'd left them in, three olive
army-issue footlockers, the lid of each stenciled with the name
BENÉT W.F.—the accent applied by hand with a soft-point pen—
and each one heavily padlocked.

Having had no word as to the keys to these treasures, he left
that matter for another day and did the next indicated thing,
which was to travel to the embassy in Manila in a staff car almost
entirely filled with his uncle's project. There he was instructed to
keep the car and travel some forty miles beyond the capital to
Clark Air Base, where he'd board military transport for South
Vietnam.

Tomorrow was New Year's Eve. His itinerary would have him
taking off on New Year's Day from Clark Field for the airport at
Tan Son Nhut, outside Saigon.

At last! Feeling as if he'd already taken to the air, he sat in the

staff car on Dewey Boulevard watching the sun quiver on Manila
Bay, and by its glorious light, in order to calm himself, he glanced
through his mail. An alumni newsletter from Bloomington.
Newsweek and *U.S. News and World Report*, both many weeks old.
In a large manila envelope he found his final batch of California
mail, forwarded from there through his APO address. These letters
had chased him for two months. From his Aunt Grace and Uncle
Ray—the eldest of his father's four siblings—came a greeting card
envelope with something whacking around inside it, one of the new
John F. Kennedy half dollars, it turned out, and a Hallmark card, to
which the coin had evidently been taped before coming loose on
its ten-thousand-mile journey. Skip had turned thirty on October
28, and in commemoration of this milestone here came fifty cents,
double the usual, no more quarters for such a big boy.

Also, quite a rare thing: a letter from the widow Beatrice Sands,
Skip's mother. It felt thick. He didn't open it.

And here was a letter from Kathy Jones. He'd received several
in the last year, each one crazier than the last, had saved them all,
had ceased answering.

Are you finally here in Vietnam? Maybe in the next village?
I welcome you to the Bible in Panavision and Technicolor.
But here it's good not to be from your United States of
America. Too many resentments. They don't mind the
French so much, though. They beat the French.
  Do you remember Damulog?

From the next paragraph the word "affair" leapt up at him, and
he stopped reading.

Nothing further from the colonel.

He hadn't seen his uncle in over fourteen months, had concluded that one or both of them had been sidelined owing to the
questionable business on Mindanao. Something, anyway, had
kept them both from the action. He'd taken his course in Vietnamese at the Defense Language Institute, and what started by

looking like the sensible prelude to a Saigon posting turned into
eleven baffling months spent with a crew of three other translators, not one Vietnamese national among them, working on a
project of doubtful utility, that is, pursuing a patent folly—to
extract an encyclopedia of mythological references from over
seven hundred volumes of Vietnamese literature, an endeavor
waged mostly in three basement-level offices of the Naval Postgraduate School in Monterey and consisting mainly of the listing,
categorization, and cataloging of fairy-tale figures.

This he understood to be his uncle's contribution to the
Psychological Operations Group of the Military Assistance
Command–Vietnam, for which the colonel now served, Skip further understood, as chief CIA liaison. In fact, all but officially the
colonel ran Psy Ops for MAC-V, according to an Agency officer
from Langley named Showalter, who checked in with Skip's translation team on a more or less monthly basis; and before long Skip
would help the colonel run it. "When does he want me there?"
"January or so." "Outstanding," Skip said, completely infuriated
by the delay. This conversation took place in June.

The fanciful project ended with sudden postings to other
places for all the participants, who boxed and shipped to Langley
the useless material.

He opened the letter from his mother.

"Dear Son Skipper"—her hand rounded, slanting, large, covering several pages of six-by-eight-inch stationery bond:

I'm sure not much for writing, so first thing, nothing's
wrong. Wouldn't want you to think it's only bad news
would get me to sit down and send a greeting to you. It's
really the opposite, a really fine day of Indian summer.
The bluest sky, not a dab of a cloud anywhere up there.
The trains go by with a different sound due to leaves
turning on the trees, it's a happy greeting now, pretty
soon we'll hear that lonely sound of a whistle in bare winter. This afternoon it's warm enough you want a breeze

through the house. Open the windows and hear the red-wing blackbirds calling. And the grass is still coming on, you can see where it needs one more cutting before the fall is really official. When I saw how pretty the day was I thought, "I think I'll write a letter!"

Thank you for the money. I bought a new drier to go with the washer. Got it full of clothes right now and going round and round. But in fine weather like this I like to put the big things like the sheets and bedding out on the line and dry them in the world, and that's just what I've done. Got the sheets on the line like in the old days. Yes, I ordered a drier, I didn't get a TV. You said get one, but I didn't. When I feel like I need entertainment I go to the shelves and take down The Old Curiosity Shop or Emma or Silas Marner and read just any old part and nine out of ten times I have to go back to the beginning and read it all. I just have to. Those are good old friends.

I told you about old Rev. Pierce retiring. There's a new man at the church, Pastor Paul. Pretty young. His last name is Conniff, but he goes by Pastor Paul. He puts his new slant on things. He kept me interested, I went every Sunday all last winter, then the weather relents, the sun shines, things get busy, and I haven't been since early April probably. No TV, but I try to keep up with the news. Isn't it terrible news? I don't know what to think. Sometimes I wish I could talk to somebody about what I think, then I think I better not. I know you joined the government to be of service to the world, but our leaders are sending good boys to wreck another country and maybe lose their lives without any sound explanation.

Well, a half hour's gone by since that last sentence. That new drier ding-donged and got me running to do the folding while it was still hot. Excuse me for the things I say. Maybe I'll just say what I want and go back and write this letter over, cross out the bad parts and just send the nice parts. No, I better not. War means something different to me than it does to generals and soldiers. As of next December 7 twenty-six years will be gone since we lost your father, and every day I still miss how it was. After a while I had boyfriends after your father, and really spent some time with Kenneth Brooke before he took a job with Northwest Airlines, but it was a little too soon for us before we'd gotten it all sorted out what we'd do, Ken and I, so when he moved to Minneapolis, that was that. Otherwise I think we would have gotten engaged, which means you would have had a stepdad. But that's off the subject. What <u>was</u> the subject? Goodness, I better not send this letter! I don't know if you even knew it was a little serious between me and Ken Brooke. Do you even remember Ken at all? Every other Christmas he and his family come back home to visit his folks and his sister. The other Christmases they go back to his wife's home town, I don't know where that is. Boy, am I having one of those days.

I'd better get out that old push-mower and do the yard one last time for this year. I'll have to oil it up. Had it done by the kids all summer, one or other of the Strauss kids, Thomas or Daniel, but they're in school now. They took turns with their Dad's big noisy gas-powered monster. Made two dollars each time. That old push-mower is an old friend of mine. Remember how I used to do the yard—"And stay away from those blades with your fingers!"—that's what I hollered, like those blades would jump up and bite your fingers off, even with nobody pushing. Then one day I hear those blades whirring and look out the window and here comes Skipper in his teeshirt with his skinny arms, pushing past the window like The Little Engine That Could. Did the whole yard on your first try. I hope you remember, because I remember so clearly. I hope you remember how good you felt, and I will too.

   I appreciate the little notes you send. People ask about you, and it's good to have news to relate. Attending the Language Institute, attending the Naval Post-Grad, attached to U.S. Embassy, pretty impressive, makes me feel like a star.

   We've had a beautiful day all day, but here about three PM it's gusting up a little, gets the sheets waving and slapping at the wind. That's the whitest they can get, when they're dried in the sun and the breeze. And we're lucky about that breeze, because the tracks aren't far, but the breeze is always the other way, no grit coming down. Makes me glad we live on the "other side" of the tracks! I remember when I saw you go by that window. I saw your strength of character in a flash. I thought when I saw you, He's a goer like his Dad, he'll get himself through college on jobs and scholarships, nothing's stopping that little lad. And now more study, more grad school. Army, Navy, Embassy, seems like everybody needs you.

Here, six lines from the finish, he had to stop reading and curse himself. He'd spent fourteen months in the States, could have arranged a visit home before he'd left again. But he'd ducked her. Sure: war, intrigue, the fates—certainly, he'd face them. Just, please, not Mom. Not her laundry flapping in the sorrows of autumn. Not Clements, Kansas, with its historical license to be tiny, low, and square. Here, in Manila, at approximately fourteen degrees latitude north and fifty-seven longitude east, he couldn't get much farther away. But it wasn't far enough. It hurt him to think of her all alone. Particularly after his time at the Language Institute. True to the colonel's word ("I'll send you to the school, we'll work that out"), he'd been posted, just before that Thanksgiving of 1965, to the institute on a high bluff overlooking Carmel. The view was that of low fog hunched over the coast, or higher fog wrapped around the grounds, or, on the clear days, the pure Pacific heartrendingly removed from him while he underwent his total immersion course in Vietnamese, which meant four weeks' confinement to the facility followed by four weeks with weekend passes only. On his first leave he took Communion a few miles down the coast at the Sisters of Notre Dame de Namur, a nunnery open to the public for Mass on Sunday mornings. The laity faced the altar, and the sisters, cut off by their vows from the world, sat or stood, no telling which, behind a wall, hidden even from their families, some of whom sat in the pews to glimpse the upturned palms of the cloistered acolytes reaching through a small window to receive the Body of Christ. Watching them that morning, thinking of them now, eased his bonds. Had he taken a vow of separation? No. Whatever his circumstances, he was free, and fighting for the freedom of all. But his mother: Some sort of vow undertaken there. Some sort of walling-in acceded to.

Skip, I pray for you and for the whole country. I'm going to start up with the church attendance again.

I'm sorry I hardly ever write, I do appreciate your notes, but it takes a certain kind of day to make me get out the pen and paper.

Well, there you have it, another letter or something!

Thinking of you,

Mom

Having proved himself with this one, he felt he might face the letter from Kathy Jones. But it had grown too dark to read.

He'd spent some considerable time with these communications, and his taxi hadn't moved half a block. "Is there a problem?" he asked the driver. "What's wrong?"

"Something is delaying," the driver said.

Far around the curve of the boulevard as it followed the contours of the bay, he saw the lights of traffic moving freely. But here they were stuck. "I'll be back," he said. He got out and walked toward the trouble, skirting the stalled cars, wending among the rancid puddles. A large city bus held up the flow, stopped by a single man who stood lurching in the middle of the street, drunk, his face covered with blood, T-shirt ripped down the front, weeping as he confronted this vehicle, the biggest thing he could challenge, apparently, after somebody had beaten him in a fight. Horns, voices, gunned engines. Keeping to the shadows, Skip stood and watched: the bloody face, deformed by passion, shining in the bus's headlights; the head back, the arms limp, as if the man hung by hooks in his armpits. This reeking desperate city. It filled him with joy.

At the beginning of James's furlough his mother took three days off from the McCormick Ranch, and they spent the time watching television together in the small house at the edge of the desert. The day he got back she unpacked his Class A greens and straightened the creases carefully with her steam iron. "Now you're doing something for your country," she said. "We have to stand up against the Communists. They're Godless." It might have meant something, if she didn't say the same about the Jews and Catholics and Mormons.

After the old woman went back to work, James saw a great deal of Stevie Dale. The afternoon of Christmas Eve the two of them drove in his mother's pickup out to the edge of the hills on the Carefree Highway, to the site of a one-car accident in which the driver had been killed.

"See there?" Stevie said. "He hit a saguaro, then a paloverde, then that big rock."

The blackened wreck had been pried away from a boulder by emergency crews some days earlier, but hadn't yet been removed. The car had turned turtle and burned.

"He must've been flying."

"Only one in the car. Only car on the road."

"I guess he was late."

They popped a couple of beers each, and quickly Stevie got tipsy. They sat looking at the wreck like a charred, upturned hand.

"The driver burned to death inside," she said.

"I hope he was knocked out," James said. "For his sake."

The car had been red, but the flames had melted its paint. Now it showed several patches of bare, bright metal. It might have been a Chevrolet, there was really no telling.

"Every single thing in the world is slowly burning up," she said.

"Yeah? Is it? I don't get you."

"Everything's oxidizing. Everything in the world."

He gathered she'd come by this news in her chemistry class.

During basic he'd thought of her continually, but it was nothing personal. He'd thought just as often about at least seven other girls from their high school. Being with her here, even surrounded by these unbounded spaces, he felt trapped in a vise.

He said, "Can I ask you something? The first time we did it, were you—you know—a virgin, or something? Was that your first time?"

"Are you *serious*?"

"Uh. Yeah."

"Are you *kidding*?"

"Yeah. I mean no."

"What exactly do you think I am?"

"I was just asking."

"Yes, I was a virgin. This isn't something you do every day, or *I* don't anyway. What do you think I am," she said, "some motorcycle mama?"

That made James laugh, which in turn made Stevie cry.

"Stevie, Stevie, Stevie," he said, "I'm sorry." He was glad it was Christmas Eve. She'd spend tomorrow with her family, and he wouldn't have to see her.

But it was only the beer working on her, and in two minutes she'd accepted his apology. "The sunset's always beautiful when there's clouds," she said.

In the dusk it would cool off quickly now. He felt a breeze

starting, the day's last warm breath as it ended. Stevie kissed him · many times.

In South Carolina they'd treated him like a beast, and he'd survived. He'd grown bigger, stronger, older, better. But having returned to the world he'd grown up in, he had no idea how to sit in a room with his mother, or what to say to this sixteen-year-old girl, no idea how to get through a few days in his life until he shipped to Louisiana for Advanced Infantry Training, until he got back where people would tell him what to do.

Stevie said, "I guess we'll open presents and all that stuff pretty early," and placed her loving fingertips on the back of his neck. "What time do you want to come over?"

As he considered this simple question, it seemed to widen until it split his very thoughts open.

He wrenched at his door's handle and got out into the air and walked past the exploded wreck and stood bent over with his hands on his knees, barely keeping upright, his gaze lifted toward the winter horizon. He wanted somebody to come out of the faint pink and blue distances and save him. Far away he saw the ripples of a mirage—either a horrible burning death in Vietnam, like that of the man pried from this charred Chevrolet, or a parade of years filled with Stevie's questions and her fingers touching his neck.

Sands stayed overnight in a private room with a bath at Clark Field's Bachelor Officers' Quarters, most of which was devoted to dorm-style living in a collegiate atmosphere, with doors opening and closing and half-dressed young men shouting up and down the halls and the sounds of showers and Nancy Sinatra tunes warring with Stan Getz bossa nova instrumentals, and the stink of Right Guard spray deodorant. He arrived around eight at night. He and the driver got his footlockers into his room. He spoke to no one, turned in early, got up late the next day—New Year's Eve—and

boarded the base shuttle bus and asked the Filipino driver to let
him off wherever he could find some breakfast.

Thus Sands found himself at 9:00 a.m. on December 31, 1966,
at the snack bar in a bowling alley filled, even at that hour, with air-
men pursuing improved averages in a clattering atmosphere. He
ate bacon and eggs off a plastic plate at a table alongside rows and
rows of bowling balls and watched. Despite the general noise there
was a kind of tiptoe stealth in the approach of some of these athletes, a stalking, bird-dog concentration. Others lumbered to the
line and flung like shot-putters. Skip had never bowled, never
before this moment even observed. The appeal was obvious, the
cleanly geometry, the assurances of physical ballistics, the organic
richness of the wooden lanes and the mute servitude of the
machines that raised the pins and swept away the fallen, above all
the powerlessness and suspense, the ball held, the ball directed, the
ball traveling away like a son, beyond hope of influence. A slow,
large, powerful game. Sands determined he'd give it a try as soon as
his breakfast settled. Meanwhile, he drank black coffee and read
his letter from Kathy Jones. She wrote in a neat hand, apparently
with a fountain pen, in blue ink, on flimsy, grayish, probably Viet-
namese-made onionskin. Her first few letters to him had been
direct, chatty, lonely, affectionate. She'd wondered if they might
meet in Saigon, and Sands had looked forward to that. Now these
recent letters, these confused ruminations—

> I've dealt with jokers all my life. Just jokers. No aces, no
> kings. Timothy was the first ace and he introduced me to
> the King—Jesus Christ. Before that I went to Minneapo-
> lis for college. But I lost my drive so I quit and worked as
> a secretary and went out for cocktails every night with
> young guys who worked downtown, young jokers.

—they might have been torn from a journal, addressed to no one.
He could hardly stand them. He'd stopped looking forward to seeing her again.

These people here in these lands we're visiting—look at
these people. They're as trapped by circumstance as
criminals are trapped by prison. Born and live and die
according to the dictates of how things go—never say, I
want to live in that place rather than this place, I want to
be a cowboy rather than a farmer. Can't even be farmers,
really—they're just planters. Tillers. Gardeners.

In the beginning her communiqués hadn't been long, generally
two sides of a page, and had ended, "Well, my hand's getting
tired! I'd better sign off. Yours, Kathy" or "Well, I see I'm down to
the bottom, I'd better sign off. Yours, Kathy." In the beginning
he'd replied, always very briefly. Not, he hoped, curtly. But he
hadn't known what to say. The nature of their connection, clear
enough in the heat of it, had become mysterious.

When it comes to the contrast between having a choice
and no freedom to choose whatsoever—here's where it
gets as stark as it can get. You, America, your forces are
here making war by choice. Your enemy doesn't have a
choice. They were born into a land at war.
    Or maybe it's not that simple—U.S. vs. North
Vietnam—no, it's the young men who get this war forced
upon them versus the ones who choose this war, the
dying soldiers vs. the theorists and the dogmatists and
the generals.

Here was clumsy thinking, and Sands had long ago lost patience
with it. Would she like to see a bust of Lenin by the door of every
public school? See the Statue of Liberty toppled in an obscene
ceremony? Of course she would. And that wrongheadedness
appealed to him. Always the sucker for sardonic, myopic, intellectual women. Women quick-witted and congenitally sad. In
her face a combination of aggression and apology. Kind brown
eyes.

Remember asking me about a place in the Bible claiming
there are different administrations on the earth and I said
I didn't think so? You were right—First Corinthians 12:5–6
etc. "And there are differences of administrations, but the
same Lord. And there are diversities of operations, but it
is the same God which worketh all in all."

That must appeal to a G-man like you! (I still don't
believe you work for Del Monte.) If you want to believe
that different angelic departments sort of run different
parts of the show down here on earth, I don't blame you.
Just going from the Manila airport to Tan Son Nhut airport in Saigon I'd be almost ready to call it diversities of
deities, diverse universes, all on the same planet.

Come to think of it, in North America various Spanish
priests (the Catholic Church itself?) must have believed
that some areas are under control of the Devil—or of
Christ—thus places called "Mt. Diablo," "Sangre de Cristo
Mountains," and so on.

He slipped the letter under his coffee mug. No concentrating
on it now. Travel excited him. This world ending, the next emerg-
ing, the bowlers surrounding him with motion and noise, flinging
out black planets, smashing the constellations of wooden pins.
Back in his room, other things to set moving: the monster of the
colonel's files, and a duffel bag packed with two pairs of walking
shoes and four changes of machine-washable clothing—no suit,
no dress apparel—also a small crate woven of cane, a basket,
really, but quite sturdy, packed with dictionaries in several languages. Skip had been trained to remember that he came as a
civilian and must dress like one, avoid khaki or olive garb, wear
brown shoes rather than black, brown belts as well. He'd left
behind his custom-tooled carbine and traveled with a secret
agent's kind of weapon, a .25-caliber Beretta automatic conceal-
able in a pants pocket. His mind raced over all of it, a result of too
much coffee. He gave up the idea of bowling, left the lanes, and

went striding through the tropic noon until his brow thudded and his wet shirt clung to him.

The base library looked open. The air conditioner roared on its roof. He approached the door and saw people within beneath fluorescent lights, but the door wouldn't budge, and he had a moment of panic in which he felt himself locked out and gazing helplessly on the land of books. A man coming out opened it with some effort—just stuck in its frame, swollen with damp—and Sands gained entrance. Jangling from the coffee he flitted from stack to stack and looked into a number of books, never taking a seat. In a copy of Twain's *Pudd'nhead Wilson* he read all the chapter epigraphs, looking for one he thought he remembered—something to do with the treasure of a life spent in obscurity—but it wasn't there. In the children's section he found some volumes of Filipino folk tales. Nothing from Vietnam.

He was delighted to chance, next, on a book about Knute Rockne. He sat down and turned its leaves until he found on page 87 a photo of Rockne on the fields of Notre Dame in 1930 with the last team he'd coached; and among them, in the middle of the third row, with more abundant hair and his wrinkles erased and the familiar, eager sincerity on his face: Uncle Francis. A second-string freshman, but nevertheless one of Rockne's blunt, confident young men—chests out, chins up, peering ahead no further than two or three minutes into the life to come. Francis's older brother Michael, Skip's father, had graduated from Notre Dame the year before and moved to his bride's hometown of Clements, Kansas. Francis would join the army air force and leave it in 1939 to fly with the pseudo-civilian Flying Tigers in Burma. Michael would grow restless selling farm equipment and join the navy in 1941 and go down six months later with the *Arizona* in the first few seconds of the attack on Pearl Harbor. Death had too often visited prematurely among his father's people—wars and accidents. The colonel had a daughter, Anne; a son, Francis Junior, had drowned one Fourth of July while sailing in Boston Harbor. A brother and a son, both claimed by harbors. There had been brothers and sisters and plenty of cousins, and many children from those sources, and everybody had somebody missing. It was a loud, sad family.

Skip stared at the ranks of the players. Men who raced from the benches to collide with one another in joyful bloodshed. Who let themselves be hammered and rounded into cops and warriors and lived in a world completely inaccessible to women and children. They stared back at him. An old ache sang its song. Only child of a widowed mother. Somehow he'd entered their world without becoming a man.

He shut the book and instead opened the fragile pages of the letter from Kathy Jones:

> They were born into a land at war. Born into a time of trial that never ends.
>
> What I don't think has been talked about is the fact that in order to be Hell, the people in Hell could never be sure they were really there. If God told them they were in Hell, then the torment of uncertainty would be relieved from them, and their torment wouldn't be complete without that nagging question—"Is this suffering I see all around me my eternal damnation and the eternal damnation of all these souls, or is it just a temporary journey?" A temporary journey in the fallen world.
>
> And I might as well tell you, my faith has gone dark, because I started reading Calvin, wrestling with Calvin, and I lost the fight and got dragged down into Calvin's despair. Calvin doesn't call it despair but it's despair all right. I know that this is Hell, right here, planet Earth, and I know that you, me, and all of us were made by God only to be damned.
>
> And then suddenly I scream, "But God wouldn't do that!"
>
> —See? The torment of uncertainty.
>
> Or I guess as a Catholic, you might ask yourself if this is a journey through Purgatory. You'll sure ask yourself

that when you come to Vietnam. Five or ten times a day
you'll stop and ask yourself, When did I die? And why is
God's punishment so cruel?

He spent the afternoon in the cool of the library and rode the
shuttle bus back to the BOQ.

He'd hardly been back in his room a minute when somebody
knocked at the door, a man about his own age, wearing civvies,
holding in each hand a bottle of San Miguel beer.

"These are the last in the bucket, my man."

The quality of the man's smile was disconcerting.

"The Skipper needs a beer."

Skip said—"Hey!"

"Quantico!"

He accepted a bottle and they shook hands, Skip flushing with
a warmth of recognition, although the name escaped him. They'd
done a twenty-one-day ciphers program together at Quantico just
after his training at the Farm—never buddies, but certainly, now,
well met. They sat around chatting about nothing, and after a few
minutes Skip felt the moment for getting his friend's name had
slipped past. "Where's your home station now?" he asked the man.
"Still Langley?"

"They've got me stashed in the District. At the State Department, the big building, Pennsylvania Avenue. But I make the
rounds—Saigon, Manila, DC. What about you?"

"I'm being transferred. Saigon."

"You get a good deal in Saigon—share a house, servants, that
order of existence. Run of the place whenever you can get away.
Hell—every weekend. Most weekends."

"I hear it's a beautiful country."

"Surprisingly beautiful. You step out of a hooch to take a leak,
shake off the last drop, and look up—God, you can't believe it,
where'd it come from?"

"Just like here, in other words."

"Considerably more dangerous. You do earn your hazard pay."

"I'm looking forward to it."

"You're in Operations, am I right?"

"Right," Skip said. "Officially. But I seem to work for Plans."

"Well, I'm in Plans, but I seem to work for State."

"What brings you to the base?"

"A free ride back to the war at twenty hundred hours. The clock's running out for me, son. Last chance for a San Miguel. Wish I could take a keg with me."

"Do they sell San Miguel by the keg?"

"Come to think of it, I'm not sure. But they sell it by the bottle at the Officers' Club. Let's go."

"I'm all grimy. Should I meet you?"

"Should I wait?—Or what about going into town?"

"Well," Skip said, "if you're leaving at twenty hundred—"

"Or we could swing by the Teen Club, find out what the officers' kids are up to."

Skip said, "What?"

"Say, that reminds me—I mean, speaking of officers' kids. Aren't you related to the colonel himself?"

"Which colonel, now?"

"Aren't you close to the colonel? The colonel Francis Xavier?"

"I'm one of his favorite people, if we're talking about the same guy."

"There ain't but one Colonel."

"I guess not."

"I took that Psy Ops course of his. He's a man with a message."

"He's got vision, all right."

"You took it too? He titled it wrong. 'Reminiscing and Theorizing' would be more like it."

"That's the colonel."

"He's put some of his thoughts in an article for the journal. Have you read it?"

"In the journal? You mean in *Studies*?"

"Yowza."

They referred to the Agency's in-house organ, *Studies in Intelli-*

gence. The colonel's thoughts in the journal? What to say to this? Nothing.

He gulped his beer and wiped it from his mustache. He'd gone through the bushy Kennedy phase. Now they were all back to crew cuts again, flattops—proving they weren't the Beatles. But Skip had kept his mustache. It was luxuriant.

"Do you read the journal much, Skip?"

"I catch up in Manila. We didn't have it in the boonies. I was up in San Marcos."

"Oh, yeah—the Del Monte place."

"Ever been there?"

"No. You haven't read his piece?"

"I can't believe he'd get anything into shape for actual publication."

"It hasn't been published. It's just a draft."

"How did you happen to see it?"

"I wondered if you'd seen it in a rough form."

"Man, I didn't know he ever put a pen to the page. How'd you get hold of it? Are you with the journal?"

"So you haven't seen it."

Skip now felt his heart coming to a halt. "No," he said, "like I said."

"Well, I'll be open with you. The piece is a little puzzling. One explanation is it's meant to be satire. But if he's submitting satire to the house organ, that's puzzling in itself. That's troubling too; that in itself is puzzling."

"I see," Skip said. "Look, obviously I remember you, but I've forgotten your name."

"Voss."

"Rick, right?"

"C'est moi."

"The face was familiar, but—"

"I'm getting porky."

"If you say so."

"I got married. We had a kid. I got fat."

"Boy or girl?"

"A little girl. Celeste."

"Nice name."

"She's eighteen months."

"That makes it hard, huh? Traveling and all."

"I'm glad I travel. I'm like the moon, I come and go. To tell you the truth, I don't think I could take it day after day. Women and children frighten me. I don't understand them. I'd rather be somewhere else." He'd been sitting on the bed; he got up and sat on one of the footlockers. "And whose gear is this here?"

"I'm just delivering it."

"Who's W. F. Benét?"

"The recipient, I guess."

"Or maybe the sender," said Voss.

"I'm actually not familiar with the name."

"What's the W for? William?"

"Beats me," Skip said.

"And what about the F? What's his full name?"

"Rick . . . I'm just a blind courier on this one."

Voss said, "Wanna arm-wrestle?"

"Uh, no," said Skip.

"If we arm-wrestled, do you know who'd win?"

Skip shrugged.

"Do you care?"

"No, I don't," said Skip.

"Neither do I," said Voss. "We don't need muscles. We've got a private army now. These Green Berets are like human tanks. They're death machines. One of them could tear the two of us to shreds, huh? And they work for the Agency. Well, the point is, from here on out we're gonna keep the tough guys in uniform. They don't graduate from the field, they don't get behind a desk and start running things. This ain't the OSS. That war is history."

Skip clinked his bottle against Voss's. Both bottles were empty. "If we were halfway through a case of this stuff," he said, "I'd just figure we were having a bull session. If it was four a.m. and we were half sloshed."

"But we're not."

"No."

"Yeah."

"When are we gonna get those beers?" Skip said.

"Well, how about right now?"

They both stood up.

Skip said, "Oh, drat. Wait a minute."

"What."

Skip said, "My watch is stopped. What time is it?"

"Fifteen-twenty."

"Darn, I've got a little briefing in forty minutes. I'd better get my gear in order."

"Then what? Right to Saigon?"

"As far as I know."

"I'll probably see you there."

"All right," said Skip, "and then we can have those beers. What do they drink in Saigon?"

"Tiger Beer. Then they puke."

"Good enough," Skip said.

Voss stared at the floor and concentrated before raising his gaze, preparing to speak.

"You'll be heading off, then," Skip reminded him.

Voss stood up. "Rain check," he said, and as he departed Skip sent him half a salute.

The colonel had always said: When you hit the wall, take a shower and change your clothes.

Skip did both, and then he took the day's apparel downstairs to the laundry room with the intention of traveling to his new post completely clean. For over an hour he sat on a plastic chair among the thudding machines—hiding, essentially, evading scrutiny—in a rising tide of confusion and dread. He climbed out of it momentarily to fold his clothes and was dragged back down. He sat upright in his chair, back straight, hands in his lap. He remembered that his life was nothing. He focused on that point on the horizon, the solid, the fixed, the prominent goal: the defeat of Communism. The panic subsided.

Soon he stood out front of the BOQ under a dark but rainless sky. Shuttles came four per hour. He boarded the next one and traveled at the base limit of "15 MPH/24 KPH" through this town of green buildings with identical corrugated roofs, out to the last stop just inside the gate, and then in a taxi into the town of Angeles, a main street of asphalt, tangled dirt lanes, bars and brothels and shanties. "Would you like to meet some ladies?" the cabbie asked. "No, thanks." "Then will you go to the carnival?" Yes, why not, he'd go to the carnival, what had he come to town for anyway? Two acres of dirt was all this carnival needed for its mildewed brown tents with shuddering frayed hemp ropes, its half dozen rides, its loudspeakers playing the local radio station, its grand, faded murals raised up in front of the sideshows. As he paid his driver, pleading children boxed him in, and angry vendors chased them away. He bought peanuts wrapped in a page from a magazine. Liked the look of the Mermaid of Sulu on a mural and went in to see. He was the only patron. She had long black hair tied back with plastic flowers. Her small breasts were cupped, clasped, by a bikini top. Of what material the tail? He couldn't see, some kind of cloth. It didn't swing like a fish's. With her arms she shoved herself back and forth in a glass tank about four feet high and eight feet long, set on a platform three feet above the earth. She came up for air, went down, back and forth, back and forth. Broke the surface again and reached for a white towel hung on the tank's rim, dried her hands and face, took cigarettes and lighter from their perch beside the towel, lit a Marlboro skillfully with damp fingers, smoked a minute, waved her hand at him to leave, to go away, and turned her back. He left and made for another tent—the Five Dwarfs of Bohol. Where was Bohol? Somewhere in these islands, he assumed, he'd look at a map sometime. For now he'd only meet some of its citizens, the small, jolly, bearded men depicted on a huge banner stretched above the entrance, two of them working their gold mine with their glinty-pointed picks, the other three hauling a barrow heaped with winking nuggets — Franco, Carlo, Paulo, Santo, Marco, odd names, magical men. But inside were not these men. In five large bassinets the dwarfs lay in dirty diapers, blind, spastic, comatose, with their names, ages, and weights displayed on cards. Between seventeen and twenty-four years old. Twenty-eight, twenty-nine, thirty-three pounds . . . Not beards, but long filaments of peach fuzz never trimmed. Their limbs jerked, their milky eyes shivered in their heads . . . Flies landing on them . . . Sands limped outside and boarded the roller coaster, nothing too impressive, the kind of thing disassembled and trucked from town to town, and yet what it lacked in height and depth it made up for in speed and torque, and as the cars swooped down an incline or rammed into a bend, as the whole structure lurched and swayed, death stopped his throat, for who oversaw the assembly, who looked after this ride, who vouched for its safety? — No one. Expect a tragedy. Good and dizzy, he descended from this amusement and stood once more in front of the tent of the mermaid, the wet prisoner. Sunset now. New Year's Eve. Throughout the afternoon, fireworks had sounded sporadically, now more and more. Not whistles and bangs. A peripheral crepitation, pops and bursts from off somewhere. On the tall poster the mermaid smiled and didn't seem the type to smoke Marlboros. He had an impulse to go in again and further oppress himself.

An air force jeep pulled up quite near, driven by an airman. Voss was the passenger. He disembarked and they stood together before the gigantic discolored illustration. "Was this your appointment?"

"Yes."

"Your briefing?"

"Right." Feeling frightened, hilarious. "Do you want to go in?"

"Actually, I was here a couple of days ago. You go ahead."

"I've already been," Skip said sadly.

"Let's talk a little more."

"Sure."

The two Americans sat at a vendor's linoleum table, each with a bottle of San Miguel. Looking most out of place. Voss wore a pin-striped shirt, brown slacks, brown wing-tip shoes. He looked like a Bible salesman. So did Skip.

Skip said, "So this isn't a coincidence."

"Surely you understand I have a purpose here."

"Yeah. I just said so."

"I'm here to shake you up."

"You haven't succeeded."

"Good enough," Voss said. "I just hope I've been heard."

"All I've heard is a lot of ungrateful nonsense."

"What's that supposed to mean?"

"Look, I agree there's such a thing as evolution. Things are changing, we're a new generation, but—what have you got against the old guard?"

"Nothing at all. They're running the show. But not the colonel, right? The colonel's a show unto himself."

"Do you know him at all? Aside from the course of his you took?"

"I know him. I worked for him."

"Really?"

"All last summer and fall. Old F.X. He kidnapped me. Had me doing research."

"Research on what?"

"Anything and everything. He called me his clerk. I think his idea was if he had to be a prisoner in Langley, he'd better take a prisoner of his own, you know? But I owe the guy. I've gone up two grades since then."

"Wow."

"Since June."

"That's fast."

"Like lightning."

"He did that for you?"

"Skip, no. It wasn't the colonel who got me promoted. But after I'd been with him, folks took an interest."

"Good. That's great."

"No, no, no. You're not picking this up fast enough."

"What. Tell me."

"Folks took an interest in me because folks have taken an interest in the colonel."

Here was a moment for staying still, betraying nothing. ". . . An interest?"

"Now you're getting it."

"I mean, when you say he was 'a prisoner' in Langley . . ."

"Now he gets it."

The next question would have to be whether the colonel had landed in real trouble, fate-provoking, career-wrecking difficulty. But the question to follow that one was whether the colonel still had trouble, and then, after that: Who else has trouble? Am I, for instance, in trouble?

Therefore he swallowed all questions.

And Voss was spitting them out now.

"What happened in Mindanao fourteen months ago?"

"I guess you must have seen the report."

"I read it. I did the decode. I was sitting right by the telex when it came in 'Eyes Only.'"

"Well, if it came in Eyes Only, why did you decode it?"

"Eyes Only is not a legal classification, I'm sure you know. It's out of James Bond."

"Well, still—as a courtesy."

"As a courtesy to whom?"

"As a courtesy to me, and to the recipient."

"We look at everything directed to the colonel. Or from the colonel."

"Then you know how things went down there."

"Yeah. The colonel botched it."

"That's not what my report says, Rick. Read it again."

"Can you tell me why he's wasting valuable time and resources trying to run down newsreel footage of a ball game?"

"No, I can't. Baseball?"

"Football. A football game. He tried to commission a transpacific flight for some cans of film. Does he think he's the president?"

"The colonel has his reasons for whatever he does." His blood roared. He was ready to hit Voss with a bottle. "What football game?"

"Notre Dame versus Michigan State. The one last month."

"I have no idea."

"The colonel's collecting more intelligence on the Notre Dame–Michigan State game than he is on the enemy." Voss looked at his watch, signaled the airman.

"Are you carrying his football film to him?"

"Skip. Skip. Nobody's giving him any football film." He stood up and held out his hand. As firmly as he could, Skip accepted it. "Look," Voss said, and as he searched for words his eyes broadcast human sympathy. "See you in the war." His jeep was running. He turned away.

Sands drank two more beers, and when darkness had fallen he wandered away from the fun and ate fish and rice in a café. Through the doorway he watched a minor spectacle in the street, a drunken young man with one burned and bandaged arm in a sling, who nevertheless was able to light a succession of firecrackers and toss them at the feet of leaping, squealing passersby. By 9:00 p.m. the town rattled all over with celebratory explosions. Independence Day in San Marcos had impressed him, but this was wilder and decidedly more dangerous, full of actual gunfire and large booming cadences, as if the entire night were under attack. He thought he'd probably find it more peaceful in South Vietnam. He strolled into the red-light district—Angeles consisted of little else—the slop, the lurid stink, the thirsty, flatly human, open-mouthed stares of the women as he passed dank shacks beating with rock 'n' roll music, as hot and rich with corruption as vampire mausoleums. The wanton mystery of the Southeast Asian night: he loved it as passionately as he loved America, but secretly, with dark lust; and he admitted to himself without evasion that he didn't care if he never went home.

Beginning two days after Christmas, James ceased calling his friends, stopped taking Stevie's calls. He spent the days watching cartoons on television with his ten-year-old brother, Burris, sharing as best he could in the serenity of a mindless childhood.

On New Year's Eve he went to a party. Stevie was there. She was angry, and she left him alone. She stayed out back in the dark with Donna and her other friends, the alternate cheerleaders and future runner-up prom queens, huddled under a cloud of resentment. Good. The one he'd really always wanted was Anne Vandergress, who'd come to Palo Verde High School the same year as James and who stood now in the doorway of the kitchen looking beautiful, talking to a couple of guys he'd never seen before.

He drank rum. He'd never before tasted it. "We call this a three-oh-two," somebody said.

If he was going somewhere to be blown up by a mortar or something, then he wished he'd never started going around with Stevie Dale.

"Well, hell. That three-oh-two goes down easier'n beer does," he agreed.

"Now put you some in a Coke."

It was Anne Vandergress talking. She was a honey-blonde who always wore nice makeup, and he'd never approached her because to him she'd seemed too young and pure and elevated, then his last full year in school he'd heard she was dating a football player, a senior, Dan Cordroy, then another one, Cordroy's buddy Will Webb, then half the goddamn team, all seniors, and he'd heard she was putting out for every last one. "You're so fucking beautiful, you know that?" he said. "I never told you that," he said, "did I ever tell you that?"—though it seemed to James she was a little less beautiful than he remembered, a little heavier, thicker in the face. More grown-up, but not in a good way; instead in a way that reminded him of middle age.

One particular swallow of rum stalled in his throat and nearly gagged him, but then it went down all right, and after that his throat felt numb, and he could have swallowed nails or glass or hot coals.

He rushed through an hour like a physical thing, a hallway. His lips turned to rubber and he drooled while saying, "I've never been this drunk in my life."

People seemed to be circling him, laughing, but he wasn't sure. The room tilted sideways and the very wall knocked him on his ass. Hands and arms grappling him upright like the tentacles of a monster . . .

He arrived in his body from some dark place, and he was standing outdoors holding a cigarette in one hand and a drink in the other.

Donna loomed like a wreck coming at you. Mad as *fire*. "Why would you say that? Why would anybody talk that way?" Stevie in the background with her head bowed, weeping, girls around her patting her hair and smoothing away the grief.

Rollo held him upright in the yard. Donna dive-bombing him, you couldn't shake her. "Donna, Donna—" Rollo was laughing, snorting, barking—"He can't hear you, Donna. Stop the lecture."

"Stevie was almost pregnant. Don't you realize she was just about pregnant? How can you act like this?"

"Almost pregnant?" Rollo said. "*Al*most?" James was on his knees with his arms around Rollo's legs.

"She *thought* she was pregnant, okay, Rollo? Okay? He can't just spit her out the last night he's in town and just go to Viet-*nam*. Okay, Rollo?"

"Okay!"

"Tell him that!"

"Okay! I'll tell him! James," Rollo said, "James. You got to talk to Stevie. You sure hurt her feelings, James. Stand up, stand up."

His legs rolled him over to Stevie standing by a stone barbecue pit with a fire in it. He said something, and Stevie kissed him—her soggy teenybopper breath. "And you're smoking a cigarette," she said, "and you don't even smoke."

"I smoke. I always did smoke. You just didn't know about it, is what."

"You don't smoke."

"I smoke."

Something else happened and Stevie disappeared and was replaced by, or turned into, her friend Donna. "You've hurt her for the last time, James."

"I smoke," he tried to say. He could neither shut his jaws nor raise his chin from his chest.

He was back inside the kitchen, where Anne Vandergress seemed no longer beautiful. She seemed old and worn-out. Her hair was frizzy. Her face was flat and red and sweaty and her smile looked dead. She laughed along with everybody else while he announced she was a whore. "It took me a while—but you're a whore. You're a whore, all right," he said very loudly. "I just want you to figure that out like everybody else already did," he said, "that you're a complete, slutty whore." Anne laughed grotesquely. She looked like she'd been pulling a train all night. His mind was stuck in a warp and he kept saying, "What a whore—what a whore—what a whore—"

They threw him on the ground and hosed him down. The dirt turned to slime around him and he crouched in it, flailing, trying to stand upright.

This was not vastly different from certain moments of his basic training. His feet splayed and he flopped on his face and ate mud, thinking: All right, men: here we go.

1967

On the afternoon of January 1, 1967, Nguyen Hao drove to Tan Son Nhut Airport with Jimmy Storm, a man very close to the colonel. Jimmy Storm almost always wore civilian clothing, though the first time Hao had seen the lad he'd been squatting on his heels outside the CIA–Psy Ops villa taking a break, smoking a cigarette, in U.S. Army fatigues with the hash marks of a sergeant.

This afternoon Mr. Jimmy wore this same uniform, and the entire distance to the airport, Mr. Jimmy, or Sergeant Storm, sitting rigidly upright, with his cap on, in the backseat, where he'd never sat before, said nothing at all—possibly a little nervous, Hao thought, about greeting the new arrival.

But this silence might have come from anywhere. Mr. Jimmy Storm was a strange and complicated young man. By the time they saw William Sands coming down the gangway of the Air America DC-3, ducking his head a bit against the noise of jets and the onslaught of damp wind, Mr. Jimmy had recovered all his volubility and spoke with Sands cheerfully, and too rapidly for Hao to follow.

They put two footlockers in the trunk of the black Chevrolet, and the third had to go in the backseat with the newcomer, who asked his hosts to call him Skip.

"Right, right, right," Mr. Jimmy agreed, and then he disagreed: "But let me call you Skipper. Skip's too short. It just skates past." Now Mr. Jimmy sat up front with Hao.

Hao said, "Mr. Skip, I'm glad to welcome you. Your uncle knows my nephew. Now I know your uncle's nephew."

"I have something for you." The newcomer handed over a carton of cigarettes. From the box they looked almost like Marlboros, but they were the other kind. Winstons. Hao said, "Thank you so much, Mr. Skip."

A bicycle approached on their right as they waited for traffic. Mr. Jimmy rolled down his window rapidly and said, "Diddy mao!" and gestured, and the rider veered off.

Mr. Skip said in Vietnamese, "May I speak Vietnamese, Mr. Hao?" and Hao answered in Vietnamese, "It's better. My English is that of a child."

"Today is our New Year," Mr. Skip said. "Soon I'll be celebrating another, your Tet."

"Your pronunciation is quite good."

"Thank you."

"Have you come many times to Vietnam?"

"No. Never."

"That's surprising," Hao said.

"I took an intensive course," Mr. Skip said, using the English words for "intensive course."

"So there it is, huh?—all seven hundred pounds," said young Mr. Jimmy, reaching back to place his hand on the footlocker. "The keys to the kingdom of the Duke of Earl."

Hao was suddenly convinced that despite never having met him, Jimmy Storm floundered in a deep hatred for Skip Sands. Skip, for his part, seemed suspicious of Storm and hesitated slightly before saying, "More like two hundred pounds."

Sundown, and the bellies of the clouds flared red. They entered Saigon and passed along a street of homes where kids played jump rope in the twilight, and snatches of the jumpers' magical chants reached their ears. Then over to the GI streets, the avenues of wretched commerce, past doorways like mouths, each delivering its music, its voices, its stench, and then across the river and into what was officially Gia Dinh Province and down Chi Lang Street to the CIA–Psy Ops villa where nobody lived for very long, only Jimmy Storm in his cluttered bedroom with its chugging air conditioner, just off the parlor with its rattan tables and kapok-cushioned sofa and nearly empty bookshelves and its bamboo bar—no stools—and a framed painting of horses in a stable on one of its pale yellow walls.

The black Chevrolet stayed at the villa. Hao helped the Americans with the unloading—Mr. Skip's duffel and his cane basket and the three footlockers—and said goodbye and walked home along the broken pavement beside a sewage canal, seeing his way by a flashlight.

They lived above and behind the family's defunct shop, he, his wife Kim, and occasional relatives. The shop had come from Hao's family; the relatives were Kim's. It had been dark for an hour when Hao entered by the alley, but he heard her sandals scraping in the concrete court out back as she puttered among the fruit plants she raised in large pots. Hao turned on the overhead fluorescent light in the parlor to summon her.

He wanted to talk. It seemed to him that having been asked to meet a member of the colonel's family on his arrival, he'd now solidified an alliance and crossed a river in his life, which was also hers. She had a right to form some general appreciation of their circumstances.

He sat in his chair before his red plastic electric fan. Quite soon Kim came in, middle-aged, splay-footed, a stick frame with fat daubed onto it, wiry arms and bowed legs with a jutting paunch. Her face had become somewhat like those on the stone frogs in gardens, and somewhat like that of the Buddha's—jowly, pop-eyed. She sat catching her breath and said, "I'm fine today."

"It's a miracle," he said, because he knew she liked to use such terms.

"I took the asthma remedy from the old story."

"Ouch," he said, "that's a crazy idea."

"But it worked. I'm fine."

"Let me get you a checkup with an American doctor. I'm sure Mr. Colonel can arrange it."

"Leave me alone," she said, as always, "I'm the only one going to fill my grave."

She took good care of things and was a fine friend to him. He held her dear and wished her a long life. But her health wasn't good.

They sat together while the red fan whirred and the tabletop hummed underneath it. Kim shut her eyes and breathed through her nose, this on the recommendation of yet another practitioner.

It had really been a very long illness, complicated probably by the loss of her nephew some years ago—four years? Often she came back to the topic of Thu's suicide. Hao could see how she looked somewhere else, longingly, while something, maybe just the sound of her own voice, dragged her down into the discussion against her will: Do you think it could have been an accident, do you think he could have simply been experimenting, wondering, looking, smelling the fuel, I don't know. And Hao would say, I don't know either; but Thu had to go to some trouble to come into possession of the gasoline. I don't like Buddha, she would say. There are many gods, she would say, with Buddha things are too simple, just look around, do things look simple? No, no.

Because in order to talk to her he must enter her world, he asked, "What do your dreams tell you lately?"

"That my breathing will stay clear and my cousin will be married soon."

"Cousin? Which cousin?"

"Lang! Do I have to take you to the side room and show you Lang sleeping on her pallet?"

"I forgot which one was staying with us."

"There are two! Lang and Nhu."

"It's time to talk about our situation."

"Talk."

"You realize Mr. Colonel has a project near Cu Chi, around Good Luck Mountain."

"It's dangerous to help him. Can you dodge the wind?"

"I'm already helping him. I've talked to several headmen, I've marked the location of tunnel openings on his maps."

"If you take sides, what will happen to us?"

"I've taken a side. I believe we have to consider what happens when the country's reunified. I think we'll have to leave."

"Leave?"

"Leave the country. Emigrate. Go to another country."

"But we can't!"

"What keeps us? There's nobody left in the household."

"There's nobody left because you don't have work for them. Why did you sell the other two shops when this one was already closed? Anyway, there's Minh."

"Minh has his own opportunities and will make his own arrangements."

"You mean sooner or later he'll be killed."

"Wife, please, it's time to consider these matters carefully."

Often when they spoke of things that upset her, she stood up and moved around without realizing it. Picked up the pillows and tossed them between her hands and clapped the dust from them, or used a knee-high whisk to stir the lint on the wooden floor. Hao's mother had used such a broom. His grandmother too. There'd been one in every household he could remember having entered.

"I met Mr. Colonel's nephew. His name is Skip. Let's have him to dinner."

"It's not good to have Americans in the house."

"If we don't choose sides, neither side will trust us. We'll be the people in the middle. That kind of person is eventually put into a camp somewhere, no matter which side wins."

"So you've joined the Americans. If the Americans win, we can stay."

"No. The Americans won't win. They're not fighting for their homeland. They just want to be good. In order to be good, they just have to fight awhile and then leave."

"Hao! Then why help them?"

"They can't win, but they can prove themselves a friend to their friends. And I believe they're honorable and will do so."

"But you have friends in the Vietminh."

"They're called the Vietcong now."

"Trung. Trung Than is your friend."

Hao said, "I don't want to talk about the Vietcong. The Communists believe only in the future. In its name they'll destroy everything, they'll fill the future with nothing. I want to talk about the Americans."

"Talk. I can't stop you."

"If I help these Americans, we don't have to be refugees, they'll help us get away. Maybe to someplace like Singapore. I believe it can be done. Singapore is a very international place. We won't be made to feel like outcasts."

"Have you talked to them about Singapore?"

"I'll talk when the time is right. There are other places too. Manila, maybe Jakarta, maybe Kuala Lumpur. As long as we don't have to be refugees in a camp."

"I'll pray the Americans destroy the Vietminh."

"I don't hold any hope, Kim. There's an old saying: The anvil outlasts the hammer."

"Which one are we? We're neither one. We get smashed between."

"And another: Every cock fights best on his own dunghill."

"Hah! Here's one more old saying: A rooster is a chicken, but men are like a bunch of hens."

"I never heard this saying."

She laughed with delight, heading toward the kitchen.

"I know," Hao called, "you're happiest when you make a fool of your husband." But it warmed him to hear her laugh, she did it so seldom since Thu had gone. She'd treasured Thu as a gift. The two brothers had come from her dead sister. They were all she had. Now she had only Minh.

In the kitchen Nguyen Kim lit the Primus stove under the teakettle. Paused before the shelf and uncapped, one by one, her small bottles of fragrances and inhaled from each. The therapy of breath occupied her much. These days rosemary in particular intrigued her. She wanted to blend it with the extract of patchouli, not as a curative but just for the perfume, and she couldn't find a way; concocted, they seemed to produce a third fragrance, not entirely pleasant.

Her asthma remedy had been delivered to her in a dream. She hadn't told him that. And she used a syrup from a Chinese herbalist in the Cho Lon District. He wouldn't say what it was but she'd heard they used the meat and skin of the gecko. Hao disapproved of these things.

Kim viewed her husband as a gambler and a dreamer. He'd surprised them all by selling two of their dry-goods stores and leasing the third to a man who'd quickly lost the business. Now her relatives camped among its naked shelves. Rather than putting his money into something else, Hao used it to meet their daily needs and had instead invested all his time, his very soul, in these Americans. Did he think that wasn't clear? Did he think she had to be told?

She appreciated the two girls living with them, Lang and Nhu, they helped out, cousins from her ville who couldn't be called servants. She had no way of telling them that under certain circumstances she wished they'd behave like servants. But it was no good unless they understood this, unless their good-for-nothing mother, her aunt, had already told them this—

She steered her mind away from ungenerous thoughts.

She believed that when the blood exhaled a disease it took with it certain spiritual impurities, and the convalescent experienced a fleeting state of purity.

In such a state, she believed, clear thought was possible. Even inspiration, perhaps.

Hao didn't discuss finances with her other than to say if they didn't make major purchases, they could go on as they had before. That was good enough. Gambler, dreamer, yes; but he was a dependable man, and she respected him. His father, bringing native goods down the Saigon River to trade with the French, had built a good business. Hao—cursed with a childless marriage, the scion of a dwindling line—Hao had overseen its slow destruction. She wouldn't ask him to stay here. If he wanted to run, they'd run. And why cry about tomorrow? Maybe long before they had to tear up their roots they'd be dead.

She carried the pot and two cups out to him where he sat with his hands on either arm of the chair, his eyes closed, meditating in the breeze from his electric fan.

She settled herself and poured for them both. "I need an oath from you," she said.

"Tell me."

"I want you to promise me that whatever happens, you will take care of Minh."

"I promise."

"Too quick!"

"No. Understand me, wife: when I said Minh had his own opportunities, I meant he's already making his way. He no longer flies jets, you know. He flies U.S. transport helicopters—only for transport, and only for the colonel. He's already safe. And Mr. Colonel and I will keep him safe. Hear me again, wife: I promise."

"And one more."

"How many more?"

"Only this: If we leave, will we ever come back?"

"If it's possible."

"Promise me."

"I make this vow to you. If it's possible, we'll come back home."

"Even if I come back as ashes," she said.

To hear Kim speak openly of her concerns surprised him. She'd never said anything like this, was careful always to hide her best hopes from the scrutiny of the powers, from the vague assembly of her innumerable gods.

The conversation thrilled him. She was more than considering the move, she was bargaining over it, compromising, as with something inevitable. They went upstairs, and despite the heat, which always stayed a bit longer in the top of the house, he embraced her and held her until she slept. War and war and war like a series of typhoons against their lives, and now, on the other side of it all, a distant peak of safety, a place to travel toward. And Kim's breath came quietly, just as she'd claimed, no more of the wheezing, at least not tonight.

He moved to his own bed, putting his clothes and his sandals on the floor just outside the net—his plastic sandals, which said on the instep, in English, "Made in Japan." The high walls between cultures were dissolving. Collapsing as mud. He and Kim might go anywhere. Malaysia. Singapore. Hong Kong. Even Japan was possible. He laughed to think he could walk out into the road now and remark to someone, "Japan is possible."

Kim woke him in the night. He looked at the clock's radium hands. Quarter to four. "What is it?"

She said, "Dogs were barking down the lane."

"Sleep. I'll listen for a while."

Until she slept again he lay quietly, watching the tiny ember of insecticidal incense burning on the dresser across the room.

From out in the lane he heard Trung—of course it was Trung, who else could it be?—imitating a gecko's warble.

Trung had never before arrived this late. But a cautious man would vary his approach.

Hao reached down and drew up the netting and swung his feet out. He took his trousers, shirt, and Japanese sandals to the head of the stairs and dressed there and stood in the darkness hearing nothing, tasting his own breath. Headed downstairs as softly as he could. The cousins slept right below his feet, in the shop of which the staircase made the slanting ceiling. There was no way to go quietly, every tread had something to say. At the bottom he waited until he was sure he hadn't wakened the two girls.

He made his way into the kitchen, to the window behind the gas stove, and turned the clasp. As soon as he opened it he heard a small cough just outside.

"Trung?"

"Good morning."

"Good morning."

"I'm sorry to disturb you."

"I can't offer you anything hot. Would you like a glass of water?"

"Thanks for your kindness, but I'm not thirsty."

"I'll come outside."

He went out the kitchen door into the tiny courtyard, where Trung stood by the wall in the dark.

"My cigarettes are upstairs," Hao said.

"I don't think we should smoke. We might be seen."

The two men squatted side by side against the wall beneath the kitchen window.

Hao said, "You take a chance coming into the city."

"It's a risk to be anywhere now. Just a couple of years ago, I could travel in a wide area. Now we're fugitives anywhere in the South."

"And coming to the house, it's a risk for both of us."

"More of a risk for me, I'd say."

"I'm protecting you, Trung Than. I give you my word."

"I believe you. But it's best to assume the worst."

"Trung, I understand completely that you have to feel protected every step we take."

"Don't push ahead too fast. I don't yet agree we're taking steps."

"Each meeting we've had has taken us a little farther, don't you agree?"

"Farther toward an understanding, maybe. But we haven't actually taken any steps."

"Are you ready to change that?"

"No."

A ploy, in Hao's opinion, and not an actual refusal.

"Before we go any farther," Trung said, "I have to make sure I'm understood."

"Please tell me. I'm listening."

"It took three days to go north on a Russian ship. That was in '54. They said we'd come back to a reunified country in two years."

"Go on," Hao said.

"Six years later it took me eleven weeks to get back by Ho's trail, and on the way I nearly died a hundred times."

Hao said, "I'm listening."

"In '64 I realized I'd been waiting ten years to come home. And yet by then I'd already been back in the South for four years."

"In all these numbers I hear the massing of resentments. You're dissatisfied," Hao said.

"I've been living a contradiction. It isn't going to go away."

"I see."

"I've been a coward. I have to resolve this for myself."

"I'm here to help you any way I can."

"I know that," Trung said. "But what do you want from this?"

"I want to be helpful to an old friend."

"We need to talk honestly. You say you want me to feel safe, and then you lie. Tell the truth: What do you want from this situation?"

"The survival of my family."

"Good."

"And what do you want?" Hao asked.

"The survival of the truth."

What now? Philosophy? Hao said: "How can the truth be threatened? It's the truth."

"I want the truth to survive inside *me*."

Hao thought, I'm a businessman; let's talk profit and loss. But said only, "I'm trying to understand."

"I don't think words can take me any farther in explaining what I'm doing. I just want you to understand that nothing forces me. I'm not in any trouble. I don't need money. I just need to steer closer to the truth."

Hao disbelieved him. He was betraying his comrades, what could be the motive for that? Not philosophy.

Squatting at Hao's side, Trung leaned his head back against the wall and sighed. It seemed he might make his farewell. "All right," he said instead, "let's have a smoke together."

Hao crept back upstairs and found his cigarettes and his American Zippo lighter. At the head of the landing he got two going and brought them downstairs, wondering if the Monk would still be waiting. There he was. Very good. Tonight they'd take important steps.

Hao said, "He wants to meet you."

"He wants too much."

"He's willing to protect you."

"As long as he can't identify me, I won't need his protection."

"He wants to protect you from his own people. From his side, not from yours."

"I'll be the one to worry about both sides."

They smoked, each with his hands cupped around the glow, Hao thinking, I can't even light a cigarette for my friend, he can't survive a light on his face. It's years since I've seen his eyes.

"Trung, in order to get where you're going you need a protector, and this protector has to trust you."

"It's not time yet." His friend scraped the ember from his cigarette and put the butt in his shirt pocket.

Hao said, "Three years ago, shortly before you first contacted me again, my nephew burned himself alive behind the New Star Temple."

"I know about it."

"Is that what you're doing too? Destroying yourself?"

What a slow, thoughtful man the Monk had become. He'd always had a dogged sincerity, but this was deeper. His silences were searches. They were inspiring. "There's been a lie told. I've told it. I'm going to let the truth reclaim me. If I can't survive that process, so be it."

"We have to express a more intelligible motive."

"No. The truth. They'll assume I'm lying anyway."

"It takes time to gain trust. They'll need something. Can you give me something?"

"This time I'll tell you something they probably already know. Next time a little more."

"Ah. We're going to cross, but we're not going to jump."

"The ones returning from the North say a big push is coming. Not soon. Probably around the next Tet."

"I've heard nothing about this."

"Your colonel has. Surely he's heard rumors. But I'm telling you it's not a rumor. Everyone can feel it. It's coming."

"He'll want to debrief you. A few days' interrogation. It's standard."

"Don't expect me to be stupid."

"Forgive me."

"I'm the one controlling the process. I have to be."

"As you say."

"I need time before I give him something specific, something he can confirm."

"All right."

"I need time. I'm not ready to cross."

The neighborhood roosters crowed for the third time. Trung had just the frailest dawn by which to make his way out of Hao's neighborhood—fruit trees, dirt yards, wood homes, fluorescent lights glowing in the kitchens of the early risers, a sewage ditch winding down among the yards. He envied his friend this simple peace.

When he reached the thoroughfare he paused to light his

cigarette butt and watch a couple of baker's boys on their bikes, gliding by in the silence with the morning's bread.

He remembered walking arm in arm with Hao at just such an hour in quite another universe: reeling and wild, two lads too drunk on purloined rice brandy to care how Master might punish them. Remembered precisely the size and color of that night's moon and the unbounded friendliness of the young world, and their voices singing an old song: "Yesterday I followed you down the road . . . Today I chose a flower for your grave . . ."

At lunchtime on January 2, his first full day in-country, Skip Sands waited for his uncle at the Club Nautique beside the Saigon River. Junks and sampans and shanties choked the opposite bank downstream, but not much moved on the brown water. He studied the menu, all appetite gone, and played with his utensils and listened to a loud miscellany of birdcalls, some of them almost sentimentally musical, others angry. Sweat trickled down his spine. His eye fell on a patron at the next table, an Asian man with an incomprehensibly large black growth descending from his scalp and covering the nape of his neck. Across from this man sat a woman with a monkey in her lap. She scowled, the monkey gave her no cheer, the menu made her unhappy.

A single very loud blast—mortar? rocket? sonic boom?—caused a lot of consternation. The monkey lunged to the end of its leash and danced from side to side under the table. Several patrons stood up. The tables went quiet, and waiters gathered at the railing to peer up the river toward downtown. Someone laughed, others talked, the dinnerware clinked again on the porcelain, the moment resumed.

Colonel Sands was just entering the terrace and said, "My boy, settle yourself."

The colonel had traveled by chopper from Good Luck Mountain, so Sands understood. Red mud speckled his canvas combat boots and his cuffs, but he wore street clothes and looked alarm-ingly usual, as if all he cared about were the local sights and the golf. Already he had an amber highball in his hand.

Sands took a seat across from him.

"Is everything good? You're stashed at the billet."

"Yes."

"When did you get in?"

"Last night."

"Seen anyone from the embassy?"

"Not yet."

"What are we having today?"

"Colonel, let me start right out by asking you something about San Marcos."

"Before we eat?"

"I need to clear something up."

"Sure."

"Were you passing orders to the major?"

"The major?"

"Aguinaldo? The major?—the last time we saw each other."

"Right. The Del Monte House. San Carlos."

"San Marcos."

"Right."

"Aguinaldo? The Filipino?"

"Yes. The Filipino. No. I wasn't running any Filipino."

"What about the German? Was he yours?"

"It's the Political Section in Manila runs everybody. I'm not the Political Section. I'm just a sick dog they can't force them-selves to shoot."

"All right. Maybe I won't press it."

"No, no. You've started, so don't quit. What's the problem?"

"Maybe I'm out of line."

"Come at me. We work together. Let's get it done."

"Fine. Then what about Carignan?"

"Who?"

"Carignan, sir. The priest on Mindanao."

Now, he sensed, his uncle appreciated how serious he was. "Oh, yes," the colonel said. "Father Carignan. The collaborator. Somebody put him out of his misery."

"Which somebody?"

"If I remember right, that operation originated with the Philippine Army command. That's how we understood it from the report."

"I wrote the report. I rode a donkey all the way to the VOA substation near Carmen and sent a coded report to Manila to be forwarded to you, as instructed. And I only mentioned the local army—barely mentioned them."

"I believe it was a Philippine Army operation. And I further believe it was run by our friend Eddie Aguinaldo. And we had every reason to believe that this Carignan was involved in the transfer of weapons to and among Muslim guerilla groups on Mindanao."

"The priest was killed by a dart. A sumpit, they call it."

"It's a native weapon."

"I've never seen one except in the hands of that German at the Del Monte House."

"I see."

"You weren't running the German."

"I've said I wasn't."

"That's good enough for me."

"I don't care if it is or it's not."

"Fuck you, sir."

"I see." While the colonel considered a reply and ran a finger, a trembling finger, around the rim of his highball, Skip wilted. He'd armored his soul for this assault. But he hadn't expected to strike flesh. "Well," the colonel said, "I'm repeating myself, but what's the problem?"

"I just worry," Sands was able to say.

For the moment the colonel said no more. Skip's fire was out. Why hadn't he known he could hurt this giant? So ignorant of these older men: Why don't I have a father?

The colonel said, "Look. These things happen rarely, but they happen. Somebody's name gets mentioned by more than one source, somebody gets a notion, somebody issues a report, somebody wants an adventure—you know how that one goes, don't you?—and pretty soon there we are. That you've witnessed this kind of cock-up will turn out to be an invaluable experience, Skip."

"I'd say I was more than just a witness."

"My point is you see the power of the beast we're riding. Take care how you prod it." His bulldog face seemed to speak of a special sadness. He sipped from his drink. "Are my files secure?"

"Yes, sir, they are."

"How did you like Monterey?"

"Unbelievably beautiful."

"Order me a hot dog in Vietnamese."

A waiter was pouring water. Sands spoke with him. "He says it's buffet-style, please be his guest."

"Remarkable. But I did understand 'buffet.' And you met Hao Nguyen."

"Hao? Oh, right."

"He picked you up at Tan Son Nhut. Did you speak Vietnamese to him?"

"Yes, sir, I did."

"Are you hungry?"

"I might order off the menu."

"Skip."

"Yes, sir."

"Are we going to feel bad about talking frankly to each other? Because I don't want that. We can't have it."

"All right. I appreciate that."

"Good." The colonel took himself to the buffet.

When he rejoined his nephew he carried a bowl of crab in a white sauce; he sat down and forked and swallowed several bites, hardly chewing. He took a slug of his drink. "What about Rick Voss—Voss? Was he at the house last night?"

"Rick Voss? No."

"You'll meet him soon enough. Too soon."

"I met him at Clark before I left. He came looking for me."

"He did?"

"Mainly to ask about you."

"And what was the line of inquiry?"

"He wanted to talk about an article you'd submitted to the journal."

"I don't give a curse for some of these young pups coming up. Present company excepted."

"I hope so."

He thought he heard his uncle sigh. "I tell you, Skip, the world has turned and carried me into the dark. I got a letter from your cousin Anne just last week"—Anne the colonel's daughter—"and she's taken up the anthem of the college leftists, can you believe it? She writes, 'I think you should look at the motives of our government in Vietnam.' She's dating a beatnik, a mulatto. Her mother was scared to tell me. I had to hear about it from your Uncle Ray. 'The motives of our government'? Jesus Christ. What better motive can the government have than to defy Communism at every turning?"

Skip remembered Anne Sands squatting flat-footed on the sidewalk in a checkered sun suit, bouncing a tiny red ball and scooping up jacks from the pavement; he could summon effortlessly the picture of Anne skipping rope, braids flapping, devoting herself to chants and flying footwork. To hear of her letter made him angry, but her loss of patriotism was secondary—her offense was in passing beyond the clichés of girlhood . . . A mulatto beatnik?

"Now," the colonel said, "let's cheer up, and meet someone."

He pointed to this someone as he approached, a skinny young man in army fatigues from the waist down, yet sporting a colorful box-cut madras shirt, open and displaying his olive undershirt.

"Sergeant Storm," Skip said.

"You know him?"

"He met me at the airport last night."

"Yes, yes, yes," the colonel said. "Jimmy, sit down. Do you want a drink, either of you?"

Skip said no and Jimmy said, "American beer." Skip was seeing Jimmy for the first time by daylight. A sun-browned face and bright, small, earnest eyes, the same color as Skip's own — categorized on his IDs as "hazel." He had spectacular tattoos and a couple of teeth. Stenciled on his undershirt: STORM B.S.

The colonel signaled for a waiter and ordered a beer and a high-ball and said, "Well, now, here's a respectful gesture: Jimmy's buttoning his shirt for us. I think you're committing a brig offense with that shirt."

"I'm fashionably insane."

"And you're appearing in public with your pant legs unbloused."

"I'm not in uniform."

"I think that's the offense."

Storm said, "Did you eat already, Skipper?"

"Not as yet," Skip confessed.

"Skip says you were there to welcome him last night. I thank you for that."

"Not a problem."

"And Skip says he met Voss. Voss found him at Clark before he even got here."

"Don't ruin my beer with funny talk," Jimmy said.

"Voss asked him about an article I've been working on." To Skip the colonel said, "I've withdrawn that piece. It lacked an organizing theme, to say the least. I was just flailing at the pond of my notions with a fat paddle and going in circles. Making much spray. What did he talk about? — Voss."

"I kind of shook him off before much got said."

"Did he describe the article?"

"No, he didn't. Can I get a look?"

"Why don't you help me write it?"

"I don't know. If I see the draft—"

"If I can find the draft. It was a garbled mess. I picked it up after a year in a drawer, and I couldn't follow my own ideas."

"Well," Jimmy said, "that's what you get for spending a year in a drawer."

"Look, I didn't submit that draft to the journal. Voss undertook that on his own."

"Isn't that overstepping?"

"Goddamn right it's overstepping. It's an act of sabotage. What else did he say? I mean at Clark."

"Well, let's see," Skip said. "He talked about your interest in a football game."

"Notre Dame–Michigan State. Incredible game. Very instructive. I'm trying to get some film of it and work up a lecture. I'd like to take it around to the troops. Morale in this theater is dismal. The land itself sends up a scent that drives you crazy. Skip, it's not a different place. It's a different world under a different God."

"This is getting to be a regular philosophical obsession," Jimmy said.

Skip said, "Philosophical obsessions win wars."

"Touché," Jimmy said.

Sands said, "Touché?"

"How's the French coming?" the colonel asked.

"I'm always at it," Sands assured him.

"Skip and I got to reminiscing," the colonel said. "I haven't briefed him."

Jimmy said, "Can I get some of this chow first?"

"Go to it. I'll visit the gents'."

Both men excused themselves, and Jimmy soon returned with a plate in one hand and a large bread roll in the other. While Storm tried to eat, Skip quizzed him in the Agency's sweat-room style: let your man have a cigarette, but ask questions so fast he can't smoke it.

"Where are you from, Jimmy?"

"Carlyle County, Kentucky. Never going back."

"Your name is B.S. Storm?"

"Correct. Billem Stafford Storm."

"Billem?"

"B-I-L-L-E-M. It was my grandfather's nickname. My mother's father, William John Stafford. It doesn't really solve the puzzle, man, it just puts in a crazy piece that doesn't fit. You start out confused and end up mystified."

"And they don't call you Bill."

"Nope."

"Or Stormy."

"Jimmy's good. Jimmy gets you a response."

Skip said, "Are you army Intelligence?"

"Psy Ops. Just like you. We want to turn those tunnels into a zone of psychological mental torture."

"The tunnels?"

"The VC tunnels all over Cu Chi. I'm thinking: odorless psychoactive substance. Scopolamine. LSD, man. Let it seep through the system. Those bastards would come swarming out of those holes with their brains revved way past the redline."

"Gee."

"Psy Ops is all about unusual thinking, man. We want ideas blown up right to where they're gonna pop. We're on the cutting edge of reality itself. Right where it turns into a dream."

"Rick Voss isn't Psy Ops, is he?"

"Nope."

"But you deal with him as a regular thing?"

"'Keep your friends close. Keep your enemies closer.'"

"Who said that?"

"The colonel."

"Well, but he's quoting somebody."

"He's quoting himself."

"He usually is."

"Voss is an evil prick."

"Then it's good he's on our side."

"Whose side? In a liquid situation, the sides get stirred together."

"He's quoting Attila the Hun, or Julius Caesar."

"Who? Voss?—Oh."

"The colonel."

"Right. So those files, man. Is that the whole kaboodle? The whole Tree of Smoke?"

"Oh, a little of everything."

Skip let him eat. Storm was having the crab, and thin, delicate fries, which he ate with his fingers. He broke a small silence by saying, "Do you think the guys who dropped the bomb on Hiroshima, did they ever feel bad about it later?"

"No, they didn't," Skip said quite confidently.

"Here comes the chief."

As the colonel rejoined them Skip said, "Jimmy tells me he's interested in tunnels."

The colonel held a can of Budweiser and an empty glass. He carefully poured one into the other and sucked the foam away and took a long draught before saying, "Right-o. Now for the skinny. Sergeant Storm is the Psy Ops liaison with CDCIA, and I am the CDCIA liaison with Psy Ops. Together the sergeant and I run a very small, tight program called Labyrinth. Mapping tunnels. I'm sure you know about the VC tunnels."

"Sure."

"Today they're VC tunnels. When we have them mapped, their status changes."

"Mapping. That sounds more like Intelligence. Or Recon."

"Well, now," the colonel said. "I describe Labyrinth as tight, but our mission parameters are very elastic. I'd say we're operating without benefit of any clear parameters at all."

"But—Psy Ops?"

"Matter of fact, we do have a Recon platoon. And a permanent LZ, which we're not allowed to call a base."

"Who does?"

"I do. And a real nice bunch of infantry looking after it."

Skip's blood leapt. "Naturally I'm at your service." His hands tingled, and suddenly he wasn't sweating at all.

"William, I believe we have something in process now that you'll be a very important part of. A crucial part of. But your part doesn't begin anytime soon. I'm afraid what I'm going to ask you to do right now involves a whole lot of waiting."

"Waiting where?"

"We've got a little villa in the boonies."

Skip's joy died in his heart. "A villa."

"This is something I wouldn't ask anyone else to do."

Skip forced himself to say, "I'll go where you put me."

"I think we like this guy," Jimmy said.

"We'll have you all set up within the month. In the meantime, if any of our bunch want you here in Five Corps, you're at their service, too."

"Very good."

Jimmy said, "We want to turn those tunnels into a region of hell."

"Jimmy went to mining school."

"You're kidding."

"It's all part of a master plan," Jimmy assured him.

"Did you graduate?"

"Fuck no," Jimmy said. "Do I look like a graduate of anything?"

After coffee, during which Skip had his lunch—a sweet roll as pallid and lumpy as his spirits—Storm drove them in the black Chevrolet to the Continental Hotel, where the colonel kept a room on the ground floor, in the back, removed from the noisy lobby. Evidently he kept it permanently—boxes of books and record albums, a typewriter, a phonograph, a desk for working, another desk that served as a bar. The colonel set a record spinning. "This is *Peter Paul and Mary in Concert*. Listen to this one." And he bent over the player and squinted and with his thick fingers set its arm down on the trio's rendering of "Three Ravens," the melancholy ballad of a fallen knight and his doomed lover. They sat in silence, Skip and Jimmy each at one of the desks, while the song played and the colonel changed his pants and shirt. His mood, the mood Skip had put him in, had passed. He sat on his bed and slipped his feet into a pair of loafers while saying, "That Mindanao mission. That was a good report. Do you know what I liked most about it?"

Then he paused.

"No," Skip said, "I don't." It annoyed him, the colonel's habit of waiting for answers to rhetorical questions.

"What I liked about it was you didn't mention me."

"I think I had legitimate reasons for being less than complete."

"I think you have an instinct for discretion," the colonel said.

"I assumed you'd be the first to read the report."

"The first and last, my boy. That was the intention, anyhow."

"I assumed you'd let me know if you required more detail."

"This guy has his jive down," Jimmy said, resting his arm on the back of Skip's chair. "He knows how to skate."

The colonel looked very directly at Jimmy and said, "This man is family in every sense of the word."

"Message received," Jimmy assured him.

"All right, then." The colonel stood and said, "Guess who flew over with me from Cao Phuc? Our good lieutenant."

"Screwy Louie," Jimmy said.

"Now, now. Disrespect."

"That's how his tag should read. The grunts call him 'Screwy Loot.'"

"He's probably in the lobby."

"Screwy Louie went blooey."

"Now, Skip, we are dealing with the American infantry. Let me suggest that we take our allies as we find them."

"He's talking about the lieutenant," Storm said, "not about me."

"I've got nothing against the army. I'm an old army air force man. But the infantry isn't what it used to be."

"At least he didn't burn up one six-month ticket and leave," Storm said.

"It's true, he's been with us. Screwy Loot, is that what they call him?"

"He's a psychological operation all by himself."

"Now, young William," the colonel said, rummaging in his desk drawer, "I've got your document." He tossed his nephew a maroon passport.

Skip opened it to find his own face looking out at him over the name William French Benét. "Canadian!"

"Your rent's paid by the Canadian Ecumenical Council."

"Never heard of them."

"They don't exist. You're out here on a grant from the council. Translating the Bible or something."

"Benét!"

The colonel said, "Come on, Benét, let's get some coffee."

In the large, frantic lobby they sat in rattan chairs under one of a multitude of whirling fans. Around them beggars and urchins crawled at the feet of exiles and campaigners—at last, a wartime capital, a posh lobby full of sagas, busy with spies and cheats, people cut loose and no longer accountable to their former selves. Deals struck in a half dozen languages, sinister rendezvous, false smiles, eyes measuring the chances. Psychos, wanderers, heroes. Lies, scars, masks, greedy schemes. This was what he wanted—not some villa in the bush.

Sadly he asked the colonel, "Will I be seeing you out in the boonies?"

"Sure thing. We're getting you all set up. Anything special you'll need?"

"Just the usual. Pens, some paper, that sort of thing. The usual."

"Paper cutter. Rubber cement."

"Very good. Wonderful."

"I'll get you a typewriter too. I want you to have a typewriter. And lots of ribbons."

"I'll write your memoirs for you."

The colonel said, "The heat's got you all prickly."

"Can I be disappointed for a half hour or so?"

"Come on, it would be worse if you stayed in Saigon and

worked for our bunch. They've got fifty interrogation stations in the South. That's one mighty mountain after another of reports to go through. It all stays in-country. They'll put you in a hole and have you cross-indexing references till you're shitting five-by-eight cards. You'd rather be out there in the villes getting to know the people—the land we're at war in. We're getting you squared away someplace nice, never fear. And eventually you'll do important work for us."

"I believe you, sir."

"Any questions at this point?"

"In the files."

"Shoot."

"What is the significance of the phrase 'Tree of Smoke'?"

"So you've come to the *T*'s in the files."

"No. I just heard the phrase today."

"Jesus," Storm said. "I mentioned it, but I thought we were all kind of sharing our germs and diseases here, you know?"

"He's family," the colonel reminded him.

"So what's the meaning?" Jimmy said. " 'Tree of Smoke.' "

"Oh, God, I wouldn't know where to begin. It's embarrasingly poetic. It's grandiose."

Skip said, "That doesn't sound like you."

"To be poetic and grandiose?"

"To be embarrassed."

Jimmy said, "Here's a question: Who said, 'Keep your friends close, keep your enemies closer'?"

"Is this an interrogation?" the colonel said. "Then let's have cocktails."

Cocktails were served in a succession of louder and danker establishments mostly on Thi Sach Street, tavern darknesses where during a single play on the jukebox whole eras passed before the vision like scarves. In each one Skip nursed a beer and tried to stay alert, taking it in, though there was nothing to take in but pop tunes and small joyless go-go dancers. He felt dazed, didn't know why he didn't go home. At some point, he hadn't noticed when, the lieutenant had joined them, the one they called Screwy. He certainly seemed it—his tense face, his eyes deliberately widened, as if his message to the world were, Look at me, you've made me a frightened child—certainly inviting no conversation. Meanwhile, "I'll tell you what tells me about Voss," the colonel was saying. "First time I met Voss we sat down for San Miguels in Manila. He ordered one and he never once touched it. It sat at his feet like a prize."

Skip said, "In my presence he drank half a beer," making sure he followed this statement by taking a sip of his own.

The Screwy Loot seemed hypnotized by the knees of a go-go girl skipping, four feet away, to the Caribbean rhythms of Desmond Dekker while Sergeant Storm shouted in his ear, "Ain't no big shit whether we win or lose this thing. We live in the post-trash, man. It'll be a real short eon. Down in the ectoplasmic circuitry where humanity's leaders are all linked up unconsciously with each other and with the masses, man, there's been this unanimous worldwide decision to trash the planet and get on to a new one. If we let this door close, another will open." The lieutenant paid no mind.

The colonel also seemed deaf to Jimmy's nonsense. He drank deeply of his zillionth highball and announced, "The land is their myth. We penetrate the land, we penetrate their national soul. This is real infiltration. It may be tunnels, but it's in the realm of Psy Ops most definitely."

Skip couldn't tell if they were being serious, or just having fun with the lieutenant.

"Hey," Jimmy said, "I want to get into sounds. People can be allergic to sounds. Can't a whole genetic substratum be allergic to one set of vibrations?"

"Excuse me," Skip said, " 'substratum'?"

The colonel said, "I myself am allergic to gunfire in certain calibers. Helicopter blades at certain rpm's."

The lieutenant suddenly actually spoke: "Do you know what makes me bitter above all? The heretofore unattainable level of bullshit we're now all forced to engage, and I do mean non-fucking-stop."

"Excuse me," Skip said, " 'heretofore'?"

"Something's warping you," Jimmy told the lieutenant. "Maybe it's your perception of how the brass will see you—but they're not seeing you at all right now, so it's a perception of a nonperception, man, which is a perception of nothing, which is nothing, man."

The colonel complained of marital problems. "She calls our fighting 'domestic disputes.' It's obscene—isn't it obscene?—to take something that reaches down and rips at your heart, and call it a 'domestic dispute.' What do you think, Will?"

Never had he seen the colonel so drunk.

At some point in the zigzag procession of events a woman gripped his arm high above the elbow and said, "Strong! Strong! Let's go fuck, okay?"

What about that? How much did she charge? But he imagined her sad thinness, her genial kiss-ass terror, or her bitter terror, depending on how she cared to mask her terror . . . Another danced slowly beside the jukebox, hands hanging, chin dropping to her chest, not even trying to sell herself.

"No, thanks," he said.

The colonel's face arose before him like a diseased moon. "Skip."

"Yes."

"Did I promise you a shot?"

"Yes."

"Are you getting a shot?"

"Yes."

"Cheers, then, sir."

"Cheers."

A flashbulb popped in a corner. The colonel seemed to recognize the photographer and went in his direction. They were in a semi-elegant, air-conditioned place. The lieutenant took notes on wet cocktail coasters with a ballpoint pen while Jimmy spoke

earnestly at his ear. The colonel returned with a camera in his
hands. "He'll give us copies when he gets the film back. Sit up, Skip.
Up straight, now. Young lady, move out of my frame, please. This is
for the family." The flash, the moon drifting. "I'll send it to the family. Your Aunt Grace was asking for a photo. They're all very proud
of you. We all loved your father very much," he said, and Skip
replied by asking, "What was my father like?" and suddenly they
were having one of the most important conversations of his life.
"Your father had honor, he had courage," his uncle said, "and if he'd
lived long enough he would have added wisdom to those. If he'd
lived I think he would've gone back to the Midwest, because that's
the place your mother loves. I think if he'd lived he'd have become a
businessman, a good one, a driving wheel in his community. I think
he would definitely have stayed out of government." Yes, yes, Skip
wished he could say, but did he love me, did he love me?

While the jukebox played something with trumpets by Herb
Alpert, the colonel ignored its music and raised a song in a
whiskey baritone further roughened by his cigars:

> She buried him before his prime,
> Down a down, hey down, a down
> She was dead herself ere evening time,
> With a down.

> God send every gentleman
> Fine hawks, fine hounds, and such a lovely one,
> With a down, derry, derry, derry down.

Skip stepped from the evening's perhaps eleventh tavern and
ended his first day in Vietnam walking away from Thi Sach with
only a general idea where he lived, amid the swarming throng,
through the gritty diesel smoke, past the breath of bars and their
throbbing interiors—what songs? He couldn't tell. There—a
recent hit stateside—"When a Man Loves a Woman"—then the

music twisted around on itself as he passed the anonymous doorway and it might have been anything. He bartered with a cyclo
driver who took him across the river and dropped him on Chi
Lang Street. Here among the quieter lanes he breathed the fumes
of blossoms and rot, smoldering charcoal, frying food, and heard
the distant roar of jets and the drumming of helicopter gunships,
and even the thousand-pound bombs exploding thirty kilometers
away, not so much a sound as an intestinal fact — it was there, he
felt it, it thudded in his soul. What must it be like under those
bombs — or above them, letting them loose? To the west, red tracers streaked the sky. This was what he'd wanted. He'd come for
this. To be shoved into the forge, an emphatically new order — so
to speak a "different administration" — where theories burned to
cinders, where questions of morality became matters of fact.

At Ton Son Nhut the previous afternoon he'd witnessed unbelievable airborne activity, an array of fighters and bombers landing
and leaving, and cargo planes the size of mountains disgorging
heavy armaments as big as houses. How could they fail to triumph
in this war?

He found the villa's door. It wasn't locked.

Inside, behind the bar, stood Rick Voss, who said, "Welcome
to our demented little show."

"And good evening."

"You found us."

"Are you staying here too?"

"Always, whenever I'm in the Twilight Zone. Martini? I've got
the makings."

"I just spent half the night not getting drunk."

"Welcome to the second half."

"I'm ready to turn in."

"Been clubbing with the colonel?"

"Just a wee skosh."

"Has he snagged you? Did he put you on a task?"

"Not as yet."

"I have something for you. Just busywork."

"Thank God," Skip said.

"Just keeping you close," Voss said, and mixed him a surprisingly cold martini.

Assaulted by the scalding damp, their free hands thrown up against the rippling glare, they wrestled their duffels down the gangway onto the tarmac, PFC James Houston and two other new men of Echo Recon, and made their way to a staging area in a large open hangar where they sat on their gear and drank Cokes until a couple of spec fours came in who seemed to understand who they were.

Neither man actually greeted the three privates. They went on with their conversation as they guided the new arrivals to an M35 carryall big enough to haul a platoon, one saying to the other, "Who I specifically asked for was Carson, but who did he put in my ride? You. And now that means I'm saying, yes, fuck you, stay out of the Long Time, that's my bar."

"You mean you're the only person in hell gets inside the Long Time. You're their only customer on the planet."

"No hard feelings."

"Yes hard feelings, shit hard feelings."

"Well, then, hard feelings, then. But stay the fuck out of my bar. Are those your orders?" he continued, now addressing the three new ones.

James had collected the papers for all three of them and held them in a tight sweaty grip.

"You realize your pay's gonna be hung up, right?"

"Why? What's wrong with our papers?"

"Nothing. They're all fucked up."

The other one said, "It all gets routed around the world, down your throat, and up your ass."

The two hosts rode up front in the cabin and the new ones in the back, in a canvas-covered cavern, as far from the open end as they could manage. They bumped forward as the view of the air-field behind them, the jumble of crates, Quonsets, vehicles, air-craft, then the city, the wildly colored buildings, the streets full of people who didn't know how strange they looked, gave way to a general vegetation. James had trained for jungle environs in South Carolina and in Louisiana, but only during the fall and winter. His feet steamed in his boots. He took off his helmet. The day was cloudy, but the glare of it behind them through the open tarp made it impossible to keep his eyes open. He nodded forward into a brown stupor and slept until the truck jumped and explosions roared around his head. Fisher and Evans had already flattened themselves on the deck among their duffels. James fell on top of them. The truck had stopped. The doors slammed. The two from up front now both stepped up on the rear bumper and peered in at the tangled grouping. "I told you they were queer," one said. The other held his cigarette aloft and touched to it what turned out to be the fuse of a string of fire-crackers, which he pitched in beside them. Another deafening, rattling burst. The two captors disappeared. The vehicle resumed its motion. The three privates were horrified at the callousness of the joke. James almost wept from fear, and Evans said, "If we had guns we could shoot that guy in the back of his head and leave him laying, doesn't he know that?" "Jesus God!" Fisher shouted. He kicked viciously at the wall of the cabin. The truck stopped again. "Now see what you done!" Houston cried. "These bastards are gonna kill us now!" Only one—Flatt—popped up at the rear. "GI!" he shouted. "GI motherfucker! Incoming!" One at a time he tossed in three cans of Budweiser beer. "That was a stupid gag," he admitted.

"Goddamn right," Fisher said.

"Well, anyway, those are real-ass stateside cans of Bud with pull tabs. Eat up them beers, and no hard feelings."

Fisher continued as spokesman: "*Yes* hard feelings! Jesus God! What *are* you, a goddamn NVA Vietcong *spy*?" He popped his beer and foam sprayed everywhere and he cried, "Fuck!"

"We're taking an R-and-R detour," the man said. "Have you ever had sideways pussy?"

The three had rearranged themselves now on the benches. Nobody replied.

"I repeat: Have you ever had sideways pussy?"

They continued pondering the question.

"I believe I have your attention now," Flatt said, and he hopped off the bumper and they recommenced their travels.

"Jesus God!" Fisher said.

"Don't say Jesus God no more," Evans said.

"What am I supposed to say?"

"*I* don't know. How am *I* supposed to know?"

James held his beer can down by his feet as he popped it. He dropped the tab into the can and turned it up to his face and guzzled warm Budweiser till the tab hit his tongue, and still he sucked at the opening.

A storm came over, fell like a cataract for five minutes, and subsided. Then it was foggy, hard to breathe. James slid himself along the bench to the end of the carrier and ventured to look out at the Vietnam War—rain dripping from gigantic leaves, deformed vehicles, small people—the truck gearing down, engine bawling, mud boiling under the big tires—barefoot pedestrians stepping away from the road, brown faces passing, rut after rut after rut, the beer lurching in his stomach. He mopped his face with the hem of his shirt, shielded his brow with his hand, and watched the sunset, as it fell below the level of the clouds, turn the colors of the world both somber and powerful. They'd joined a highway. All the roadside vegetation looked dead. The concrete pavement had acquired a reddish tint from all the mud rubbed into it. All kinds of vehicles used this road, bicycles and motor scooters and larger contraptions apparently created out of exactly such two-wheeled conveyances, and oxcarts and pushcarts, as well as half-naked pedestrians in conical hats, bent down by large bundles. The truck pushed east along the road with much honking, much zigging and zagging, braking and gearing. For a while they moved so slowly a cart behind them was able to keep pace, and James stared for a long time into the stupid, deeply sympathetic face of a water buffalo.

The dark came abruptly. For a while the traffic got very sparse, and then it appeared they were slowing, they were in, or near, some kind of town. The carrier stopped before a structure made mostly of bamboo, with a sign out front dimly lit by a red bulb and saying COCA-COLA and LONG BRANCH SALOON. Floating in its red cloud, the place looked hot, damp, mysterious, lonely. Music thudded within. Houston leaned out and peered frontward and could see quite a lot of doings ahead, shadowy structures and the tiny moving lights of bicycles. Between here and there, however, lay a long patch of darkness.

Their hosts, or captors, approached. Flatt said, "Get out of my truck."

"Really?" Houston said.

"Give them a break, Flatt. Come on."

"All right," Flatt agreed. "I'm sorry I been fucking with you. You guys are the best thing happened all week. Your ride coming in so late means we should really, really in the interest, you know, of the wisest judgment, spend the night here in Bien Hoa. So you and Jolly entertain yourselves, and meanwhile, I gotta go in here to the Long Time and see a couple important enemy spies."

"We're coming with you, right?" Evans said.

"No. You can't go in there."

"We can't?"

"No, it's off-limits."

James said, "Well, ain't you going in yourself right now?"

"I'm on official business," Flatt said. "You guys better just find another spot up the street there. Go over to the Floor Show."

"Up the street?" Fisher said. That's not a street. It's dark."

"Corporal Jollet will escort you into town."

"All right—shit. Fine. Shit. I'll take over," said Jollet. "All aboard, let's go."

"Oh no you don't. The truck stays here."

"It's near a klik to anyplace else!"

"Men," Flatt said, "carry on. Move in single file and pray your asses don't get ambushed your first night on the ground. You got any money?"

"Shit," Jollet said. "They don't have any money."

"You keep saying 'Shit' like it's my name," Flatt said. "Stop saying 'Shit' like it's my name. How much you guys got? Because in this wacky-ass modern world where we're living," he explained, "you can't get laid without no money. You got enough for a beer?"

"How much is a beer?"

"I got a couple bucks," James admitted.

"U.S. cash or MPC?"

"Regular dollar bills."

"Corporal Jollet, take these new guys to the Floor Show."

Flatt and Jollet, both bumping into each other and getting in each other's way, giving off an aura of mutual dependence and resentment, like brothers, placed their M16s in the carryall's tool compartment. Jollet said to the privates, "Where's your weapons?"

"Jesus God!" Fisher cried out. "I TOLD you!"

James said, "We don't have no weapons."

"How bizarre," Flatt said.

"Are we gonna get some?"

"Yes, I believe we can furnish you all the weapons you want," Jollet assured them. "This is a war."

Flatt went into the Long Branch Saloon, leaving them with Jollet, who said, "I'm not actually gonna say it, but I feel like saying, 'Shit.'"

He turned and headed toward the town. They could only follow.

"Where are we?"

"Bien Hoa. We don't go past the edge. It's all air force in there."

It was dark. This was Vietnam. "Goddamn," James said, trying to keep his voice as soft as the darkness.

"The point being?"

"The point being is, it's darker'n hell."

"They should show you a picture of how dark it is here before you sign up at the recruiters," Evans said.

"I didn't sign up," Fisher said. "They drafted my ass. And I qualified for chopper training."

"Then what are you doing here?" Evans asked.

"What are *you* doing here?"

"I volunteered," Evans said. "Why? Two things: curiosity plus stupidity. What about you, Cowboy?"

Having mentioned that his mom worked on a ranch, James Houston had become a cowboy. He said, "Just stupidity all by itself, I guess."

Fisher said, "You think they have any mines around here? Mines on this road? Booby traps or anything?"

"Shut up, all of you," Jollet said, and instantly they shut up.

James smelled cook-smoke, greasy vapors. They walked toward the vague dim lights, not very far off now, their boots creaking and their canteens ticking. He would never top this feeling, he was sure of it: scared, proud, lost, hidden, alive.

Fisher broke the silence. "Can you please just tell us where we're going?"

Jollet halted to light a cigarette, sending over the region a glow from his lighter. "To this place called the Floor Show. The floor shows used to be very weird, due to a lack of music." He waved the lighter and the flame went out. "See? No snipers."

"What do you mean 'floor shows'?"

"They should be improved considerably. I heard they got a jukebox."

"What's on it?"

"Songs, man. Tunes, you know?"

"Where'd they get a fucking jukebox?"

"Where do you think? Some NCO club someplace. Somebody sold it out the back door."

"And you don't know what's on it?"

"How would I know that, Private? I got no fucking idea."

"But, I mean—just a general idea."

Jollet halted, his face toward the sky. "DEAR LORD. I HAVE NOT *BEEN* TO *SEE* THE FUCKING THING YET."

"Well, okay."

"I AM ON MY *WAY THERE* RIGHT FUCKING NOW."

"Okay. Okay."

"I AM ON MY WAY THERE *WITH YOU*."

A broken-off sign out front of the place said FLOOR SHOW. It looked like a barn, only inside instead of goats and chickens there were people, mostly small women. Behind the plywood bar a green neon sign said LITTLE KING'S ALE. There were lava lamps. "Sit here," Jollet instructed them. They sat at a table. "You, sir. Your name is what?"

"Houston."

Jollet said, "Buy me a beer, Houston."

"I'll buy you just one, and that's all."

"Yow, daddy! Yer scratchin' my number."

"What does that mean?"

"That means I need two dollars."

One of the women approached. "You want floor show?" She seemed to guess Jollet was the one to talk to, maybe because he hadn't sat down. She smiled at him in her tight, short blue dress. She'd lost a front tooth.

"No floor show. Beer now, floor show later."

"I be your waitress," she said.

"Give me two dollars," he said. "Four beers."

James said, "Lemme have a Lucky Lager."

"No Lucky. Puss Boo Ribbon."

"Pabst? Nothing but Pabst?"

"Puss Boo Ribbon or 33."

Jollet said, "Bring us 33."

"I want Pabst," James said.

"You want the cheapest," Jollet said. "Bring it in the bottle. Don't bring me no dirty glass."

She took Houston's money and departed.

Looking terrified, Fisher said, "All righty, then!"

"Fellers," Jollet said, "I'm gonna sky on out of here."

"What?"

"Got errands to run. You children stay put."

"What? How long do we stay here?"

"Till I get back."

"How long is that, man?"

"Corporal Jollet," said Fisher, "please. We just came from the States. We don't know where we are."

"I know where you are. So just stay where you are till I get back."

The woman returned carrying four bottles by their necks, two in each hand. Jollett intercepted her, took one, said, "Thank you very much," and disappeared.

And here they sat while the woman wiped the sweat off their beers with a bar rag. She was very small and wore a lot of makeup too white for her dark complexion.

"This beer tastes like pimple medicine," Fisher declared.

Evans said, "What was the name of this town again?"

James tipped his beer to his mouth and guzzled and tried to think. He drank half of it down, but no thoughts came. The beer tasted like any other. "We didn't need them Yankees anyway," he said.

"*I* needed them. I'm *lost*," Fisher said. "I'm a Yankee too," he pointed out.

The woman said, "You want floor show?"

"Beer now," Evans said. "Floor show later. Okay?"

She leaned down and said directly to James, "You want bo-jup?"

"What did she say?"

"'Scuse me," James said, "did you mean to say, you know, *blow* job, are you saying?"

"Bullshit."

"That's what she said."

"Oh, holy Jesus God," Fisher said.

"How much is it?"

1967

"One time right now two dollar."

"Can you believe this?"

"Somebody loan me two dollars," James said.

"You're the one with the money."

"I ain't got it," James said.

"What's your name?" Evans said.

"My name Lowra," she said.

"That means Laura, right?"

"I give you good bo-jup."

"Beer now, bo-jup later," Evans said. He looked pale and amazed.

Rapidly James finished his 33 beer, the only thing in this environment he felt qualified to deal with. In a corner at several tables shoved together sat a gang of youngsters in white uniforms, sailors from a foreign land, all holding or wearing berets of a color indeterminate in this dimness, most of them with whores in their laps. Nearby the famous jukebox throbbed redly like a forge. In a central spot three couples slow-danced, hardly moving, to "You've Lost That Lovin' Feelin'." A tall GI kissed his partner in an endless, terrifying kiss, enshrouding her in his arms, hunched over her and devouring her face. The couples continued in exactly the same fashion while the machine stopped its music, while it whirred and deliberated. When the Beach Boys' "Barbara Ann" came on, the foreign sailors sang along sloppily. James felt like joining in, but he was too shy. Whatever the rhythm, the dancers stood like zombies grappling in a trance. "I think those sailor-looking guys are French," Evans said. "Yeah, they're French."

The three men of the infantry sat watching the dancers while the jukebox played some woman singing "Makin' Whoopee" and then another doing "The Girl from Ipanema."

When Laura came around and asked again about a floor show, Fisher said, "Voulez vous coucher avec moi?" and she said, "Mais oui, monsieur, boo-coo fuck-you," and the three broke down in hilarious embarrassment, and she left them with a quick, dismissive air.

"Buy me a beer, Houston."

"I done bought you one. Buy me one now."

Evans said to James: "You dildo-sniffer."

"What's that? What's a dildo-sniffer?"

"I think it's fairly obvious."

James thought not. "What's a dildo?" he asked Fisher.

"You got any money?"

"Where's my two dollars?"

"Ask them."

"Don't I get no change back?"

"Ask them."

"I ain't asking anybody anything."

"Shut up," Evans said, "let me count. You know what? In this room there's more women than guys. There's fifteen women."

"Would you fuck one?"

"What do you mean? Of course I would. I'd fuck all of them."

"They're kind of ugly," Fisher said.

"Kind of, yeah," James said, "but not exactly." He stared at one across the room—pug-nosed, sexy-lipped. Her flat, noncommittal gaze provoked him.

"I'll buy, and then you buy," Evans told Fisher.

"Deal."

"Deal."

"So go get them."

"You go get them."

"You're buying, so you get them."

"Fine, fucker," Evans said. "Is everybody twenty-one? Can I check your ID?"

"Are you gonna get them beers or not?" James said.

"Yes." Evans crossed into the smoky gloom as if moving forward out of the trenches, as if this were finally the war.

When he got back he seemed happy with himself. "One more beer and I'm ready to dance. But really. Houston. Hey. How old are you?"

"I don't know."

"You don't know? You don't know? I'm nineteen. There, I told you, so you tell me."

"Eighteen."

"Eighteen?"

"Me too," Fisher said.

The jukebox started playing "Walk on By" by Dionne Warwick.

A fat whore who seemed to be dancing all by herself nearby turned slowly, and in doing so revealed a short man almost dangling in her embrace, his head on her breast. Two-inch heels on his cowboy boots made his rear end jut like a woman's. Fisher started laughing at the couple and showed no ability to restrain himself.

The man disengaged himself from his partner and came to their table. He was smiling, but when Fisher stood up, the little man said, "Do you want to get knocked down?"

"No."

"Well, don't stand so tall-up and so bloody fucking close, then. How tall are you?"

"Tall enough."

"Tall enough to get knocked down," the man said, mainly to the others. He wore jeans and a madras shirt. He was short, wide, round-headed. "How tall?"

"I don't know."

"How many feet and inches, Yank?"

"Six feet five inches."

"Jesus bloody hell."

"You couldn't knock me down," Fisher said.

"He's just being friendly," James put in.

"I'm just saying what I think," Fisher said, "about knocking me down."

"Sounds like you've grown your beer muscles now, mate."

"I'm just stating a fact."

"Oh, yeah, he's got his beer muscles right big all over him!"

"Who *are* you?"

"I'm Walsh of the Australian merchant marine. I'm nine stone in weight and one hundred fifty-two centimeters tall, and I'll fight all four of you all at once, or one at a time. Let's start with the toughest. Who's the toughest? Come on. You the toughest?"

"I don't think so," said James.

"You don't want to be taking me on, if you're the toughest or not," the Aussie said. To Fisher he said, "How about you, big fella? Think you can just throw me up on the roof, big fella?"

"You're a ornery li'l shit, but I'll throw you up on the roof," Fisher said, laughing.

Little Walsh was outraged. "You'll throw me up on the roof? Get out here. Get out here. Come and throw me up on the roof, come on outside." He wheeled and headed for the door.

Fisher followed him, somewhat baffled. "Oh, shit," he said, "I'm going to get beat on by a midget wrestler."

Houston and Evans went too. Outside in the muddy street, where they got no light except what fell through the doorway, Walsh primed himself for battle by working his shoulders, flexing his hands, arching himself backward, bending over forward, touching his palms to the dirt. "Come on." Fisher stooped with his arms outstretched, as if preparing to lift a child. His opponent weaved left and right, bobbed his head, dropped his left shoulder in a quick feint, shot out his right hand, and apparently threw dirt in Fisher's eyes. Fisher stood upright, blinking, squinting, openmouthed. The Aussie kicked him in the groin, ran around behind him, and lashed out with the bottom of his foot twice, rapidly, first at the crook of Fisher's knee and then at his spine, and sent the big boy sprawling on his face with his hands wrapped around his crotch.

The Aussie bent over him and shouted, "Wake up, ya lazy bastid!"

By this time the French sailors and their girls had come out to watch, but it was already over.

Walsh helped Fisher to his feet. James and Evans lent a hand. "Come on, get up, get up. Enough of our shenanigans, it's time for a hefty lager amongst us boys."

Inside, he joined the youths at their table, pulling his fat whore onto his lap. "Don't fight the little fella. Never fight the little fella. We're here amongst you giants because we've survived, and we've survived because we're tougher than God. All right, then! Beers for everyone! Christ!" he suddenly shouted. "I smell cherry! Who's cherry here?" He looked around among their blank faces. "Have none of ya never had a fuck? That's all right. The beer's on me, boys. I bullied you, I snookered on ya shamefully, and I'm a bastid of the low degree. But Christ, I only weigh nine stone. And I'm hung like a hummingbird. Right, honey? Tiny-tiny!"

His girl said, "I like tiny-tiny. I don't like bick dick."

Girls surrounded them. A girl sat in Fisher's lap. A girl stood beside James's chair, playing with his ear. She leaned down and whispered, "Let's go fuck." The one in Fisher's lap said to him, "I like bick dick." Her zoris dangled from her toes above the floor. She had a funny face. Huge slanted cheekbones. She looked like an elf. He told her, "Get off me. My balls hurt. I don't love you."

"I'm fifty-nine and three-quarter inches tall. Survival is my chiefest consideration at this altitude. I've got to be aggressive." Walsh pushed at his woman's rump and said, "I want beers all around for these brave lads of the American Army. Did you brave lads see the sign out front? In the days of yesteryear this place was called Lou's, and there was a big Coca-Cola sign that said 'Lou's,' and the small sign out front said 'Floor Show Any Time.' But one night a drunken Aussie of the merchant marine karate-chopped the sign and broke it off. Me. Yeah! That was me gave this place the famous name. Where's your home, big fella?"

"Pittsburgh. And I wish I was there."

"You're a game lad, Pittsburgh. Here's my hand in friendship. Never fight the little man. He's learnt to bring you down. I've been around the world in ships, and I've learnt to bring the victory home. I'm one hundred fifty-two centimeters in height, and shall never grow another. And the floor show's on me."

James tried dancing with his woman. She came close against him, soft and hot, and her hair was stiff and she smelled like baby powder. When he asked her name she said, "I make my name for you"—her ripe, sassy lips. The rhythm was driving, but they slow-danced together in the ruby light of the jukebox. Walsh paid for the beers. They sang songs with the French sailors, one of whom danced on the table in his underpants while the others shook up their beers and sprayed him with foam. Walsh arm-wrestled the table and beat them, every last one. He paid for the floor show, but they had to pay a man in a striped gangster suit two dollars extra, he said, "for the jukebox." They went to a bedroom in the back of the establishment and sat on the floor and a woman came in, shut the door, pulled her dress off over her head without taking her cigarette from her mouth, and stood before them naked in red high-heeled shoes, puffing on her smoke. Her body was utterly perfect in every part. "What what WHAT is your name?" Evans cried out, and she said, "My name is Virgin." Out in the bar the jukebox again struck up "You've Lost That Lovin' Feelin'," and the naked Virgin began to move. "I'm horny tonight, so horny, so horny," she wailed. James couldn't feel his hands, feet, lips, or tongue. Standing less than one meter from his face she danced for a minute to the music, then sat on the bed, parted wide her knees, and inserted her cigarette's filter tip between the lips of her vagina and puffed away, blowing smoke from her crotch while the juke-box in the next room played "Satisfaction" by the Rolling Stones. Now James felt as if his head had been chopped off and thrown in boiling water. Virgin lay back, the bed supporting only her head and shoulders, her high heels planted on the floor, her torso gyrat-ing to the rhythms of "Barbara Ann," and they all sang along . . . God almighty, some part of him prayed, if this is war let peace never come.

The three Kootchy Kooties came around for one of their consul-tations. They kept to themselves and hogged the shade beside Bunker One this sunny morning, and none of Echo Recon thought of crowding them. The black guy was especially scary. He'd done a tour with a Long-Range Reconnaissance Patrol squad who traveled the nights completely jazzed on uppers taking the life of any man, woman, or child they encountered. His hair grew out in an explosion of savage curlicues and he painted his face like an Indian and went around with the sleeves of his uniform torn off. In comparison, the actual Indian among them, diminutive, wiry, bowlegged, from somewhere in the Southwest, appeared quite sane. The third guy was of Italian or even more foreign extraction, Greek maybe, Armenian. He never talked, not even to his operational superior, the colonel.

Meanwhile, at the moment, Colonel Sands wouldn't shut up. And he wasn't a real colonel, he was more like a Southern honorary fat-boy colonel, and the men called him "Colonel Sanders" behind his back and referred to these rare morning assemblies in the encampment on the west side of Good Luck Mountain as the "Hour of Power."

But the colonel wasn't a fool. He had an eerie sense for what you were thinking: "You men realize I'm a civilian. I confer with your lieutenant; I don't pass orders to him. But I do direct our operations in a general sense." He stood right in the crashing-down light of the tropical morning with his hands on his hips. "Twelve weeks ago, last November nineteenth, my alma mater, Notre Dame, played what should have been the bloodiest game in its history against Michigan State. Both superb teams. Both undefeated. Both raring for a fight." The colonel wore canvas boots like their own, stiff new Levi's, a fisherman's vest with a lot of pockets. White T-shirt. Aviator sunglasses. From his back pocket jutted the blue bill of a baseball cap. "A week before the game the Michigan State students leafleted the Notre Dame campus from an airplane. The leaflets were addressed to the 'peace-loving villagers of Notre Dame.' They asked, 'Why do you struggle against us? Why do you persist in the mistaken belief that you can win, freely and openly, against us? Your leaders have lied to you. They have led you to believe you can win. They have given you false hopes.'"

What was he rattling on about? The colonel was part joke, part sinister mystery. Sometimes he sounded like a cracker, other times like a Kennedy. He liked to have the Screwy Loot drive him around the mountain in a jeep while he chewed cigars and sipped from a pint of whiskey, clutching an M16 between his knees, hoping to shoot at tigers or leopards or wild pigs.

"Now, this Notre Dame–Michigan State game I'm telling you about is already being called the Game of the Century. It's important to me not just as a former tackle for the Fighting Irish, but as an enemy of the Vietcong right here and now. I've been trying to get hold of the films of this game. I'd like every soldier in this theater to study what happened. I hope I can get some film of the train ride our Fighting Irish took to the Spartan Stadium in East Lansing, Michigan. People standing in the cornfields and dairy farms beside the train rails holding up signs saying 'Hail Mary, full of grace, Notre Dame's in second place.' I'd like to show every one of you what the Irish saw, heading into a stadium full of seventy-six thousand people chanting and rocking and swaying and hollering. I wish we could all sit down together and watch the kickoff.

"The Irish played under a cloud of misfortune. Our main pass receiver—Nick Eddy—slipped on the ice getting off the train and wrecked his shoulder before the game even started. Next setback, after the first play of the game our best center left the field on a stretcher. Then our quarterback Terry Hanratty went down in a pile and *he* was dragged off with a separated shoulder. Well into the second quarter, Michigan State was tromping us ten to nothing. But this young diabetic second-string quarterback name of Coley O'Brien somehow tossed a thirty-four-yard touchdown pass to a second-string receiver named Bob Gladieux—not even an Irish name—and then the Irish held Michigan State off until our kicker made a field goal right at the start of the fourth quarter.

"And there you are, a tie game, ten to ten. One minute thirty seconds left. Irish have the ball on our own thirty-yard line. There's the field. There's the goal. Here are the men.

"But the head coach, Coach Parseghian, elected to run the

clock out and take the tie. Elected to leave the field without a victory.

"Now, why was that?

"It was because taking the tie didn't diminish their chances of winning a national championship. A tie still left them in first place, nationally. And a couple weeks later they did, in fact, take the national championship. They trounced USC fifty-one to zero.

"Now, do you think I'm going to tell you that was wise? Well, maybe it was. Maybe it was wise. But it was wrong.

"Because that day in East Lansing, against their bitterest foe, they left the field without a victory."

The sweat poured out of his silver flattop down his face, but he didn't wipe it away. He removed his hands from his hips and slapped his right fist into his left palm, a fist as broad across the knuckles as any heavyweight champion's. "By God," the colonel said, "I'm going to get the film of this game. We're going to sit down and watch it together right here in this camp.

"Now, listen to me. I don't want you to get confused why I'm telling you this. I'm telling you this because it's exactly what we ourselves, right here, are always up against, invariably. Invariably we are up against a stretch of ground and an enemy. And to give up the stretch of ground in pursuit of some theory about the future is not the way we do things here. Now, your mission is to keep this hill secure for our LZ up there, and to check out tunnel entrances and mark them on the map. You do not have to go down inside those tunnels. We have people for that job."

Indeed, there were people for that job: the badass Kootchy Kooties. These guys slithered down face-first into dark holes in the earth with a pistol in one hand and their balls in the other and a flashlight in their teeth, anywhere in the Cu Chi region. "Kootchy Kooties" was a fabulous name. As for Echo Recon, they didn't have a flashy call-name, but owing to their proximity to Cao Phuc they couldn't avoid being known as the Cowfuckers, a stupid bit of luck. They didn't even get to paint it on anything because it was dirty language.

"We will win this war." Was he still talking? "And the efforts of this particular platoon will be instrumental in that. Think of us as infiltrators. This land under our feet is where the Vietcong locate their national heart. This land is their myth. We penetrate this land, we penetrate their heart, their myth, their soul. That's real infiltration. And that's our mission: penetrating the myth of the land.

"Questions?"

There came a long pause during which they listened to the birds down here and the whack-whack-whack of a helicopter up on the mountain.

The colonel removed his sunglasses and succeeded in staring the whole platoon in the eye at once. "Here's what we said about tie games when I played for the Irish: we said a tie game is like kissing your sister. I didn't come out to Southeast Asia in 1941 to kiss my sister. I came to Southeast Asia to fly missions with the Flying Tigers against the Japanese, and I stayed in Southeast Asia to fight the Communists, and I now tell you something, men, with all the solemnity of the deepest kind of promise: when I die, I will die in Southeast Asia, and I will die fighting."

He looked to the Screwy Loot, and the Screwy Loot said, "Dismissed!"

They moved to their respective duties. Screwy and Sarge and the Kootchy Kooties congregated over by Bunker One with the colonel. In general the platoon resented this civilian, but they were youngsters, after all, and they acknowledged his experience and had a vague superstition that he brought a blessing on them, for there were some—like Flatt and Jollet, at the moment MIA but probably just AWOL—who'd done a whole tour and upped for seconds and had still never once taken enemy fire.

Around eleven hundred hours—fifteen hours late—they heard the M35 pulling in: Flatt and Jollet bringing three replacements, one short, one medium, one tall.

Sarge was standing there to greet them, Staff Sergeant Harmon, a sunburned man with his sleeves turned up to his biceps, his leggings tucked meticulously, his blond, almost white hair neatly trimmed. He appeared never to sweat. "I consider you to be just coming back from AWOL with a government-property vehicle."

"No no no no no no no no," Flatt said, "no, Sarge, it ain't like that at all. These guys can explain."

"You two's the ones going to explain," Sergeant Harmon said.

"Whatever you say, Sarge."

"You men stow yourselves in Number Four," Harmon told the replacements, and took Flatt and Jollet into Bunker One.

As soon as they'd gone from sight, Private Getty, who was as usual very upset about something, slapped his helmet down on the wet ground outside the showers and sat on it with his feet apart and his knees together like a little girl, holding his sidearm in his lap.

Somebody yelled, "SARGE . . ."

Getty raised his weapon overhead so they could all see it and promised to kill the first motherfucker who got within six feet of him.

Sergeant Harmon came back out to find the three replacements watching Private Getty undistractedly.

"Steer off that man," the sergeant said.

The tallest one was upset, almost tearful. "We don't even know that guy. We just got here."

Getty shouted, "I just want everybody to realize!"

The sarge turned on Flatt and Jollet, now squatting by the door of Bunker One. "Ease up on him some."

"Aaah —"

"He was fine till you turned up just now. Quit riding on him."

"Listen, Sarge."

"You already made me say it twice. I'm done telling you."

"Yes, Sarge."

"No response required. I'm gon' watch how you do."

The sarge was one of those casually shining, exemplary guys, tall, strong, relaxed, very blond, with blond eyebrows, even, and disconcertingly blue eyes, blue from fifteen feet away. A scarred, seasoned lifer, a survivor of Pork Chop Hill, one of the Korean War's most heroic battles, later a movie starring Gregory Peck.

"Lost your guns," he said.

The three new men kept silent.

"Y'all pacifists?"

"Sergeant, we got routed all wrong. We went to Edwards instead of San Diego and we went to Japan someplace instead of Guam."

"They put us on a cargo plane, Sarge."

"Nobody gave us any weapons. Nobody said a word."

"I'm just fooling with you. We have weapons for you. What I don't have is time to sit waiting for my truck. Why did it take you fifteen extra hours to make your way sixty-eight kliks on good roads?"

"We got routed completely wrong."

"And the plane was late, real late."

"We spent hours and hours in Japan."

"I think my watch is stopped. Yeah—see? It's stopped, Sarge."

"We don't even know what town we're in."

"Or which province."

"Or even what a province is."

The platoon waited to see how the three would handle this inquiry. It appeared they couldn't remember whatever they'd been coached to say by Jollet and Flatt. But they continued in this way, making nothing clear.

"Listen up."

"Yes, Sergeant."

"This is Cao Phuc where you're currently at, Echo Reconnaissance Platoon of Delta Company. We're at the southwest corner of the Cu Chi District of South Vietnam—district, not province. You heard of the Iron Triangle? We are not in the Iron Triangle, we are southwest of there in a friendly zone. We keep this region secure for the LZ established on top of the mountain which we are not allowed to call a base for reasons of military protocol.

Echo's down here, the rest of the company's up top. They give you that whole 'don't be no pin-on-no-map sermon? Well, this here's a pin on the map. We don't call it a base but this *is* a permanent base, and we have two types of permanent reconnaissance patrols. Around the mountain then over, or else over the mountain then around.

"We're good for shares down here. We got fourteen guys and three share-heads, but no chemical latrines. So you dig your own kaibo over in the bush, and keep your business covered. Don't want no stink up my nose. We got no mess, it's all rations down here. Mess is up the mountain, two hot meals daily, you rotate one of those, one hot meal per day, you work that out with the guys as to your rotation, and if I get a lot of whining in my ear about people coming up short on the hot meals and I have to work out a complicated schedule, I'll be pissed off and looking to make life hell. If you're easy on me, I'm easy on you, that's the system here. You keep yourselves sorted out and squared away and I will be just no more than a presence. Questions. None. Good. Now.

"There are outfits all over this theater living in open rebellion against their officers. This ain't one. I am here to carry out the orders of Lieutenant Perry and see to it that y'all do the same. Do you hear my words?"

"Yes, Sarge."

"I come in slow and easy, but I mean what I say."

"Yes, Sarge."

"Now, Private Evans, Private Houston, Private Fisher. You have just received the speech. Do you have any current questions? No? I am available for all questions at all times."

"What's shares?"

"Shares? Shares. Look at my mouth—showers. Do you have any further questions?"

"What's a kaibo?"

"That's your to'let-hole, Private. I think it's Filipino."

"Sarge, we need shut-eye."

"Good deal. Sack out. I want your bodies on stateside time,

because I want you up nights. You gon' be pulling guard for a while. Stow yourselves in Bunker Four. If you want to sling yourselves a hammock in the trees, that's fine. Never no Charlie around here. See Corporal Ames for hammocks and weapons."

They couldn't find any Corporal Ames. In their new quarters, a tarp-roofed sandbag bunker smelling of dirty socks and bug repellant, they found four cots, three of them free of clutter. Evans brushed dried mud from one and sat down and said, "Only three hundred and sixty-four more days of this shit."

As they sorted themselves out, their friend Flatt appeared at the entry. "Welcome to World War Three. Hey, I'm sorry about that fucked-up little thing I did with the firecrackers. Come on over to the Purple Bar and I'll buy you one."

"The Purple Bar."

"If it's purple, I ain't going."

"Are you scared of purple people eaters?" Flatt asked.

"I ain't scared. I'm tired," Private Houston said.

"Okay. But I owe you one." Flatt gave them the middle finger and departed.

Elongated Fisher, the high school basketball center, rubbed his head back and forth on the plastic ceiling. "This ain't bad," he said.

They lay on their cots, not moving. After a while, Houston and Evans discussed how to get a Coca-Cola. An overwhelming sense of embarrassment and self-consciousness kept them from moving. But they didn't sleep—they heard Flatt's voice outside, and all three rose and followed him to the Purple Bar.

The roadway, roughed out by bulldozers and ruined by jeeps, was so rutted they couldn't walk on it. They kept to the margin. A jeep from the LZ up top passed them by and honked. "Don't wave, don't wave them down," Flatt said. "They never stop." He kicked at the bumper as the vehicle blew by in a gust of exhaust.

Many of Cao Phuc's villagers, considered untrustworthy, had been loaded into trucks one day and moved God knew where. The paddies had gone to hell and herbicides had turned the trails into swaths of desolation. Now the ville was a ramshackle camp for displaced Friendlies dominated by the New Star Temple in the southern hamlet, and in the north by the Purple Bar.

"You wait out here," Flatt said when they'd reached the Purple Bar.

"Why, goddamn it?"

"Just kidding!"

The sarge had business up the mountain, and half the platoon was here. They all sat around two tables shoved together. On paydays there were lots of women, but today just one, with black high heels and red toenails, sitting at a table with a newspaper, wearing pants and a shirt. Flatt said, "Four beers, hon," and she said, "I not your slave," and the papasan, who was always there, brought them the beers from a freezer full of cakes of yellow-brown ice. Before popping his beer Flatt poured iodized water from his canteen over the top, and the others copied him, muddying the straw beneath their feet. Skinny dogs watched them through the entry.

The replacements tried to ask Flatt what might be the purpose, the mission, of their outfit, and Flatt tried to tell them it was mainly a kind of wide-perimeter security for the landing zone. And somebody else said, "We work for the CIA."

"I thought this was a Recon unit."

"This is not a Recon unit. We don't know what we are."

"If I work for the CIA, then where's my green beret? Them's the assholes work for the CIA. The Green Berets."

And just that quick—probably not yet sober from the night before—the new guys were drunk in the Purple Bar.

"One thing about you, Houston, you're sort of a cowboy, but one thing about you: You got class. You got style."

"Thanks, pardner."

"No, I mean it. I mean it. I'm drunk, but—you know what I mean."

"I do. I do. I do. You mean you're a queer and you want to blow me."

"Shut up. Who farted?"

"What do you mean? The whole country stinks."

"He who smelt it, dealt it."

"He who detected it, ejected it."

"He who sensed it, dispensed it."

The guys living up the hill around the helicopter bull's-eye were always covered with dust; they kept their heads nearly shaved rather than deal with filthy hair. Flatt introduced the replacements to a couple of men from the LZ by saying, "Ask them their name."

"You mean, both of them?"

"Yeah, asshole, both of them, both of them."

The cowboy said, "Hey, now, listen: I am not your asshole."

There was a pause. Then they all burst out laughing, the cowboy too.

He said, "Okay. Who are you?"

"Bloodgutter."

"Bullshit."

"Nope. Bloodgutter."

"He is. That's his real name."

"Bloodgutter? What a cool fucking name, man. That is the coolest name in the world."

"It's not as cool as this guy's name."

"What's his name?"

"Firegod."

"*Fire*god?"

"Yep. Joseph Wilson Firegod."

"Wow."

"And his name is Bloodgutter," Firegod said.

"Wow."

"So we are asshole buddies," Bloodgutter said, "we hang around together. It just stands to reason."

Private Getty came in and sat by himself.

"Gettys-bird, where's your big old forty-five?"

"Sarge took it," Private Getty said.

"Where'd you get a forty-five, Private Getty?"

"Traded for it."

"Traded, fuck. You stole it."

Private Getty went into one of his trances where he acted deaf and talked to himself. "I don't know why I'm remembering so hard about home."

"Pay no attention to Gettys-bird. He crazy. He dinky dau."

Everybody, including Getty, stopped talking when the three Kootchy Kooties came in. The three pulled chairs around the table and sat down, and one belched loudly.

It was best not to talk until they talked, but Flatt seemed driven to ask, "Hey, is the sarge back down the hill?"

"Sarge still up there," the black savage said. "You still safe."

Flatt couldn't shut up. "You're a Indian," he told the Indian tunnel rat, "and this motherfucker Houston right here is a cowboy."

"You're a cowboy?"

"Not back home I ain't. Just here."

Off by himself Private Getty was still trancing—"I'm on the wrong ride. I'm on the wrong ride. The—wrong—ride"—expressing this thought over and over and nothing else.

The other two just drank their beers, but the black Kootchy glowered at Private Getty. "Busting me down with his jive. Busting cracks inside me."

Flatt said, "Aw, he don't mean nuthin."

"I know he don't mean nuthin. I won't hurt him. Do I look like I'll hurt somebody?"

"No."

"No? I *feel* like I'll hurt somebody."

A second jeep stopped out front. One of the new guys said, "Shit—Lieutenant Perry."

"Sarge ain't with him, so fuck him."

They insulted the lieutenant wholesale as he breezed through with a false, wise smile saying, "I suggest you discontinue fucking with me," and tossing out plastic dosers of talc that turned to sludge all over you in four minutes if you used it, but all of them used it.

He got himself a bottle of Coke and sat by himself, the same way Private Getty did. From time to time he fed rum out of a chromed flask into the mouth of his Coke. At one point he turned to them all, trying to look like a man of the world, and pointed at the cowboy and said, "You. Do you know what reality is?"

"What?"

"Wrong answer."

He was like that, that's all, mostly when he drank, which was most of the time; otherwise he was just mostly young and mostly stupid, like most of the rest of them.

Later he said, looking at no one at all, "I will fuck the Reaper. But I won't kiss my sister." Nobody answered him.

Cowboy said, "He's goofy, ain't he?"

"What is he?"

"He's goofy."

"What is he?"

"I said he's goofy, he's all screwed up."

"That's it! You got it! That's the Screwy Loot!"

When Screwy Loot stood up to leave he looked over at the replacements, in particular Fisher, the tall one with a front tooth chipped from playing basketball, and said, "The movie's not over till everybody's dead." He walked out with an uncoordinated, bouncing step.

And then they sat around letting the new ones in on things little by little:

"Do we work for the CIA?"

"You're working for Psy Ops."

"Does Psy Ops work for the CIA?"

One of the new ones, Evans, was very plastered, saying over and over again only, "Let's face it. Let's face it. Let's face it."

"Do you understand what's happening? The rest of the Third are getting chewed up alive. The rest of the whole Twenty-fifth Infantry."

"In fact, when they get chewed up alive, they're dead."

"Shut up. But that's right. They're dead, like I would hate to be."

The Purple Bar was made of bamboo poles and thatch. A layer of some kind of straw covered the floor. Underneath that, dirt. It didn't have walls, only bead curtains painted with various faded tropical scenes—palm trees and mountain ranges. A deep ditch on three sides protected the Purple Bar from flooding when the rain poured down on the town. It was really just a large hooch furnished with collapsible tables and chairs, all U.S. government–issue. A loud MASH generator outside ran the juice for the Purple Bar. Three table fans along the west side turned their faces left and right as if following the conversations.

"Yeah. Yeah. Yeah. Let's face it."

"Here's to the Lucky Fucks."

"Who's the Lucky Fucks?"

"We're all the Lucky Fucks because we pull about five patrols a month in a totally friendly zone."

"About once a week, yeah, and the rest of the time we just stay out of everybody's way."

"That is our sacred duty. Gimme a toke."

"A what?"

"A token? A cigarillo? Of the smoking variety? So I can smoke it?"

"Okay. You call them a token?"

"The trouble is, when you don't pull duty, you spend your pay—that's actually a horrible drawback."

"Because—I mean—let's *face* it."

A table by the freezer served as the bar. On it were a portable record player, a stack of albums, and a bar toy called a lava lamp, an amber jug in which you could observe the unfathomable almost cyclical but unrepeating lit-up movements of liquid wax in warm oil. The girl with red toenails controlled all the records. No requests allowed. If you asked her name, she said, "What name you like? I make my name for you."

Blackflies and mosquitoes clouded the air. The papasan chased after them with a swatter and a can of Raid.

The tunnel rats got drunk and bought a few rounds in a

friendly manner that made them no less scary. Only one was black, but they all talked like spades. They had eerie stuff to say. Philosophers. All God's chillun got tunnels. Everybody got a tunnel to be motorvating. They drank and drank, drank until their eyes went completely flat and blind-looking, but they didn't appear drunk otherwise, except that one of them when he had to piss just unzipped and did so right there at the table, in fact right on his own boots . . . You didn't often see blacks and whites hanging around together . . . People kept to the categories . . .

Minh understood Skip's disappointment, but life came as a storm, and the colonel, Skip's uncle, was the landscape's dominant figure. It made sense to take shelter in him. If the colonel wished his nephew out of the way, well and good. Thanks to the colonel, Minh himself no longer flew jets and had reason to hope he might survive this war. Nowadays he flew only helicopters, and only for the colonel. He went about often in civilian dress and spent many days free in Saigon. He had a girlfriend there, Miss Cam, a Catholic, and he went to Mass with Miss Cam on Sunday mornings and spent Sunday afternoons at her home in the company of her large family.

Flying took concentration, it wore on the mind. He enjoyed this ride as a passenger in the black Chevrolet. Nothing to do but look out at the murdered landscape off Route Twenty-two and wonder about Miss Cam.

Uncle Hao had warned Minh that Mr. Skip spoke Vietnamese. While driving the American to his new quarters in the region of Forgotten Mountain, therefore, he and his uncle didn't speak much. Minh sat up front, Skip in the back with one of his footlockers. Uncle drove the car, both hands at the wheel, head forward, concentrating deeply, his mouth open like a child's. The rain clattered on the Chevy's black roof, a storm out of nowhere, a bit early this year. Uncle Hao tried speaking English, but Mr. Skip didn't answer much. "Perhaps we shouldn't talk."

"Ah, my friend Hao," Skip said, "the rain is making me sad."

Minh tried some English himself: "It's good to learn to be happy in the rain. Then you'll be happy a lot, because there's a lot of rain." In English it didn't sound very clever.

Uncle braked, and Minh braced himself against the dash—a water buffalo crossing in front of them. A cargo van coming the other way ran into the animal and seemed to carom from its thick hide, stopping sideways in the middle of the broken pavement.

The buffalo put its head down as if trying to remember something, stood still a few seconds, and walked off into the tall grass wagging its horns from side to side, its rump rocking like two fists alternating in a paper sack. Hao maneuvered the Chevy around the stalled van as the beast faded away among the sheets of rain.

Once they'd left Route Twenty-two all the roadways were bad, almost impassable, but as long as Uncle kept the wheels turning they'd avoid getting mired. "When we come to the big dip," Hao said, "I will go down fast, because we have to get up the other side."

"The big dip—what is that?"

"A hill down and then a hill up. There's mud at the bottom."

"I understand." They were speaking Vietnamese.

Uncle Hao headed the black Chevrolet into the long drop and they splashed through the mudhole at the bottom and climbed up the other side, steeply, until the top was nearly theirs and only sky was visible in front of them. The tires broke traction and howled like tormented ghosts while the Chevy slowly slid backward. They rested at the bottom in a foot of gumbo. Hao switched off the engine, and Mr. Skip said, "All right. Here we are."

Minh removed his sandals, rolled his cuffs above his knees, draped himself in his clear plastic poncho, and waded to the house of the nearest farmer, who followed him back to the car, yanking his water buffalo along by the nose ring, and hitched a rope to the front axle and hauled them out of the bog.

Skip peered through the rear window at where they'd been and said in English, "Out of one hole and into another."

It wasn't so bad where Skip was going. He would have a gas stove, some form of indoor plumbing, probably a couple of servants. A hot bath when he wanted one. The villa, Minh understood, belonged to the family of a Frenchman, a physician, a specialist in hearing disorders, now deceased. As far as could be ascertained, this Frenchman had been fascinated with one of the area's tunnels, had gone exploring, had tripped a wire.

The drumming of the rain lightened to a tapping on the roof. Minh opened his eyes. He'd been asleep. Uncle had stopped the car again. The road seemed to end here, to dive into a creek overrunning its banks, and Minh wondered if now they'd wait for some hooded skeletal boatman to ferry the American across this river to his state of exile. But Hao inched them forward. It wasn't a creek at all, just a wide rivulet escaping from some creek they couldn't see.

The rain ceased as they wheeled slowly into the village of Forgotten Mountain. The afternoon sun glittered on the wet world, and already the people moved around outdoors as if no storm had ever visited, carrying their bundles along the road, clearing palm fronds from the front of their homes. By the dirt lanes, in the shaded, drier places, children skipped rope using pale plastic chains.

They stopped in the driveway of the villa, and Minh hardly had a minute to take it in before getting involved in a small adventure—a lot of yelling from behind the house, then an old man who appeared to be a houseboy or papasan ran into view waving a rake over his head and yelling about a snake. Minh leapt to follow, Uncle and Skip close behind, and they came on a monstrous constrictor zigzagging across the backyard, a brindle python longer than any of them, longer than all of them together. "Let me, let me," Minh said. The old man swiped his rake at it one more time uselessly and gave up the weapon to Minh. What now? He didn't want to mar the valuable skin. The snake headed for the bank behind the house. He ran after and brought the rake down hard, hoping to trap the reptile's head, but sank the splines rather farther down its spine, and like that, with frightening energy, the snake wrenched the handle free of his hands and swiveled off wildly, still skewered, dragging the rake into the brush. Minh and the houseman gave chase, beat the wet bushes with their hands, both men sopping now, and the houseman yelled, "Here is the monster!" He came up behind a dripping poinsettia holding the tail. "It's almost dead!" But it was still writhing and got away from his grip. Minh managed to catch hold of the rake, step on the snake's spine, extract the weapon from their prey, and bring it down several times on its skull—surprisingly fragile, easily pierced.

The old man's face positively broke open, all smiles. "Come, come, we'll take it to my family!"

The region's Catholic priest had turned up to greet them. He spoke in English to Skip: "It's not necessary to kill such animals. Many people keep them for a pet. But it's big enough to take the skin. Too bad it's not more colorful. Some of them are red and sometimes orange." A young man in nice clothes, probably from the city, wearing the priest's collar. "You must visit my residence," he said, and Skip said he would.

Then Minh and the old man paraded their catch down the main street through the ville, Minh at the head and his friend at the tail and fully four meters of snake bridging the distance between them, their free arms outflung to counter its dead weight, and little children running after, yelling and singing.

Mr. Skip had stayed at the house with the priest, or Minh at this moment would have assured him, "Here is a wonderful omen for your arrival."

William "Skip" Sands of the U.S. Central Intelligence Agency arrived at the villa in Cao Quyen, which meant "Forgotten Mountain," with his duffel and his uncle's three footlockers at the very moment a hard rain gave way to fine, sunny weather in which he didn't feel a participant.

Voss had claimed to have something for him, had claimed he'd keep Sands close. It had come to nothing, he'd kept Sands stashed, not at all close, in an air-conditioned Quonset hut in the MAC-V compound at Tan Son Nhut, as part of a short-lived project devoted to collation of a superabundance of trivia called the CORDS/Phoenix file system, which amounted to every note ever jotted by anybody who'd seen or heard anything anywhere in South Vietnam. The project group, roughly eighteen men and two women, all drafted from the personnel pool, spent most of their energies trying to characterize the dimensions of the material delivered onto the site—boxes of pages that would make an eight-and-one-half-inch-wide path four-point-three times around the earth's equator, or completely blanket the state of Connecticut, or outweigh the pachyderms in seventeen Barnum & Bailey shows, and so on. Shock and despair. An appreciation for the victims of sea catastrophes as the cataracts thundered into the hold. One day instructions came to put all the boxes on handcarts and push them along a cinder path under the tropical sun to a storage facility in the same complex. End of project. History.

Next, the waiting in Cao Quyen—"Forgotten Mountain," "Mountain of Forgetting," or "Forget This Mountain"—which he thought of as "Damulog II," once again beyond the last reasonable stretch of roadway and past the end of the power lines.

He and Hao and Minh were served a meal of rice and fish by the Phans, the elderly pair who looked after the place and whom he would address as Mr. Tho and Mrs. Diu, and then his companions abandoned him with promises that Hao would return every week or ten days with mail, and books, and commissary items for the pantry.

Skip's new home had running water from a tank on its roof as well as indoor plumbing, a bathroom downstairs with toilet and sink, and upstairs another with toilet, bath, and bidet, and wallpaper depicting mermaids, burnished by a strange mold. When he opened the shutters in this bathroom, half a dozen moths flew out of the toilet bowl and attached themselves to his scalp.

Nothing electric. He had butane lamps with copper shades, and rooms of rattan furniture shedding its finish in flakes. If rain came, and it would come daily for months now, there were wooden louvers to wind shut. Small leaks came down through the upstairs into several lacquer bowls set around the parlor. But the house was well situated for the breezes and had a homey feel. Things were sensible here. They spooned the salt and pepper out of tiny cups, like sugar, rather than clumping it into shakers; and his bed upstairs took up a screened corner of the house just off the modest master suite, open to every movement of the sultry night atmosphere.

By the day's last light he toured the villa, a two-story structure mainly of a damp, rough material like concrete or adobe. Small black wasps crawled in and out of bullet holes in the outer walls—during the time of the French, the region had seen battles. A concrete gutter ran around the foundation of the house and carried off the rain into a fat, slow creek in a gulley behind the grounds. He had a look down there: adventurous children sailed past on water wings patched together out of absolutely any buoyant thing—kindling, coconuts, palm fronds—calling out to him.

The villa's owner, a French physician, had passed away leaving, as Sands understood it, no trace of his physical body other than a film on the walls of a tunnel, but his shoes stood by the front door in a row, three pairs, sandals, slippers, bright green rubber boots. His walking shoes had disappeared with the rest of him. The physician, a Dr. Bouquet, had arrived from Europe early in the 1930s with a wife who had returned, according to the papasan, Mr. Tho, very shortly to Marseilles, and of whom no evidence remained anywhere in the house, unless she'd chosen the wallpaper in the upstairs bath, the innumerable tarnished mermaids. But the absent doctor constituted a pervading presence; since the day of his death nothing had been done with anything, all of it waited. In his high-ceilinged study off the living room the surface of his massive mahogany desk hid under books and journals held down by a porcelain model of the human ear—inner and outer—with detachable parts, an inkwell, an ashtray, and so on, his rack of three meerschaum tobacco pipes turned at a slight angle, shreds of newsprint or coarse, beige toilet paper marking places in several books stacked beside it, one of these pages surely holding the last word he'd read before he'd set his glasses aside, gone out walking, and been vaporized. Except for the clutter of his studies the office was clean and neat, the furniture draped with pages of the Saigon *Post* and *Le Monde* and the shutters closed. Skip pried gently under the covers of the books, careful not to shift their places, as if the owner might come checking. The physician had been cruel to the pages—tea stains, inky fingerprints, lengthy passages outlined boldly. Each volume bore inside its front cover the inscription "Bouquet" in an identical hand above the date of its purchase. He failed to find a single one without it. In addition the doctor had collected seventeen years of *Anthropologe*, a book-sized periodical, sixty-eight numbered issues with paper covers of heavy stock, all beige. And several scholarly reviews, each bound by year in the same brown paper. A damp, burgundy-cloth-bound *Nicholas Nickleby* was the only book in English. Skip had read it in college and could remember nothing about it except that somewhere in its pages Dickens called human hope a thing "as universal as death."

In a week Hao came out again, as promised, delivering many flattened cardboard boxes for Dr. Bouquet's effects, along with Skip's mail. He was glad for the boxes—he hadn't asked for them, Hao had just guessed. There was a crazy, despairing letter from Kathy Jones. Apparently these days she acted as liaison between the ICRE and several orphanages, and her life now, the things she witnessed, had turned her Calvinist fatalism—or, Skip thought, her fatal Calvinism—completely black:

> Maybe I shouldn't read certain things. But I might as well tell you I came to believe in it some time ago, even

before I learned for sure that Timothy was dead. Certain people are fated from the foundation of the world to spend eternity in Hell, and I say they never even get a taste of regular life, but just begin their Hell right at birth, we've seen that, you've seen it at least in Damulog, I know, and if you've come to Vietnam, you're seeing it in technicolor no doubt and I pity you, but I laugh.

Maybe some are in Heaven, some in Hell, some in the Limbo Zone, or maybe the worlds get separated geographically—in fact, did I tell you I found the reference to "different administrations" you asked about when we made love night after night in our own little psychedelic passion pit in Damulog? First letter to the Corinthians, was it Chapter 12?

Right—I've checked now, 12:5&6.

But I didn't recognize the quote because it's from the King James and I'm used to my Revised Standard which says, "And there are varieties of service, but the same Lord; and there are varieties of working, but it is the same God who inspires them all in every one." So "administrations" is more properly translated as "service"—it doesn't refer to some angelic governmental ordering, get it?

I wish you were here to talk to, but we didn't talk much, did we? Every time we got together we ended up quickly "getting together." I hardly know you. But I write to you.

Are you even reading this?

As a matter of fact, no. No.

Between downpours a breeze off the creek cowed the bugs and kept the study cool. He spent the evenings in the doctor's shot-silk robe, inquiring among the doctor's library of some eight hundred French titles, and, at first, hardly ever ventured beyond the grounds.

He busied himself recovering to the third dimension the flattened cardboard boxes. Also Hao had brought a roll of gummed
paper tape, turned by this weather into a solid wheel, all stuck
together, completely useless. Since Marco Polo, he thought, this
climate has defeated Western civilization.

He sent Mr. Tho to the village shop for string and told Mrs.
Diu he was heading to the local priest's for tea.

Père Patrice's small house lay a hundred meters off the main
street, down a pathway marked by tattered boards bridging the
puddles.

Père Patrice traveled around the district a lot, and Sands
hadn't passed much time with him. Sands hadn't revealed himself
as a Catholic. Perhaps he wouldn't. Maybe, he thought, I'm tired
of my faith. Not because it's been tested and broken, like Kathy's.
Only because it's gone unexercised. And the small open-air
church, a tin roof on wooden poles on a concrete slab, is this
where the drama of salvation plays out? Sands found the priest, a
tiny man in his tiny garden. Père Patrice had a round, simian
face. More nostril than nose. Huge reptilian eyes. Beyond exotic,
he looked like a man from outer space. He brought his guest hot
tea in a water glass. They sat in the garden on damp wooden
benches while the recent rain dripped from the tall poinsettias.
Sands tried his Vietnamese.

"Your pronunciation is good," the young man said, and then
spoke incomprehensibly for half a minute—Skip had already
practiced his Vietnamese with the villa's two servants and found it
hopeless.

"I'm very sorry. I don't understand. Can you please speak more
slowly?"

"I will speak more slowly. I'm sorry."

There was a silence between them.

"Will you kindly repeat your statement?"

"Yes, of course. I said I hope your work will go well here."

"I believe it's going well, thanks."

"You are with the Canadian Ecumenical Council."

"Yes."

"It is a project of Bible translation."

"We have many projects. That is one project."

"Are you one of the translators, Mr. Benét?"

"I'm trying to improve my Vietnamese. It's possible I'll help later on with translation."

"Let's speak English," the priest said in English.

"Whatever you like."

Père Patrice said, "Shall I hear your confession?"

"No."

"Thank God! You're not Catholic?"

"Seventh-Day Adventist."

"I don't know about Seventh-Day people."

"It's a Protestant faith."

"Of course. God doesn't care who is Protestant or Catholic. God himself is not Catholic."

"I hadn't thought of that."

"What is this universe to God? Is it a drama? Is it a dream? Perhaps a nightmare?" The priest smiled yet seemed angry.

"That's a big question. I think it qualifies as a mystery."

"I'm reading a most wonderful book."

Skip waited for him to finish, but he didn't say anything further about the book.

"I have met Mr. Colonel Sands, there at your villa. He's your friend? Your colleague?"

"He's my uncle. Also my friend."

"The colonel fascinates me. I don't understand him. But I don't think we should talk about him, do you?"

"I'm not sure what you mean."

"I believe that we should confine ourselves."

Sands decided that the priest was a subtle man unable to complete his thoughts in English.

"Can you help me collect folk tales in the area?" he asked the priest.

"Folk tales? Fairy tales, perhaps?"

"Yes. It's a hobby, a personal interest of mine. Not associated with my work."

"Not associated with your Bible work?"

"Well, of course it helps me as a translator. It helps me to understand the language of myth."

"But do you say that the Bible is a myth?"

"Not at all. I say it's in the language of myth."

"Of course. Surely. I can help. Do you like songs also, perhaps?"

"Songs? Of course."

"I'll sing you a Vietnamese song," the priest said.

He gazed into Skip's eyes. His features seemed to clarify. His look became earnest. For almost a minute he sang quite beautifully in a clear, strong voice, unabashed, completely unselfconscious. The tune was high and struck a note of yearning.

"Did you understand the song?"

Skip was speechless.

"No? For three years, he is a soldier at the outpost, far from his village. He's very lonely and he works hard to cut bamboo all day. His body hurts. He eats only bamboo shoots and some fruit, and his friends are only the bamboo. And he sees a fish in the cistern, swimming by itself, also with no friends. I think we are like this— Mr. Bénet and Père Patrice. Don't you think so? I'm far from my home in my village, and you are far from Canada."

He said no more.

"Is that the end of the song?"

"The ending. He sees the fish swimming alone."

"I think you've got a little Irish in you, sir."

"Why?"

"The Irish love to sing."

"Sometimes there are singing competitions, and I place very well. It's also my hobby, like yours. Here in this district, every man must sing. We must sing to the demons."

"Really?"

"Mr. Bénet, it's true, the demons live here."

"I see."

"If you do something disrespectful, for instance if you relieve yourself in the forest, you will suffer some tricks from them. Trees may fall on you, huge branches may break off and hit your head, or you might fall in a crevasse and get a broken bone. It might be a shocking way to learn there are spirits here in the forest."

Skip said, "Yes, I'd be shocked if that happened."

"Certain Chinese doctors in this district practice their medicine here. They know about these spirits. I'll take you to the shop sometime. Would you like to go? They keep many fascinating things. He keeps practically all parts of a tiger in jars and tiny boxes. If he grinds the bones and feeds to a dog, that dog will become fierce. Did you know that even the wax from a tiger's ears can cure you of something? And the tough hairs from the elephant's tail can ease the woman while she gives birth. They also grind the teeth and bones of the elephant to rub on certain kinds of lesions to cure it. They grind the horns of the deer and mix it up with alcoholic beverage to make an evil kind of drink. It makes a man too powerful in sexual matters. Other animals too. Many snakes, many kinds of animals. Perhaps insects, I don't know. The Chinese doctor knows these things."

"I'd probably enjoy seeing a collection like that."

"Everything is not merely superstitious with these people. Some things are already verified. The tribes make shrines and altars in the forest. A tiny house for the spirits from bamboo, perhaps the coconut shell. The spirits are there, they live there, I must believe it from the evidence. As in the case of a young man who scornfully urinated in front of an altar in the forest, and then he suffered a complete mental breakdown."

"Shocking."

"My name is Thong Nhat," said Père Patrice. "I hope I will be your friend."

"I look forward to it," Skip said. "Please call me Skip."

So it went—tea with the priest, walks when it didn't rain, a program of calisthenics. He took to puttering among the dead physician's French magazines, translating passages the physician had underscored. He tended the colonel's files. Sometimes he heard distant choppers, fighters, bombers, and felt himself captured in a rainbow bubble of irrelevance.

Next visit, Hao brought a letter from Major Eddie Aguinaldo, forwarded by the embassy in Manila to the Saigon Embassy's APO address in San Francisco.

I've decided to marry myself to a certain young and quite beautiful woman. Indeed! I knew you'd be amazed. I can see you before me right now with your mouth dropped opened. Her name is Imogene. She is the daughter of Senator Villanueva. I intend to become some kind of politician of a local sort, not too corrupt, but certainly rich, and you can depend on me to help you make money if you come back to our fair land.

I have had a somewhat curious visit from a "Mr. so-and-so" from your Political Section in Manila. I hesitate to refer to him more specifically. He expressed considerable interest in our friends and relations, that is, my friend and your relation. I hope you'll understand the reference. Mr. so-and-so's intensity was very uncharacteristic of people from your crowd. I must say he left me feeling a little shaken. When he was gone I went immediately to the sideboard to pour myself something stiff, and now I've sat down to write this letter to you at once. I am feeling some urgency. I can't be depended on to know everything, but I convey my sense of things to you that our friend and relation should be talked to about this right away. About the violent interest shown in him, about an adversarial tone on the part of someone supposed to be our friend and relation's colleague. I believe you should immediately warn him to begin casting the occasional glance behind, even when he feels the safest.

Skip, in Mindanao that was a botched thing. An intol-
erable mistake, and very much regretted. I cannot say
anything past that.

Yours Quite Sincerely,

—"Eddie," in a flourishing hand.

James dreamt of firefights: shooting useless bullets from an
impotent gun. Dreams send you messages, this he knew. He disliked these particular messages, warnings that in battle he'd have
no power. Not that he saw battles anywhere outside his night-
mares.

The choppers in and out of LZ Delta carried strictly supplies,
no battle teams. Once in a while somebody hurt had to touch
down in a shot-up chopper that couldn't make it farther, but Echo
only heard about these things.

James didn't mind the patrols. A patrol took two days. Your
squad went west up the zigzag track, through the LZ, and around
to the south—along an old track through the open farms, into a
patch of jungle, and out into the craggy wasteland made by
herbicides—and back to Echo Camp; or you went around to the
north, then east up through the LZ, then down the mountain and
back to Echo. On the way you camped one night. Nothing ever
happened.

On the west side of Cao Phuc it was still Vietnam, untouched
by herbicides and full of jungle and paddies where enemy might
easily hide in ambush. The west side should have been scary, but
it wasn't. The farmers strung along the hillside, hacking away at
their terraces, always waved. Word was their families had never
had trouble with the French or the VC or the GIs.

Nothing happened on the north side either, but it was unin-
habited, rocky, plunging, cut by ravines, and often a leaf turned
wrong caught the light and looked like a flash of white up above a

cliff—like somebody hiding there—and terrified him. Any fallen log looked, at first glance, like a sniper in the undergrowth.

"What's that there?"

"That's a elephant turd."

"You suppose they booby-trap them things?"

"Oh, yeah. Oh, yeah. Oh, yeah. They'll booby-trap any kind of motherfucker."

Black Man said, "That's buffalo shit. No elephants around here."

"There's plenty of elephants."

"Not on this mountain. That's buffalo shit."

"It's big."

"Buffaloes are big, fool."

"What's that growing out of it? Mushrooms?"

"Mushrooms will grow out of any kind of motherfucker. Shoot right up," Black Man said, "grow so fast you can watch it. Hormonally and such, it's a trip."

"Well, anyway, there wasn't no shockers in that batch."

"That's one batch of shit we foxed."

"We aced that shit pile."

"Only seventy-six more million to go."

"Yeah," Black Man said, "lotta boo-shit coming at you, ratshit, bat-shit . . . But you don't take it, you just deflect that shit with your Maximum Mind."

Right now Black Man was the only soul brother in Echo Platoon. Black Man did this. Black Man did that. Black Man had a name, but it was secret. "I don't want nobody calling me nothing but Black Man," he insisted. "I won't live by the slave name the white man gave my forefathers." He'd placed adhesive tape over his name patch, wouldn't tell anyone what it said.

Black Man told them, "I'm a black man with a black dick. But it ain't that big. Lotta guys wanna brag on their Big Ten-inch. But if they had ten inches like I have *six* inches, this sorry-ass world would be blown in two. That's how much power I got in my Little Six-inch."

Fisher and Evans were James's only friends, friends for life. He thought, also, maybe Sarge approved of him. As for the rest of Echo Platoon, they spoke a strange language, and most of the time James felt scared and angry and left out.

He hurt for home. Now he understood what it must have meant to his brother Bill to dial a number in Honolulu and make the phone ring in his mother's kitchen. He repented his casual gruffness with his brother when he'd called. Fantasies of talking and laughing with his brother, talking with his friends, dominating these assholes of Echo, dreams of not being here, being anywhere but here, being somewhere that was elsewhere, of never having heard of this place.

You could draw leave and hitch a ride over to the Twenty-fifth Infantry's big base or all the way into Saigon on one of the trucks from the LZ. Trucks went every day.

The sarge, Sergeant Harmon, wasn't as different from the others as he'd seemed at first. He swore, he drank beer, though only one or two at a sitting, and his only other vice was chewing tobacco, snuff; some of the guys called it snoose, and they did it too, out of admiration for the sarge. He was older and had these war-movie looks—very light blond hair, sky-blue eyes, and a tanned face, and a grin that crawled up on one side like Elvis Presley's. One of his dog-teeth on that side was chipped, but his teeth were very white, and it didn't look that bad, and James almost felt he wouldn't have minded having a tooth chipped like that, like Sarge did. Fisher had a chipped tooth too, but his chip looked like you'd want to get it fixed. And the sarge's fatigues fit him very neatly. He made it appear as if the tropics weren't really hot.

Flatt had predicted their pay would never find them way out here in the shadow of Good Luck Mountain, but he'd been wrong, and well into May James sent part of each paycheck to his mother in Phoenix. Once she sent him back a small note in a big envelope, her greeting scrawled on a page of pink stationery she must have stolen somewhere. She thanked him and said, "We're getting on okay, the Lord is making ends meet."

The second Friday in June was a little different. James's birth-day had come the day before. He and Fisher and Evans left Echo Camp on a legitimate pass and got as far as the ville. Evans had decided they must all get laid. "Come *on*," Evans said, "we're in a *war*. We're *men*."

"I don't see no war."

"It's all over the place, or at least somewhere around here, and I don't want to die in it till I get laid."

They went to the Purple Bar, and on straw-filled sacks in a row of hooches behind it Evans and Fisher lost their virginity, and James betrayed Stephanie Dale with a girl who at least did not have terrible teeth, or any teeth at all, that he could see, because she didn't have to smile or talk, and therefore no dishonesty was required to get things started, and no sincerity either, and she moaned like a savage and whirled him upward through a cloud of joyful lust.

The three privates met afterward in the bar. They still had six-teen hours' leave, but they'd done all there was to do in the world.

Evans raised his glass: "Git some!"

"Come on."

"What."

"Don't say 'Git some.' It's so posed, man."

"The fuck it's posed. It isn't posed. It's who I am."

"You are who? You are 'Git some'?"

"Lemme tell you something, man, lemme tell you something, fucker." Evans wiped beer from his chin and said, "All right, okay, I was cherry, I hereby admit it. That was my first time ever."

They stared at him until he was forced to ask, "What about you?"

"Yeah, me too," Fisher said.

"Well? Cowboy?"

"No. I wasn't."

"You're sticking to that lie."

"Yes, I am."

"Fine. You always were a little more advanced."

"But there's one lie I'm done with. Today's not my nineteen birthday, it's only my number eighteen."

"What?"

"What?"

"You just turned eighteen?"

"Yep."

"You mean you *were* . . . *seven*teen?"

"I sure was."

"My God! You're a *child*!"

"Not no more I ain't."

Evans reached across the wobbly table to shake his hand. "You're more advanced than I even suspected."

In honor of his birthday, James bought several rounds. He was happy and high and laughing. Now that he'd come to where the humidity was awful and the beer cheap and infinite, he really understood beer's meaning and its purpose.

They drank until night fell. Fisher, a Catholic, came under a black cloud of penance. "I'll get VD for sure."

"VD can't get through a rubber."

"Yeah," guilty Fisher said, "that's if you can get the packet open."

"What?"

"I didn't use it! I couldn't get the little packet open! My fingers were too goddamn nervous!"

"Use your teeth next time, you pitiful fool."

They walked home in the dark. Fisher refused to be consoled. "I'm gonna get VD from God."

"Are you gonna go to confession about this?"

"I have to."

Evans said, " 'Catholic' sounds very close to 'cuntlick.' "

Fisher seemed wounded. "That's a really evil statement."

"Do you have a religion?" Evans asked James.

"Now I do, I sure do. Now I worship the Holy Fuck."

None of them had his flashlight. They couldn't see. The dry mud was like concrete and they stumbled in the ruts. Evans shouted, "We did it!"

"I know! We did it! It's like . . ." Fisher was speechless.

"I *know*!" Evans said. "It *is*! God-DAMN! I shot my wad so hard I almost exploded the top of my penis off."

Fisher begged, "Come on, you guys, for real—did you use a rubber?"

"Hell, yes, I used a rubber."

"You better use one next time," James told Fisher.

"What next time? I'll never do it again."

"Bullshit."

"I just hope to God I don't get VD. It hurts like hell to piss, then the shot hurts too."

"That shot's supposed to be like a knife in your butt."

"It's the next worst shot to rabies."

"At least you can't get rabies from a whore."

"Can't you?"

"Shit. I don't know."

"Not unless she bites you!"

Coming back into camp they tried to keep it quiet, but as they found Bunker Four, Evans whispered loudly, "I can't believe it! If I'm gonna die, at least I'm not gonna die a virgin."

Fisher sat hunched on his cot. He sounded seasick. "I feel so evil. I never should've done it. My first time, and I paid for it."

Evans fell back on his cot, fondling himself. "Man, I just want to kiss my own dick cuz I'm so in love with it for being able to FUCK!"

Somebody in another bunker shouted, "Well, fuck YOUR-SELF and SHUT THE FUCK UP."

Fisher went to his knees in the dark. "Please, God, please, Holy Mary and Jesus and the Saints, don't let me get VD."

"I don't know how to describe this," Evans said, "but after I fin-ished, I was lying on top of her and she kind of put her legs together and kind of . . . rubbed her legs together. And it felt . . . real good."

James said, "I've been scared so it don't let up, like I have a sore stomach all the time, right here." He touched himself below his breastbone. "But for once in this God-fucked shit-hole I feel like I don't have to be scared no more. Because I'm so goddamn drunk, and I'm finally eighteen."

"Oh, man," Fisher said. "She took my shit. She took my powers. They're working for Charlie. Those whores are working for Charlie."

In June, during the rains, a man named Colin Rappaport rendezvoused with Kathy Jones on the highway not far from her nursing station in Sa Dec on the Mekong Delta. He had the use of a Land Rover. Making a tour of things for World Children's Services, for whom he worked these days. He helped her get her knapsack and her rattling black bicycle in the back of his vehicle, and they headed for the orphanage eight kilometers down the American-made road.

She'd met him several times in Manila long ago. Colin had been skinny then, now he was portly, having lived in the U.S. the last year or more. While he drove he set aside his straw hat and mopped his crown with a sopping hankie. He'd always been bald. You couldn't get much balder than Colin Rappaport.

"How are you liking your visit?"

"Jesus, Kathy, I thought poverty was bad enough."

"Isn't it?"

"I mean, I've never wondered about what a war could do."

"After a while it just gets funny. I'm not kidding. You get so sick in the head you just start laughing."

When they arrived at the Emperor Bao Dai Orphanage, ragged attendants were cutting up a handful of rotten vegetables into a cauldron of steaming rainwater. "Here's Van," she told Rappaport as a young man hurried over wiping his hands on his T-shirt. "Miss Kathy, so good to have a visit, come, I take you," Van said, shaking hands with Rappaport, guiding them up the dark staircase of this former factory to the building's third level,

where in six chicken-wire pens on the vast open floor lived two
hundred children, segregated by age. The place was thick with
flies and the smell of piss and offal. Van made the eight-year-olds
rise and stand in rows in their frayed and filthy cotton shorts and
shirts to sing a song of welcome, throughout which Rappaport
stood still with a glazed smile, and then Kathy led him back down
the stairs and out to the malaria bay, a tin-roofed shed where a
dozen patients lay in darkness and silence. Kathy moved among
them propping open eyelids and mouths. "Nobody's dead," she
told Colin.

When they came out two attendants were hoisting the cauldron between them and heading for the main building, one with
a ladle in his free hand.

"Oh, Lord," Colin said. "It's their food."

She took him under a tree and they sat in the dirt.

He said, "I thought it was garbage. Dishwater."

"We in Purgatory sing fondly of Hell."

"I think I get you."

Van came over with two glasses of tea.

"Go ahead, they boil it," Kathy said.

Colin set the glass between his feet. He took a cigar from his
left breast pocket and a lighter from the right. "It's a mess, isn't it?"

"The whole planet. The days are evil. — I'm sorry, am I talking
kind of crazy?"

Obviously he thought yes. "I had no idea how overwhelmed
you are."

He said no more while he finished his tea. He smoked most of
his cigar, carefully shaved away its ember by rubbing it against a
tree root, and replaced the rest in his breast pocket.

Soon it rained hard, and they sat in the Land Rover while the
downpour splashed on the asphalt drive and turned its surface to a
bed of glassy spikes. "I'll see if we can't get you supplies here," he
said. "I'd like to divert a whole planeload for you. I think I can do
it. I'll see."

"Good. Thanks."

"Is there anything else I can do?"

"Can I have the rest of your cigar that's in your pocket?"

"Are you kidding?"

"No."

"You smoke cigars?"

"Once in a while."

"I guess we'd better let you do what you want," he said. "Jesus Christ, we've got to get you some help."

She said, "I've got Lan and Lee."

"Who?"

"You'll meet Lan. She and Lee mind the shop when I'm gone."

"Oh. Right. Are they trained?"

"They're a great help. Not formally trained. Very competent."

"Kathy, this is why I left ICRE. They just drop you down in the jungle with a map and a compass."

"We get help from all over, though. The GIs give us stuff. We do what we can."

"The GIs help you?"

"I got a half liter of Xylocaine last week. I spent yesterday and this morning pulling teeth. They love the Xylocaine. Otherwise they go to the local yanker, who gets it with a big pliers and the flat of his foot on their chest. And if he's not around they dig it out by themselves with a nail. Carpenter's nail. It takes all day to do that. They're very stoic."

"Not like the Filipinos, huh?"

"The Filipinos have a lot of pride, but they're not stoic."

"They're never ashamed of their agonies."

"Believe it or not, I like it better here. In this country there's nothing left but the truth."

"Well then," Colin said, and by his tone she realized she must be talking crazy again.

Back at the nursing station that evening she dispatched her assistants to their homes and boiled some rice on the Primus stove. For the last two days a sick child had been occupying her hammock. She mashed up rice in a bowl with the heel of her hand and fed the patient mush from her finger, cradling the head in her other hand, the head like an empty eggshell. Nothing went down. She tried rice water and Coca-Cola in a baby bottle, but the child, a boy, was five or six and had no sucking reflex. Tomorrow morning or the next the child would likely be dead. And if he lived?—one of the cages at Bao Dai.

She sat in a large rattan chair and smoked the butt of Colin Rappaport's stogie. The village was dark. Children moaned and dogs barked and the small voices of women called out. A few bicycle headlamps moved here and there far up the road. She puffed the cigar until she felt woozy and green-faced and threw it down, then took her chair back inside, near the mosquito coil, next to the stertorously breathing child in the hammock, and fell asleep. In her dreams people spoke very clearly in Vietnamese and she understood all they said.

Next morning the child held its head up on its own and sipped water and Coke from a cup. Survival was a breeze that touched some and not others. Neither hope nor hopelessness had anything to do with it. She fished the cigar butt from the dirt where she'd tossed it, brushed it clean with her fingers, and smoked it in celebration.

M. Bouquet, the brother of the deceased Dr. Bouquet, putting the doctor's estate in order, came to the villa with a van and a driver to claim the late doctor's effects.

Sands had arranged to be off visiting the villages with Père Patrice, but when he returned at the end of the day the brother was still there, an almost elderly Frenchman, husky, lantern-jawed, dressed as if for a day of angling, in olive short-pants and a matching vest with many pockets, fanning his face with a canvas hat with a chinstrap. Sands and he took tea together. His English was better than passable. He spoke at first not of his brother, but of women. "As I get older, the older females have more attractions.

Flesh which used to be ugly, now it can seem charming. The thin
purple veins, you know, so frail. It's a beautiful mystery. The new
kind of grace—the grace of a calm woman, it's even more erotic.
Now I come to adore the women of the Renaissance painting.
Very full, very soft from the inside. Have you a native concubine?"
    Sands had no answer.
    "No? I don't know this country. But I thought it's customary
here to have a concubine. I prefer a widow. A grown woman, as I
have been telling you. She has experienced love, and she realizes
how to behave in bed."
    "I've been curious about your brother," was all Skip could say.
    "Claude was my twin. Fraternal—we didn't look alike. I got
the information that he is dead, and I didn't cry about it. I suddenly thought, Oh, no no no, I didn't know him, even not a little.
We grew up together, but we never talked about anything, we just
lived there. As far as I was concerned, he was like a visitor. But not
coming to visit me—coming to visit my parents, my sister, something like that. Now, this morning, seeing everything, this house
where he lived, I know more about him than I knew from many
years of youth spent side by side. Looking here, I wondered if I
would find a certain print of a certain painting we had in our bedroom in those days. Yes, I know, it makes no sense that he would
have it after all this time. *The Clown in Repose*, or some similar
name. A clown with his eyes closed—Dead? Unconscious? Why
closed? He had it on the wall above his bed for many years. It
frightened me as a child. And the fact that the clown didn't
frighten Claude—that was frightening even more. And he stayed
here so many years in this place, and he wasn't frightened. I am
frightened." M. Bouquet sighed. "We've loaded the boxes, as you
see. Thank you for packing so much for us. I'll leave the furniture,
and those kinds of things. Someone from the family will live here
again sometime—when the Communists are finished. When you
have defeated them. For now I'll go on renting the house to your
Ecumenical Council and"—He looked at Skip anew. "You're not
with the CIA or something like this, perhaps?"

"No."

"Okay." He laughed. "I'm not concerned!"

"No need to be."

Skip had kept aside a few fragile items—let the brother take responsibility for packing them. M. Bouquet elected to leave the doctor's delicate representation of the human ear, the porcelain bones. "They came so far to here. It's pointless to take them back, it's sad to take them. We must rescue the books and papers for the family library. Our sister makes it her passion. The papers, the papers. For her it's our only legacy, but I say to her, Why must we have any legacy at all? Things are destroyed over and over, the good things and bad things. So many wars and storms on the earth. Destruction on top of destruction. What happened to Claude? Poof, exploded, nothing left. The same thing for all of us—ashes, dust, poof, that's our legacy. No. I don't take this one. It's too breakable." With his thick fingers the brother detached and examined each part—the outer ear with its Pavillon and Lobe, then the Conduit and Tympan and then the Labyrinthe Osseux with its Vestibule and Fenêtres, its Canaux semi-circulaire and the Nerf auditif, the Limaçon, the long tube of the Trompe d'eustache heading into the skull. Even the minute inner bones had been fashioned and labeled—the Marteau, Enclume, and Étrier—and the spongy-looking Cellules mastoïdiennes. "Ah! So small, so perfect, an antique—it comes from his school days, perhaps, I think. Claude took his certification in 1920 or 1921." He said suddenly, "Do you know the tunnel where Claude was blown up? Have you seen it?"

"No, I'm sorry, I haven't."

"Avez-vous Français? Un peu?"

They switched to French, and the conversation quickly became trivial. Apparently this large, solid man enjoyed his frankest exchanges in a language in which he wasn't facile enough to camouflage himself.

Sands encouraged M. Bouquet to stay until morning, but he seemed fearful of spending the night here, though the roads would be dangerous. Everything was in the van. He left as the dark fell.

Weeks earlier, M. Bouquet had sent a letter to the phony Ecumenical Council's mail drop, naming this day of his arrival. In the meantime, Sands had grown attached to certain of the dead man's texts—a few obscure quarterly magazines and dusty books—and he'd placed these in his footlockers, hidden them from the doctor's relatives and heirs. The brother left without them.

And weeks later, Sands still worked to translate paragraphs the Doctor had underlined—bits of philosophy by French intellectuals Sands had never heard of, abstract passages that unaccountably inflamed him, one, for instance, from an article called "D'un Voyage au Pays des Tarahumaras" by somebody named Antonin Artaud:

Que la Nature, par un caprice étrange, montre tout à coup un corps d'homme qu'on torture sur un rocher, on peut penser d'abord que ce n'est qu'un caprice et que ce caprice ne signifie rien. Mais quand, pendant des jours et des jours de cheval, le même charme intelligent se répète, et *que la Nature obstinément manifeste la même idée* ; quand les mêmes formes pathétiques reviennent ; quand des têtes de dieux connus apparaissent sur les rochers, et qu'un thème de mort se dégage dont c'est l'homme qui fait obstinément les frais—et à la forme écartelée de l'homme répondent celles, *devenues moins obscures*, plus dégagéls d'une pétrifiante matière—des dieux qui l'ont depuis toujours torturé ; quand tout un pays sur la Terre développe une philosophie parallèle à celle des hommes ; quand on sait que les premiers hommes utilisèrent un langage des signes, et qu'on retrouve formidablement agrandie cette langue sur les rochers; certes, on ne peut plus penser que ce soit là un caprice, et que ce caprice ne signifie rien.

With a pen and blank paper and a stack of dictionaries, he waded into battle against its horrific vagueness:

When Nature, by an odd caprice, suddenly portrays in a
boulder the body of a man being tortured, one can think at
first that this is just a fluke and that this fluke means nothing. But when, during days and days on a horse, he sees the
same intelligent charm repeating itself, and *when Nature
stubbornly manifests the same idea*; when the same pathetic
forms return; when the heads of known gods appear in the
boulders, and when there emerges a theme of death for
which man obstinately pays the price; when the dismembered form of a man is answered by those—*become less
obscure*, more separate from a petrifying matter—of the
gods who have always tormented him; when a whole region
of the earth develops a philosophy parallel to that of its people; when one knows that the first men used a language of
signs, and when one discovers this language enlarged formidably in the rocks; then surely one can no longer think that
this is just a fluke and that this fluke means nothing.

Yes, the intent of the mysterious M. Artaud was unspecified, as
was the location of his Country of the Tarahumaras, whether
somewhere in the New World or only in the head of this Artaud;
but the doctor's reasons for selecting the passage were obvious: the
pale traveler, the indecipherably alien land.

The doctor, himself, was a cipher. Apparently he'd stopped
practicing medicine long before his death, but wouldn't go home.
Sands thought he understood.

And Sands had kept, in addition to the several publications,
one of the notebooks, the doctor's private jottings. Stolen it. The
doctor's notes stood up in a strong, square script which Sands was
translating, along with the doctor's favorite passages, into a notebook of his own.

Dear Professor Georges Bataille:
    In March of 1954 I read, in manuscript form, your
essay "Prehistoric Painting: Lascaux, or, The Birth of Art"

in the offices of the Library of Fine Arts at the Sorbonne, where my brother's wife is employed. I was visiting my homeland from Indochina, where I have resided for nearly thirty years.

Skip recognized the title—*Lascaux, ou, La Naissance de l'art*—a big, beautiful volume with color plates of the paintings on the walls of a cavern system in France's Lascaux region; he cursed himself for letting the book go, but it had seemed too valuable for stealing.

I have recently acquired the book, with the photographs. Of course it is superb.

May I direct your attention to a book by Jean Gebser, an Austrian "professor of comparative civilizations"—*Cave and Labyrinth*? I quote:

"To return to the cave, even in thought, is to regress from life into the state of being unborn."

"The cave is a maternal, matriarchal aspect of the world."

"The church of Saintes-Maries-de-la-Mer in the Camargue of Southern France in which the gypsies worship Sarah, the black Madonna."

(M. Bataille: In Spain, 3,000 gypsies live in caves near Granada.)

(M. Bataille: Is the mind a labyrinth through which the consciousness gropes its way, or is the mind the boundless void in which certain limited thoughts rise up and disappear?)

(M. Bataille!—We think of things in caves as black, but aren't they pale, almost translucent, very pale . . .)

"Theseus by entering the labyrinth is re-entering the womb in order to gain a possible second birth—a guarantee against the second, irremediable and dreadful death."

(M. Bataille: In the year 1914 Count Bégou'n discovered the Trois Frères cave in the Pyrénées—here a tunnel that can only be wriggled through like a birth-canal ends in a massive chamber covered with Paleolithic 12,000-year-old images of the hunt, including fantastic were-animals. This chamber was used for initiating adolescent boys into the ranks of manhood in a ritual of death and new birth.)

"If the cave represents security, peace, and absence of danger, then the labyrinth is an expression of seeking, movement, and danger."

(—Seeking an exit, M. Bataille, seeking an escape? Or seeking a secret at the center of things?)

(After longer than sixty years of life, I see myself.)

(Chaos, anarchy, and fear: This drives me: This I desire: to be free.)

Yes!

The body of Bouquet's unfinished letter to the scholar Bataille— impassioned, intricate, verbose—Skip was still working on.

After a month in his burrow he let Père Patrice lure him out into the weather to view the tunnel into which Dr. Bouquet had disappeared. They walked through the village and out the north end and along a trail to the west, hardly half a kilometer. At the base of a rain-eroded hillside lay a scoop in the earth, no more than that. The fatal blast had undermined the entrance, and the rains had caved it in. As with so much else in this country, its depths were denied him.

"This is not a critical area," the priest announced. "The tunnel was not used."

"Who laid the booby trap?"

"He took his own dynamite, I'm sure. Some dynamite to get past a cave-in, perhaps. Then—he exploded himself."

On the walk back Skip told the priest, "I'm glad I didn't have to go inside."

"Inside the tunnel? Why did you want to go in?"

"I didn't."

"I beg your pardon?"

"I'm a coward, Père Patrice."

"Good. You'll live longer."

The priest had come many times to the villa for supper. If his duties to the parish hadn't taken him far and wide he'd have turned up every night. The cuisine was marvelous. Mrs. Diu, it turned out, knew omelets, sauces, dainties, anything you could name in French, and though she didn't often have exotic ingredients, still she served simple, delectable meals of fresh fish or pork with rice and wild greens, and local fruits for dessert. She baked delicious dinner rolls and golden loaves: here, Sands felt, he could have made it on bread and water.

In these ten rainy weeks, the colonel hadn't visited. Except for the priest two or three times a month, and Nguyen Hao about as often, Skip stayed friendless and returned to his natural solitude—he knew this about himself, the only child of a working mother, a widowed mother—to the solitude of rainy school-day afternoons. In the smallest of the three upstairs bedrooms he pursued his calling as an arbiter of fragmentary histories in his uncle's "2242" file. A languid pursuit. He could only stand so

much at one sitting. The colonel's file cards had been alphabet-
ized according to the names of people either questioned or mentioned in interrogations between 1952 and 1963 throughout
what was now South Vietnam. He'd passed the cutting and pasting stage and begun making new headings for each of the nineteen thousand duplicate cards and arranging them according to
place names mentioned, so that someday—not soon!—it would
be possible to look at this information as it related to district, village, or city. Why hadn't it been kept to these categories to start
with? And why should he care? As with CORDS/Phoenix, officers had ventured out, asked questions, made notes, gone on to
other posts. He longed to trip on a clue and follow it to some rav-
aging discovery—Prime Minister Ky spied for the Vietcong, or an
emperor's tomb hid millions in French plunder—but no, nothing here, all worthless; he sensed it with his fingers on these
cards. Not only were the data as trivial and jumbled as those of
CORDS/Phoenix, but also their time had passed. These three-
by-five cards served only as artifacts. In this they held a certain
fascination.

At the beginning of August, Hao brought him a bigger French-
English dictionary—Skip's request—and a packet of photocopies
from the colonel: a somewhat famous article from *Studies in Intelligence* called "Observations on the Double Agent," by John P.
Dimmer, Jr.; and a partial draft of the colonel's own article, the
one that had made some trouble for him, seven typed pages with
handwritten notes—ideas more inflaming than French texts,
more sinister than Eddie Aguinaldo's cryptic warnings. On the
one hand completely reasonable, on the other alarmingly disloyal.

The colonel had clipped a covering note to Dimmer's "The
Double Agent":

Skipper, refamiliarize yourself with J. P. Dimmer, and
have a look at these pages from my draft. I've got more,
but it's a mess. Will dribble it out to you. Or you'd go
crazy trying to sort it out.

Sands well remembered the afternoon in which he'd last heard mention of "Observations on the Double Agent." Remembered it not for the mention, but for other remarks the colonel had permitted himself.

Along with Sergeant Storm he'd come to rescue his nephew temporarily from CORDS/Phoenix. Once in a while the colonel took him to lunch, today on the terrace of the New Palace Hotel. At the top of the stairs a sign announced today's FESTIVAL OF HAMBURGERS. Skip remarked that again it was overcast, and Jimmy Storm said, "Ain't no sky in the tropics." Jimmy wore civvies, he was zingy; Skip suspected he took Benzedrine.

The colonel, his chair cocked, his right hand on the railing, sat with the eastern half of Saigon spread out behind him and before him a long buffet, the Festival, apparently, of Hamburgers. His left hand gripped a cocktail. "The Agency is in a state of shock. The Kennedy thing and the Bay of Pigs business have left us quaking. We don't know how to behave, how to carry out our mission. In Cuba we're blundering around—we as an agency, and we as a nation. We're the Russia of the Western hemisphere."

Sands said, "And how do you see things working out for us here? At the moment?"

"It depends on the Vietnamese, Skip. We've been saying 'It depends on the Vietnamese' so long it sounds like bull, but it's the truth. The question is, how do we help them? You, me, us, sitting at this table. I mean the three of us. I think we take a new approach. We've got to be more aggressive in handling the data."

"Aggressive?"

"The three of us."

"Us?"

"The question about intelligence-gathering is where do you stop taking the initiative? Do we get out there and beat the bushes aggressively, accumulate everything aggressively, and then passively leave it to others to sift? No. A sifting goes on continually, at every level."

Jimmy: "A selection."

"And I don't like the goddamn selection, Skipper. What gets sifted out, among other things, is that one particular piece of information that's going to make life unpleasant for us by troubling our superiors. And what's left over is a lie that lands on the desk above, a happy lie, a monstrous lie."

Jimmy: "A happy monster."

"The lies go up, and what comes back down is poor policy, mistaken policy. Stupid ideas get generated out along the designated paths, and way out here, in the field, our limbs start jerking in a crazy way. Then when so ordered we file a report that says with care and deliberation we thrashed around causing havoc. You know how it works, Skip: Mindanao. We swing from being tepid and ineffectual to being ardent and silly."

Jimmy: "Ardent—that's a good word."

The colonel said, "Why should we wait for the silliness from the center of the hive? Why not generate our own scenarios?"

At this point Jimmy Storm took notice of a patron sitting down to another table, a rather tall young Asian woman, prepossessing, strikingly kempt, sheathed in a glamour of silk, and said, "I'd like to get into her groovy gravy."

The colonel laughed. "HAH!"

His jester picked a bit of meat from its sauce with his fingers and slurped it into his jaws. "Or maybe Skip wants to."

. . . The article's draft began with a handwritten note—the colonel's block printing—photocopied:

WE DON'T HAVE AN INTRO YET

Want to revitalize the distinction between analysis and intelligence—clarity of thought, purity of language, correctness of speech, etc, clarity of fact—appreciating how a lack of clarity has led to the complete perversion of the intelligence function of our Agency. Its motives and its purpose. And its means. Its methods.

Let's hit that as the main thing—the distinction between analysis and intelligence.

> *Orwell—"Politics and the English Language"*
> *As far as intro—*
> BASICALLY TO SAY HERE THAT WE'RE TALKING ABOUT
> TWO FUNCTIONS OF THE CLANDESTINE SERVICES—
> INTELLIGENCE AND ANALYSIS. AND THE BREAKDOWN
> OF BARRIERS BETWEEN THE TWO ETC

On the next page began the typed material. Skip anticipated an embarrassing mess. By the third sentence he could see the colonel must have had assistance:

Cross-Contamination of the Two Functions

Our figures of speech with regard to the process of communication give us our model for this discussion. We speak of "lines" of communication and "chains" of command, reminding ourselves that data move in a linear and linked fashion through the ranks of those interpreting it. In the case of the functions of our intelligence services, we view this movement as originating in the field and terminating in archives, in plans, or in operations. Hard data collected by the officer in the field slows down as it trickles up the chain, and eventually finds itself stalled by considerations as to its impact—on other operations, on the goals of higher-ups, and even on the career-path of the person passing it along—until related data climbs up parallel structures to corroborate it, or—most unfortunately, perhaps dangerously—until command finds a need for it as justification for political policy, and those in possession of this data sense this need.

This hesitation and doubt is an indication that the intelligence function has been polluted by the analysis function. Data is being interpreted, albeit unconsciously, perhaps, and its effects on command anticipated. We speak of "command influence" on the intelligence function, and the fact that we possess a term for it acknowledges its existence; however, we have thus far failed to grapple with the operations, the mechanics, of command influence.

This paper suggests, in broad outline, that "command influence" operates through the cross-contamination of the two functions of the clandestine services: intelligence and analysis.

Cross-Contamination of the Two Categories

As data hesitates on the chain, awaiting (1) the accumulation of pressures to drive it upward and (2) the corroboration of related materials, the segregation of human intelligence from documentary intelligence is threatened and finally gives way. Simply put, the need to examine the veracity of sources yields to the pressures of process. The result is cross-contamination: data from human sources, notoriously undependable, become the support for doubtful interpretations of documentary sources, and these interpretations come to be seen as shedding light, in turn, on data from human sources.

The cross-contamination of these two categories, human intelligence and documentary intelligence, is a sub-process of the broader breakdown between the two functions of intelligence and analysis.

Cross-Contamination of the Two Waves

Meanwhile, the interpretive process, we remember, is always subject to appropriation and enlistment in the service of policy. Cross-contamination renders data vague, malleable, and eventually useless as anything but an ingredient of internal bureaucratic and political chemistries.

A detailed examination of the processes by which the needs of command are communicated downward along the chain must wait for another occasion. At this point let it be enough to acknowledge that a sense of the needs of command does travel downward through the chain in the same kind of wave action by which data are communicated upward. The result is cross-contamination of the two waves.

It is to be stressed that this process is of an entirely different nature than the intelligence-gathering process of our Agency in its earliest incarnation, the Office of Strategic Services (OSS). There the function of Intelligence remained almost untouched by policy, because policy is the game of peace, whereas the OSS served a command structure pursuing the objectives of war. From that era we have allowed to survive the old model of field-to-archive, field-to-plan, field-to-plan-to-operation. However, that model no longer serves us well.

The model of a chain on which two waves of data under pressure cross-contaminate one another is truer to the actual processes of our Agency today. The downward pressure derives from the needs of command, while the upward pressure derives from the need to satisfy command.

At this point in the discussion let us again acknowledge the process's lack of utility, as we have now illuminated the category of service in which intelligence becomes useful, that is, in the pursuit of the objectives of war.

Cross-Fertilization of the Two Goals

This paper will leave open the question of how we shall apply the lessons of this improved model to our contemporary wartime situation, i.e., in South Vietnam. However, some thoughts assert themselves for consideration:

Groups wage war either with the goal of achieving

political aims, as in the case of revolution, or with the goal of ensuring survival, as in the case of counter-revolution. (A long parentheses: We leave aside the instances in which the two goals become blurred, for instance when nation-states engage in empire-building, in market-building, or in defense against these two aggressions. And we deliberately forgo the elaborations and subtleties that would result from bringing Clausewitz and Machiavelli to the table. We reiterate: our focus is on using an improved model to consider the role of intelligence in our contemporary wartime situation, and thus we simplify.)

Here an arrow in the margin led the reader to a handwritten note at the bottom of the page:

> V—So far so good. The end part is just to say we're inviting further thoughts from all comers. Main thought to end on is that Vietcong-NVA goal is political revolution cross-fertilized by national survival. Inviting thoughts as to where USA stands as far as goals—what are we doing? And what is role of intelligence in that? And how do we get back a sense of wartime objectives and wrestle a whole Agency around to reviving the original role of an intelligence service?

The Necessity of Insulated Activity

The United States, on the other hand, even in this wartime situation, does not enjoy the clarity of warlike goals. Ours is, in effect, a pawn's game played out with the not-quite-expressed priority that the back ranks, the powerful pieces, the world powers, should never be brought into play. For entities in the intelligence community this circumstance suggests that insularity must be established in order to create an arena of activity in which the true and original purposes of intelligence are recovered and re-engaged. We use the term "arena," but let us say, instead, that a length of the communications chain must be insulated against the pressures from above and below—the pressures of "subordinate prudence" from below and the pressures of "command influence" from above. Such insulation is hardly likely to result from an order from command itself, and must instead come as a result of the initiative of this Agency or members of it.

In the margins—

V, please fix this to be less uppity, more vague—'He who hath ears to hear, let him hear.'—FXS. But V—time is of the essence. MOBILIZATION-LOSS DICHOTOMY my man.

Who had helped? Who was "V"?—Voss, he had to presume. On the last page, another note in the colonel's hand:

Tree of Smoke—(pillar of smoke, pillar of fire) the "guiding light" of a sincere goal for the function of intelligence—restoring intelligence-gathering as the main function of intelligence operations, rather than to provide rationalizations for policy. Because if we don't, the next step is for career-minded power-mad cynical jaded bureaucrats to use intelligence to influence policy. The final step is to create fictions and serve them to our policy-makers in order to control the direction of government. ALSO—"Tree of Smoke"—note similarity to mushroom cloud. HAH!

Then the typewriter again, Voss:

One might hypothesize a step beyond the final one. Consider the possibility that a coterie or insulated group might elect to create fictions independent of the leadership's intuition of its own needs. And might serve these fictions to the enemy in order to influence choices.

—HAH! He could hear his uncle laughing. As on the terrace of the New Palace he'd laughed at Jimmy's crude insinuations. While Jimmy slurped at his fingers, the colonel said to Skip, "Do you remember J. P. Dimmer's piece on the double agent?"

"I read it a thousand times."

"Suppose you have a double."

"Have we got a double?"

"Suppose."

"Okay."

"And suppose you want to give him some bogus product."

Skip said, "Bogus product? I don't remember any discussion of it in the Dimmer."

"Get him a copy, please, Sergeant."

"Get him a copy of what?"

"It's an article called 'Observations on the Double Agent.' In my stack of *Studies in Intelligence*. Winter issue, '62."

"What a memory."

"Suppose Hanoi believed that an insubordinate element in the U.S. command had decided to blow up a nuke in Haiphong Harbor."

"Are you kidding?"

"Wouldn't that mess with Ho's thinking just a little? If he thought a few lunatic bastards had decided to finish this thing without asking permission?"

"We're speaking hypothetically, I hope."

"Skip. Have you got a nuke in your pocket?"

"No."

"Know where to get one?"

"No."

"No. This is Psy Ops. We're talking about unbalancing the enemy's judgment."

"We have no borders to the thinking process," Sergeant Storm announced. "It's almost like yogic or spiritual work."

He remembered another of the pronouncements of Sergeant Storm: "We're on the cutting edge of reality itself. Right where it turns into a dream."

After his first time at the Purple Bar, James just wanted to go back the next possible minute and drink beer and get laid, and go back again after that, and he couldn't imagine any higher aim.

He didn't forget his mother. His first few paychecks, he sent her half. After that he had nothing to send. He'd spent it all on riot.

April wasn't springlike, just hot. All summer came a torrent of rain. October and November felt cooler and drier. James couldn't eat the Thanksgiving turkey they served up at the LZ base. Other messes had real turkey, but this stuff came bleached and water-logged out of a can. "Christmas," Fisher said, "is gonna break everybody's heart."

At first James sent Stevie numerous short, tortured messages, mailed her trinkets he picked up in Saigon, cherished her letters to him, tried to imagine her face and voice when he read her words. Then one day he couldn't seem to remember her. For the other guys this wasn't true. As their tours stretched out they only grew more obsessed with their girls back home, and as their time grew short they counted the days and rhapsodized about getting white meat, white meat, white meat. But James only wanted more of what he got at the Purple Bar, whatever color of meat it was.

Communications from Stevie came relentlessly, usually brief notes she jotted in typing class, exactly the kind she might pass surreptitiously to anybody else in school, as if James were sitting two aisles over from her, dozing, and not opening his pants in a bunker, shining a flashlight onto his bared crotch and staring at a horrendous purple-red region of jock rot—in the quivering beam a volatile, almost green color. "You don't get it from whores, you don't get it from whores," said the other men, the men he asked over and over, "it's just a thing, a sweaty jungle horrible thing, and the shit they give you makes it go away eventually. And you don't have to shave your balls. So don't worry. And don't shave your balls." Stevie's letters, their *i*'s dotted with little circles, terrified him as much as jock rot. He hardly ever answered.

I could only lead you halfway to love, he wrote her once, quoting one of Evans's poems to his own girlfriend.

I will wait for you always, she wrote in return, I am loyal to the end.

He wanted to write back saying, Don't be loyal, because I'm not loyal. Instead he simply didn't answer.

At Christmas he got a card from his mother and felt sick about opening it—suppose she sobbed about money? But she'd only written, "Love, Mom" at the end of a Hallmark verse about the Savior and the manger and the shepherds and the wondrous star-filled first Christmas Eve.

The Screwy Loot took a squad on patrol, and the first thing his bad luck did for them was to run them across a spider-hole with two dead VC down in it. Screwy found it all by himself when, leaving the trail to get around a fallen tree, he plunged his foot through the thatch and onto the head of a corpse. Several of Echo pushed the tree trunk aside and pried up the broken lid of bamboo and grass to find the dead men, one on top of the other, water-logged and stinking, their eye sockets swarming with ants. The tree had toppled over to trap them inside and the groundwater had come up during the night, had risen so fast, apparently, they'd hardly begun digging their way out before they were drowned. Screwy Loot wanted to question everybody in the area. The first man they approached, coming back from the field with a bundle of kindling on his shoulder, threw down his load and took off running with two of Echo on his heels. The others squatted on their own heels and waited. "This mountain is taking a shit on us," Screwy Loot said. Most of them hadn't been around long enough to appreciate the changes in the air. With Flatt and Jollet gone and people transferring in and out, the platoon's oldest were Specialist Fourth Class Houston, known as Cowboy, and Black Man, the nameless sergeant. By now there was another black guy too, Everett, a PFC, who answered to his name, but who spoke only to Black Man, and very softly, so nobody else could hear. "Speaking of taking a shit," said Screwy Loot, and headed off behind a bush and was coming out buckling up when the two runners returned, without the local.

"No luck?"

"He's gone."

"He's underground, sir."

"We think he is."

"There's a tunnel, sir."

"Fuck. Don't tell the colonel," the Loot said.

"It's right over here."

The whole squad stood around what certainly looked like a two-by-two-foot opening to the world beneath. Screwy Loot got on his knees and poked his flashlight down into it and got up quickly. "Yeah, that's how they are. They go three feet, four feet down and take a header. Back off," he told them, and unpinned a grenade, rolled it into the hole, and ran like hell. The bang sounded small and muffled. Dirt erupted and rained down. "Fuck if I know," he said. He put two men on the hole, and he and the others returned to the corpses.

Here on the mountain's south side they patrolled what amounted to a roadway. For five kilometers a D6 bulldozer had been able to widen the trail out of Echo Base. After that it was cliff and ravine, impassable by vehicle. Screwy Loot radioed for Sergeant Harmon, who drove out in a jeep. "I don't want these dead fuckers here," he told Harmon. "Drag them away. If there's Charlie on my mountain, I want him to wonder did we take these guys alive. See," he told the others, "that's Psy Ops: fuck with Charlie's brain."

He and the sergeant sat in the jeep eating C-rations until the others hit on the notion of blowing the local man out of the tunnel—if he was in there—with gasoline.

Three men hoisted a fifty-five-gallon drum, half full, from the rear of the vehicle and rolled it off the trail and over to the tunnel's entrance, the barrel zigging and zagging, the men swearing and hacking at vegetation. All the others came to observe. Two men tipped the container over the hole and the third rapped on the bung with the butt of his M16 to loosen it.

Screwy Loot marched over quickly as soon as he saw this. Let his mouth drop open slightly and jutted his head, chastising without speaking.

"We are in a process of elimination," the man explained.

"Wayne, your weapon is not a sledgehammer."

"Sorry, sir. But I just mean we're gonna blow that Gook fucker out of there."

They unscrewed the bung and emptied the acrid contents into the hole, and PFC Wayne, a big, empty-headed boy from Iowa, straddled the darkness, struck a match, and dropped it in. The force of the blast shot him into the air, over their heads, and down through the treetops, howling like artillery.

"Who's next?" Sergeant Harmon said.

PFC Wayne's two partners rushed to find him. He came limping back between them.

"You forgot to say, 'Fire in the hole!'"

He didn't seem seriously hurt. "I'm famous now," was all he said.

"The colonel won't like it you fucked up his tunnel," Black Man said to Screwy Loot.

Screwy Loot put his arm around Black Man's shoulders, while the sarge came around facing his front.

"Somebody should check on the status of that hole."

"Why don't you go down, Black Man?"

"Me?"

"Yeah. Nip down there, take a look-see."

"See is it the one you don't come out of."

"Ain't no tunnel left, Lieutenant, sir."

Screwy Loot drew Black Man close by his shoulders and said, "All god's chillun got tunnels."

Cowboy spoke up: "I guess I'll go on down."

The squad looked at him—all heads turning. Then all looked elsewhere. Up, down, over there somewhere.

"Got us a volunteer," the sergeant said.

Screwy Loot told Cowboy, "We'll make the colonel happy."

These days Echo didn't see much of the colonel. The new ones had only glimpsed him from a distance. Cowboy asked Harmon, "Is he a real colonel?"

"Well, he ain't just a figment of my mind."

"What's that supposed to mean?"

"I guess that means he's real, sojer. I guess if he stepped on your fingers, you'd yell out."

"I don't know about that," Cowboy said. "I've sat on Santa Claus's lap more times than I've laid eyes on that colonel. So to me he ain't as real as Santa Claus, now, is he?"

"Here." Harmon handed him his own flashlight. "Take an extra along."

Cowboy turned on the light and went down headfirst, the way some of them had seen the Kootchie Kooties do it.

When he'd gone all the way in, when there was nothing left of him to see, the others stood around and waited. Going down into that worldwide mystery had to produce some respect, if not for his prudence, at least for the level of his insanity.

There were stories that the tunnels went for miles. There were monsters down there, blind reptiles and insects that had never seen the light, there were hospitals and brothels, and horrible things, piles of the offal from VC atrocities, dead babies, assassinated priests.

"Get my feet," he shouted from down in the mouth.

They pulled him out by the ankles. He hadn't been able to turn around. "It's caved in about twenty yards along," he told the Loot.

"Nobody in there?"

"Not since I came out," Cowboy said.

She woke about five in her room in the back of the house. The windows were closed but she heard coyotes yipping and weeping in the distance, to the east, toward the Superstitions. No work today. She lay in bed and prayed. May Burris start the New Year with better intentions toward school, and may he find the Lord in his heart. May Bill find joy in his duties, and may he find the Lord in his heart. May James be kept safe in war, and may he find the Lord in his heart. The coyotes sounded like hurt dogs. They agitated plainly for Christ's return. May they not be heard. May Christ stay his feet till the last soul on earth be saved. The last soul saved might be one of her boys. Of that there was every indication.

She put her feet on the floor and put on a flannel shirt over her nightgown. Still well dark. She lay back down and a bit later realized she'd slept again. No extra dreams. The clock ticked. Its radium dials said not quite six. She rose and found her slippers.

In the kitchen she put down a few drops of Carnation milk in a saucer for the cat. May the coyotes not get her. Or the toms. They didn't need kittens around here . . . Still dark. Burris had been up half the night watching fright shows on the television. There was nothing she could do to keep him from the snares.

She lit a Salem off the burner on the stove. She boiled water for powdered coffee and sat at the kitchen table, a collapsible card table, set the cigarette in the ashtray, and pulled her shirt neck closed with one hand while she brought the cup to her lips with the other. Greenish streaks of light to the east. The window was dirty. Prayer was all she had. Prayer and Nescafé and Salems. This was the one time of day she didn't feel crazy.

She spilled some coffee when the phone rang on the wall. God be with us all. She went to the wall and lifted the receiver wanting words to plead for mercy from whatever was coming. Before the terrors of possibility she only knew how to say, "Hello?"

"Hi, Ma. It's James."

"What?"

"Ma, it's James, Ma. I'm calling to say Merry Christmas. Guess I'm a little late."

"James?"

"It's James, Ma. Merry Christmas."

"James? James? Where are you?"

"I'm in Vietnam, like before. Like always."

"Are you all right, James?"

"I'm fine. I'm perfect. How was Christmas for y'all?"

"Are you all right? Are you hurt?"

"No, no. I'm fine."

"I'm scared to hear you calling me."

"I don't mean to be scary. I just thought I'd say hi."

"But you're all right."

"I'm just fine, Mom. Don't be scared or nothing. Hey, I just sent you another money order."

"I'm very grateful."

"Sorry I slacked off there a little while."

"I know it's hard. I don't count on it, I just say it sure helps us along."

"I'll try to do a little better. I truly will. How was your Christmas?"

"It went all right, James. It went just fine. I've got to sit now. Let me get a chair. You scared me."

"Nothing to scare you about, Ma. I'm doing pretty good here."

"Well, I'm glad to know it. Did you call Stephanie?"

"Stevie?"

"Stevie. Did you call her yet?"

"I mean to ring her right up. She's next on my list tonight."

"What time is it there?"

"Just about eight p.m. We call that twenty hundred hours in the military."

"It's six-oh-eight in the morning here in Phoenix."

"There you go."

"Get off, sweetie," she said. "Not you—I got this old cat here."

"You still got that cat?"

"No. Another one."

"What happened to that other one?"

"Run off."

"Coyotes got it."

"I expect."

"Well, you got you another one."

"James—" she said, and her voice broke.

"Now, Ma."

"James."

"Ma. Ain't nothing to worry about."

"I got to worry."

"It's not like you're thinking it is. We're very safe where we're at. I haven't seen one bit of fighting. It's just patrols. The people are all friendly."

"Are they friendly?"

"Yes. They sure are, Ma. Everybody's nice."

"What about the Communists?"

"I've never seen a one. They don't get around our part. They're scared to."

"If it's a lie, I appreciate it."

"It's no lie."

"And I expect you'll be home soon. How long will it be?"

"Ma, I'm calling to say I'm signed up for one more go here."

"One more?"

"Yes, ma'am."

"One more year?"

"Yes, ma'am."

She didn't know what to say, and so she said, "Do you want to talk to your little brother?"

"Burris? Okay. Right quick, though."

"He's in trouble at school. The teachers have told me he wanders. One minute he's there, next thing he's gone."

"What does Burris say?"

"He says he doesn't like it at school. I told him to go anyhow. Nobody likes it, or they wouldn't give it away free."

"Put him on."

"He's sleeping. Just a minute."

"Never mind, then. Just tell him I said he better get his tail in gear."

"Thank you, James. I'll tell him what his brother says."

"Well, I'm talking on a radio unit, so I better let you go."

"A radio unit?"

"Yes, ma'am. Up at the base camp."

"You're on the radio? And I'm on the phone!"

"Happy New Year's, Ma."

"Same to you."

"Have a happy New Year's, Ma."

"I will. You do the same."

"I sure will. All right, then, so long."

"So long, James," she said. "I pray for you day and night. Don't listen to what they say. You're doing the Lord's work to keep his faith alive in a world going dark. It's one of them Old Testament times."

"I know. I hear you, Ma."

"Communists are atheists. They deny the Lord."

"That's what they tell me."

"Look at the Old Testament. Look how many slain in the name of the Lord. Look at First Samuel, look at Judges. Be the Lord's smiting hand if you have to be."

She heard him sigh.

"I just mean to take your arm and buck you up. Read your

Bible daily. There's doubters and demonstrators and God knows
what. Traitors is what they are. If you hear about those people,
shut your ears. Thank God they don't come around Phoenix. If I
saw a demonstration I'd get in a truck and come through that pack
like a boulder down a mountain."

"They're telling me my time's up, Ma, so I better say 'bye, so—
'bye."

There had been a washing sound coming over the phone. It
stopped when her son rang off. "Well," she said to nobody.

She rose and put the phone back on the hook.

A rare, brilliant morning. Nguyen Hao stayed in bed late, watching feathers of mist turn in the light outside the bedroom window,
thinking what it meant to do battle with—no, not to fight against,
but simply to face unwaveringly—the dragons of the Five Hindrances: lust, aversion, doubt, sloth, restlessness.

Sloth kept him in bed awhile. Restlessness drove him downstairs to the tiny court behind his kitchen, where the sun made
more mist. Under its warmth everything gave off ghosts. They
woke from the bricks, rose with a deep reluctance, disappeared.

Hao spread his white handkerchief on the stone bench, seated
himself carefully, and tried to find some quiet in his mind.

At nine-thirty, Trung rattled the back gate. Hao got up and
found the key and opened the padlock. The Monk possessed forged
papers now. He walked around Saigon with impunity. He looked
healthy, even happy. They sat together on the marble bench as
they'd done many times, never, in Hao's opinion, making any
progress. Anywhere ahead lay the turning point.

"Are you all right?"

"Kim is sick. Worse than before."

"I'm sorry."

"I've been thinking about the Five Hindrances."

"Sometimes I do too. Do you remember a poem? — 'I'm caught up in the world like smoke blown everywhere.' "

"The dragons have defeated me," Hao said. "They've driven me so far into the world I can't get back to the silence."

The Monk appeared to be thinking about it all. Hao was too weary to prod him. After a while the Monk said, "I try to get back too. I want to find the silence again. But I can't get back."

"Will you stop trying?"

"I think I have to finish the life I've lived. I've been very confused."

"I'll be honest. You've confused me too."

"Do you criticize me for taking so long?"

"I've spoken to the colonel about you many times. He suspects you might be taking our money falsely. But you keep turning up. I've told him you're worth supporting because you keep coming back."

Trung said, "I remember when the cadres came to my village in 1945 and read Ho's speech to us. A young woman got up and read in a voice like a song. The world rang with Ho's words. In the girl's beautiful voice he talked about freedom, equality. He cited America's Declaration of Independence. He won my heart. I gave everything. I left my home behind. I spilled blood. I suffered in prison. Can you criticize me for taking so long to betray all of that?"

Hao was shocked. "Your language is strong."

"The truth is strong. Put it this way: the people's thirst for freedom has driven us to drink bad water."

Whether or not he lied, here was a story the colonel would understand. "I'll put it in exactly those words."

"The negotiation is over. I've come to ask, and to give."

"What do you ask?"

"I want to be done with this life. I want to go to the United States."

Hao couldn't believe it. "The U.S.?"

"Can it be done?"

"Of course. They can manage anything."

"Then let them take me there."

"What do you offer?"

"Whatever they want."

"But now. Immediately. What?"

"I can tell you the rumors are true. There's going to be a big push at the New Year. Everywhere in the South. It's a major offensive."

"Can you give specific information? Places, times, and so on?"

"I can't give you much, because it's mostly NVA. But in Saigon it's us. Our cell has been contacted. We'll be working with a sapper team. They're planting charges in the city. We'll probably have to guide them to two or three locations. As soon as I have the locations, I'll pass them to you right here."

Hao could hardly respond. "The colonel will value information like that."

"I'm almost certain they're laying these charges for the big push. I believe it's coming exactly on the day of Tet."

Four years dancing on the doorstep, and now all this in less than twenty minutes. Hao couldn't keep his hands in his lap. He offered Trung another cigarette, took one himself, held the lighter for them both. "I respect your courage. You deserve the truth from me. And so I tell you this: The colonel is interested in the possibility that you'll double. That you'll go back north."

"I could probably go back. There's a program to take tribesmen north for education and indoctrination. The idea is to send them back home afterward, to organize. I've had some involvement with the program."

"You'd really go back north? Why?"

"I despair of explaining."

"What about going to the States?"

"Afterward."

After going north as a double agent? Hao doubted the existence of any afterward. Something gripped his heart. "We've been friends," he told Trung.

"When peace arrives, we'll still be friends."

The two men sat together on the smooth marble bench, and smoked.

"There—all right?" Trung said. "We've crossed over."

From Dr. Bouquet's notes:

Night again, the insects are loud, the moths are killing themselves on the lamp. Two hours ago I sat on the veranda looking out at the dusk, filled with envy for each living entity—bird, bug, blossom, reptile, tree, and vine—that doesn't bear the burden of the knowledge of good and evil.

Sands sat on the veranda himself in the heat of the afternoon with the doctor's notebook in his lap, while behind him moldered and loomed the house full of codes and files and words and referents and cross-referents, examining an illegible line in the doctor's jottings, the notebook hastily closed on wet ink, the line blotted out. No matter which way he turned the page—

~~Lkjflkjlsd kjsfld Lkjflkjl sdkjsfl Lkjflkjl~~

And the strange thing is that those who travel through this region, as if seized by a sleepy paralysis, shut down their senses in order to remain ignorant of everything.

When Nature, by an odd caprice, suddenly portrays in a boulder the body of a man being tortured, one can think at first that this is just a fluke and that this fluke means nothing. But when, during days and days on a horse, he sees the same intelligent charm repeating itself, and *when Nature stubbornly manifests the same idea*; when the same pathetic forms return; when the heads of known gods appear in the boulders, and when there emerges a theme of death for which man obstinately pays the price; when the dismembered form of a

man is answered by those—*become less obscure*, more separate from a petrifying matter—of the gods who have always
tormented him; when a whole region of the earth develops a
philosophy parallel to that of its people; when one knows that
the first men used a language of signs, and when one discovers this language enlarged formidably in the rocks; then
surely one can no longer think that this is just a fluke and that
this fluke means nothing.

1968

Three weeks short of his scheduled release from the navy, Bill Houston had a fight with a black man in the Yokosuka enlisted mess, in the kitchen, where he'd been detailed with three other sailors to paint the walls. Houston's unvaried style of attack was to come in low and fast, get his left shoulder into the other man's midriff while hooking his left arm behind the man's knee, and upend them both so that Houston came down on top, driving his shoulder into the solar plexus with his full weight behind it. He practiced other moves as well, because he considered fighting important, but this opening generally worked with the tough opponents, the ones who stood their ground and raised their dukes. This black man he was having it out with caught Houston a blow to the forehead as he rushed for the man's legs, and Houston watched stars and rainbows fly as they both fell onto a five-gallon bucket of paint and spilled it all over the place. He'd never gotten into it with a black guy before. The man's middle was as hard as a helmet, and he was already squirming away as they slid across the tiled floor on a widening pool of institutional-green enamel. Houston tried to right himself as the man hopped up as lightly as a puppet and aimed a sideways kick from which Houston's skull was saved only because the guy slipped and went down in the goop, his left hand stuck out to catch the fall. But his hand slipped too, and he made the mistake of going onto his back in the effort to get himself up again, and by that time Houston had his bearings and jumped on his stomach as hard as he could with both feet. This maneuver was called the "bronco stomp" and was reputed to result in death, but Houston didn't know what else to do, and, in any case, while it ended the altercation and gave Houston the victory, it didn't do much more than knock the wind out of the guy. Six men from the Shore Patrol arrested the combatants, two green bipeds now racially indistinguishable. As the SPs wiped them down, laid tarps across the seats of the jeeps, and led them away in handcuffs, Houston determined that if they did a stretch in the brig together he would avoid a rematch. Officially he'd put the guy away, but Houston was the one with the great big bruised knot between his eyes, somewhere under all this paint. "What was the fight about?" a patrolman demanded, and Houston said, "He called me a dumb-ass cracker." "You called me a nigger," the guy said. "That was during the fight," Houston said, "so that don't count." Still excited from the battle, proud, happy, they felt friendly toward one another. "Don't call me that no more," the black man said, and Houston said, "I wasn't going to anyway."

Thus Seaman Houston received an early general discharge, and spent his last ten days in the navy not as a sailor but as a prisoner in the brig of the Yokosuka Naval Base.

On his release he was issued a voucher for a commercial jet flight to Phoenix. Traveling by air made him miserable. His ears popped like a hammer on his skull, he felt dizzy, the air tasted dead. The first and last plane ride of his life, this he swore. In the LA airport he balled up the Phoenix portion of his ticket and tossed it in an ashtray, changed into his uniform in the men's room, and, impersonating a sailor, hitchhiked home with his duffel on his shoulder through the clarity of the Mojave Desert in January. He encountered the outskirts of Phoenix sooner than he'd expected. It was much more of a city now, tires wailing on Interstate Ten and loud jet airliners coming in overhead, their lights shimmering in the blue desert twilight. What time was it? He didn't have a watch. In fact, what day? Houston stood at Seventeenth and Thomas under a broken streetlamp. He had thirty-seven dollars. He was twenty-two years old. He hadn't tasted beer in almost a month. Lacking a plan, he phoned his mother.

A week later, sitting in his mother's kitchen drinking instant coffee, Bill answered the phone: his younger brother James. "Who's that?" James said.

"Who dat who say who dat?" Bill said.

"Well—I'll be."

"How's that Saigon pussy?"

"I guess Mom ain't sitting right there."

"Done left for work, I think."

"Ain't it six a.m. there?"

"Here? No. Closer to eight."

"It ain't six a.m.?"

"It used to be. Now it's eight."

"What are you doing there at eight a.m.?"

"Sitting here in my Jockeys, drinking Nescafé."

"You done with the navy?"

"Done with them, and them with me."

"You living at Mom's?"

"Just visiting. Where are you at?"

"Right this minute? Da Nang."

"Where's that?"

"Down deep somewhere in a bucket of shit."

"I haven't seen you since Yokohama one year ago."

"Yeah, that'd be about right."

"That's funny to say."

"Yeah, kind of."

"'Haven't seen you since Yokohama.'"

James said, "Well . . ." and there was a silence.

Bill asked, "You getting any pussy?"

"Oh, yeah."

"How is it?"

"'Bout like you'd think."

Bill said, "Did you know your gal came by?"

"Who?"

"Stephanie. Your little gal that you dated. Yeah. She paid a visit."

"So what?"

"Bothering the old woman about you."

"About what?"

"Says you don't answer her letters no more. Wants to know how you're going along."

"Are you living there now, or what?"

"I just thought you should know. So now you know."

"So now I know. Don't mean I care."

"You're a funny feller. Yeah, she's all upset about you doing another tour."

"Are you living there for sure?"

"I'm just visiting a few days till I get squared up with a job."

"Good luck."

"I appreciate it."

"Where's Mom? She at work?"

"Yeah. What time is it there?"

"I couldn't care less," James said. "I'm on leave. Three days."

"It must be seventeen or eighteen hundred."

"I couldn't care less. Not for three days."

"And it's already tomorrow, ain't it."

"It ain't never tomorrow, not in this fucking movie. Never ain't nothing but today."

"You seen any actual combat yet?"

"I been in them tunnels down there."

"What'd you see?"

His brother didn't answer.

"What about the fighting? Have you been in battles?"

"Not so's you'd notice."

"Really?"

"It's sort of off over there somewhere, never right around where you're at. I mean, I seen dead guys, hurt guys, guys all tore up, over at the LZ, the landing zone."

"No shit."

"Yeah. So, yeah, there's shit going on all over. But it never gets to right here."

"You're probably lucky."

"That's about it."

"What else? Come on."

"What else? I don't know."

"Come on, brother. Tell me about that pussy."

His young brother's voice came small and echoing over the wire, seven, eight thousand miles. Anybody's voice. Talking about the one thing. "It's all over hell, brother Bill. It's falling out of the trees. I got one I keep in a hooch over at the ville. I never seen anything like her, I mean never. Her ass never once touches the bed while I'm on her. She couldn't weigh more'n eighty-two pounds, and she keeps me lifted up halfway to the roof. She must eat atomic fuel for breakfast. Listen: I don't think I could take her in a fight."

"Goddamn. Goddamn, little James. I don't know how I'm gonna get laid now I'm back at home. I don't know how to talk to a natural white woman!"

"You better get back with the navy."

"I don't believe they'll have me."

"No? They won't?"

"They got a little tired of me, seems like."

"Well . . ." said James.

"Yeah . . ."

During the silences came a faint wash of static, in which you could almost hear other voices.

"How's old Burris?"

"He's all right. He's a funny feller too, just like you."

"Mom doing okay?"

"Just fine."

"Runnin' with Jesus."

"Sure enough. Did you get my postcard that she sent?"

"Yeah, that postcard? Yeah."

"I was in the brig when I sent that."

"Uh-oh."

"Yeah . . ."

"Listen, don't tell that Stevie gal I called."

"Stephanie?"

"Yeah. Don't tell her you talked to me."

"She said you don't answer back when she writes you."

"Everybody else just thinks about their girl back home, that's all they think about."

"What do you think about?"

"Sideways pussy."

"Whorehouse pussy. Paid-for pussy."

"Nothin's free on Planet E, brother Bill."

Dead guys, guys all torn up. In this James could have been lying. He might have felt pressured, in an overseas long-distance phone call, to produce experiences worth telling. Bill Houston had heard there wasn't much fighting over there. Not like Iwo Jima, anyhow, not like the Battle of the Bulge. Bill Houston saw no point in calling him on his bull. James wasn't his little punk brother anymore. You didn't want to kid him and keep him in his place.

"I got to go, brother Bill. Tell Mom I love her."

"I'll pass the word along. What about your Stevie gal?"

"I done told you," James said, "just don't mention me."

"All right."

"All right."

"Keep your head down, James."

"It's down and staying down," James said, and the phone clicked dead.

January came and nearly went before Bill Houston found work in the rural environs outside Tempe, near Phoenix. He took a room on South Central Street he could pay for by the day, week, or month, and bused back and forth. At 10:00 p.m. each Tuesday through Saturday he arrived in darkness at the gates of Tri-City Redimix, a sand-and-gravel outfit, for his duties as night cleanup man. By ten-thirty the last of the second shift had left and he tossed aside his mandatory hard hat and presided over fifteen acres of desert—mountains of crushed rocks sorted by size, so that each mountain was made bewilderingly of the same-sized thing, from fist-sized stones down to sand. From one hopper leaked a thread of fine dust that made a pile at the end of a tunnel some twenty feet long; for each shovelful he crept down its tight length toward a distant lightbulb burning in a hemisphere of wire mesh, holding his breath and approaching, a mist of dust exploding in slow motion when he jabbed the blade into the pile, backing out step by step carrying the one shovelful and tossing it to the chilly currents circling the earth. He washed the concrete troughs under the crushers' conveyor belts with a violent fire hose and scraped each one clean with a flat-nose shovel. The nights were wild with stars, otherwise empty and cold. For warmth he kept fifty-five-gallon drums full of diesel-soaked sand burning around the place. He made a circuit among the maze of conveyor belts under gargantuan crushers and was never done. The next evening the same belts, the same motions, even some of the same pebbles and rocks, it stood to reason, and the same cold take-out burger for lunch at the dusty table in the manager's trailer at 2:00 a.m.; washing his hands and face first in the narrow john, his thick neck brown as a bear's, sucking water up his nostrils and expelling the dust in liverish clumps. Not long after his lunch the roosters alone on neighboring small farms began to scream like humans, and just before six the sun arrived and turned the surrounding aluminum rooftops to torches, and then at six-thirty, while Houston punched out, the drivers came, and they lined their trucks nose-to-ass and one after another drove beneath the largest hopper of all to wait, shaken by their machines, while wet concrete cascaded down the chute into each tanker before they went out to pour the foundations of a city. Houston walked a mile to the bus stop and there he waited, covered with dirt and made sentimental by the vision of high school punks and their happy, whorish girlfriends walking to class, heading for their own daily torment, sharing cigarettes back and forth. Houston remembered doing that, and later in the boy's bathroom . . . nothing ever as sweet as those mouthfuls from rushed, overhot smokes . . . stolen from the whole world . . . In his heart—as with high school—he'd quit this job on the first day but saw nowhere else to go.

Screwy Loot stopped his jeep, signaled to one of the new guys. New guy ran over to the jeep, came back humping two clanking double basic loads of magazines and threw them at James's feet and ran back toward the jeep, saying, "He's calling me."

"What's all this ammo for?"

"Fuck if I know! He's calling me!" The new guy returned to Screwy Loot's jeep, listened, came back humping two jerry cans.

"Burn 'em, burn 'em, burn 'em!"

"What?"

"Burn the hooches! He says we gotta burn 'em."

"Why?"

"I don't know. Something very fucked-up is going on."

"What do you mean?"

"He says there's an attack!"

"*Where?*"

"I don't know!"

James gripped a handle and as panic rode over the back of his skull down his spine and up his ass they both flicked the cans at the nearest hooch and dabbed it with fuel. From somewhere over the hill came deep, repetitive explosions.

The new private pulled a Zippo and the spark blew the vapors and the explosion sent them backward, but it wasn't as loud as the booming from over the hill. He said, "It's all a *thing*, man, it's all a desperate, fucking *thing*."

James circled one hooch and then a second, sloshing gas until the can was empty. He tossed the can into a burning dwelling and the flames found it and ignited the vapors inside and it whooshed loudly and whirled and took a hop. "Did you see that?" James shouted, but the roof's thatch fried so loudly as it burned he couldn't hear himself talk.

He shouted, "What are we doing this for again?"

"Fuck if I know!"

"What's your name again?"

"Fuck if I know!"

James said, "That's kind of fucked-up," but couldn't make

himself heard. He heard gunfire nearby. A noisy chopper floated past overhead and laid a pair of rockets down on the other side of the draw, out of sight, where James was sure there'd never been any people or structures. Black smoke and orange light leapt out of the earth. Had he ever seen any people there? Maybe somebody was dug in. Tough titty, they were on fire now.

The private yelled, "Psycho-delick!"

The structures collapsed quickly. James looked inside a hut as it burned. It was empty. Not even a piece of trash or an old cigarette pack remained. The roof began falling in, and he drew back.

"This is the shits, man," he explained to the private, "because we knew them. I mean, I've seen those people before. We pass by here a lot."

"I've still got gas."

"Let's pull back to them hooches over there."

Keeping low, they ran to a copse of huts in a small basin.

It was empty of life.

"Where's our guys, goddamn it?"

The private said, "Fuck if I know."

"Go tell Sarge."

"I ain't going over that hill—there's people shooting over there!"

"That where it's coming from?"

"Yeah. They'd just as soon shoot me as Charlie."

"I thought it was coming from around to the east."

"Damn. They're shooting all over."

Sergeant Harmon came ducking and running over the lip of the basin. He stood upright as he came down their side.

"I want you two dug in over here."

"What happened? Seems like we were just about in a firefight."

Sarge said, "Did you fire your weapon?"

"No."

"Then you weren't in no firefight."

"Who was it?"

"Could have been our own fucking guys!"

Sarge said, "This whole mountain's under attack."

Huge booms from straight up the hill.

"What is that?"

"Mortars?"

From the east boomed something bigger.

"What is *that*?"

And from behind them, too close, came more. "Where *are* they?"

"Right around us. Them's mortars," Sarge said. "Listen up. I want you dug in here. You hear me?"

"Yes," the new guy said.

"We're in a mess here. If we do this right we can fall back, we can cut around west and skedaddle around them up the hill. I want both ends holding while we fall back from the center real quiet and they don't know. If they flank us on the west, we're fried. Or east. Either way. You've got cover on your west. And you are the cover for the east, you hear me? Charlie comes around that hill, don't cut and run. You hear me?"

"Yes, yes."

Sarge threw down a bindle of twenty-shot magazines. "Keep your switch on semi-auto. You hear me?"

"Yes. Roger."

"There'll be more strikes coming. Stay put. Do not move or you'll get our own rockets up your ass."

"Roger. Roger."

"If we do this right, we'll come around from their backside and you'll be fine going up the hill. On my flare. When you see my flare from the west, you head up the hill to the LZ. Only on my flare."

He put his hand on James's shoulder and shook him until James said, "Roger. On your flare."

The sarge headed back west, over and down into the draw.

On a hooch's south side, in its shadow, they enlarged a rain ditch with their trenchers, cringing at every boom of mortar and artillery. As big as the biggest thunder James had ever heard.

"I'm doing this a lot faster than I did in training," the private said. They flopped into the hole, and he said, "Fuck if I know . . . Gimme an M&M."

In his web belt, in the place of one of his ammo clips, James carried a bag of M&M's candy. "Gimme a handful," the private said.

"I will if you quit saying 'Fuck if I know' all the time."

"It's a habit. I don't say it that much."

"Say 'For all I know' or say 'Jesus God' or 'Kiss my ass.' Just mix it up some."

"Roger, Corporal."

"What's your name?"

"Nash."

"Goddamn!" James cried. Rounds tore through the huts, knocking bits of thatch everywhere.

He'd had basic training, weapons training, jungle training, night training, survival training, evasion and escape; but he now appreciated that no one could train for this in any way that counted, and that he was dead.

He lowered his voice. "Them aren't 16s," he said. "Them are AKs for sure." Zip, zip, zip, the bullets overhead like poisonous insects, zip, zip. Dust and shreds of thatch whirling in the air. Fronds fell from palm bushes only meters away.

"They're killing everything!" Nash said.

"They don't know we're here," James said, "so shut up, okay?" Neither man fired back.

A racket of automatic fire erupted from the west. A voice screamed, "COVER ME, COVER ME, COVER ME, COVER ME!" James rose up and saw Black Man coming down the basin's west side, now screaming, "SHOOT SHOOT SHOOT," and James began laying down fire to the east. Black Man carried on his shoulder an M60 machine gun and dragged behind him a fifty-kilo box to feed it from. He dove into their trench right on top of them and blew their eardrums out letting loose with it and yelling, "Nobody gets past this motherfucker!" He raised up on his knees firing, and the dirt splashed off the higher ground ahead of him. He was leveling the basin's lip like a bulldozer. "Gennemuns, I got ammo enough to kill the human race."

I will never call nobody no nigger again, James promised in his heart.

He thumbed his selector and fired off a full magazine on auto. The mortars began again up the hill.

"Do you believe this shit?"

"What the fuck? WHAT THE FUCK?"

"Sarge said this whole mountain's under attack!"

"Folks misbehaving," Black Man said. "They usually don't attack in daylight."

"Goddamn it," James said.

"What is it?"

"I don't know. You're making me laugh."

"You're making *me* laugh."

"Why are we laughing?"

They couldn't stop. The whole thing. It just made you feel so happy you couldn't stop laughing. James said, "Fuck if I know!" and reloaded and the three of them laughed and fired until James had gone through two more clips, and Black Man shouted, "STOP STOP STOP CEASE YO FUCKING FIRE."

The immediate area was quiet, though they still heard artillery or mortars from up the hill somewhere.

"Gimme a M&M," Black Man said.

"Hell, yes." James gave him the whole pack. Black Man upended it into his mouth and chewed fast.

A chittering came from vegetation that only minutes before had jerked and flown apart under gunfire.

"What's that? A Vietcong squirrel?"

"A monkey."

"A gibbon," James said.

Black Man smiled with chocolate-smeared teeth and said, "There's the flare. Here we go."

"Where we go?"

"We're moving up."

"Moving 'up'? Ain't no 'up.'"

"We moving soon as my gun cools off. Can't touch it now."

"What's happening around here?"

"Touch it. Fry your finger right off your hand."

"I ain't touching shit."

"Put you another clip in, both of you," Black Man said. "We got to go up that hill."

"Those were *mortars*, man."

"Got to go. Let's get our feet under us."

Black Man headed uphill with his gigantic machine gun balanced on his shoulder like a miner's pickaxe, cushioned by an olive towel and gripped by its bipod. Houston followed Black Man, and Nash followed Houston.

Above them paddies terraced the hillside. They moved along the dikes and trudged generally upward.

From nowhere came the racket of gunfire, bullets jerking the small shoots and chirping in the water.

They raced without speaking over the dikes and flopped on the dry side and crawled along until they found a gulley and dropped into it and scrambled away from whoever was trying to kill them.

"You don't understand," Nash said. "I'm not ready for this at all. I only been here three days!"

"I just took a second tour," James said. "I don't know which one of us is the stupider shit."

They passed burning hooches and empty hamlets and never saw any people. By their complete absence they seemed to suggest themselves vividly. But there was activity ahead. They heard shooting. At one point they heard a voice crying in a foreign language. They came on a hamlet whose dwellers had just cleared out minutes ago.

They'd even left an animal picketed in a garden, a goat with his neck stuck out as if offering it to the axe, but he was only shitting. Right in the middle of a war.

The three soldiers climbed on toward the peak.

By sundown they'd traversed seven kilometers of mountain full of people trying to murder them. To James the ascent seemed to have taken no time at all. The sky was pink and purple as they climbed the last half kilometer to the LZ. Coming into the perimeter they saw a prone figure in a U.S. uniform, half of it torn away down the side, and hardly any head left. James wasn't sure it was a body, because no one was even looking at it.

By the bull's-eye some medical corpsmen waited for the return of a chopper, which they said had turned around and left due to reported missile fire. "It might've been just flares," a corporal explained to Black Man. "One got in through the port and had to be kicked out." Still no one mentioned the corpse. James stayed with Black Man and Nash. They sat on a sandbag wall and looked down the mountain they'd just spent five hours climbing in a crazy zigzag. The east valley lay in a cool shadow.

"What was that all about?"

"I have no idea."

"They attacked us. We are their enemy."

"I'm not anybody's enemy."

"I don't want to be friends, or enemies, or anything."

"Where's the sarge?"

"Where's Echo?"

A captain James couldn't remember having seen before came up to them, red from head to toe with rotor dust, chewing on a cigar stub, and blinking at the sweat in his eyes. "This is an established base camp." A bug flew into his forehead—"I want this whole area secure."—swooped around, recovered, was gone.

"Captain, we're looking for Sergeant Harmon."

"Where's Echo Platoon?"

The captain pointed at Black Man and his big gun. "Find a placement for that 60." He left. The three didn't move.

A hippie-looking corpsman with a long mustache and a blue bandanna tied around his head brought them three hot meals stacked on top of one another, and they thanked him sincerely, though Nash said, "You got one of them crawly-caterpillar mustaches."

Toward all these men around him James felt goodwill at an unprecedented depth. The corpsman said they'd had one KIA in a mortar attack. James said, "I seen that guy! I seen a dead corpse. But I thought it was something else."

"Something else? What else could it be, man?"

"Right, yeah," Black Man said, "we seen him."

"I'm not figuring this out," James said. He still couldn't determine whether he'd just fought a battle. "Was this whole mountain under attack or not?"

He ordered his memory to produce some sort of history of the afternoon. It was all very vivid and disordered. He knew one thing. He'd never moved so fast or felt so certain of what he was doing. All the bullshit had been burned away.

It seemed to be over. There was no explanation. No guerrilla activity had ever troubled this mountain. Suddenly the west-side people had dematerialized, and then these VC, and now the VC too had gone up in smoke. James hunkered down and ate his franks and beans. His fatigues still dripped with sweat. Nash, he noticed, was also completely sopped. James said, "How you doing?"

Nash said, "I'm doing fine, man. Why? Don't you believe me?"

James was nonplussed and could only say, "Yeah. I believe you. Sure. Yeah."

Nash said, "My *balls* are sweating, that's all. It ain't piss."

In the dusk the medic took them along a zigzag path to a glen where shirtless youngsters bathed themselves above the waist. Somebody squatted on the bank, squeezing out his socks over the muddy creek. They were all pumped up, laughing, whooping. Boots off, shirts off—a legitimate swim call meant it had to be over, they were definitely safe. In the dying light James felt jazzed and happy and every blurred young face he looked at gave him back a message of brotherly love.

"You boys from Recon travel light."

The speaker was new, perhaps; he didn't realize Echo was a joke. They did travel light. James himself no longer carried a rucksack, just a Boy Scout knapsack holding a poncho and entrenching tool, seven twenty-round magazines, a few sentimental talismans—rubbers, poker chips, and candy—and dosers of insect repellent and bandannas soaked with the stuff. He'd concluded that wanting something was generally less painful than hauling it.

Somebody said, "Well, the war's over. I'm going down to the ville and get laid. The whores give it away free on Tet."

"What's Tet?"

"It's the Hooky-Gooky new year, asshole. Today is Tet."

"Tomorrow is Tet. It's January the thirtieth, man."

"When?"

"To-*day*. Jesus."

One of the grunts from the LZ came into the clearing and said, "Goddamn! Goddamn!" James realized he himself probably looked like that—sweaty, dirty, wild in the eyes. "Shit! Shit!" the boy said. He ran to the clearing's edge and faced the purple distance, the shadows of other mountains. "SHIT."

One of his friends said, "Shit what?"

The boy came back and sat down shaking his head. He took both his friend's hands in his own as if in some foreign style of heartfelt greeting. "Shit. I killed a guy."

"I guess. Shit."

The boy said, "It ain't no different than shooting a deer."

"When did you ever shoot a deer?"

"I guess I had it mixed up with the movies. But this was just— bing. And now it's over."

"It don't sound like it's over, Tommy."

"Hey. Half his skull flew up in the air. Is that over enough for you?"

"Lay it down. You're losing control of yourself."

"Yeah, okay," Tommy said. "I gotta lay it down."

"Hey, let go of my hands, you fruit."

James had killed someone too. He'd seen a muzzle flash, tossed a grenade into a small garden, and after the bang two VC had dragged a man out of the place and into the bush, and he hadn't looked too alive. James had been so shocked he hadn't fired at the two rescuers. Who may or may not have been VC.

He'd been in possession of five twenty-round magazines and the lieutenant had brought twenty-eight more. He'd fired over three hundred rounds and thrown two grenades and traveled ten kilometers and killed one possible VC.

The others watched while Tommy took a cigarette and a Zippo from his breast pocket. He lit up and blew smoke with a certain authoritative air and said to his friend, "Did you kill any of them?"

"I think I did."

"Which one?"

"I don't know which *one*. How the fuck would I know that?"

James had done a whole tour without injuring a single person, and here he'd just said yes to his second trip around and already people were dead—and this guy, Tommy, singing a happy song about it.

The medic went into the trees with a couple guys and pretty soon the smell of green reefer came wafting over, but that was all right, let them wreck their minds, this was war.

The sun, falling farther to the west, came from behind a mountain and shone down the valley. Beyond the paddies the jungle boiled with soft colors. From far below came the squeals of a pig being slaughtered in preparation for Tet. One boy sang new words to a Beatles melody:

> Close your eyes, spread your legs,
> And I'll fertilize your eggs—

Another boy said, "Shit, you guys were fighting? We patrolled halfway down the mountain and back up again and never saw fuck-all, never pulled the trigger. We heard rockets, man, jets, choppers, bombs—never saw shit. We heard mortars, man. Never saw shit."

A youngster came among them saying, "Hanson enters the area bringing good cheer to all," and breaking up a six-pack of Budweiser among the nearest, who came at him like wild dogs.

"Who's Hanson?" James asked.

"Me! I'm Hanson!"

He pictured Hanson's head blowing apart. In basic he'd heard about people just dropping dead of a random bullet or hidden enemy sniper: thinking a thought, saying a word, dropping dead. Bending to tie your shoe, your head flying apart. He didn't want to drop dead and he didn't want to be around anyone else who dropped dead.

Black Man addressed them all. "You got to watch your karma in a time of war. You don't rape the women or kill any of the animals, lest you get fucked around by the karma. Karma is like a wheel. You turn a wheel below you, it turns a wheel above you. And I'm beside you. Your karma touches mine. You must not, no never, disturb any of the karma."

"What is that, a Black Muslim thing?"

"I am not a Muslim. I just been around and seen."

He was talking complete shit that he would never have applied to himself. But it made James's skin crawl all over to hear these warnings.

As soon as dark came to hide them from their superiors, the three from Echo found unoccupied hammocks in some trees on the perimeter's east side, as far as they could get from where the enemy had come that afternoon, and fell out still wearing their boots and web belts. Until the owners came to turn them out, this was home. The night came down. If he lay on his side and looked at ground level, James made out bits of phosphorescence in the foliage; otherwise he'd have thought he'd gone blind. Mosquitoes

whined at the netting. He positioned his repellent-soaked bandannas wherever his arms or cheek might touch it as he slept.
Things crawled in the underbrush. Night was always like this.
He'd killed someone today. Less than eight hours ago. During
basic he hadn't thought about killing anyone, only about getting
killed, about cars he wouldn't race and women he wouldn't conquer, because he was dead. He heard a couple of guys talking over
there. Too jazzed to sleep. When death was around, you got right
down to your soul. These others had felt it too. He could hear it in
their voices.

In the night James unzipped the netting and rolled out thinking it was because he had to pee, but then realized the mortars
had started somewhere down the mountain again. He heard
voices saying Fuck, Shit, saying, Go, go, go. Flares dangled in the
night to the east, and in their dim amber illumination down the
hill he saw the nude crags made by herbicides dancing with their
own shadows. He saw muzzle-flash and heard the pop-pop-pop of
AKs and the racket of M16s. He heard jets. He heard choppers.
He heard rockets. He froze beside his hammock with his weapon
in his hands, scared and weepy, stupid and alone. Now he saw
what a mortar explosion looked like—a red-orange splash as big as
a house, and one second later the boom so loud it hurt his sinuses.
And another hit him, and another, and one more, coming closer.
Weapons fired all around him. A round ricocheted off his helmet
and rifle.

"HEY HEY HEY!" Something had him by the belt and
yanked him backward. It was Black Man. "What you doing?"

"Oh, no. Goddamm, goddamn, goddamn."

"You running right at them! Get down, get down!"

"Sorry, sorry, sorry."

"Oh, shit! He's signaling."

James said, "What?"

"Let's go, let's go, let's go."

Black Man moved, and James tried to grab him by the back of
his shirt, but he was gone, moving back. The whole perimeter was

moving back. Nash was beside him, a ghost in the light of flares.
"Stop shooting! That's us! That's us!" Was I shooting? James
asked, but heard nothing. It was all mental telepathy. He moved
without touching the ground. To where? To here, right here. Still
with Nash and Black Man. Nash said, "Who *are* these people?"

"They's a spotter on that other peak," Black Man said. "They
stair-stepping those mortars on us."

Voices: "Where's my RTO! RADIO RADIO RADIO!"

"Here here here!"

"Tell them up there we're hot. Nobody comes down!"

"Say again say again!"

"Stay off that bull's-eye! We're hot! We're hot!"

James lay on his belly clutching at dirt. The earth bounced
beneath him. He couldn't stay on it. He could hardly breathe.

"What do these motherfuckers want!"

James asked, am I moving? The dark was thick enough to
drink and streaked with the afterimages of tracers and muzzle-
flash. Now it was quiet. Not even a bug droning. In such unprecedented silence James could tell just from the tiny sound his clip
made as the sling ticked against it that the clip was empty, whereas
only two minutes ago the surrounding noise had been so magnificent he couldn't hear his own screaming. In this new silence he
didn't want to replace the clip for fear all the senses of the enemy
would lock on to the sound and he'd be shredded, shredded,
shredded.

Two kilometers east across the darkness lay another mountain,
he didn't know its name, he'd never thought about it, but now
there was gunfire over there, a rippling, insignificant sound. More
on a hillside below, still not in his world, but closer, crisp and dis-
tinct. His hearing was clear as long as he didn't have to fire himself.

From the west came jets. "These fuckers are dead fuckers
now," somebody said.

Rockets lit up the whole mountainside beneath them and the
ceiling of foliage above their heads.

"Don't shoot, don't shoot!" somebody yelled, thumping over the ground. "It's just Hanson!" This person flopped out next to James and said, "Hanson says fuck this shit."

As far as James could tell there were six of them, counting this Hanson, laid out on their bellies in the bush, just above a drop.

In the silence between air strikes below on the mountain he spoke quietly, like a golf-game announcer during a tense moment on the putting green: "Hanson keeps low. Hanson feels the sweat running down his backbone. Hanson's thumb is on the safe, his finger's on the trigger. If it comes, the enemy will feel sincerely fucked with. Hanson will explode their faces. Hanson's finger licks the trigger like a clit. Hanson loves his weapon like a pussy. Hanson wants to go home. Hanson wants to smell clean sheets. Clean sheets in Alabama. Not them stinky sour ones in Vietnam."

Nobody bothered Hanson about it. They realized the enemy were killers, they themselves were just boys, and they were dead. They were glad to hear Hanson's voice talking about this very moment as if it could be understood and maybe even survived.

"Where's my Echo people at?"

Sergeant Harmon came up behind them, walking upright in the sudden glory of another rocketing down below, and they knew they were saved. "How many of us here?"

Black Man's voice came: "Five Echo and one loose screw."

Sarge said, "We have activity right down this slope about two hundred meters. We gonna close that to fifty meters and lay down fire. Come behind me. When it's bright you flop down and look, and when it's dark you move where you looked." He bent and touched James's shoulder. "You're breathing too deep. Make it quick breaths through your nose, and that's all you need. Just don't start hyperventilating in these situations, or you'll cramp up in your hands and fingers."

"Okay," James said, although he wasn't sure what they were talking about.

"'S'go!" Sarge said, and moved out. Over the valley flares hung by their flickering tails of smoke, detached from them, and drifted down, and as James moved forward he could see his feet in a smoky half-light. As long as he moved forward nothing could kill him. Each moment came like the panel of a comic book, and he fit perfectly inside each panel. Air strikes lighting up the night, flares swaying in the heavens, and black shadows dodging all around him. "Black Man!" James yelled. "Black Man!" He heard the big gun ahead and scrambled on elbows and knees toward it. Rounds ticked through the leaves on all sides of him. Somebody was hurt, bawling, howling without letup. Just ahead, a guy kneeling with his helmet shot off, scalped by a head wound—no, it was the hippie doc with his kerchief tied around his head, a couple morphine syrettes clamped between his lips like cigarettes while he knelt over the screamer, who was the sarge. "Sarge, Sarge, Sarge!" James said. "Good, good, talk to him, don't let him go," the doc said, and bit a syrette and drove the point right into Sarge's neck. But the sarge kept bawling like an infant, emptying and filling his lungs over and over. "Lay some down, will you?" the doc said. James crouched and duckwalked toward Black Man's position, firing down the hill at muzzle-flash. He knew he was killing people. Moving, that was the trick. Moving and killing he felt wonderful.

Since three that afternoon Kathy had attended a difficult birth. By five, only the crown had breached. Atop the crown, a face, eyeless, earless. The tiny mother had labored since then to bring forth her deformed child, but nothing yet. The family couldn't afford a midwife. A British doctor was on the way from the Biomedical Centre, where he studied monkeys. Kathy would assist him, perhaps in a Caesarian. She had morphine and she had Xylocaine. She hoped the doctor had something better.

The French doctors were saying the defoliants caused these monstrous births. The people themselves explained it otherwise, called on gods offended by misconduct to stop punishing the innocent babes. What misconduct? Thoughts of the heart. A woman bearing young like this must have succumbed to horrible images inside. Dreams or yearnings or unclean thoughts. On her pallet in the low hooch the youngster appeared free of any thoughts at all, legs akimbo, her hands white and cramped. The effort, the breathing, the body—was it in Colossians?—something about the body knit together and having nourishment ministered by joints and bands. This one seemed nothing more than that. The war had stricken many of the children she worked with, one or both legs amputated, one or both arms—faces burned, sightless. And orphaned. But now this big-headed, half-faced tragic miracle stuck in the breach, coming out already ravaged by the strife.

By ten or so it was clear the doctor wouldn't get there. Soon the infant's heart stopped. She sent the family out and dismembered the stillbirth and delivered it in bloody pieces, cleaned up as best she could, and shortly after midnight called the family back in. She lay down among them, beside the girl. Out in the night firecrackers banged for Tet, and the hands of celebrants waved gunpowder sparklers. She fell asleep.

Then much, much larger blasts. A storm, she thought. God with his big white thoughts. But it was fighting, some to the east and some to the south, like nothing she'd heard before in her time here, explosions like firecrackers in a trash can, only of a size to rival natural thunder, at a bone-ringing depth. She counted the seconds between flash and boom and judged some of them to be falling about a kilometer away. The household was awake, but no one lit a lamp. Far out over the paddies a helicopter sent out its white search beam amid a rising swarm of orange tracers and loosed a terrible downpour from its glittering port guns. The battles went on for hours, the torn spirits flailing in the storm. It stopped. Occasional eruptions followed. By dawn things had settled down. The cicadas started, and a slow sweet light saturated the atmosphere. A gibbon called over the treetops. You'd think there wasn't a gun in the world. A small rooster came and stood in the doorway, raised its beak, and crowed with its eyes closed. You'd think it was Peace on Earth.

Next she was called to a nearby village struck by incendiaries, whether from South Vietnamese fliers or American wasn't clear, but in either case by mistake. Kathy had seen burns, but never a place of burning. She arrived in late afternoon. A black splash the size of a tennis court took in, at one edge, about half of the ville. Ashes where a few huts had been, and a paddy with its marsh boiled away, its shoots dematerialized. The smell of burnt straw, everything tainted with an odor of sulfur. It likely hadn't been napalm, she saw, but rather a white-phosphorous bomb. At the sound of low aircraft the villagers had raced for the cover of the jungle. Several had been killed. One, a young girl, still survived, deep in shock, extensively charred, naked. Nothing could be done. Kathy didn't touch her. The villagers sat surrounding her in the dusk. The pallid green shimmering of her burns competed with the last light. She looked magical, and in Kathy's exhaustion and in this atmosphere of aftermath and silence the scene felt dreamed. The girl was like some idol powered by moonlight. After all signs of life had ceased, her flesh went on glowing in the dark.

She stayed in the ville until morning and then headed on her bicycle for the Biomedical Centre. Word had come last night that the facilities there had been struck. Destroyed, came the word. The boy who'd brought the news, who couldn't have been more than ten and yet traveled by dark shouldering a machete like a lumberman's axe, led her in the dawn light to a shortcut through paddies and fields, and Kathy drove her pedals hard along the path, in a hurry to get to the monkey couple right away. The shortcut led her alongside a narrow channel lined with homes and along the dikes through a wide flatland of delta paddies. In the distance a U.S. helicopter, lit up pink on one side by the sunrise, hunted over the river. Here and there peasants worked the paddies even at this hour, even on such a day, bent over with their hands among the shoots, straight-legged, straight-backed, hinged at the hips, while around them loitered ducks and chickens, huge water buffalo,

fawn-colored, starved-looking Brahman cattle, bag-of-bones
ponies, all behaving as if war were impossible.

Not long before noon she climbed a low rise and found desolation on the other side. She stopped at the top of the burned hill
with smoke still stringing from its soil and looked down at the Biomedical Centre. The wing housing the monkeys had been razed,
but not the living quarters. She walked her bike over the black
ground and down to the building. Shrapnel had gouged at its
walls but had missed the windowpanes. A boy squatted flat-footed
by the doorway with one hand around an upright rifle, spitting
between his feet. He looked up at her and smiled brilliantly as she
passed inside.

In the front room she found Mrs. Bingham, a thin, almost elderly woman in a khaki outfit stained with blood, her hair cut like a
boy's, cigarette jutting from her lips while she knelt diapering one
of many elfin, simian creatures laid out on an army blanket on the
low coffee table. Bloody rags and bandages surrounded her. She
paused and took her cigarette from her mouth and gave Kathy a
kind of smile or grimace, very simian in itself, while tears welled
in her eyes. "What do I say now? Come in." She waved her cigarette around helplessly. "Be alive."

Viewing the destruction, Kathy had feared for the medicine.
But she saw two refrigerators in the kitchen.

Kathy sat down and said, "It's terrible."

"These were all that survived, as far as we know. We had all
four subspecies of langur. Now we have two." Inexplicably she
laughed, finishing the outburst with a wet smoker's cough.

Kathy said, "It's horrible."

"We're in a horrible place."

"It's a fallen world."

"I can't contradict you. That would be stupid."

There seemed to be ten or so monkeys recuperating on the
blanket. All wore cloth diapers.

Mrs. Bingham said, "Sorry we didn't make it last night. Did
things turn out? Better not answer."

"The mother's fine."

"The baby perished."

"Correct."

"Sorry. We've had our hands full. There's been a little flu epidemic here. But it doesn't matter now, does it?"

Kathy placed her knapsack on the table and opened it. She carried a plastic baggie full of loose GI cigarettes to give as gifts, and she passed them all to Mrs. Bingham. "Some of them look broken, eh?" she said.

Mrs. Bingham held the tiny monkey on her knee and both she and the big-browed creature looked at the baggie without comprehension. "We had eleven bassinets," she said, "but they all burned."

They're only monkeys, it was all she could do to keep from shouting, monkeys, monkeys.

In the kitchen was a maidservant—young, in high-heeled sandals and a short skirt—who stopped washing tiny diapers at the sink in order to see to Kathy. "What can I get?" she said.

Mrs. Bingham said, "Get out of my sight," and the girl returned to the kitchen.

"Is the doctor around?"

"We're waiting. Some may have escaped. He's looking for survivors."

"Can he find them? Can he catch them?"

"If they're hurt. This is a golden-head." She replaced the wounded langur on the blanket. It lay back looking upward with its black eyes and seemed to be furiously thinking. "The others are probably dead. It could have been all of us. The bastards. They're psychotic. Oh, well," she said, "we've all been driven mad, haven't we, whether we realize or not."

Soon the doctor came in and gestured at the assemblage of battered animals.

"Behold the Vietcong."

"Anything?"

He shook his head.

Kathy asked, "Was it mortars?"

"Rockets," Dr. Bingham said. "Planes. And not just rockets."
"Napalm?"
"Probably."
"It must have been." His wife broke down weeping. "The screams are still in my head—just now as I'm talking. You've no idea. You've no idea."

"You just don't know," the doctor explained to Kathy. "I'm sorry, but you can't possibly."

"Mimi," his wife said to the servant, "bring Miss Nurse a Coca-Cola, please."

The servant gave her a Coca-Cola in a glass with ice and they sat in the living room under generator-powered lights while Dr. Bingham spoke of monkeys. The four subspecies of langur had come to be regarded as two separate species, one of which was divided into three subspecies. Of these, the golden-headed *Trachypithecus poliocephalus* had grown, in his words, "excruciatingly rare," with an estimated five hundred individuals remaining. And now so many less. They allowed Kathy to put the nipple of a baby bottle into the mouth of one of the langurs and hold it while it guzzled formula. The creature was appealing, but blue snot bubbled from its nose, and she wondered if she'd catch her death.

The couple behaved most hospitably, but when the doctor, a large, bearded man in early middle age, a most prepossessing figure, a real jungle bwana, Kathy had always thought, noticed her open knapsack sitting on the coffee table, he said, "What is that?" very coldly, very hatefully. Most strangely.

"It's a blood pressure device."
"It's a tape recorder."
"It's a blood pressure gauge."
"You're recording this," he said.
"Dear, it doesn't look anything like a tape recorder."
The doctor's lips were pursed and bloodless. He breathed hard through his nose.
Kathy said, "I've turned it off now."
"See that it doesn't go back on."

"He thinks it's a tape recorder," Mrs. Bingham said.

Kathy reached for the glass of Coke resting on the floor by her chair. Fire ants covered it, rolling in from the blazing day in a phalanx about six inches wide and God knew how long.

"Have you listened to the radio?" Mrs. Bingham said. "The North is attacking all over. They hit the American Embassy."

"Really."

"They've been repulsed, it seems. So the news reports say. But it's the American station. They'd want to sound victorious, wouldn't they? Dear," she said to her husband, who ministered to one of the small creatures, "she's dead. Dead."

"I was arranging her arms."

"Leave her alone."

The servant girl attacked the ants with brisk strokes of a short-handled broom, driving them out the front door. The boy guarding the entrance edged a couple of feet to his left. The girl looked Chinese, taller than most, quite tall, with a very short black skirt and long legs.

Kathy asked, "Will you stay on?"

"Stay on?"

"Can you repair things, do you think you can rebuild the facility?"

"What else can we do? Who else would take care of them? There are only seven, but, I mean, nevertheless. Seven left out of one hundred sixty."

"One hundred fifty-eight," the doctor said.

"You had a store of antibiotics, didn't you? I wonder if that's still true?" She knew they had antibiotics—the second refrigerator.

"Goddamn them, who do they think they are, what are they trying to do? You're Canadian, aren't you? You're not American."

Kathy said very evenly, "I'm wondering about your antibiotics now. Now that things are so different."

"Oh, for God's sake," Mrs. Bingham said.

"I wondered why you'd come around."

"I know. I'm sorry. I know," Kathy said. "It's just the way of things. It would be such a help."

"Do you have cold storage?"

"I was thinking of the Bao Dai facility. We have a couple of Frigidaires. It would really help. It truly would. Two hundred children, more or less."

"We had one hundred fifty-eight," Mrs. Bingham reminded her.

"Yes," Kathy said, longing to strike her in the face. She asked them again: "What will you do?"

"We'll probably stay on."

"Yes. We'll stay on," Mrs. Bingham said, staring at the maidservant as she rinsed out rags at the sink.

"Your generator is working well."

"Yes, yes. We still have power."

The doctor said, "Who do you really work for? What are you after?"

His wife leapt to her feet. "Do you want medicine? Do you want medicine?" She ran over to the girl at the kitchen sink and pulled up her skirt from behind. Underneath the girl went naked, she wore no panties—"There," Mrs. Bingham said, "will we stay on? How could we leave!"

"Let her have the medicine."

She opened one of the refrigerators wide and shrieked, "Take it over my dead body!"

"Give it to her. She needs it," the doctor said.

"It was stupid of you to come," Mrs. Bingham said.

"Take it," her husband said. The girl went on washing at the sink as though none of this were happening.

Above Echo Camp as the sun rose the mountain disgorged black smoke like a volcano. The paddies on the west side, untouched by two wars, were now a wasteland, destroyed by NVA artillery or VC mortars, whichever it was, and by U.S. incendiary ordnance and rockets. Echo Camp lay untouched. Mortar blasts had dug craters a hundred meters off, nothing closer. The ville of Cao Phuc too was safe. But it appeared many of the villagers had been warned—that the VC had warned them—that they'd been contacted, cultivated, turned. The place had been strangely quiet the afternoon preceding the onslaught. The Purple Bar had been inexplicably closed. Before dawn Tuesday came the attack; by mid-morning Tuesday the population had crept back home, though some still came, without bags or bundles, as if they'd only been gone a few minutes.

At dawn the colonel had arrived by chopper and come down the mountain in a jeep and toured the area with Screwy Loot and two men from Psy Ops—Sergeant Storm and a civilian the little sergeant referred to as the Skipper.

"Boy, boy, boy," Screwy Loot said, "those F-16s sure tore the shit out of our mountain."

The colonel said, "This is just the start. From now on all hell is going to rain down from these skies. It's a goddamned shame." The colonel was beside himself. During the fighting these villagers had disappeared, but the farmers on the mountain's other side had not—except in flames. He slapped at the heads of several local men who sat on their rumps in the dirt in a line, legs straight out with their ankles trussed together and their wrists bound behind their backs. The Kootchy Kooties had captured a man, a VC, they said, who'd come at them with an AK and blown the Indian's rucksack to shreds, right on his back. The Indian took hold of their blindfolded prisoner's bound wrists and dragged him backward over the earth into the brush where the Kooties had pitched their tents. The little man grimaced so hard he seemed to unhinge his jaw as his arms popped out of their sockets at the shoulders, but he didn't make a sound as the Kooties hung him by the wrists from the lopped-off branch of a banyan tree, his toes six inches above the earth.

Echo was messed up over Sarge, who'd been taken to Hospital

12 with wounds in his neck and spine and belly and waited there in a state of paralysis, too critical to be moved stateside. Most of Echo sat in the Purple Bar saying nothing, drinking only a little, silly with grief and nauseated by the violent power of fate. The new black guy sat among them telling whopping lies about people he claimed to know personally back home. He was able to talk because his heart wasn't broken. He'd never really known the sarge. He came from the boonies in Louisiana and seemed both shy around these men and excited to talk about his home. "I been rode on by a witch before. I know a witch rode me all night once because I woke up tired and dirty with bloody corners on my mouth where I bit on the bridle. You can hang a horseshoe over your bed to keep witches off. Before she can come in your house she got to walk down every single road where that horseshoe been walking. My uncle fetched a rock and broke the arm on a witch one night and next day I swear on Jesus it was Sunday and old neighbor lady singing hymns in church got bubbles outa her mouth and fell down rolling and preacher say Take up her shawl and they took up her shawl and there was her arm bust and bone sticking out right where my uncle broke that witch's arm and preacher say Drag her to the pit and they dragged her to the pit and preacher say Burn the witch and they burned her up right there in the pit. I swear it's true. Don't nobody back home say it ain't. My uncle told me and everybody knew about it." He was a pie-faced black youth, very black, the color of charcoal. Nobody stopped him and he might have gone on talking forever, but Nash came in and interrupted, saying, "Hey, you gotta see this, the Kooties are messing with that Vietcong and he's all fucked up, I am not shitting you, man, you really gotta see this."

Outside, Black Man watched while eating a mango, peel and all, with his hands. There were always mangoes around—bananas too, sometimes papayas. He said, "Those Lurps all janged up on bennies and goofballs. Zippy zoodle."

One of the Lurps, in fact the most randomly unhinged of the colonel's Kootchy Kooties, the savagely dressed black guy, stood in a bloody puddle in front of the hanging prisoner, spitting in his face.

Screwy Loot stood watching too, along with Sergeant Storm from Psy Ops.

The colonel observed from the shade, from a seat on an old connex crate shot full of holes, with chickens living in it. He and the Skipper didn't seem interested in making their presence known. The lieutenant went over to them and said, "Well, now, it's like this, the thing about this kind of thing . . ." He didn't finish. He frowned. He chewed his lips.

The black Kooty seemed to be lecturing them while he dug at the man's belly with the blade of a multipurpose Swiss Army knife. "They are kicking our ass and we gonna find out what's what. They attacking all over the South. The American Embassy compound even."

Sergeant Storm from Psy Ops said, "Man, no, don't," but not very loudly.

Cowboy says, "Give it to the motherfucker. Make him holler. Yeah, motherfucker. That's how Sarge hollered. Make him holler." His face was purple with rage, and he wept.

"There's something I want this sonabitching muhfucker to *see*." Now the Kooty went at the man's eyes with the spoon of his Swiss Army knife.

"Do it, do it," Cowboy said.

"I want this muhfucker to get a real . . . good . . . look at something," the Kooty said. "Oh, yeah. Sound like a baby girl," he said in answer to the man's screams. He dropped his knife in the gore at his feet and grabbed the man's eyeballs hanging by their purple optic nerves and turned the red veiny side so that the pupils looked back at the empty sockets and the pulp in the cranium. "Take a good look at yourself, you piece of shit."

"Jesus Christ," the skinny little sergeant said.

The colonel hopped down off the connex crate and walked over to the scene unsnapping the flap on his holster and motioned Cowboy and the Kooty out of the way and shot the dangling prisoner in the temple.

Sergeant Storm said, "Goddamn fucking right."

Cowboy put his face directly in the colonel's. "You didn't hear the sarge crying and bawling till he lost his voice," he told him. "One or two things like that, and this shit ain't funny no more."

The corpse went limp instantaneously and a rag of brain flopped down the side of its face.

Young Captain Minh, as a Viet Nam Air Force pilot, had directed ordnance against countless targets and, from the cockpit of his F-5E fighter-bomber, must himself have finished the lives of hundreds, but these had ended in obscurity, beneath carpets of fire and smoke, and Minh had never seen anyone kill anyone before.

It was a sunny morning. Almost noon. Already uncomfortably hot.

The colonel holstered his weapon and said, "There is a great deal I'll do in the name of anti-Communism. A great deal. But by God, there's a limit."

Minh heard the colonel's nephew laughing. Skip Sands could hardly stand up, he was laughing so hard. He put a hand against the tent and almost pulled it down. Nobody paid any attention to him.

The black Lurp stared at the colonel and cleaned the blood from his clasp knife ostentatiously with his tongue before tromping off toward the north hamlet and the Purple Bar.

Minh took the attitude that all this destruction wasn't happening, that a foul wind of illusion blew through, dragging behind it an actuality of peace and order. The village of Cao Phuc, for instance, what had happened here?—the Echo camp a small base, now, with Quonset huts, latrines, two big MASH generators; the temple still dominating the south hamlet but resting now on a thick concrete slab with a tiled entryway; the north hamlet overrun by a compound of refugee housing resembling crates and

coops—all these changes in the couple of years he'd been flying
the colonel back and forth. The Purple Bar was the same over-
sized hooch, a loitering place for dull-faced prostitutes, waifs
whose families had perished. No local girls entered there.

"Jesus Christ," Jimmy Storm said, "that is one fucked-up nigger."

"And who fucked him up? We did," the colonel said. "History
might forgive us for what's going on around here. But that man
never will. He'd better not."

Minh didn't know this black Lurp who'd cut the prisoner's eyes
out. When the man wasn't around, everybody spoke of him. He
slept on his poncho on the ground, and only in the day. At night
he moved through the world, no one said where. His hair grew out
in wild foot-long clusters. He'd cut the sleeves and most of the
pant legs away from his uniform, and nothing kept the vermin
from his flesh but the bright designs of red, white, and blue paint
streaking his face and limbs.

A little after sixteen hundred hours Minh and the three Americans went back up the mountain and on to Saigon in the colonel's helicopter, a Huey modified with two extra seats and without
a machine gun, on loan to the colonel from the VNAF, though
the colonel himself had arranged for the VNAF to have it in the
first place. On the colonel's orders Minh took them to several
thousand feet and kept up a speed of nearly a hundred U.S. miles
per hour. Sergeant Storm, sitting on his helmet with an M16
across his knees, his hair raked back by the deafening winds, occa-
sionally raised his weapon to fire a burst down into the world
below. The colonel's nephew sat next to the sergeant, staring out
the open portal at the jungle and the paddies, the flicker of fires,
man-destroyed badlands from which smoke ascended like steam
through rents in a cauldron's lid. Two fighter jets passing close
underneath actually drowned out the incredible racket of the
chopper's motors. The craft came very close. F-104s. Minh could
almost make out the emblem on one pilot's helmet.

Skip Sands often smiled, and always Skip Sands joked, but
Minh had hardly ever heard Skip Sands laugh. Why had he

laughed at the poor tormented man? Certainly nobody could have found it funny. But something had struck him as hilarious.

The colonel, wearing his headset, sat next to Minh and studied the horizon and seemed to have forgotten the terrors of the morning. Skip, for his part, looked as if they'd never leave him. The colonel hadn't mentioned his nephew's behavior. Maybe it didn't bear mentioning. Perhaps Skip thanked his God right now that he had no headset and that their transport was too loud for talk. But who can look into another's thoughts? And Minh often felt of the Americans that behind their actions lay no thoughts anyway, only passions. But he'd seen Skip's face as his uncle had helped him aboard and he believed completely that this American was thinking only of the murdered man.

For a brief period Minh let the colonel take the controls. It wasn't safe, but the colonel did what he wished, and nothing could hurt him. The colonel had seen war at its worst and had once made to Minh a sad confession: in order to save his fellow prisoners from a massacre, the colonel, at that time a young air force captain like Minh himself, had killed one of his own comrades in the dark hold of a Japanese POW ship, had choked him to death with his bare hands. The colonel often shared such stories, possibly because he didn't think Minh comprehended. Minh's English, however, kept improving. He could speak confidently about matters within the realm of his duties and sometimes followed whole conversations among Americans, though the subtleties eluded him and he couldn't hope to participate with any skill. And Minh thought he was probably the only person who knew that the colonel kept a wife in the lower Mekong Delta and frequently traveled to visit her in this very helicopter.

The airfield at Tan Son Nhut in Saigon had come under rocket fire three times since the initial predawn assault, but no attack was under way at the moment, and they were permitted to land. They left Minh with the craft and crossed the field through an oily wind under gray skies. Outside the terminal Hao waited with the Chevrolet, just beyond the concrete barricades.

Skip thought he should demonstrate some minimal interest in where they were going, but he had none. Storm, however, demanded to know, and the colonel said, "Hao better have that figured out." Skip and Storm in the back, the colonel up front beside Hao, who smoked a long cigarette and worried its filter tip with his thumb, dotting his pant legs with ash, and peered out myopically and drove without certainty. The city echoed with small-arms fire and the drumroll of helicopters and, somewhat curiously, firecrackers. They passed several unclaimed corpses at the side of the street but saw little real damage, saw people carrying on as usual, walking to and fro, sailing out on their small motorcycles. The colonel said, "Do we have a good enough fix on where we're going?" but Hao didn't seem to get the question, and the colonel said, "Hao, I don't think we know where we're going."

"He tell to me the location. I will find it." A few minutes later he said, ahead of the colonel's next question, "Cho Lon is too big. Too many street."

"There — there — those jeeps."

Hao stopped the Chevrolet near a trio of ARVN jeeps parked randomly around the dead bodies of two Vietnamese men.

"Stop. Stop. Go ahead and kill it," the colonel said, and as Hao cut the engine he said, "Hao, we're going to see some dead VC up here. I want you to look and make sure none of them is our friend."

Hao nodded.

"You know who I mean?"

Hao said, "Our friend."

"I don't think he's here. He shouldn't be. But I want you to make sure. All right — let us proceed."

They all got out of the car.

The two corpses lay side by side in the middle of the street with their arms stretched above their heads. Each had been shot a great number of times. A squad of nine or so ARVN infantry sat in or leaned against the jeeps. Nearby a small ARVN officer smoked a cigarette, standing almost at attention with one hand on the butt of his sidearm.

"Major Keng?"

"C'est moi."

"I'm Colonel Francis Sands.—Skip, can you get the drift for me? This is Mr. Skip, my nephew and colleague. Skip, thank him for coming out. Thank him for keeping this under guard. Tell him I'm the one his information originated from."

The major closed his eyes and smiled. "No need for that, Colonel. I get you."

"No," Skip said. "Your accent is terrific."

"Keng is a Chinese name. Incidentally, I am not Chinese."

"How many languages do you speak?"

"French, English, Chinese. And my own, of course. What can I do for you, Colonel?"

The colonel said, "Did it all go like we told you?"

"Like a charm," the major said. "We ambushed them."

"Did they have explosives?"

Major Keng tossed away his cigarette and beckoned them all over to a jeep on whose rear seat lay four satchel charges. "Red China," he said.

"What time did they come here?" the colonel asked.

"Three a.m. on the dot."

The colonel said, "Everything like we told you?"

"Everything was correct," Keng said, "to the tee. Oh three hundred hours." He swept his hand out at the corpses. "Two VC. As promised."

"What was the target?"

"To destroy the traffic bridge there," Keng said.

"Is this stuff big enough for the job?"

"I will give you my best guess: more than enough."

"No IDs, I suppose."

"No identity cards." Keng shook his head.

"Major, we won't trouble you further. I just wanted to be sure our information was correct. We'll take a quick look at this overpass and be on our way."

Storm and Skip followed the colonel over to the traffic overpass evidently targeted for destruction by the two guerrillas, and stood atop it. Buzzing motor scooters echoed below them. "I'm not sure I see the point," the colonel said. "I suppose it would have tied up the street down there. But I'm not sure I see the point." He headed back to the car.

Storm walked beside Skip and said, "I can tell by the way you move, you like it here. You walk very softly and you don't get your body hot for no good reason. You use the air around you." Making this remark he seemed strangely shy, not at all the tough little lunatic. "You know what I mean?"

"Sort of."

"You blend with the air like a native," Storm assured him.

After Colonel Sands had shaken hands with Major Keng and invited him out for supper and drinks and been politely refused, the colonel sat in the Chevy's front seat maintaining a zealous poise and told Hao, "Out Highway One. Let's get a drink."

Hao executed a lurching U-turn and they left the corpses behind.

"Goddamn it," the colonel said, "we are in business with a double."

They were somewhere out on Highway One at a restaurant-tavern in an unpaved cul-de-sac, the Bar Jolly Blue, a place mainly, it seemed to Skip, for whores and gangsters. But it was the Saigon watering hole of Echo Platoon and of many serving the Cao Phuc landing zone, none of them present now, as today no soldier in the country took leave, not in the northern army or the southern, not the Vietcong or the U.S. forces. Skip, Storm, and the colonel sat in deck chairs under an awning in the cooling dusk, and they kept the Chevy's radio tuned to AFVN and stayed on top of things. Skip hadn't slept since he'd left Cao Quyen almost forty-eight hours earlier. He assumed the colonel and Storm were equally exhausted, but none of them wanted to go down before they knew what had happened, what might happen next, how things stood with this unprecedented monster push, which seemed, at this point, to have been a disaster for the enemy.

Between hourly radio news dispatches the colonel made phone calls from a pimp's room to the U.S. Embassy and got a wealth of confusing and contradictory reports.

"Coordinated attacks all over Quang Tri Province. At least that far north."

"How far south?"

"They hit Con Mau down there."

"On the peninsula? Jesus."

"They're all over. And being slaughtered in swarms."

Combined NVA and Vietcong forces had assaulted nearly every sizable population center and military installation in the South. "Bold and crazy," the colonel said at first, and then as reports accumulated he said, "Bold and crazy and stupid." While the overall offensive was stunning in its orchestration and its suddenness, its fierceness and grandeur, the individual attacks seemed to have been mounted without clear planning or adequate support.

The colonel poured drinks from a fifth of Bushmills—out of a case of it that rode with him everywhere in his Chevy's trunk. "We're bombing Cu Chi nonstop already. Any square inch where a GI isn't standing is going to be a crater. I told you all hell would rain down. I consider this hasty. We had plans for those tunnels."

"Just to get down to the actual facts," Jimmy Storm said, "I don't care about the tunnels."

"We're casting about for some other approach to combating this enemy. Anything but what we've got," the colonel insisted.

"I started out with a red-hot desire to fry their minds. Now I spend my day trying to keep my own mind from exploding."

Skip had spent half a year in exile, missing this, longing for it, and it seemed he hadn't missed a minute, had taken up exactly in midconversation with the red-eyed colonel and the quivering bird-dog sergeant. It seemed the two held forth on parallel tracks, confident of meeting somewhere in infinity. Skip's esophagus burned. He drank 7Up. In his mind the day's truest fact was that the bleeding, gouge-eyed man his uncle had dispatched so readily was a human soul in a family of others who had known him by name and held him in love, and he, Skip, a spy for history's greatest nation, was troubled that this should trouble him.

"What did I tell you," the colonel said, "about centralization? The VC and the NVA are controlled from a single source."

"Most elegant."

"Probably unbeatable. We can't win like this. Our young foot soldier this morning phrased it correctly. This shit ain't funny no more. This shit is a mess. This shit has got to stop."

Skip had never heard from the colonel any statement even remotely like this one. It was all wrong. It was completely false because it offered entrance to far too much that was true.

"If we can't be centralized, if we're going to flounder around like ants in molasses, then we as individual floundering ants can't wait for orders from above."

Storm said, "What's the skin, daddy-o?"

"The skinny is we've got ourselves a double, and we'll work him very carefully. But we have a lot of planning and thinking to do, and none of that begins today. Let's just be happy we don't have to sit on our asses while Uncle Ho executes one grand strategy after another until something works. This time it didn't work. This time they tossed themselves into battle and just pointlessly expended themselves."

Jimmy Storm laughed with a kind of exhausted abandon while Skip and the colonel watched. He got control of himself. "Jesus, how can you go forty-eight hours without sleep and then come up with this eloquent moonshine? KEEP THESE HARLOTS AWAY FROM ME," he shouted at the mamasan waiting tables. "All right—you," he said, "you can come here," and he snapped his lighter open for the cigarette of a petite woman with fat thighs encased in a black miniskirt, explaining, "This one's a lying psychotic whore. Good people. My kind of people."

The colonel took a light off the same flame. He was smoking Players cigarettes in the flat pack—the brand, if Skip remembered, of James Bond.

"What's this, now—no cigars?"

"Some days they taste a little scummy. You still don't smoke."

"No."

"Don't start." He smoked. "It's a war, Skip."

"I understand."

Skip got up and wandered around the place. He looked into the vague interior of the Bar Jolly Blue. Standing in the doorway he could feel it was ten degrees hotter inside. It was empty except for three girls and the mamasan behind the plywood bar, who called, "Yes, sir, you want beer?"

"I'm hungry."

"You want soup?"

"Soup and a baguette, thanks."

"I bring you. You sit down."

"Let me introduce you myself," one of the girls said, but he turned away without answering.

He went around to the concrete trough looking out on a dark plain of elephant grass behind the sex rooms. He pissed, washed his face from the spigot at the cistern, retucked his sweaty shirt, told himself: It's a war, Skip. Vanquish fear.

He made his way back to his comrades.

At their table the colonel was telling Storm, "Eggs were hard to come by. We pooled things like that, eggs and any meat we'd trapped, and the docs, the medical people, such as we had, the docs decided who ate what from the food store. We caught dogs, monkeys, rats, birds. We had a few chickens cooped up." He said to Skip, "I'm telling him what Anders Pitchfork did for me in the prison camp. I was sick, and Anders fed me a hard-boiled egg. Anders was allowed an egg every day because he was on a hard detail and needed the protein. And he gave one to me because I

was laid out sick. And I didn't say pish posh, no thanks—I gobbled
that egg down quick before he changed his mind. If Anders Pitchfork walked in here and asked me to cut off my hand for him right
now, I wouldn't hesitate. My severed hand would lie here on this
table. That's what war gives you. A family deeper than blood. Then
you go back to peacetime, and what do you get?—backstabbing
enemies in the office down the hall. Guys like Johnny Brewster.
Brewster is a thoroughgoing asshole, and he's permanently pissed
off at me. Do you know him, Skip?"

"Not personally. What did you do to piss him off?"

"The question is, what did Brewster do to me? Got me stuck
behind a desk almost six months last year and answering a lot of
questions. They tried to make it look like some sort of health
inquiry. But I knew what it was about."

"And what was it? Not the business in the Philippines?"

"Hell, no. About Cao Phuc. About my helicopter, about my
platoon. And I put him on his ass, and do you know what? The
questions stopped. The interlude was over, and I was back here
again."

"Put him on his ass, did you say?"

"Last June," said the colonel, "I knocked him out."

"What?"

"You heard right. I invited him to play handball. We suited up
in the locker room, we stepped onto a court, and I walked over
and I socked him on the chin. Ask any boxer: you don't want to
take a blow to the point of the chin. The first thing they teach you
is—tuck your chin. I laid him out, sir, and I don't regret it,
because he's a slimy, oily, politicking—have you got a thesaurus?
I'd have to hunt through a thesaurus to give you Brewster's full
description."

"I never heard anything about this."

"I don't know that he ever told anyone. How could he? No way
of putting a good face on it, running to the brass and whining that
he got his ass kicked."

"Have you ever arm-wrestled this old thug?" Storm asked.

"No," Skip said.

"I didn't hurt the SOB. Johnny Brewster's a strong and agile man. He parachuted into northern France for the OSS. But he spent too much time with the Resistance, and they turned him pink. Made him a leftist sympathizer. And he's an elitest. Wants to get rid of us old thugs. The war shook quite a few of us toads in amongst the goldfish, and they'd like to get us sorted out."

He signaled to Hao, who sat in the Chevy three yards away with the radio on and the door open. "Hao, Hao. Come on." Skip saw by the way his uncle cocked his head and waved his fingers that he was drunk now. "Do you need anything? When was the last time you ate? Sit down, buddy, sit down."

"I can get something in the bar."

"Sit down, we'll get you something, sit down."

Hao sat down and the colonel waved at the mamasan and said, "Actually, I don't play handball. Those noisy acoustics, and the ball whacking and the rubber shoes squeaking—never play it. It's harder on your ears than the target range. It's as deafening as artillery." The mamasan approached and he said, "Get him something to eat. What can we get you, Hao? What are you hungry for?"

"I will talk to her." Hao rose and walked off toward the barroom with the mamasan.

"John Brewster," the colonel said, "wears socks with clocks on them and thinks Washington, DC, is slightly bigger than the universe. What are they going to do to me? Fire me? Jail me? Kill me? Will, young Will, you know something of my history. What can they do to me now? I was a prisoner of the Japanese. What is there left in human experience that they can hope or expect to scare me with?"

The mamasan came over with four bowls of soup and a plate of baguettes on a tray. The colonel tore a baguette in half and said, "I tell you this sincerely: there'd better not be a man at this table who in any way fears death."

"Hear, hear," Skip said.

"It's all death anyway," Storm said.

"Oh, I forgot," the colonel said with a mouthful of baguette, "Mr. Jimmy thinks he's a samurai."

"I'm just moving through the motions, Papasan. Death is the basic condition."

"What do you know about it really?"

"No. No. The universe had to come from somewhere, right? Wrong. It had to come from nowhere. The Big Nothing."

"Mr. Jimmy follows the Buddha."

"I follow a completely different mode of Buddhism."

"Mr. Sergeant Jimmy studies the Tibetan."

"I study the knowledge of the moves after death. The realm of the Bardo. What to do at each part of the journey after you die. It's full of wrong turns leading back here, man. Back to Planet E. I'm not coming back. It's a shit-hole."

"It's a shit-hole with fireworks," the colonel said.

"Come back if you want. But don't expect your current rank."

That his uncle would tolerate, even celebrate this fool.

"You tried some meditation over in Cao Phuc—at the temple, didn't you, Colonel?"

The colonel squinted at Storm as if trying to summon an answer and after a considerable pause said, "I don't play handball. Although it's an ancient game. Sport. Pastime." He sat back comfortably. "Venerable Irish pastime. Came from Ireland. Came over from Ireland." His head nodded forward, and he was deeply asleep.

In this way began the Year of the Monkey.

Kathy traveled to Saigon to seek help from anyone she could, starting with Colin Rappaport at World Children's Services. Vietcong and even stray NVA regulars marauded in the Sa Dec area, the Americans and ARVN had grown ruthless and undiscriminating in the pursuit, supplies weren't getting to the Bao Dai Orphanage, soon it would all be impossible.

The American helicopters strafed anything moving on the rivers. To reach the road to Saigon she pedaled her bike along the paths by the canals, hard going, not muddy, but unresisting, slowing the tires—how pliant this land, how rich and soft, how deceptive—and out onto the dikes, in the open. A wind came rolling over the paddies and sunlight moved in the green shoots like a thrill under the flesh.

She waited in a dirt-floor café. Tin-roofed, straw-paneled. Sat at a table drinking hot tea from a tin can, awaiting transport across a river about a hundred feet wide. At her feet a little kid played with a bright green grasshopper half the length of his arm. She left the bicycle with the café family, who told her no helicopters had shown in the area since early morning. A sampan woman wearing pale violet formal-gown gloves and a pink face-cloth ferried her across. On the other side lay houses and gardens . . . A girl in a beautiful dress in a tiny plot of graves, prostrate on one of the tombs in the dappled shade . . . Kathy caught a lift with a farmer in a three-wheeled truck bearing old rice sacks full of duck feathers toward Saigon. A few miles southeast of the city their ways parted and he let her out.

She wore a calf-length skirt, sandals, no stockings. Sitting in a thatched teahouse beside Highway Seven she felt the sweat running from the crooks of her knees down her calves. She opened her knapsack and took out her Bible to read, but it was already too dark. She held it in her lap, flicking at the bookmark with her finger. Somewhere in the Psalms it said: Against You, You only have I sinned. For a few minutes as the explosions came particularly close the night of Tet she'd felt all pride crushed, all knowledge stopped, all desire, had existed only as naked, abject subjugation. Her sin had seemed small, her salvation or damnation seemed small.

Night came. A man set out red chairs in front of the teahouse.

She took a cyclo into the city. She stayed at a hostel of sorts across from the green-shuttered Jamia Mosque on Dong Du Street. She lay on a cot for half an hour but couldn't sleep.

She went walking. It was nearly eleven. As she waded through the traffic, a cyclist bearing on his shoulder a three-meter-long sheaf of lumber seemed about to make a turn and possibly knock her head off with the ends of his boards. She stepped backward and was almost run down by a U.S. jeep—they called them "Mutts"—the tires screeched, and one wheel went up over the curb. "Sorry about that, ma'am," said the wild-faced young infantryman driving.—So; nearly dead. She didn't care.

She walked down a red-lit alley. In a window—a soldier slapping his woman while a child up on its knees on the mattress howled out of a face like a fist . . .

Through the doorway of a tavern—a couple of sad-drunk infantrymen dancing in the jukebox glow, each alone, chins down, fingers popping, shoulders working, heads bobbing, trudging like carriage horses toward some solitary destiny. She stopped to watch them. In the songs on jukeboxes or on radios tuned to AFVN she often heard God calling out to her—"Love me with all your heart"—"This guy's in love with you"—"All you need is love"—but tonight the voice sang only to the soldiers, and its message didn't reach the street.

She passed a recruit with his head hanging, one hand guiding his stream against the wall. He raised acid-bright eyes to her and said, "I been pissing for a thousand years." His friend beside him was bent over puking. "Don't mind me, ma'am," he said, "I'm high on life."

The Vietnamese were restful to her eyes. She had no background with them. The American soldiers seemed far too much like Canadians—pulling her heart out in an undertow of joy and sorrow, guilt, anger, and affection. She watched the broad backs of these two as they tottered away from her.

They threw hand grenades through doorways and blew the arms and legs off ignorant farmers, they rescued puppies from starvation and smuggled them home to Mississippi in their shirts, they burned down whole villages and raped young girls, they stole medicines by the jeepload to save the lives of orphans.

The next morning in the offices of the World Children's Services Colin Rappaport said to her, "Kathy. Please. Let me find you a bed in one of the hospitals."

"This isn't the conversation I came here to have."

"Do you realize the shape you're in? You're exhausted."

"But if I don't feel tired, it doesn't count."

"But you realize."

"I realize," she said, "but I don't feel tired."

At the start of February, James Houston, in his dirty jungle fatigues, caught a ride with a water truck from Good Luck Mountain down to Highway Thirteen and then with a jeep into Saigon. He could have stopped—had meant to stop—at the big base to look in on Sergeant Harmon at the Twelfth Evacuation Hospital. But the boys in the truck were heading all the way, and he simply stayed aboard.

The sarge, very soon, as soon as they got him to the point he could be moved without killing him, would be taken to Japan. If James wanted to visit him, he'd better do it now. This according to Black Man. According to Black Man the sarge was seriously hurt, hurt permanently. Something big and possibly from their own side had hit him from close range, hit him square in the belly, above his pelvis, and Black Man had promised James he wouldn't like what he'd see.

From a vendor on Thi Sach Street James bought a stick of chewing gum and a fake Marlboro cigarette. His second tour had entered its third day. He was sober, AWOL, and virtually broke.

James's two friends Fisher and Evans had shipped out the day before. Tall, chip-toothed Fisher had shaken James's hand and said, "Remember our first night here?"

"The Floor Show."

"Remember the Floor Show?"

"I sure do."

"Remember that first time getting laid at the Purple Bar?"

"I sure do."

"When the world ends, and Jesus comes down in a cloud of glory and all that shit, it'll be the second most incredible thing that ever happened to me. Because I will remember that night at the Purple Bar."

They embraced one another, and James put all his concentration into damming back the tears. They all swore to meet again. James assumed they never would.

In the Cozy Bar on Thi Sach James bummed another cigarette from an airman who revealed he was a Cherokee Indian and the descendant of chiefs and who refused James a second cigarette and seemed on the brink of ditching him until James, finally taking the stool beside him, rearranged the gun under his shirt, at which point the airman said, "What's that there?"

"It's for tunnels."

"For tunnels?"

"Thirty-eight automatic. Got me a suppressor back at camp."

"Do you mean like a silencer?"

"Yep. Christ almighty—what smells like gasoline in here?"

"I pump jet fuel all day long."

"Is it you?"

"I don't smell it no more myself."

"Whoo. You're making me dizzy. Buy me a beer, would you, please?"

"No can do. You know, there's a jeweler right on Thi Sach. I sold him a forty-five this morning."

"He buys weapons?"

"I sold him a forty-five."

"You think he'd like a thirty-eight?"

"I bet he would."

"I bet I know where he can get one."

That afternoon, drunk, AWOL, flush with Vietnamese piasters on the smelly street—odor after odor and the hiss of frying gunk—James stopped at a shop and bought himself some imitation Levi's denims and a red T-shirt and a shiny yellow tour jacket illustrated with a naked woman that said "Saigon 1968." It was far too hot for such a jacket, but he wore it anyway because it put him in an excellent mood. He bought two packs of real U.S. Marlboros and got a haircut from a street barber—he'd never had his hair cut anywhere but at the big base, but he was drunk enough to try something different—and afterward purchased a pair of flimsy blue-black loafers. He changed in the street while people very carefully didn't look at him, and carried his fatigues in a brown paper shopping bag with string handles.

He thought he'd better get sober before he went to see the sarge, and before he got sober he'd better get drunker. Around eleven that night he bartered with a cyclo driver to get him to a cheap hotel in the Cho Lon District, but somewhere en route they revolutionized the plan and instead traveled in the unsafe hours of darkness nearly sixty miles to the shores of the China Sea and to a whorehouse James had heard of called Frenchie's, a place with its own legend. At two in the morning they reached it, a scattering of shacks near a fishing village. He woke up a papasan napping on the bartop in the café who understood a little English and could guess the rest, and who, when James asked, "Are you Frenchie?" said, "Frenchie coming," but Frenchie didn't come. No exterior lights. He heard no generator. Saw no girls anywhere. No other GIs. Nor anyone else at all. The melancholy old papasan led him by flashlight to a bungalow no better than a hooch in a row of several just like it. Somebody else's pubic hairs dotted his bedding. He stripped off the sheet. The thin mattress was stained, but the stains looked less recent than the pubic hair. For this room, including a battery-powered bedside fan, he was paying about a dollar a night. He didn't bother letting the net down. He didn't see any mosquitoes.

In the glow of a kerosene lantern he found his clasp knife and

almost cut away the legs of his fatigues; but thought better of it and
shortened his fake Levi's instead. By the time he turned in, his
drunk had become a hangover.

He rose around noon and went to the sand-speckled café,
where a woman served him an omelet, hot tea, and a small
baguette. Then he told her to bring him the same thing all over
again, only with a beer, no tea.

He wasn't the only customer. A one-legged GI in cutoff jeans
and rip-sleeved fatigue shirt, a towhead with sunburned flesh and
aviator sunglasses, sat a couple tables away drinking beer and eating nothing, most of the time holding a nine-millimeter pistol
with his thumb on the ejector button, dropping the butt of the clip
into the palm of his hand and slapping it back in, ejecting it, slapping it back in.

"We all die," he said. "I'll die high."

James didn't like this at all and got up and left.

He headed for the low seawall and the rumbling shore. The
beach was narrow and the sand was brown. He sat on the rock
wall and smoked a cigarette and watched a drowned rooster
rolling in the surf. This wasn't the Frenchie's everybody talked
about. Everybody said Frenchie sold only 33 beer—that much
seemed correct—and also Spanish Fly. Also girls—but they were
peasants—but they were girls. And everybody said there were
Old West–style gunfights out front almost every night. And said
the cyclo drivers never went near there after dark, or their little
machines would be commandeered for races up and down the
beach and usually out into the sea.

The noise of a single gunshot stopped his thoughts, and he ran
to the café to look at the disaster, but nothing had happened. The
towheaded boy sat alone there.

"HEY EVERYBODY," the boy cried, though nobody was
around. "This guy thinks he's figured out some shit!"

James stood in the entry and went no farther. He would have
liked a beer, but the lady had run off.

"You want to play 'Spin the Browning'?"

James said, "No."

"You better get your shit-proof Playtex pants on, señor."

James took the chair across from him and sat with his hands at his sides.

The boy stopped playing with the gun and scratched the puckered end of his stump with his fingers, then resumed ejecting the clip into his palm and slapping it back in. "Don't sit at my table if you don't want to play my game."

He'd obliterated the name on his name tape, apparently with the burning end of a cigarette. Instead of dog tags, from a string around his neck hung a rusty-pointed can opener.

He set the gun before him on the table next to a pack of Parliaments and a Zippo lighter.

"You like these things? Parliaments?"

"Not much," James said.

"More for me."

He tapped out a cigarette, put it between his lips, and fired it up, using only his right hand for these proceedings, resting the left on top of the gun.

James told him, "I can't watch this."

"Fine. This ain't the circus."

"How do I get a ride out of your insane asylum?"

"Just start humping down the road."

"I can't walk to Saigon."

The boy scratched his scalp with the gun's muzzle. "No, man, no. First motherfucker who sees you, he'll be right up your ass with his scooter. Or his cousin will." He kept the gun pointed at his scalp.

"Put that sucker down, would you?"

"We all die, man."

"Ain't you even got a name?"

"Cadwallader."

"What about just putting it down for a minute? Then I could have a beer with you."

"I told you my real name. Big mistake."

"Why is it a mistake?"

"People know your name," he said, "and it hurts."

"I realize you got tore up," James said. "It's the shits."

The towheaded boy closed his eyes and sat without a twitch, breathing through his nostrils. "Oh, man," he said after a long time, "all you zombies."

The buzz of a two-stroke engine approached and stopped outside. Cadwallader lowered the pistol to the tabletop. "The French have arrived."

In came a skinny man dressed in Scotch-plaid Bermuda shorts, zoris, and a long-sleeved shirt. A white man, blue-eyed and baldheaded. Pulled up a chair as if to sit, but hesitated, noticing the weapon.

"It's for you," he said, and set down a cardboard packet next to Cadwallader's hand.

Cadwallader dropped his cigarette and let it burn on the floor. He stripped a side away from the packet and spilled a dozen or so large tablets onto the tabletop. He plunked four down the spout of his 33 beer, and the mixture began to foam. He toasted James. "Time for a change."

James said, "Frenchie."

"C'est moi."

"You speak English?"

He shrugged disinterestedly.

"This motherfucker's fixing to do himself harm."

This time a complete body shrug—hands, shoulders, lifting himself on his toes—with a little grimace of the face.

"Why don't we get us a couple of girls?" James suggested.

Cadwallader watched the tabs fizz and dissolve in his beer. "You can't just paint everything with your mind to make it look like it makes sense."

"Don't pussy make sense no more?"

Frenchie swung his seat around, straddled it backward, and sat with his stringy legs sticking out and his forearms resting on the back of the chair.

Cadwallader floated his hand above his leg as if conjuring up the missing portion. "This is the only thing in the world I've ever seen that isn't bullshit."

"I hate to be the one telling you," James ventured to say, "but that shit ain't nothin'. There's guys with a whole lot worse been done to them."

"Here's the explanation, Frenchie. We all die, right? Fuck you." Cadwallader swirled his potion and drank it off in several pulls. He sat back and began cleaning under his fingernails with the pointed end of his church key. "Go ahead and go for that gun."

The old man didn't move. "Do you say I need a gun? Don't you know I'm French? Our war is lost."

"There's only one happy ending, man. If I don't blow this world away, then I'm a coward and a bullshitter."

"Catch you later." James got up slowly and with, he hoped, a harmless air.

"I didn't hurt nobody. So don't tell me about karma."

"I wasn't."

"Then don't."

"I don't even know what karma is."

"You're better off."

"I'm going somewheres. I'm going for a swim. So if you end up doing something, there won't be nobody here to care."

"Frenchie's here."

"Frenchie don't care," James said, and went back down the path to sit on the seawall.

In only a couple of minutes the towheaded boy came after him. Having jammed the index finger of each hand into the mouth of a 33, he was able to carry two dangling bottles while humping on crutches. He stopped. Hung on his struts like a scarecrow, flicking drops from the mouth of one of his beers, with his thumb, directly into James's face. "As the recipient of a Purple Heart I can fuck with you all I want, and it's tough shit."

"The fuck it is."

"You can't attack a pitiful cripple."

"The fuck I can't."

"Hold these 33s for me." He dropped the left crutch, and lowered himself down the other to sit on the sand before letting it fall.

James gave him back one beer and kept one.

"Peace and love, my fellow Americans."

"All right, then. Peace and love."

"I got all sideways."

"It ain't nothin'."

"Sorry 'bout that, I guess."

"Is your leg hurting you?"

"I can call you a dumb fuck for asking a dumb-fuck question, and you can't do shit, because I'm crippled. You want some pills?"

"Not just now I don't."

"There's thirty milligrams of codeine inside every one of these things."

"I tried pot a few times . . . Hell, I been drunker'n that."

"My invisible foot hurts."

"What area is this?"

"We're in Phan Thiet. Or Mui Ne."

"I never seen boats like that before."

"Those are dinghies. The real boats are out fishing."

"They look like bowls for soup."

"What are you? Absent without leave, missing in action, or deserter?"

"AWOL, some."

"I'm a deserter."

"I'm just AWOL. Anyways I think."

"Thirty days and it's desertion."

"I ain't up to thirty yet."

"My leg deserted. So I followed the example. Cut out from China Beach."

"Didn't you like it?"

"That smiley gung-ho physical therapy? Fuck no. I like to drink and cry and take pills."

"I don't need telling."

"Yeah. Sorry 'bout that, GI. I got seized up in a mood."

"So this is Phan Thiet, you think?"

"Yeah. Or Mui Ne."

"And this is really the worl' famous whorehouse? I heard this place jumped."

"It's been like this for the last two weeks. It don't jump since the big push. The enemy triumphed over Frenchie."

"Where'd everybody go?"

"Mostly people went back to their units, or somewhere else, I don't know. You're coming the other way."

"I guess I am."

"You bug out at the height of the action, boy, that's desertion."

"Why are you trying to convince me that I deserted?"

"I'm philosophizing, brother, not convincing. Hey, if they were shooting at me, I'd leave too—Wait! I already did!"

"I didn't desert for that."

"Then why?"

"I had to see a feller."

"Who is it?"

"A guy supposed to be at Hospital Number Twelve over there."

"So you cut out to go see him?—or you cut out so you don't have to?"

"Yeah, funny. What's your name again?"

"Cadwallader."

"Don't rag on me, Cadwallader. I got twice as many legs to kick with."

"What am I gonna call you?"

"James."

"Not Jim?"

"Never Jim."

They finished the beers and flung the bottles into the surf.

James went among the coconut palms down the beach, Cadwallader following with great, three-legged strides while James turned upright one of the odd round boats—giant baskets six or

seven feet across, of woven thatch and batten, coated with something like lacquer—and dragged it in heroic, lurching fits toward
the surf. Little naked children came around to view the struggle.
If there were any grown-up people in the hooches beyond the
palms, they didn't show themselves.

He stopped for breath, still many yards from the water.
"Where's your mighty weapon at?"

Cadwallader pulled up his shirtfront. The gun butt protruded
above his waistband.

"If you're riding with me, it's liable to get wet. 'Cause I'm liable
to sink us."

"Lift up that boat over there."

James raised the edge of another of the overturned boats, and
Cadwallader wrapped the gun and his cigarettes and lighter in his
shirt and tossed it under. James did the same with his Marlboros
and in one last explosion of effort got the craft out into the waves.

Up to his chest in the mild surf, Cadwallader laid his crutches
in the boat and clambered aboard. The craft had one paddle.
"Rock and roll!" cried Cadwallader while James nearly capsized
them. "If we get in the wrong current we'll never see land again.
Do you care?"

James tried paddling on alternate sides. He didn't know where
to stand, or whether to stand at all in this rocking hemisphere.
"This ain't working. How do they make these things go?"

"Gimme that paddle. I'm a sailor in my blood."

The children stood on the shore and watched the boat drift
away. Goats bleated in the coconut grove. Soon James heard nothing but the surf behind them. Beyond the shore the grove, beyond
the grove the hooches of thatch and straw ... They go up like
matchheads, he thought.

"We're lost at sea!" Cadwallader cried. "My head is *swimming*
from the *symbolism* of it."

"You remind me of my little brother."

"Why—what about him?"

"I can't put my finger right on it. You just do."

They floated around and the current took them away from Vietnam.

"Well, James, you gonna stay awhile?"

"Maybe. I don't know."

"I can talk to Frenchie about a discount."

"I got money. I don't need a discount."

"That's kind of a strange attitude."

"I'm just saying I don't need no favors."

"Where are you at in your tour?"

"A little ways into number two."

"You're just a mess of strange attitudes. I don't get why anybody would go around a second time on this hog."

"Ain't no reason for it," James admitted. "Are you short?"

"Not that short."

"How far along are you?"

"Eight months. Six months and eight days when they hurt me. Halfway and eight. It's fucked up."

"Just as fucked up to eat shit if you're the new guy."

"Yeah. It's always fucked up to eat shit. That's part of the plan."

Cadwallader rose storklike on his single leg, tipped sideways, and rolled into the water. James was entirely alone in the ocean until Cadwallader broke the surface, blowing and spitting.

"Hey, man."

"Hey what."

"Get back in the boat."

"What for?"

"At least stay there."

"I am. You're the one moving."

"I can't paddle this thing. Come on, I'm about to lose you."

"Yeah?"

"Cadwallader. Cadwallader."

"Adios, motherfucker!"

"It's a mile to shore."

Cadwallader floated on his back a hundred feet away.

"Cadwallader!"

James paddled hard but he didn't know how it was done. He could glimpse the boy now only when the low swells dipped. Cadwallader floated on his back, staring upward and kicking. "You're coming the right way!" James shouted, but Cadwallader didn't hear or didn't care. James believed one of them was making progress toward the other, and this inspired him. The paddle seemed to function better if he worked it back and forth like a fishtail out behind. The work exhausted him. Cadwallader came near and James grasped at his hand, but he fended him off. James clutched at his hair. Cadwallader yelped and took hold of the side. James didn't have strength to haul him aboard. He had no breath left even to swear at him. His chest heaved and the coppery taste of fatigue filled his mouth.

Cadwallader kicked away, turned over, and began swimming overhand toward shore. James paddled after. The current seemed to be with them now.

The teacup craft scraped bottom and the small surf pitched it around. James got out and dragged it to land.

Cadwallader lay flat on his back a hundred yards off. James trudged toward him, dragging a crutch by either hand and leaving two lines behind him in the sand. Meanwhile, the waves had reclaimed the boat. It bobbed in the foam and seemed to be heading out to sea.

"You're fucked up, man. You're all wrong inside."

"Obviously."

"I've had it, man."

"Gimme my sticks."

James flung each one as far from him as possible. "Get your own goddamn sticks."

He shuffled to where they'd stashed their gear and retrieved it and examined Cadwallader's gun, a Browning Hi-Power.

"Hey," he called. "This is officer's issue. Are you an officer?"

Cadwallader crawled bitterly across the sands like a cinematic Saharan castaway.

"Are you an officer?"

"I'm a civilian! I'm a fucking deserter!"

He dragged himself to James's feet. James ejected the Browning's magazine and yanked back the slide to clear the action of the last bullet and said, "Now you can play all you want."

"Fuck you. I got plenty of ammo."

"Enjoy it, then, and I'm taking the weapon."

"Gimme back my boom-boom."

"Never happen, or you're gonna kill yourself."

"You're stealing my gun."

"Looks like it."

"Fuck your cracker ass. That's my ticket to Paradise."

They both lit cigarettes off Cadwallader's Zippo, and James said:

"I gotta go."

He turned and walked off.

"Halt. That's an order. I'm a lieutenant, man."

"Not in my war," James said over his shoulder.

As he headed through the chink in the seawall he heard Lieutenant Cadwallader calling, "Kill me a Gook, man!"

James caught a ride in a Mutt with two men of the Twenty-fifth from downtown Saigon out to the big base. They dropped him right in front of the Twelfth Evacuation Hospital in its fog of rotor dust and he went inside without talking to anyone and was instantly lost amid all the wards with their sickly hush and medical stench. He'd had a lot of beer that morning and felt irritable and hollow. First they told him Ward C-3, then no, C-4, and the nurse for C-4 guessed Ward 5 or 6, and finally a nurse in 6 gave him a doughnut and said she cared for the expectants and some of the bad ones and brought him to a curtain around a space in a kind of alcove and said to him, "Jim? Do they call you Jim?" She didn't move the curtain.

"I go more by James."

She moved the partition aside a bit. "Sergeant Harmon?" the nurse said. "James is here. James from your unit."

The sarge was in no kind of shape. James stood beside the bed and said, "Hey, Sarge," and tried to work up something further, but failed. James wanted to say The guys are gonna drink without you around and say They were shooting the place up a while ago and say I was shooting the place up too. He was angry at somebody around here and possibly it was the sarge, who looked not very different from dead, certainly past provoking by news of undisciplined conduct. He looked like the Frankenstein monster laid out in pieces, wired up for the jolt that would wake him to a monster's confused and tortured finish. The sarge even had gleaming metal bolts like the Frankenstein monster's coming out the sides of his head—for what purpose? A sheet covered him up to where his navel would have been, if he'd had an abdomen instead of something that looked put together out of scraps from a slaughterhouse. A machine beside the bed made a regular hiss and thunk. Red numbers on a monitor's screen told his pulse: 73, 67, 70.

"What's that tube out of his mouth for?"

"James, the sarge isn't breathing entirely on his own yet."

The nurse moved a chair for him, and he sat beside the bed and took Sarge's hand. A bubble traveled up the drip in the sarge's wrist. "Sarge."

The sarge's very blue eyes, free-floating in their sockets, drifted toward James and stopped. Sarge made a ticking noise with his tongue against his palate.

"Do you see me?"

The sarge clicked his tongue again, *tsk tsk*, as if he were scolding a kid, *tsk tsk*. The lips white and cracked, flaking.

James leaned close and looked down into the sarge's eyes. Eyelashes shellacked together by tears, radiating out in a burst, as in a child's drawing. Beautiful blue eyes. If they were a woman's you couldn't stop looking at them.

"What's that sound he's making?" he asked, but the nurse had gone. "What are you trying to say, Sarge?" He wiped his own tears and sucked and spat in the brown waste can full of swabs and slimy tissue papers. "I just came by," James said. "Just to say hi. See if you need anything. Shit like that."

Every few seconds, that ticking sound. Was it Morse code? "Sarge, I forgot my Morse code," he said.

Two nurses came in and moved James aside and drew the tube from between Sarge's lips and stuck another tube deep down his throat. The tube made a scouring and sucking noise and the numbers on the monitor rose rapidly—121, 130, 145, 162, 184, 203. After a minute they replaced the tube and the sarge was able to breathe again and the numbers descended slowly.

"Goddamn," James said.

"We're keeping his lungs clean," one of the nurses said.

"You didn't even say hello," James said.

"Hello, Sarge," the nurse said, and they departed and James sat down again and took the sarge's hand.

The sarge's eyes floated there burning and pleading. Everything coming out of his eyes. James wept like a barking dog. The reality and the rightness pouring off him, the purity of weeping, just crying, and who gives a shit—this is bigger than any of your games. The tears ran backward from the sarge's eyes over his temples and into his ears, but he made no sound other than by clicking his tongue.

"This is James, Doctor," the nurse said. She'd come back with a happy-looking medical man. "James is from Sergeant Harmon's unit."

"How we doing today, Sergeant?"

"What happened?" James said.

"What do you mean?"

"What happened? What happened? How'd he get hurt?"

The doctor said, "What happened to you, Sarge?"

The sarge moved his flaking lips and clicked his tongue.

"He makes that noise," James said. "Can you hear it?"

"What happened to you, Sarge? Do you remember? We talked about it yesterday?"

The sarge timed the movement of his lips with his machine's

exhalations, and he said, "I—I—" or moved his lips so it looked like that's what he said.

"Remember what we talked about? We said you might've got hit with a flare? Hit in the back?"

"I thought he got hit in the middle, the belly, I thought—"

"The flare entered below the solar plexus and headed up the spine, as far as we can tell. Laid him open all up his backbone."

"He got hit with a flare?"

"Correct."

"You mean a flare. A signal flare."

"Correct. Lotta damage. Muscle, lung, spine. Spinal cord all the way up to the second vertebra. Lotta damage, huh, Sarge?"

Moving his lips. Trying to produce sounds with the saliva in his throat, trying to shape a statement. As far as James could make it out, the message was, "I'm a mess."

The lines for the phones ran ten deep, but there were three other phones just for the use of officers at the Officers' Club, and he went there. After he'd dialed for the operator he kept his right hand on the butt of his new pistol and locked eyes with anyone who got near. He had all three phones to himself.

He gave the operator Stevie's number, an unforgettable series of digits, he'd dialed it hundreds of times thousands of years ago, in high school.

Her mom answered—"Hello?"—sleepy and maybe frightened. He hung up.

A captain brought him a Budweiser. These guys weren't so bad. He took his hand off his gun and lit a smoke, and then called home.

"What time is it there?" his mother said.

"I don't know. In the afternoon."

"James, what did you decide? On the business of staying on? What did you decide about it?"

"I put a little extension on my visit here."

"Why would you want to stay on? Don't you realize you've done your service to your country? As much as anybody ever *has*."

"Yeah . . . It felt like it wasn't over yet."

"Don't you dare sign away for no more of it after this one."

"I been shirking my duties. They might not even want me no more."

"Well, I wouldn't be surprised. You're probably shell-shocked."

"Suppose they cut me loose—maybe I could come to Phoenix."

"Well, yes, yes, hon. Where else would you think of to go to?"

"I don't know. Some island maybe."

"What do you mean, a island? We don't live on a island."

"How's everybody? How's Burris?"

"Burris takes drugs!"

"Jesus."

"Don't swear!"

"Jeez. Jeez. What kind of drugs?"

"Whatever kind he gets his hands on."

"How old is he?"

"He's not even twelve!"

"What a little punk. Well—well—what do you hear from Bill Junior? Anything?"

"Bill Junior was away almost a month."

"Away where?"

"Away. Away. Away is all."

James paused to take the last drag and put out his cigarette. "You mean jail?"

"One on drugs, and another off to jail!"

"What for?"

"I don't know. Some of this and some of that. He got in jail one week after New Year's Day and didn't get loose till February tenth. They had him for three weeks. He had to plead guilty and get two years' suspended sentence or they'd-a kept him and kept him. These folks are tired of the misbehavior."

"Is he in Arizona?"

"Yep. Suspended sentence. If he strays in his behavior they'll put him in Florence with your Dad. Like father, like son."

"Ain't that sweet."

"Don't be smart about it. The Holy Spirit's been battering away at the souls of the men in this family for generations. But do you think he's ever made so much as a dent?"

"Yeah—you know what? Maybe the Holy Spirit ain't so holy."

"What on earth do you mean?"

"You been to Oklahoma, ain't you, and Arizona. And that's all."

"What do you mean by saying that?"

"I don't know. Just you need to get around a little more, before you start talking about the Holy Spirit."

"James, do you go to church?"

"No."

"James, do you pray?"

"To who?"

His mother began to weep.

"Woman, let me tell you about the Holy Spirit. He's crazy."

"James," she said.

He really felt nothing, neither sorrow nor satisfaction, but he said to her, "Mom, okay, sorry 'bout that. I'm sorry."

"Will you pray? Will you pray with me now, son?"

"Go ahead."

"Dear Lord, dear Redeemer, dear Father in Heaven," she said, and he removed the receiver from his ear thinking if the Holy Spirit ever came to South Vietnam, he'd probably get his balls shot off.

Over at the bar he saw men drinking whiskey from glasses with ice. An officer in fatigues stared down at his fingers while they shredded his cocktail napkin.

At this moment he thought suddenly of Sergeant Harmon:

Oh, my Lord. He wanted water.

"Son," his mother said, "are you still there?"

The dry, cracked lips—thirsty, parched. Signaling with his tongue.

"Thanks for the prayer, Ma," he said, and hung up the phone.

He tipped his beer and drank it away and sucked out every last drop. It was the best he'd ever tasted. The worst and the best.

James dreamed he couldn't find his car. The parking lot changed into a village of narrow curving streets. He didn't want to ask for help, because he carried his M16, and these people might arrest him. Time was running out. That's what he remembered when he woke on the mat in his saturated civvies, though the dream had held a million peripherals, avenues of twisted events and unspoken complications. He dreamed a great deal each night. It felt like work. Sleeping made him tired.

He got up to start the air conditioner, but there wasn't one. A jukebox downstairs thumped under his feet. A mosquito net hung from nails over the open window. He'd thought it was day, but it was only the yellow bulbs of a sign outside. He found his blue-black loafers and went down the stairs on the side of the building for a beer. This was a cul-de-sac, unpaved, and he had to watch the mud. The Bar Jolly Blue. He sat with some guys, also from the Twenty-fifth, also Recon, but bad boys, Lurps. They gave him some speed and he woke right up. There weren't any women with them. Their eyes shone like animals'. These guys took acid, things that kinked up their nerves, turned their brains inside out. "Come with us. We just go. We run the night. We take speed. We fuck. We kill. We destroy." He wanted to make things happen but he couldn't. He realized he would just have to go with these guys, go LRRP, transfer over. And his eyes would be transformed like theirs. He said, Do you know Black Man? "Yeah," they said, "we know Black Man, he runs with us." He can show me how to transfer, James said. "Then do it, do it, haven't you done everything else but this?" Yeah, sure, he said, it's time to get it on with the monsters.

"You got some time to go?"

"I'm in my second tour."

"They give you home leave?"

"I don't want home leave."

"Don't you want to see home?"

"This war is my home."

"Good. Go home you end up playing Solitary till you wear the faces off. Deck after deck. Sitting in the window doing it."

"Ninety-nine percent of the shit that goes through my head on a daily basis is against the law," one said. "But not here. Here the shit in my head *is* the law and nothing *but* the law."

"They got theories of war, man. Theories. We can't have that. Can't have that here. We got a mission. Ain't no war. *Mission.*"

"Moving and killing, right?"

"You got it. This motherfucker has got it."

"Fucking A."

"So keep it."

"You know what a double veteran is? You fuck a woman and then you X her."

"Everybody here is double veterans."

"Yeah?"

"Here's to every dead motherfucker."

They left, and he drank his beer and watched a go-go girl with bruises on her legs. Couple of mosquitoes bumping stupidly along the wall beside his head. Otherwise he had the moment to himself. The music pounded, country stuff, psychedelic stuff, the Rolling Stones. On the bar, and behind the bar—the slow humping dance of a lava lamp, a scintillating waterfall in a Hamm's Beer sign, a kaleidoscopic clock face broadcasting the minutes, the little lit shrines to the religion.

I can't figure out is it too real, or not real enough, said James to someone . . . or someone to James . . .

Then in comes the colonel, the civilian, the good-as-CO of Company D, the more or less stepdad of Echo Recon.

He filled the doorway, shirt open, breathing convulsively.

Arms flung around two small whores who smiled showing gold bridgework. He didn't look at all squared away. "Help me, sojer."

"Sit him over here."

They helped him into the mashed seat of the only booth—everything else was tables. He signaled for a drink. Insofar as the somber light allowed, his face looked purple and then very pale. One of-the girls squeezed in beside him and opened his shirt wider and wiped at his pale sweaty chest, covered with silvery hair.

"I'm in a coronary medical situation."

"Should I get some help?"

"Sit down, sit down. I'm having a medical situation but mostly I'm overheated and poisoned by this goddamn rice brandy. You ask for Bushmills, they hand you Coke full of rice brandy. That concoction ain't for drinking. It'll sure kill warts, though."

"Yes, sir."

"I'm old army air force, but I respect the infantry."

"I know you, sir. I'm with Echo Recon."

"It's honorable to be a foot soldier."

"I gotta believe you."

"If you ever get a wart, nick it with a razor and soak it ten minutes in rice brandy."

"Yes, sir, I will."

"Yes, indeed. Echo. Sure thing. You're my tunnel man since I lost the Kootchy Kooties."

"Well, I went down in a couple tunnels is all, seems like. Three tunnels."

"That counts. Three's a good number."

"It ain't much."

"Jesus, you're the biggest tunnel man I've ever seen."

"I ain't that big."

"For tunnels you are."

"Sir, do you know about Sergeant Harmon?"

"He's been hurt, I understand."

"Yes, sir, paralyzed clear up to his neck."

"Paralyzed? Jesus God."

"Clear up to his neck. He's tore up from the floor up."

"It's a goddamn shame."

"I'm going to shift over to the Lurps. I mean to hurt these bastards."

"There's no shame in hating, son, not in a war."

"I ain't your son."

"Forgive the presumption."

"I'm drinking too hard tonight."

"I feel for your loss. The sergeant's a fine man."

"Where'd the Kooties get to, sir?"

"I'm denied the use of them. A couple rotated out. The whole LZ is gonna go. No more Kooties. No more chopper."

"I thought so. I wasn't seeing you awhile."

"It's all collapsing. At home and abroad. At home I believe my wife and my little girl are banging the same mulatto activist beatnik peacenik."

"I'd just as soon hang around this mess."

"I'm sorry. I'm drunk and sick and embarrassing.—I was saying . . . hatred. Yessiree. It's love of country that sends us forth, but sooner or later vengeance is the core motive."

James assumed the colonel knew his subject. Here was a fat-ass civilian discussing warts, and here also a living legend—a life of blood and war and pussy.

"Did you go to tunnel school?"

"No."

"You want us to send you?"

"I want Lurp training."

"How long have you been around?"

"I'm one month into my second tour. Into number two."

"If you take the training, they'll probably want you for a third tour."

"That's fine. And can you fix this AWOL thing?"

"AWOL?"

"I'm three weeks missing, is the truth of it."

"You go back to your platoon tomorrow, first thing."

"Yes, sir."

"Get cleaned up and go back."

"First thing tomorrow. Yes, sir."

"We'll fix it and put you on the LRRP training."

The summer rains had held off. But today it rained.

Skip walked several kilometers alone from a village he'd visited with Père Patrice. Not quite 10:00 a.m. now by his air force wrist watch, a gift from the colonel in his boyhood . . . Martin Luther King had been killed. Robert Kennedy had been killed. The North Koreans still held hostage an American naval vessel and her crew. The Marines besieged at Khe Sanh, the infantry slaughtering the whole village of My Lai, hirsute, self-righteous idiots marching in the streets of Chicago. Among the hairy ones the bloody failure of January's Tet Offensive had resounded as a spiritual victory. And then in May a second countrywide push, feebler, but nearly as resonant. He devoured *Time* and *Newsweek* and found it all written down there, yet these events seemed improbable, fictitious. In six or seven months the homeland from which he was exiled had sunk in the ocean of its future history. Clements, Kansas, remained as it had been, of that he could be confident; to Clements, Kansas, only one summer could come, with its noisy locusts and blackbirds, and the drifting fragrances of baking and soap suds and mown alfalfa, and the brilliant actuality of childhood. Gone, stupidly gone—not the summer, but himself. Departed, exposed, transfigured. Overridden and converted, if it came to that. He loved and fought for a memory. The world inheriting this memory had a right, he couldn't help seeing, to make its way unbeholden to assassinated ideals. Meanwhile, the air around him glittered with an invasion of delicate insects. Closer to the ground the population thickened—ducks and chickens, children, dogs, cats, tiny potbellied pigs. He'd ridden out on the back of the priest's motor scooter after stories and sayings among the scattered parishioners. He'd collected a single tale from an old woman, a Catholic, a friend of the priest. Père Patrice had continued west while Skip headed home on foot.

A half hour along the rain caught him and he sheltered under the awning of a tiny store whose leather-faced papasan smoked a cigarette with exquisite languor and had nothing to say. When Skip smiled at him the old man's face broke open in an exalted smile quite full of healthy-looking teeth. The storm was a harmless roaring downpour interrupted, however, by startling gusts that tore at the vegetation and furrowed the large puddles in the roadway. Skip bought a "Number One" soft drink in one of its several unidentifiable flavors and drank it rapidly. He addressed the old man in English: "Do you know what I think? I think maybe I think too much." The rain stopped. Across the road in front of a small house a young woman played peekaboo with a child just walking, who lurched on tiptoes while a slightly older sister danced a solitary improvisation, with sweeping, parallel gestures of her arms, all three of them smiling as if the world went no farther than their happiness.

That morning he'd been very moved by the tale he'd learned, which began: Once upon a time there was a war; a soldier left his wife and baby son behind and went off in defense of the country. The young wife looked after their house and their garden and their child. Each evening at sunset she stood by the river behind their home and looked for her beloved husband to come sailing on it back into their lives . . .

One night a storm burst over their little home and snatched at the roof and battered the walls. It blew out the lamp, and the little boy wept in terror. The mother held him close and relit the lantern. As she did so, her shadow leapt up on the wall by the doorway, and she comforted her son by pointing at it and saying, "We have nothing to fear tonight—see? Daddy stands by the door." Immediately the child was comforted by the shadow. Every evening after that, when she came back into the house after standing by the river and longing for her husband to return out of the last rays of the sun, her little boy called for his daddy, and she lit the lamp, and every evening he bowed to the shadow on the wall and said, "Goodnight, Daddy!" and slept in peace.

When the soldier returned to his little family, his wife's heart nearly burst with joy, and she wept. "We must give thanks to our ancestors," she said to him. "Please prepare the altar and look after your son," she said, "while I get food for a thanksgiving meal."

Alone with his child, the man said, "Come to me, I am your father." But the child said, "Daddy's not here now. Every night I say goodnight to Daddy. You're not Daddy." As he heard these words, the soldier's love perished in his heart.

When his wife returned from the market, she felt a cloud of death in their home. Her husband refused to give her even a word. He folded up the prayer mat and refused her the use of it. He knelt in silence before the meal she prepared, and when the food was cold and no longer worth eating, he walked from the house.

His wife waited many days for his return, standing by the river as she'd done when he was a soldier. One day her despair overcame her, and she took her child to a neighbor's house, kissed and embraced him one last time, and ran to the river and drowned herself.

Word of her death reached her husband in a village down the river. The shock broke the ice in his heart. He returned home to look after his son. One evening, as he sat beside his son's pallet and lit the oil lamp, his shadow leapt up on the wall beside the door. His son clapped his small hands together, bowed to the shadow, and said, "Goodnight, Daddy!" At once he realized what he'd done. That night as his child slept he built an altar by the river and knelt by it for hours, making it known to his ancestors how deeply he regretted his failure. Just before dawn he took his sleeping son to the riverside, and together they followed his faithful wife into the waters of death.

The old woman had relayed the tale without any expression or detectable interest. It gripped his heart. The child and the mother alone in their life. The man and the woman who misunderstood

one another, the shadow who was a father. The river that washed
away their histories.

He entered a valley with a wide flat creek running down its
middle, and this time was caught in the downpour. He walked
through it under a black umbrella. The creek foamed under the
battering rain. Afterward it rolled along swiftly, brown and muscular, with scummy whorls. He came again onto the level ground,
carpeted with paddies, that predominated the landscape around
Cao Quyen.

He passed the dwellings, not peasant hooches but small homes
with gardens out front, and behind them the rectilinear tomb-
stones over the family graves with their half hoods, like large stone
bassinets. Here and there along the road ahead people had set fire
to small wet neighborhood trash piles that sent up a smoke dis-
orientingly reminiscent of the autumnal perfumes of his childhood.

The old woman had added a coda to the tale: After the tragic
deaths, the sky rained among the mountains. The river that had
drowned the family swelled, its waters grew angry, even the biggest
stones in it wobbled from side to side, and the noise of its outrage
never again abated. Even in the dry months, when its water moves
along calmly, the river still roars. A bit of sand scooped from it and
held in the hand makes a loud noise. Drop the sand in a pot and
fill the pot with water; in a minute it boils.

When he got back to the villa the black Chevy sat out front, and
his uncle lay inside on the divan in the living room, while beside
him, on the floor, lay a dog who'd been around the place lately.
The colonel lifted his hand from the dog's head and waved at Skip
and said, "I'm being digested by your couch." Skip helped him sit
upright. "By these pillows." He appeared flushed, and yet, beneath
that, pale. "Your silken pillows."

Nguyen Hao occupied a rattan chair beside the low black lacquer coffee table. Sitting right there but managing to seem much
farther away, he said nothing, only nodded and smiled.

"What time is it?" the colonel asked.

"Almost one. Are you hungry? And welcome, incidentally."

He'd been told to expect the colonel sometime after the rainy season, and that was all. Been told in fact by the colonel.

"I ordered coffee," the colonel said.

The dog attacked its privates with a volcanic, ecstatic grunt-music.

"Got yourself a dog."

"It's Mr. Tho's. I think we might eat it."

The toilet flushed in the downstairs bath. Jimmy Storm came out in clean fatigues. Adjusting the hem of his shirt, he stared at the masturbating animal. "I think your dog's in love."

"My dog? I thought he was your dog."

Storm laughed and sat on the couch and said, "You're a fool-hardy moocher of a mutt." He scratched the dog's head and then smelled his fingers.

"Why didn't you take the chopper?" The sight of Jimmy Storm made him speak brusquely.

"The chopper's no longer mine."

"Oh. Whose is it, then?"

"It still belongs to our allies, but they've put it to better use. And we're breaking down the LZ—that's official now."

"I thought all this was happening months ago."

"The gods move slow, but they never stop moving. No more Cao Phuc, as of this September first."

"I'm sorry."

"Fortunes of war," the colonel said. "In any event, I wouldn't have taken the chopper today. This is an unofficial visit. Just family."

"Tho can bring you a beer. Or what about a drink?"

"He's making coffee. Let's talk with our heads clear. I'd like to conduct some business."

"Well, okay. I'm not here for the free doughnuts." It was something his mother sometimes said, and it sounded silly to him.

"Have you thoroughly reread the Dimmer article?"

"On double agents. Yes, sir."

Storm said, "Jesus Christ."

"What."

"I read that thing."

"What."

"Nothing what. It's not applicable."

"Sergeant."

"Colonel, if you want to assassinate the Virgin Mary with Oswald's Mannlicher, I'll spot for you."

"You're saying we're not within the guidelines."

"Yeah. Adapt and improvise."

"Skip? What say?"

"I'll drive the getaway car."

"We're not shooting the Blessed Virgin."

"Should I wait to be told? Or should I ask?"

"We're here to discuss a hypothetical."

"Not an assassination."

"No. God, no."

"Along the lines of a deception operation?"

"So you remember our previous chat about this kind of thing. Our hypothetical chat."

"You talked about a double. A hypothetical double."

Mr. Tho came in with a tray of cups and two pots and poured coffee for the Americans and tea for Nguyen Hao. As he departed he herded the dog from the room with the side of his foot.

The colonel worried his coffee with the spoon. "What is this stuff?"

"Creamer? That's powdered creamer."

"Powdered cream?"

"No—'creamer.'"

"Lord, it doesn't dissolve. What is it made of? Clay?"

"Hao brought it. I assume Mrs. Diu asked for it."

"Jesus Christ. It tastes like somebody's armpit."

"Seems like it's been around for years," Storm said. "It kind of snuck up on civilization."

"Engineers could build a substantial dam out of this stuff.

They could hold back mighty waters. Now. As to our ruse de guerre. The operation."

"The double. The hypothetical double."

"His status has shifted."

"How much can you tell me?"

"He's a walk-in. He had his toe in and out for quite a while. But when Tet came, he dove headfirst. He's ours. If we use him, we use him long-range and short-run. So we can keep this a family op. Are you needing some information?"

"Family op. The family is . . ."

"Just the three of us here, and Hao's nephew Minh, my helicopter pilot. Lucky. You've met him. Lucky, and the three of us."

Storm said, "And Pitchfork."

"And Pitchfork, if we need him. Pitchfork's in-country."

"I thought the Brits were out of this."

"They've got a couple of SAS teams here in New Zealand uniforms. And a few specialists wearing Green Berets. So Anders is here. He was SAS for years."

"Now, 'long-run but short-range'—what does that mean?"

"Long-range, I said, but short-run. We'll send him back north for a onetime op, delivering some deception material. This is the operation I brought you out for, Skip. Operation Tree of Smoke."

The colonel waited for Skip to adjust to this news.

Skip experienced no excitement. Only the lethargy and sadness of a man freezing to death. "How far outside the guidelines are we?"

"Guidelines don't apply to hypotheticals. We're brainstorming."

"Then you don't mind if I play the role of Dimmer a little?"

"Go ahead. We need a Devil's advocate."

"I think in this case, the Devil is you."

Storm said, "Skipper's on the side of the angels."

"He's asking the hard questions. Somebody has to. Go ahead. What would Dimmer say?"

"I can tell you exactly what questions he'd ask. Or anyway the important ones—the ones that leap out at me."

"For instance."

"Can you control his commo both ways?"

"No. We won't even try. This is a onetime, one-way operation. He can blow this particular op and nothing else. We give him nothing else."

"And if he blows it? If he's a fake?"

The colonel shrugged. "Nothing ventured. Next question."

"Has he told you everything? Or at least enough to start testing him by polygraph? How's your information?"

"Nebulous at this point. We're still in the process of initial assessment. You'll be the IO on this one."

"Me?"

"You're not here for jollies. You're the interviewing officer."

Skip took a deep, involuntary breath and let it out. "So."

"So—next question."

"I guess this one's already been answered: How far along is the process? Has he been polygraphed? But we'll do that later."

"I don't want polygraphs. I don't trust those things."

"Dimmer says to test continually. 'Polygraph early and often.'"

"No polygraph. There's only one way to vet a man, and that's with blood. He's given us the blood of his comrades. That's better than any machine can tell us."

"Why not both?"

"Only blood will tell. He needs to feel we trust him. And do you trust me? Can you go with my judgment on this?"

"Yes, sir. No polygraph."

"Thank you, Skip. It means a lot." The colonel wiped his upper lip with a finger. By a kind of inner wilting, and a sinking of the sun in his expression, he managed to convey that trust in his judgment was at a premium. "What else?"

"The jackpot question."

"Shoot, sir."

"Have you reported the case?"

The colonel shrugged.

"Let me get the article." Skip rose to his feet.

"Up jumped the Devil," Storm said.

Though it was classified, he kept it on the desk. "He's got a list of do's and don't's," he said when he returned. "Number Ten."

"Don't stand, please."

Skip resumed his seat. "Number Ten: 'Do not plan a deception operation or pass deception material without prior headquarters approval.'"

"This is what I'm talking about," Storm said. "But what the fuck."

"Twenty: 'Report the case frequently, quickly, and in detail . . .' Let's see here. All right, the Devil speaks loud and clear: 'The service and officer considering a double agent possibility must weigh net national advantage thoughtfully, never forgetting that a double agent is, in effect, a condoned channel of communication with the enemy.' What we're discussing amounts to an unauthorized liaison."

"I like 'self-authorized.'"

"A self-authorized liaison with the enemy."

The colonel said, "Hao, will you get me some real milk somewhere on earth, please?"

Hao left the room.

The colonel sat up straight, hands on his knees. "Nobody in this room has ever met the hypothetical fella. No liaison as of yet, as such."

"Colonel, sir, as long as it's just us for a minute."

"Right. Go ahead."

"I understand it's a family op and all that. But should we necessarily be talking in front of Hao?"

"Hao? At this point Hao knows more than we do. He brought our man in. He was the initial contact."

"What do we really know about him?"

"Really? What do we really know about anybody in this hall of mirrors?"

"Really nothing."

"Ten-four. Here's a rule of thumb: trust the locals. Have I ever told you that?"

"Plenty."

"You can't trust everyone in this country, but we've got to trust somebody. We go by our guts. And I can tell you this," he said, as Hao returned with a small pitcher, "I just asked for milk and here it is. And that's how everything always works with Mr. Hao." Hao sat down and the colonel said, "Mr. Hao, we're planning a self-authorized national deception operation. Are you with us?"

"'Zeckly," Hao said.

"Good enough?" the colonel asked Skip.

"Plenty good."

"More questions?"

"That's the lot," Skip said.

"Fine." The colonel took from his breast pocket a half dozen three-by-five note cards of the kind Skip had handled all too often, and began a presentation. "It's out of the bag: a national deception operation. But it can't be any kind of op unless it comes with a plan. Let's move to that phase of the hypothetical. How do we get bogus product credibly into the hands of the enemy? Specifically into Uncle Ho's hands? Through a plant who allows himself to be captured and tortured? Through a double who 'steals' phony documents? An almost impossible task, but a combination of those two would be nearly ideal. Coming from separate sources, its credibility would be enhanced."

"Is all that written on those little cards?" Storm asked.

"Jimmy," the colonel said, "you make me tired."

"All this is hypothetical," Skip felt it necessary to be assured.

"Yes, yes, nothing's figured out. We don't know what we're doing yet. Thus the coming debriefing. And you're the debriefer. The man's name is Trung. You have some Vietnamese. He has some English. You both have some French. Right, Hao—he's got some English?"

Hao spoke his first complete sentence since entering: "No, Colonel, excuse me. He doesn't speak English. None."

"Well, fine. That's why Skip spent a year in Carmel."

"We'll work it out," Skip promised.

"I know you will. Mr. Tho!" the colonel called.

Tho appeared with a dishtowel in his hand. He was probably in his sixties but seemed physically no more than middle-aged—although philosophically seasoned, imperturbable—and he smiled radiantly because the colonel smiled at him first.

"Mr. Tho—break out the Bushmills."

They all took Bushmills mixed with water. Even Hao accepted one and held the glass with both hands without drinking from it. The potion banished the colonel's paleness, and halfway down his highball he seemed rescued from any symptoms of his illness. And clearly he was ill.

Without any bitterness that he could, himself, detect, Skip said, "Do you wonder what I've been doing?"

"The same as all of us—waiting while a viable strategy emerges. Meanwhile, what are you doing to keep busy?"

"Nothing. I'm wasted here. I'm a pogue."

Storm said, "That's jarhead terminology."

"It applies."

"Up until this stage we're entering," the colonel said, "the candidate has to set the pace. And look—the most convincing thing about him is all this delay and this reluctance. It says to me he appreciates what a step this is. And he's honest with us about being doubtful."

Hao spoke: "Yes. He is honest. I know him."

"But now he's committed," Skip said.

"He's come over. That's right. That's the situation," the colonel said. "Now he's ours and I want him here with you. I don't want him in Cao Phuc or in Saigon. I want him where he hasn't worked before."

"But what's the delay?"

"He can't just disappear. He's part of a cell. The cell is part of a network. He can't just go on vacation. He's offered credible reasons for relocating to this area, or he assures us he has, but it takes time. He says it takes time and I believe him."

"Meanwhile, I'm a pogue. Reading Dickens, as you know."

"And Ian Fleming. Sorry I couldn't get the Tolstoy."

"Anything big and fat, or full of suave secret agents."

"Have you read Shell Scott?"

"Sure. You mean the series. Richard S. Prather."

"What about Mickey Spillane?"

"Everything. A dozen times."

"Henry Miller?"

"Can you get Henry Miller?"

"He's legal now. He went to court. I'll get you Henry Miller."

"Get me *Tropic of Capricorn*. I've read *Tropic of Cancer*."

"I didn't like *Cancer*. Boring. *Capricorn*'s really good."

"Wow. I didn't know you stayed so current."

"They were written in the thirties, man. Mr. Tho!" he called. "Do I smell food?" He drained his glass. "Let's get out while lunch cooks. Let's take a drive."

"Or walk," Skip said. "There's a tunnel just down the road."

"You're kidding. Here?"

"We've got all the latest stuff, Uncle."

"Let's explore," the colonel said. "And don't forget the bottle."

The outing was a failure. They followed a zigzag course down the main road, walking around the puddles. "Don't talk to me about current events," the colonel said. "That's all I ask. Jesus Christ, another Kennedy. Can't somebody kill Uncle Ho? These folks mean business." He stopped as if to make his next point, but more likely to catch his breath. "You whack them down in January, they're back all bright and shiny next May, ready for more of our terrible abuse. Is that the tunnel?"

"What's left of it."

The colonel waited silently ten seconds before persevering

over the last twenty yards to stand before the tunnel, now an
eroded delve in a small bluff.

"Well, no, Skip, no. I don't think so. Have you seen the tunnels in Cu Chi? You haven't, have you?"—pronouncing it the
native way, so it came out *Goochy*.

"No, sir, I haven't."

"This isn't a tunnel, Skip. It looks more like the man's own
excavation. More like he was excavating a cavern or something—
but the geology doesn't seem the kind where you'd find caverns—
don't you need limestone for that?"

"A cavern?"

"Maybe there's a subterranean crevasse here. A crevasse in a
buried rock."

"Okay. Yeah. He was definitely fascinated by caverns. Possessed. I looked at his notes."

"Sure. But it's not a VC-type tunnel in the least. The VC tunnels aren't like this at all. The entrances go straight down. Makes it
harder to breach one." Skip couldn't tell if the colonel was disappointed in the tunnel alone, or also somewhat in his nephew.

They left the mystery behind and went back to see about
lunch, Skip dealing with his irritation—the tunnel wasn't a tunnel. Nor even, probably, a cavern. He felt jilted by the dead man.
Bouquet had let him down.

At the villa's low gate the colonel reached for Hao's elbow.
Clinging to the smaller man's arm, he stooped to pick up a tree
limb thrown down by the recent storm as if he'd grown interested,
suddenly, in jetsam, and leaned on it as a staff as he took the last
few steps to the entry.

Mrs. Diu had lunch ready. They went directly to the black lacquer dining table, where Tho officiated, Skip thought, with a certain air of accusation: in sixteen months, except for the priest, these
were his first guests to a meal. Local fare today, beef noodle soup
with mint leaves and bean sprouts. But American-style sliced bread
fresh from the oven, and butter too. And Bushmills throughout. No

chopsticks, not even for Hao. And no Bushmills for Hao. Dessert was a kind of pudding made from guava.

"To the Irish," the colonel suggested, having cracked a second fifth, or, Skip feared it possible, a third.

"The name Sands isn't Irish," Storm said.

"We don't speak of it," Skip admitted.

The colonel said, "We don't?"

"Well—I didn't think we did."

"We started out Shaughnesseys. All of a sudden on the boat over it was Sands."

"That's what Aunt Grace told me. All my life my mother treated it like some great mystery and scandal."

"No, it's just a source of amusement and minor shame. How's the news from your mom?"

"All good, I guess. I get letters from her. I send back postcards."

"Anyway, fellas, I wasn't toasting a whole nation. Just my old team—the Fighting Irish of Notre Dame. I'd say they're the majority of them Polish. At least we were when I was on the squad—look at Skip. Look at his face. He thinks the old man is about to start."

"Go ahead, Uncle. I'm drunk enough, if you are."

"Yes yes yes, I'm full of hot gas. You could raise a balloon with my reminiscences. Go ahead, change the subject."

"Your paper for the journal: I didn't understand your paper."

"I didn't either."

"This isn't exactly changing the subject—if the subject is hot air."

"I'm impervious to criticism."

"Lotta wild terms in there. 'Insulated activity.'"

"Insulated activity: showing initiative, i.e., taking the bull by the horns while the brass sits on its ass."

"And others."

"What others? I'm your glossary."

"I can't remember."

"Jargon is important. Consider the potential audience. These folks are all about mumbo-jumbo. Have you read 'Politics and the English Language'?"

"Um—George Orwell. Yeah."

"Have you?"

"Yes. And *1984.*"

"Well, 1984 is coming. And it won't take seventeen years to get here."

"Anyhow," Skip said.

"More like sixteen," Storm announced.

"Sixteen what?"

"Sixteen years till 1984."

"Wait a minute. Eighteen. Eighteen."

Storm laughed, waving a slice of bread around beside his crew-cut head.

"Men," the colonel said, "the enemy isn't doing this."

"Doing what?"

"Adding and subtracting, Sergeant."

"What's the enemy doing, Colonel?"

"They're cutting up our dud ordnance and blowing off our testicles with it. They're living in holes in the ground. They're not having pudding. They're eating their children in the name of victory. That's what they eat for lunch. So let's get with it. We've got one of them on our side now. He could whip half our infantry by himself. He's come in by every gate—you know the VC's 'three gates'? Blood, imprisonment, and time in the North, he's done all three. Hao can tell you—this guy's been fighting since the French. He was a prisoner on Con Dau. He went north and was reindoctrinated after the Partition. He came back down on Uncle Ho's trail and he's been doing his worst ever since. Couple years ago in Cao Phuc he tried to assassinate me."

"You're kidding."

"About a year after Kennedy died, so late '64, I'd say. Two and a half years ago. He admitted it to Hao."

He turned to Hao, who'd remained invisible despite his presence at the table, and Hao confirmed it. "He said to me, yes."

"Tossed a grenade into the temple when I was visiting. He's the real McCoy. Lousy Chinese grenade."

Skip felt his mouth hanging open as he regarded his uncle—drunk, obsolete—absolutely unkillable.

"Question is, with that kind of commitment, what's making him turn? What does he say, Mr. Hao?"

"I don't know," Hao said.

"That's the part I don't like. Don't like it at all."

"I don't know," Hao said.

"Listen, listen," Skip said, suddenly buoyant, "we've got to create the bogus thing, the fiction. Maybe I can help with that."

"That's what you came seven thousand miles for. Suppose this. Suppose in the embassy bombing last year some papers got loose in the wind. A transcript, say—minutes of a meeting of a few old pirates who think they've got a nuclear weapon they can divert. These horrible folks want to smuggle it into Hanoi and put a stop to the nonsense. What they see as nonsense. Which actually *is* nonsense."

"Wait," Skip said, "not a meeting actually about the, the—whatever you call it—the plot, not the plot itself. The meeting was about trying to *stop* the plot. These are not the plotters, in other words. They're the ones trying to investigate the plotters."

"I get you."

"I don't," said Jimmy Storm.

"The papers aren't the minutes of people actually conspiring," Skip said, his ears buzzing from the Bushmills, "not of the actual conspiracy, but of folks assessing the, the"—marshalling his powers—"the progress of the conspiracy. So there's this coded transcript—"

"Not in code. Just some torn fragments that survived the bombing. A few shreds—" The colonel's thoughts continued without speech.

Skip regretted getting back to this subject now. The colonel had been right to postpone drinks until they'd discussed it. Now they were discussing it again, and he, for one, didn't know what he was saying. But the colonel lifted another sip of whiskey to his lips, and it was over. "Give me giants!" he said. "I mean, for the love of—Johnny Brewster? He's spent the whole war in Washington batting a handball around and scheming how to break up the operation at Cao Phuc. And now it's broken up—September first, all over, no more. Fucker was OSS. He fought a war: he knows, or once upon a time he musta known—John Brewster must jolt upright in bed some nights and think, Wait a minute, wait a minute, wasn't this about something else? But before he can remember it's about the survival of freedom, and human salvation, and the light of the world—the pettiness and bullshit of his dreams drag his head back down to the pillow, and he's snoring away again. And next morning it's just about Langley. The war is in Langley, and it's between guys like him and guys like me, and it's all about the Agency. I knocked that sonofabitch on his ass. Goddamn these fuckers. What do guys like that think the United States of America is trying to do in Vietnam? Now, wait—and these fuckers in Langley, these fuckers at the Pentagon. These fuckers! They don't know. They just don't know."

He bowed his head.

"Colonel," Jimmy Storm said.

The colonel raised his head.

"Colonel."

"Yes."

"You fuck me up," Storm said.

"Is that a compliment?"

"Fuck yes."

"Get me out to the car," the colonel said.

Hao stood up. He took no initiative beyond that.

"Hey, guys, hey—why don't you stay the night?"

"No, Skip, no. Best be going back."

"Take me with you. Let me hang around Saigon. Just for the weekend."

"We can't have you in the city, Skip."

"Come on. I was there for Tet."

"I took pity. No more of that. You're a soldier."

"Hang around. Please. We can play some poker."

"You got cards?" Storm said.

"Yes. Yes. Stay."

"No. We've got to get back."

"I'm a pogue."

Storm said, "He thinks he's the lost beautiful child."

"Wow," Skip said, "it's the American Century."

Storm said, "Rock 'n' roll is here to stay."

Good and drunk, Skip Sands of the CIA stood and aimed himself at the stairwell. He felt steady enough to climb the stairs and find his room but too dizzy to lie down in it, and so sat in a chair with his feet resting on the wave-flung, heaving bed.

He woke from an hour's nap and went to the veranda to drink hot, strong coffee less reviving than his thrilling vertigo before the vista of his mistakes, all this wrongness he'd wandered into on the tails of his uncle, the aboriginal Man of Action. Neanderthal, had been Rick Voss's term. Mr. Tho came out with a burning mosquito coil in a dish and set it on the arm of the opposite chair, and there you are, simplicity itself, the ember of the foul-smelling incense, orange bead tunneling along its spiral path toward extinction and nonentity. He felt surrounded, assailed, inhabited by such serpentine imagery—the tunnels, Project Labyrinth, the curling catacombs of the human ear . . . But over all loomed the central and quite different image: the Tree of Smoke. Yes, his uncle meant to unfold himself like a dark wraith and take on the whole Intelligence Service, the very way of it, subvert its unturnable tides. Or assault it on the handball court.

For its nourishment, he'd asked for real milk in his coffee. It tasted pretty much like the chalky substitute. The new dog came between his knees and shoved its snout into his cup and went at it with a vocal, snarfing sound.

Uncle F.X., pillar of fire, tree of smoke, wanted to raise a great

tree in his own image, a mushroom cloud—if not a real one over
the rubble of Hanoi, then its dreaded possibility in the mind of
Uncle Ho, the Enemy King. And who could say the delirious old
warrior didn't grapple after actual truths? Intelligence, data, analysis be damned; to hell with reason, categories, synthesis, common
sense. All was ideology and imagery and conjuring. Fires to light
the minds and heat the acts of men. And cow their consciences.
Fireworks, all of it—not just the stuff of history, but the stuff of
reality itself, the thoughts of God—speechless and obvious: incan-
descent patterns, infinitely widening.

At any point before now, he realized, he might simply have
told his uncle he wanted to go home. But he couldn't slip out
from under this far along, this deep in, and collapse the sky on his
uncle's anvil head. He wouldn't see that head bowed low.

He called Tho to the veranda.

"What's the story on this dog?"

Tho said, "Le médicin."

"It's a doctor's dog?"

Tho nodded, gambling on agreement, and retreated.

Soon Mrs. Diu came out. "Mr. Tho says the dog has the spirit
of Dr. Bouquet. When the doctor die, after one year the dog is
coming."

"Dr. Bouquet was reborn as this dog?"

"Yes. Dr. Bouquet."

"Mrs. Diu."

"Yes, Mr. Skip."

"Why won't Tho speak English to me?"

"He doesn't speak."

"He doesn't speak English? Or he doesn't speak at all."

"Yes, sometimes," she said. "I don't know."

"Good," he said. "I hope that clears things up for you."

The dog was in the yard now lifting a leg at one of three papaya
trees. Nearby Mr. Tho supported himself with the handle of a
rake as he crouched to put a match to a pile of household rubbish.
Skip admired the papayas with their slender forms and tufted

crowns and the fruit clustered around their throats . . . The old papasan stepped back and watched, making sure of the flame while his reconstituted employer, curled tightly as a doughnut, bit at vermin around the base of his tail.

"Excuse me, Mr. Skip." Mrs. Diu was still at his shoulder. "You want supper?"

"Let me think about it. I'll be there in a minute."

One thing at a time. Maybe he'd send for Père Patrice, have him to supper. As a kind of penance, in the presence of the priest, he would force down a sickening meal. But he'd nodded off, and reached this decision while dreaming. He woke at 9:00 p.m. by his air force wristwatch. Dark like a velvet gauze, the burn pile's embers, the canine Bouquet snoring at his feet. He was hungry, but life was ludicrous. He went to bed.

The Cherry Loot was a tight, muscular, earnest youth with the shirt of his fatigues tucked and the waist pulled up too high. He didn't smoke, and he drank very frugally, with suspicion. He talked a lot about microbes. Tropical diseases occupied his mind. Apparently he'd read a book about swift, horrific things they couldn't vaccinate against. As for the enemy, he hardly believed in their existence. They didn't frighten him at all.

Cherry Loot told Sergeant Burke, "I'm gonna make the best of this fuck-a-monkey show. Don't mean fuck to me if it's illegal, unjustified, and sinful. Today we're heroes, tomorrow we're the Nazis. You never know. Nobody on this ball knows shit." It was an attitude refreshing if not outright inspiring. Everybody else was headed the other way. "I was dating Darlene Taylor until this hippie named Michael Cook took her to a party and gave her drugs and fucked her and turned her into a hippie, and if Michael the evil hippie is against this war, then I am goddamn for it. That's all I have to know." The Cherry Loot didn't seem the least bit cherry. He didn't know what country he was in, but he was at home in the universe.

He was fast, precise, devoted. It took him two days to catch up to the time zone, and on the morning of the third he sprang awake, looked around with clear eyes, and demanded to have brought before him any material and personnel that might enlarge his understanding of the local VC tunnels. This came down to a few of the guys and a couple of wrinkled drawings the Cowboy Corporal had made for the old, the previous, the former, the Screwy Loot.

Screwy Loot, it was said, had gone to Tan Son Nhut, hitched a ride on a MAC flight to Honolulu, and melted away into the gigantic heaven of stateside.

Cherry Loot spent a morning in his Quonset hut with the Cowboy Corporal's drawings spread out on the collapsible table serving as his desk. He demanded creative input from his sergeant. "Isn't there some radar or sonar we can use to deal effectively with this shit? I mean, we only want to know where these tunnels are located. We don't have to crawl around inside to figure that out, do we? Are we bugs or snakes or some shit like that? Or are we upright rational humans on two legs with brains so we can attack this problem?"

"I don't think we really have to do this, sir."

"What?"

"I don't think we actually have to map these holes."

"I'm under express orders to accomplish this. It's our whole purpose for being here. Otherwise you know what we do? We get down along Route One and breathe some stuff's gonna kill us. That's the alternative assignment. Clouds of God-knows-what that's gonna fuse up your lungs and no doubt sterilize your balls."

"Express orders, sir, I mean, sir, do you mean written?"

"I mean they are clearly expressed inside my mind as I interpret them. Do you want me to hassle somebody to clarify in writing? Because ROTC didn't teach me fuck-your-mother about how to survive one day in this shit but they did teach me not to go yanking the coat of my superiors or catch their attention in any way."

"I encourage you to make that policy, sir," Burke said. "But there's squads they call them tunnel rats will go down in there for you. I can check if they can get assigned over here."

"We're under Psy Ops–CIA till September first, then there's a chance we all go home. I'm saying a chance."

"Sir. Consensus is that Colonel F.X. has ripped his stitches."

"Leave it alone. You don't know the history of this thing."

Cherry Loot paced the camp hatless under the smoldering clouds of noon. He seemed profoundly afraid, but not of the war or of his responsibilities in it. Of something bigger. Cosmically worried.

Echo found very irritating the difference in the way litter was handled by Screwy Loot and by Cherry Loot. Screwy had just let the trash scatter itself around until the sergeant, at first Harmon and then Ames and finally Sergeant Burke, hustled them to police the area, but Cherry wants it done by the clock, everything tick-tock, wants it all relentlessly squared away. In a number of ways the Cherry Loot was screwier than the Screwy Loot. Screwy Loot hadn't been entirely irrational about garbage. Just extremely twitchy about all else.

Black Man was snapping his fingers, wrinkling his face, squinting his eyes, then popping them wide—all ripped up over whatever he was trying to get across even as James was still approaching the Cherry Loot's Quonset hut—saying to James:

"And you go up against Mr. Charlie, right into him, right *through* each other, and you swap yourselves and it ain't you coming up here with us, man, with your buddies. It's him. And it ain't him coming up over there and getting with the other Charlies, squatting down and shovel that sticky rice up into their face, man, it ain't him. It's you. Oh, they just mickey mousing us every which goddamn way."

"Black Man."

"Yeah, baby."

"It's me."

"Oh. Oh. Shit, yes. Yes, it is. You going in to see the new boy?"

"Looks like it."

Black Man chewed his lips nonstop today. "He's cherry but he act like he don't know it."

James said, "How's it going?"

"Okay. Okay. One or two demons have quit eating me."

James hadn't seen Black Man in a long time. Since Tet.

"I thought you were gone."

"It wasn't nothing. All that blood turned out to be from one lit-tle vein or something. Shit. Didn't you hear I was dead almost?"

"You got hit?"

"No. I got cut over there at the Tu Do Bar. Nigger followed me in the john."

"You got in a *knife* fight?"

"Muhfucker broke a bottle and jabbed my shoulder right here while I was pissing."

"You get a Purple Heart for that shit?"

"Almost ate it for my muhfucking country, now I'm back here smelling you. And you stink."

"I didn't know nothing about it."

Black Man's eyeballs were shaking in his head.

James said, "I saw the sarge. Remember Sergeant Harmon? Staff Sergeant Harmon?"

"Yeah. Harmon. Sarge. Yeah. You saw him? Just now?"

"No. Right after."

"Right after the bad thing?"

"Yeah," James said.

They stood in the parallelogram of shade on the Quonset hut's eastern side. James sat down and leaned back against the wall, but Black Man couldn't sit.

"Hey, man. Tell me your name."

"You dreamin'!"

"Please tell me at least your first name."

"Charles. Charles Blackman."

"Blackman?"

"That's what I mean. That shit right there. Name like that."

"Gah-damn. Name like that."

"You going in to see the New Loot?"

"I guess."

"He got some moves, baby."

"Yeah, he's a little ball of fire."

"Yeah. Ball of fire."

"Charles Blackman."

"See?"

"I guess there's white guys named Whiteman."

"Yeah, yeah. But I don't hear the laughter, you dig?"

James said, "I'm laughing at you, but you're making me kind of sad."

The door banged. The little sergeant from Psy Ops strode from the Quonset hut and sat down facing James like an Indian at a powwow and said, "Another perfect day. Whether we know it or not."

"I don't think so."

The sergeant read James's name tape and said, "So—Houston, J. What's the J for—jerk-off? I'm just kidding. Sorry. I'm an idiot this morning again oh shit. And I bet you never been to Houston."

"Nope. I'm from Phoenix."

"It's hot there. What's the J for?"

"James."

"They call you Jimmy?"

"Sometimes, but I tell them don't."

"They call me Jimmy. But don't call me James. I like Jimmy. Don't ever call me James. Let's keep it loose. It's hot in Phoenix. It breaks a hundred there. One-oh-two, one-oh-three, one-oh-four."

"You that guy from Psy Ops?"

"Yeah."

"Jesus."

"What."

James just shook his head.

Jimmy lay back and pulled his cap down over his face. "It's hot here too. Vee-yet Nam. It means 'permanent sweat' in their fucked-up language."

Once again the door banged. A guy came out and walked off toward the latrines without greeting them. Storm hopped upright. "Phoenix Houston's turn."

He followed James in and stood beside Sergeant Burke and said not a word while the Cherry Loot took his turn.

"Corporal Cowboy."

"Yes, sir."

"Did you think I wouldn't get around to you?"

"Matter of fact, sir—"

"I saved the worst for the last."

James looked around for a chair, but Cherry Loot had the only one in the room.

"We got sixty-six days left on this thing."

"Yes, sir."

"Before we have to break this thing down and we all go back to the regular Twenty-fifth Infantry."

"Yes, sir."

"We had ninety days and we've wasted twenty-four out of ninety. Speaking of which," the lieutenant said, "you were AWOL twenty-one days last February. I know your history. Where were you—demonstrating at the Democratic Convention?"

"The who?"

"The Democratic National Convention?"

Sergeant Burke said, "Sir, the Democratic Convention was last week."

"Where'd you run to, Corporal?"

"I was on a special assignment."

"No. You were drunk and running, and the colonel fixed it with my predecessor. Say yes, sir."

"Yes, sir."

The lieutenant looked at the sergeant from Psy Ops as if expecting comment. None came. The lieutenant said, "We want focus, which means we want mission, which means we want goals. Otherwise we get pulled and sent thirty kliks over that way, to the most horrible place on earth. Have you seen that wasteland along Route One?"

"Yes, sir."

"Our mission is mapping the local tunnels. You're the one jumped down in there."

"Me?" James said.

"You went in there."

"Just to sort of, you know," James said, "sir."

"Well, what's your report?"

"I don't know. Like what?"

"What did you see?"

"Just tunnels."

"What about it? Tell me something."

"The walls are very smooth."

"What else?"

"It's small in there. You can't stand up."

"You have to crawl?"

"Not exactly crawl. Just stay bent over is all."

"You must be insane," the Cherry Loot said.

"No argument there, sir," James said.

"I'd like to put you back in those tunnels. Get those suckers mapped in detail. Not these raggedy drawings. You kind of like it down there, don't you?"

"It ain't exactly that."

"Well, no, shit no, nothing ain't exactly nothing no more. But you kind of like it down there."

"You can go ahead and volunteer me if it gets you all hard," James said.

"Look, sojer, I want to create an environment about two-by-two kliks that I know every single thing inside it that lives and breathes."

"You know, there ain't but six tunnels around here. I been in them all and they don't go nowhere. The real tunnels are north of here. Northwest."

"Don't tell me that. You take away my reason for living."

"I want reimbursement for my kit."

"Your kit, is it."

"I paid two-eighty-five for the gun and the silencer and the headlight. Seems like I should've been issued one, but if I'd waited on the army I'd still be waiting this minute."

"You mean two hundred and eighty-five dollars?"

"Yes, sir."

"What's that on your hip?"

"Hi-Power."

"Where's your .380 for tunnels, then?"

"It's kind of complicated."

"Is it? Is there anything not kind of complicated in this fuck-a-monkey show?"

"Never happen."

"Two-eight-five?"

"Thereabouts."

"If I could put in for actual cash money, I'd get a whole bunch for myself. I can put in for a tunnel kit, maybe. That much seems reasonable."

"Put in for one, then. I can sell it and break even."

"Are you going to make me an accessory to black marketeering now?"

"Just thinking out loud is all."

"I can't have people thinking. I can't have it."

"Yes, sir."

"Meantime for sixty-six more days you hit the ground running every day and all day you bust hump for Echo Platoon. No leave no furlough no beer at the Purple Bar say yes sir."

"Yes sir."

"Dis-missed up and at 'em rock 'n' roll."

James turned to go.

"All right. Wait."

"Yes, sir."

"After I chew you up for sixty-six days, what's your plan?"

"I'm over to Nha Trang for Lurps."

"No shit. The recondo school? That's on-the-job training, man."

"I know it."

"You know who they do their training maneuvers against?"

"Yeah."

"The NVA Seventeenth Division. They just put you on patrol and see who eats who."

The little Psy Ops sergeant laughed happily. "You fuck up in training you'll be dead, and mushrooms," he said, "will be growing outa your ass."

"Shut up, Sergeant—please. Corporal, this your second tour?"

"It is."

"They're gonna make you do your third."

"Fine with me."

"Dismissed," the lieutenant said. "Good luck. Dismissed."

He woke in the late afternoon to the quarreling of birds. Gave himself a sponge bath of water and, for its cooling effect, rubbing alcohol at the bowl in the upstairs bathroom. Put on his army surplus bathing trunks and zoris and went downstairs. "Mr. Skip, it is tea?" Mr. Tho said in English. "S'il vous plaît," he said. He sat at the desk and went to work on the passages of text even before his tea had arrived or his head had cleared of dreams, for he'd often found this a favorable state in which to come by the meaning of a foreign phrasing, to catch its glimmer. He kept the lamps off and worked in a kind of twilight. During pauses he peered at the porcelain model of the human ear, running his finger along the delicate Labyrinthe membraneux—the Utricule and Saccule, the Canal endolymphatique and Nerf vestibulaire, the Ganglion de scarpa and Ganglion spinal de corti—and

Si incroyable que cela paraisse, les Indiens Tarahumaras
vivent comme s'ils étaient déjà morts . . .

"Incredible as it may seem," Sands had rendered it, "the
Tarahumara Indians live as if they were already dead . . ."

Il me fallait certes de la volonté pour croire que quelque
chose allait se passer. Et tout cela, pourquoi? Pour une
danse, pour un rite d'Indiens perdus qui ne savent même
plus qui ils sont, ni d'où ils viennent et qui, lorsqu'on les
interroge, nous répondent par des contes dont ils ont égaré
la liaison et le secret.

It required a definite act of will for me to believe that something was going to happen. And all this, for what? For a
dance, for a rite of lost Indians who don't even know who
they are or where they come from and who, when questioned, answer us with stories of which the thread and the
secret have drifted from their grasp.

Each afternoon he followed a long nap with this game of
translation, while outdoors the birds continued, some insistent,
others probing, interrogatory, grandly ecstatic, troubled—more
intelligible, at least in their intent, than the mysterious song of M.
Artaud:

Il me sembla partout lire une histoire d'enfantement dans
la guerre, une histoire de genèse et de chaos, avec tous ces
corps de dieux qui étaient taillés comme des hommes, et
ces statues humaines tronçonnées.

I seemed to read everywhere a story of childbirth in war, a
story of genesis and chaos, with all these bodies of gods
which were carved out like men; and these truncated statues of humans.

This Artaud sounded tough. Maybe he was in earnest, maybe
he was actually after something. But E. M. Cioran. The Cioran. It
was decadent. It was — unproductive, and delicious:

Cet état de stérilité où nous n'avançons ni ne reculons, ce
piétinement exceptionnel est bien celui où nous conduit
le doute et qui, à maints égards, s'apparente à la « sécher-
esse » des mystiques.

This state of sterility in which we neither advance nor
retreat, this peculiar marching-in-place, is precisely where
doubt leads us, a state which resembles in many respects
the "dry places" of the mystics . . .

. . . nous retombons dans cet état de pure indétermina-
tion où, la moindre certitude nous apparaissant comme
un égarement, toute prise de position, tout ce que l'esprit
avance ou proclame, prend l'allure d'une divagation.
N'importe quelle affirmation nous semble alors aven-
tureuse ou dégradante; de même, n'importe quelle néga-
tion.

. . . we relapse into that state of pure indetermination
where — since any certainty whatever seems to us a lost
turning — each resolution, all that the spirit advances or
announces, takes on the aura of a divagation. Then any
affirmation, no matter what, seems foolhardy or degrading;
the same for any negation.

He would seek out an English translation, if such existed. To read
and feel the meaning erode under the work of his mind — he was
hungry for that pleasure. He thought of writing a letter to a friend
saying: I think I might be bad, I could actually be evil, and if
there's a Devil it's possible I'm his ally . . . Right at the heart of my

ability to grasp the truth, I want to be paralyzed, I want to swoon . . . I want my mind to fail before the truth. I want the truth to flow over me only as something sensual and as nothing else. Want it to wet me—to be real, to be a thing . . .

He never wrote it down. He didn't know who the friend was. He had no friend in the world but E. M. Cioran:

> Le détracteur de la sagesse, s'il était de plus croyant, ne cesserait de répeter : « Seigneur, aidez-moi à déchoir, à me vautrer dans toutes les erreurs et tous les crimes, inspirez-moi des paroles qui Vous brûlent et me dévorent, qui *nous* réduisent en cendres. »

> The detractor of wisdom, if he were a believer as well, would never stop repeating, "Lord, help me to fall, to wallow in every error and every crime, inspire me with words that scorch You and devour me, which reduce us *both* to ashes."

No wonder Bouquet had written in his notebook:

> In the glory of war, in the bliss of combat, in the truth of war we see that might makes right. And that our respect for principles is based on eloquence and superstition.

He'd actually finished with the colonel's files. A momentum had developed. Pointless labor, useless trash, but for the bureaucrat nothing's trash until he affronts his soul by throwing it out.

Why was he not off meeting with villagers in the region, collecting folk tales? Why did he send Tho out to tell Père Patrice he had a fever when the priest came to beg a hot meal?

> Sans rime ni raison, remettre toujours tout en question, douter même en rêvê !

Without rhyme or reason to keep putting everything in question, to doubt even in dreams!

Reading Cioran he was revisited by the revelation he'd had as a ten-year-old, when a railroader's son had showed him a small photograph of a woman fellating a large black penis, only the man's torso visible, the woman's sickly-happy eyes flirting with the camera—that his curiosity about such acts wasn't an alienating treason, that it was known, gauged, understood, that others would feed it.

Le doute s'abat sur nous comme une calamité ; loin de le choisir, nous y tombons. Et nous avons beau essayer de nous en arracher ou de l'escamoter, lui ne nous perd pas de vue, car il n'est même pas vrai qu'il s'abat sur nous, il était *en* nous et nous y étions prédestinés.

Doubt collapses onto us like a disaster; far from choosing it, we fall into it. And try as we will to pull out of it, to trick it away, it never loses sight of us, for it is not even true that it collapses onto us—doubt was *in* us, and we were predestined to it.

He'd come to war to see abstractions become realities. Instead he'd seen the reverse. Everything was abstract now.

Alone in this house, alone in this war, with the likes of E. M. Cioran . . . No wonder Bouquet had gone out to the veranda . . .

Night again, the insects are loud, the moths are killing themselves on the lamp. Two hours ago I sat on the veranda looking out at the dusk, filled with envy for each living entity—bird, bug, blossom, reptile, tree, and vine— that doesn't bear the burden of the knowledge of good and evil.

The abyss is full
of reality, the abyss experiences itself, the
abyss
is alive

Between jobs Bill Houston mooched off his mom, living with
her and also with Burris, his twelve-year-old brother, which put
him on the same level, it seemed to him, of this strange pre-
teenager, a problem child like the elder two, a flunker and a tru-
ant, a glue-sniffer, pot-puffer, drinker of cough-control medicines.
A test of faith, the old woman said, a call to prayer. In August, in
answer to prayers of his own, Houston got a job on the west side
loading raw linseed into semi trucks and soon took a room in the
region dominated by Second Street and known as the Deuce, in
whose skid-row atmosphere he felt he could forget his mother and
wrestle unobserved with his confusion. He'd have headed for the
ships again, if not for the general discharge. He wondered about
the Merchant Marine, but he believed they wouldn't have him
either. Houston thought of his younger brother James, facing war,
assaulted by experience, pulling ahead of him somehow. The
whole world had left him in its wake, while at Roy Ruggins Seed,
as so often in his work life, he earned his pay performing the same
motions over and over. Up before the sun and then hiking a lot of
miles in and out of those fifty-three-foot trailers, back and forth, a
long way up the ramp and all the way to the front, dragging two
eighty-pound sacks with hay hooks. Here and there little points of
daylight in the cars' leaky interiors. Stacking the sacks in each layer
at a right angle to the sacks in the layer beneath. Eight layers high.
Linseed had a peculiar, sick-making smell. They worked deep-
desert summertime hours, five to nine in the morning and five to
nine at night, taking eight hours off during the hot of the day.
Between shifts trying not to get drunk. Or anyway not too drunk.

After he lost that job he gave up his room and tried the Salvation Army, who rigorously insisted on sobriety, however, and who couldn't be fooled for long. Expelled for liquor breath, he would have made it all right sleeping daytimes in the square downtown and tramping the streets at night, but a person had to eat, and from the New Life Mission he got only one peanut-butter sandwich at noon and franks and beans for supper, both meals with a cup of reconstituted chocolate milk. While he waited for this fare twice each day in a line of losers, life laughed at his hunger, and he wished he was in a situation with a roof and a kitchen, the navy once again, or again the Salvation Army—even jail. He'd passed three weeks in the Phoenix lockup awaiting trial on a charge of assault and found nothing behind bars to complain about. They served you three meals there and the people were decent—criminals, maybe, but sober and well-fed criminals didn't behave too badly. Anywhere but his mother's house. Her zealous hope of Heaven made it hell there.

In a tavern on Central he met a chubby adorable Pima woman who called herself a half-breed. She took him out to the desert on the reservation way east of town and they sat on the hood of her rattletrap Plymouth in the cooling dusk while the sky turned a nothing-colored shade of blue. They hit it off fine, he and this warm-hearted woman with a brown front tooth in her happy Eskimo face. Short and fleshy. She was in actual point of fact spherical. She took him home to her shack east of Pima Road, just inside the reservation, and within days he married her in a ceremony conducted by a wizened old cretin who claimed to be a medicine man. Houston and his new wife lived in bliss for two weeks, until her darkly, poisonously silent brother showed up and moved in. While she napped one afternoon Houston took six dollars and six cigarettes from her Plymouth's glove compartment—six, his lucky number, and lucky for her it wasn't in the double digits—and rode back to the Deuce on a bus. Did he need a lawyer? He doubted it. The woman had burned her way into his heart, but two weeks hardly counted. He didn't intend to complicate the adventure with a divorce.

After October, after the rainy season, many mornings in Cao Quyen came with sunlight before the inevitable dull afternoon— he thought sometimes of a remark of Jimmy Storm's: "Ain't no sky in the tropics"—and with this gift came certain regions of beauty into the villa's eastern rooms, solid-looking slats of light between the louvers upstairs, the kitchen filled with pinpoint reflections among the utensils, the murky office's shutters fiercely outlined, also the large rectangular vents near the parlor's ceiling: flat, stark planes like a painter's small exercises in perspective . . . And then the afternoon's perpetual, uniform, businesslike illumination from overcast skies sank his soul. In the morning he saw it: options always waited open. By afternoon he couldn't take steps, the ground was gone, doubt had dissolved it.

Mrs. Diu said, "Lady to see you, Mr. Skip."

He rose from the desk, entered the parlor, and encountered a female stranger, freckled, brown, stringy, in a white blouse with front pockets, a man's khaki trousers, and he said, "Kathy," before he realized he knew her.

In Damulog she'd had none of the flushed and frightened— hysterical, or haunted—leaning, overheated look of so many jungle missionaries. She had it now. One hand gripped the rim of a peasant's conical hat—the nong la. He took it from her and set it on the coffee table in the parlor and she followed it to stand there a little out of breath, keeping her hat near.

"I was told about a Canadian."

"I can get us some tea. Would you like some tea?"

"Is it you? You're the Canadian?"

"Speak up, now, ma'am. Tea or no?"

"How about some of that incendiary compound you drop on the villages?"

"I'm, I'm—I'm all out."

"I might have known. I did know. AID! Del Monte! Canadian! What else? Toronto Symphony Orchestra?"

"Seventh-Day Adventist."

"All of you, oh, my Lord. You're too laughable to laugh at."

"I'm translating the Bible, I'll have you know."

"It isn't funny."

"Don't you think I've caught on to that? I lost my sense of humor a long time ago. Now, will you have tea with me, Kathy? Or isn't this a social call."

"I'm calling on a Canadian."

"But socially, right?"

"Yes. I'll bet you've got honey."

"No. Condensed milk, the sugary stuff."

"No honey?"

"Nothing like that."

"No? Maybe you thumbed your nose at McNamara. Is that the one?"

"The Secretary of Defense?"

"Yeah. He must've put you in exile as a punishment, huh?"

"I like it here very much."

"You spies are always so perky and so chipper."

"Have a seat." With all that had come along to disillusion him, the dismal realities of his work, it lit up his heart to be called a "spy."

She sat on the edge of a chair and looked around wildly.

"All right, now," he said, "tea."

"How are things in Canada?"

"Come on. Please."

"I don't know what to say. I don't know what to say. I'm just, I'm quite simply—I'm angry." She got up without any purpose in her face. "I'm leaving now." As if getting the idea from having expressed it, she went quickly through the entry and out, slapping her hands onto the bicycle she'd parked out there and kicking at its kickstand, a black bicycle.

"Kathy, come on, wait," Skip called, but he didn't go after her. She'd said she was angry. He didn't think she very often felt any other way.

He sat on the divan and leaned forward, elbows on his knees, looking at the magazines on the coffee table—*Time*, and *Newsweek*, a cover photo of two black American Olympic athletes raising the single-fist salute of the Black Power Movement. In Mexico City, he believed, but didn't know, because he'd stopped reading them.

Back she came. "I never heard from you."

He waited until she took hold of the large chair facing him, dragged it a little distance away in a show of dissent, and sat down on its creaking rattan. "Well?"

"Well, I sent a few cards."

"I wrote a slew of letters. I even mailed a few. Do you know why I cut off communication?"

"I hope you'll tell me."

"Because when Father Carignan died—did you know he died? Of course you know he died—because news came to us that the priest near Carmen had drowned, and you were the one who brought the news to the diocese, and we were together three weeks, as lovers, and you never mentioned it!"

"Didn't I get a letter from you a year ago? A long time after the priest, the business there, the drowning."

"It took a while, but I finally figured it out: liars aren't worth talking to."

"Maybe not," he said. "But I appreciated the letters."

This seemed to give her pause. "You never really answered. Cards don't count."

"Maybe I didn't want to lie." True, but not truly the reason for his silence. He'd thought her letters crazy. "Or, well, no—letters are hard. That's closer to the truth."

"A phony Canadian talking about truth. Incidentally, what name do you go by?"

"Skip."

"Skip who?"

"Benét. But mostly Skip. Still Skip."

"Alias Benét wants to talk about truth!"

"We can't always tell the whole story about ourselves. As you once said to me yourself."

"I don't remember ever saying that, but it's certainly true when it comes to somebody like you, it's certainly true in your case."

"So then—you'll stay awhile."

She glared, eyes watering. Her wrath went out of her in a gusty sigh, and he could tell she was glad to see him.

As for the spy, he was thrilled, his hands shook with joy. He found Mrs. Diu and asked for tea, fruit, bread, returned to his guest to say, "Just two minutes," and went back to hang around the kitchen, terrified of facing Kathy without things to eat and drink, while Mrs. Diu prepared them. He brought the tray himself.

She too appeared suddenly shy. "This dog," she said, "just wanders all around."

"That's Docteur Bouquet. He used to own the place."

"He acts like he still does."

"He's reincarnated."

"Really. He sure picked the wrong country to be born a dog in."

"But I'd say just the right household."

"He'll end up in somebody's chopsticks."

"I think he's too old now."

He started to scratch the dog and realized it would dirty his fingers. "Hey," he said, "I can't really ask you to stay. I'm not in a position to entertain. Not at all. Not these days. Buried under work."

"What?"

"Well, *that's* insane."

"Yeah. It is. I mean to say—"

"I thought I was rolling with it, but I guess I'm in a panic here."

"Do you want me to stay, or do you want me to go?"

"I want you to stay."

He fumbled and dropped a small baguette, and Docteur

Bouquet trotted off with it. He watched it go, a man without graceful reflexes. "I've been calling him Docteur Bouquet, but I think it
should be 'Monsieur.' His degree wouldn't stay with him into the
next life, would it? What are you doing up here in Cao Quyen?"

"What am I doing here?"

"Yes. More or less."

"I'm with WCS now. No more ICRE."

"WCS?"

"World Children's Services is a network of nearly sixty agencies around the world, providing social services to children and
their families since 1934."

"I'm sure it is."

"Adoption assistance is the core service of WCS. In several dis-
tricts, including this one, we're doing what we can to coordinate
efforts on behalf of children without families."

"I wouldn't doubt it."

"Stop it. So I was visiting the missionary family in Bac Se, and
they told me about you. The Thomases."

"I never met them. Never heard of them."

"They heard about you from a priest."

"Thong Nhat—Père Patrice."

"I wouldn't know. I just know I came out of my way to say hi to
a fellow Canadian, and instead I find you. The Quiet American."

"Oh, well," he said, "thanks for not calling me Ugly."

"You wouldn't hear it anyway. You're deaf. We all know that
about you by now, all but you Americans yourselves."

"It seemed like we were getting along there for a second."

"Sorry."

She ran out of things to say and gazed at him pitiably.

"Qué pasa?"

"'Qué pasa'? You talk like a GI."

"I know. Qué pasa?"

"I'm all worn out."

"I'm sure you are."

"I mean—I'm the ugly one. It's worn me down, hasn't it?"

"Look," he said, "I'm so glad you came. I'm so happy, Kathy."

"Really?"

"Do I have to make a fool of myself?"

"I wouldn't mind," she said.

Fortunately, the dog was back for more. Skip roughed his fur and fed him bites of mango. "And you're here about orphans, I guess. For WCS."

She nodded her head, slice of mango speared on a fork and upheld like a flag, mouth full of bread roll. Swallowed the bread, the mango, almost the fork too.

"Now it's me who's sorry. I wasn't thinking—do you want a regular meal?"

She shook her head, still chewing. "No, thanks. Yes—I mean, yes, adoption. We're an umbrella organization for adoption agencies."

"If every family in North America adopts one Vietnamese, we win the war."

"Something like that. I wouldn't mind clearing the country out and just leaving it to the killers."

"Are you guys as hard up as ICRE?"

"Oh, sure—relative to the size of our effort we are. But as I once heard Mayor Luis say—'We will find the money, we will kneel to many people.'"

"You're good. You sound just like him."

"Have you been in touch?"

"No."

"Me neither."

"Let's get back to the other thing," he suggested. "Where you said you wouldn't mind if I made a fool of myself."

"Let me eat first."

In a few minutes he showed her to the upper rooms. From what he could see, climbing behind her up the stairwell, she'd kept a little weight in her hips and thighs, but she'd called it right, the life had worn her down. He himself had gone the other way.

He didn't have a scale, but his bathing trunks fit him tighter and he wore them lower, beneath the belly roll. No scale, but he'd been provided a stethoscope and a blood-pressure gauge. A dozen rolls of bandage, no adhesive tape. Wartime supplies were like that—all cocked up. These were the thoughts that ravaged him as he tried to figure out how to deal with his overwhelming happiness and lust, his buzzing fingertips, clenched heart, dizziness. Not that he thought she'd mind a pass, but she was nuts—at the very least complicated—hidden-wounded, phony-cynical, overpassionate. Definitely angry. And all of it inflamed him. And she was the last woman he'd slept with, one of five in thirty-odd years of life. Men with graceful reflexes don't interrogate their opportunities. Men without them should stop the questions. And of the five, she was the only one he'd slept with more than once. He led the way into his bed suite, turned to her, and—nothing. No reflexes.

"I said I wouldn't mind," she said, and they commenced with an awkward kiss.

"Mr. Benét, do you have any wine?"

"I do. Thank God, I do. And half a fifth of Bushmills."

"Sounds like a party," she said, and laid two fingers lightly on his forearm. Taking the fingers in his hand, he led her to the double-sized bed, where he put to use what he'd learned from Henry Miller's daring passages, from small obscene photographs, dorm-room bull sessions. As in the time in Damulog, they didn't speak. Everything they did was a secret, especially from each other. As she'd said, she didn't mind, and at the very last part she gazed upward at something on the ceiling and cried out. And for an instant he thought, I am James Bond, before he dropped again into gray doubting—Artaud and Cioran, the dog, the weather, the point of it all, waiting for contact with a supposed double agent, the thing he'd been brought here nearly two years ago to accomplish. And it was folly. The wild-card operation and the war itself—folly on folly. And this woman beside him with whom he'd just made love, perspiring like a handball player.

There was a little contest, then, it seemed to him, as to who was going to talk first.

"It takes a fire to make hot water," he said, "but if you want a shower—"

"Oh, come on! I'll take it cold."

"I'll pee," he said. "And then you can have the shower, okay?"

While she showered he wiped himself down with the bedsheet and got back into his bathing trunks. He thought he might look at a book, but the weather was ominous and he had only the rumored, greenish daylight from storm clouds to see by. All the books, he thought, are downstairs. There's nothing to do, he thought. Nothing to be done. He sat at the little tea table staring at his knees, his bare feet.

She came back with a towel wrapped around her and her hair slicked back, the high pinks visible even in her sun-browned cheeks. She had sad, pouched knees. Holding the towel to her breast she stretched, extending only her left arm, keeping the towel close. Across from him was a chair, but she sat on the bed. "Those look like the first clothes I ever saw you in. You were wearing an odd sort of bathing suit, just like that, with pockets."

"The very same pair, actually. They're sturdy as hell."

"What about your wild Bermuda shorts?"

"They fell apart, I guess."

"There was a storm then too."

"The first time you saw me I wore pants. That restaurant in Malaybalay, remember?"

"I refuse to remember."

She'd come at just the right time. This was her atmosphere. This was the light for her, for sad, pale skin below the tanned neck and above the rough elbows, for a virgin martyr's poise, for her unexpectant waiting—her right calf, rather thick and like a peasant's, dangling from the bed and the foot plunged into shadow near the floor, which was of old wood, the other leg akimbo and the sole of its foot against the other knee, making a number 4 with her legs as she lay back on the bed, her hand across her breasts, the other behind her head — pond-light, church-light. Had she known how he stared, she'd never have allowed it. But she turned her eyes to him and looked at him full on as if he didn't matter, without any change of her expression. She wasn't, herself, beautiful. Her moments were beautiful.

The room darkened and gusts carried voices from the ville and the rattle of things shaken, though just before the rain the wind let off, and what came down might have fallen any summer's day in New England.

"You're really staring."

"You are a goddamn relief. You're making everything go away."

"Everything such as?"

"Boredom. Boredom. And too much thinking. Cabin fever."

"Oh, we know all about cabin fever in Manitoba. Come spring, guys jump in their trucks and drive a hundred miles for a shot of whiskey."

"Speak of the devil. You want some Bushmills?"

"We forgot! For gosh sakes — what are you staring at?"

"Isn't that allowed?"

"Not when it's me. I'm an old crone. This sun roasts you like a marshmallow. I'm all beat-up."

"You just wear the badge of your adventures."

"Malarkey."

"No."

"You think this place is an adventure?"

"Sure."

"It isn't fun, though. It's an adventure, but an adventure isn't fun till it's over. If then."

This impressed him as a truth. He poured two shots of luke-warm Bushmills and brought them to the bed. Scooting back against the wall, she held the small glass in both hands and sipped.

"Do Seventh-Day Adventists usually drink?"

"Some do, some don't. Here in this mess I'd say all of us do when we get the chance."

"Where were you? On the delta."   •

"A ville called Sa Dec. But I had to leave. It's different around there since Tet. Everything's chewed up by big American bullets. Everybody has to be careful. Disaster's just around the corner. For a lot of people it's already here. It's a terrible, terrible situation. You get used to it and plod along, then one day you wake up and you're not used to it anymore. Then after a while you get used to it all over again."

"So you're here looking for orphans?"   ·

"We don't have to look."

"Right. Right."

"We're just liaisoning with missionaries. If we can, we want to get something going, something better. Bigger. The existing facilities are terrible, every one of them." At the moment terrible things didn't interest him. As she spoke he studied her head and wondered what Rembrandt might have tried in such lackluster, truthful illumination.

Kathy said, "And your camera."

"Camera."

"I remember you had a camera. Do you still have it around?"

"I gave it up. No more photographs. It turns the world into a museum."

"Instead of?"

"Instead of a crazy circus."

He kept photographs in his dresser drawer, next to the Beretta pistol he'd never used. "Look here." He handed her a dozen or so.

"Emeterio D. Luis!"

"Not a single one of you."

"A jeepney! I miss those things."

"Nearly fifty people riding on it."

"No wonder the tire popped."

A knock. Mrs. Diu asked admittance. "We'll be down for supper," Skip called through the door.

"I have the incense. You want?"

"All right."

She came in with three sticks fuming sweetly in her hand and said, "Yes, good evening," and placed them in their holder on a high shelf across the room. "Okay. Supper later. I will tell you," she said, and went out closing the door softly behind her.

The rain had stopped. Through the screened view, in the two minutes of dusk before black nightfall, he watched Tho ascending one of the papaya trees behind the villa. Because they jutted over the bank and the creek the old man couldn't simply knock the papayas down, but had to walk up to them on the flats of his splayed bare feet with a kitchen knife in his teeth, clinging to the trunk with both hands, cutting one of the fruit away one-handed and clutching it under his arm, descending backward, and taking the last two feet in a weightless hop to the earth.

"Can I have another drink?"

"By all means, comrade."

"Just a wee splash."

Skip felt a little irritated, suddenly, that Kathy had first wrung apologies from him—though he'd made jokes, belittling his atonement—and she'd now forgotten it all. And it occurred to him that the months of solitude had taught him to read himself, to parse himself like a scholar; that one person on this earth had become known to him.

It rained again, and then it was night. She couldn't return now to the missionaries in Bac Se. They slept together side by side, without sheets, she in one of his rough hand-washed T-shirts and he in boxer undershorts. Following breakfast the next morning she left for Bac Se on her black bicycle, and Skip never saw her again.

1969

When the three Americans appeared at the front door of his home to take him to the Armed Forces Language School, Hao felt uncertain as to the nature of the encounter. The only one of them who spoke, a black man, did so politely, introducing himself as Kenneth Johnson from the American Embassy. They drove downtown in a closed, air-conditioned Ford with diplomatic plates, Hao in the back with one of the two younger men.

At their destination the two younger men both got out, and each opened one of the doors for the passengers. Hao and Kenneth Johnson proceeded alone past the concrete barricades toward the fine new building. Its predecessor had been wrecked in the Tet attacks the previous year. Two or three thousand members of the Vietnam military studied English here. The interior smelled of fresh paint and sawn wood.

As far as he knew, the building housed no prisoners.

Johnson led him down a stairwell to the building's basement, where a uniformed marine fell in with them. The students thronged the upper stories and their footfalls vibrated in the ceiling overhead, but in this basement hallway Johnson, Hao, and the marine walked alone. At the corridor's end they came to a door with something like a small adding machine fixed to the wall beside it, four or five buttons of which Johnson now pressed expertly, and the door lock hummed and clacked.

Johnson said, "Thank you, Sergeant Ogden," and he and Hao entered a hallway lined with closed doors. Here it was quiet, air-conditioned. Johnson led him through the only open door into a small lounge furnished like any parlor with a couch and padded chairs, also a large electric-run cooler, red, with the words "Coca-Cola" on it. The room had no windows. This basement must be far underground.

"You want a Coke?"

Johnson lifted the cooler's heavy lid, took out a dripping bottle, and, levering off its cap on an opener attached to the cooler's side, handed the drink to his guest. It was very cold.

Feeling obligated, he took a sip. He pursed his lips and sluiced it down the right side of his mouth and swallowed. He had a bad tooth, a left molar. The colonel had spoken of a dentist.

"Have a seat," Johnson said, and Hao sat himself on the edge of the couch's cushion with his feet poised under him like a runner's.

Johnson remained standing. He was small for an American, with big stains in the armpits of his white shirt. Hao had never before conversed with a Negro.

They'd taken him an hour or so after Kim had left for the market. That meant they hadn't wanted her to see. That they cared to keep this visit a secret. That no one knew where he was.

Johnson sat down comfortably in the chair across from him and offered him a cigarette. Hao accepted it, though in fact he possessed a pack of Marlboros, and lit it with his own lighter and dragged deep and blew smoke out through his nostrils. Nonfilter. Delicately he spat out a shred of leaf. The fact that this man's forebears had been a race of slaves embarrassed him.

Mr. Johnson returned his cigarettes to his shirt pocket without taking one for himself, and stood up. "Mr. Nguyen, will you excuse me a minute?" While Hao tried to make sense of the question, the black man went out without shutting the door and left him alone with his thoughts, which weren't happy ones. He dropped the last of his cigarette into the bottle and it hissed, floated, darkened, sank halfway to the bottom.

Through the open doorway Hao saw his wife Kim, accompanied by another American, passing along the hall. A fissure opened in his soul. She watched her feet as if negotiating a rocky path. Apparently she didn't notice him.

The black man came back. "Mr. Nguyen? Let's relocate the

discussion, do you mind?" Johnson hadn't sat down. Hao understood that he didn't intend to, that he himself must stand up. He
let himself be guided only a few steps along the hallway to a second windowless room in which sat a thin, angular, youthful man
with reading glasses far down on his nose, one ankle crossed over
his knee, looking down and to the left at the contents of a manila
folder opened on the table beside him. He smiled at Hao, saying,
"Mr. Nguyen, come on in, I want to show you this thing," and
Hao searched for hope in his almost sociable tone of voice. On
the table were arranged devices and wires like an elaborate radio
system.

"I'm Terry Crodelle. Everybody calls me Crodelle, and I hope
you will too. Okay if I call you Mr. Hao?"

"Okay. Yes."

"Sit, sit, please."

He sat in the hard wooden chair beside Crodelle's. A third
chair waited, but Mr. Johnson remained at attention. Here were
two very different American types, both dressed the same in their
somber slacks, their brilliant shoes, white short-sleeved shirts: Johnson standing, extraneous, mildly uncomfortable, brown-skinned
and black-headed, Crodelle relaxed and in charge, with pale,
freckled skin, and hair the color of straw.

Mr. Johnson said, "Do you want Sammy?" Crodelle gave no
answer.

"Mr. Hao," Crodelle said, "we're going to keep this short,
never fear."

"That's good."

"You'll be back home within the hour."

"Today we'll plant a tree for the Tet."

"Do you understand my English?"

Hao said, "Sometimes I don't understand many things." He
still held his half bottle of Coke with its drifting cigarette butt.
Gently Crodelle took the beverage from his grip and placed it on
the table.

"Another drink?"

"No, thank you. But it's quite good."

Crodelle put his glasses in the pocket of his shirt and leaned in to contact Hao's gaze without hostility or guile, but studiously. He had stubby eyelashes the color of his hair, and irises a pale blue. "I don't want an interpreter in here. Can we talk without an interpreter?"

"Yes. My English is not good to speak, but I understand better."

"Good enough," Crodelle said.

And Johnson said, "Good enough," and left the room, shutting the door behind him.

"Do you know what this contraption is?"

"Maybe a radio."

"It's a machine that can tell who's lying and who's telling the truth. Or so they claim."

Did the machine transmit this news about himself now?

"How can it work?"

"It's not my area. We won't be using it today."

Hao said, "I am searching true peace. I cannot wait for you to make the peace. I cannot wait for you guys."

Crodelle smiled.

"War is not peace."

Crodelle rose and went to the door and opened it. "Ken?" he called, and then said, "Excuse me, Mr. Hao."

It was Johnson who appeared.

"We need a translator."

Johnson left the door ajar. Crodelle arranged the third chair, saying, "Just someone to help us get things across."

He sat down and again crossed his ankle over his knee.

Hao wondered if they'd let him smoke in here.

"When was the last time you saw the colonel?"

Hao patted the Marlboros in his shirt. Crodelle produced a lighter and held out the flame while Hao steered the tip of his cigarette into it and puffed, reflecting that life in this city of feints and reversals called for nimble steps and a long view, and he lacked this combination. He found himself unable, for instance, to cope with his wife's brother, who owed him money, who had lived in Hao's father's house since the old man's death, when it became Hao's property, but who refused to acknowledge his debt. Relatives and business: he'd failed to navigate between them. And since his father's death he'd run the family's enterprises into the ground. He couldn't handle the day-to-day of simple commerce; much less whatever these people had in mind for him now. He inhaled delicious smoke and said, "Not for a long time."

"One month? Two months?"

"I think maybe two months."

Johnson had returned. "Here's Sammy," he said, and a very young Vietnamese man dressed in slacks and shirt just like the Americans' sat in the third wooden chair while Johnson left again and Crodelle spoke rapidly, looking at Hao.

"Mr. Hao," the boy translated, "we've invited you here instead of arranging an apparently chance encounter in a public space. I will tell you the reason."

"Tell me," Hao said in Vietnamese.

"Because we want you to understand that this inquiry has the weight of the United States government behind it."

In English Hao said, "I'm a friend for the United States."

"Do you have a lot of friends?"

Hao asked the interpreter, "What does he mean by such a question?"

"I'm not sure. Do you want me to ask him to explain?"

"Why did they bring me here? Why do they ask if I have a lot of friends?"

"That's not my business."

"Sammy," Crodelle said, "just ask him the questions. I talk to you, you talk to him. He talks to you, you talk to me. You two don't sit back chatting."

"It's best just to speak to him, and not to me," the boy suggested to Hao.

Hao held his cigarette almost vertically so as not to lose the two-inch-long ash and put his lips under it to get a puff. Crodelle said, "I forgot the ashtrays. I don't actually smoke myself."

Sammy said, "Can I get one?"

"An ashtray? Please, if you don't mind."

Now he was alone with pale Crodelle again. A lot of friends? Not a lot. Perhaps the wrong ones. He'd clung to the colonel as to a mighty tree, expecting it to carry him from the tempest. But a tree isn't going anywhere.

Sammy knocked and came back in with an ashtray as well as his own burning cigarette, put the tray on the table in front of Hao, dipped his own ash. "It's all right?"

"Smoke away," Crodelle said. "Smoke like Dresden, man," and Hao brought his Marlboro gently above the ashtray and let fall the pendulous ash.

"American cigarette," he said. "I like it better than Vietnam." He stubbed it out and sat back.

"Who's the friend who visits you? The VC."

A simple enough question. But the route to the answer started some distance from it and passed through a thicket of irrelevant histories. He spoke of his training at the New Star Temple. Of how the tenets had seemed, in a way, cowardly excuses for old men to hide behind, but afterward, in middle age—now—had begun to reveal their importance. He spoke of the Five Hindrances—they did, indeed, hinder—and the Four Noble Truths—they were actually true. When he'd run out of things to say, the translator Sammy dragged from his cigarette and said: "Buddhist."

Crodelle said, "To each his own. I'm not here in the name of any particular outfit except Five Corps. So your friend's name is Trung, correct?"

"Trung. A very old friend. We went to school at the New Star Temple."

"What name does he travel under now?"

"I don't know."

"What's Trung's full name?"

"I don't know."

"You went to school with him, and you don't know his full name?"

Hao said in English: "Wait one minute, please."

"Mr. Hao, his name is Trung Than."

"I think so."

"When was the last time he came to your house?"

"Please wait one minute."

—And Kim, in the hallway, her head down. Had they arranged it that way? Possibly. Probably. To what end? He didn't want to think this out too far. He hoped he understood his position. He hoped he had a grip on his goals. He said, in English, "I want to go from here to a good place. To Singapore."

"Singapore?"

"Yes. Maybe Singapore."

"Just you?"

"My wife also, please."

"You and your wife want to emigrate to Singapore."

" 'Zeckly."

"Is that your first choice?"

"I want to go to the United States."

"Then why did you say Singapore?"

"The colonel says I can go to Singapore."

"Colonel Sands?"

"He's my friend."

"He doesn't know what he's talking about. Malaysia's a better bet. —That is, if we're the ones helping you."

Hao didn't want their help. But the choice seemed help or harm.

"We're getting ahead of ourselves. Do you understand the expression?"

"Sometimes I don't understand."

"We need to talk later about things like where we put you. Right now we need to become friends. Nothing more."

"It's bad stuff."

"What's bad stuff?"

"Now."

"Now is bad stuff? Here and now?"

"Yes. Please. I am the colonel friend."

"You have the wrong friends."

"No. He is a good man."

"Certainly. A good man. Yeah—you have to wonder how many operations have been code-named 'Labyrinth.'" The boy didn't translate. "Do you want another Coke?"

"No, thank you. Sorry. My tooth has a sore."

"Hao, it's not bad stuff. In fact, if I can't pour another Coke down your gullet, I believe we're finished for today. I just wanted to introduce myself. I've done that, and I really don't have much else to say. Except I hope we can be friends. Once in a while I'll contact you, bring you down. We can talk. Get further acquainted, have a Coke. That okay with you?"

"Yes. A Coke," Hao said in English.

"Does Sammy need to translate what I just said?"

"No, it's okay. I understand."

"I guess we've lost the car. Let me give you some cab fare. You're planting a tree for Tet?"

"Yes. Every year, each year."

"Kumquat? With the orange fruit?"

"Kumquat."

"They're beautiful."

"Yes. That kind."

"Like the ones you have now in your front yard."

"Yes."

"You plant one every year? How many have you got?"

"Ten."

"And this one makes eleven."

"Yes. Eleven." Eleven years since my father died.

Crodelle seemed to study the lying device, which was made up of several components laid out on the tabletop. "Jesus, will you look at all these wires." He'd said nothing about keeping this visit a secret from the colonel. It probably suited their purposes either way. Or they guessed he'd never mention it because it could only lead to questions, and he'd be grappled down by lies. But Trung— should he tell Trung?

Crodelle said, "What on earth is all this for? . . . This thing obviously attaches to your finger . . ."

He'd wait for the next time Trung sought him out, and at that time he'd decide how much to tell.

Crodelle said, "One of these days you and I and a technician will sit down and find out how all this works."

Hao said, "It's the same."

"The same?"

He meant it's all the same, it doesn't matter, everybody's lying.

Kim waited out front of the house beside the tree, its roots wrapped in newspaper, until her husband came home in a cyclo cab. She watched him climb from the cart and pay and come at her smiling, as if nothing had happened.

"Those people asked me about Trung," she said. "Your friend."

"They asked me too," he said.

"Did you see me there?"

"I saw you in the basement."

"What do they want?"

"It all concerns Trung. I think he's in trouble."

"They said he comes here to visit us."

"No, Trung doesn't come here. Have you ever seen him here?"

"No. They asked me if he comes here, and I said no."

"They asked me too, and I said no, he doesn't come to my house."

"Good. If my grandmother's ghost chases you tonight howling at you, I'll tell you what she's saying: Don't scatter your kindnesses."

"That's the end of it," he said. "No trouble."

"This one's exactly the same size as most of the others," she said, meaning the tree. "I went to the market on my way home."

"Kim," her husband said, "listen to me: You know who I am."

"I can't find the shovel," she said. "Do you expect me to dig with my hands?"

"You know me," he said.

"Don't make trouble."

"I want peace."

"Then listen to my grandmother. She always told us, Don't scatter your kindnesses in the forest. Plant them where they'll grow and feed you."

"Good advice."

"Are those Americans angry at you?"

"No. Everything's good."

"Did they give you money for a cyclo?"

"More than enough."

"Me too. Where's the shovel?"

"I don't know."

They went to the edge of the low ironwork fence, and there, using the corner of a small board and his hands and fingers, he scraped out a hole, and they put the tree in it. From the next street over they heard singing, firecrackers, the cries of children. With the side of her foot she kicked the dirt into the hole, careful to get as little as possible on her sandal. Her husband stared at this operation as if wishing he could grow tiny and throw himself in.

Tomorrow she'd have her fortune told. She'd been looking forward to it. Now it seemed a punishment.

"Ah," he said, "I remember."

"What?"

"The shovel is in the . . ."

"Where?"

"No, no. It's not there," he said.

———

The double had arrived.

He came to the villa in the black Chevrolet, with an entourage, Hao, Jimmy Storm, the colonel, even Hao's young nephew Minh, formerly the colonel's helicopter pilot, now back with the Viet Nam Air Force but not, today, in uniform. To Skip it seemed a gathering unnecessarily inclusive.

They all sat in the parlor—the double Trung on the divan, between the colonel in his loud Hawaiian shirt and the uniformed Jimmy Storm—and Sands ordered coffee and studied this person he'd waited two years to get a look at.

Trung was about five-six, and bowlegged. He could have been any age between thirty and fifty, but Skip understood him to be Hao's old schoolmate, which would make him just past forty years old. He didn't grease his hair; it spiked upward in the middle of his scalp. He had dark skin of the kind in which miscellaneous shallow scratches left scars. Thick eyebrows came together sparsely over the bridge of his nose. He had large ears, a weak chin. An ugly face, but friendly. He wore Asian-looking, strangely tinted blue jeans and a green T-shirt a little small for him—both quite new-looking—and black high-top tennis shoes, also apparently Asian-made, also new, and no socks. He kept his hands on his knees and both feet on the floor. Between his feet lay a forest-green knapsack, probably new; collapsed, probably empty. In a kindly way, Trung met his stare. The whites of his eyes had a yellow tint. Maybe his relaxed manner came from illness.

At this moment, the most genuine and legitimate in Skip's journey as a Cold Warrior, his uncle seemed distracted, wouldn't sit down, walked from window to window looking out, and failed to make introductions.

"Skip, come with me. I've got some news. Come out front with me."

They stood outside the entry in the muggy morning, Skip thinking he should go upstairs and get into something besides

bathing trunks and a T-shirt, and the colonel said, "Skip, I've got
bad news."

"It looks more like good news."

"Yes, that's him, that's our man."

"That *is* good news."

"No. Yes," the colonel said. "Now. Skip. Your mother has died.
Beatrice. Bea."

The statement struck him like a blow to the chest. Yet its
meaning eluded him completely.

"What the *fuck*?" Skip said.

"The timing's terrible. And the cable is three days old."

"No. I don't believe it."

"Skip, sit down. Let's sit down." They rested themselves on the
step. Cool, worn granite. His uncle was reaching into his breast
pocket with his right hand. He placed his left on Skip's right
shoulder. Now Skip held in his hands a pale yellow piece of paper.
Whenever afterward he reviewed this moment he was unable to
suppress these details, he had to include them.

The colonel said, "I'll be back with a drink," and left him
alone with the cablegram. He read it several times. In it his
mother's pastor explained she'd passed away due to complications
following a routine radical hysterectomy. Whatever that meant.
The pastor offered his sympathies and above all his prayers.

The colonel returned with a glass in his hand.

" 'Routine radical,' " Skip said. "How do you like that?"

"Here. Please. Here. You need a good stiff shot."

"Jesus, okay."

His uncle stood over him holding out the glass, but Skip failed
to accept it. Palms up, he held the cablegram like a big delicate
ash. "I'll miss the funeral."

"It's bad stuff."

"I hope somebody's there."

"She was a fine woman. I'm sure she has many mourners."

The colonel drank away half the glass he'd carried here for his
nephew. "The cable came three days ago. I was in Cao Phuc.

They radioed me that a cable had come, and I meant to get in touch with somebody and find out the content, but I failed to make it a priority—there's so much cable traffic, and it's generally so picayune, as you know . . . And in all honesty, Skip, I was distracted."

"Well, no, you don't need to—you know."

"It's all done. No more Echo. Courtesy of Johnny Brewster, probably. But maybe not. For all I know, they're just getting us out of the way so they can carpet-bomb the place."

"Jesus."

"So I'm sorry about the delay. When I got back, Trung said he was ready to move. In all the excitement about losing Cao Phuc, I'd almost forgotten him entirely."

"The funeral is day after tomorrow."

"Go, if you feel you have to."

"Obviously, I can't."

"The folks back home understand. They realize you're off to war."

"Can I have my drink?"

"Oh, shit."

Skip drained the glass.

"Skip, I'm going to leave you a few minutes to collect yourself. Then we'll need you back inside ready to do your work."

"I know. Jesus. Both in one day."

"I'm sorry, but that's how it is."

"Sure. I'll be in."

Skip watched the road beyond the gate. Not thinking about his mother at all. He supposed he'd think about her later. He couldn't predict the order of these emotional events, his mother had never died before. Nor anyone close to him. His father had gone before he could remember. His Uncle Francis had lost a young son, drowned while sailing off Cape Cod, to say nothing of all the comrades fallen in war. Skip himself had watched his uncle shoot a man who hung from a tree branch. Guess what? People died. He wished he didn't have to take this moment alone.

It was useless to him. He was glad when his uncle returned and sat by his side.

"Well, Uncle. I'm your orphan nephew."

"Beatrice was a wonderful wife to my brother. I never thought of it before, Skip, but he must have died in the midst of his happiness. It was short, but she made him very happy."

"They killed her. The butchers."

"No, no, no. They know their stuff. You've seen what they can do. You bring in a foot soldier in half a dozen pieces—a year later he's ready for the parade."

Skip folded the cable in half and again in half but couldn't choose which one of his pockets to defile with it. He tossed it overhand toward the road.

"You know what? Your dad knew what counted. He married early. He wasn't like the rest of us. Hell, in our family none of us is like the rest of us. I'm five-foot-eight with shoes on. Your Uncle Ray is six-four."

"Is he your senior?"

"Ray? He's two years younger. Two years and three months."

"Oh."

"The point is, you've got family. You're not an orphan. I guess that's the point."

"Thank you."

"I mean it. But you know that. You always have. Now, listen, it's bad stuff, and the timing's terrible . . ."

"I'll be fine. Let's go in."

Mr. Skip had said the local priest might know where to buy a certain kind of powdered bark from which Kim wished to brew a medicinal tea. These days her health seemed good. But herbs and medicines still enthralled her. Hao and his nephew left the Americans and went looking for the priest's house, taking the creekside path for only a couple of hundred meters, passing behind a series of small yards, each with one or two or three monuments covering family graves, and entered the Catholic domain by the back garden.

In the homes up and down the creek old women boiled the day's rice over charcoal or sticks of kindling, but no smoke came from the priest's. Minh had to whistle twice. The little man came from the back of the house barefoot, cinching his belt, buttoning a long-tailed American-style shirt hanging nearly to his knees.

Hao felt irritation at finding him home. He'd only wanted to talk to his nephew about the family business.

"Yes, I know you," the priest said when Hao began to introduce himself, and Hao explained he needed herbs for his wife. Also, perhaps, something for a bad tooth.

"I can give you directions, but I can't escort you."

"That's fine."

"I'm not going out today," the priest said. "I'm staying in. I had an important dream."

Minh asked, "Did the dream tell you to stay indoors today?"

"No, I just want to be quiet and remember and understand."

Hao wished he didn't have to talk to such people. But his wife—ghosts, dreams, potions, every kind of nonsense. So here he was. "Do you know of an herbalist or not?"

"Take the road north out of town. The third hamlet you reach, ask for the Chinese family. They're not really Chinese," he added.

"Thank you."

They walked back to the villa by the roadway. Hao decided this quest for phony remedies would end here. No enchanted powders for Kim. He'd make up a lie. "It doesn't matter," he told his nephew. "I only wanted to talk to you. We haven't seen you for weeks. Three months, at least."

"I'm sorry, Uncle," Minh said. "I'm the general's slave. I can't get away."

"And the last time you visited you didn't even stay for tea. It wasn't us you came to the city for. It was your woman friend."

"It's difficult, Uncle."

"I asked the colonel to bring you to my house today, or you probably wouldn't have come."

"And the colonel brought me here."

"Is it such an inconvenience?"

"It's a journey. I'm not necessary here, but I like to see you, and it's good to see the colonel."

"There's a problem with my wife's brother. Huy."

"I know about it. Uncle Huy."

"It's impossible. Do you have guns on your helicopter?"

"It's General Phan's helicopter."

"What kind of guns?"

"One machine gun."

"I want you to attack the house."

"Uncle Huy's house?"

"He doesn't belong in it. It's my house. He owes me eleven years' rental."

"You want me to strafe the house?" Minh said, using the English word.

"No," said Hao in English, "not strafe. Not strafe. Destroy."

"With much love and respect, Uncle, that's not a good idea."

"You see how angry I am."

"I see."

"Then go back home to Lap Vung. Talk to your Uncle Huy, tell him how angry I am. Will you go home for Tet?"

"No, I can't go. I'll go for my aunt's birthday."

"His wife?"

"In March."

"What date exactly?"

"March eighteenth."

"Talk to him, please."

"He's a stubborn man. I don't want to ruin Aunt Giang's birthday."

"Ruin it. I don't care. You see how angry I am."

They'd arrived at the low iron gate of the big villa in which his old friend Trung, surrounded by Americans, gambled negligently with his future. So. Trung had all along been completely sincere. Hao had never believed him.

Inside, the colonel was talking, seated on the divan next to Trung with a teacup in one hand and the other hand on Trung's shoulder. Hao had seen little of the colonel lately, and in any case was terrified of him now. On Trung's other side sat Jimmy Storm, his arms crossed in front of his chest and an ankle resting on his knee, as if someone had tied him in a knot and left him helpless. Trung, however, seemed completely at ease.

Hao and Minh took chairs at the border between parlor and office, not quite in nor out of the gathering. The colonel stopped talking to Skip in order to interrupt himself, saying, "It's two families helping each other. In the end it's all about family. Do you have family, Mr. Trung?"

Trung looked confused, and Hao translated.

Trung told Hao, "I have a sister in Ben Tre. My mother died a long time ago. You remember."

Hao spoke Vietnamese: "The colonel's sister-in-law just died a few days ago. The mother of his nephew here."

"This man with us now?"

Hao nodded once.

"Sounds like he's got family," the colonel said.

Hao told him Trung had one sister whom he hadn't seen for several years.

The colonel caressed Trung's shoulder. "This guy's the goods. He's been on board since '46. Twenty-plus years."

Mr. Jimmy hadn't said a word. Hao disliked the way he stared.

Trung said, "This young man's mother just died?"

"His uncle brought the message this morning."

"Please tell him I'm sorry."

But the colonel was addressing Skip: "What I want you to apprehend above all is that you're not running this man. In a sense you're not even collecting data. Definitely not interrogating. Definitely not. Just serve as a sponge."

"I understand, sir."

"If you regard yourself as learning, just getting his story in general, we'll all be much better off."

"All right."

"And I don't want you sweating under any elaborate fiction, either. Whatever he asks you, I want you to be completely honest with him—long as you're sure he's not digging for product."

"All right."

"But, I mean, if he asks about your background, your family, your life—everything, tell him all of it."

"Very good."

"What is he saying?" Trung asked Hao.

"He's giving instructions. He told his nephew to be honest with you."

"Will you say for me that I'm grateful?"

Hao wanted to shout: I'm lying to all of you.

"You two, you'll have to work out your commo," the colonel told Skip.

Skip said, "We'll get along."

Going back to Saigon, Minh rode in the backseat with Jimmy Storm. Minh didn't know why he'd been asked along on this outing. Because they were two families helping each other, he understood this, but still, he played no role. As short as a month ago he'd have resented the time out of his furlough, but Miss Cam, his girlfriend—her father had turned cold toward Minh, the house was closed to him, and she refused to meet him secretly. Apparently the father had depended on marrying his family to Uncle Hao's wealth. He must have learned there wasn't any.

His uncle's problems had crushed the good sense from his head. The preoccupation with the house on the Mekong and the rental he surely knew he'd never see, and the suggestion Minh murder the whole bunch, it was all too silly. Meanwhile, Hao hadn't even mentioned the colonel, particularly not the change in him. The colonel was pale, breathing was work, all morning he'd sipped his Bushmills rather than gulping it, and he'd held the glass with his fingertips rather than in his fist. And Jimmy Storm had kept unusually silent, unaware, or pretending to be, of the colonel's deepened loneliness.

Minh himself had seen little of the colonel since his C&C chopper had gone back to the Viet Nam Air Force, and Minh with it, still its pilot. Except for the .30-caliber machine gun his uncle was so anxious to have him turn on his own family, the craft carried no assault equipment; he was spared combat and remained an aerial taxi driver, now for General Phan. The general had given him an unprecedented week's furlough. He felt grateful, but saw the leniency as part of a new pattern. The military's attitude had changed. He didn't like it. The fire had died.

"Hao," the colonel said, "stop the car."

They'd reached Route Twenty-two by now. Hao pulled to the side of it and the colonel got out, in order to relieve himself, Minh presumed.

But he only stood beside the vehicle, fixing his attention, it seemed, on a solitary cloud in the sky ahead of them like a small, wispy moon perhaps many dozens of kilometers distant, perhaps poised over the China Sea, which was invisible to them. The colonel moved toward the front of the car, knuckles of one hand resting on its hood, right hand on his hip, and waited in the brown landscape of dirt, once thick jungle and paddies, now poisoned rubble, nothing but jags and skeletons, and glowered at the cloud as if trying to influence its activity, staring down this thing of nature until its drift had taken it some ways southward out of their path.

He got back in the car. "Okay. Roll on."

No one else spoke. Even from the sergeant there came only silence. Minh had once felt himself acquainted with the rhythms of these two comrades. He sensed a blank space where Storm should have made a dry comment, or one of his jokes.

Skip realized he'd overprepared. What had been left to him these past two years but to memorize the labyrinths of doubt and J. P. Dimmer's "Observations on the Double Agent"?

"Experience suggests," Dimmer warned his readership, that some people who take to the double agent role—perhaps a majority of willing ones, in fact—have a number of traits in common . . . Psychiatrists describe such persons as sociopaths.

- They are unusually calm and stable under stress but cannot tolerate routine or boredom.
- They do not form lasting and adult emotional relationships with other people because their attitude toward others is exploitative.
- They have above-average intelligence. They are good verbalizers—sometimes in two or more languages.
- They are skeptical and even cynical about the motives and abilities of others but have exaggerated notions about their own competence.
- Their reliability as agents is largely determined by the extent to which the case officer's instructions coincide with what they consider their own best interests.
- They are ambitious only in a short-range sense: they want much and they want it now. They do not have the patience to plod toward a distant reward.
- They are naturally clandestine and enjoy secrecy and deception for its own sake.

The double who'd never encountered J. P. Dimmer said to Sands, "Your tea is delicious. I like it strong."

Skip carried a pair of dictionaries from his study and laid them on the coffee table. He assumed this man waited for instructions he couldn't give him, while he, Skip, the officer-on-site, wanted what? To stop waiting. To serve. To make himself indispensable in putting this man to use against his own people. To know this man, and his uncle was right, you won't map a traitor's mind with thirty yes-or-no answers and three lines traveling a polygram. Better the floundering and backtracking and getting lost, bilingual dictionaries and mismatched goals. And even with these difficulties and with his bridges on fire behind him, this Trung savored his tea, allowed himself to be completely caught up in Mrs. Diu's shortbread pastries, and enjoyed his introduction to M. Bouquet and recommended roasting the dog on a spit rather than boiling him in pieces. No slippery gaze, no tenseness about the knuckles, nothing like that. Where was Judas? Skip began to wonder if this wasn't perhaps some off-course neighbor of Hao's, here by some ludicrous miscommunication. The double had only a little English, and Skip's Vietnamese was simply inadequate. Both spoke French with slightly less than true facility. In all three languages they might make zigzag progress toward crossed purposes.

"In the United States we don't eat dogs. Dogs are our friends."

"But you are not in the United States now. This is Vietnam. You're far from home, and this is a sad day. Mr. Skip, I'm very sad for you. I wish I came on another day."

"You understood my mother passed on?"

"My friend Hao explained it. I'm very sad for you."

"Thank you."

"What was your mother's age?"

"Fifty-two."

"I came back from the North in 1964. After ten years in that place. The march home was very hard. All the way I thought about my mother, and my love for her came to life again strongly. I remembered many things about her that I didn't know I remembered. I was very sad to think she'd be an older person when I returned to her. I wanted my mother to be young again. But when I reached Ben Tre she was dead for six months. She lived to be almost sixty. Her name was Dao, which is a kind of blossom. So I cut the dao blossom for her monument."

"Do you have a wife? Children?"

"No. Nobody."

"And your father?"

"He died when I was a small child. Killed by the French."

"Mine too. Killed by the Japanese."

"Any wife for you? Some children?"

"Not yet."

"So it's very hard. I see it. Very hard when the second one goes away. How did your mother die?"

"I'm not sure. Some surgery that went wrong. How about yours?"

"An illness. My sister said it lasted for almost four months. Our mother died while I myself was very sick and I had to stop along the way down from the North. A fever came over me. Not like malaria. Something different. I lay in a hammock for two weeks. Other sick comrades came and strung their hammocks in the same place and we lay there without anyone to help us. After a few days some of the hammocks held corpses. I survived my illness and waited to feel my mother's arms around me again. I was very sad to find she'd died, but in those days I had strength, and my passion for the cause was much bigger than my sadness. I was sent to Cao Phuc, where one of my first orders was to assassinate your uncle. But I didn't kill him. My explosive failed. Aren't you glad?"

"Very glad."

"If it had functioned, my friend Hao also would have died. But the cause meant more than Hao. I'd already lost many comrades. You bury a friend—that gives you an enemy. It calls you more deeply into the cause. Then the time comes when you kill a friend. And that might drive you away. It can also have the oppo-site result—to deafen you against your own voice when it wants to ask questions."

"And you began to ask questions. Is that what brings you to us?"

"I had questions from the beginning. I didn't have ears to hear them."

"What changed for you, Trung?"

"I don't know. Perhaps my mother's death. For a man without children, that's a big change. Then the time is ready for your own death. Any time it can come, even before your body is killed."

"What exactly do you mean? I don't think I understand."

"Perhaps you don't want to."

During supper, when his lousy Vietnamese kept the talk to a minimum, Skip observed his environment anew—wondering what the visitor must see—fine old mahogany and rattan furniture, an imposing front door where normally in this region the home's entire face would stand open to the air, protected at night by iron gatework; and plastered walls decorated with paintings on lacquered wood, brushstroke pastorals: studious, silent scenes with sawtoothed coconut palms in a world without a soul to be torn. Mrs. Diu served a beef-and-noodle soup, greens, steamed rice. This morning she'd placed small yet striking arrangements of blooms around the house. Skip realized she did it daily. He'd hardly noticed. She and Mr. Tho lived just upstream from the villa in a hooch surrounded by palm and frangipani trees with white blossoms . . . At one point the double covered his mouth with a hand and yawned.

"Are you sleepy?"

"Not yet. Where will I sleep?"

"I have a room ready upstairs."

"Anywhere."

"It's not elegant."

Trung then either asked for a pistol or declared he possessed one.

"Excuse me?"

He said it again, in French: "Do you have a pistol for me?"

"No. Nothing like that."

The request called him back to the situation. He'd ceased thinking of this man as anyone in particular. A guest, someone deserving of hospitality, nothing more.

"For protection only."

"You won't need protection. You're safe here."

"All right. I believe you."

For dessert Mrs. Diu served a delicate egg custard. Trung and Skip got out the dictionaries. "Sorry about my Vietnamese. I've studied, but I can hardly make out a word you say."

"People tell me I picked up an accent from the North. But I didn't pick up much else there. In the North we southerners stuck together. We have a style down here. It's very different from up there."

Skip said, "That's true in our country too."

"What are the southerners like in your country?"

"They're known to be very gracious and slow of speech. Among their families and friends they're very open with their affection. Whereas in the North we're thought to be more restrained, more cautious, we give less of ourselves. That's how we're known. But there are exceptions. A person's birthplace can't tell you everything. And you know, we had a civil war too. The North against the South."

"Yes, we know your history. We study your history, your novels, your poems."

"It's true?"

"Of course. Even before your military came to Vietnam, America was important in the world. The world's major capitalist nation. I like Edgar Allan Poe very much."

Next they talked of the mistake of the war, without mentioning whose mistake it was. "In Vietnam," Trung said, "we have the Confucian mode for times of stability—for wisdom, social conduct, and so on. We have the Buddhist mode for times of tragedy and war—for acceptance of the facts, and for keeping the mind single."

"Yes, I've heard that said."

"The war will never stop."

"But it has to."

"I can't expect to see the end. I want to go to the United States."

"We understand that. And it can be arranged." He pictured this man standing on a corner in San Francisco, waiting for a sign that said WALK. Some of Skip's childhood schoolmates had come from immigrant parents, Scandinavian, most of them. He'd visited their stuffy homes, felt his lungs clutched by alien odors, looked at unimaginable bric-a-brac and cloudy photographs of military men with feathers jutting up behind the brimless caps of their uniforms, and heard the parents fumble the grammar and drop small words, thick-spoken and sincere, everything about them an affront to their sons, who endured the fathers in silence and rushed past their mothers' offerings: "Yes, Ma—okay, Ma—I gotta go, Ma." Naturally at his age Skip had overlooked these grown-ups, heroes of dogged risk, ocean-crossers, exiles. With their little questions they touched the walls of their children. On the other side, this child for whose sake they'd wagered their lives rolled his sleeves up tightly above his biceps, plastered back his hair with Wildroot Cream-Oil, lied about girls, performed surgery on firecrackers, golf balls, dead cats, propelled loogies of snot at lampposts, laughed like an American, cursed without an accent. But his best friend in the seventh grade, the Lithuanian Ricky Sash—probably from Szasz, come to think of it—said "please" and "thank you" as much as "fuck you," and tied his shoes with a big double knot. Nothing else gave him away. Asians wouldn't have it so easy. "Certainly," Skip said, "we've wondered about your motives."

"Do you want a practical reason?"

"Can you give me one?"

"No."

"You understand: for us, it's an important question."

"You need something simple. You need to hear me say I stole some Communist Party funds or I'm in love with a forbidden woman and we must escape."

"Something like that."

"It's nothing like that."

"Can you tell me?"

"With every gesture I make in betraying my comrades and my cause, I feel pain in my soul, but it's the pain of life returning."

The poignant shreds of a torn heart, or high-minded sewage?

"Trung, you say you want the U.S. But you say you'll go north."

"First the North. Then the USA. I know a way north."

"The colonel mentioned you worked with primitives."

"Some boys from Ba Den. It's true. There was a program to enlist the tribes, or at least indoctrinate them. I don't know what happened to the program. There's so much wasted effort. And pointless death."

"The colonel is interested in such people."

"It's true, he wants me to accompany a group to the North again."

"Why would you go back north?"

"The question is why didn't I get out a dozen years ago, when I went to the North and hated it there? In 1954 some people stayed in the South because they knew the party expected nothing in two years, no election, no reunification. The rest of us weren't so smart. We boarded the ships for the North with our eyes put out by hope, and saw nothing. They took us north to make us forget our homes, our families, our true land. But I only remembered more clearly. I remembered the red earth of Ben Tre, not the yellow earth of the North. I remembered the warm southern days, not the chilly northern nights. I remembered the happiness of my village and not the rivalry and thieving of the kolkhoz. The life of the family, the life of the village, that's the communal life—not the kolkhoz. You can't throw people together and forbid them to leave and tell them they're a commune united by doctrine. I thought Marx would give us back our families and villages. That's because I only thought of the end Marx talked about: I don't know the English or the French, but he says that at the end of the future the state is like a vine that will die and fall off. That's what I expected. Do you know Marx? Do you know the phrase?"

"I know the English." Together they paged through the dictionaries and Sands devised an equivalent for the expression "the withering away of the state."

"Yes. The withering away of the state. And when it withers away, it leaves my family and my village. That's what I saw at the end of the future: the French are gone, the Americans are gone, the Communists are gone, my village returns, my family returns. But they lied."

"When did you realize they lied?"

"Soon after I came to the North. But it didn't matter to me then that they lied. The Americans were here. First we must deal with the Americans, then we can deal with the truth. I was wrong. The truth is highest. The truth first. Always the truth. Everything else comes after the truth."

"I agree. But what truth are you talking about?"

"The Buddha describes four truths: Dukkha, Samudaya, Nirodha, Magga. Life is suffering. Suffering comes from grasping. Grasping can be relinquished. The Eightfold Path leads to this relinquishment."

"You believe it?"

"Not all of it. I can only tell you my experience. I know from experience that life is suffering, and that suffering comes from clinging to things that won't stay."

"Well, those are facts. What we in America would call 'the facts of life.'"

"Then what is the truth for you in America?"

"Something beyond the facts. I suppose we'd call the Word of God the truth."

"And what is the word from God to America?"

"Let me think." He laid his hand again on the French-English volume. But he was tired now. Ten minutes' conversation had dragged them through a hundred dictionary entries and taken nearly two hours. He knew only the Word as imparted by Beatrice Sands, his Lutheran mother: This life, she'd wanted to tell him at moments that transported her, moments that embarrassed him because he viewed her as a woman unworthy of them, a woman trapped by clotheslines in a yard of tall grass by the railroad tracks, this life is but the childhood of our immortality. Mother, now you know if it's true. And I pray to God you weren't wrong. And as for America—inalienable rights, government by consent, parchments, mountains, elections, cemeteries, parades . . . "Well, all of it can be debated," he said in English. "In any language it can all be argued about. But the facts you name can't be argued with. But there's something beyond that." He tried French: "There is a truth, but it can't be told. It's here."

"Yes, there's nothing else. This place, this moment now."

"And now I'm very tired, Mr. Than."

"I am too, Mr. Skip. Have we done enough today?"

"We've done enough."

He put Trung upstairs, across the small hallway from his own quarters, in the room full of the colonel's files, among which he hoped the double slept soundly. Skip slept, but not soundly. He woke in the dark and looked at the iridescent dials of his watch: a quarter after two. He'd dreamed of his mother Beatrice. The details evaporated as he tried to remember them, and only his grief stayed, and a certain excitement. He'd been everything to her. That could stop now. No longer a widow's only child—once on the long train ride to Boston he'd looked out the car as it moved slowly through downtown scenes—Chicago? Buffalo?—to see two boys on the street outside a small grocery, eight- or nine-year-olds, ragged, sooty, smoking cigarettes, and had assumed they must be orphans. Hereafter, that's who he was.

Then remorse crushed him physically, the blood pounded in his head, he struggled for breath—he hadn't called, hadn't written, left her to ride to her death on a gurney all alone in helplessly polite apologetic midwestern confusion and fear. He flung the netting aside, put his feet on the floor, straightened his shoulders, raised his face, and drew air in short gasps. Maybe a drink.

———

Trung turned in upstairs in the big house in a storeroom filled with boxes, on a bed made of boards stretched between two foot-lockers and covered with a Japanese straw tatami. The CIA's rep-resentative had given him a butane lamp, and he had a socialist-realism novel in Vietnamese which he didn't care to fin-ish and a copy of *Les Misérables* in French. He'd read it so many times it no longer interested him. He lay in the dark feeling the house around him and wondering if he'd ever slept in a dwelling this large, outside of the New Star Temple of his boyhood.

He heard the hallway's other door open. With the soft tread of bare feet Mr. Skip passed the storeroom and took the stairs down to the rest of the house.

What now? Grief, sleeplessness, Trung believed. Noises from the kitchen—It's best to leave him alone. His mother is gone.

Mother, I grieve for you still.

He lay in the dark ten minutes and then got up and followed. Downstairs he found the American in shorts and T-shirt, sitting beside a hissing butane lantern in the study with a book, and a glass with ice in it beside the lantern. "Did you get some sleep?"

"Not yet."

"I'm having some Irish whiskey. Can I get you some?"

"All right. I'll try it."

Mr. Skip started to rise, and then said, "We have glasses in the kitchen," and settled back in his chair.

When Trung had found a glass and returned, the American was paging through one of his phrase books. He reached to the floor beside his chair and raised his bottle of liquor. Trung held out the glass and he poured a little into it.

"Do I drink it fast or slow?"

"How do you drink rice brandy?"

"A little slowly," Trung said, and sipped. Musky and medicinal. "It's quite good."

"Please. Sit."

Trung took the chair at the desk, sitting sideways.

Mr. Skip said, "I've been looking for your name." He closed his phrase book.

"'Than' means the color of the sky, and there's a flower that color also, with the same name."

"I don't know it. You mean the blue of the sky?"

"Blue, like the sky."

"And 'Trung' means 'loyalty,' doesn't it?"

"Loyalty to the country. It's humorous today that I have this name."

The study was lined with shelves, the shelves full of books. Tight netting covered the two windows, also the eaves in the main room and the ironwork on either side of the wooden door to the outside. Nevertheless small bugs attacked the butane lamp and died.

"You have a lot of books."

"They don't belong to me."

"Who lives here?"

"Just me and a ghost."

"Whose ghost?"

"The previous owner. The man who built the house."

"I see. I thought perhaps you meant me."

Mr. Skip emptied his glass and poured a little more whiskey over what was left of his ice. He didn't speak.

"Perhaps I'm intruding."

"No. I appreciate the company."

The American finished his drink. "I thought you'd be Judas," he said, "but you're more like the Christ."

"I hope that's good."

"It is what it is. Do you want some more?"

"I'll finish mine slowly."

The American said in English, "You've gone there. You're there, aren't you? What is it like to carry two souls in one body? It's the truth, isn't it. It's who we really are. The rest of us are just half of what we should be. You're there, you're there, but you killed something to get there. You killed—what." Trung couldn't follow.

And the resignation to the truth, the final resignation, the despair that breaks into liberation, where was the word for that in all these books?

In silence the American poured another for himself and drank it slowly. Trung stayed, though it was clear the American didn't want conversation.

Next morning his friend Hao came again. The woman served breakfast, and he and Skip and Hao sat down to eat, but Trung sensed some trouble.

Mr. Skip asked them about their days at the New Star Temple. They told him about the times they'd stolen brandy during the Tet celebrations, told of laughter and singing; all three conducting themselves like students in a foreign-language exercise called "Breakfast with an American."

"Trung, the library's all yours today. I have to go to Saigon on an errand. I'll be back around noon tomorrow."

"I'll stay by myself?"

"If you don't mind."

Trung walked them to the black car. He detained Hao a minute. "What is it about?"

"Only a quick meeting."

"Tell me."

"I can't. I don't know."

"Nothing serious?"

"I don't think so."

The American had heard them. Standing on the other side of the car, he spoke across the hot metal roof. "A friend has invited me to lunch. A colleague. I think I'd better see what he wants."

"Perhaps there's a safer place for me until you come back."

"No, no, no. Nobody knows you're here."

"But they know that you are here."

"That's not a problem," the American said. Trung disbelieved him.

Dietrich Fest of Department Five of West Germany's Bundesnachrich-tendienst boarded a night flight at the National Airport near Washington, DC, and for eighteen hours had nothing to do but read and nap and nothing to think about other than his father's medical crises. Seven, eight months since the old man had seen the outside of a hospital. Gallbladder; liver; heart; a series of small strokes; hemorrhaging in the bowels with massive blood loss and transfusions; a feeding tube in his stomach; latest of all pneumonia. The old man refused to die. But he would. Perhaps already. Perhaps earlier while I dozed with a sagging head. Perhaps now while I look at a stupid mystery book. "Claude," the old man had called him when he'd visited in October—wires and tubes exiting from him everywhere, blue eyes shining into space. "Look, it's Claude," he'd told the urine-smelling, otherwise empty room, and Fest had said, "No, it's Dirk," and his father's eyes had closed.

At 3:00 p.m. local time Fest landed in Hong Kong. He gave his cabbie inaccurate instructions and was forced, some blocks short of his hotel, to get out of the taxi and continue on foot. Even this tiny vehicle was too large for these tiny streets. With his one bag Fest climbed a steep stair-stepped alley jammed with doorless shops selling nothing but junk.

On a larger thoroughfare he hailed a pedicab and rode behind a stringy old man wearing a kind of diaper who pedaled him swiftly to his hotel, which was right there, looming three blocks straight ahead, as the old man might easily have told him. Two minutes after climbing aboard the strange conveyance, Fest had arrived. A printed notice posted just behind the bicycle's handlebars listed the official rates, and for a journey of this small distance Fest owed four or five Hong Kong dollars; but the old man smacked fist on fist and shouted, "Tunty dollah! Tunty dollah!" Fest didn't begrudge him. At his age, the old man deserved whatever he could get for such labor. But Fest believed in fair dealing in business. He refused. In seconds he was hemmed in by pedicabs and besieged by diapered drivers of all sizes, babbling, frothing. He thought he saw a knife. An angry bellboy came out and drove them all off with magical outward-chopping gestures of his hand. The old man remained. He'd rather die. Fest turned over the twenty dollars. He went upstairs and slept through the afternoon, woke at 2:00 a.m., and read a short novel—Georges Simenon, in English. He called the hotel's operator and asked about overseas calls to Berlin, but his mother's number was somewhere in his bag, and he let it go. He'd called her frequently of late, almost daily in recent weeks, while she dealt with his father's failing health.

At eight he showered, dressed, and went downstairs to the lobby to meet his contact. They drank coffee, sitting across from one another in large uncomfortable mahogany chairs. The contact was an American, youthful, impressed with his assignment, a little pious about his role. At first he told Fest only where he was going. Of course he knew where he was going, he had the ticket in his pocket.

"Do you have the ID materials for me?"

The young man lurched downward to rummage in his leather briefcase, clasping it between his shoes. "We have two versions for you." He handed over a manila envelope. "While on assignment you use the one with the predated entry visa. Destroy it before you leave. For your exit use the one with the postdated visa."

"How long is determined for this assignment?"

"You mean according to the visas? The postdated one says you entered on—what does it say? February eleventh, I think. So you'll have to stay in-country till then, at least. But the visa's good for six months."

He didn't like the sound of six months. But the purpose of a visa postdated by two weeks was to say he'd entered after the period of the assignment. He took it, therefore, that they'd planned for no more than two weeks' duration.

Fest laid the envelope across his lap, pinched together the clasps, opened the flap, and raised its open end to peek within. Two German passports—he took one out and read the bearer's name—Claude Gunter Reinhardt.

"Interesting. My son is named Claude." After the old man. And my dead heroic brother.

"Whatever's on top of the stack."

"Of course. A coincidence."

The face was his own. He'd always looked somewhat like a spoiled boy, but the beard covered the softness and made him look, he believed, a little like Sigmund Freud or Ernest Hemingway. In clothing, perhaps, he appeared portly, but he felt solid. Even in the States they'd kept him taking courses, including physically challenging operational training. But he was thirty-six and two months. This couldn't go on. In fact he'd thought it was over with the American posting.

"You enter on your own passport. Whatever you're traveling with now."

"Of course."

As the man paid for their rolls and coffee and rose to go, he assumed an insufferable casualness and mentioned, as if in afterthought, the pass-signs and the time and place arranged for Fest's briefing in Saigon.

Fest distrusted Hong Kong's drivers now. He skipped lunch and left for the airport two hours early and arrived without trouble and sat watching his fellow passengers assemble for their journey home, cheery affluent Asians returning from holidays in Hong Kong or Bangkok or Manila with pastel shopping bags, smiles, even laughter. He didn't know what he'd expected—the beleaguered members of a ravaged populace, hunched shoulders, tight faces—he hadn't thought much about this war, had never expected to come to it, had been sent, he was sure, ill-advisedly, like everybody else. The stewardess gave him a purple Vietnam Airlines traveling bag and he held it empty in his lap looking down at the clouds and nodded off until late afternoon, when the same stewardess touched his shoulder to tell him they were descending toward Tan Son Nhut.

In a deteriorating terminal crowded with soldiers both

American and Asian, the floor piled with boxes and baggage, he
found his man, a Negro holding up a small sign saying MEEKER
IMPORTS. "Mr. Reinhardt," the man said. "I'm Kenneth Johnson.
Anybody else?"

"I don't know."

"Me neither. But we'll take all comers." A man of good cheer.
There was nobody else.

"How was the flight?"

"All flights end on the ground."

"That's what the ducks say. Jesus," he said, "who thinks up
these pass-signs?"

"I don't know," Fest said, and added nothing, though he understood this was probably the moment for a joke.

They came out through the front entrance to a line of taxis
whose drivers leapt up waving, and Johnson said, "You're all set up
under the name of Reinhardt at a place called the Quan Pho Xa.
You're papered for Reinhardt, right?"

"Correct."

"All right. Off you go, Mr. Reinhardt."

"I don't understand."

"This is as far as I go. I'm just verifying arrival."

"I see."

"You'll get a glimpse of me tomorrow. Just a glimpse."

"At the briefing?"

"Yes. Just a glimpse."

"Will I use the same pass-sign?"

"No. I'll be there to introduce you."

They shook hands, and Kenneth Johnson put him in a cab
and spoke to the driver briefly and was gone.

"Do you speak English?"

"Yes, sir. Little bit."

"Do you know where my hotel is?"

"Yes, sir. Hotel Quan Pho Xa."

"What does it mean?"

He got no answer. The taxi entered the city proper, passed down an avenue crowded with buildings painted pink or blue or yellow, and slowed, stopped, moved a couple of car lengths, stopped. The driver told him it was the New Year. Everyone was going somewhere. "What is New Year this time?" Fest asked. "Year of Dog? Year of Goat?" The driver said he didn't know. A buzzing tide of motorbikes flowed around the larger vehicles. One went past with a woman passenger seated sidesaddle, ankles crossed, reading a magazine. Engines coughing out exhaust. The palms looked none too healthy. He watched a foursome of street boys who lounged on the pavement playing cards for cigarettes.

Why had they stopped him in Hong Kong to pick up documents prepared in Saigon?

The traffic moved again. On gravestones in a tiny cemetery he saw emblems in a swastika shape, and swastikas carved on the door of its small temple. The sight shocked him. Years since he'd seen one, except in photographs. Including two or three taken of his father. Fest watched for street signs and landmarks, trying to inscribe it all on his mind, to locate himself. He checked his watch. In nineteen hours he'd be briefed as to schedule and method. The brusque treatment at the hands of Kenneth Johnson told him much. His colleagues wanted him only at a distance. Possibly he'd been sent here after an American—even Kenneth Johnson himself.

It was raining lightly but felt no cooler when he got out of the cab at the hotel. A woman sat on her sandals outside the entrance. He guessed Americans didn't stay here—she was its only protection.

While he checked in, the two girls downstairs in the lobby, the receptionist and her assistant or her friend, sang unintelligible lyrics along with their radio.

"What is your name?" he asked the clerk.

"Thuyet."

"Thuyet, can I make an overseas telephone call?"

"No, sir. Only cable. Only the telegram."

She wore a blue skirt and crisp white blouse. She interested

him. Bizarre and delicate of face. No jewelry, no paint, but probably all of them were whores.

He showered and changed and went down to the street, wondering where he'd find an overseas telephone to call his mother. It
was night now. In the distance above the city, helicopters tore up
the air with their rotor blades, and tracer bullets streaked upward
into the darker reaches. From over the horizon, bombs thundered.
Down here, innumerable little horns and small engines. Radios
playing silly local music.

Sandbags lined the curbs. He walked along the fractured sidewalk, picking his way among holes and people's outstretched feet
and parked motorbikes, chased by beggars and pimps and snide,
sassy children who offered him "cigarette, grass, boom-boom,
U-globe, opium."

"Bread," he said.

"No bread because of Happy New Year," a vendor explained.

He gave up hope of a telephone and had dinner in a place
with hostesses wearing fringed red miniskirts and small red cowboy hats and fancy plastic gun belts with empty holsters. The waitress said because of the New Year they had no bread today.

Fest had seen the signs and banners saying "Chuc Mung Nam
Moy" and gathered they wished him a Happy New Year, though
they could just as easily have meant The Plague Is Terrible.

He woke in the night, as he'd done the night before. He heard
gunfire outside. He fumbled with the bed net, and keeping low he
crossed the room and chanced a look over the windowsill. A
woman walked along in the glow of a paper lantern. Her hand,
swinging the light by its wire haft, looked like a claw. Children
chased past her in the street, setting off firecrackers. He heard
music, and voices singing. He went back to bed. His pattern
hadn't changed yet, he wouldn't sleep again tonight. He had two
books and he'd read them both. The ceiling fan whirred at its top
speed but didn't cool him. Out the window the madness continued. It seemed to him absurd that people surrounded by warfare
should entertain themselves by lighting off explosives.

He stayed in bed rereading Georges Simenon, fell asleep at dawn, and woke around ten in the morning.

Not long before his lunch date, he took a cab to Sung Phoo Maps and Charts, only, as the driver had assured him, a few blocks from the hotel, but hard to find. Inside, a brisk young man greeted him in English. When Fest explained he wanted the most current available map of the region, the young man led him up narrow stairs into a chamber full of women seated at drafting tables under circular white neon tubes, and very soon he stepped back into the Saigon morning with three scrolls wrapped together in brown paper and tied with twine: hand-colored, French-language maps: North Vietnam; South Vietnam; Saigon.

The day was sunny, clear, hot, bright, with black shadows on the pavements under the trees. He walked a block and hailed a taxi. The cabbie said because of the New Year he couldn't turn the meter on and would have to be paid copiously. Disgusted, Fest got out and took a cyclo to his rendezvous and arrived, by his watch, four minutes early at the Green Parrot Restaurant, a very narrow establishment much like a locomotive's dining car with tables for two—no more than two—along either wall, and an aisle between. No maître d' greeted him, only a young man behind a cash register, who raised his eyebrows.

"Do you speak English?" he asked the cashier.

"Yes, please."

"Do your facilities have a flushing device?"

"Sorry, I don't understand."

"Plumbing with water."

"I don't know what you say."

"Where is your bathroom?"

"Yes, sir. To the back."

He took a seat. Almost everyone in the place was Vietnamese.

Only three tables away, alone, sat an American he recognized from the earlier assignment in the Philippine Islands, the nephew, he believed, of the bullish colonel who'd so enjoyed joking with Filipinos. His contact? A flush of warmth, familiar ground under his feet, a friend to work with, or anyway an acquaintance.

Basic craft required they not greet each other without a pass-sign. Fest headed for the men's room, passing close to the American's table as he made his way. He leaned his tubular parcel against the damp wall, washed his hands, and waited three minutes, until exactly twelve-thirty. When he went back out the American was gone and a different American waved to him from a different table—Johnson, who'd picked him up at the airfield yesterday and so quickly disappeared. A Vietnamese officer in uniform, wearing aviator's sunglasses, sat facing the Negro; nothing before him on the table but a pack of cigarettes.

Johnson rose as Fest approached. "Mr. Reinhardt, meet Major Keng."

"It's a pleasure," Keng said, and reached up to shake hands.

"Where can I sit?"

"Take my place," Johnson said. "I'm running late. You're in capable hands."

"It's local business?"

"What's that there?"

"Maps of the area. I just bought them minutes ago."

"Walk me to the door."

At the entrance Johnson handed him a business card on which the name was Kenneth Johnson, of Meeker Imports. "In the event of something unforeseen, go to the basement of the Armed Forces Language School. I've written the street address on the back there. The basement, okay? You'll be greeted by a U.S. marine, so hand him this card."

"Many thanks."

"That's only as a last resort. Only and absolutely."

"Yes. I understand you. A last resort."

Once again the black man vanished like a fugitive.

Fest placed the card in his money clip, taking extra time for

himself. Another native handler. That meant the same kind of
business as in the Philippines. Over at the table the Vietnamese
had removed his sunglasses to look at the bill of fare. His khaki
uniform looked slept in, but his black boots shone brightly. Local
business. Fest didn't like it.

He took the seat across from his contact.

"Mr. Reinhardt, what will you eat?"

"Nothing."

"Nothing? Some tea?"

"Tea, all right. And bread, if possible."

"Of course it's possible. I'm having pho-ban, some beef soup
with noodles. It's very inexpensive here."

Without the sunglasses Major Keng's eyes seemed small and
black and polished. As Fest looked at the faces around him they all
had their differences, but all the faces, including this man's, were
identical to his recollection of, say, the face of the desk clerk Thuyet,
or any others he'd seen in this city. Their language sounded impossible. Fest observed he was now the establishment's only white patron.

He remained stubborn and had only bread and weak tea. The
major asked him what he'd seen of the city, shoveled into his noodle soup a salad of greens and pallid sprouts, and slurped viciously
at it, using enameled chopsticks for everything, including, somehow, the liquid, and spoke of his university days here in Saigon.

"Do you like your baguette?"

"Yes," Fest said sincerely, "it's wonderful."

"Many things survive from the French."

"I see. Of course."

Keng pushed his empty bowl aside, took a cigarette from his
pack, and brought a lighter from his tunic. "May I offer you a cigarette and also a light?"

"No, thank you."

With a look Fest interpreted as one of light contempt, or disappointment, the major produced a flame. "It's a Colibri of London.
Butane."

"Is this a good place to discuss business?"

"Of course. That's why we're here. I have some things for you."
He reached for the floor between his feet, almost laying his chin
on the table's surface, and sat back with a brown briefcase in his
lap. "I have the goods." It was a parcel wrapped in brown paper
and string. "Now you have two packages. Did you say you have
some maps there?"

"Yes."

"I worried that perhaps a rifle."

"No. Is this the pistol?"

"Yes. Use the silencer."

"Is it as I requested?"

"It's a three-eighty automatic."

"I asked for twenty-two caliber."

"We don't have anything that small."

"Do I have surveillance photos?"

"At this time there has been no surveillance."

"What can you tell me about the target?"

"Not yet identified to me. You'll be told."

"How long can I expect to stay in Saigon?"

"At this time the schedule is uncertain."

"I was told I'd receive the timetable at this meeting."

Keng made a long business of finishing his cigarette and stub-
bing it out in a small dirty ashtray. He folded his hands in his lap.
"We lost him."

Fest believed this man was amused. What now? Even to
remark on such incompetence seemed pointless. "I am here as a
courtesy only."

"We'll find him."

"Can you understand me? If I stay or go, that's completely up
to me. My decision. That is my brief."

"I can only give you the facts. Then you must make your own
decision," the major announced, as if Fest hadn't just said precisely the same thing.

"All right, give me facts. Who is the target?"

"A Vietcong."

Fest kept silent.

"You don't believe me."

"There are a couple of armies here for killing Vietcong."

Keng lit another of his cigarettes with his marvelous silver butane. "A couple of armies, yes. And today also one extra guy, eating lunch with me. Reinforcements."

Now Fest believed him. This man was angry. Possibly the extravagance of this operation insulted him, and he'd decided to view it as an entertainment.

"I can tell you it's simple to find him. The Americans are working on it."

"So you know him."

"I can be a little more specific. The truth is that we don't have his location, and we are trying to get more specific information without causing alienation of the source."

"You have a source, but you don't want to jeopardize."

"Correct. We have to be careful. We can't put a gun to someone's head in this case. Do you see what I mean?"

"This is not my area, Major."

"We need our sources for future use."

"I understand."

"In the meantime, we have a secure drop point for communication close to your hotel."

"I want another one."

"Two drops?"

"No. Just one. The lavatory of this restaurant. On the underside of the sink."

"You're going to check it every day? It's a lot of trouble to get here."

"No. You will check it in three days. The message will give you the location for a new drop."

For a full minute the major didn't reply. "I'm not going to fight you," he said at last. "But don't make the new drop too far from here."

"Then we're agreed?"

"We are agreed, Mr. Reinhardt."

They parted, and with his maps and the weapon in their two brown packages Fest charged down the walk looking for a cab. He perspired heavily but kept his pace, daring anybody to block his course, the beggars rushing at him to display their stumps, their crumpled heads, their stick-figure infants blotched with ulcers, and what does this one want—attacking my flank with offers of opium, U-globe, grass, and what is U-globe? It was 3:00 p.m. before he reached the Quan Pho Xa.

The next morning he moved. The small desk clerk Thuyet was on duty downstairs. "Checking out?" she said when she saw his valise, and he said he was. As he waited for transportation, he asked her about the name of this hotel. "It means 'Around the Town,'" she said.

"I see."

"Are you leaving for the Europe?"

"I have to do a lot of traveling."

"Okay. It's good for your business."

"This is the New Year."

"We call Tet."

"Happy New Year."

She laughed, as if surprised by sharp wit. "Happy New Year!"

"Is it the Year of the Dog? Goat? Monkey?"

"Not now. The Year of the Monkey is finish. Now will be the Year of the Rooster."

An hour later he checked into Room 214 at the Continental Hotel. This place was famous, and somewhat expensive, and it had air-conditioning. He took lunch in a restaurant downstairs full of Europeans and Americans. Afterward he went down to the square out front, where seven or eight celebrations seemed to be taking place, each oblivious to the others, all under the eyes of armed figures in a variety of uniforms and helmets—local police, American MPs, American and Vietnamese infantry.

Fest spoke with a cyclo driver, who walked with him to a side street and introduced him to a girl in a café and then proposed to escort them both to a room in a hotel Fest had never heard of.

"We'll go to my room."

The driver explained this to the girl, and she nodded, smiling, and wrapped Fest's upper arm in a full embrace and put her head on his shoulder. Her deeply black hair smelled like vanilla extract. Perhaps she used exactly that as a perfume. He didn't want her, but something like this was necessary. He'd learned on these operations that he came as a predator, he must violate the land, he must prey upon its people, he must commit some small crime in propitiation of the gods of darkness. Then they'd let him enter.

Richard Voss spent the morning at the embassy reading and sorting cables that had come in over the weekend designated "Classified," which meant almost everything. Anything of importance had already been dealt with, but somebody—anybody—from Internal Ops had to see every word, that was the rule. "Send it Classified," his first boss at Langley had once told him, "otherwise they won't read it." He didn't mind being shut away. He preferred it to drinks with foreign diplomats and Vietnamese semi-dignitaries, and if Crodelle stretched their lunch with Skip Sands far enough into the afternoon, he could return here, look over the new cables, and find some excuse for hanging around through the cocktail hour.

At noon he left the embassy and made his way down the block and across Tu Do, through the mass of vendors and celebrants who all week had made the thoroughfare impossible for four-wheeled traffic. He found a taxi on a side street. For this short trip he'd allowed thirty minutes; even so he was ten minutes late when they came into view of the Green Parrot.

Skip Sands stood out front in the noon sun wiping perspiration from his eye sockets and looking confused—and don't we all these days, Voss thought. Skip had gained weight. And haven't we all done that too. Aren't we all fat and sweaty and confused.

Voss opened the cab's door and beckoned him in. "Long time, my man! Come on—I thought of a better place."

"Good. Scoot over." Sands climbed in beside him. "I saw a guy I don't like."

"Who?"

"A guy from Manila. Let's move, okay? I need a breeze."

"Cross the river," Voss told the driver.

"What about the Rex?"

"We can't go downtown," said Voss, "they've got checkpoints everywhere. Uncle Ho won't catch us sleeping! We are absolutely thoroughly prepared for one year ago."

"What's going on across the river?"

"Not a thing, brother. It's like real life. Some nuns opened a French place last month."

"Nuns? Can they cook?"

"Outrageously well. Nobody goes there yet, but they will."

The driver said, "One bridge no good. I take other bridge."

"Go ahead, make a buck," Voss said.

Sands said, "How's the family?"

"They're great. Haven't seen them since April. I missed Celeste's birthday."

"How old is she?"

"Jesus . . . No, wait—four. What about you? Still solo?"

"Afraid so."

"Completely? No fiancée in the States?"

"Not yet. Completely single."

They crossed the bridge to the east side, where junks and miscellaneous unsinkable wrecks jammed against the bank.

"Jeez, the river stinks worse than ever."

"Welcome back."

"Thanks. I think."

"No, I'm serious. It's good to see you," Voss said, and he meant it. "How long have you been gone?"

"I'm in and out."

"So you've been gone all this time?"

"I'm just back for a week or two. Collecting stories. How goes the fray?"

"Oh—we're winning."

"Finally someone who knows."

"You're collecting stories?"

"Stories, yeah—folktales. Fairy stories."

"Well, you've come to the right place for *that* stuff." Neither of them laughed. "Folktales."

"Yeah—remember Lansdale."

"I never knew Lansdale."

" 'Know the people'—songs and stories."

Voss heard himself sigh. "Hearts and minds."

"Yeah. It's for a project at the Naval Grad School."

"Over there in—where."

"Carmel."

"I've never been there."

"A beautiful place."

Small talk, Voss thought, in the Terminal Ward. He had to take over directing the driver, and he was spared.

Only a few blocks across the river, and not far from the neighborhood of the old CIA–Psy Ops villa where for several weeks Voss and Skip had lived together, they found the Chez Orleans. "I like these vines," Voss said of the incredible overgrowth almost extinguishing its façade. "You can hardly see through the windows. Privacy." I sound like a fool.

"Do you still stay at the old place?"

"The old place is no more. I think the army got it. I'm at the Meyerkord."

The vines continued around the building and flourished over lattices to make relatively cool shade for the flagstone patio. Music emanated from a burlap-wrapped PA high in the coolest corner of the trellis—flamenco, classical guitar—and beneath the speaker, near the small fountain, three officers with large yellow Fifth Cavalry patches on their sleeves ate without speaking. Otherwise not a soul. They sat down and Sands ordered 7Up and grenadine. "I'm having a martini," Voss said.

"I don't like olives," Sands said. While Voss wondered how you reply to such a statement, Sands went on: "I didn't mean to sound cynical a while ago."

"I'm the one who sounded cynical. And I kind of think I meant to."

"No, no, I understand. We've all got questions."

"Yeah, and the left thinks we don't, we're all brainwashed and stupid, we have to have somebody shouting up our ass—do they think they're intellectuals? Who wants to be an intellectual? Who cares how powerful your equipment is if you can't safely operate it? What have the intellectuals got?"

"Chess."

"Cross-eyed Communism. Unhealthy unsatisfying perverted sex lives."

Sands said nothing. He seemed as clear-eyed as ever, and just as blind. Where, Voss thought, is the fun in this? Crodelle, you're a shit.

"Skip. Skipper. What's the matter?"

"My mom died."

"Oh, shit."

"I just got the news yesterday."

"I'm sorry."

"Well, I'm dealing with it."

"I guess you have to."

"I know. What can you say? Let's eat."

The lunch menu was light, salads, crepes, and sandwiches, and Voss recommended the salade niçoise, which he promised was made with real tuna and which Skip declined because of the olives. Sands asked instead for the salade d'epinard et crevettes, and they spent the interval looking over the dinner menu with

admiration: filet de porc rôti, carré d'agneau aux pistaches, thon
aux pignons de pin, these nuns had it all—and privacy—if in fact
the management were nuns. He'd never seen any nuns here. "Better than the Yacht Club," he told Sands, "and cheaper, man." He
was hungry, and he took his salad as a reprieve. But Sands, after
going at his shrimp and spinach for several bites, drifted visibly
from the scene and began poking with his fork, stirring whorls in
his orange-and-caper sauce, and Voss felt terrible about Skip's situation and said, "It's hard to believe people back home can pass
away. It gets so you think we have all the dying right here. All the
death in the world."

Skip looked up in surprise and said, "That's true. I've felt just
that very thing."

"We all do. Remember last Tet?"

"Yeah."

"You were here?"

"I was around."

"Cao Phuc?"

"Off and on."

"You've been getting mail pretty regularly at the embassy."

"Oh. You keep track of those things?"

"Every little thing, somebody keeps track of it. But who's keeping track of who's keeping track? So Cao Phuc. Yeah. You guys did
some nice work on Labyrinth."

"Yes, thanks—do you really mean that?"

A cab stopped out front, and even through the viney lattice
Voss could see who it was.

"Well, Skip," he admitted with sudden irritation, "no. Not really.
What the heck do I know about Labyrinth? I'm just being—you
know—generally and vaguely complimentary."

"Okay. Generally and vaguely thanks. Look, Rick," Sands said,
"maybe we can talk straight."

"Always. Always."

At this moment Crodelle made his appearance, moving
directly toward their table as if he'd consulted a map and planned

the route. Tall, angular—not tall enough for college basketball, but surely pressed into it in high school. Physically he looked the drowsy, slouching intellectual. A misapprehension. He had a redhead's characteristic fire. Voss had led himself to believe that redheads outgrow their freckles with childhood, but Crodelle still sported several across his cheeks. Voss was aware that he considered these things too often, that they'd lodged as irritants in his thoughts—Crodelle's height and type, his intellect, his freckles—because Crodelle frightened him.

"I want soup!"

Sands said, "I'm not sure they have soup."

"Bizarre. No soup?"

"Not for lunch."

"Terry Crodelle."

The two shook hands. Voss said, "Skip Sands."

Crodelle sat down and said, "Indeed," and called across the room: "Martini? And a salad"—he pointed a bony finger at Voss's plate—"comme ça."

"And some tea," Sands said.

"And tea, please."

Sands said, "Were we expecting you, Terry?"

"I'm stuck this side of the river. Nothing on the other side but banners and flags and firecrackers. So—you're back in Cao Phuc? Or you were never gone."

Sands kept good control of his physical presence, but couldn't hide his surprise. "I assume you're working with us."

"Us who?"

"We. Us. The outfit."

"I'm with the Regional Security Center."

"Stationed here?"

"Visiting. A visitor to your charming planet."

"First time in-country?"

Crodelle blinked and stared. "I've been in the region off and on since '59. I'm pre-Kennedy."

"Wow. You look younger."

"I looked in on Cao Phuc once or twice. How's the scene there these days?"

"A lot quieter. Quiet."

"Have they broken down that relocation facility?"

"I don't know the official status of that endeavor."

"But what do you see?"

"It's hard to tell what stage they've reached"—Sands looked up and around as if seeking their waiter—"whether they're breaking it down or if it's just been more or less abandoned. But I'd say the Buddhist temple is pretty much the center of things again."

"Are the VC moving in?"

"I haven't been bothered."

"What have they got you doing over there?"

"Collecting stories. Folktales."

"Gimme a break! Rick, here, thought you'd left the country."

"I'm in and out."

"So the base is broken down?"

"We didn't call it a base. Landing zone." Sands seemed inexplicably content.

"Did you ever get over to the Purple Bar once in a while?"

Skip laughed. "Only at the legitimate cocktail hour."

"You know what, Skip? I'm glad we finally meet."

"Hey, you guys," Voss said, and excused himself.

He went to the restroom and found its urinal filled with ice cubes, a fascinating extravagance.

Voss wished Crodelle had stayed away from lunch longer. Maybe some straight talk after all, he and Sands—who can you talk to but a man on the way out? He'd worked in intelligence for only six years, but he would have liked to crawl out of its waters and into a cave and confess to some giant mollusk. Absurd, yes. But it had the right elements. Air and drowning. Darkness, damp.

What a monstrous stupid fucking mess.

One of the army officers joined him in the bathroom, hawk-faced, crew-cut, major's bars on his shoulders and the yellow sleeve patch of the Fifth Cavalry, a man without secrets, a man who relieved himself in front of others. While the major pissed meditatively down onto the piled ice, Voss washed his hands and dried them on one of the cloth napkins stacked beside the sink and tossed the napkin into a wicker basket. This place had class. Above the cloudy yellowish mirror that gave his face back as if he were the victim of some viny invasion of hepatitis were painted in a precise, feminine, nunlike script the words:

Bon appétit!

When Voss returned to the table they were already on the subject Crodelle wanted to raise, at least to begin with—the colonel's insane article—and Crodelle was showing off. He managed to seem blithely expert on any area that strayed into his conversational grasp. Voss didn't mind it so much, but he minded that at this moment he was bullying Sands. This business of tracking "command influence," Crodelle wanted to know—had the colonel considered how tricky the whole idea was? Hadn't the Mayo brothers written of Dr. Gorgas, "Men who achieve greatness do not work more complexly than the average man, but more simply?" Wasn't the problem with trying to show "command influence" through experiments just that almost all such experiments, those Crodelle knew of anyway, had been carried out to determine the impact of an intervention, a treatment, a new drug, rather than to prove the presence or absence of a causative factor?—like Lind's eighteenth-century tests with treatments for scurvy, or, a more recent instance, the Salk vaccine trials? On the other hand . . . was Sands maybe familiar with the nineteenth-century Yellow Fever Commission and the then-new science of bacteriology?—with the efforts of Walter Reed and James Carroll? Maybe trials could be run, but what would serve as the experimental "marker" for "command influence"? And the struggle against malaria and typhoid and yellow fever, hadn't that been as

much a war as this one?—hadn't Jesse Lazear died a martyr's
death in a sick ward in Havana, cut down by the disease he was
helping to conquer? Wars demanded new ideas; and maybe the
colonel had landed one: could we maybe, just maybe, inject the
elements we think would provoke "command influence" into pre-
selected information channels? Crodelle's curiosity overpowered
him, an earnest wish to communicate charged his features, he
held up his hands before his face, fingers splayed, head forward,
taking careful and passionate aim, as if each of his concepts were
a basketball—but, come on, who was the colonel in all this, Walter Reed the careful investigator, or Guiseppe Sanarelli, the guy
with the quick answer to the wrong question? The colonel needed
an Aristides Agramonte to get in there and dig into the corpses.
Did Skip know the work of Agramonte? Did Skip know, come to
think, that with that mustache and high forehead he resembled
Agramonte?

This last question seemed other than rhetorical. Crodelle
stopped. He waited.

Voss couldn't tell whether Sands was a fool, or the Buddha
himself. From where came this poised, shiny-eyed amusement?

Sands said, "Jesus Christ."

"Yeah. It's pretty wild."

"What is your interest in all this, Terry?"

"Purely academic. Disease control was a passion of mine in
college—premed. Then I dropped out and wandered into our
world, and I never thought I'd see anything from *that* field that
applied to *our* field, the field of intelligence."

"It's just a draft. He'll never finish it."

"What you need to do is prove the existence of 'command
influence.' What you need to do is isolate these different channels
running up the chain of command, and randomly inject information among these channels to see how much they get distorted.
How do you, so to speak, 'clean' a channel? You need channels
you affect and channels you keep unaffected. This isn't new. Yellow fever again, polio, et cetera. What you'd really need is two or

more unconnected intelligence organizations—get some of our allies to participate. It would be interesting. It might get us somewhere. It might bring on a revolution. But do we need to start one until we *need* to start one?"

"I'm not sure what you mean by that."

"It's just remarkable he's opened the whole question. The colonel. I mean, is it possible to create markers, intelligence markers, and follow them up and down the chain of command and out through the lines of commo, and draw conclusions about the way we do things? It's pretty wild, man. Your uncle's a wild revolutionary."

"Have you met him?"

"Once or twice. I enjoy the colonel. He's a sizable personality. I mean, Cao Phuc—case in point. As far as we can trace things he talked someone, some drunken commander of one of the helicopter assault groups, into securing a landing zone on that mountain in '64, then when the Twenty-fifth Infantry arrived he sort of borrowed a platoon and kept them out there twenty-four months, on one pretext after another, and had the Twenty-fifth serving that LZ as if it were a base. Then he sold the ville as the world's best place for a relocation camp. At the peak he had half a dozen platoons running up and down that mountain, and his very own helicopter. That is one impressively large personality, man. Unfortunata*men*te, during the Tet thing he took casualties and lost a whole platoon we can only hope are POWs now, and folks started asking what in tarnation is going *on* in Cao *Phuc*. If it wasn't for last Tet, by now he'd probably have his own brigade. And he's not in any way connected to the military!—except as liaison to Psy Ops, hardly any of whom have actually personally encountered the guy, ever. He did it all on his personal authority. I mean, man, he did it all on balls and bullshit. Can you believe it?"

"You seem to know more about him than I do."

"There's a lot to admire there. He's a warrior—"

"A genuine war hero, Terry."

"Of course, let's say a hero, he's got medals up the ass, okay—but he's not a spook, he's not that type. He *suspects* everybody's against him, but he *acts* like he hasn't got an enemy in the world. You know what a guy once told me about the colonel? 'His enemies are only friends he hasn't defeated yet.'"

"John Brewster, right?"

"Who?"

"You heard me."

"Matter of fact, it might have been John. I don't remember. Look. Come on. Look . . . your uncle has something to teach us, which is: Trust the locals. He's never separated himself from them. He works with them, he's joined to them. But in doing that, he separates himself from us, his people."

Skip said, "I think you're misinterpreting the facts, and then exaggerating your own misinterpretation. Or at least you're just allowing your interpretation to enlarge itself."

"Have you read *The Quiet American*?"

Skip said: "Boo-coo fuck you."

Voss said, "Boy, this is quick. I thought we'd shoot the shit awhile."

"Yeah. Yeah." Crodelle blinked. Nothing more. "He was living at the Continental when he wrote it."

"Graham Greene. Next door to the colonel."

"Skip . . . a man outgrows his mentors. It's inevitable."

"Look," Skip said, "I get it."

"Then explain it."

"You explain it."

"I've *been* explaining it. If the colonel wants to make empirical sense out of his theories, then let him propose a random-assignment study using two systems—a control, and a system into which he introduces some agent or catalyst whose effect he can measure against the control system *without* the agent. Think back: the old proposals for the cause of polio, the days when they were just banging away with any idea that came into their heads—dog feces, for Christ's sake; injecting polio patients with their own urine. That's the colonel, man. Shooting piss into the intelligence apparatus. I mean," Crodelle said, "even in Washington he was legendary for his three-hour hydraulic lunches."

Sands turned to Voss. "Fuck you too, Voss." He stood up. "Speaking of shooting piss. I gotta whiz."

"Melt yourself some ice," Voss said.

"What?"

"You'll see."

He left, and Crodelle watched him until he'd gone inside the restaurant.

"Gee, Terry. What took you so long?"

"Rick? Do you know your role?"

Voss didn't answer. He watched Crodelle sip from his martini.

"Is there a window in there?"

"He's not going out the window."

"How do you know?"

"He's having too much fun."

"Are you?"

Voss thought of ordering another drink, but felt the remark about hydraulic lunches had rendered such a thing inadvisable.

"If he pushes, I'm gonna push back. Just to keep the balance in my favor, okay? And things are gonna speed up."

"They certainly are."

"Fine with me. And you do have a role to play. When the balance tips too far, you jump on the teeter-totter—on my side, incidentally."

"I'm clear on that."

"On the way here I picked up something at the shop."

"What shop?"

Crodelle convulsed into life again. "Will you look at this?" He took from his breast pocket what looked like a large cigarette lighter. Holding it in his palm, he pressed its side with his thumb. "Open it up, and—zow." Two tiny reels within. "The tape is—you see it? That little wire? That is one one-thousandth of an inch in diameter, man."

People from Manila's Regional Security Center showed up in town regularly and Voss thought he knew them all; Crodelle wasn't one of them. He'd set up a shop in the Language School's basement, and Internal Ops had been told to give him what he needed, and today he needed a twenty-first-century recording device.

"You guys have all the nifty stuff."

"These things have been around for a dozen years."

Sands was back. He sat down, and Crodelle held out the recorder, its face still open. "Behold."

"Where's the tape?"

"The light has to be right. See?"

Voss said, "One one-thousandth of an inch."

"Is it on?"

"Why the hell not?" Crodelle said, and shut its lid and left it between them on the green linen tablecloth. "Let's give it a whirl. We're here at the Aragon Ballroom with bandleader extraordinaire Skipper Sands . . . Sands. German? English."

"No. Irish."

"Irish?"

"My great-grandfather came from the Shaughnesseys. Apparently he started calling himself Sands on the ship over."

"A bit of a turncoat."

"I never met him. I wouldn't know."

"Was he in trouble?"

"No. Can I ask you something?"

"Sure."

"Am I?"

"The Aragon Ballroom is a place of music and frolic. No one's in trouble here."

"Hell. Why not polygraph me?"

"That's not out of the question."

"I mean right now, Crodelle."

"No, Skip. Not right now. We'll need to prepare you if we want to end up with a decently conclusive polygram."

"Any old time."

"Sure. Noted."

"What about Crodelle? C'est Français?"

"I don't know. Yeah, French. It may be a misspelling of 'Cordelle.'—Where's Uncle Francis, Skip?"

"I don't know. Right here in town, I assume."

"Do you know he was recalled to Langley seven weeks ago, eight weeks ago—anyway, early last November?"

"I didn't know that."

"No, because he never went."

"He goes where he wants to."

"Yeah. And when he wants to, he'll just whip out a pistol and shoot a bound prisoner."

"Really, now."

"Didn't he execute a prisoner at Cao Phuc during Big Tet?"

"I don't know anything about it."

"Well, it's known you know something about it. We know you know."

"I'm pretty sure you're confusing a story from World War Two."

"He executed prisoners back then too? We'll have to look into that. But you're located at Cao Phuc right now, right? And last Tet too? Is Cao Phuc your station, more or less?"

"In-country, yeah. I'm in and out. Mostly out. I keep some stuff there."

"Well, you spend a lot of time there. You're bound to have some stuff. When we say you keep some stuff there, we're including some of the colonel's stuff, right? His footlockers and such."

"Footlockers?"

"You know, here's the crux of it all. I think these guys we admire so much, I believe that every one of them has fallen away from the faith, each in his own way. We fight Communism, but we ourselves exist in a commune. We exist in a hive."

"You think they don't believe in freedom anymore?"

"I think they've just gotten numb."

Silence.

Crodelle said, "What do you think, Skip?"

"I think it's too complicated for discussion."

Crodelle said: "What's in the footlockers?"

Skip kept his peace.

"Why the silence?"

"Am I supposed to answer suddenly just because you ask suddenly?"

"Three of them, three footlockers. You had them at Clark Field on December thirty-first, 1966, and they arrived with you at the CIA villa right over here on Chi Lang Street on New Year's Day."

Sands hadn't once touched his teacup. His focus was amazing.

"I'd like to ask what you're doing in Cao Phuc," Crodelle said.

"Well, I don't think you should even be wanting to know."

Crodelle stared. "Gosh-darn it."

Sands stared back.

"You're in business. You're running something. Something or somebody."

"Who, exactly, are you?"

"All right. Let's get ourselves identified. I'm Terrence Crodelle, Regional Security Officer."

"Congratulations."

"Your turn. The Saigon base has two branches, designated Liaison Operations and Internal Operations. Which are you, Skip?"

"I Ops, working mainly with military Psy Ops."

Crodelle sat back and sighed. "I Ops with Psy Ops," he said, and Voss thought: I believe you're on the ropes.

With an actual mounting nausea, Voss forced his own face into the muck: "You remember the footlockers? Those three footlockers? Sure you do. I don't think you would've forgotten those footlockers. Do you remember the name on those footlockers?"

"No, I don't."

"Can I ask what name you're here under?"

"My name is William Michael Sands."

"What's the name on your passport?"

"That is the name on my passport."

Crodelle said, "Where's the colonel's hideaway?"

"He's got a room at the Continental, last I knew."

"I understand he has some associates on the Mekong Delta. One in particular. A female."

"That's news to me."

"Near Binh Dai."

"Further news."

A vehicle stopped outside. Skip rose, went to the patio's edge, and spoke through the vines: "Hold that cab for me, please."

He still had his napkin tucked into his belt. It was the only off move Voss had seen him make all day.

He came back and laid his napkin on the table and said, "Lunch is on you guys," and walked out.

Certain that he was spending too much, that the GIs and local businessmen got lower prices, Fest passed the afternoon with the young woman whose hair smelled of vanilla, who charged him thirty dollars for four hours in his air-conditioned room. She huddled under the blankets, she insisted on using the phone many times, though he didn't think she knew anyone to call and was only pretending to have conversations, she plucked at his beard and the curls on his chest, and tried to squeeze the blackheads on his nose—in fact she played constantly with his nose—delighted with its European dimensions, and in general behaved like the stupid harlot she was. Just as Fest was a stupid customer. He ordered champagne for the room and she refused it—chattering, giggling, fearful—as she might the offer of a particularly nasty bedroom game. Fest drank it all himself. She wouldn't eat. He showered while she fraudulently telephoned. His greatest hope for this hotel had been extinguished—that its phones reached Berlin,

and news of his father. Cables were no good. He had to keep his
whereabouts to himself. Apparently it was possible to call Berlin,
but not from the hotel. The concierge had promised to arrange it,
to take him somewhere personally. Meanwhile, the old man
would die. Perhaps already. Perhaps yesterday while I bought the
maps. Right now he's dead while I shower in tepid, diseased water
and a whore stinks in my bed. People die when you're thinking of
something else. That's the way of it. Claude had done so; shot in
the throat by a sniper of the French Resistance. Their father had
been a strong man, a patriotic German, an acquaintance of Hein-
rich Himmler. His older brother had been an officer of the Waffen-
SS. These were facts. They were not to be disputed, covered over,
or despised. And Claude had given his life for the Nazis, another
fact. But Claude was more than a fact: the family legend, constantly on his father's lips; dead, yet throughout Fest's youth more
alive to their father than Fest himself. He gave the girl some Vietnamese money, he didn't care how much, and sent her away.

While celebrants out in the square produced the music and
explosions of warfare, defeat, and victory combined, he took dinner in his room and prepared to turn in early. He had a drop
point, a point of rendezvous, and a point of last resort. As of this
moment, no one could find him, in particular not his local handlers. The champagne left him with a headache that kept him
awake. He sat at the writing desk of Room 214 and broke apart
and examined his equipment. The gun had been ramped and
throated, he saw. It wouldn't jam. He reassembled it. Both clips
went into it smoothly and the bullets cycled through it almost
without sound as he worked the slide backward and forward.
Both the silencer and the barrel to accommodate it were factory-
made. Somebody was paying attention. But the pointless meeting in Hong Kong, his quick treatment at the hands of Kenneth
Johnson, the sense he was being passed from cousin to cousin,
always farther from the source . . . And that he was being used at
all. Not that work for other services was unprecedented. Nine or
ten years ago an Algerian in Madrid; and a man on a yacht in

Como, Italy, whom Fest thought might have been Mafia. And the Philippines, the American priest. Not one of them an enemy of his homeland. Eleven operations in all, counting this one. Showalter had described it as "a hurry-up," and yet Showalter had entertained them for a couple of weeks before ever mentioning an assignment, and next not another word until a month ago, and even then no discussion of scenarios, and now the gun was in his hands . . . And would they even have picked me if I'd taken the family to Berlin on our summer leave, if I hadn't avoided, like a coward, another look at my father's deathbed, if I hadn't spent my leave showing New England to young Claude and Dora from the small windows of a rented caravan? In Cape Cod they'd parked behind Showalter's summer place. Both families knew each other well, considered themselves friends, in fact, but he'd never been associated with Charles Showalter on any kind of operation. He was a superior, that's all. Showalter displayed no illusions, none tainted him, that's why they liked each other. That's why Fest trusted him. Stay another week, stay another day—of course they'd stay, he was a superior. Meg too— even after two weeks with cords going out the window from her kitchen outlets, three guests running down the hot water and wetting all her towels, Dora complaining about Langley, holding forth in her fluent English about American idiots, young Claude nibbling out of her fridge, talking about school and sports because Meg was beautiful and because she listened— Meg too: Stay a while, we love it, it's rather lonely here in the sandy woods. Two weeks along, Meg's smiles turned brittle, mixed with invisible perspiration. The stress brought out her strength and grace, and seemed to underscore her intelligence. Charles took Fest to the cape's Atlantic edge, only the two of them, to show him a beach house he thought of purchasing. Fest praised it but wouldn't have lived there. The panes rattled in a relentless wind and the surf ate at the shore only yards from the supporting posts. Showalter stood on his future balcony before his future Atlantic, his gray locks snatched up in all directions like a poet's. "There's some business in Saigon. I'd like to put you on it. It's a hurry-up job."

"In Saigon?"

"Or the environs."

The Philippines, and now this. And why send him across the world on a single operation when whole armies crawl over the region?

"It's ten thousand miles to there," Fest said.

"That's nearly accurate."

"Are you assigning me to the Phoenix Program?"

"It's not Phoenix, and it's not ICE-X. We don't want our people to know about this."

"It's quite a sensitive target, perhaps."

"I guess," Showalter said in a way that meant he thought it, perhaps, not so much a sensitive target as a senseless operation. "He's been promised our protection."

"I see. How much more can you tell me?"

"Nothing. We'll talk more in Langley. When we're back on the clock."

"Will I hear from my people first?"

"Consider that you're hearing from them now."

"No need to check about that."

"No need. And—Dirk."

"Yes, Charles."

"It's a war. Go ahead and use a gun."

He now possessed a .380 automatic, a very American and warlike weapon. With it he could probably put together three-inch groups at forty feet. Beyond that range he found it unpredictable. Not quite as good as the sumpit, the blowgun. But how would he know until he aimed and fired?

No team, no discussion of scenarios, no drilling with the weapon.

Why couldn't they have given him U.S. documents here in Saigon, official passports with genuine Vietnamese visas? Why stop in Hong Kong for German ones?

Because the documents were forgeries. The BND had no part in this. Yet Showalter had more than implied BND endorsement. Without the invisible stamp of the BND he was nothing more than a criminal.

There was a line. He'd crossed it. But the Communists had crossed it too. Criminals? In China, in the Ukraine, they'd done more killing than the criminal Adolph Hitler would have permitted himself even to contemplate. That couldn't be said aloud, but it had to be remembered. Sometimes, perhaps—in order to grapple with such an enemy—one crossed to his side of the line.

His own cowardice revolted him; it hurt him physically, in his stomach. If he'd gone to Berlin in the summer instead of to New England . . . If he hadn't avoided a last moment with his father, who didn't love him . . . Just the same, I stand beside you. Old Father, you fought the Communists, and I fight them too.

Skip Sands rode out of Saigon on Route One in a commercial van and caught a ride to Cao Quyen with a motorbike hauling a tiny trailer full of eight-foot boards, this latter leg taking nearly two hours.

Halfway along, he was surprised to see the colonel's black Chevy coming the other direction, and he waved both his arms, nearly losing his perch behind the young cyclist. Too late. The Chevy went on. Sands recognized Hao but couldn't see his passengers.

At the villa he found a white Ford sedan parked out front. The colonel waited inside, on the divan in the parlor, sipping from a coffee cup and looking at a book.

"Where's Trung?"

"Gone," the colonel said. "We had to get him out of here."

He couldn't understand his own crashing disappointment. Moving the double for a few days was what he would have suggested himself.

"Where did he go?"

"I don't believe I can tell you."

"All right, I agree, as a temporary measure—"

"It's not temporary. It's over."

"You're shutting it down?"

"It's over for you. As far as your participation."

"But *why*?"

"Quit acting the fool."

Skip had no response.

"Sit down, Skip. I have some things to say to you."

Apparently the colonel had brought some mail: a couple of envelopes on the coffee table. "Is that my mail?"

"Take a seat, please."

He sat in the facing chair. "What's the book?"

His uncle turned up its face: *The Origins of Totalitarianism.* "Hannah Arendt."

"The woman who reported from the Eichmann trial."

"When I can't sleep, I read. And I haven't slept in an impressive interval, my man. Not a wink. Hold this book in my hands and watch the words go by." He let the pages fall open and read aloud: '. . . in the final stages of totalitarianism an absolute evil appears absolute because it can no longer be deduced from humanly comprehensible motives.'" He tossed the book onto the table. "There's something to shrivel your balls on every page. These Jews are obsessed. As well they should be. Obsessed with their fate. But . . . they're telling the truth about what we're up against. Absolute evil."

The colonel's cup, he saw, held black coffee. He might be sober—Skip smelled no liquor—but he seemed quite drunk.

"Your Aunt Bridey wants a divorce from me."

Skip said, "But she's Catholic."

"Nobody's Catholic anymore. Not really. I haven't been to Mass in years."

"And so—have you lost your faith in God?"

"Yes, I have. Haven't you?"

"Sure."

The colonel drew a breath deeply, as if he would sigh, but he only stared at Skip. "Mr. Trung, I admire you," he said.

Skip looked over his shoulder. They were alone.

"She wants a divorce? She actually said that?"

"She left McLean when I did. Last year. Year before last. The year before Tet. Do you remember how we used to mark time as since JFK's assassination, and now it's since Tet?"

"And she told you then?"

"She told me, but I didn't believe her. Now I do. She's engaged an attorney and instituted a suit for divorce. Good for her. I won't contest the thing."

"Did she give any reason?"

"God knows she has reasons enough."

"But specifically? — or it's none of my business."

"She says I'm in this war to run from my failures in life. And she's right about the running. I'm here because I won't go back to my homeland. Go back to what? A bewildering place full of left-leaning feminine weirdos. What if I do go back? What then? Retire to North Carolina and die and get a forty-foot bridge over a creek named after me. Anyway, she's right. A war with absolute evil is one hell of an excuse to turn your back on the rest of it. So she's divorcing me."

"And it's got you down," Skip said, "it's really got you down."

Now the colonel let himself sigh deeply. "A lot of trouble around here lately. My own load of crap, this business with Trung . . . your mother and all. I'm sorry . . . Skip, I'm sorry."

"About my mother? Or about the trouble in general?"

"About all of it. About your mother, sure . . . About whatever part of it I can be blamed for. Which is most of it. But none of us are going to come out of here any too happy. We've lost this war. We've lost heart."

Speak for yourself, Skip had an impulse to say, but recognized it instantly as reflexive optimism. He said, "Do you want a drink?"

"No, I don't want a drink."

"All right."

"You go ahead."

He called for Tho. The colonel said, "Mr. Tho made coffee and I sent him home."

Skip went to the kitchen and poured himself a shot and drank it off in a single pull. He poured another and returned to his seat to face his uncle, all his movements weakened by dread. He saluted with the glass. This second swallow brought tears to his eyes, and the colonel said, "That'll straighten your hairs!" with such brittle falseness he himself seemed brought up short by it. He sat with his coffee cup in his grip, squinting, against what light Skip couldn't say, as the day was nearly down . . . "I would not be comforted by angels," he said.

Skip was aware of feeling as a child before an adult—before his mother, for instance, in her fits of loneliness—of wanting only to get through the moment, waiting to hear, That's all, you can go, waiting for an end to this violating intimacy.

For many seconds his uncle stared as if they'd never met before. "Did you hear Nixon's inaugural address?"

"No," Skip said. "Parts of it."

"He talked about keeping commitments, preserving our honor—not about winning. Not about the future of Vietnam or the future of the kids we see around here. Nixon. I don't care what he says, you can see it in his eyes: he's played the whole game out in his mind, play by play, and we lose. That's how he sees it. Who did you vote for? The Democrats?"

"Nobody. I forgot to get a ballot."

"I've always voted with the Democrats, this time reluctantly. Humphrey would have pulled us out even quicker, I think. The big boys see the big picture. So we lose. In the big picture it doesn't matter. When it comes to geopolitical balance, just the fact we've fought the war is enough. For the United States it'll all be fine in the end. But I'm not fighting for the United States. I'm fighting for Lucky and Hao and folks like your cook and your housekeeper. I'm fighting for the freedom of real individuals here on this ground in Vietnam, and I hate to lose. It breaks my heart, Skip."

"You think we'll actually lose? Is that what you think, ultimately?"

"Ultimately?" His uncle seemed surprised by the word. "Ultimately I think . . . we'll be forgiven. I believe we'll wander in the darkness for a good long time, and some of what we do here will never be made right, but we will be forgiven. What about you? What do you think, Skip?"

"Uncle, we're in a mess. A mess."

"Half the Agency stayed out of this war. I as much as offered you Taipei, Skip. I could have made it happen."

"I don't mean the American effort here. I mean us, we, you, me, these other guys. We're in trouble with our own outfit."

"Really? That's fine. I've never felt any loyalty to organizations, Skip. Just to my comrades-in-arms. You fight for that guy on your right and that guy on your left. It's a cliché, but clichés are mostly true."

"I feel that too."

"Do you?"

"I mean about who you fight for. I truly do."

"Will . . . what were you doing in Saigon?"

"Yes," Skip said, "that's what I was telling you."

"No, you weren't."

"I mean I started to."

"Then finish, okay?"

"Yes. Rick Voss sent a note out in the mail packet. He wanted to see me. I thought I'd better go. So . . ." He wished he hadn't added, like a schoolboy, the last dangling word.

The colonel made as if to get up but instead remained there, caught in his own tides, rubbing at his face with his fingers. "I had dinner with Pitchfork the other night. I don't think we passed two words of conversation. Just sat there on the terrace of the Yacht Club letting the river go by. Didn't talk. Didn't have to . . .

"One day in the camp, in Burma, in Forty Kilo, there in Burma, when I was down with a fever and it was assumed I would die, he gave me an egg. Boiled it and peeled it and fed it to me bit by bit. One of the finest things anybody's ever done for me. An act of profound generosity. But he doesn't remember it. Thinks it must have been somebody else. But it was him. I remember who it was. Anders Pitchfork gave me an egg.

"To outlive those terrors together and then just to sit and share a meal at a place like the Yacht Club, to share a bit of comfort—you have no idea. It's better than when my little daughter, little four-year-old Annie, would reach up with her little hand and—walking along holding my little girl's hand, Will, and I'd look down and see her looking up at me. The love among comrades is that intense.

"And all I can say is, Fuck Rick Voss. Fuck Voss for what he's done. I can't do anything else. I can't show him even a hint of what he's missed. He'll never know. All I can do is say, Voss: Fuck you."

Sands waited to be sure he was finished.

"Colonel, you and I are friends."

The colonel said, "Yes, Skip, you and I are friends."

"We're together in this."

The colonel lifted his coffee cup and held it in both hands. "You told Voss everything, right?"

"I did?"

"Didn't you?"

"We had lunch."

"What did he ask about?"

"I think he was curious about where I've been, but I didn't give him a chance to ask. I'm too confused, to tell you the truth."

"And did you leave him to enjoy a similar state of confusion?"

"Yes, sir, I'm pretty sure I did. There was another guy, Crodelle."

"I don't know him. Crodelle?"

"RSC."

"Who else?"

"Nobody else was there. We had lunch. But I saw the German."

"What German?"

"The guy from San Marcos. And Mindanao."

"The so-called attaché? From the BND?"

"Wherever he's from, he's in Saigon now."

"Then something's up. All the more reason to get Trung out of here. The German was with Voss?"

"No. I saw him earlier, before the lunch."

"The German."

"Right. He was alone. He may have nothing to do with us."

"If he's not with us, he's against us." He looked hard at Skip. "Let's just assume that about everybody."

"I haven't given anything away."

"What were you doing with Voss?"

"We had lunch, lunch, lunch, that's all."

"This man Crodelle. What did he want?"

"He's after your head. All our heads."

"And they let you go?"

"Yes, sir."

The colonel got up decisively as if in need of something but only stood by the window looking out at the yard, his knees locked, stringy calves outlined against the back of his slacks, big belly jutting forward, both hands way back on his hips, on his rump, nearly on his spine. An old man's pose. Hard, sharp breaths. Suffocating with great emotion.

Skip said, "I sort of felt a certain sympathy on Voss's part."

"No, you didn't. Don't be fooled. With all respect to Rick Voss's mother and with hope for the fate of his soul, that man is a goddamned son of a bitch."

He sat down again on the divan and hiked the cuffs of his slacks. Brushed invisible crumbs from the fabric over his thighs. "Skip, listen to me. There's no traveling side by side in the narrow places. In the narrow places you climb alone. It has to be enough to believe there's somebody behind you."

"I'm right behind you."

"No. I think you've already started the process of saving your own ass. Go ahead and finish. Save yourself."

"Uncle . . ."

"I think I'll head back to the States. I was called back weeks ago."

"I know. Crodelle told me."

"I'll do my best to keep you out of it."

"Uncle, stay here."

"I've put my hand to the plow. No turning back."

"I mean here, right here, the villa. They don't know about this place."

"If they know anything, they know about this place—because you told them."

"They never *asked* me. They only talked about Cao Phuc. As if they thought I was based there."

"So you say."

"They don't know about Cao Quyen at all. Nothing. Whoever snitched us, he hasn't told them."

"Skip, I think it was you."

"Uncle, no, no, no."

"Then who? Not Storm."

"I wouldn't think so. But I don't know."

"No. He wouldn't feel the pressure. He's a monkey. That's what we like about him."

"Hao?"

"Hao's a good man. And Trung's his friend. Never happen."

"What about Minh?"

"Lucky? He doesn't seem positioned to be pressured either. And I've known him since he was a pup."

"Then why do you accuse me? You've known me all my life. My father was your brother."

"I can't explain it, Skip. There's just something about you. You have no loyalty at all."

"Uncle. Colonel . . . I didn't betray you."

"Am I just a fool?"

"Uncle," Skip said, "I love you. I would never do such a thing. I do love you, Uncle."

"That may be right. That may just be right. But love and loyalty are two different things." He gazed at Skip with a terrifying need in his eyes. "What do I think ultimately, finally? I think a young man finds his fortune in war. And I'm goddamn glad you made it, Will." He sat back comfortably and sighed. "Talk to my ass: my head aches."

Sands's duties—though he had none—prevented him from attending the colonel's memorial services, neither the one for the family two weeks later in Boston nor the military one the following month in Bethesda, Maryland. The colonel had been stabbed to death in Da Nang by a prostitute—the colonel's throat had been cut by the brother of his Vietnamese mistress on the Mekong Delta—the colonel had suffered tortures unto death or been assassinated by enemy agents—so the story of his passing evolved through a series of reports into something not unrespectable.

When Sands learned of it he was out behind the villa watching three young boys harry a water buffalo from its rest in a mudhole across the creek. One kicked at its rump with the heel of his bare foot while the other two stung its spine with small switches. The ox, or the indications of it, its nostrils, its rack of horn, the bony hips and the peaks of several vertebrae, made no move. A woman, their mother, someone in authority, appeared from the blossoming bougainvillea above them and tempted the beast with a swatch of greens, and like some geologic fact it developed massively out of the ooze. Sands had heard a vehicle's engine, and slamming doors. He realized it after the fact. Going toward the house he met Hao and Minh coming out to find him. Hao clutched several items of mail. Something in the way Minh held himself back, some mournful acknowledgment of a need for privacy between his elder and the man of the house—and Skip asked, "What is it?"

"Mr. Skip, maybe it will tell you that the colonel is dead."

"Dead?"

"It's bad stuff. We heard it from Mr. Sergeant. He passed me a letter for you."

Without any power of speech Skip led them to the dining room and the three sat down at the table. One of the envelopes came minus a stamp. He cut it open with the blade of his Boy Scout pocketknife.

Skip—
Some boys from the Top Three Floors dug me out of a hole to ask questions. Looks like the worst kind of news. They say the colonel's gone. He didn't make the mission.

Somebody put his lights out but they don't know who. So they say.

That's all I've got. I'll get more. As soon as we find out who and what I'll pass you the word and I swear to Fuck I will get dirty as hell. I will drink the motherfucker's blood.
                                                BS Storm

"I don't believe it. I *can't* believe it." But he believed.

"Mr. Jimmy said it."

He sought for words and heard himself say, "Mrs. Diu is making lunch."

Neither Hao nor Minh replied.

"Where's Trung?"

Hao said, "He's on the Mekong. We took him."

"Does he know about this?"

"Not yet. Minh will go there."

"I can give you some money for him."

"Just a little will be good."

"All right."

"Mrs. Diu is—have you eaten? I'll tell her. Some soup. I'll tell her."

In amazement at the power of tiny necessities to surmount such a moment, he ordered that soup and rice be brought to the table. His guests ate slowly, and as quietly as possible, while Skip ignored his meal and opened the other two envelopes, which in fact contained three letters, and a poem:

Jan. 30, 1969

Dear Skip,

Pastor Paul here, from the First Lutheran Church here in Clements. I hope I can call you "Skip" and I hope you don't mind if I write you a few words about your wonderful mom. I'm sitting at my desk right now, and she used to visit me and sit in the chair right beside it. I can almost say she's here right now, at least in spirit. I just came from her service. To discover how many people she's touched, how many lives she's enriched, in her very quiet and modest way, is truly inspiring.

I haven't met you, but your mother was a woman very dear to us at the church. She wasn't always a Sunday person, but she visited me once or twice a week at the office. She came in the afternoon just to say hi and chat, and often asked me about the sermon I was preparing for the next service. When the conversation turned to what I was thinking and what I was going to say, it generally meant I could expect to bring something more heartfelt to my congregation the following Sunday. She just naturally contributed in that kind of way. So although I call her not a Sunday person, she was present with us many Sundays in spirit. And her spirit abides.

In the last three months or so your mother was very spiritual. She seemed to have a spiritual turning. She seemed to sense something, it was almost as if her spirit sensed that her journey was turning for home. I hope I'm not forward to say this, or sort of "out of line," as the kids say.

I'm enclosing this note with something she was about to mail you. I found this folded and ready to mail. The envelope wasn't sealed, but it's addressed to you, so I'm pasting on a stamp and sending it on. (I didn't read it.)

Paul Conniff,
Pastor
Clements First Lutheran Church
("Pastor Paul")

Dear Son Skipper,

It's Sunday today. I read a poem in the Kansas City *Times* Sunday section by a poet who died six years ago, and I never heard of him. I would clip it to send to you but I want to keep the printed version, so I'll copy it out and you'll have to read it in my handwriting.

I've written you three or four letters I had to throw away, because I thought they'd sound discouraging. I know you're doing what you feel is best for your country. I hope so anyway. I hope you aren't just stuck. People can get stuck in things and not find the right way to get themselves out. And there I go again. That's enough of that.

I have two doctor appointments on Monday and Thursday next week. They love to give you tests. Nothing serious. But ever since the change-of-life I've had little problems. You get good medical attention there, don't you? I'm sure they provide the best.

Okay, here's the poem. It doesn't rhyme, and to get the feeling of it you have to read it several times over and over. I warn you it's kind of sad.

THE WIDOW'S LAMENT IN SPRINGTIME
by: William Carlos Williams (1883–1963)

Sorrow is my own yard
where the new grass
flames as it has flamed
often before but not
with the cold fire
that closes round me this year.
Thirtyfive years
I lived with my husband
The plumtree is white today
with masses of flowers.
Masses of flowers
load the cherry branches
and color some bushes
yellow and some red
but the grief in my heart
is stronger than they
for though they were my joy
formerly, today I notice them
and turn away forgetting.
Today my son told me
that in the meadows,
at the edge of the heavy woods
in the distance, he saw
trees of white flowers.
I feel that I would like
to go there
and fall into those flowers
and sink into the marsh near them.

I warned you! It's very sad! So I won't send it. I read it
and I sat by the window with my hands in my lap. I cried so
hard the tears fell on my hands, right down on my hands.

And I thought, well, that is a poem. A poem doesn't have to rhyme. It just has to remind you of things and wring them out of you.

Thinking of you,
Mom

Dear Skip,

I guess you've heard the worldly life drags down the spiritual life. That's what everybody tells us. What they don't seem to realize is that it works the other way round, and that the spiritual life ruins the worldly life. It gives every pleasure a bad aftertaste. The only thing that feels right is the pursuit of God, although that doesn't always feel pleasant, or even natural.

So one minute I want to be a natural woman, and ten seconds after I've been one, behaved like one, I want to run away to God. Whom I don't like that much. I like you better.

But I have to seek God's will. God's will for me is whatever's in front of my feet to do. Romance isn't part of it. Running off for an affair. Running off to Cao Quyen—

Do you get the message? Maybe you do. Maybe you don't.

I could say more but I'd just be repeating myself in different words.

Kathy

P.S.: I flipped a coin and I'm addressing this note to the name William Sands. Maybe you'll get it and maybe you won't.

He examined the envelope. The letter had come through the American post office in San Francisco.

Goodbye to the women in his life. And so much else.

"Are you sure the colonel's gone? Dead?" he asked Minh.

"Yes. If he was living, I can still feel him." Minh set down his chopsticks and touched his breast gently to indicate where.

"I know what you mean."

"Colonel is dead. My heart can feel it."

"Yes. Definitely. I feel it too."

Skip turned his eyes anywhere, to the tiles of the floor, the walls, the cobwebbed vents in the eaves, seeking a clue as to the character of coming days.

Everything he looked at was suddenly and inexplicably smothered by a particular, irrelevant memory, a moment he'd experienced many years ago, driving with fellow undergraduates from Louisville to Bloomington after a weekend holiday, his hands on the wheel, three in the morning, headlights opening up fifty yards of amber silence in the darkness. The heater blowing, the boozy odor of young men in a closed car. His friends had slept and he'd driven the car while music came over the radio, and the star-spangled American night, absolutely infinite, surrounded the world.

On the morning of March 17, a day before his Aunt Giang's birthday, Viet Nam Air Force Captain Nguyen Minh sat with a bowl of noodles at one of the many tables under the awning at the big bus station in the Cho Lon neighborhood of Saigon. He was hungry. They were delicious. He shoveled them at his face with the chopsticks and sucked them down, wiping his chin with a white handkerchief after each mouthful.

The steaming pots of rice and shrimp, all these buses, all this diesel smoke, the horns were driving him crazy . . . Perhaps he felt the tiniest bit more sensitive because he didn't like going home.

Two U.S. noncoms sorted out the Vietnamese infantrymen patrolling the Cho Lon bus station. They'd doubled the patrols since last May's Communist offensive, coming just five months after the big Tet push. The two sergeants gathered with the patrol commander and went down on their haunches to converse. Minh's people squatted on flat feet, their arms around their knees.

Now the colonel was dead over a month. Minh hadn't seen him much during the past year, but the colonel had remained, for him, a great fact. Without the fact of the colonel looming between his sight and these Americans, they stood up clearly as empty, confused, sincere, stupid—infant monsters carrying loaded weapons. The idea that they fought on anyone's side was foolish.

On the bus he chose a window seat and opened the glass a bit and buttoned his shirt at the neck. The vehicle left the city on High-way Seven, a good road, American-built, past donkey carts, cyclos, small three-wheeled vans, past paddies where buffalo dragged furrows in the mud with single-blade plows and where herons and egrets jutted from the shoots of nearby sections already planted, past women selling petrol in glass jars, past stone ovens in which kindling smoked, turning to charcoal for the kind of cooking his aunts and cousins even now probably labored at in preparation for Aunt Giang's birthday feast. His Uncle Hao wanted him to settle the question of ownership and rental of the house there, a matter that had lain for years, but now his uncle was suddenly anxious that it be finished with. And he had to speak with the man Trung, send him to Saigon.

And why ride a bus?—His uncle still had use of the black American Chevrolet, they could have driven together in the car. Because his uncle was a coward whom Uncle Huy would chop up with his teeth. Hao had avoided his brother-in-law on the last trip. Dropped off the man Trung, settled him in a room above a café, and a month now Trung had languished there a stranger, if he hadn't run off.

Minh disembarked at the roadside and bought a roll and a cup of tea in a store whose proprietress remembered him and asked about his family and said the water taxis were running again these days, but not many. The ville lay two miles down the brown river. He walked. After the city, things smelled different here. The reeking water. The smoke from the burn piles of deadfall and trash had the odor of legend, the chicken droppings, even. Everything carried him off—where? To here. But not to this moment. Here he had fished from the back of a buffalo while beside him Brother Thu had held the string of a kite surging in the winds above . . . even then their lines plumbing opposite depths. One to high school and the air force, one to the monks.

He saw little traffic on the water. An old woman with an old woman's mashed-in face poled past in a skiff keeping to the shallows, every push of the pole threatening to steal her last breath.

Minh walked under a gray sky, sorrow biting at his throat. He stepped into a banana grove and tore off three of the fruits and ate, tossing the peels in the water as he and Thu had done in a better world.

He imagined his brother burning—he often did—Thu's body in the flame, dreadful pain outside, going up his nostrils and in. And then as a monkey holds two branches for an instant, lets go of the first and clings to the new one, he was no longer the body, but the fire.

Lap Vung was more than just a ville. An extensive pier, a market, several shops, everything the same, all of it.

He found Trung Than taking his lunch at the café's only table. The daughter of the proprietor sat across from her guest without food herself, staring at him, her face empty.

"Hello."

"Hello."

"Is your room all right?"

"Come and see."

They went out and up the stairs at the side. At the landing overlooking the back, Trung said, "The room is small. Let's talk here."

"Good."

"I shouldn't stay here any longer. There's VC activity here. By now the cadres must have been told about a single male making a vague agricultural study."

"Hao wants to see you."

"He's here?"

"In Saigon. He'll meet you there tomorrow."

"Will I travel with you?"

"No. Tomorrow morning go to the highway and take the earliest bus to Cho Lon. Hao will meet you at the depot."

"As long as I leave here. That girl wants to marry me. Every day she serves me lunch and asks what I studied out in the countryside. It's a crazy lie. Too vague. I stay up all night reading, and in the morning I dress, take breakfast, and go out to sleep in the fields till noon."

"Are you afraid?"

"I'm thinking of the mission."

Minh believed him.

"Mr. Than, the colonel has died."

Trung said, "Would you like a cigarette?"

"Thank you."

They smoked for a minute while Trung deliberated and at last said, "He was your friend. It's sad for you."

"It's sad for me, and it means your operation won't be completed."

"Something else. Another operation."

"Hao will take care of you."

"What is the plan you have in mind for me?"

"My Uncle Hao has arranged a meeting. Hao has instructed me."

"Do these instructions come from the other American?"

"Skip Sands? No."

Trung was silent.

"What's the trouble?"

Trung tossed away his cigarette and composed his face and ignored the question, but Minh knew the trouble. Trung had

settled his mind, marched across the bridge, and found the colonel dead on the other side.

"Mr. Than, I believe my uncle has several American contacts.
I know your friendship is strong. Hao will look out for you. Hao
will take care of you." He knew he shouldn't be talking like this,
but the man's strength aroused pity.

Minh left the double to his fate and took the path along the old
canal. Ahead of him an old man jerked a water buffalo along by its
nose ring, and Minh followed, the animal lurching in a jungle
rhythm, full of fellow suffering. The same thick smoke from the trash
piles, the same thatched houses, and then his uncle's home with its
orange clay shingles tarnished with mildew, the low gate left open,
the meter of cinderblock topped by green ironwork, pointed fleurs-
de-lis topping the rusty bars—rustier now—the waist-high chain-link
dividing this household from the neighbors' on either side, the front
garden with its small wooden shrine and a dozen or so ornamental
Bong Mai trees, said to bring good luck, but they hadn't, and the
same pillared front porch of shiny tile a shade of gray-violet he still
found very soothing.

As he came through the gate three children ran from him as if
he had a gun. He slipped his feet from his shoes and removed his
socks and placed them by the entrance before walking through
the house.

Two girls, cousins he didn't recognize, worked at washing
clothes in a cauldron over a fire out back. Aunt Giang was cooking in the kitchen shed. The children's yelling brought her to see,
and she came across the yard wiping her hands on her shift and
took his wrists in a strong grip.

"I told you I'd come."

"No, you didn't tell me!"

"I wrote you a letter."

"That was a long time ago! I believe you now."

"I kept my promise."

"I'll wake your uncle."

His aunt led him into the parlor and left him. The same shrine
in its sky-blue box atop the same black lacquerware chiffonier,
taller than he by a couple of feet. Mirrors painted with geometric
designs. spangled the shrine's inner surfaces. Beside it the same
huge candelabra, bowls of fruit, long sticks of incense in a brass
burner shaped like a lion, an array of small votive candles, and a
small Bong Mai tree growing in a vase, perhaps the same Bong
Mai from his childhood, he couldn't be sure.

His uncle came from the good bedroom, the one inside the
house itself, looking sleepy and harmless, skinny and brown, hardly
changed at all, buckling the belt of his long pants and buttoning his
dress shirt and saying nothing. Aunt Giang followed, patting her
husband nervously on the head. A small head, a round face, his features rushing toward its middle. As ·ever, he maintained a blank
expression.

They all three sat on the tiled floor barefoot, drinking tea and
eating candy from a big golden plastic bowl modeled after a king's
fairy-tale crown. Aunt Giang asked him about his love life and his
prospects for marriage, about the air force, about the great General Phan, and never about her brother Hao. Uncle Huy hardly
spoke. Minh saw no need to mention the house, the unpaid
rental. After so many years away, he could only be back because
Hao had dispatched him here on business.

After half an hour Uncle Huy said, "What about the food?"

"I'm going," his wife said, and they all three got up from the
floor.

Uncle took him around by the paths and introduced his
nephew proudly to people Minh had known since childhood.
Everyone asked why he wasn't in uniform today, the anniversary
of his aunt's birth. At the home of Huy's youngest brother the
women left them alone while several male relations gathered to
greet the returning pilot. This brother, Tuan, though called
Minh's uncle, was not Minh's blood. Tuan seemed to have
changed. Nothing about him was right. Maybe he'd suffered a

stroke. On his right side he looked melted—eyelid, shoulder, his right leg seemed to cave at the knee. His left eye seemed propped wide open. Maybe he'd been wounded. The VC, according to the Americans, operated all over the Mekong ever since the Tet push, though Minh wasn't so sure. Perhaps his Uncle Tuan was VC. Minh didn't mention his disability. No one did. The men smoked cigarettes and drank tea from demitasse cups. When one of the men asked Minh about his aunt and uncle in Saigon, Uncle Huy interrupted Minh's polite description of their happiness: "He rents me a house without land. I have to rent land from old Sang. Sang gets forty percent of my crop. And Hao thinks he suffers."

They went back to the house, and Minh lay down for a nap in the bed of his childhood.

He woke up confused. Somewhere a descendant of the roosters of his childhood yodeled like a strangled infant, and for a second he thought it was dawn. The voices of children laughed and called. The family had arrived—it must be late afternoon. The room, tin-roofed, of rough boards, was more window than wall, and he swept the bed net aside and sat up to see, meters away, the monuments covering two of his great-uncles. In this bed he'd slept with his little brother. The sheets smelled new and clean but they covered the same bedding and its musty tang of old perspiration and feathers, and overhead was the same baking galvanize under which he and Thu had come to live when their mother had died, in the family that wasn't their family. To be outsiders had made them close as only children are close, without any sense that time could shake them loose from one another.

At 5:00 p.m. Minh's Uncle Huy called the family together in the front room.

They waited while he lit candles at the shrine out front of the house, moving among his avocados and kumquats, past the neighbors' pants and blouses and T-shirts drying on colorful plastic coat hangers on the chain-link fence. He offered his obeisance, came into the front room greeting no one, and went through the house to stand out back before the grave monuments, and afterward came back in and placed two pillows on the floor at the head of the parlor. He crossed his legs and lowered himself to sit straight-backed before them all. The others, the children, the aunts, the cousins, the family of which he was the head, sat against the walls, the littlest ones just beyond the bounds of the room, circling the two porch pillars with their backs against them, like prisoners tied to trees. The family listened without a word. It was Minh whom he addressed. "My sister and my sister's husband have always been unfair to this family," he said. "You, also, are unfair to this family. Your father went to high school while I plowed and harvested. When he died they called it a sickness that he got from visiting the mountains, but I believe it was a direct blow from the spirit of our father, who died of his labors rather than give up the rice paddies where his son, my brother, your father, should have worked instead of going to high school. My sister married your Uncle Hao, a businessman, in order to give her sons a life in the city and an education in the schools and make them ready to prosper. Her husband, Hao, had no use for this house. His father left it to him. My sister's husband, Hao, never lived here. He visited as a child, and then he stopped coming when his grandparents died. Then this house was empty. Then Hao's father died. My sister's hus-band, Hao, is the last of that family. He had no sons to prosper after him. He has no family anymore. He calls us family, but treats us like horses and buffalo. The people you see here in this room looked after this house for my sister's husband, Hao. This house would have crumbled and washed away in the monsoons, the vines would have broken the walls, nothing would be standing now if not for our labors every day. Do you see the pads on my hands? Do you see my wife's crooked back? Did you see my wife brushing the dust from the walls this morning after she walked to the paddies and back? Did you see her cooking you a wonderful meal to share with all of us? Do you see the table laid out? Can you smell the delicious soup? Look at the chicken, the dog, the fruit, and smell the steam from the rice — do you see the sweat on her face from the steam? Everyone you see in this room works every day like that so the rest of you can live in the city. We do not pay rent. That is our arrangement with my sister's husband, Hao. My sister's husband told us our care for the house paid the rent. We've all worked more than we should have. Instead of working like horses and buffalo we should have paid rent and let the building fall to pieces around us. I am planning to set fire to this building. I will burn this building down. This man Hao sends you to tell me I have to buy my own house, and you come without any honor or love for your family to give me his message. This is a time of wars. We have nothing to count on but our family. You are a person without love, without honor, the son of a thief who robbed me of my chance at education and the lackey of a thief who robs this family of our home. Everyone here will die when I burn this building that is not a home because he steals it. Your aunt made you a wonderful meal. Eat a meal under this roof and then go back to the city and tell the man my sister married that he has no family except his wife because this building is ashes, and every one of us is dead."

His uncle uncrossed his ankles and rose to his feet, his hands folded before him.

Minh said, "Thank you, Uncle."

Uncle Huy clapped his hands together and proceeded to the table and picked up a china plate from the stack. The others followed him in silence, filling their plates or bowls from the massed fruit, the steaming rice and the soup, the shreds of dog and chicken.

Some of the children were too small to have understood the speech. They ate fast, left their bowls on the floor, ran in and out of the yard laughing, returned for more food. Older children began to play too. The adults talked of other things, first out of graciousness and embarrassment, then with true interest, finally with a certain enthusiasm. The young women sang songs. His uncle suggested to Minh that perhaps he could tell Hao the house and it occupants had been destroyed by an American bomb. Minh thanked him once more.

When he woke the next morning, his uncle had already gone to the paddies. Minh had coffee with his aunt and some cousins, one by one embraced them all, and set out along the path beside the canal toward the road to the city, where he'd have to explain to his Uncle Hao that getting money out of Uncle Huy looked like more trouble than it was worth.

Skip on his knees at an open footlocker, lifting out the troughs of card files—a musk of paper and glue, slight nausea, anger, those many months with these odors in his mouth, all of it a waste—and found the *T*'s and flicked through the cards by their edges and plucked out three entries in his uncle's block printing:

ToS

A pillar of smoke stood above the Ark like a cedar tree. It brought such a beautiful perfume to the world that the nations exclaimed, "Who is this that cometh out of the wilderness like a tree of smoke, perfumed with myrrh and frankincense, with all the powders of the perfumer?"
Song of Solomon 3:6

ToS

And I will give portents in the heavens and on the earth, blood and fire and palm trees of smoke. The sun shall be turned to darkness, and the moon to blood, before the great and terrible day of the Lord comes.
Joel 2:30, 31

ToS

"cloudy pillar"—Exodus 33:9, 10. literal—"tree of smoke."

Six weeks now in the Villa Bouquet since the colonel's death, a state of disarray and pointless aftermath, a new flavor to his imprisonment. Hao came once a week with magazines and cards of sympathy for the death of Beatrice Sands. No movement from RSC, or whoever Crodelle worked for, as to the question of Skip's participation in a doubtful scheme. Surely with the principal schemer dead and gone, some sort of pardon approached. He waited for Hao to bring a summons. No word from anyone in power.

Sands thought it fitting, in the meantime, that he compile notes for some sort of biography for the Agency's *Studies in Intelligence* organ, something more extensive, more deeply illuminating of Colonel Francis Xavier Sands than the single-paragraph death notice in *Newsweek*'s "Milestones" ten days ago. He sat at the desk in the upper room occupied lately by the colonel's double agent Trung and opened a notebook to a blank, lined page. What did he know that *Newsweek* didn't? Bits from here and there. His Aunt Grace, who'd married into the family, said they were Shaughnesseys out of the County Limerick, and why his great-grandfather Charles Shaughnessey had elected himself a Sands, and whether, actually, he'd even been a Charles, had never come to light. Charles had arrived in Boston on an American ship, because everyone did, Aunt Grace had explained, because planes, she informed young Skip, weren't invented then; maybe the new immigrant had come ashore with the crew and presented himself as an American citizen, borrowing the name of the captain. He'd worked on the docks, married as soon as he could, fathered two children, a girl and a boy, and died in his thirties having seen no more of the country than Boston Harbor. Fergus, his son, Skip's granddad, had worked harder than Charles, made more children—Raymond,

Francis, and William, and then two girls, Molly and Louise—and lived longer, into his fifties. The three boys had all attended the St. Mary's grade school, and here the family's history, as Grace retailed it, had become mainly the history of Francis, the middle brother. Francis had been expelled for unnamable mischief and banished for a couple of years to a public school also unnamable, then returned for high school to St. Mary's, where he played line positions on the football team, behaved honestly, studied hard, and gained admission to Notre Dame. By his plunge and redemption Francis had rendered himself a bold figure, the one to watch, the one to follow, the one who fell on his face and got up and headed for Notre Dame.

The colonel's own reminiscences weren't histories, but merely anecdotes. They didn't constitute a biography. He'd entered Notre Dame, if Skip remembered correctly, in 1930 or '31. Again good grades, a freshman tackle for Notre Dame during Knute Rockne's final year as its football coach. Of Rockne he hadn't told much, and Skip had gathered the famous coach had paid no attention to the freshman squad. Francis had moved to the first squad halfway through his sophomore year. He'd graduated high in his class, having done nothing, up to this point, to distinguish himself from any number of strong, earnest young men, save in his education, which placed him beyond the obvious choices of his lower-middle-class Boston origins—the docks, the police force—but which he seemed to shed with his graduation gown, striking out after adventures.

Whatever Francis had met with to make him a madman and a hero had found him sometime, Skip concluded, between 1935 and 1937, a period of biographical darkness. Apparently he headed west. Skip had heard mention of freight cars and hobo camps, mention of a rodeo, a Denver whorehouse, a prison term, a brief mysterious marriage—most of this from Skip's mother Beatrice, none of it from the colonel himself. More than once, however, the colonel had alluded to experiences with aircraft—engine work for barnstormers and crop dusters, work around airfields and hangars, nothing he seemed to think worth elaborating on—and to some association with Chinese laborers in San Francisco during this same period, when Japan was making war on their homeland. Whether some person among the fliers or some event involving the Chinese had caught him by the head and pointed him toward the rest of his life Skip simply didn't know; at the end of 1937, however, young Francis, now about twenty-six years old, had returned to Boston, found work at the docks, and enrolled at the City College for night courses designed to assist in passing the army air force's aviation cadet exam. He entered the army, trained in Tennessee on Stearman biplanes and in Mississippi and later Florida on low-wing Vultee Valiants, and by 1939, with a rank of captain, was flying P-40 Warhawk fighters and training, when he might have slept, for larger aircraft, including bombers.

In 1938 he married Bridghed McCarthy, a childhood friend. By 1940 he had a daughter, Anne, and a son was on the way— Francis Junior, who drowned in the summer of 1953 while sailing in a race from Boston Harbor to Nantucket. Not once had Skip heard his uncle mention the tragedy.

Early in 1941 Captain Sands resigned from the military under an arrangement among the Chinese, the U.S. government, and the paramilitary Central Aircraft Manufacturing Company to fly, along with nearly a hundred other American pilots, as a mercenary for the Republic of China Air Force in Claire Chennault's American Volunteer Group, known as the Flying Tigers, with a mission to protect the Burma Road supplying Chinese troops. Each American volunteer was promised eventual reentry into the military at his former rank and paid $600 a month in salary and $500 for each Japanese plane he shot down. Here the captain flew his P-40 on over a hundred missions, and earned his share of the bounty. However, in December 1941—days after the death of his own brother at Pearl Harbor—having offered to replace a comrade down with malaria as pilot of a modified DC-3 on a parachute run of British commandos, among them Anders

Pitchfork, the captain had been surprised on the return trip by
fire from a rare Japanese antiaircraft battery and had crashed in
the paddies, but not, he claimed, until the second wing had been
shot off. Despite help from the locals, he'd been captured by the
Japanese and forced—along with Pitchfork, also captured, and
sixty-one thousand other prisoners—into labor on the Siam-
Burma railroad: sickness, beatings, torture, starvation. Once he'd
been given an egg. Inexplicably placed on a ship out of Bangkok
for transfer, perhaps to Luzon, possibly to Japan itself, the captain
had escaped overboard off the coast of Mindanao by a terrible
ruse. A fellow prisoner had gone mad during their confinement
in a nearly airless hold belowdecks, and their captors had promised to shut the hatch and suffocate them all if his cries didn't
cease. Captain Sands, chosen among them by lot, had strangled
the man to death. Escape was forbidden; those left behind would
be punished; but the captain, having soiled his soul in aid of the
others, demanded the right to make an attempt by having himself
handed up through the hatch along with his victim's corpse. If
the Japanese threw him overboard for dead, as he hoped, his
escape would go undetected. The ruse worked. Though weakened by a year's mistreatment and hard labor he swam for miles,
subsisted for weeks in the jungle, and lived for two years in a
series of island villages in the Sulu Sea before managing to get
space on a freighter that took him to Australia. Immediately he
rejoined the U.S. Army Air Corps and returned to Burma for
secret aerial missions, often with British commando units. He
earned impressive citations, rose rapidly in rank, and came out of
the war a colonel, *the* colonel, the iron figure that had broken the
hammers.

The colonel viewed violence as inevitably human and warriors as peculiarly blessed. The peacetime military must have
galled him. Not long after the war the promotions stopped.
Another dark patch. For a career officer an end to steady advance-
ment was a bad sign, tantamount to firing. The specific cause of

his trouble with the military—the transgression or infraction, the misstep—never found its way into his record, but the general why of it was plain enough. The colonel knew how to lead, but he couldn't follow.

As Skip understood it, the colonel had applied to the CIA as soon as Truman had formed it in 1947, but was passed over for several years, during which he'd served on many southern air force bases, an interim that had warped his Boston accent into something unique and hardened his drinking habits. The Agency took him on in the early fifties, a latecomer among that first generation, an outsider without any OSS background but with loads of experience in Southeast Asia, over which Red China was rising. On to the Philippines, Laos, Vietnam, and, sometimes, at the beginning, in Malaya with Anders Pitchfork and the Malay Scouts, just for fun—always in a quasi-military role, generally outside the scrutiny of Langley, focused as it was on Eastern Europe and the Soviets.

On Luzon he'd worked extensively with Edward G. Lansdale combating the Communist threat there, the Hukbalahap guerrillas. The prison camps had shaped his character: belief in himself, learning on the run, fighting without thought of surrender, the stuff of heroes. Lansdale had shaped his methods: trust the locals, learn their songs and stories, fight for their hearts and minds. Curiously, perhaps mysteriously, the colonel seemed to have had no contact with General Lansdale while in Vietnam.

Vietnam had been the colonel's apex, and his undoing. Left to himself there he might have won the campaign single-handedly, but now the Asian threat was taken seriously, Langley paid attention, Congress took a hand. He was vocally bitter that the promised elections were canceled, the promised reunification postponed. As the U.S. Army arrived in stronger force, it found the colonel waiting. The Green Berets hadn't succumbed to him— too broad in his focus, maybe, the sources of his authority too hazy. He made himself indispensable to certain helicopter assault

groups, then, in 1965, to the Twenty-fifth Infantry. The King of
Cao Phuc. Psy Ops. Labyrinth. And the Tree of Smoke.

More than anything else, the colonel's time with Lansdale in
the Philippines had determined his vision. Won over by the
power of myth, he became one himself, somewhat in life but
especially in his death. According to Nguyen Minh, the young pilot the colonel had called Lucky, the colonel kept a wife in or
near Binh Dai, a ville on the Mekong Delta. After the colonel's
capture and death at the hands of the Vietcong, his body had
been returned to the ville either as an example to others or in
honor of the manner in which he'd withstood his final
torments — delivered to his widow with its digits, eyes, and tongue
torn away and all its bones broken. The people of this ville,
which had once been a Catholic parish, buried the corpse in the
earth of the chapel yard — the chapel itself had been mainly bamboo and nothing by then remained of it — in a casket of thick
rough-cut mahogany sealed with tar. Immediately afterward,
before the concrete slab could be poured to anchor it, the rains
came, days on end, very rare this time of year. Under the downpours, with no roots to hold it together, the freshly churned red
earth of the burial pit turned sufficiently liquid that three weeks
after it was hidden in the ground the coffin heaved to the surface,
and Colonel Sands came back from the underworld. The villagers pried the lid and found a beautiful black-haired American
pilot with his fingers and toes intact, a naked young Colonel
Francis unblemished, unmolested. They surrounded him with
stones, pierced his vessel with holes to let the water in, and sank
him again in his grave. Still it couldn't hold him. More rain, the
canal nearby had climbed its banks and delved away the barren
churchyard and scooped up the colonel in his casket. It was witnessed on its way down the Hau River; they saw the coffin in An
Hao, Cao Quan, Ca Goi, heading out the Dinh An mouth into
the South China Sea.

Jimmy Storm, immediately as he'd heard the rumor, had traveled to this ville. He'd found a woman who seemed to have been

the wife of an American, and the villagers escorted him to this American's grave site. It lay apparently undisturbed. But as for who rested there, how long, and all the rest of it—Storm had gone alone, none of them spoke English, their French was bad, his French was worse—he left knowing nothing. And Skip had this account through veils upon veils, through Hao, from Minh, who'd directed Storm to the village with the grave.

Skip, however, had word from Aunt Grace, as well as the assurance of *Newsweek*, that the colonel had been buried in Massachusetts—without military honors, in accordance with his wife's wishes. Skip preferred the myth. It told the truth. In this world his uncle had stood out grandly, even more so set against the landscape of his own imaginings. Skip regretted the role handed him at the end, that of traitor to the rebellion. At the end the colonel had sought reasons not just for an operation gone wrong, but for the breaking of his own heart, had looked for betrayal at the very center of things in the shape of some classical enormity, and what could have been more enormous, more darkly Roman, than betrayal by one's own house, by his nephew, by his own blood? A soul too wide for the world. He'd refused to see his downfall as typical, refused all collaboration with the likes of Marcus Aurelius: "You may break your heart," the old emperor had written, "but men will go on as before." He'd written himself large-scale, followed raptly the saga of his own journey, chased his own myth down a maze of tunnels and into the fairyland of children's stories and up a tree of smoke.

The summons came in a reusable interdepartmental envelope addressed to him care of Psy Ops, eight weeks after the colonel's death. Lunch again, Voss again. Sands expected Crodelle too.

He asked Hao to leave him at the traffic circle near the river and walked several blocks to the Continental and entered perspiring heavily. In the lobby, Rick Voss sat in an elaborately carved and japanned chair. Unaccompanied. Voss stood up and shook Skip's hand with a certain weariness, as if he'd walked here himself over rivers and mountains. "I'm sorry about the colonel."

"He was something."

"God, yes. And I'm sorry."

"So am I."

"We all are. Lately we are one sorry bunch."

It was only 11:00 a.m. Sands said, "Are you hungry yet?"

"Let's call this a prelunch. I wanted to get ahead of things here."

"Ahead of things? Why don't I like the sound of that?"

"I need to eat a little crow."

"No need. Should we sit down?"

"Hang on. We've got about five minutes."

"Where are we going?"

"Let me talk, will you?"

"Sure. You bet."

"Thanks. Thanks. Look," Voss said, "here's the speech. From the minute I heard the colonel was gone, I've been feeling like a royal piece of shit. Some folks think he was a swashbuckler, a Neanderthal. Not everybody shares that opinion of him. Some of the bunch think he was a pretty great man. I didn't start out one of them, but that's where I ended up. And this is an apology, for the little it's worth. I was wrong to pass along that draft of his article. First of all, it wasn't really his. I wrote ninety percent of it, and I didn't mind making him look bad. And I think I passed it along just to curry favor with some people who didn't like him, who I now believe to be absolute assholes. And I am fucking sorry, Skip."

"Apology accepted."

"Well, look," Voss said, "here's the problem. That article set the machinery in motion. So now he's gone, so—let's hope that's enough, right? But the machinery has to do some chewing before this business winds down. Things just have to complete their run. Can't cut it short. So you're being called back to Langley."

"Do I interpret that as an order?"

"Correct. We're sending you home."

"Okay. Will Station want to talk to me first?"

"I suspect you'll get a little going-over."

"I'm not really attached to Station. I'm Psy Ops."

"You're in-country, that's all. You're in this theater of ops. They'll want everything before you give it to Langley."

"Who's They?"

"Terry Crodelle."

"Sounds like a party."

"He wants a polygraph."

"You bet. Whatever's most helpful," Skip said.

Skip guessed most of the equipment on the conference-sized table comprised the polygraph machine. A microphone on a stand faced him, beside it a large tape recorder. Skip watched the revolutions of its reels, one fast, one slow. Beside the tape recorder rested Crodelle's green beret. Crodelle wore the battle dress uniform of the Special Forces, a captain's bars on his collars.

"Well, this is, I think, is—I don't know what it is."

"It's what?"

"I said I don't know."

"You said you had a thought."

"A thought?"

"You said you thought you knew what it was."

"When did I say that?"

Crodelle thumbed a lever on the tape recorder and found the place, Skip's voice saying Well this is I think is—"there."

"That's just—I'm stuttering."

Captain Crodelle paused and stared a few seconds before saying, "Good enough. Very good. Just checking."

He held down a button while depressing a lever and the reels began again.

"Are you actually Special Forces? Or is it a costume?"

"It's a uniform."

"Whose store is this?"

"We're with the RSC, more or less."

"I thought the RSC was Manila."

"It's a temporary shop."

"And you're a real live soldier."

"Come on."

"I did come on. I came. I'm here. The question is, where are you?"

"Sometimes you're behind the desk, sometimes you're in the field—but this stuff, this Tree of Smoke, it's neither desk nor field. It's somewhere out in the jungles of romance and psychosis." Crodelle stopped the recorder and said, "Your shit is a mess," and started it again.

"It was just a hypothetical exercise. A scenario. Psychological warfare."

"Jousting with terms. You're not going to help yourself."

"Captain, I'm not here to help myself. I'm here to help you."

"How are you covered here in Five Corps? What's your name?"

"I'm using my own documents."

"No cover."

"It's just me, fellas."

"I want you to clarify a few terms for me from this article entitled—well, no title. But clarify a few terms."

"By all means, to the extent I'm able. If it helps."

" 'Insulation'—that just means sticking your fingers in your ears when somebody issues an order."

"That's a simplification, but that's the gist of it."

"Basically cutting oneself out of the chain of command."

"Again, that's simplifying."

"Without chain of command, what we get is feudalism. Now, of course we speak figuratively of bureaucratic fiefdoms. But in this instance we believe the fiefdom to have been actual. We believe your uncle, the colonel, to have been the fief."

Skip said, "I believe we've reached a linguistic impasse."

"I'm as much as suggesting renegade activity."

"I believe we're staring into a linguistic abyss."

"The 'mobilization-loss dichotomy.' "

"The what?"

"Mobilization hyphen loss."

"Oh! for goodness' sake. 'Move it or lose it.' He says it all the time. Said it, that is."

"Without chain of command what you get is warlordism. He was running his own little agency."

"And the phrase 'move it or lose it' proves that?"

"The article proves that he considered it his duty. He was running his own operations branch—assassinations in Mindanao, for instance. And his own private, personal double agent right here."

"Where?"

"Here? You know—little place called South Vietnam?"

"What double agent?"

"Skip—I don't mean you!"

"Now you're making me sick. Literally ill."

"We aren't accusing you of treason."

"Then what? If there's an accusation, tell me what it is. Don't tell me what it isn't."

"We just want a name. If it's the name we already have, then you'll have verified it."

"Give me the name you have, and I'll give you the verification if I can."

"Skip. You work—for *us*."

"Yes, I do. And proudly, but—"

"Well then, Skip."

"You can understand my reluctance."

"No, Skip, I can't."

"From where I'm sitting, the area you're delving into, the parameters, if any—it all seems a little amorphous. I feel an obligation to get assurances from you we're going to keep things . . . in the arena of relevance."

"Assurances? What? Me no speakee."

"I don't want to jeopardize overlapping interests, let's say."

Crodelle again stopped the reels. "What interests?"

"If any."

"What a load of shit."

"That's just what I'm thinking."

"All right. Fuck." Crodelle frowned, stared at the floor for a good thirty seconds before raising his head again. "I'm willing to drop this line. Just assure me, *you* assure *me*, that no unauthorized operation is in process."

"It was a hypothetical exercise. If it were actual, it would actually be over. You have my assurance of that."

"It's all over."

"As over as it would be if it never existed."

"All right. Let's stop giving each other headaches." Crodelle resumed the recording. "As for this hypothetical exercise in psychological warfare code-named Tree of Smoke. In our last conversation, you and I talked about some files."

"Files?"

"Where are the colonel's files?"

"Files."

"The data apparatus for Tree of Smoke."

"Where are you getting all this?"

"What a silly question."

"I don't know about any files."

"What a silly answer."

"Describe what you mean. I'm here to help."

"What bullshit."

"I'd say the bullshit's all yours."

"His three-by-five collection."

"Oh. Yeah. Those were archives. I don't know where they got to."

"When did you last see the material?"

"In the PI—I was cataloging some of it, then he took it away. Check with the RSC up there. Maybe somebody knows. Check at Clark Field. That's where I last saw the stuff."

"Voss saw those footlockers here. In Saigon. At the CIA bungalow right after you arrived."

"That can't be true. Or it's very doubtful. They were taken off my hands at Clark."

"They were here."

"Then they were shipped here after they were taken off my hands."

"Skip. What kind of career path do you believe yourself to be following?"

"Kind of a corkscrew one. Pointing down. Can I tell you about the files? The files were archival in nature, very out of date, of no current interest. If I had them I'd have no reason to hide them, no motive. If I had them, I would turn them over to you immediately."

"You know what I like about your style? We catch you lying and you forge right ahead."

"Hook me up. I'll pass."

"Oh, we'll hook you up."

"I'll pass. Get to it."

"And a UA."

Skip said nothing.

"A urinalysis?"

"Oh. That's fine."

"Lot of narcotic use in Five Corps. Can't tell who might be caught in the snares."

"Bring me a jug and I'll piss in it."

Crodelle stopped the recorder, stood up to lean over it and grip its cord and pull the plug from the wall. The plug came flying at his face and he dodged it and hesitated, blinking, before he sat back down to say, "Skip, I don't believe this. I've never seen anybody fuck himself so thoroughly and so completely. And for no good reason. What's the point?"

"I don't know, man, there's just something about you that pisses me off."

"You're pretty good at this. I wish you were working for our side."

"I'm not going to touch that crap."

"Excellent. Let's meet the machine. I'll be back." He went out, leaving Sands alone.

Within seconds Sands heard activity in the hall. Escorted by a black civilian, Nguyen Hao passed the open doorway.

For ten minutes Sands sat alone at the conference table with his thoughts banging against nothing.

Crodelle came back with a middle-aged man, apparently civilian, and introduced him as Chambers, the technician. "Chambers has been doing this longer than any of us have been telling lies."

"Is that true?"

"Twenty-plus years," Chambers said.

"I'm down the hall if you need me," Crodelle said, and went out while Chambers sat next to Sands and peered beneath the table.

When he sat up again he said, "You've been polygraphed before."

"Yes. One time. What's under the table?"

"Just making sure it's unplugged."

"Oh."

"This is the dry run."

"Oh."

"So you've been polygraphed. Just the once?"

"Yes. For clearance."

"All right, now, this exam. We'll probably be taking you through the same steps you went through when you were polygraphed originally for your security clearance. What we're after is minimal exam-created stress. In other words, ha-ha, relax, buddy."

"I'm relaxed."

"Sure you are. So, okay. Couple questions."

"Okay."

"Have you been schooled in methods for evading the truth while being polygraphed?"

"I've been told. Not schooled. I've just—it's been mentioned."

"You haven't been trained, using an actual machine."

"No. Never."

"After the session, you'll be examined physically. We'll check your tongue for signs you've been biting it, palms for nail marks, and so on."

"I've heard about those things, but I don't remember when you're supposed to use them. Whether it's when you're lying, or when you're telling the truth, or—"

"Have you been schooled in techniques for slowing your breathing, staying calm under stress, that kind of thing?"

"Not for these purposes. Not schooled. Just—'Keep a tight asshole when the guns go off, breathe shallow when your heart beats too fast,' that kind of thing."

"So, first step: This test consists of twenty questions. I have the questions here, and you will read them silently to yourself. We do this in order to eliminate any reaction of surprise from the graph. Do you understand the purpose of seeing the questions in advance of the test?"

"Yes. We're eliminating reactions of surprise."

Chambers opened his manila folder and handed it over. The questions were typed on a single sheet of paper bound to the inside cover by a paper clip. Sands looked them over.

"At this point, is there anything you need clarified about the process?"

"Will there be more tests? Subsequent to this one?"

"Oh, right, good. The exam itself consists of four tests, each with different questions, although some questions may be repeated in subsequent tests or in all four tests. Sorry. I forgot to say that. Anything else you need clarified at this point?"

"I don't think so."

"Anything you need clarified at any point, just ask. Now. In order to familiarize you with the procedure in advance, I'm going to hook you up without turning on the machine. The machine will not be operating. Do you understand that the machine will not be operating?"

"The machine's off. Yes."

"When the machine is operating, this scroll will be moving along, and these three needles will move up and down to create lines across the graph."

"I understand."

"I've got to ask you to remove your shirt, please."

Sands complied and laid his shirt across the arm of his chair.

"And the watch. Just lay it on the table. Are you right- or left-handed?"

"Right."

"Will you place your right arm here on the table, please? Lay it out flat." Chambers wrapped a blood-pressure cuff around Sands's bicep. "We'll record blood pressure, and breathing, and galvanic skin response. If you'll lean forward, please." Sands leaned forward and Chambers wrapped a beige rubber tube around his chest and joined its ends together with a small metal clamp. "Too tight?"

"No. I don't know. You're the technician."

"These clips go on your fingertips here. That gives us skin temperature." After the finger clips, Chambers touched the attachments gently, the cuff, the tube, the clips, making small adjustments, and sat back in his chair. "Comfortable?"

"Definitely not."

"Well, nobody ever is. You've read the questions, correct?"

"Yes."

"To you some of them seem stupid, probably, and some seem irrelevant. Others seem obviously true or obviously false. That's how we get a reading of your response to different categories. I'm just assuring you it all makes sense."

"I understand."

"Very good. At this point in our dry run, I'm going to read the questions to you so you hear them in my voice and we eliminate the random stress of any surprises. You don't answer the questions. I just read them. You can stop me at any time to discuss any question." Chambers picked up his manila folder and opened it on his lap. "Ready?"

"Begin."

"Is your name William Sands? . . . Were you born in Miami, Florida? . . . Do you know the whereabouts of footlockers contain-

ing the files of Colonel Francis Xavier Sands? . . . Did you graduate from Indiana University?"

"Excuse me."

"Yes."

"I have two degrees, a BA from Indiana and an MA from
George Washington. So I wouldn't know exactly—"

"Okay. Bachelor of Arts from Indiana University, correct?"

"Correct."

"All right. The question will read as follows: Do you have a
Bachelor of Arts degree from Indiana University?"

"Okay."

"Okay. The queries continue as follows: Do you know Trung
Than? . . . Are you the nephew of Colonel Francis Xavier
Sands? . . . Am I wearing a shirt with short sleeves? . . . Do you
enjoy telling lies?"

"Wait."

"Yes."

"The one about whether I'm a nephew—I assume I'm someone's nephew whether they're living or dead."

"Hm. You know what? I have to check on that one. Excuse me."

Chambers stood and left the room, taking with him the manila
folder.

Sands waited and watched the door left open, past which he
now believed any of his acquaintances might be seen drifting,
Minh, Storm, Trung, his mother, uncle, father, a parade of ghosts.

When Chambers returned he said, "We've changed two
queries. I'll continue with my little recital here, and then you can
read it all to yourself again, okay?"

"Yes. Okay."

"Do you know the whereabouts of Trung Than? . . . Were you
born in the month of December? . . . Are you stationed in Cao
Phuc, South Vietnam? . . . Do you know the whereabouts of files
compiled by Colonel Francis Xavier Sands? . . . Have you ever
met a man named Trung Than? . . . Do you have a son named

John? . . . Are the lights on in this room? . . . Has Trung Than ever
been a VC operative? . . . Did you ever witness Trung Than having direct contact with Colonel Francis Xavier Sands? . . . Do you
know where the colonel's files are at this time? . . . Do you have a
master's degree from George Washington University? . . . Do you
know the probable whereabouts of the colonel's files? . . .

"That's it. Let's get you unhooked." As Chambers removed the
cuff and chest tube and finger clips and Sands slipped his arms
into his shirtsleeves, Chambers said, "I'll leave the query sheet
with you for a bit. Look over the questions again while I excuse
myself again."

Sands sat looking over the questions without seeing them.

"If you button your buttons," someone said, "we can go to
lunch."

Crodelle and Voss stood in the doorway with something of the
air about them of older brothers who'd just paid his fare at a
brothel.

"What?"

"Lunchtime."

"Lunch?"

"It's two-fifteen," Crodelle said. "Are you hungry?"

"You mean go out?"

"Yeah. The Rex or someplace. Let's go to the Rex."

"All right."

"All right?"

"Fine with me."

"It's a lull. You'll read better if you hear the questions and then
forget about them awhile."

"Forget about them. You bet."

He followed them down the hall past the marine sergeant and
the digit pad and the electric lock and up the stairs.

Before descending the steps outside, Crodelle stopped to place
his green beret on his head and get it snug. The beret-flash was
one Sands hadn't seen before, black and white and gray, edged

with yellow. They walked toward the concrete traffic barricades and Skip said, "Your hair's a little long for uniform, isn't it?"

"I'm not often in uniform."

"What's your insignia there," Skip asked, pointing at his beret-flash.

"JFK Special Warfare Center," Crodelle said.

"Where's that located?" Skip asked, and as they stepped beyond the barricades he took off running, pounding along in a full-out sprint until he came up against a cross street, heading right, continuing along the path of least resistance. Where a woman guided her two children into the motor traffic he slowed to a walk and joined them and they threaded themselves through the deranged flow of small vehicles to the other side, and he ran again, following a series of right-angle zigzags through the city for half a mile, not once looking back. On Louis Pasteur he took to the park under the massive trees and adopted a pace he'd learned in the Boy Scouts of America, fifty paces walking, fifty paces jogging.

He observed the activity of the streetside beyond the trees and saw no one but the denizens of Saigon, gripped by a lust for survival, making their way through the moments. To reach here he must have leapt over sandbags and in and out of the street, must have paused, reversed, dodged left and right like a linebacker, and knocked some of these fine people to the pavement, but he kept no impression of any of it.

Coming out of the park he hailed a cab and collapsed perspiring in the backseat and sent the driver to the Cho Lon depot. This late in the day the buses had probably already stopped running. Until they started again in the morning he'd take refuge in a barroom. Or in a temple or a church. A whorehouse, an opium den. A fugitive, a traitor.

His cordovan shoes stank of the gutters he'd run through. He cranked the window down.

He regretted having to miss the exam. Of the questions they'd prepared for him, he saw one as relevant:

"Do you enjoy telling lies?"

"Yes," he would have answered truthfully.

Generally Dietrich Fest took his lunch at a soup place on the far side of Tu Do Street, the big thoroughfare a couple of blocks from the Continental. For supper he'd found better places, nothing with a German flavor but good enough that he worried about his weight. By now he was familiar with every restaurant he could walk to. He didn't like the taxis. He dealt more easily with the cyclo boys.

He used the message drop in the Green Parrot's lavatory only once—to change the location of the next drop. He chose a restaurant across the plaza from the Continental where he could watch the people going in and out. Only Major Keng used the drop.

He told the management his room was too small, and they moved him to another on the western side that got too much sun in the afternoon. That night he put the air conditioner at its coldest setting, and by morning its labors were muffled and its vents clogged with frost. He called downstairs to complain. Two workmen arrived and said if he set the controlling dial at medium the ice would melt and the machine would work better. They went away talking to one another in a language he found twangy, shrill, grating, a kind of buzzing whine.

He'd planned on a couple of weeks in Saigon. He'd been here almost two months.

Every few days he came to the management with a reason to move to another room.

His target lodged in a room in a mixed Chinese-Vietnamese neighborhood at the edge of the Cho Lon District.

Across the street from the site of completion, a single shop sold fabric and perhaps also made women's dresses. On that side the rest of the block presented closed doors and a couple of alleyways in which noisy women and children appeared to pass most of their daily lives: crates for tables and boxes for chairs, fuming hibachis and leaking wooden tubs and lines of washing. Fest could watch a little, but there was no café on the street, no excuse for his presence. He stood next to the fabric shop as if waiting for someone.

The hotel's entry matched every other wooden door on the block. Next door at street level the owner ran his business in a glass-windowed office and kept charge of the rooms upstairs. Major Keng had referred to this man as "a trouble agent." Alone, smoking a cigarette with an air of tender introspection, the trouble agent sat between two electric fans positioned on the counter expertly so as not to disturb his papers. Fest could only guess at his profession—broker, lawyer, lender—identified as it was only by Chinese characters painted on his windows. While Fest stood across the street watching, a man arrived clutching a pasteboard portfolio under his arm and sat in a chair before the counter with his knees pressed together and his package in his lap, handing over documents one by one.

After ten minutes Fest felt conspicuous and left the neighborhood.

By their fourth meeting Fest had determined that communication with the Americans ran in only one direction. Possibly all commo had ceased. In any case Major Keng had no method of getting back to the Americans with Fest's concerns. Either that or Keng simply didn't care about the operation.

"I do not like our scenario. It has too many contingencies."

"There are always problems."

"I went to view the location. It's difficult. I'm not able to keep an eye. There is no café on the street and no rooms for rent where I can take up an outpost. I can't be sure of my ground."

The major frowned. "Mr. Reinhardt. Parlez-vous Français?"

"No."

"Your English is not so clear to me."

"When I enter the room, I must be sure he's alone."

"He's alone." The major was smiling. "He is unarmed. He was brought to the location by a contact he trusts. He's not going to stir from it until he is told. This contact has given us the keys. One to the street door, one to the room."

"Then give me the keys, please."

"It's better if I give them four days from now."

"Do you have the keys?"

"I will have the keys four days from now."

"When is the time for completion?"

"One week from now."

"Can you put some people to watch the location? We must be sure of our ground."

"What do you mean? He can't go out. It's the only safe place for him. That is his belief. You can be confident."

Little brown clown. You tell me to walk through a closed door with a gun in my hand and be confident.

"May I make a suggestion?"

"Of course, Mr. Reinhardt."

"Let me take him outdoors, away from his room."

"Take him? Do you intend to kidnap?"

"Call him to a meeting in a location we can monitor. Perhaps his contact can arrange it. We'll monitor in advance of the meeting. Then the ground is ours."

The major pursed his lips as if considering the angles. "It makes cleanup perhaps difficult."

"The site must be cleaned?"

"Not by you, Mr. Reinhardt! That's all in place. Everything is in place, Mr. Reinhardt."

"You're saying it's too late to change the plan."

"We shall go forward with confidence."

On the way back to his room he stopped at a stall in the square and, without bargaining over the price, bought a large English dictionary of some two thousand pages. At the Continental's desk he asked for his valuables from the safe, and the clerk brought his Vietnam Air Lines flight bag. Upstairs he took the equipment from the bag and turned the room's radio up loud. It was 2:00 p.m.; the U.S. military station delivered the news of an imminent journey to the moon. He affixed the silencer to the pistol, placed the dictionary in his bathtub, and fired four shots into it from a distance of one meter.

The first unblemished page was numbered 1833. As he'd expected, at close range the weapon would produce an exit wound. More nonsense. I ask for a twenty-two, and you bring me a howitzer. I can't call Berlin, while astronauts aim at the moon.

The phones worked, he'd gotten through, his father was dead.

Two years he'd waited to hear it, yet the news had absolutely stunned him. The old man had won his way forward breath by breath through so many ailments it hadn't seemed possible he'd ever be stopped. Nothing in particular had beaten him. He'd died in his hospital room while napping after breakfast. On the phone his mother had sounded tired but otherwise unaffected.

He'd called Dora as well, and he'd broken down weeping as he told her of his father's death. "I'll call again soon. The phones are working." It must have sounded as if the good news about the telephones had broken his heart.

Because a Chinese travel broker ran this four-room hotel, Trung assumed Chinese businessmen used the establishment.

Daytimes the street outside was noisy, and after 9:00 or 10:00 p.m. fairly quiet—distant traffic, distant jet fighters, helicopters much closer, over the city itself. He'd never before stayed in a rented city room. He had possession of a key to the street entrance and a key to his own door, both attached by a string to a scrap of wood with the numeral 1 scratched into it.

The door on the street opened onto a narrow stairwell leading up into a narrow hall with high ceilings and plaster walls and two rooms on each side and a bathroom at the end of it—a sink; a tub; a toilet that flushed when he pulled a chain. In the mornings he heard feet stomping along the hall and his neighbors running the water and hocking and spitting in the bathroom and at night he heard the man next door coughing and treading from his bed to the window to spit down into the alley.

The place was wired for electricity. At the top of the stairwell and also in the ceiling above the bathroom hung fluorescent tubes that burned all night, but his room had none. He had a butane lantern, a thin mattress on a bamboo frame, a circular, domed bed net, and a small square table on which rested the lantern, a box of wooden matches, and a large clamshell for an ashtray.

Each night he took his supper at a café one street over and bought food to last him through the following day. Hao had given him money and told him to stay indoors as much as possible until the Americans, probably within a week or so, accomplished their arrangements. But he had to make this outing every day. He wouldn't deprive himself. He'd been in Saigon four days.

He didn't have to be told to keep out of sight. If anybody recognized him it was over. The cadres understood him to be visiting family in Ben Tre for the Tet celebrations, for only a few days; he'd been out of touch now almost two months. No explaining such an absence, no lie would spare him a "workout"—hours of group discussion, until more than anybody else in the room you yourself believed you'd crossed the line, and you demanded to be punished. He'd make sure the Americans understood this problem. Maybe the Americans knew other turncoat VC who could devise a story—he couldn't imagine what, a bout of illness, or a wound—and vouch for his whereabouts during his absence.

I won't have rice again today. Noodles, if they still have the hoisin sauce. They had it yesterday, but I used the last.

These past few weeks, first in the room above the café on the Mekong, now in the room above the travel broker's, had been a form of incarceration, but under conditions happily very different from what he'd learned to think of as prison. In the cell in Con Dau he'd slept on a stone floor with a dozen other men, sometimes on a concrete slab to which his ankles had been shackled. The guards patrolled on catwalks crisscrossing overhead—pissing down on them sometimes, or tossing offal from a bucket. The cell itself had been not quite long enough for two men end to end, about half that in width. The prisoners had all looked out for each other, nothing but death could separate them from the cause. Then the end of the French, liberation, the journey north by ship, and the kolkhoz, the communal farm—the citizens of the Collective Future, generally tense, sometimes erupting, always desperate, living in stupidity, anger, and submission. The citizens of the future had found little to say to him. He was older and had come in by all Three Gates—prison, blood, self-denial—each a stage deeper into the lie that trapped them all. And the last gate, the one that didn't get a number: renouncing friends and relatives, the gate to true imprisonment. Once you mix in your blood, your strength, and your days, then you belong to the cause. But betrayal is the main thing.

The happiest days of his life had been those spent coming down out of the Truong Son Mountains, ambling homeward in good weather after the weeks of climbing through rain on the uphill northern side, after the plague that had nearly killed him, after the camps of deserters all shivering with fever, after the grave mounds of piled boulders bristling with sticks of incense or dug up and scattered and the corpses chewed to pieces by hungry tigers, and now the easy downhill journey toward Ben Tre, the breath of the south in his lungs, the sunshine falling in shafts through the jungle's canopy, and the flowers with his mother's name. But I entered a land where my mother was dead and all the others pretended not to be. My legs carried me over the mountain, but I never got home.

Betrayal had fueled the trip out. Betrayal would bring him back.

In his olive bathing trunks, bare-chested, Sands sat in the wicker chair on the small back porch taking the breeze from the creek and drinking something made with sugar and coconut milk and things he probably didn't want to know about. All this trash smoke, the creek's stench wrung his stomach, the bugs were driving him crazy. Screeching cicadas. Tiny winged creatures flailing at his face.

He heard a vehicle coming up the lane and recognized the sound as that of a military jeep.

Four days since his getaway, and no one had come until now. The gods ground slow. Or they realized he'd fled without a plan, without money, leapt from the window into the wild night, and what—loitered in the dark, waiting to be arrested.

When he heard the jeep's brakes out front he got up and entered the house.

This time of day, with the heat, Skip hung mosquito netting over the front door and left it open. He watched through the open doorway as Jimmy Storm, in fatigues and a brown T-shirt, let himself through the low gate and walked up the steps.

Sands pulled the netting aside and let it drop closed behind his guest.

Storm clutched a bundle of mail against his chest. He did not say hello. "Voss is no longer a contributor."

"Pardon?"

"He didn't make the mission."

"You're saying he's what, he's—"

"Tagged and bagged. He fucked the monkey."

With his free hand Storm hit Sands with an uppercut deep to the solar plexus. His lungs emptied, his diaphragm seized, nausea blinded him. He collapsed forward onto his knees, and then the side of his head smacked down onto the tiled floor.

He came to some form of consciousness, breathing again, as Storm prodded his ear with the toe of his canvas boot.

"I could kick my foot through your head now, you know?"

"I know," Sands managed to say.

He tossed things down one at a time into Skip's face, first reading each one: "Here's your *Newsweek*. Here's your *Time*. What's this?—fucking *Sports Illustrated*."

"Storm—"

"You've got us in a skinny little crack. You've got us in a real tight little fuck."

"Storm—let's talk."

"What makes you think I'd talk to you? What makes you think I'd discuss the game with a pogue rolled up on the floor in a fetal ball?—Is that what they taught you in unarmed combat school?"

As a matter of fact, the student was advised when tackled by a gang to curl the skeleton around the vital organs and "pray for the cavalry." Not, however, when downed by a lone attacker. A man solidly on the ground could find an advantage over a man balanced on one leg while kicking, so went the wisdom. Sands didn't care to test it.

"And don't say you did what you had to do. That's bullshit. Just say you did what you did, man. Just say you did it."

"I haven't said anything," Skip said, "about doing anything."

"You and me have to talk on some other level, man, because you won't get *down*. You won't get *down*. This is what's *happening*. So *fuck*." He was kicking Sands in the head as he spoke.

"Are you done? I'd like you to be done."

"Yeah. I'm done. No, I'm not done." He kicked Sands twice in the ribs.

He turned to leave, got as far as the door, and came back.

"Do you think I really give a fuck? So we lose this war, so

what? Will the little kiddies of America be going to Uncle Ho
High School and memorizing the Gettysburg Address of fucking
Lenin? Will Charlie be raping our women in the streets? Fuck
no. The whole thing's bullshit, man. Win or lose, we're gonna be
fine. But we're here. You and me and these other assholes. It's our
shit to deal with. So why the fuck not? The all-important underly-
ing reason is, 'Fuck it, let's just do it.' Either you understand that
or you don't."

"Yeah. That was more or less my uncle's theory."

"The colonel's alive."

"He is?"

"Isn't he?"

"No."

"Yes, fucker."

"That's just bullshit."

"Yeah, it is. But you don't get it. That's exactly what runs the
reactors. The fragrance of bullshit."

"Are you going to let me get up?"

Storm sat on the divan, breathing hard.

"Fine, I'll just lie here. I'm tired."

"You put down what we're doing. To you, Psy Ops is baby food.
I'm telling you, man, this is where it's won or lost. In the realm of
bullshit. It doesn't matter how bad we kick their asses on the bat-
tlefield or vice fucking versa."

"The colonel's dead."

Storm said, "Yeah. You are a pogue. You just stay here all
curled up like a piece of popcorn in your little womb. Your traitor-
incubator."

By painful stages Sands got himself standing and made his way
to a chair and collapsed again.

"How are you feeling, Skipper? Like shit, I hope."

"Jimmy."

"Yeah."

"Is Rick Voss dead?"

"Very very much so."

"Did you . . . You killed Rick Voss?"

"No, fucker. The VC killed Rick Voss. Somebody shot down his helicopter. They think. Anyway, it went down."

"Rick Voss is dead?"

"Everybody aboard. Poof."

"What was he doing in a helicopter?"

"Diddling around like a dick, like always."

"Jesus Christ. He had a wife and kids."

"Well, he don't no more, Jack. Pretty soon some other guy'll have 'em. That's how the shit goes."

Voss had a little girl, Skip remembered. He leaned forward and retrieved his coconut drink from the table and held the cold glass against his pounding cheekbone.

"So, little Skippy. Where were you last Thursday?"

"Saigon."

"Where else?"

"Taking a polygraph."

"Yeah. You sure were."

Sands leaned forward in his chair. He kept his .25-caliber Beretta in a dresser drawer upstairs and had an impulse, momentary but almost irresistible, to go up and get it and shoot Jimmy Storm in his face. When the wave had washed over he felt weak to the point of paralysis. He put his face in his hands. "Listen. Are you leaving, or not?"

"Yeah, I'm going. I just came to let you know karma turned your good buddy to soup."

"Jesus Christ. Poor Voss."

"Yeah, Poor Voss. I wish I could be the one to tell his wife. I hope he had beautiful little kiddies. I hope he thought about them while he was going down."

Suddenly Sands clutched up some ice cubes from his drink and flung them at his face. "Aah, shit," Jimmy said. "I'm sorry. Come on, throw some more." His eyes cried out for it, for punishment. "The first time I saw you I thought, This guy is looking fucking sketchy. Sifting through ashtrays for a snipe. He's got that how-do-I-get-your-wallet look. He's here on a kiddie-cruise. He's here to play Spooks and Gooks. You came here to troll the drag and show off your fucking hot rod."

"If you're all done stomping me, I'd like you to leave."

"Stomping? Fuck you. Right now the colonel is being tortured. Right now they're breaking every one of his bones."

"Jimmy. Goddamn. Come on."

"You remember how he ditched the Japs in World War Two, man?—he played fucking dead."

"Good for you. Keep the legend alive."

"I'm not the motherfucking voice of reason. I soak shit up, I process it, I feel the facts. It's visceral. There's not enough of that going on around here."

"Jimmy, the colonel died. And everything fell apart."

"What did he say? What did he say a thousand times? 'How do we get bogus product credibly into the hands of the enemy? Specifically into Uncle Ho's hands?' Scenario one: through a double who so-called steals phony documents. Number two: use a real live American, a plant who gets himself captured. But his favorite idea was using both. Coming from separate sources, you enhance the credibility level."

"Jimmy. Focus."

"No, man, this makes too much sense. It's just too lined up and laid out. He faked this shit, and he didn't tell us. He's on a mission, and we're fucked. We can't help him. Something cold is happening, extremely cold. And we're the niggers."

"Why would he pull a ruse without letting us in on it?"

"Why? Because you're a fink. And a pogue. And a queer. I should screw you in the ass."

"Focus, will you focus? Who told you they picked me up?"

"I know things."

"Hao told you."

"Fuck you."

"Storm—it's Hao. It's Hao."

"What about him?"

"The rat. The fink. It's Hao."

"Fuck you. Nice try."

"Jimmy, it's Hao."

"Watch your karma. Behold your karma. Observe while it eats you slow-motion from the toes up, fucker."

"They polyed me at the Language School. Hao was there."

"Bull—shit." Storm took a second to consider the assertion. "Right at the party?"

"No, but I saw him in the hallway."

"Maybe he's taking classes."

"They've got a store in the basement. RSC or somebody. Hao walked past the door while I was sitting there. They wanted me to see him."

Storm regarded him for some seconds. The human polygraph. "What did I tell you? This is a rock 'n' roll war. Motherfuckers do not understand that shit." He stood up and wiped his face with the hem of his shirt, exposing the reddish legs and green skirt of a hula dancer tattooed on his chest. "Fuck, fuck, fuck."

"Leave Hao alone. He's just staying alive."

"Yeah. Fuck. This place is Disneyland on acid. Have you taken that shit yet? Acid?"

"Haven't had the pleasure."

"Stay away from it, Skipper. You're too flaky."

He had a location. He had access to it in the form of two keys. He had a weapon, a timetable, and a point of last resort. He lacked what he needed most.

He had no team. Too much had been left to him. He had to watch the drop point because he didn't trust his own handlers, and he had to do what he could to monitor the site. Even if there were three of him, his cursory training in surveillance probably wouldn't

serve. He was, in plain American, only a "triggerman." He operated the weapon.

The target had spent almost a week at this location. Fest sur-
mised that unless the target had his meals delivered he would
sooner or later have to go out for food, and probably in the dark. In
any case, nightfall was the only time for observation. A shadow
among shadows. Nothing last night, at least not before ten or so,
when Fest had given up his post. He came a bit earlier this evening, at sunset, and walked around the block waiting for darkness
that would hide a stationary figure.

Duskfall had little effect on the life of the alleys. If anything
the children howled more loudly, and the men, sullen or noncommittal, back from wherever they spent the daytimes, seemed
by their presence to make the women even more shrill. Fest
missed his comparatively quiet family. Dora talked too much and
Claude perhaps talked foolishly, but not in tones that rivaled the
noise of city traffic. Fest missed his family altogether. Why not?—
the old man's death had made him mawkish and philosophical.
At first the news had rocked him, but he'd quickly adjusted to a
loss so long expected. A few days later sorrow attacked him again
as he realized the old man was still dead. As if some part of him
had believed his father could die and later one could visit him and
talk about it.

He'd determined not to regard this operation as some sort of
sentimental monument to his father's anti-Communism. An operation so unprofessionally structured and unnecessarily hazardous
would stand as a ludicrous memorial to a man who'd seen his
duty clearly and lived by it.

As he circuited the block a fourth time and came around the
corner he saw a man leaving the rooming house by the street door.

This had to be the one. Others he'd seen coming out had
worn dress slacks and shirts or, in the case of a couple of old
men, the long shift and loose pantaloons of comic-book China-
men, and more importantly they'd moved where they wanted,
crossed the street, if that's what they wanted, immediately on

coming out of the place. This one wore jeans and a T-shirt and kept close to the walls, in the shadows, until he reached the end of the block. As he crossed at the corner, Fest began walking. The target continued up the perpendicular block and Fest turned the corner in time to see him turn right at its end. Fest broke into a trot, keeping close to the walls himself. As he took the same right, he slowed to a walk. The man was only twenty yards ahead. Now they traveled on a street parallel to the one the man lived on. He turned into a lighted entrance. Fest continued past it and saw him sitting at a table in a café talking to the papasan. When Fest reached the next cross street he turned around and walked by the café again. The man sat inside with a bowl and chopsticks and a teapot.

Fest walked briskly to the corner, turned left, and broke into a trot again. He had the keys in his pocket.

At the end of the block he crossed the street, stood in a shadow, and observed the windows along the second story of the rooming house. None on this side were lighted. In the distant sky beyond, the orange tracers streaked upward. The show came nightly, a kind of parody of the aurora borealis. The noise of helicopters and jet engines came and went. The general din of the city floated over from busier streets. A couple of cyclos passed, and pedestrians, but the block, except at the lurid alleyways, was quieter than most of Saigon this time of night.

He took out the gun from the belly holster under his shirt and the silencer from his trouser pocket and fitted them together. He needed no weapon now, but tomorrow night he would have it in his hand from this point forward. He perspired heavily. Tomorrow night he'd bring two handkerchiefs and thoroughly dry his palms before handling the equipment.

At the street door he held a key in his left hand and the gun in his right and gave the key a try. He'd chosen the right one. He placed it in his left back pocket and went inside. He left the door unlocked. Under a naked fluorescent tube dotted with insects a narrow stairwell led upward. He tried a switch on the wall to his left, produced a couple of seconds of total darkness, and raised the switch. The light flickered back to life. He took the second key from his front pocket and climbed the stairs without muffling his steps, like any patron, and inserted the key into the lock of the first door on the right. It opened inward and rightward. He pushed it wide and stepped back and sideways, holding the gun ready. The interior was dark, as he'd expected. He heard no sound from within. Across the room a single window faced the wall of the adjacent building.

He worked the door open and closed. As it passed about sixty degrees of arc its upper hinge whined. The door lock, too, could use some oil, but he hadn't thought to bring any—didn't they know he was only the triggerman?

Leaving the door open, he stepped inside. Without light from the hallway it would be impossibly dark, and yet in order to complete the operation he'd have to put out the hallway lights before entering. He felt the wall either side of the door for a switch and found nothing. He holstered the weapon and took his penlight from his shirt pocket to send its small circle about the room—no switch on the wall, no lamp in the ceiling.

A narrow bed with a mosquito net knotted above it, a table with a lantern and a large seashell resting on it. On the floor beside it, a folded pair of pants and a T-shirt, a knapsack too, which he rifled quickly—two books, a pair of boxer undershorts. He lifted the thin mattress and through widely spaced supporting boards ascertained the floor beneath the bed was bare. He lay on his side and shone his light on the undersides of the boards and the small tabletop— nothing secured in either of those places. He got to his feet.

He went about the room with the penlight, feeling the plaster walls, studying the floorboards in particular, looking for any loose ones.

The pane of the single window was raised, the building outside so close he could touch it. God knew what lived in the narrow space between. He put his hand out and felt below the sill. Nothing affixed to the wall outside, no cache of any kind.

There was absolutely no other place to keep a weapon. Either the man carried one on his person, or he had none, as Keng, the major, had promised. As for something improvised—if the man woke he might use the table, or the seashell, which seemed to serve as an ashtray.

He'd been emphatically assured the man was unarmed. But anybody could buy a knife. Or carry a length of rope for a garrote.

By the glow of the penlight he made a careful examination of the mattress. Discolored at one end, probably where the head would rest.

The problem, as Fest saw it, was that a prudent man, and on top of that a man made sensitive by stress and strain, would wake at the slightest sound and rise from bed and ready himself for anything.

Insane simply to walk through a door. Assuming he could get up the stairs noiselessly, still too much depended on the man's sleeping while Fest turned the key.

Why not take him now?

In ten or fifteen minutes the man would come through this door, having finished his supper. He could kill him and go directly to the Armed Forces Language School to explain he'd been forced to improvise. Adapt and improvise, the bywords of the trade.

But until forced, one sticks to the plan of operation, or its semblance, or its shreds. He'd always kept to the plan. And no plan had ever failed him.

Major Keng had stressed that it must come tomorrow night, precisely at 2:00 a.m. One hour later the site would be cleaned, the body disposed of. Apparently that part of it was fixed. He had to work around it. Fest resented that the scenario seemed to center on the cleanup operation rather than on the actual killing.

But suppose tonight the man ate quickly—suppose he'd already finished, suppose he came up the stairs, imagine right now he stands in the doorway—I'd kill him. And if I choose to wait here fifteen minutes, and that very thing happens? What difference

whether the moment was selected by prudence or forced by circumstance?

Again he went over the walls and the floorboards, aware of taking longer than needed, inviting a change in plan, daring fate, the
target's fate. But the man took his time, apparently savoring his
excursion—who wouldn't?—and in five more minutes Fest closed
and locked the door behind him and descended the stairs with the
gun pressed against his right leg, as he would tomorrow night, and
exited onto the street. He put away the gun and locked the door
behind him without glancing around and walked directly across
the street and waited in the shadow of the fabric dealer's entrance.

He'd waited fifteen more minutes when the target returned
along the opposite side and went through the building's street door.

Fest recrossed the street and stood at the narrow space between
the buildings to watch the windows above him. Less than a
minute after the little man had entered, a small glow in the nearest window gave way to a brighter one as the man lit his lantern.

That was the right window. He had the right man.

Suppose tomorrow night the man went out for supper and died
as soon as he returned, rather than at two in the morning? Suppose
the body lay in the room for several hours, rather than sixty minutes? Rigor mortis might present a problem for the disposal team,
but Fest doubted it. The trade-off in assurance of completion made
the change well worthwhile—the difference between entering a
pitch-black room in which anything could be going on, or waiting
in a pitch-black room for a man who thought it was empty.

At this time tomorrow he'd come again. If the man went out,
Fest would greet him when he returned.

Trung Than sat on the bed finishing a warm Coca-Cola. Without a clock or a watch he knew only that it was later than 3:00
p.m., not by much. A full two hours before the dusk came and
released him.

He tried sitting straight-backed on the bed and attending only to his breath, only to his breath.

Holding still, when I want to act, and letting my impatience be crushed, is a thrill that feels almost illicit because of the slight nausea it includes. Like stolen brandy. When Hao stole the bottle from the old man's hooch. The old man hid it in the ashes of the stove because his wife was dead and he never cooked for himself. Almost half of it left in the bottle, and we drank it all without even rinsing away the soot, and with black hands and black faces we walked on a cloud, singing wonderful songs. The master laughed. He always called me the Monk. The master thought I'd stay.

In those days he'd known how to sit still. He'd learned to live a good part of each day in the silence under the world. Now the world lived in his mind, it colonized his solitude like a virus, thoughts crawled, shot, rained through his meditation, and every one pierced him.

He tried meditating on his knees on the floor, but that only slowed the passage of time. It was still light, still well before 5:00 p.m., when he heard feet on the stairs and a knock at the door and unlocked and opened it to find the sharp-faced, feline American sergeant standing before him.

"Double-oh-seven! Remember me?"

He moved forward as he spoke, and Trung stepped aside but didn't shut the door until the American gestured that he should.

"How goes it, brother? Still laughing?"

Trung recalled his name was Mr. Jimmy.

"Oh, yeah," Mr. Jimmy said, "it's like jumping into a shit-pile of diseased spiders and I love it."

Embarrassment caused Trung to smile.

"Where's Hao?" The American looked at his watch. "The fucker's not here, is that the message for today?" Mr. Jimmy strode four paces to the window, put his hands on the sill, and stuck his head out to look down the narrow space toward the bit of street visible to him. He turned to Trung. "Well, I hate to inject a negative strain. I'm not gonna say it yet. But I'm gonna say it: that little fucker isn't coming. Which means we are either partially fucked or completely fucked. You got another Coke?"

"No, thank you."

Mr. Jimmy crossed the room again and sat beside the door with his back against the wall and one leg straight and one knee raised. Apparently he meant to stay. "You smoke?"

"I like cigarette."

He went into his shirt pocket and lit a cigarette and tossed Trung the pack and the lighter.

"Marlboro."

"Yeah. I'm trying to think. So let's shut up."

Trung got up and locked the door and sat on the bed smoking, dipping his ash down the neck of his empty Coke bottle.

"When I take the last drag on this mother, that's it. I get the fuck out, or I'm here for the duration." The sergeant drew deeply on his cigarette. "Fuck it. I'm here for the duration."

They finished their cigarettes in silence and Trung dropped his into the bottle while the sergeant placed his own under his heel and ground it into the floor. At that point Trung realized he hadn't offered him the ashtray, or used it himself.

"Listen, guy. Is Hao your friend?"

"Hao is my friend."

"Good friend?"

"Good friend."

"True friend?" Mr. Jimmy clasped his hands together tightly. "True like right down the line and all the way to hell?"

Trung felt he perhaps comprehended the question. He jutted his lips and held out his palms and shrugged his shoulders, the way he'd seen Frenchmen do.

The sergeant leapt up, but he wasn't leaving. He came to Trung with the cigarette pack outstretched and the disease of terror in his eyes. "Double agent? What a fucking joke. In the shitbucket of South Vietnam, every living thing is double."

Trung accepted another cigarette but raised his palm and

shook his head at the sergeant's lighter. He set the cigarette on the table.

"You probably figure I snapped my twig. I'm with you there. I have to agree. But I'm still listening to my own shit, comrade, because it's the only thing happening."

"Mr. Jimmy. Please speak slowly."

"Do you speak English?"

"A little bit. Number ten."

"We are not getting through to each other. No commo, savvy? I don't have the names for the entities in your language. You have all the names. You got it concerning your basic whereabouts. What you don't understand is how it all floats in a region that's completely basically dislocated from natural laws. That is, all the *laws* do apply *inside* Vietnam. But from the rest of planet Earth, those laws don't apply *to* Vietnam. We are surrounded by a zone or a state of dislocation, and you kind of graduate up from knowing the names around here to being able to *suck up* from that zone. You *suck up* from that zone around us and *they cannot touch you.*"

Trung listened closely, trying to feel the man. He sensed panic and anger. "What, please?"

"Who can't touch you?"

"What?"

"Everything that's got its shitty fingerprints which I can see smeared all over you and glowing like a motherfucking, Bozo-the-Clown goddamn *target*. Every bad fucking thing. So suck up from the zone, Agent 99. Shit's about to rain."

He sensed fear and bravado.

"And—the colonel—the process, okay, dig—you're a participant. You're a contributor. This is a thing. We're part of it. The colonel, man. The colonel."

"Colonel Sand."

"Very much boo-coo Colonel-san. He's jerking the strings, and we are dancing like one-legged women."

"Okay," Trung said hopelessly.

The sergeant made his hand resemble a mouth opening and closing rapidly. He placed it to his ear. "Hao told me. Hao. A man will kill Trung. Un homme. Assassiner."

If Hao said it, it could be trusted. "Tonight?"

The sergeant stood and thrust his wrist at Trung's face and pointed at the dials of his watch. "Two a.m."

"Two o'clock."

"Oh two hundred."

"Two o'clock morning."

"Unless the little double-fucker's set us both up to get DX'd by a whole team or something. But I'm not gonna run around nowhere like a squirrel on a wheel about it—or—fuck yes, yes, I am, let's not bullshit each other. But I'm not leaving. I do not intend to boogie. What comes is the coming thing. I just look on it like whatever madness takes a dump on me, it must be a lesson, man, a lesson some random-ass sadistic Hitler-God wants me to learn. That's why I don't like it. Because I don't like learning, I don't like school, I don't like lessons. The idea of discipline scares the crap out of me and pisses me the fuck off. But Hao said he'd meet me here at four p.m. with money, and Hao lied in his teeth. Hao is one absent motherfucker. Hao is nobody's friend. That little Gook is a straight-out demon. I would've snapped his neck and fucked his corpse if his wife hadn't been home. And he knew it. But it was a semi-public situation. Fuck, I should've done her too . . . Yeah. So this is a weapon."

He lifted the hem of his shirt and took an automatic pistol from his belt. "Special delivery for Señor Mister Trung."

Trung stepped back and raised his hands slightly.

"No, man, no. Fuck! Learn English, will you?" He held the weapon out sideways, turning it this way and that. A Vz 50, of Eastern European make.

He went to stick his head out the window again. He jammed the gun in his belt and lit another cigarette and tossed the match over the sill. "All right, fuck, yes, okay," the sergeant said, "look. I'd like to ambush this fucker down in the street, but I don't know who the fuck he is. We don't know shit till he knocks on the door. We're dealing through the dark. Situation normal." He smoked and looked around the room at nothing in particular. "No fucking pillow. I envisioned a pillow. Fuck! Don't you have any pillows?"

"Mr. Jimmy. Please speak slowly."

"We have to make this thing quiet. Pillows. Quiet." He mimed the gun jerking in his hands while he placed a finger to his lips and made a sound: "Ssshhhh."

A knife, then. Trung clenched a fist and thrust it at him.

"Where's your dagger, man? Show me your stuff."

Trung shrugged.

The sergeant dug in his pocket to produce a clasp knife. "This is maybe a three-inch blade." He opened it. "It's got a spoon and fork too, man. Afterward we can eat him."

Trung held out his hand for it.

Trung laid the open knife beside him on the mattress. He held out his hand. "Weapon."

The sergeant drew the gun from his belt and handed it over with a certain air of relief. Trung ejected the clip, cleared the chamber, and thumbed out the bullets onto his mattress: nine 7.65-millimeter rounds, counting the one from the chamber.

"That's a reliable Communist weapon. VC-type weapon. Boo-coo bucks."

Did he indicate he wanted money for it? Trung determined any statement less than clear was best ignored. Sitting on the bed, he reloaded and inserted the magazine, cocked a round into the chamber, and depressed the safety. When the hammer fell, the little sergeant jumped and said, "Fuck me!"—apparently he didn't know about a decocker safety. The gun, therefore, didn't belong to him.

Trung ejected the magazine and placed the gun, magazine, and chamber round on the table.

"Excellent. The secrets of the machine."

"Quiet," Trung said, and tried French: "Silence."

"You got it. We're fucking bilingual here."

He handed the sergeant the empty Coke bottle.

"That's not the kind of deal I make. Way too lopsided."

Trung laid the gun on the mattress and picked up the knife and ripped a half-meter-long gash in the mattress. Setting the knife aside, he plucked tufts of kapok from the tear and pushed them down the Coke bottle's neck with his fingers while the sergeant held it. "Silence."

They spent forty-five minutes rigging a muffler for the pistol, attaching the stuffed bottle to the muzzle of the gun using four small bamboo splints from the bedstead and strips of bedsheet and mosquito netting. The young sergeant sweated a great deal. He removed his flower-print shirt. A large incredible tattooed illustration of a woman in a grass skirt covered his bare chest.

They laid the muffled weapon on the mattress. It resembled a great cocoon from which emerged, backward, a small pistol rather than a moth.

Trung tried in many ways to get the idea across: "One silence. One. Seulement. Only one."

"I get it."

Trung determined how he'd deploy the weapon, supporting the muffler by one hand mittened with his own T-shirt.

He would have to do this left-handed. He positioned himself to the left of the door with his back to the wall and practiced his movements.

"You are a nasty little fucker. Jesus Christ." Mr. Jimmy seemed excited and happy. Trung knew the feeling, had experienced it strongly before operations in the early days. Even at this moment a little of it sparked in him.

Trung stood to the left of the door with his back against the wall and his left hand raised and its forefinger pointing. "I. Me." He stepped forward, brought the finger down to the level where the man's head should be, jerked it once, and stepped back three paces. He repeated the motions, pointing at his feet and making particularly sure the sergeant understood exactly where his movements would take him.

"You. Mr. Jimmy." Trung moved to stand with his back to the wall at the right of the door, reached out with his left hand, and pulled it open, stepping once to his right in the process; then stood frozen: "Arrêtez. Stop."

He put the sergeant against the wall in the same position and had him go through the movements to open the door wide and get out of the way of fire and stop cold.

"Gah-damn," the sergeant said. "I'm gonna need to get fucked-up drunk after this shit."

Trung shrugged.

"I'm a thinker, man. I'm not an assassin."

Before Trung began the drilling in tandem, he made sure one more time:

"I . . ." He put a fingertip to his temple. "La tête. One."

"Yeah. La tête. One shot."

"You . . ." He opened the door.

"C'est si bon."

It seemed possible to Trung that if they crosscut the head of the bullet it might not exit the skull and make a lot of mess. Did the sergeant want no trace afterward? The question was too complicated to ask in grunts and signs. If their fortunes permitted, they'd deal with the mess when the time came.

Can I depend on this man?

At bottom, Trung doubted the sergeant. If he failed to control his movements, there was no small chance Trung might put a bullet in the man who'd come here to save him. He made certain the sergeant knew he must take one step when opening the door and move no more.

They went through it together. Storm opening the door, stepping well out of the way, and standing absolutely still. Trung stepping forward, pulling the trigger, taking three steps back.

They heard the street door open downstairs. Mr. Jimmy's

mouth also opened. Trung attempted to smile reassuringly and stepped into the hall.

At the bottom of the stairwell the travel broker who owned the building stood reaching his hand to the wall switch. The hall lights came on fitfully. Trung said, "Good evening," and the man raised his hand both in greeting and farewell and stepped out and shut the door.

Dusk had come. Trung lay the bulky weapon on what was left of the mattress and lit the lantern and turned up the hissing gas so the wick flared white-hot.

"Mr. Jimmy. I go."

The idea seemed to puzzle the sergeant deeply.

"I go out."

"You're going *out*?"

"I go. Yes."

"Well, what's on for tonight, man? Is there a mah-jongg tournament we just can't miss? Because this is not the time for excursions."

"Mr. Jimmy. I food. Hunger."

"Stay here. I'll go."

"Stay here. I go."

"Jesus Christ."

"I come back." Gingerly Trung pointed at the sergeant's wristwatch. He moved his fingertip over its face to indicate thirty minutes. "I come back."

"This is bullshit."

"No, Jimmy." A great storm of frustration brewed inside him. In Vietnamese he said, "I need to get out. I need to think. I need to breathe. I need to go. I need to move." He seized the bulky weapon and reinserted the magazine, pulled the slide to bring a round into the chamber, ejected the magazine, loaded into it the spare round, and reinserted the magazine. Cradling the weapon in both hands, he presented it to Mr. Jimmy, who set it down on the mutilated bed before pointing at his watch.

"Thirty minutes?"

"You wait."

The American took a billfold from his hip pocket and gave him several bills. "Get cigarettes. Marlboros. Real Marlboros."

"You wait."

"Real Marlboros. Don't bring me no fake Marlboros."

"Marlboros," Trung assured him.

On the street Trung kept close to the buildings, but after crossing at the corner he walked openly. What use caution?

Hao had betrayed him.

Or Hao had saved him. Or both. Under the circumstances it wouldn't get any clearer than that.

When he reached Anh Dung Street he stopped a vendor for a pack of Marlboros, the good ones. The American wanted the good ones, he understood that much.

In the café he sat at his usual table. It wasn't the old Chinese man tonight. It was some woman instead, nearly as old, maybe the wife. "Noodles, please," he said, but she shook her head. She didn't speak Vietnamese.

All right—he didn't see any noodles. Let it be rice again. He went to the counter and pointed to the kettle of rice on the stove, pointed above it to the teapots on a shelf. She nodded some kind of assent, and he took his chair again.

He watched people passing on the street. Surrounded by souls he didn't know he woke to the world in its true scale, not a room with a window that looked at a wall, but an entire world in which he was lost. Whatever the details of the situation, whatever the nature of the problem, whoever had let him down, he was lost.

And to think how careful he'd been, and how pointlessly. It wasn't that he regretted the mistake. He regretted the hesitation. Doubt is one thing, hesitation another. I waited three years to decide. I should have jumped. Doubt is the truth, hesitation a lie.

The old man came into the café. "You want two Coca-Cola? And the bread?"—his usual day's supply. He didn't suppose he needed it, if he was about to run. Run where? Where could he go? Once there, what would he do? And why wait around to ambush the assassin? Why not disappear quickly and fight another day? Mr. Jimmy recommends fighting now—insists on it. And who is Mr. Jimmy? By appearances, an ally. And on what basis to proceed, now, other than on the basis of appearances?

But Hao—enemy or ally? Trung doubted he would ever know.

The sergeant might know, but the two of them couldn't communicate. This led him to think of Skip Sands with his terrible pronunciation, his phrase books and dictionaries, an American he could talk to. But for all he knew, Skip Sands had arranged this. The colonel was dead; perhaps his contacts had become liabilities and were being eliminated. To seek out Skip Sands was not advisable. To trust anyone on earth was ill-advised.

He felt the weight of innumerable griefs—but so many people had just as much to carry, and even more. But this one. This one was very lonely.

The old woman brought the bowl and a teapot, came back again with a teacup and two sauces. He smelled each decanter. One was hoisin. He poured it over the rice. No sticks. He waved his hand at her and rubbed two fingers together. She brought him lacquered sticks ornately decorated. Good luck, bad luck, but hunger visits each day. He bowed his head, lifted the bowl to his face, and fell to.

Though perfectly visible in the last light, Fest stood out front of the fabric shop without any pretense. Let them wonder why. Whatever happened, this was his last evening on the post.

If the target doesn't go out by ten or so, after the cafés have closed, if I'm sure he isn't leaving, if I can't get inside to wait for the man—that's it. I won't go in at all.

He would instead go directly to the Armed Forces Language School and report his failure and demand extraction. And if the school was closed at night—if that contingency, like so many, had been overlooked—he'd go to the American Embassy and present Kenneth Johnson's business card to the marine guard. If they turned him away he'd take a cab to Tan Son Nhut and wait there for the first plane going anywhere.

The darkness fell, the woman who ran the shop locked the door from within and turned out the light. She must spend her nights somewhere in the squalor of the building's recesses. He stepped farther into the doorway, and he was hidden.

The street door to the rooming house opened fifteen minutes after nightfall, and the target headed diagonally across the street without keeping to the shadows. Fest waited until the man had rounded the corner and followed at a trot as he had the night before, and did the same at the next corner, when the man turned right to head, perhaps, for the same café. At the end of the block Fest couldn't turn to follow—the man was stopped, talking to a street boy. Fest continued across the street, heading into the tide of honking motorbikes without pausing, as he'd learned to do. They knew how to keep from hitting pedestrians.

From the other side Fest looked back. The man was buying cigarettes or gum. Then he went on into the café.

Fest turned and made his way back to the street of the rooming house. At the first patch of darkness he came to he stopped and caught his breath. He took out a handkerchief and wiped his hands, replaced it in his back pocket, and repeated the process with a second handkerchief. He drew up his shirtfront and took the pistol from the belly holster and the suppressor from his front pocket and fixed them together and took the key from his left pocket and walked immediately to the building's front door and opened it. Locking it behind him, he pocketed the key, took the other from his right-hand pocket, and proceeded up the stairs.

His hand in its wet envelope of heat inserts the key. He opens the door and removes the only assumption left: that in thirty-odd years of life he's learned something that will be of help in this region where the grown-ups are all dead.

Inside, the lantern was burning. A shirtless man, a white man, unmistakably American, stood beside the bed holding out a rotund package.

He'd departed from his instructions. What had he done?

In English Fest said, "Excuse me."

Simultaneously the entire building turned on its end. The hallway's ceiling passed overhead, the stairs rushed up behind him and struck him in the back, the street door came to a stop upside down, hanging above him.

Blows struck his chest. He had a question, but he couldn't draw a breath to ask it. The street door above him flew open, and a person was sucked up through it into the enormous darkness beyond. Something unbelievable began to suggest itself.

Approaching the corner of his street, Trung noticed a man on a motorbike stopped there, one foot on the pavement, his machine idling as he watched something over his shoulder, in the direction Trung himself was going. Trung rounded the corner cautiously.

In front of his building stood several men all shouting at once in Chinese. He stayed on the opposite side. In the first alley he passed, a few locals attended to small tasks with studious preoccupation. He saw no children among them. Down the block, more stopped motorbikes, people looking back at his own front door, which lay open. Among the men gathered around it he recognized the building's owner.

He walked past rapidly, glancing across the street only once to see a man flung out on the stairwell as if he'd fallen backward, one arm twisted under him and the other reaching out behind. Trung had seen corpses. The man was dead.

The man wore a white shirt or perhaps a blue one, soaked now with blood.

As far as he remembered, Mr. Jimmy wore a bright flowered shirt and in any case had been bare-chested when Trung had left him.

He couldn't risk slowing his pace to see better. He kept walking, absolutely without a destination.

Sands sat at the dining table of a villa with its rent most probably in arrears, finishing a fine lunch prepared by servants he couldn't pay, and considered that if he still had a job his salary would never find him. And that these were his smallest problems.

When he heard a vehicle in the road he stood up quickly. A white Chevrolet Impala stopped out front, Terry Crodelle at the wheel.

Crodelle rolled down the car's front windows six inches or so, probably to let the breeze through, and got out. Today he wore civilian garb, including a yellow cardigan sweater, and he carried a briefcase which he switched from hand to hand while removing the sweater and tossing it onto the front seat and kicking shut the driver's door. Sands watched him coming alone through the gate and considered that from the loneliest outpost on earth Cao Quyen had become the Crossroads of the Far East. In his manner of mounting the granite step onto the porch, clutching his briefcase, and peering at the house, Crodelle projected some of the doubt and hope of an insurance salesman.

As Sands pulled aside the netting for him, all uncertainty dropped from Crodelle's face. Immediately inside he stopped. "The prey in his lair."

"You want a drink or something?"

"Put me where there's a breeze."

"There's a veranda out back, but I think it's still getting the sun right now."

"Right here's just fine."

In the parlor Crodelle set his briefcase on the coffee table and

sat down in one of the big rattan chairs. "Maybe a large glass of
cold water. I don't want to lose my cool."

"Reassuring news."

Sands went to the kitchen and found Mrs. Diu seated on a
stool with her feet on the rungs shelling snow peas into the lap of
her skirt and tossing the rinds in a galvanized tub. That's the kind
of work he wanted. "Will you make us some tea and sandwiches,
please?" She scooped the peas from her lap onto the counter
while Sands poured a big glass of water from a pitcher in the
fridge. Dread weakened his hands. Water splashed on the tiles.

Crodelle didn't look over his shoulder as Sands came back into
the parlor to sit facing him.

"What's in the briefcase, Terry? A tape recorder?"

"Better than that."

"A super-miniature polygraph?"

Crodelle gave him the finger.

"You found me. Excellent work."

"You've got snitchy friends."

"You don't have to tell me."

"Nice place."

"It's haunted."

"It feels like it. Yeah. A little.—Jesus, Skip, what happened to
your ear?"

"I got beat up."

Crodelle sat back in his chair and crossed ankle over knee.
"You're an interesting character. I should have been visiting you a
lot more often. And there's a sense of quiet here."

"I try not to move around and break a sweat. There's no air
conditioner."

"Rick Voss went down in a helicopter. He's dead."

"I know. It's terrible."

"Thanks for your sympathy."

Quite against his will, Sands heaved a quavering sigh. "What
about Hao? Dead too?"

"Nguyen Hao? Not quite."

"Listen to me, please. If he's your guy, you'd better look out for him."

"Hao does a hell of a job looking out for himself. A hell of a job."

"He isn't safe, Terry, I mean it."

"Hao and his wife are on their way out of the country."

"Wow. No. Are you serious?"

"What's serious is that Rick Voss is dead. He was on his way to see you in Cao Phuc. Now he's dead."

Sands had no idea what to say. The pulse in his battered ear tormented him. The kettle began whistling in the kitchen. "So I pack up and we go?"

"More or less."

"Why don't you have a couple embassy marines with you?"

"It's not a pick-up. If you had a phone, I could've just called you and invited you in. Look, Skip," Crodelle said, "I'd like you to send the servants home."

"Their home is about sixty feet away."

"Just so we have some privacy."

"Their home is a little building right out the back door."

Crodelle merely stared at him.

"Can we get some tea and sandwiches first? She's making them now. Are you hungry?"

"Sure."

"They're good. She cuts the crust off."

"Just like the Continental."

"Yeah, man. You can get crust if you want it—"

"No, thanks."

Mrs. Diu was already bringing the plate of sandwiches. Skip leapt up and went to get the tea. When Mrs. Diu joined him in the kitchen he said, "Now I'd like you to take the rest of the afternoon off."

"Off?"

"Yes, please. We need the house to ourselves."

"You want me to leave?"

"Yes, just—to the house. I'm sorry, just go home."

"You don't want me to clean the lunch?"

"Maybe later."

"Yes, sir."

"I'll clean it up."

"Okay."

"It was very good."

She left by the back door. Sands placed the sugar bowl, spoons, two cups, and the teapot on a tray with handles too small for his fingers and brought it all into the parlor to find Crodelle staring at his plate of crustless sandwiches. He hadn't touched them. "It's just the local tea," Skip said. "No milk today."

"You don't have milk?"

"I mean it's just the weak stuff—you know. Watery. The way they make it."

He poured tea and watched Crodelle devour several sandwiches in two bites each. He realized he was sitting forward tensely and sat back and pretended to relax. He checked a midwestern impulse to urge on his guest more sandwiches, and more—chicken, pork, a little butter. "Good bread," his guest remarked. Neither spoke again until Crodelle had wiped his hands on a blue linen napkin.

"I believe," Crodelle said, "your last words to me were a question as to the location of the JFK warfare school."

"Fort Bragg. Yeah. It came back to me."

"I'm with the Fourth Battalion. MOS training."

"And MOS, what's that?"

"Military Occupational Specialty."

"Well then. Who do you train?"

"Guys. Fellows."

"Really. What's your specialty?"

"Psychological Operations."

"Captain Terry, you seem a little miffed with me."

Crodelle smiled, but only slightly. "So we couldn't interest you in a polygraph."

"No. I would have lied on the control questions anyway."

"Why would you do that?"

"Just to mess up the first-round results."

"Skip, you're not expected to behave when we're questioning you as you've been taught to behave when being questioned by the enemy. We are not the enemy."

Skip said, "'Enemy' is no longer a term I'd use in any case. Ever."

"Why not?"

"It's just stupid, man. Have you looked around yourself lately? This isn't a war. It's a disease. A plague. And that was my preliminary round the other day, with the phony polygraph. And this is the second round. Correct?"

"No. Incorrect. This is just a pick-up. Sort of. I mean, it's just time for you to wrap up here, that's all, so I'm here to get you."

"Then why are we sitting around?"

"Intellectual curiosity. It's always my downfall. Who *was* the colonel? What was he doing? I mean, his little article was an act of professional suicide, but the assertions are hard to refute."

"Voss told me he wrote most of it."

"The ideas came from the colonel. The semi-treasonous ones anyway."

"He was a great man," Skip said, "and he wasn't in any way treasonous."

"We all want to believe that, Skip."

"He was a force of nature, Terry, and now he's gone. I'm confused and you're confused. He's suddenly absent. It's disorienting as all get-out."

"Then let's orient ourselves, Skip, and deal with the colonel's mess."

"You misunderstood him completely."

"Oh no you don't!—you don't turn this into a movie about Walt Whitman or somebody—the shortsighted, narrow-minded boobs lynching the golden-boy visionary. You don't turn this into the crucifixion. I'm asking you who *was* this guy, and you're singing a bullshit movie theme song."

"Hold on, hold on. I'm just trying to tell you something you don't understand. I knew him all my life, and I swear to you, Crodelle, the colonel was exactly who he looked like. He really was this madman flying a plane with one wing blown off and smoking a cigar and laughing at death and all that. But he had this second side. He wanted to be intelligent, he wanted to be erudite, he wanted to be the suave bureaucrat. I'm surprised he didn't take up smoking a pipe. He wanted to intellectualize, he wanted to monitor information systems, he really—somewhere inside him was this librarian, hidden away."

"And that's the part that fucked things up for us, Skip. Let's deal with that part."

"Deal with it?"

"Come on, Skip, come on, work with me. We need to get everything back under the light. The colonel didn't share. He didn't lend his efforts to the general endeavor."

"So?"

Crodelle poured the dregs from the teapot into his cup.

"Look, Terry, am I supposed to be getting something right now? Because I don't."

"I want to ask you about these files."

"They're right upstairs. Take 'em."

"Really?"

"Yeah, take 'em. They're shit."

"You realize at this point you don't need to lie."

"I realize. The files are upstairs. The files are worthless. That is the absolute truth."

Crodelle relaxed, as if perhaps he believed. "The guy was really something. Really something."

"Yeah. Yeah. He was a lot of things."

"How did he characterize his relationship with John Brewster?"

"Brewster?"

"Yeah. I'm curious. How were their relations?"

"Strained. Brewster had some concerns, and put him behind a desk."

"Hah! Concerns?"

"About his health."

"His health. You mean about his heart, and his drinking, and his tendency to suddenly slug people in the jaw."

Skip said, "His heart?"

"Isn't that what killed him?"

"I have no idea how he died. I heard he was assassinated."

"I've heard all that nonsense too. The colonel threw a coronary upstairs at the Rex. In the swimming pool. Or in the restaurant or somewhere. Anyway, he didn't go down defending the Alamo."

"Oh—oh, *wow.*"

"What."

"You're Brewster's boy."

"I resent that."

"Yeah, but I repeat it: you're Brewster's boy. Brewster wants to look at the files before anybody else finds out about them. Right?"

Crodelle smiled.

"Don't leer at me like I'm an idiot, Terry."

"I can't help it."

"This isn't about any crazy unauthorized op. This is just about a bunch of note cards that might make somebody look bad. Somebody who probably hasn't done anything to worry about."

"That's nonsense."

"Yeah, it is, it certainly is. I mean, considering the fucked-up nature of the files. But that's what's going on here, isn't it? Jesus Christ. Come on, let's look at them."

"Yeah?"

"Come on."

Crodelle followed him up the narrow stairs. This time of day the villa's upper regions trapped the heat like an attic. Sands pointed at the spare room and opened his own bedroom door to get what they might of a breeze. Crodelle stood looking into the spare room. "Where are they?"

Sands pushed past him and raised the lid of one of the footlockers. "Cleverly hidden."

"That's them?"

"They're all in alphabetical order. And cross-referenced. Go ahead, look up Brewster."

"Come on. If the old man was serious, they're coded."

"It's not in code. Look up anything that might cross-reference with Brewster. Place names, something like that."

Crodelle raised the lid of another and stared down into it. "You're willing to turn these over to us?"

"Do I have a choice?"

"Let's load these babies in the buggy. If we stack things properly, we can get them all to town in one trip."

"To the Language School, or where?"

"The MAC-V compound. Tan Son Nhut."

"MAC-V's not there anymore."

"There's a little facility there."

"Oh, fuck," Skip said.

"What?"

"I'm not going anywhere with you."

Crodelle looked at him with raised eyebrows, and Sands gauged the redhead's size, considered taking a page from Jimmy Storm's book and throwing an uppercut into the man's middle, just below the sternum, but thought against it. Having recently lost one fight, he didn't feel like starting another one.

"Hang on," Skip said. "I'll get dressed."

He went across the hall and into his own rooms, and Crodelle followed him and watched as he changed his shorts for long slacks, put on socks and shoes and a shirt. What else? He wouldn't be returning. On his dresser, a stack of photos from the Philippines. He put half a dozen in his pocket.

From his dresser drawer he took his watch, his passport, and his .25-caliber Beretta. "Shit," Crodelle said. "Never happen."

Sands pocketed the passport, put the watch on his wrist, and stepped forward and put the gun against Crodelle's forehead.

"Okay, okay, okay. Is the safety on?"

"No." Sands tried to think. "Here's where it gets tricky."

"Just put the safety on, and step back, and let's talk."

"I do all the talking. You do what I tell you. I don't have to shoot if we do this right."

"I'm with you," Crodelle said.

"Stand there."

"I'm standing." Crodelle stood very still with his hands raised to the level of his chest and his fingers splayed. "Just put the safety on, that's all I ask."

"Not one more word."

"Fine."

"I mean it. Sit in that chair."

Crodelle drew a chair from the tea table and sat. Sands opened his dresser's top drawer and with one hand pulled out socks and underpants, feeling for his first-aid materials. He placed several rolls of gauze bandage on top of the dresser. "Stand up. No talking."

Crodelle stood. Holding the gun against his spine, Sands pulled the chair closer to himself. "Sit down." Crodelle sat. "Cross your arms behind the chair. Open your mouth. Wider." He jammed a sock into Crodelle's mouth. Pulling the clasp from the roll of bandage with his teeth and managing as best he could with one hand, he wrapped Crodelle's face and neck with the gauze and then girded him around the chest, going around him several times until he'd reached the end of the roll and pinned his arms behind him to the back of the chair. With one hand he was able only to make a rudimentary knot. He felt apologetic about his materials. An electric lamp cord would have been just the thing. Not possible in a house out past the power lines.

Crodelle seemed, by the pattern of his agitated breath, to attempt some commentary on the process, which Sands repeated with two more rolls in order to bind each of Crodelle's legs to a chair leg, providing the commentary himself: What are you doing? What comes next? How do you tie a Green Beret to a chair with gauze and no tape? You'll have to tie a knot. Don't you need two hands to tie a knot?

"I'm putting the gun on the dresser while I get you tied down tight," he said. "You can try something and see how it all turns out, or you can sit still." Crodelle made no movement while Sands used two rolls to tie his wrists together and secure his arms to the back of the chair with a proper trucker's-hitch knot. Sands knelt in front of him with the four remaining rolls and tied each leg firmly in place as tightly as he could without concern for his prisoner's circulation.

Without speaking to Crodelle he left the room to find some packing tape across the hall. When he returned Crodelle hadn't, as far as was discernible, made any movement to escape. Sands wound several yards of tape around his mouth, chest, and legs, covering the knots he'd made. "I'm taking the files downstairs. I'm going to be up and down the stairs and I'll be checking on you. If I think you've been fooling around here trying to get loose—I swear to God, that's it. I'll kill you."

On his last trip up the stairs he leaned close to Crodelle's ear, breathing hard from his exertions, and said, "I'm going to burn the colonel's files. Do you know why?" He paused, as if the red-head might answer through a suffocating inch of gauze. Crodelle only kept his eyes shut and concentrated on breathing through his nostrils. "No? Well, think about it." The speech disappointed him. He left the room feeling embarrassed and went out back of the house to Tho's burn pile, where he'd assembled a mound of cards and papers five feet in circumference, perhaps, and a couple of feet high at its peak, a paltry monument, he thought, to the work of two of his years and God knew how much of the life of Colonel Francis Xavier Sands. The breeze blew strongly, and some of the note cards fluttered away to land in the creek.

He was out of matches before the pile had caught. He went into the kitchen for something more incendiary and heard

Crodelle upstairs thumping around on the floor overhead, progressing over it, perhaps, in the manner of a monkey hopping on its ass. It didn't matter.

He carried a full box of matches outside and went past the burn pile and shouted for Tho, who came from his house barefoot, in long pants and a T-shirt. "Mr. Tho, where's the kerosene?"

"Kerosene? Yes. I have."

"Get the kerosene, please, and burn those papers."

"Now?"

"Please, yes, now."

Tho went to the side of the house and came back with his battered two-gallon can of kerosene and doused the pile while Skip knelt and struck matches at its base. The fire blazed up, and he stepped back. He stood with Tho and watched a minute. Across the creek and downstream a ways, above the coconut palms and papayas, gray and brown smoke also rose from some neighbor's pile of trash.

Jesus, he thought, what a fool that old man was.

Tho went for his rake. Skip returned to the house.

He was astounded to find Crodelle in the kitchen, still in the chair, bent forward, his hands free, cutting away with a bread knife at the windings that still bound his left leg.

Sands dug in his pocket for his Beretta and pointed it as Crodelle stood up.

Immediately he sat down. "You don't have to shoot me! You don't have to shoot me!"

"Do you know what I'm doing? Can you smell that smoke? I'm burning the files."

"This isn't about the files! God*damn*, man. You don't have to shoot anybody."

"What happens if I don't?"

"I can pretty well assure you that's the end of it. I want to move my hands. I want to rub my legs. They're dead, you cut off the blood. Jesus. What a fucking asshole you are. Go ahead and shoot me. I've got six thousand dollars for you. Fuck you."

"You've got what?"

Crodelle leaned forward and spat bloody drool onto the floor. "A really fucked-up thing has happened, Skip. A BND operative got X'd the other day in Saigon. A man named Fest."

"For God's sake," Sands said. "I know that guy."

"Dietrich Fest?"

"Not by name, but I met him in the Philippines. And I'm pretty sure I saw him at the Green Parrot—the same day I met you."

"Well," Crodelle said, "it's a screwy deal. It blew up. We should have stopped it, but things develop a momentum. And it was a legitimate VC target."

"Oh, shit. Trung Than?"

No answer.

"Trung killed the German?"

"Your unauthorized double."

"So where is he now?"

"Who."

"Trung Than, goddammit."

"Wandering the earth."

"Alive."

"That's the assumption."

"Jesus. A man without a country. How must he feel?"

"You tell me. About like you do."

"And going after Trung was your affair? Your responsibility? Who ran the operation?"

"That will never be known. All that will ever be known is—you caused it."

"Where did the authorization come from?"

"Authorization is a concept. Not always concrete."

"So it's about renegade ops after all. Yours and mine and everybody's."

"We all messed this thing up. But you're the one looking at prison. Prison and disgrace. Have no doubt of that, Sands. When

somebody starts an investigation, you're the one guy we're all willing to point to. So how's this for an idea?—go away."

From behind the house there came the sound of an animal
yelping. Sands tried to ignore it and get the situation in his grasp
by jabbing the gun in Crodelle's direction, but he felt helpless.
"Are you bastards going to get me out?"

"No. You have a passport. I give you the cash. Hop a plane."

"Jesus Christ! A plane where?"

"The money's in my briefcase."

The yelping out back had become a screech, drawing nearer.
Through the frame of the screen door Père Patrice came into view
dragging the dog Docteur Bouquet by the ear and calling out
above the dog's protests. "Skip! Your dog! Your dog, please!" He
opened the door and dragged the animal inside with him.

"Give him to Tho."

"Tho says to put him in the house." Taking in the kitchen fes-
tooned with streamers of white gauze and the two Americans, one
gripping a pistol, the priest took a deep breath. "Tho says to put
him inside the house." He let the dog loose and it ran off and
scrabbled up the stairs. The little priest had not released his
breath. He reached backward as if to push open the screen door
behind him, but his hand didn't actually contact its object, and he
stood holding his arm out as if it provided him balance. "He is not
a problem, but he might attack my chickens there. It's better to
keep him here." Perhaps because his voice seemed to have
stopped the progress of a tragedy, he continued. "I had a dream
about you, Skip. You were not in the dream, but it was a dream
about the President of the United States. Usually the French, the
Americans, the Communists—they don't come to the world of
dreams. They go there, but they don't believe in it so they are just
only ghosts." A form of hysteria seemed to rise in him as he spoke.
"I will tell you what happened to a man of my home village
named Chinh. He left our village when his father died and credi-
tors took his land. Chinh became poor at that time, he became

destitute. He had to go away to travel on the coastline and if possible learn to fish. It was a desperate journey because he had no money. He slept in the bush as he traveled. One night Chinh had a dream telling him to sleep in the Catholic churchyard of a certain town. The French were there. The outpost commander found him and turned him out. But Chinh says, I am asleep here because a dream told me to come. You are a fool believing in a dream, this is what the French commander says, don't you know we all dream each night? Last night a dream told me in fact that seven pieces of gold are buried beneath the biggest banyan along the river—do you think I went digging? Don't make me laugh. And he drove Chinh from the town. On his way downriver Chinh found the biggest banyan, dug all day around the base of it, and found seven gold coins exactly. He returned to my village and lived prosperously. This is a true story. I told it to a French priest. He said it was a lie. He said Chinh stole the money and explained it with a dream. But, however, I pointed out that Chinh lived long and prospered. A thief who lies and steals cannot prosper from the money he stole. The story is quite true. A few years ago Chinh died, incidentally. Sick people come to his grave to be healed, especially people with some malaria."

"Thong Nhat."

"Yes."

"Stop."

There came a silence, the first the room had enjoyed since the priest had entered.

"Skip," the priest said as if touching on a matter of explosive delicacy, "something is wrong."

"Jesus H. Christ," Crodelle said, and began to laugh.

"I'm sorry about the excitement, Nhat. Will you do me a favor?"

The priest seemed unwilling to answer.

"There's a briefcase on the coffee table in there. Will you bring it to me, please?"

"Of course. But I'm worried about you today."

"Where am I?" Crodelle said. "Where in God's name am I?"

"Nhat, will you get me that briefcase?"

Skip watched the priest move cautiously into the parlor to stand before the coffee table touching his hands together at the level of his breast and wondered if he was praying.

Crodelle, still laughing, spat on the floor again.

"Are you all right?"

"Minimally banged up, just minimally."

"Tell me something. If you're willing. How did you get down the stairs without breaking your neck?"

"I hopped and hula-ed as far as the staircase and fell over sideways and slid down. Sort of."

"And not a bruise. No Purple Heart."

"I believe my right shoulder was briefly dislocated."

"Good."

"I need to be sure you understand this business about the BND man's murder. Do you get it?"

"Sure. I'm the fall guy."

"You're Lee Harvey Oswald, baby."

Père Patrice had found his strength. He stood beside Skip holding out the briefcase with both hands. Skip set it on the counter and thumbed the button, and the brass clasp snapped open with a shudder.

"Whose briefcase is this?"

"All yours. Complimentary."

The briefcase held only an empty manila folder and a sheaf of U.S. currency circled by a red rubber band.

Doubt and fear possessed him suddenly.

"So you, what—stuck your hand in your pocket and out comes a wad of getaway money just like that?"

"Yes, indeed. Chop-chop. We're very efficient."

"Not too often, Crodelle. Mostly you're incredibly inept. And stupid. Why didn't you just come in and say, Here's the situation, and hand me the cash?"

"Well, you seemed completely in love with this idea that your

silly files are the reason for everybody's breakfast. I kind of hoped
we could let it go at that."

Sands held his hand out. "Give me your car keys."

"Never happen, son. You don't get a vehicle. I'll take you."

Leaning toward Crodelle close enough to breathe in his face,
Skip placed the gun's muzzle against Crodelle's knee. "Three—
two—one—"

Crodelle slapped his pants. "Right here."

"Let's have them."

Crodelle turned over a single ignition key wired to a paper tag
from the embassy motor pool.

With his free hand Sands reached into the briefcase and
pinched a half dozen twenties and shook them loose from the
stack and laid them on the counter. "This is for Tho and Mrs.
Diu," he told the priest. To Crodelle he said, "I'm going out the
door. If I even think you're moving around in here before I'm
down the road, I'll come back and shoot you. Happily. I mean it,
Crodelle. It would make me happy."

He left by the back door as Crodelle called after him, "I don't
care about your fucking happiness."

As he started the ignition, Père Patrice came out by the front
way. Sands reached his left hand out the window and the priest
took it and said, "It's too late for traveling. Near the Route Twenty-
two it's a critical area. You know this."

"Thon Nhat, it's been good knowing you."

"Will you come back?"

"No."

"Yes. Perhaps. Nobody knows."

"All right, nobody knows."

"Mr. Skip, until I see you again, I'm going to pray for you each
day."

"I appreciate it. You've been a wonderful friend."

He engaged the clutch and set off bumping over the rutted
road. In the rearview mirror he saw Crodelle join the priest to

stand out front of the villa's gate with his arms crossed on his chest and his legs in the at-ease position, projecting an air of defiance and nonchalance.

Beside him on the seat he found Crodelle's yellow cardigan sweater. He threw it out of the car, rolled up the windows, and turned on the air conditioner.

World Children's Services had rules, procedures, requirements, including a bimonthly visit to Saigon for Reports and Recommendations. In the hostel on Dong Du Street if the frolic of the later hours didn't wake her then the moaning of dawn prayers from the mosque would manage. Tonight the horns and go-go music turned her out of bed.

In these damp nights the temperature of human breath she felt a moldering and sleepy grief born, she was convinced, of self-infatuation—a slow, hot, tropical self-pity. She needed to turn outward, to find others, she needed her duties in the countryside. Or she'd sink. Rot in the underneath. Be devoured by this land. Flower up as new violence and despair.

Here in the city the empty striving compressed itself into a solid thing, and she longed to give herself up to a monstrous suffering, wanted to be torn by every pain.

She started across the street, stepped back for a little Honda pulling an eight-foot-long trailer heaped with cheerful fresh produce. In the city too many of them kept their headlamps switched off. Go-go music boomed from a doorway behind her. She needed a cold drink, but in there it was ten degrees hotter and full of twenty-year-old men on fire in their souls. She went inside anyway. The tavern stank of beer and sweat and bamboo. She clutched her purse tightly and swiveled toward the bar through the crowd of men.

A couple of women danced on a stage hardly bigger than two soap crates. "What's yours?" a GI said to her at the bar. With the red light of the stage behind him he had no visible face. "You there—pretty lady." A youngster's voice, but the crown of his head was bald.

"Pardon?"

"What's yours? Because I'm buying."

"I wouldn't mind a beer. How about a Tiger?"

"Coming at you. Don't go away." He moved sideways behind the men at the bar in pursuit of the Tiger. Kathy looked left to see a little harlot resting her elbow on the bamboo bar, her hip cocked, silver smoke rushing from between her lips. But—wasn't it Lan? But it couldn't be. But it was. "Lan," Kathy called, but Lan couldn't hear.

Kathy walked over. "Hi, Lan."

Raising her cigarette to her face, Lan moved to a barstool just vacated. She'd assisted Kathy her first year or so in-country, at Sa Dec, then trouble had called her back home, the relocation of her village, and now she sat with a stare and a red mouth and her legs showing up to the crotch of her panties. "How are you, Lan? Do you remember me?"

The girl turned to speak softly to the bartender.

"What you want?" the bartender said. Kathy didn't know how to answer. The girl—was it somebody else, not Lan?—swung around and leaned her elbows back on the bar and stared at the GIs who danced in the crimson glow with frail women, clutching them tightly to their chests and hardly moving.

Kathy's own GI was back. "Honey, I'm getting the beers," he said. "Don't you believe in me?"

"I'll be right back." Holding on to her purse with both hands, she skirted the dancers and went outside. The damp stink of the street felt fresh now. She walked a few paces and entered a café and sat down. Drank two beers one after the other and turned her chair with its back to the wall and asked for a third. From her purse she took her notebook, flopped it down in the stains and grease, and found a pen. Sitting sideways at the table, one hand resting on the page, she wrote:

Dear Skip,

Ho-ho-de-ho-ho. That's what my Dad used to say when he was drunk, or tipsy. He didn't get drunk. Not even tipsy, just

The mamasan slid over in her flip-flops and said, "You waiting for the bus?"

"There's no bus this time of night."

"No bus now tonight. You take a taxi."

"Can't I stay? May I have some tea, please?"

"Sure! Sure! Take a taxi later, okay?"

"Thanks."

happy. Sociable you know. So much for the family history. Next up I've got a few opinions for you.

Opinions concerning America's enlarged adrenal cortex and its sacramental lie. Dear Skip: You'd best be careful now of your human heart or you're liable to break it permanently. Lending your efforts to the cruel mad devastation here.

You may find no place of repentance though you seek it carefully with tears. Where is that from? Somewhere in the Bible. There I go again! Carefully with tears.

The day I left Damulog with Timothy's bones I saw you at the spring having a bath.

—She'd gone to say goodbye to him as she headed off for Davao City and then Manila. From down the dirt lane she'd seen him come out of Freddy Castro's three-story hotel, walking through the yard in zoris and checkered boxer shorts, carrying a white towel over his shoulder and a saucepan in his hand. She'd left him to his bath, had headed for the entrance of Castro's to say goodbye to the family, but had heard the cheering voices of little children and gone after all into the small glen to see Skip Sands

bathing before a crowd of urchins. The pipe came from a rock
and spilled its water into a large natural basin and the children,
perhaps three dozen, had arranged themselves around it as in a
small stadium, in the arena of which the young American soaped
himself and poured water from the saucepan over his head, chanting back and forth with his wild audience:

"WHAT'S YOUR FAVORITE SHOW!"

"THE SKEEP SANDS SHOW!"

"WHAT'S YOUR FAVORITE SHOW!"

"THE SKEEP SANDS SHOW!"

Kids all around you, making them laugh. That was kind of
a golden era.

She put away the pen and paper and drained the bottle and
returned to the club.

With three beers in her head the ruckus seemed more uniformly unintelligible and pointless. The woman who might have
been Lan wasn't there, only the skewed off-speed voice of Nancy
Sinatra and these chirping whores and bullshitting men of the
infantry all at least as woozy as herself—as tipsy as herself—as
happy.

"You were gone long enough!" It was the same bald GI.

"I've been here all along."

"Really? Never happen!"

She went around him to stand so his face caught the light. He
looked vacuous and friendly. He might have been a noncom, but
he wore civvies, and it was only a guess. He didn't want anything
from her. If he wanted a woman there were women all around
him. He told her as much. He had a woman in Pleiku. He paid
her an allowance. She wasn't a prostitute. She was his girlfriend.
Her family had been killed, all but one nephew who'd been left
with only half a face. The boy's brain was damaged. There was a
concrete cistern out back to catch the rain. Sometimes the kid
climbed up on the cistern, nobody knew why, and fell off and hurt

himself. Several families lived in the building, a glorified hooch, but it had two stories, and stairs leading up outside, stairs of rough lumber without a railing, hardly more than a big ladder. At night the boy had to be tied by his leg to a nail in the floor because he wandered, he walked in his sleep, he could pitch over the side and break his neck. Well, you were sad about the kids for a while, for a month, two months, three months. You're sad about the kids, sad about the animals, you don't do the women, you don't kill the animals, but after that you realize this is a war zone and everybody here lives in it. You don't care whether these people live or die tomorrow, you don't care whether you yourself live or die tomorrow, you kick the children aside, you do the women, you shoot the animals.

1970

He crouched by the window and listened shuddering to the sound of ripped high-voltage wires out there stroking the darkness, humming closer and farther, feeling along the darkness after fear. The voltage sucked along the shaft of fear toward any heart emanating it and burned the soul right inside it. That was the True Death. Thereafter nobody lived in that heart, nobody saw out of those eyes. The stench of such burning floated in and out of the room all night.

As soon as a little daylight came up, the flies started taking off and landing around the room. The radio on the windowsill said, "I've got the guys here today from the Kitchen Cinq. You've heard the music of the Kitchen Cinq, known primarily for their 'happy sound.' Fellas, what about the name? Where did the name come from?"

"Well, Kenny, the name was brewed up for us by our manager, Trav Nelson. And we just kind of liked it, so—"

"And how about the way you spell it? C-I-N-Q, that's unusual."

"That spelling means the number five in the French language. And there are five of us, and the way it's pronounced in French you say 'sank.' And we're all from Texas, so we pronounce it kind of like that too—'Kitchen Sank.'"

"And you're known for your 'happy sound.'"

"I'd say that's just a result of various personalities, Kenny, because we're all generally pretty happy folks."

"And I'd be happy to talk all day with you, but we're gonna say goodbye, stay happy, and thanks.—The Kitchen Cinq. Five happy guys. This is Kenny Hall and the 'In Sound,' for the Military Radio Network."

"So long, Kenny, and thanks to you too."

"Let's get back to the music."

He let the music play.

"What's burning?" he asked, although he knew.

"I don't want you to mention burning ever again. You're on that twenty-four hours."

"Very good."

"It's the fucking punk, man, the Mustique. You gotta know that's all it is."

"Got it. Mustique."

"The fucking green spirals they set on fire for the mosquitoes? Somebody's burning it downstairs. Okay?"

"Okay."

"Okay, James?"

"You're doing fear," James warned him. "Hear the hum?"

"Oh, man."

"Vanquish fear."

Joker sat beside him on the bed.

"I think I have to say this: you are fucking fucked-up, man."

"Giant discovery."

"Well, I mean—can't you cool it down?"

James shrugged. No profit in continuing this stupid little conver-sation.

Ming came in from another universe somewhere and said, "You want noodoos?"

"No, I don't want no fucking noodles."

"Can we go noodoo place?"

"No, I said no. You think I want to watch a pack a Gooks eating with their faces?"

"I need some money, Cowboy."

James said, "Goddamn slippery fucking wiggly fucking noo-dles."

Her stare was like a lizard's. "Gip me money, Cowboy. Tell him gip me money," she said to Joker, "my sister is so hungry, and her stomach is hurting."

Joker took the little girl on his knee and said, "You're just as pretty as two new aces."

The kid said something in Gook and Ming answered in English: "He kill some people."

James told her to quiet her kid down.

Ming said, "Boo-coo fuck you," and took the kid outside somewhere.

Joker said, "That ain't her sister."

"She says it's her sister."

"It's probably her kid."

"Either way it ain't no thang." He stood and walked over and unzipped his fly and made water into a blue chamber pot with red flowers on it in the corner. There wasn't any indoor plumbing. He didn't see where she made water. When she wanted to piss she went downstairs someplace.

Joker said, "Let's go. Listen to me, man—Cowboy? Cowboy?— I know how this shit goes."

"I gotta believe you."

"There's a difference between downtown and the bush."

"Whichever one, it ain't real life."

"I didn't say that. Will you listen to what I'm saying? You can't come downtown no more."

James headed for the door. "Take the wheel, baby! I got no hands!"

It was dark, but it wasn't that late. Joker watched over him while they walked a long way to the Red Cross and stood in line a long time. When it was James's turn on the telephone, Joker left him alone while he talked to his mother. He'd hardly said hello before regretting he'd called. She sobbed in torment.

"We haven't heard from you in I don't know how long. I don't know if you're alive or dead!"

"Me neither. Nobody does."

"Bill Junior's gone to prison!"

"What'd he do?"

"*I* don't know. A little of everything. He's been there almost a year, since last February twenty."

"What month is it now?"

"You don't know what month you're in? It's January." She sounded angry. "What are you laughing over?"

"I ain't laughing."

"Then who was it just now laughing in my ear?"

"Bullshit. I didn't laugh."

"Don't use that toilet-talk on my telephone."

"Don't it say 'shit' somewhere in the Bible?"

"Get your tongue out of the toilet. I'm your mother telling you. Your mother who doesn't even know where you are!"

"Nha Trang."

"Well, thank the Lord," she said, "that he delivered you out of Vietnam."

Now somebody laughed. Possibly himself, though nothing was funny.

Early in the morning of February 20, 1970, Bill Houston cruised in a state-owned van with two corrections officers and three other miscreants down Route Eighty-nine toward Phoenix, having served twelve months of a one-to-three-year sentence of incarceration in the Florence prison, not at all clear in his mind as to why, exactly, he'd been jailed, or why released. Apparently since the day of his homecoming from the navy a pile of charges had stacked up: a term of probation for stealing a car, a suspended sentence for assault, which meant getting into a fight when cops were around to arrest you for it, and a warrant out for failure to appear on a shoplifting charge; and then the theft of a single case of beer, twenty-four cans, had crashed it all down on his head. Drinking, strolling through an alley off Fourth Avenue, he'd seen the rear door of a tavern propped open by a delivery of Lucky Lager, and he'd taken a case off the top. This was supposed to be his lucky beer, but it had brought him horrible fortunes. He'd been two blocks away, waiting at a DON'T WALK sign like an honorable citizen—shifting the case from his left to his right shoulder, and plotting where to find refrigeration for these things—when the squad car caught up to him. A couple of hearings, a month in County, and off to live behind walls fifteen feet high.

Heading for prison one year ago, carried in perhaps this very van with these same officers toward the just reward his mother and teachers had promised him, he'd felt excited and grown-up. Was it true they tried to stab you and rape you in the joint? Then why hadn't he seen such stuff in the Maricopa County Jail? Not that he worried. He'd never lost a fight in his life and looked forward to beating up as many people as tried to make a punk out of him. On the other hand, these were killers and such, and they had nothing to do but exercise and train in there, if that's what they wanted. Best to keep his head down. Learn a valuable skill. Maybe he'd take up leather tooling, belts and moccasins, cigarette cases. After all, he was known on the street as Leather Bill. Did they let you make sheaths for knives? He had doubted the possibility.

Assigned to the medium-security barracks, he found the inmates no meaner than those he'd bunked with in the sheriff's jail and the food a little better. They had a quarter-mile track for running, as well as an extensive set of weights. His second day there he played left field in a ball game and drove in two runs and hit a homer. Nine full innings—only eight men to a side, but they had all the equipment, including headgear for the batters and full protection for the catcher.

By the third month inside he felt at home. From this distance, the things he thought he'd miss looked small. His jobs had demanded his soul and in return had given him poverty, the women he'd dealt with had quickly turned to irritants. Liquor had brought him high times but propelled him often into the arms of the police. Among free citizens his stomach had ached constantly. He hadn't felt like swallowing anything but booze. But from the day of his arrival he was hungry and focused like a hound on each coming meal. He put on fifteen pounds, all muscle—push-ups and sit-ups every morning, fifty of each. Four days a week he lifted weights. On Saturday afternoons he boxed, and a couple of former pros had taught him that brawling was an art. His wind was good, and he could take a punch. He was the best Bill Houston he'd been since he'd left the navy.

Westward now, home to Phoenix, back the way he'd come. The rising sun at his back, he sailed toward a life he couldn't imagine. They'd given him the phone number of his parole officer, a check for twenty dollars, and the clothes he'd been arrested in thirteen months before. He surveyed the road ahead, the desert frozen in morning light, flat and green after the winter rains, the highway black and perfectly straight through the van's front window, and felt an adventure moving beneath him, as when he'd watched the southern California coast growing insignificant from the railing of his first cruise at age seventeen.

In Phoenix he entered the first bar he found and got with the first woman who was halfway nice to him. She said she was an epileptic, and that seemed about right. Every couple of hours she took a pill, a downer, Seconal. She had several bottles of them all to herself and claimed they were prescribed. It took her only two beers to get tipsy. He had to talk to her for a long time.

They ambled along the streets. She wanted him to walk on the outside, the curb side, because, she insisted, if he put the lady on the outside that meant he was pimping her. She seemed to know all about that, but she didn't ask for money. When they went up to her room in a hotel overlooking the Deuce, the neighborhood around Second Street, it turned out her Seconal was undependable. In the night the bed started shaking. He said, "What is it?" She said, "I had a seizure." She seemed confused about who he was. He said, "Is there any beer left?" They'd bought only one six-pack; he found its cardboard carrier flattened under his naked ass. "I'd better go see my family. I just got out of prison," he said.

The night had cooled off. He walked through the Deuce. He would have sat down for a nap, but by now the dawn was near, the pavement had grown chilly, and the bums who'd slept on the sidewalk with their heads resting on their arms were already stirring

awake, commencing to walk through the silent streets without a destination. Bill Houston joined the parade of souls waiting for the sun.

He walked himself sober and stayed that way until after his first
meeting with his parole officer in a building downtown on Jeffer-
son Street, abstinence from alcohol being a condition of his early
release. No one was checking, however, and he soon fell back into
his old ways, pulling himself together on Tuesdays for the weekly
confrontation with the man who could send him back to prison
with a phone call. His PO, Sam Webb, a portly young citified
rancher type, who called Houston "a downtown cowboy," got him
employment as a trainee. Two months into his freedom Houston
showed up for the meeting with whiskey on his breath, but Webb
only sneered at the offense. "I could get you jailed for the weekend," he said, "but they'd just let you go again. They need the cells
in Florence for the meaner boys."

Houston finished his training and began drawing full wages.
He drove a forklift at a lumberyard, the biggest such concern in
the Southwest, it was claimed, not counting California. All day
from massive trucks to massive sheds he moved tons and tons of
puke-smelling fresh-cut boards, and he never built anything but
rectilinear stacks, and little by little he dismantled them. Others
put the wood to use. He just watched it go by. Hardly socializing
though drinking plenty, staying out of trouble, living almost as a
solitary, feeling reluctant, somehow, to become himself again, he
worked at the lumberyard well into the spring until his longer and
longer absences rendered him nearly useless, and they fired him.

The mission had made sense until it had been accomplished.
They'd turned up nothing. They sought a secure place to spend
the night. An encampment of Special Forces had turned them
away. In all likelihood, the presence of Special Forces alone had
cleared the area of activity, but no one had been briefed as to their

presence. On the basis of obsolete intelligence the six Lurps had dosed up and fared forth when they should have been sleeping in Nha Trang. The mission made no sense.

The incident was more of an assassination than an ambush. For the last half kilometer James had taken point. The night was starless, but the darkness knew what it knew. He followed it. After a few hundred paces more the darkness would widen and they'd have reached a place they knew about where they could break and wait for dawn, possibly call for extraction.

A gun opened up behind him in three short bursts. He fell and crawled back the way he'd come, but stopped a few yards along because his life forked sharply leftward exactly there. Leaves fell down on him as the others returned fire. Feet pounded on the trail. A grenade banged into the trees and he jammed his face into the dirt as it exploded. He rolled left into the bush, following the lifeline, and looked for flashes from across the trail. Nothing. The firing had ceased. The screeching of insects had stopped. The moment was strong and peaceful. The air had ringing depth. Every last particle of bullshit had been incinerated.

He slithered forward through the exhilarating lacerations of the bush until he heard one of his own crawling on the trail, and clicked his tongue. He heard a moan. He smelled shit. The moaning rose to a song but drew no fire.

"Man down! Man down!"

"On the trail! On the trail!" It was Dirty's voice. James heard boots on the trail and fired three covering bursts and stopped. A man squatted over the wounded one.

"Grab an ankle. Let's go."

"Fuck it. There's no cover."

Joker strolled up the trail as in a public park. "It's over." He put himself at the trailside with his gun at the ready. "It was just one fucker is all."

"Bullshit."

"I saw every flash. I never looked down."

Dirty said to the hurt one, "Look here, look at me!"

"I can't see nothing but bullshit."

"Bakers!"

"Who is it?"

"It's Dirty. It's me. Don't shut your eyes!"

"Fuck, I'm not in the world, man. I'm not."

"You're here. You're okay."

"I don't feel it. It's bullshit."

"You're here."

"I don't feel the world, man."

"Who threw that grenade?"

"Me," Joker said. "Fucker pulled the trigger three times and boogied."

"His eyes are empty." Dirty leaned close to smell for breath. "Fucked," he said. "Good and fucked."

All five of them were here now. James took point again and each of the others took an arm or a leg and dragged Bakers's corpse to the clearing they knew of three hundred meters down the trail.

"Tag his ass."

"He went from the feet up. He died right out of himself."

"But I like what he did, man. He stayed himself."

"Yeah?"

"He didn't bug and turn into a little child, man," Dirty said. Dirty himself was weeping.

James hadn't known Bakers too well. Gratitude and love filled him that Bakers had eaten it instead of one of the others. Especially himself.

"We'll catch somebody from one of these villes and make the message known."

"Fuck the dinks. It's them Green Berets. Do you believe that shit?"

"No, I do not."

"If they'd let us in their perimeter, this man right here would be alive. This man would be laughing."

"Let's call and get him out."

"Not yet."

"Dirty, man, it's over, man."

"Leave that radio alone." Dirty thumbed his selector loudly.

"S', señor! I will not touch the fucker."

"Who's coming with me?"

Dirty and Conrad went hunting, and the other three stayed with the corpse.

"This guy died because those fuckers wouldn't let us in their perimeter."

"Next little Beanie I see in town, I'm gonna follow him around till I can stick him in his fucking back."

"Let's call a strike on their cowardly asses."

James squatted with his back against a tree trunk and rolled a smoke with some grass in it. Licking the paper he could taste the gunmetal on his fingers.

He stood up and lit it as the others bunched around him to hide the glow.

"Did you hear what he said about bullshit? He knew. He knew."

"His back's blown out anyway."

"Good for him. Otherwise it'd be life in an electric chair. That's the sentence, man. You motorvate by blowing in a tube."

"It's lower down than that. He'd have his arms."

"I wouldn't use no wheelchair. I'd swing around by a harness in the ceiling."

James left them and sat against the tree again. He didn't want to talk about such things while his brain ballooned and finally cooled off. He put his head back and looked at the sky. Darkness, nothing, the pure nothing, just quiet electricity. The soul of everything. "I don't believe that shit," he said.

"Them little Beanies got every corner of their program stuck down real tight."

"They don't do shit. Got zero in their sacks."

"Let's call in a strike on their cowardly fucking asses."

James said, "Come here," and the others came close and squatted around him. "I need me a Chinese grenade. Soon as I get me a Chinese grenade I'm gonna frag those motherfuckers into dead red meat."

"Tonight?"

"Right as soon as I get one."

"Conrad's got one."

"I know."

"Let's put some smoke in their night. Take out about twenty a those motherfuckers."

Conrad appeared among them as silently as a thought.

"You back?"

"Just me."

"Where's Dirty?"

"He's got a woman."

James stood up. "Let me have that han'gernade."

"What."

"You know what I'm talking about. That Chinese thing."

"I'm taking it home."

"Home where?"

"Home home."

"Fuck home."

"For a souvenir."

"You can't take a han'gernade back to the world."

"Well, fuck. Anyway."

"I'll get you another one."

Conrad carried it in his breast pocket. James reached in and wrestled it out. "You coming with me?"

"Where to?"

"Back to where them Beanies are taking a snooze."

"No shit?"

"No shit."

"I will if you wait around for the interrogation."

Dirty came back escorting a small naked creature into the field of James's night-vision as into a circle of firelight. She had a shiny lower lip that stuck out as if somebody had just called her a bad name. She seemed angry enough to kill, if she'd had a weapon in her hands. They held her down and the others took turns with her, but Dirty was already done and James wanted to keep himself mean for his personal Zero Hour with the Green Berets. When the others were finished she no longer needed holding down. James fell on his knees and put the point of his Bowie knife against the woman's belly and said, "What's your rank, sojer? You ever been showed what to do with one a these, sojer? You ever seen one before, sojer? What's your rank, little sojer? What are you looking at? Do you think you're my mother? You're my mother, but who the fuck is my father?" He interrogated her until his hand was too weak to keep hold of the hilt.

Phoenix seemed to Bill Houston a much bigger city these days. Suburban developments had scattered themselves out across the desert. The traffic was fierce. Many mornings the horizon lay under blankets of brown smog. Whenever it all weighed him down too heavily he took a line and a couple of hooks and sat by one of the wide irrigation canals where catfish waited in peaceful ignorance of the twentieth century. He'd been told they came down from the Colorado River, and he'd been advised to use chunks of frankfurter for bait and a plastic bobber to keep his hook just touching bottom, but he didn't have a bobber, not even a rod or reel, and he never had any luck. It didn't trouble him. Waiting and hoping, that was the point, watching the water pass through the ancient desert, considering its travels. Often Houston stayed late spying on the folks who arrived and went in that lonely place, until he was able one night to surprise three hippies doing a dope exchange and rob them of three hundred fifty in cash and a brick of Mexican reefer wrapped in red cellophane. Staring at his trembling machete, the boys told him it was mediocre Mexican dope, regular quality, nothing special, but he could certainly have the stuff. He let them keep it, though he might have found a way to sell it himself. There was a line. He'd bully young kids and he'd steal from them, he might even have stabbed one if he'd had to. But he'd never deal drugs.

Near closing time he stood on the sidewalk in front of a bar's open doorway bathed in its warm liquor-breath, the country music from inside getting at him, cutting him. A little man came out swearing and trying to close the gaps torn in his T-shirt by an assailant. A skinny rat, too old to be fighting, with a bleeding mouth and one eye swollen shut. He smiled like a punished child. "This will cure me. This is the end." Many, many times Bill Houston had promised himself the same.

Captain Galassi expressed concerns about James's self-esteem, which he pronounced self-steam. He wasn't a boy-captain, he was the real thing, here since '63, field-commissioned and all that, but he'd let himself develop a concern for James's self-steam, and expressed it, while Sergeant Lorin sat nearby with his fists on his thighs, expressing nothing.

"What's your first name, Corporal?"

"James."

"I'm going to call you James instead of Corporal, because you'll be a civilian here pretty quick. And anyway, in my eyes, you are no soldier. You got anything to say to that?"

"No."

"They beat you up real bad, didn't they? They fucked you up pretty good. Do you think you're gonna get a Purple Heart for that?"

"I already got one. And that was bullshit too."

"See, James, those are soldiers. Those are fine men. Matter of fact, my sister married a Green Beret. They know what they came here to do, and they're getting it done. They know who the enemy is, and they're not gonna kill their own people. They're people who if their own people try to fuck them up, if an American tries to fuck them up, even throws a grenade in their lap, they don't kill that American, because that American is not their enemy. They just fuck him up some, because that American is a fucking son of a fucking bitch."

James made no comment.

"Beat you like you deserved. Are you still pissing blood?"

"No, sir."

"Can you take solid food?"

"I don't require no food."

"Are you gonna tell me you didn't toss that item?"

"I didn't throw any grenade."

"Fucker just plopped down out of the sky."

"I don't know fuck-all about no grenade. I'll tell you this about them Green Berets: they'd as soon leave their people out in the bush to get killed when people ask can we stay in your perimeter. And one of our guys did get killed. Did she divorce him?"

"Who?"

"Your sister."

"That's none of your business."

"What's your first name?"

"That's none of your business too."

"Okay, Jack. You ain't no soldier to me either. Not if you back them piece-of-shit Special Forces against your own Lurps. Fuck you, Jack."

"You know what I think? I think the sergeant and I are gonna take you out back and work some shit on you like the Green Berets."

"Some Green-Beret-style shit," Sergeant Lorin said.

"I'd just love it. Let's go."

"Apologize to the captain."

"I apologize, sir."

"Apology accepted. James, I think you have lost your control and your ability to reason in this difficult atmosphere of the pressure of warfare. Don't you?"

"I think that's real possible."

Captain Galassi lit up a Kool. The Quonset hut's air conditioner didn't filter entirely the smells from outside, good American smells, grease, frying potatoes, frying meat, reasonable-smelling latrines, not latrines full of slopehead dink Gook shit. Captain Galassi exhaled a cloud of smoke and overlaid the smells.

Screwy Loot would have offered him a Kool. James wished himself back in the days of old Screwy Loot, when the officers were the only crazy ones.

"Can I smoke, sir?"

"Go ahead."

"I'm fresh out."

"Then I don't think it's gonna be possible."

"Then I won't."

"What twisted you? Did you take a lotta Ell, Ess, Deeeee, boy?"

"I don't use no drugs. 'Cept as indicated."

"Indicated by who? Your dealer?"

"By the requirements of the mission, sir."

"You mean speed."

"I mean what I said, is all."

"You mean you're a little Speedy Gonzales. Are you aware how fucked you are? You have long-range reconned straight out beyond the borders of sanity. You gotta go home."

"I just signed on another go."

"You won't be staying. I don't want you in my war."

James said nothing.

"The knees of your pants are a mess."

"I've been digging, sir."

"Or knee-walking drunk on Trang Khe Street four nights ago."

"Four nights ago? I do not know, sir."

"How come you don't go to the Midnight Massage no more with the guys?"

No answer.

"You got yourself something steady. Little steady woman on Tranky Street. Were you on Trang Khe Street four nights ago?"

"I think so. I don't know."

"Were you?"

"I think so."

"Or were you on patrol."

"I don't know."

"What happened."

"When? On Tranky?"

"On the patrol where a woman was murdered, you fucking murderer."

James suddenly hated these two sonsofbitches because if they were going to go ahead and do this he should have been given a chair, and a cigarette.

"What happened to that local, James?"

"Anybody got wasted they were hostiles, is all."

"Were you on that patrol?"

"No."

"Four nights ago?"

"No."

"No? Address me as sir."

"Who snitched us?"

Sergeant Lorin said, "None of your business."

"Somebody's a liar."

"Somebody's a liar about what?" the sarge said.

James waited for the captain to speak.

"Did you do this?"

"I don't know."

"You don't know? Goddammit, man, you will address me as sir."

"I don't know, sir."

"Did you do this, or not?"

"I don't remember which night was what, sir. I think I drank too much beer last week."

The sarge said, "Had him a wicked jag on."

"Do you like beer, James? Well, there isn't any beer in Leaven-worth."

"Have you been there?"

"Don't sass me."

"I got friends there."

"Don't sass me."

"Apologize to the captain."

"I apologize, sir."

"What did you do to that woman?"

"She was VC."

"Bullshit."

"She was a VC whore."

"Bullshit."

"She's a whore, and this is a war. Sir."

"Don't tell me what this is. I know what it is. I think."

"So do I."

"Do you intend to do a fourth tour?"

"Yes, sir."

"No, sir. No more for you."

"Sir, I've got patrol at seventeen hundred."

"Patrol? Jesus Christ. Number one, we don't send guys with their ribs taped up and their arm in a cast out on patrol."

"It's a sling. It ain't a cast. It comes off."

"Number two: We don't send civilians out on patrol."

"I ain't a civilian."

"Well," the captain said, and such anger gripped him that he slurred his words, "do you mind if I tell you that if you're not a civilian you haven't heard the last of this? I'm gonna take stock of this, I will get back to you, you haven't heard the last of this. I will get back to you. Maybe a lot of people will be getting back to you. Maybe the whole army will be getting back to you."

"I don't think so."

"You don't think so? Are you being insubordinate?"

"I'm just saying something."

"What are you saying?"

"I don't know."

"What are you saying?"

"That you think you're gonna get back to me, but I don't think you're gonna get back to me, because she was a whore, and this is a war. And that's what happens, because this is a war, because this is not just a war."

"Well, which is it? Is it a war, or is it not just a war?"

"I'm just telling you."

"You little punk. I was in this war before you learned to jerk your meat. All right?"

"All right."

"All right," said the captain. For thirty seconds they just stood there doing nothing.

James said, "Sir, Captain, I gotta go, I gotta boogie."

"No, James, you don't. Jesus Christ. *Patrol?*"

"Yes, sir."

Captain Galassi stood up. He stepped smartly to the door of the Quonset hut, grasped the knob, and opened it wide. Outside, the dust, the noise of trucks, helicopters—a heavy, gray day— "Sergeant," he said, "speak to this man." He left and pulled the door shut behind him, leaving things relatively quiet again under the air conditioner's hum.

The sarge sat down at the captain's desk and offered James a seat. But not a cigarette.

Lorin said, "You could've wasted as many as four of those motherfuckers.—Well, I know, the only one got hurt is you." After a while Lorin said, "But this business with the woman."

"Shit goes on all the time."

Lorin just looked at him. Stared at him. Said, "James."

"What."

"No. You tell me what."

James said, "I mean, where did this shit about a woman come from, what is this shit doing in my movie?"

"You like your movie?"

"It's kind of like where I have these sensors. And the minute the shit starts my mind snaps on in Technicolor. Like I have these sensors."

"So you just want to keep on keeping on?"

"Yeah."

"Watching your Technicolor movie?"

"Yeah."

"Till you eat shit and die?"

"Yeah."

"Right there I kind of agree with you, James. I don't really think it's highly advisable to turn you loose on the United States. I'd say keep you right here till you get killed. But if it ain't bass-ackwards, it ain't the U.S. Army, is it?"

"We do it all in the dark, Sarge. Mistakes get made."

"Yeah, they do. But this little mistake with the woman is traveling right straight up the captain's ass. And then with the fragging thing, you're sticking out all over."

"Can you spare me a toke?"

"In a minute. I'm telling you something."

"Okay."

"So I think it's the real deal, Cowboy. I think you're gonna have to go home."

"Home?"

"Home where you came from."

"I don't know what to say."

"Say you're a mess."

"I'm a mess."

"If you don't want a ticket out of hell, then you ain't regular in your mind no more, are you, sojer?"

"If you're talking, I gotta listen. You always did have your finger right smack on the thing, man."

"Uncle Ho done died, buddy. You won the war. It's over."

"Yeah?"

"Pack up. Go home. Right now."

"Now?"

"Absolutely. Get to Tan Son Nhut and get on a MAC flight and go. Just go. I'll furlough you, and after you're there we'll work all the paper to make it permanent."

The sergeant took out a cigarette. He offered James one and lit

both out of a matchbook from the Midnight Massage. He said,
"It'll be honorable."

"What will?"

"The discharge."

"Oh . . . Yeah. Honorable?"

"Honorable Discharge."

"If you say so."

"I say Honorable. And I always will."

In the middle of June, Bill Houston bailed his brother James out
of jail. James had reached Phoenix a couple of weeks before but
hadn't gotten in touch with anyone until he'd been arrested for
simple assault, and then he'd called their mother. As James came
out past the bailiff's desk, he was smiling. Otherwise he looked
sketchy, like something might get him from behind.

"First of all, I ain't smiling because I'm proud. I'm smiling
because I'm glad as hell to get out."

"You're lucky I had a few bucks."

"Sorry for you spending it this way."

"Usually I'm on my ass, but lately things have been breaking a
little different for me."

"Looks like you put on a little weight."

"Well—I was in Florence."

Out on the street James ducked his head and squinted against
the light.

"I appreciate this, Bill Junior. No lie."

"Family better count for something. Because nothing else
does."

"You got that right."

"You ready for a burger?"

"Does the Pope wear a dress?" James expelled a wad of
tobacco from his mouth and it bounced on the pavement like a
small turd. "How much did you pay the bondsman guy?"

"A hundred. And if you don't do right and show for court, I owe him a thousand."

"I'll do right."

"I kind of hope so."

"I'll pay you back the hundred too."

"Don't sweat it. Just when you can."

Bill Houston reached his right hand cross-draw to dig in the left pocket of his jeans for the keys.

"You got a car."

"Yep. It's a Rolls."

"No shit?"

It was an old Lincoln with a hood like the deck of an aircraft carrier. "Yeah, it ain't a Rolls. But it rolls when you push on the gas."

He took James to a McDonald's and got him three of the biggest they had and two chocolate shakes. James ate fast and then sat there with his arms crossed on his chest, mad-dogging everybody.

"Hey."

James belched loudly.

They talked about their mother. James said, "How old is she, anyways?"

"She's fifty-eight at least," Bill said, "maybe fifty-nine. But she seems like she's past a hundred."

"I know. Yeah. She does. She has for a long time."

Bill said, "So—I'm called Bill Junior. But did something ever occur to you? It occurred to me a long time ago."

"What."

"There ain't no Bill Senior."

An old man at the next little table asked them: "How old are you boys?"

They looked at each other. The old man said: "I'm sixty-six. You know—Route Sixty-six? Like that. Sixty-six."

"Fuck yourself," James said.

Bill Houston observed James dipping snuff. He took a wad

from the tin, shoved it down inside his cheek, shut the lid, wiped
his fingers on the underneath of his pants leg.

"The bondsman said this was the fourth time in two weeks the
cops rousted you for fighting, so they finally had to charge you."

"That what he said?"

It pissed Bill Houston off, it irked him unreasonably, that
James would playact an old soldier, as if he'd explored some mysterious region and been tortured there.

"You want another burger?"

"I'm all right."

"Really? You're all right?"

"Yeah."

"The evidence is pointing the other way."

The day after James got out of jail he went to a small office where
a fat, sad man helped him fill out some forms. He said the checks
would start in about four weeks if everything didn't go too wrong.
The man told him about a place downtown that might give him
further benefits, and James went to see about it, but they wanted
him to stand in line there and fill out more idiotic forms.

For several days he was permitted to stay in a hostel on the east
side, on Van Buren Street, the street of outlaws and whores, thirty
blocks from where his mother had lived before he'd left for Southeast Asia. Perhaps she still resided there.

In the mornings he set out walking, rarely stopping. To the
west lay factories and warehouses. In other directions the city gave
way to suburban tracts, empty desert, or irrigated farmland. It was
early in the desert summer, hot, but dry. He wore a straw cowboy
hat and kept the sun behind him all day, asking in restaurants for
water. When it came down ahead of him he turned and went the
other way. Only half of him was plugged in. The rest was dark. He
could feel his sensors dying.

James didn't get in touch with Stevie. She came to see him just

before he left the hostel for good, and they went out for drinks, but
he railed at her so unflaggingly in the Aces Tavern that the bartender shouted at James to leave, and Stevie stayed, saying that
she'd seen what he wanted to show her and that she got the message and refused to go anywhere with a man who repaid her kindness with curses and abuse. As the bartender strong-armed him
into the night James looked back and saw her crying, swaying in
the light of the jukebox. Thirty minutes later Stevie found him
standing in front of the state insane asylum at Twenty-fourth
Street, looking in through the barred gate at the wide lawns,
which in the illumination of the arc lamps looked uniformly silver
and magical. She'd finished crying. She told him she couldn't
stop loving him. He swore to her he'd get a job.

He'd made it out of the war with just short of four hundred
dollars cash. He rented an apartment in a plywood sort of building
called Rob Roy Suites and bought a Harley in many pieces which
he commenced to assemble in the living room and knew he'd
never complete. He hated his neighbor across the court, a diesel-
dyke with a bad mouth. You could tell she used to be sexy but had
always hated men. James didn't know what to do. What did these
good souls want you to do? Most evenings he went to a bar just a
few blocks down the street where you could almost always get into
a fight, or he drank port wine from plastic cups in places full of
ripped-up old alcoholic men. He waited for his checks to start.
When they started, he bought a Colt .45 revolver, a real six-
shooter. He was pretty sure he would eventually shoot the woman
living across the way but he felt there was nothing any human
power could do about it.

After a month at the Rob Roy Suites he moved to the Majestic
Palms Apartments on Thirty-second Street half a block above Van
Buren. Each morning he sat by the shadeless window naked, jiggling his knees, and watched a tremendously fat black guy in a
circus-tent T-shirt cross the street from wherever he dwelt and
open up the Circle K on the corner.

James walked the neighborhood and passed the slack whores on the bus stop benches and shouldered past the old crones taking their minuscule paces forward through the intersections and observed the Mexican women in their tall spiked heels and tight pink pants, who looked for sale but really weren't.

He sits at a bus stop. He drags on a Kool. He spits between his feet. In his fingers he holds the neck of a half pint of Popov vodka, his head bowed low under the crashing irrelevance of these millions of monsters and their games.

An older guy sitting next to him with a newspaper open across his knees, reading in the glaring sunlight, squinting, began to curse these people undermining the military effort in Vietnam. "Those boys are doing right. They're our boys. They're doing right," he said. James felt as if he could sure use a cigarette, and said so. "I don't smoke," the man said. "Don't even drink coffee. I was raised as a Mormon. Yep. Raised as a Mormon. But I don't believe in it now. You know why? Because it's phony." James repeated he'd like a cigarette, and the man got up and walked away. And a dog came along and stopped and looked at him and James said, "You got a face, buddy," and he scratched its ears and he said, "Yeah, buddy, you got a face."

One night in the Aces Tavern he ran into his older brother Bill and Bill's old friend Pat Patterson. Patterson had just come out of the Arizona State Prison in Florence, where the two had been acquainted. He was a slender, erectly postured young man who looked like he'd landed here intact from the rockabilly fifties, his hair combed in a ducktail and his short sleeves turned up above his triceps, and his collar turned up too.

Bill explained to his brother a little bit about prison: "You got your guys, and they got their guys, depending on your skin color. It's not about right or wrong. It's who's who—who's the people next to you. And you owe them."

"I know about it."

"I know you know about it. You sure do. You've had experience on both sides of a gun."

"It never happened."

"But what I'm saying—you must've had a lot of experiences."

"It never happened. It never happened."

Bill Junior turned his glass in his hands and frowned. "It kind of rubs me wrong how you act, James." He cleared his throat, made sure the bartender wasn't looking, and spat on the floor. "Like, 'James is back in the world. And the world is a big old zit so James wants to piss in its face.' How long are you going to stay an asshole?"

"Till something convinces me different."

Bill drained his glass and got up and wandered out the door.

Patterson said to James, "Here's a question for you: Is this the Aces Tavern as in, Man, I got four Aces? Or is this Aces Tavern as in, This tavern belongs to a cat named Ace?" He pointed to the barmaid, saying, "She's a young, hot little machine." James agreed she was little, but she was long past young. The flesh under her arms wobbled as she plunged beer mugs into the sink and shook the drops out and placed them on a towel. James pointed it out. "I ain't watching her arms," Patterson said. "I'm watching her ass wiggle."

"I better go see what Junior's up to."

"Fuck that boy. He'll be just fine."

James went out on the sidewalk, but Bill was gone. There was only a young man out front bothering the citizens who passed, trying to sell the shirt off his back. James retreated into the Aces and rejoined Patterson, who asked if James had a gun, and James said he had one.

"Wadn't you a Lurp over there in the Vietnam?"

James said yes.

Patterson intended to rob a casino some folks ran in an isolated house out near Gila Bend and wondered if James would like to make some money. Patterson explained that robbing a casino out in the desert, in the night, would have some of the quality of warfare. James said, "All right."

————

They'd been told the patient was a child, but he was a grown man in his thirties, Vietcong, probably. At this point the men who'd brought them to the patient described him as a farmer who'd unearthed an unexploded artillery round. From the nature of the injury—one arm mutilated, the rest of him apparently shielded—it seemed likely he'd meant to salvage the device in order to turn it against its American manufacturers. How the patient had sustained his injuries made no difference to Dr. Mainichikoh, and certainly Kathy didn't care. With the doctor, in his Land Rover, she got around the villes more freely than she might have if she waited to go with any of the WCS teams, and by her assistance as his nurse she paid her fare. Among the villes Dr. Mainichikoh was known as "Dr. Mai," which, with a certain upward inflection, could mean "Dr. American," and today this had led to confusion—Kathy, clearly the Anglo, was presumed to be the physician, and the villagers took the little Japanese man accompanying her to be her nurse. Mai made no attempt to disabuse them except by seizing the situation and giving orders. She liked working with him. He was resourceful—a requirement, given the lack of resources—and good-humored to the point he seemed quite insensitive to grim facts. She understood he was rich, from a Tokyo import-export family. Whether they did business with Vietnam she didn't know.

The two men who'd conducted them here had established a kind of facility shaded by a canvas tarp. They had the patient laid out on a bloodstained table of boards and lumber rounds and told Kathy they were ready to sterilize the implements immediately. As Dr. Mai began his examination they began to grasp his true role, and they asked him if now they should get the fire going. He told them yes, right away.

Amputation had been pretty well completed by the injury itself, but the forearm remained connected by a bit of bone, muscle, and flesh below the elbow. On a day so hot and without instruments to measure at what point on the limb arterial deficiency had begun, determining what to take and what to leave was guesswork, but Dr. Mai had a deep faith in his own ability to judge the extent of devitalized tissue. "He can keep the elbow," he said. "It's a small explosive. If it's a land mine, well, you'd better take the whole limb, isn't it? Because it's going to die." She might have argued that since this was the patient's only chance for surgery, higher was better and maybe the whole arm should go, but Dr. Mai wasn't addressing her. He talked to himself habitually, always in English. "This man is quite strong. A good one. Not even in shock." The patient stared straight up at the canvas sheet protecting them from the sun and seemed determined not to lose consciousness. A dozen or so shrapnel lacerations on his face and chest had already been excised and sutured with tailoring thread. One, on the cheekbone, had just missed taking his left eye.

They had only Xylocaine, but the doctor cheerfully effected an axillary block of the brachial plexus and went to work while Kathy dabbed away the sweat on his face with a bandanna sterilized in rubbing alcohol.

The patient's two comrades squatted by a tree not far off, ready to fetch whatever might be needed, as if they had anything to fetch. The man's family kept out of the way in one of the hooches, all but a toothless mamasan who enacted a ritual of private significance only a few meters away, out in the relentless sunshine, in the smoke of the charcoal fire and the steam from the pot where the instruments boiled: a dance of ominous hesitations, and sudden leaps, and arabesques. Dr. Mai permitted the display without comment, and Kathy welcomed it as boding well for the patient. The idea that among the ragged, the crazy, the whirly-eyed, the frothing-at-the-mouth, among the sideways, among the mumblers, shufflers, laughers, a bit of loving scrutiny would turn up the blessed poor in spirit, the burned visionary, the holy vagrant—she'd always entertained it, this romance.

Dr. Mai lifted his machete from the cauldron and poured half a quart of alcohol all over it and said, "Banzai." Kathy laughed and pulled back the skin in the direction of the elbow. "In the time of your Civil War," Dr. Mai said, making the initial cut and beginning to work circumferentially through the first layer of flesh to the fascia beneath, "amputation was a very gruesome business to perform. Now we can be optimists."

"My Civil War?" she said. "Do you mean the American Civil War?"

"Yes."

"I'm from Canada," she said. "I'm Canadian."

"I see. Between the Union and Confederate."

"The Canadians weren't part of that war."

"I see—Canada."

"You know I'm from Canada."

"Yes. But I thought Canada is from the United States."

"We're north of there."

"So often north, south. Not so often east and west civil war."

She released her grip on the skin, and when it retracted Dr. Mai, pressing down with his palm on the blade's back and rocking the handle up and down, cut through the fascia and the first layer of muscle, and as each layer retracted he cut through the next. Wherever he encountered a blood vessel Kathy clamped it with thread. With her hands she applied upward pressure on the proximal muscle stump. After the deep muscles had retracted the doctor took his saw from the cauldron and went at the bone while she irrigated the site with saline from a large syringe.

The doctor brushed the severed arm from the table onto the earth between his feet and picked up the bandanna and wiped his face, while one by one Kathy pulled the major nerve stumps forward and cut them as high along as could be reached. One of the arteries still bled, and she tied it off again.

She cleaned and repacked the implements while Dr. Mai took the crazy old woman's hand and danced a little jig with her. He'd made a good concave stump—he was an excellent technician and had a genuine medical sixth sense—but Kathy wondered if they should have left so much of the arm. In fluent Vietnamese the doctor instructed the patient's companions in caring for the stump and preventing retraction of the skin by the use of adhesive tape and an Ace bandage. He just wasn't equipped to plaster-cast the arm's remainder and fashion a ladder splint and stockinette and wire retractor and all the rest, but it didn't matter. One look at the patient's face told you he'd survive. Kathy had seven one-quarter-grain syrettes of morphine in her kit and left them all with him because you could see this man would survive.

Dr. Mai stepped to the Land Rover and took his canteen from the front seat and enjoyed a long drink and brought it back to Kathy. She declined.

"I don't see you drink enough water, Kathy."

"I get plenty."

"You're well adjusted to the tropics. How long did it take you to adjust?"

"I lived in the PI a couple years before I ever came here."

"You've been here five years, isn't it?"

"Five years. Almost."

"Yes. How long will you stay?"

"Until it's over."

On a sunny November morning just two weeks before he went away to prison, James married Stevie at the courthouse.

His family came to watch. In a churchgoing dress with puffy shoulders, his mother looked like the Okie she was. Brother Bill wore a white sports coat over a white T-shirt, and as the family all stood before the magistrate he sweated as if he were on trial, while young Burris smirked and giggled like a girl, and resembled one, too, with hair grown almost to his shoulders.

Stevie's parents believed she was marrying a criminal. At first they made promises to attend, but in the end they stayed away.

As the newlyweds left the courthouse the groom could see the Deuce, the section of Second Avenue where the bums rolled in the gutters, and beyond the Deuce the neighborhood where he lived.

Afterward they barbecued small sirloin steaks in South Mountain Park. Bill Junior got red-eyed drunk, and Burris, who might
have been fourteen but looked no older than eleven, smoked cigarettes openly. Their mother stayed off in a corner, ready to preach
at all who'd listen, or rehearse the family's tragedies.

The wedding didn't change much. James kept living in his
apartment and Stevie stayed on at her parents' while James dealt
with charges of aggravated assault and armed robbery. He'd pled
innocent and made bail, but soon he'd appear again before the
judge and change his story and receive his sentence. Not much
doubt attached to his prospects. Nevertheless, his court-appointed
attorney insisted on taking the process through all its steps in
order to get the best deal from the prosecutor. James and the rockabilly Pat Patterson had done all right to begin with, but their luck
had run out and the police had arrested them without incident
outside a tavern about an hour after their fourth robbery. Patterson, a parolee, had gone directly back to Florence.

On this, his first felony offense, and thanks to his war record,
James could expect to serve no more than three years, probably
more like two. Stevie swore she'd wait. James might have run away
to Mexico, but he was tired, very tired.

Four days from sentencing, four days from prison food, ten days
married, and still never having tasted a meal cooked by his wife,
James went looking for breakfast on South Central Avenue. He
sat in a diner among a handful of demented customers, a man gri-
macing, another man swearing, and ordered an egg. The chubby
probably Chinese proprietress stood by the register having breakfast, eating her oatmeal out of a coffee mug. She tore off half a
slice of bread in her teeth and gnashed it down, carrying on with
a full mouth in what she must have thought was English, but
James couldn't understand a word — she had that whining, nasal
way of talking. Suddenly he very vividly smelled and tasted Nha
Trang.

He was distracted by the man in the booth next to his table, who sat sideways with his legs out in the aisle. "I am all souped-up on speed. Yes," he said very quietly, "I am a speedy little boy."

"I'm not in the shape of mind to find that interesting," James said.

"You know where I was seven hours and twenty minutes ago? I was home. You know where home is? San Diego. Know what I was doing? Standing in front of a mirror—full-length mirror, okay?—stark-naked, with a .357 in this hand, holding it to my head just like this. I'm gonna shoot myself. Do you believe me?"

James put his fork down.

"Yeah. Had a little problem with the gambling. Little? Fuck. It took every fucking thing I owned. Wife. Kids. House. I'm bankrupt. She got the house. And a million years of payments on it. Fuck. Ready to blow my brains all over my sister's bedroom. Yes indeed. Fuck yes. But I didn't want my sister coming home to a mess like that—or I didn't have the balls to shoot myself, let's admit it. So I'm thinking I need to come up with a way of ending this horror show that's quick and painless and they won't know I was the one who did this to myself. So I got dressed and I decided here's how I'll go out, I'll get in that little foreign job, little VW bug, small car, sister's car, ain't my car. So I got in it and fired it up and headed east on Interstate Eight, my friend, out of San Diego, and I put on my high beams and I told myself the first semi truck flashes his lights at me I'm gonna swing into him head-on, take myself out kamikaze-style. And I had both hands on the wheel the whole way, man, didn't take my hands off except to scratch my nuts or thumb the cap off a bottle of bennies and shake a couple more down my throat. And I tell you what. That whole ride, three hundred and fifty miles at least, nobody once flashed their lights at me, sir, not one person, there was not a single incident of anybody flashing their lights at me. And that's a miracle. It's a miracle I'm sitting here alive. I don't know what it means. But I'm alive. That's all I know. And I don't know anything more on this earth except that. I am alive."

He didn't appear to be on any kind of bennies. He looked very

calm and stayed quite still, with his right leg draped over his left
knee and his hands clasped gently before him on his thigh. His
eyes were red, but they brimmed with the light of love. He ordered
white toast without butter and tore small pieces from it and fed
them between his lips. Struck a match and lit a cigarette and
tossed the matchbook onto his plate.

James said, "Took you a suicide run."

"Yeah. Sure did."

"I been on a couple runs like that."

"Yeah."

"Hey. You still got your gun? You want me to shoot you?"

The man looked dapper in a tweed sort of sports jacket over a
thin beige sweater, pale blue pajama bottoms, and flimsy cloth
house slippers. He took a reflective drag on his cigarette. "I left the
gun at home," he said.

Bill Houston took his brother James out for a talk the day before
his final court appearance. He invited him to a coffee shop rather
than a tavern; James had better understand the matter was serious.
"Look, you never know. All I know is you want to stay out of max,
because somebody's always cutting up in there, and they're always
locking you down. So while they have you waiting for classification, talk about your education constantly. Any counselors, those
guys, anybody like that talks to you, you say 'education, education.' You want to finish high school, you want to learn a skill. Just
talk about stuff like that, and they'll put you in medium. Medium
is where you want to be. It's more relaxed. People aren't so crazy.
You're on the yard just about anytime you want. It's good. Believe
me, you don't want max."

"Who all's in there?"

"Where? Medium?"

"Florence. Anywheres, medium or max."

"Well—lots of folks."

"Is the old man in there? Your father?"

"He ain't my father. He's your father."

"Whoever's father. He in there?"

"Yeah. He's over in max. No. I think he got out."

"You pretty sure about that?"

"Yeah. I think he got out. She quit visiting, anyways."

"She don't go no more?"

"Not since I got out. Far as I know. So her husband must be somewhere."

"Where?"

"I don't know. Somewhere else."

Bill left his younger brother with a final handshake, not sure he'd gotten himself across succesfully, and headed downtown to check on work at the day-labor office, or hang around the park. The desert autumn had come, time for pruning the orchards. He watched men cutting away at the olive trees along the avenues with moaning chain saws and felt it all happening inside him.

He wished for a motorcycle. Wondered if stealing one was difficult. Walked around looking for one outside the taverns, then inside the taverns for happy hours and deals on port wine. As a vintage, port was nobody's favorite, but people forced to consider these things, like himself, had calculated that it offered the highest proof per penny. "Thick and sickly sweet," a middle-aged woman said, toasting him sadly. "Not you!" she said. "I mean the port. It's sweet. You look sour. I'm sour too." Her problem was, she told him, that her son-in-law had died in Vietnam. Houston said he had a brother just back from there. "No. Really? Come here," she said, "I gotta make an introduction," and led him by the hand to a booth to meet her daughter, widowed by the war after a long year's separation from the boy she'd married only a week before he'd shipped. He'd been killed near the end of his tour. Houston looked at wedding photographs. Not his idea of a party. The ladies bought a round. The young widow drank too many beers, but rather than breaking down crying, she told how she'd cried at her young husband's funeral, was glad she'd cried, had been afraid she wouldn't be able to cry. She'd spent these last ten days since the news had come in a state of relief. Now she wouldn't have to welcome him home and get to know him all over again. In her husband's absence, she'd changed a lot. She hadn't known what to do about that. At the funeral they'd presented her with a flag folded into a triangle. "Yeah, I got a flag."

"No shit. A flag? Oh, you mean an American flag. Old Glory." Houston had his leg pressed along the length of her thigh.

"Well, they don't call it Old Glory, do they? It's something else."

"It's something else, I think. Yeah."

"The Stars and Bars or something."

"My little brother was over there. Infantry. Won himself a Purple Heart."

"Really? The Purple Heart?"

"Sure thing."

"What happened to him?"

"He stepped on a booby trap in a tunnel. One of them punji sticks. Or he ran into it or something."

"Wow. Gee."

"It could've been worse. Them little VC make some wicked-ass booby traps. His was just a bamboo sliver, really. But it's a wound. It's worth a Purple Heart."

"So, wow. Was he a tunnel rat?"

"I don't know what he was. He ended up with the Lurps. Man—I used to hold him down and drip spit on his face. You know—drool it and slurp it back."

"Eew!" said both women together.

"That's how us sailors handle them Lurps."

"Eew!"

"Yeah. Ain't that the shits?"

"My husband divorced me," the mother said. "That feels the same as if he died. Except they don't give you a flag, and I still think about killing him every day."

"Is that your dad she's talking about?" Houston asked the girl.

"According to the doctors," she said.

As soon as her mother got up to visit the bathroom Houston said, "You want to go to a sleazy motel and watch some TV or something?"

"If you got the money, honey, I got the time."

"Look here. See what this is?"

"It's a Kennedy half a dollar."

"That's it, my life savings. I'll stick it up my ass for fifty more cents. I'll break a bottle over my head."

"I got the money, honey. I'm getting war insurance."

The girl leaned against him and touched her fingers lightly to his chest hair. The desert nights dipped well below fifty Fahrenheit, but Bill Houston went bare-skinned under a black leather jacket. His name on the street was Leather Bill. The rest of his wardrobe were jeans and boots wrecked by the abrasions of life.

"Better find the exit before Mom comes back," the girl said.

When he opened his eyes in the morning, it developed she'd found the motel's exit sometime earlier. A man with a mission would have rolled out first, and gone through her purse. Instead he'd snuggled down in dreams he couldn't remember.

He'd lived almost twenty-five years, his hardships colored in his own mind as youthful adventures, someday to be followed by a period of intense self-betterment, then accomplishment and ease. But this morning in particular he felt like a man overboard far from any harbor, keeping afloat only for the sake of it, waiting for his strength to give out.

When would he strike out for shore? When would he receive the gift of desperation? He stayed under the covers in the chilly, Lysol-smelling room until the management knocked on the door. He asked for ten minutes, showered, and went back to bed to wait for the knock that meant business.

James had a roommate, another veteran, a biker named Fred, and Fred's Harley, which occupied most of the living room. James noticed one day that his friend hadn't been around in a while, maybe in as long as a month or even two months, and as a way of summoning him back, if he was still alive, James perpetrated the mystical sacrilege of straddling Fred's Harley and turning the ignition key. Three kicks and it started explosively and sat beneath him growling and shuddering. He let out the clutch and it leapt straight into the wall and he found himself lying beneath it on the living room floor. He could hardly get the machine upright on his own—too much drinking and too much sitting around; he was a mess. No wonder he lost so many fights. But he enjoyed losing, enjoyed a sort of righteous lethargy while he curled in a ball and somebody kicked him in the head and back and legs, enjoyed lying with his face in his own blood while voices cried, "Stop it! That's enough! You're killing him! You're killing him!" because they were wrong. They hadn't come anywhere close to killing him.

1983

Hao brought the *New Straits Times* to the kitchen table and turned off the small electric fan in order to read. It wasn't, Kim understood, the fan's noise that disturbed him, but its interference with the pages. Each evening he sat here with Dr. Bourgois's morning edition of the *New Straits Times*, parsing out the news in English in his underwear, and, on Thursday or Friday, the doctor's *Asiaweek* as well. What was the point reading the newspaper each day in a place not your home? Even if you lived there? She didn't mind if he reported to her certain miscellaneous events, but she'd forbidden him to mention news of any obscene Malaysian celebrations. Kim was made uncomfortable by the Islamic influences around them, the crying of the mosques and the public ceremonies of circumcision for thirteen-year-old princes. However, this place suited her. Her vigor had returned—as if from her teens. Dr. Bourgois treated her with free medicines from his hospital, and Kuala Lumpur was full of Chinese herbalists who kept her in health. Several promised immunity to everything. She didn't want it. If illness didn't kill you, you died of bad luck.

Her husband stopped reading and raised his face to her. He reached for his empty teacup and looked down into it, as if a sudden need to examine it had stopped his reading.

Kim said, "What is it?"

"Nothing."

"It's something. Don't say it's nothing."

"Someone from Saigon."

She stood behind him. He covered part of the page with his hand, and she reached over his shoulder and moved it away. "The Canadian?"

"An American."

"No. It says 'Canadian.' I can read 'Canadian.' And 'Benét.'"

"He's not Canadian. And that's not his name. But I remember him. I knew him."

"Where? Here in Kuala Lumpur?"

"Back home."

"Then don't think about it."

Don't think about it? But I do. I think about luck . . . sorrow . . . gratitude . . . all mixed in a poison. And we drink it.

Luck and the sacrifice of others had brought them to live here in the servants' quarters behind the house of the physician from Marseilles. Kim did the laundry and sometimes went about the doctor's house dusting things, as she'd done all her life, though the doctor had other servants for that; and Hao drove the car. He took the girls to and from school and to piano lessons and dancing lessons. The young girls went to the American School and spoke very good English. With the parents Hao communicated in French. Dr. Bourgois walked a few blocks each day to and from the hospital where he worked as an administrator. Hao drove the wife to shopping, to the bridge club, and to the bookstores. All thanks to luck, and the sacrifice of others. But some of those others hadn't, themselves, chosen sacrifice. He'd chosen it for them. And there came sorrow. The trick he'd played Trung Than—the lowest thing he'd ever done. Yet not at all difficult. The Americans had made it easy. His most terrible crime, and where had it led? The Americans had thrown Trung into a prison camp and he'd come out a hero of the cause, with a house in Saigon and membership in the party. Historians came asking for interviews. Good for Trung. He'd dodged the wind. And Saigon was Ho Chi Minh City.

Some of those others had chosen sacrifice willingly, however, with the strength of their hearts; and there came gratitude. For the colonel. For the infantryman who'd thrown his helmet over the grenade and then himself over the helmet. And for the other Americans who'd helped them get away. The Americans had remembered, had kept their promises to him, and even to his country. They hadn't failed to keep such a promise. They'd simply lost the war.

And tomorrow, or the next day, he planned to tell Kim he'd had word from their nephew Minh—this through a Vietnamese family who ran a restaurant in Singapore, longtime emigrants who'd set a worldwide network going to make connections among scattered clans. Minh had survived—who knew what troubles he'd survived?—and lived close to Boston, Massachussets. Minh had located relatives in Texas who fished in the Gulf of Mexico, and they might be persuaded to help their Cousin Hao and his wife reach America. And there, again—luck. He'd chosen the right side. Lucky life!

His wife had started the gas, and the kettle trembled on the stove. He hadn't noticed. He'd thought she was still behind him, studying the face in the news.

She brought him the teapot. "What does it say?"

"He's in a lot of trouble."

"Is there anything you can do?"

"No. I knew him, that's all."

1/8/83

Dear Eduardo Aguinaldo,

You may have already gotten a letter from me. But assuming you haven't:

My name is William Benét. They call me "Skip." You, in fact, called me "Skip." Do you by any chance remember me? Let's just say I'm not the person I was back then, and leave it at that. But do you remember me?

I live a good deal in Cebu City. Lived. I haven't been there for two years, approximately. Around there they know me as "William Benét, the Canadian guy."

I have a family in Cebu City, a ~~woman~~ wife and three kids. Not a legal union. Look in on them, will you? Wife's name is Cora Ng. Her cousin owns the Ng Fine Store near the docks. The cousin can find her for you. Last time I checked I owned two buildings in the neighborhood. Cora can tell you which ones. She understands cash better than she understands real estate, so maybe you'd be good enough to handle the sale for her and see that she gets the money.

I know it's been a long time, Eddie. I know I'm imposing, but I don't know who else to ask. All the people I know are crooks, just like me.

If this is one of two letters you've received, forgive me for contacting you twice, but I'm not sure which one will reach you. It's no trouble for me writing an extra letter, I'll tell you that. I spend my time here writing letters I don't know how to address. The conditions are tolerable, washing up from a community bucket, eating rice with bits of fish, no maggots, the water tastes fine. It isn't exactly a Japanese prison camp in Burma. Remember The Colonel? Compared to his stories of "Kilo 40," this place is an afternoon at the Polo Club.

If you happen to run across any of our bunch from back then, I want you to tell them the Colonel never died. His body died, but he lives on in me. As for the ~~ones~~ folks who claim he never physically died and he's running around Southeast Asia with a dagger in his teeth and waving a bloody cutlass or something—they're wrong. He's definitely deceased. You'll just have to take my word for it.

These charges against me are going to stick. Whether they hang me or just keep me, I won't be running around loose in SE Asia again for quite a while. So see to my family, will you, old boy?

Your old Pal,
Skip
(William French Benét)

That he should mention the Polo Club! The letter came among a batch Eddie had taken to the club to peruse over lunch — an airletter, written in a very small hand and postmarked Kuala Lumpur, Malaysia. Charges? Hanging? For what? Eddie had heard nothing about it. He had a friend at *The Manila Times* who could perhaps see about all this. And the colonel, alive? He'd never had any report to the contrary, never any word of the colonel's demise. He wasn't in touch with any of "the bunch" from back then, but surely he would have known if the colonel had died.

How often he'd thought of Skip Sands. How seldom he'd done anything about it. He'd made no attempt to track him down. He associated Skip with the murder of the priest along the Pulangi River in 1965, by far the worst thing he'd done in his life, and the circumstances, war, duty, good intentions, made no difference.

Eddie left his table under the awning near the swimming pool and strolled through the restaurant to the bowling lanes. The man knew his shoe size without having to ask. A couple of kids bowled in the center lane, not doing too well with these duckpins, half the size of tenpins, and a ball without finger holes, held in the hand, hard to aim, and prone to little effect on the targets. After each turn a boy dropped from the darkness above the fallen pins to capture and resettle them. As a teenager Eddie had flung the ball hard and sent the pins flying in hope of catching one of those kids in the head with one, but they knew the game and stayed clear.

Eddie bowled a line in the low nineties, not unrespectable for duckpins, and drank 7Up and grenadine as he'd done when a boy. Six weeks ago, after a debauched New Year's Eve, he'd sworn off liquor.

He went up the stairs and through the lobby to the intercom and buzzed Ernesto in the drivers' shack and stood out front waiting. The grounds and the drive of the Polo Club hadn't changed in decades, and beyond the grounds, in the subdivision of Forbes Park, all was still well, but beyond Forbes Park chaos waited. The

quarantine of beautiful lawns and stately homes was massed about
with the choking city. He had plans to relocate. He was rich, he
could go where he wanted. He only lacked an idea where.

Imogene wasn't home. The children must be out of school by
now but off visiting, or looking for trouble.

In his office upstairs he sat at the desk, his chair turned toward
the window, and cradled a cup of coffee in his hands. He didn't
like coffee. He just drank it.

"A letter has come."

"What?"

Carlos, the houseboy. The formerly beautiful Imogene preferred he say "servant."

Carlos placed the envelope on his desk. "It comes from Mr.
Kingston. His driver brought it in the car."

Kingston, an American, lived nearby. The letter, he saw, came
from Pudu Prison and was addressed to Eddie care of Manila's
Canadian Consul. Kingston had clipped to it a note reading,
"This was given to me by John Liese of the Canadian Embassy. I
believe it's for you—Hank." The connection, Eddie guessed, was
that Kingston did a lot of business with Imperial Oil of Canada,
and Sands was masquerading as a Canadian.

12/18/82
Dear Eduardo Aguinaldo:

Mr. Aguinaldo, my name is William Benét. I'm currently in prison in Kuala Lumpur, awaiting sentencing on
gun-running charges. My solicitors tell me I should
expect to hang.

Mr. Aguinaldo, I'm dying and I'm glad. I imagine you at
the big window of a high-rise above the smog, looking
down on Manila floating like a dream in the fumes and
smoke, a jowly guy no doubt, big paunch, a guy I don't
know and who possibly doesn't remember me.

But I'm writing to you because you're the only one
who can deliver a message for me to the Eddie Aguinaldo

of eighteen years ago, the young Major who fought the Huks and dated rich young mestizas and who played Henry Higgins in "My Fair Lady"—do you remember?— and was the best thing in it. I've got nothing to say to anybody else. Nothing to report to the denizens of this era, the heirs to our lies. So I'm writing to Eddie Aguinaldo. The kindhearted Eddie Aguinaldo who took the time and the risk to send me a warning against the danger I'd already dived into in Cao Quyen in Vietnam, the soul-dissolving acid guys like me immersed ourselves in while we politely covered our mouths with handker- chiefs and complained about the DDT and the herbicides while our souls boiled away in something a lot more poi- sonous than poison.

I hope it surprises you to learn I lived in Cebu City from '73 to '81. Since then I've been nowhere very long- term until just a few months ago, when I was arrested in the Belum Valley, on the Malaysian side of the Thai bor- der. The wrong side, believe me, to get arrested on.

I'm currently in Pudu Prison in Kuala Lumpur. If your travels happen to take you out this way in the next few months, stop in and say hello. It would be nice to see a familiar face. You can gather I've come to end my life under a cloud. This has been embarrassing. Or it should be. But I don't feel particularly embarrassed.

Sincerely,
Skip
William French Benét

He looked again at the first letter:

. . . They call me "Skip." You, in fact, called me "Skip." Do you by any chance remember me? Let's just say I'm not the person I was back then, and leave it at that. But do you remember me?

—That one had come addressed to Eduardo Aguinaldo, Forbes Park, Makati, Rizal, Philippine Islands. No house number, no street address, but it had found him. And his name wasn't Eduardo. His name was Edward. As a kind of mockery between chums, Skip had called him Eduardo. Skip had mocked himself as well. Maybe under the Latin influence, in these islands named for a Spaniard king, he'd cultivated a silly mustache, and Eddie had called him Zorro. Certainly he remembered the young American with the crew cut and the mustache.

He stood by the window of his office and looked out on the pool, the bathhouse, the acacia dropping whirling blossoms on the lawn, and wondered if his happiest times hadn't come in his teens, when he was down here in Manila on holiday from the Baguio Military Institute, running wild in a city without limits; and in his mid-twenties, those patrols in the jungle with Skip Sands, the man from the CIA.

His window fronted none-too-sturdy-looking high-rises veiled, as Skip said he imagined, in fumes. Once the places with better views had looked out on fields of high coarse elephant grass, dirt roads, open spaces with a few tall buildings. The Rizal Theater had been visible from two miles off. All his life he'd lived in Forbes Park. At the edge of a burning field once he'd found a dead dog with newborn pups at her teats, and he'd taken the minuscule beasts home and tried to nurse them from an eyedropper. That's who he'd been once.

Recently he'd been struck with an idea for a wicked lampoon of *My Fair Lady*—a one-act, *The Wedding Night of Liza Doolittle and Henry Higgins*, with off-color lyrics set to the familiar melodies of "The Street Where You Live" and "I've Grown Accustomed to Her Face."

The trouble was that in this cultural environment such a show would be, like Liza Doolittle (as he imagined her for the purposes of this entertainment), unmountable. And for the same reasons: conformity, prudery, feminine cowardice. He felt himself unsuited for the climate of his times. He could only stand outside and laugh at his own class, the educated emulators of British and American manners—his wife, her father the good senator, all those people—a light scum of gentility floating on a swamp.

And everybody else, all his fellow Filipinos: a lot of superstitious maniacs, miracle-seekers, statue-worshippers, stigmata-bleeders, berserk flagellants running on Good Friday through province after province with dripping, self-inflicted wounds while others came out to beat them with sticks or soothe their gashes with water hurled from old soup cans, and a man in Cotabato Province who had himself crucified annually before his weeping neighbors in a church.

Skip Sands to the gallows. Me too.

Why the jolly hell not?

He thinks, I'm a jolly good fellow and an unhappy man.

Approaching the steps to Kuala Lumpur's Old High Court on the day of sentencing, Jimmy Storm looked up toward the second story and saw a number of women in bright dresses—secretaries, maybe—picnicking on a balcony, taking lunch with their rice bowls in the laps of their bright dresses. As they fed themselves they held the bowls up close to their faces, conversing, laughing, sounding almost as if they sang to one another.

On the top step he paused. He didn't know where to go. He consulted the day's printed agenda in its glass case while dropping his cigarette and grinding it out under his shoe, and then pushed through the great wooden doors of the Old High Court—Moorish in its architecture, tropic Colonial in its spacious interiors, reso-nant and shadowy, dwarfing and cooling the concerns of those who came here.

He took a seat in the rearmost pew of Courtroom Seven, where at 1:00 p.m. a Chinese gun dealer named Lau would be sen-tenced. Then, at 2:00 p.m., the prisoner calling himself William French Benét.

One yellow fire extinguisher. Twelve overhead fluorescent lights. A sign in Malaysian or whatever they spoke—DI-LARANG MEROKOK—which he took to mean "No Smoking." Eleven wall-mounted electric fans, should the central cooling fail. Storm doubted it ever would. Everything worked perfectly in Kuala Lumpur. People seemed competent and agreeable.

At the front of the courtroom, a lawyer in a gray suit sat at the defendant's table and examined the evidence against his client, spinning the cylinder of what appeared to be a Smith & Wesson Detective Special, cocking back the hammer and taking aim, for an empty, meditative moment, at the elevated bench from which, according to the agenda out front, Mr. Justice Shaik Daud Hadi Ponusammy would momentarily preside.

Except for Storm, the lawyer had the courtroom to himself. He aimed the pistol at the court secretary's empty desk, in particular at the sign on it reading DI-LARANG MEROKOK. He pulled the trigger, and the pin snapped.

Lunch was over. Storm heard footfalls echoing through the building. He stood up and went to a window with a view down into the driveway, where a blue van was arriving now from Pudu Prison. Lettering on its flank read POLIS RAJA DI MALAYSIA. Among the half dozen Chinese and Malay prisoners he could easily pick out the false Canadian Benét, his face looking white and small in the van's back window.

Storm took his seat again. A few people had scattered themselves among the pews by now, a half dozen reporters and a couple of spectators. The court's secretary came, and one security guard; and then Benét's barrister, Ahmed Ismail, entered the courtroom. He looked soft and favored, with the big, wet eyes of a child, arranging his papers before him in the shadow of the judge's looming bench. Very plush purple curtains covering the rear wall gave the courtroom the air of an old theater, and for a moment Ismail looked like a schoolboy, absurdly dressed in a black three-piece suit, coming to see a movie.

A staircase led up from the lower floor directly into the prisoner's box in the middle of the Old High Court, so that climbing it the accused, Lau, a Chinese boy looking around himself wildly, suddenly surfaced in the midst of his dilemma.

All stood for the entering Mr. Justice Ponusammy, who positioned himself behind a large ceremonial mace that rested on his desk. The prisoner leaned on the railing of his box, supporting himself with both bound hands.

All were seated.

They ran the court in English. The prisoner's lawyer explained his client didn't speak it and would use an interpreter. The boy had been convicted of dealing in firearms and of possessing a large quantity of ammunition. The judge went over the submissions, the precedents, and all the rest. The small man interpreting for the prisoner seemed nervous, sitting on his wooden chair beside the barrister and jiggling both his knees violently. When the judge addressed him he jumped up, and the prisoner also rose, though nobody had asked him to.

On hearing of his arrest, the Chinese boy's mother had killed herself by swallowing insecticide. "He does not yet know," his lawyer told the judge in English. The Chinese boy stood there oblivious. His interpreter failed to translate. "He will soon know, and that will perhaps be his biggest punishment."

Justice Ponusammy never once looked at the prisoner. He gave him six years and six strokes of the rattan cane, and three more years for the ammunition.

During the break, while they waited for the prisoner Benét to be brought up, Storm went forward and approached the lawyer Ismail. "My name is Storm."

"Mr. Storm. Yes."

"Your client. Benét."

"Yes."

"Is he coming up?"

"Yes, in five minutes' time."

"Can you give him a message for me? A message from Storm?"

"I think I can, yes."

"Tell Benét I'm completely capable of everything he fears."

"For goodness' sake, man!"

"Did you hear my words?"

"Yes, Mr. Storm. You say you are capable of everything he fears."

"Tell him I'll be at the prison tomorrow. Tell him it's Mr. Storm."

"Is it a metaphor?"

"Tell him."

When Storm had found his seat again in the back, the lawyer was still watching him.

Ismail turned away as his client Benét trudged up the stairwell from below them with his hands cuffed before him. He was in fact, and as Storm had believed, William Sands.

Like the previous prisoner, Sands supported himself on the railing of the prisoner's box as the judge entered and everyone stood up.

Sands still wore the short hair, and the mustache—no longer silly or affected, but long and derelict and grandiose, accentuating his sadness. His cheeks needed a shave. He wore a shabby blue sweater against the chill of central air-conditioning and seemed to be feeling somewhere between sulky and comatose. He was skinny and hollow-eyed and looked like he might even have a soul.

As soon as they'd all seated themselves again, the prisoner resumed his mindless down-staring. His head hanging. Really motionless. Slumped. Staring at his own face reflected in a cup of bitter karma.

For three-fourths of an hour the judge read words from a stack of documents, going over all the ins and outs, deliberating aloud to himself, from the sound of things. The Chinese youngster just sentenced had run guns for William French Benét; so had many others. The judge went over the list of counts on which Benét had been found guilty here. He referred to the prisoner as "a major dealer in illegal arms; a scourge on our lives; a trafficker in our very blood."

Storm realized the back pew was the wrong place. Nothing prevented him from getting up and sidling along the rows until he sat right behind the prisoner.

Sands turned around at the disturbance. Saw Storm. Recognized him. Turned away.

The judge looked small behind his gigantic desk. He called the prisoner "an imposter and a psychopath." He ordered the prisoner to rise and sentenced him to be bound with rope, flayed with a cane, and hanged by the neck until he was dead.

They had the Old High Court tricked out like a state capitol. But two blocks away was Little India, where Storm had taken a room. He walked upright through crowds kowtowing at his feet in the streets while public address systems screeched the Islamic afternoon prayers. Wild streetside commerce: a soothsayer lying on the asphalt on his back with a black kerchief covering his face, mumbling predictions. His partner chanted over a collection of rust-colored human bones, including a cranium, arranged on a red scarf around a white hen's egg. They were peddling tiny charms made out of gold foil from "555" cigarette packs and dirty string. The partner lifts the lid on a box, a six-foot cobra rises up, flaring its hood. He backs the cobra down with one of the powerful charms, dangling it in front of the reptile's hissing face. A man nearby displays a pile, a good five pounds, of teeth he's yanked successfully. They're all here from the demented corners of the Far East with their straw mats and immortality pills. Various elixirs for enlarging the human penis; also, for the same purpose, a somewhat frightening-looking device of belts and rings. And photo albums showing cases that have responded. Herbs, unguents. Concoctions of every sort. Medicinal roots preserved in glass jugs, floating like amputations.

He entered a small clothing store. Its atmosphere almost unbreathable with incense. Impossible to move in here without rubbing against the silk, the rugs. Outside, the mosque still shrieking. The Hindu women standing still and looking at him. Beautiful. Three of them. One stared hard and must have been the mother.

"I'm here to see Rajik."

"Mister is waiting," she said.

"Through here?"

"Yes. Again. Like yesterday." Yesterday? Her fantastically lovely face, and a deep coldness behind it. He hadn't seen her yesterday.

He passed through a curtain of painted beads, through its depiction of the god Krishna among bathing virgins at a waterfall, and into darkness.

"Come there . . . It's fine . . . Just here."

"I can't see."

"Wait for your eyes."

Storm moved with care toward Mr. Rajik's voice and sat on a cushion on a stool.

Mr. Rajik raised his hand to pull a string and ignite a constellation of dim Christmas lights behind him. He was an ordinary-looking Hindu man at a table with a tea service, no expression on his face. "I'll just make a few inquiries. Will you answer?"

"Ask me and see."

"In the period of the last week, or even a little longer . . . have you looked at any time to the place where your shadow would be seen, and yet you saw no shadow?"

"No."

"Have you seen a black bird?"

"Thousands. The world is full of black birds."

"And one that you noticed in particular? Because it didn't belong there—I might give you the example of a bird inside a house, or a black bird perching on your windowsill. A sort of thing such as that."

"No. Nothing like that."

"Have you seen something—any kind of object, any kind of . . . Again I'll use an example: You crumple up a piece of paper, and it resembles someone's head. Or a stain of some discoloration on the floor—something that resembles someone's face, the face of someone close to you in the past. Have you seen a thing like that in the last couple of weeks? A thing that suddenly showed you the face of someone close to you?"

"No."

"I am going to say a prayer for you. What will the prayer be?"

"You tell me."

"No, I can't be the one to tell you. It's not my place. It's your place to tell me what you would say if you spoke to God."

"Break on Through."

Mister was going to do a silence thing now. As if he didn't speak English.

"I can write it down for you."

Mister reached up and turned out the small lights. His hands rustled among his pockets and he struck a match and lit a stick of incense. The dark curved like a tunnel around them, like solid walls. Very sweaty nauseated hit now. "Gots to go, man, if you want to be fucking with me like this."

Mister blew out the match. Nothing now. "Your eyes." In twenty seconds the tiny red ember on the incense became visible, and the little eye that went with the voice, or the nose—this thing was the face, it was all he could see, and it was talking. "To break through—you are saying as through a boundary."

" 'Break on Through,' it's a song. It's my philosophy, my motto. You ask me for the word, that's the word I'm gonna have for you. Break on Through."

"Come back tomorrow."

"That's what you said last time."

Mister spoke without urgency, very gently. "Have I asked you for any money? Do you feel I'm not to be trusted? So I say to you, come back tomorrow. I can't give you today what I don't have today."

"Yeah. Yeah. Do what you have to do. Yeah."

As Storm came within a couple of meters of Pudu Prison's massive sheet-iron gate, he felt the heat of the morning sun banging off it into his face. The guard at the entrance slid a panel aside and peered at Storm out of the dimness of his cubicle, stared at his letter of introduction, which was in English, and made a phone call. Storm waited in the street for several minutes before the guard opened the man-sized metal door in the concrete wall.

A tall youth in civilian dress led Storm through the courtyard, where two dozen guards drilled for parade in green and purple uniforms. Ugly bastards. But soon they'd hang Skip Sands, so here's to them.

Storm stood outside the warden's office with the letter identifying him as a journalist named Hollis, the name on his Australian passport. A letter calling him a journalist wouldn't do him much good. He understood that. Storm had attached to it a note of his own, explaining to the warden that he also represented a charitable group and wanted to visit the prisoner strictly as a humanitarian, not as a reporter.

Manual Shaffee, director and warden of Pudu Prison, greeted Storm cordially. "I apologize once again very much," he said, "for our policy which prevents me from allowing you inside the prison." But Storm was already inside, here in Shaffee's office with the pictures of the nine sultans overpowering one wall, the air greenly lit by one circular neon tube overhead.

Shaffee was a little fat man of Indian descent with the pie-shaped and mustachioed face of a cartoon rodent and a jacket frogged with gold braid, and five different medallions on each mortarboard epaulet. Also, on his chest, ribbons. The impression he conveyed was one of idiotic sweetness.

"Are you a Muslim?" Storm asked.

"No."

Storm said, "I myself am a Christian, sir."

"So am I!" the warden said. "I am converted. Believe me, I don't like to hang people."

"Please give Mr. Benét this note, okay? I talked to his lawyer already, and I think I saw the prisoner give me a nod at the sentencing."

"It's completely against all regulations."

"I'm here in a humanitarian role. I'm asking you as one Christian to another."

The warden insisted Benét would refuse him in any case. He pronounced the prisoner's name as Benny. "Benny wants no visitors," he told Storm. "Benny was even rude to the Canada consul."

"What about his family?"

"Nobody comes. Canada is too far."

"Make sure he understands I'm the guy who talked to his lawyer. I think he'll see me."

"But Benny won't see you. I can only keep telling you that. Benny spit in the Canada consul's face. Doesn't that lead you to some conclusion about Benny?"

"I'm pretty sure he'll see me."

"He has refused all visitors. Otherwise I could help you."

But having fixed on this strategy, having made it Benét's refusal rather than his own, the warden now felt compelled to make Benét prove it.

"If you will please wait," he said, and dispatched a guard to talk to the prisoner. The warden lit a cigarette while Storm listened to the guards drilling out in the courtyard, in unison slamming their rifle butts down on the cracked concrete.

Sands and the guard stood together outside the door. Shaffee beckoned them with a tortured look.

Sands-Benét came in barefoot, wearing shorts and a T-shirt. And it was nice to see him looking so bad, wrecked in his eyes and skinny, nice to see him looking like a prisoner.

"Can I talk to him by myself?"

"No."

"Five minutes."

The warden's face shut, and Storm dropped it.

Storm said, "How's life?"

"Boring, mostly."

"Do you smoke?"

"I finally took it up."

"You got any cigarettes? These Malaysians smoke Three Fives, I think."

"Yeah," Sands said.

"I'll give a couple cartons to the lawyer."

"Thanks."

"He pretty good?"

"Good enough to get paid while I dangle."

"You understand the deal here. I'm just a humanitarian, a fellow English-speaker."

"I get it."

"Benny's consul came to see him," the warden said, "and he spit."

"You're my first visitor."

"Try spitting at me."

Sands stared at his bare feet.

"Warden Shaffee's a nice guy," Storm said. "That's why he's letting me talk to you. He wants to make sure you're comfortable."

"The thought of getting out of here would comfort me."

"Not possible, man. You've been found guilty and sentenced, and there's no fooling around here. Eighty-three people have been convicted under the new gun laws, and eighty-two have hanged."

"I know the numbers."

Storm asked: "And how do you feel about hanging?"

"No comments!" Shaffee said, though nobody had asked him.

Benét shrugged. "Hey, at this point, it's okay by me."

"No comments," Shaffee repeated. "But I am a Christian. I think you know my answer."

Storm took a step closer to Benét. "It's time to think about your soul."

"Don't be daft!"

"I'm offering you a chance to clear your conscience."

"I haven't got a conscience," Sands said.

"So hanging doesn't make you shit?"

"I've lived too long already."

"What about Hell, you fuck?"

"We'll have time to discuss that later. You and I. Lots and lots of time."

"Benny's got books. He has all kinds of reading matter. He has a Bible," the warden said.

Sands stared at his own ugly bare feet and spoke very softly.

"What did he say? What was that?" the warden said.

Storm said, "Tell me who to see."

"For what."

"Old Uncle."

"He's dead, man. He's dead."

"Yeah? So were you, supposedly."

"And soon I will be again."

Shaffee's unease was palpable now. He indicated the guard: "I have a witness. I am nearing retirement in a few months. I could get in a lot of trouble." But he did nothing to stop this. He seemed incapable of the slight rudeness needed, at this moment, to enforce prison policy.

Storm stepped closer. "Will you pray?" He bowed his head. "Dear Lord," he said loudly, and then more softly, "I know you've got family in the PI. And I can find them."

He stepped back and watched the prisoner shake like a toy until even the stupid warden noticed: "He's sick? What's wrong?"

"It's the power of his conscience," Storm said.

"Here," the warden said. "Sit down. Yes. The struggle."

Now Warden Shaffee and Storm stood there like a couple of prisoners, and it was Sands sitting in the warden's chair.

Sands gripped the edge of the desk with both hands and

looked back and forth from one hand to the other. "Ju-shuan, or something like that. He runs a trap up in Gerik. They call him Mr. John, or Johnny."

"Give me directions."

"You don't need directions. He grabs every Euro who comes off the bus."

"And he's the man to see."

"If you feel the need."

"See him for what?" the warden said. Not that he didn't get it. He got it, he got the whole thing, but he just wouldn't let himself see he'd made a mistake.

Shaffee had already failed to prevent this conversation. The best he could hope for now was to dominate it. "The two Australians who were executed got no help from their embassy," he remembered now. "We've had a lot of foreign prisoners—drugs traffickers and those such people," he said. "I've never seen an embassy take so much interest. The Canadians are very helpful to Benny. Benny's got books, things like that."

"You're gonna hang," Storm told the prisoner, "but life goes on and everything plays itself out. Inside of every cycle is another cycle. You know what I mean?"

"I hear what you're saying, man. But I don't know what you mean."

Storm leaned close over Sands and said, "It's just a machine. Relax."

"As long as you leave my family out of it."

Shaffee said, "We are civil servants. Please. We have our rice bowls, we want to keep them filled."

"You're not who you think you are," Storm said. "You're dead inside."

Sands said, "Look, whatever kind of revenge you want—you're not gonna get it."

"Things have to play themselves out."

Sands stood up. "We didn't pray." He beckoned him close.

The warden said, "I am a Christian too. An Anglican. I pray for Benny. He's a bit psychotic. Depressed. But he's more cheerful the last few weeks."

Sands bowed his head, almost touching his brow to Storm's, and hit him with an uppercut below the sternum. Storm's legs gave in and a lot of tadpoles raced around his field of vision. He said, "Yow, daddy."

Shaffee helped to hold him upright. "Are you sick? What is the problem sir?"

Neither the prisoner nor the visitor bothered replying.

The pause in communication seemed hard on Shaffee. He had to talk. "The Red Cross gave us the kind of report I would call useful. Yes, we have areas in this prison to be improved. Hygiene, diet, I appreciated their suggestions. But not the Amnesty International! For instance we have Chinese gangs. If we don't lock up the members without bail, they'll be out where they can reach the witnesses. The people making the report for Amnesty International didn't understand this. They gave us a very bad report. So you see why we don't want reports. Why should we allow it? We don't want you if you are a humanitarian," he said. "We don't want you if you are a journalist. You are not a Christian. I know what a Christian looks like because I myself am already a Christian." This speech had given him strength. "Get out!" he cried. He turned to the guard: "Yes! This man is not permitted here!"

Thirty minutes later Storm was eating a rib-eye steak in a place with bamboo décor but with an Anglo name—Planter's Inn Pub—listening to a wrenchingly beautiful lament played on native flutes which slowly became recognizable in its sadness as an old Moody Blues tune: "Nights in White Satin."

He'd already tried Phangan, the low-rent druggy island resort east of Thailand—but that one flopped. A lot of retrograde hippies with melted eyes, rip-off Indian ganja freaks, various bits of psychedelic European burn-off. Airheads. Just air. He couldn't deal with them.

This after his escape from the Barnstable County Jail in Massachusetts: one day a door had simply stood open—surely the Agency's doing, and likely the colonel's—and he'd walked away.

This after the great sea battle, the only firefight of his life, in which the Coast Guard had sunk his boat and many tons of Colombian ganja, and shot one and drowned another of his crew of three Colombians.

In Bangkok he'd heard the colonel might be buying and processing raw opium in the region. He moved down from Bangkok where the whores were friendly and zoned on chemicals to Kuala Lumpur where the whores performed with the bloodless efficiency of automatic shoe-shine machines. Kuala Lumpur, a name somehow connoting limpness and no warmth, like Cold Lump. A decaffeinated town, clear, acrylic brains, the precise opposite of Phangan. Air-conditioning that could reasonably be described as brutal, everybody seemed to have a respiratory condition. Very Western, very modern, kind of an Asian Akron, Ohio, with cut-rate prices, tropical fruit, and everybody driving on the left . . . He'd seen the photo of William Benét in the *New Straits Times* and had realized that along the way a sort of psychic and spiritual gravitation had guided his every footstep and that he had bested the Assassin, survived the Smugglers, transcended the Prison, wandered among the Fools, and that he would confront the Hanged Man or the Betrayer—Sands would be revealed for what he was—and that the colonel was now possible.

Storm stayed in Kuala Lumpur long enough to get a tattoo and make sure Sands really did hang. He stayed at a spittoon for humanity in Little India called the Bombay, just over a money changer's. They gave him a small blue electric fan and a white towel but no soap. He could listen to seven radios at once through the quarter-inch plywood walls.

The cheap hotels were short. You were always close to the

street in these places, almost down in it. The whistles and exclamations, the baby-voiced horns.

The hallways of the Bombay reeked thickly but not unpleasantly of curry and Nag Champa incense. In the dawns after first prayer call he could smell bread baking on the still air. Then the diesel smoke overpowered everything, rising with the urban noise. Each cycle held another cycle. You could not break out of the machine.

He spent the mornings reading from a Bible defiled by some Muslim with a Magic Marker. Or listening to the radio. In his speeches the prime minister stressed emotional tranquillity.

Or he wrote in his notebook. Efforts in verse. He admired the poet Gregory Corso, a man who spewed out genius by the ream. As for himself, a line now and then. You can't extort the Muses.

Or he read from his copy of *Zohar: the Book of Splendor*. He'd picked it up in an English bookshop years ago, in Saigon, before the fates had renamed it Ho Chi Minh City—

Rabbi Yesa said: Adam comes before every man at the moment he is about to leave this life, in order to declare that the man is dying not because of Adam's sin, but on account of his own sins.

—read until his focus loosened and the lines of text divided into duplicates and floated on the page.

Half awake, he dreams himself coming to the colonel at the end: and the colonel says: You know there is a cycle of imagining and desire, desire and death, death and birth, birth and imagining. And we have been tempted into its mouth. And it has swallowed us.

He imagined the look in the colonel's eyes as he witnessed Storm breaking a cycle just for the curiosity of breaking it.

He traveled the city not allowing himself to desire the women— their silk touching past him in tight aisles, on buses, in cafés.

On his fourth visit to Rajik, the Hindu gave Storm his answer, speaking again with an immense gentleness. "You cannot be healed. You are forbidden to hope for it. You cannot be saved."

Four days after the hanging Storm took a deluxe bus with air-conditioning and even TV to the end of the line, the end of the highway itself, in Gerik, a sizable, complicated town of wooden structures and dirt streets. It was nighttime when he disembarked. He walked among the vendors' tables in the square where the buses stopped.

Sands had been right: immediately Ju-shuan accosted him. A squat, heavy man. He wore shorts, a large T-shirt. Walked crab-footed in his zoris.

"Hey, I'm glad you came. Call me Mr. John, okay?"

"Mr. John okay."

"Want mas-sage? Want woman?"

Storm said, "Do you have boy massage?"

"Boy massage? Hah! Yes. You want boy?"

"Is that too twisted for you, Johnny?"

"Boy, girl, fine. Anything."

"Girl is fine."

"Girl massage, fine. You gonna stay at my hotel, okay? Two blocks. You are American? Germany? Canada? Everybody stays at my place."

"Let me get some food."

"I got food in my café."

"I'm gonna get some fruit."

Storm went among the vendors' tables. He bought a couple star fruits. A mango. Johnny followed him.

"You want coconut?"

"I'm done."

"Then you can have some dinner, and then whatever you want. I get you the lady for the mas-sage."

"Dinner later. Woman first," Storm told him.

As they went into Johnny's, he pointed out to Storm the

establishment next door. "Don't stay in that place," he said. "Don't go there. It's a bad place." It looked pretty much the same as Johnny's.

Johnny put him in a room with a straw tatami on its wooden floor and a Muslim toilet with a rubber hose. "Wait one half hour," Johnny told him.

"Don't bring me one that doesn't smile."

Johnny brought the girl in twenty minutes. "Smile," he told her in English.

"I think I know your friend," he said to the girl when Johnny was gone.

"Mr. John is my friend."

"I think his name is Ju-shuan."

"I don't know Ju-shuan. I never heard Ju-shuan."

She too was Chinese. Thick of flesh and friendly. She smelled of the joss-house, of incense. Possibly on the way over she'd stopped to pray, or to contribute. Not, he hoped, to consult the monks as to some ailment.

"You seem sad," he said.

"Sad? No. Not sad."

"Then why don't you smile?"

She gave him a brief, sad smile.

Later Storm ate out front of Johnny's hotel at a small wooden table under an awning, on the street itself, under a paper lantern, in a storm of moths and winged termites.

He shared the table with a Malaysian man who tried to talk to him in English.

"Don't bother me now, Maestro."

"Whatever you say. I'm all yours!"

Except for the small lantern over their heads and a few dim-lit doorways, all around them was darkness—damp, warm, stinking like breath.

Out of it materialized a skinny European, a young man with an angularity both boyish and plainly British, coming at them like a horror-film mummy, his belt cinched and his khakis puckered at the waist, the crown of his head wrapped in dirty bandages.

He sat down at the table and said, "Good evening. How can I get served?"

Johnny joined them and introduced himself and ordered food for the traveler and conversed in Malay with the other man until, after a while, the other man finished his tea and left. "He doesn't know English. He is a relative from my wife," Johnny explained. He urged on them more bowls of rice mixed with a green lemony weed and bits of shellfish, or crisp pork, Storm couldn't tell which. "What happened to your head?" Johnny asked his new guest. "You're okay now, I hope."

The young man had been going at his meal seriously, surrounded by whirling bugs. He stopped long enough to say, "Last week I was in Bangkok, just passing through, and I stepped into an open sewer."

He went back to his eating. He ate everything. They always did. In the Colombian mountains Storm had once seen a Brit eat cattle tripe tenderized in kerosene, eat it like a starving man.

"Pitch-black. Walking along. Right into a concrete ditch. There wasn't a lot of wonderful stuff in there, I might as well tell you. I've been monitoring my symptoms ever since." He spoke mainly to Storm. "I fainted right in the guck, with an open gash in my head. At this minute I picture an invading horde of microbes assaulting my skull. I took myself to the nearest surgery in a cab and the young nurse told me, You should carry a small light with you wherever you go wandering. A small light. She told me when I came, and again when I left with a head full of stitches. Wherever you go wandering, take a small light. Sounds rather like a line from a musical play."

Johnny said, "I can meet you to a healer. A woman. Mas-sage. To heal you."

"I like the Asians," the Brit said. "As a general thing I find I like them quite a lot. They don't play games the way we do. Of course,

I mean, they do the same things we do, but they aren't games. They're simply there. They're simply actions."

"This your first visit?"

"But not my last. And you?"

"I've been in and out since the sixties."

"Really. Impressive. In Malaysia, then?"

"Yeah. The general region."

"What about Borneo? Have you been?"

"Borneo is not good," Johnny said. "Don't go there. It's ridiculous."

"I've got a torch now, you can bet. And it's no small light. Look here." He dug a small but hefty-looking flashlight from the pocket of his pants. "Bore a hole in your flesh." He pointed it playfully at a little child hovering at the edge of the dark. "Bore a hole in your flesh with this one!"

"Please don't give him any coins," Johnny said.

"No, I wouldn't," the Brit assured him. "I've got too many friends in this town as it is."

"You have a lot of friends here?" Johnny said.

"I'm just playing a game," the young man said. To Storm he remarked, "You see? Mr. John doesn't play games."

Johnny asked, "Are you a sightseer?"

"I am when I haven't got thirty stitches in my head."

"You are a sightseer. I can get you a guide to the forest tomorrow."

"Give me a rest. Two days and I'm ready for Kilimanjaro."

"What about you?" Storm asked Johnny. "Do you hire out as a guide?"

"Sure, if you want," Johnny said. "But we'll go slow, and I can't climb the mountain. Just to visit the caves at the Jelai River. I'll show you the caves, and that's all."

"That might work out."

"There is one small mountain we must pass."

"I'll think about it."

"The mountain is nothing. It's just more of the same thing—up, up, up. Are you a sightseer? Maybe we'll see an elephant."

"I said I'll think about it."

The young man with stitches in his head said: "I met a missionary in Bangkok. He told me to go by Psalm 121—'I lift mine eyes unto the hills.' I told him I'm a pagan. He insisted I read Psalm 121 every day while I'm traveling. So. Was he playing a game? Why tell me something like that?" He filled his bowl once more. Storm watched him eat.

"Because it was a message."

"A message, indeed. But who was the message for?"

Storm didn't tell him who the message was for.

Johnny said, "I don't like talking about religious things. It makes two people unfriendly."

"No, Mr. John," the Brit said, "we're not going to argue, not about religion. It's too boring."

"What about a woman for you tonight? What about a mas-sage?"

The Brit looked disturbed by this talk and said, "We'll mention it later, all right?"

The next day Storm engaged Johnny to guide him into the government-owned forest. Three blocks from Johnny's hotel they stepped into an open twenty-foot motorboat and were piloted up the Jelai River through a light rain by a man draped in several clear plastic bags.

"This man is from the primitives," Johnny said. "But he is living in the city now, with us. We'll meet his relatives, his clan. The government supports them. They live like a thousand years ago."

They traveled upstream. The river flat, sinewed, brown. They said nothing. The outboard engine's small clatter. Stink of its smoke. The town receded. At first, some occasional dwellings alongside their progress, then none.

Many miles upriver the two passengers stepped from the boat onto a wooden pier that seemed to serve no nearby village or any habitation at all.

"Where the fuck is he going?" They watched the boat head into deeper water and turn back downriver.

"He wants to see his people. He will be back. When we come at suppertime, he will be here."

Storm tied a bandanna around his brow. They hefted their packs and took to the worn trail, Johnny leading, skirting frequent large cakes of elephant droppings sprouting tiny mushrooms. Somebody lived here: the wild rubber trees had been scored in spirals, and sap dripped into wooden bowls tied to the trunks at knee-level.

On the flap of Johnny's large backpack was emblazoned an American flag. Storm watched it moving through the jungle, floating over the trail. In his own small pack he carried only cigarettes and matches and his notebook and socks and bandannas, all wrapped in a plastic bag, and a flashlight. And batteries. There was no use carrying a gun. You were always outnumbered.

The rain stopped. It didn't matter—sweat or rain, he'd be wet. "Your name is Ju-shuan."

"Ju-shuan?"

"So I was told."

"Ju-shuan? That is a nonsense noise. Ju-shuan is not a Chinese name."

They were climbing, and they were breathing hard, but Johnny stopped for a quick smoke.

The trail made its way along the side of a cliff. They remained standing, looking down on the rough green canopy and the brown Jelai River cutting through it.

Johnny asked him, "What is your name?"

"Hollis."

"How old are you?"

"I'm forty-plus."

"Forty-plus," Johnny said, "forty-plus." A bit later he said, "Forty-plus."

"That means I'm more than forty."

"Forty-one. Forty-two. Forty-three."

"Forty-three."

"Forty-three years old."

"Yeah."

Johnny mashed his cigarette into the earth with the heel of his black sandal. "I know you."

"Sure you do. And you knew Benét."

Johnny's eyes searched around for a lie. He tried candor: "I knew him, sure."

"He's dead. They hanged him."

"Of course, I know, it's a famous case. That's what I mean. I heard about him from the newspapers, that's all."

He began climbing again, Storm close behind.

"Why don't you talk? I have a lot of information about the region. Why don't you ask me?"

"When I'm ready, I'll ask."

After half a kilometer they stopped again to rest. The trail was narrow here and they could only lean against the cliffside. "There is the top. Then we'll go down, and at the bottom we'll find the caves."

Storm lit a cigarette.

"I said seven and you came at seven," Johnny said. "You're very on-the-dot." His face was not the inscrutable kind. He looked perplexed and desperate.

"That's me."

"I didn't sleep correctly," Johnny told his patron. "I felt my soul departing from me in the night. Did you know that I pray? But in the past few days, nothing has gone correctly. When I pray, I see no shadow on the wall—but I am not superstitious."

"You're babbling."

Johnny pointed to an outcropping on a bluff across the gorge: "I see my father's face in that rock."

Storm made no answer, and they resumed hiking, Johnny still in the lead, his head turned three-quarters now at all times toward Storm behind him. "Look, I'm telling you two things," he said as they walked. "I don't know Benét and also my name is not Ju-shuan."

When they gained the ridge Johnny shed his pack and sat down beside it. "It's too heavy. I have a small tent inside. After the caves we can camp. I have the food. Do you want some fruit?"

Storm devoured a mango and scraped at the seed with his teeth. The clouds had parted. The sunshine crashed heavily down on them and turned the canopy below a lively pulsing green and glinted sharply on the river far below. It was his first time in real jungle. He'd never seen the bush during the war except from helicopters high overhead. Spongy and multifariously green, like this, only sometimes with tracers rising out of it, or under flares at night.

"We must get a stick. If it's too wet, we can slip going down."

Each found a staff, and they headed down to the caves. At the bottom Johnny showed him a square-meter hole in the base of the cliff. "The natives took the boys here to be changed into men. To go inside you have to be born for a second time. You'll see. That's why they chose it. You'll see. But first, are you hungry?"

They sat on a log and ate rice out of plastic baggies with their fingers while an angry monkey tossed dirt and bark down onto them from the cliff above. "It's always good to eat," Johnny said. "Now we'll go inside. We must leave our belongings."

Storm crouched before the hole. Pebbles dribbled down in front of his face—the monkey still at it up the cliff. He shone his light: the aperture narrowed within. "Bullshit."

"It's quite safe. No one is here to steal from us."

"It's a little fucking tube, man."

"We can do it easily. I will go. It turns to the left. When you don't see my light, you come, okay?" He went down on all fours grunting and crawled forward scraping his flashlight along the floor. Storm squatted at the entrance looking after him. In seconds Johnny's light was gone around a tight bend. Storm followed on hands and knees. The beam from the torch in his hand leapt at the walls and flashed up at his face. After the bend he saw Johnny's light pointing back at him. Within a few yards he had to stretch out and wriggle through the passage with his arms to his sides, flashlight directed backward, head laid flat. In Chinese Johnny talked to himself. Storm had to blow out his breath to go on, but he couldn't see how to back out, and anyway the fat bastard had made it through and he had to stay with him—he'd do anything to keep with him and reminded himself that he didn't care whether he lived or died. He slid face first through darkness, incredibly swiftly. Light bloomed around him. Johnny stood in a chamber whose walls lay too far off to see. With Johnny's help Storm rose carefully from the slick floor but could hardly keep his feet under him. Johnny whispered, "Quiet, please."

He shone his light upward. Bats covered the high ceilings like a shaggy carpet of drooping leaves. Tens of thousands of them.

Johnny snapped his fingers once, and each bat shivered slightly where it clung—the collective noise like that of a locomotive charging past. The blast died quickly, but the darkness seemed to resonate now with a certain life.

"Look where they scratched the rocks. The natives."

Storm examined a few barely discernible markings in the circle of the flashlight's glare, nothing he could make sense of.

Johnny moved his light among the vague symbols and asked, "What does it say?"

"What? I don't know."

"I thought you knew. Maybe you know about these people from your university."

Storm laughed. It came out of him like a shot, and the bats roared again.

He clutched his light in his armpit and wiped slick goo from his palms along the backs of his pants legs. "What is this shit?"

"Yes. It's the guano. From the bats."

"Goddamn. How far do these caves go?"

"This is the only cave. We can go out the other side."

"Fuck me. You mean there's an easier way?"

"Only to go out. We have to drop out a small hole, but it's easier than going back. Very easy to drop. But you can't climb inside that way. It's too slippery."

"Well, fuck, man, let's go."

"This way." Johnny moved ahead of him very slowly toward an emptiness that soon produced out of itself a wall, and next a hole in the wall somewhat larger than the one they'd come in by.

"Me first," Storm said.

They only had to duck their heads to stay moving now, but the footing was almost impossible. Storm saw no bats in the passage, though their shit was everywhere.

Johnny's light wavered and tumbled to the floor. Storm took two careful steps backward and retrieved it and found Johnny on his back and dropped the instrument beside him.

"I can't see you," Johnny said.

Storm unsnapped the knife from his belt and shone his own light on it. "Can you see this, fucker?" He crouched and raised the hem of Johnny's T-shirt with the knifepoint.

"What are you doing?"

He trained the beam on Johnny's face and Johnny squinted and looked away. "I want to know what you're doing."

"I'm going to carve some fat off your belly."

"What are you doing! You act crazy!" In the chamber down the tunnel the bats roared.

"I'm going to skin you bit by bit. I'm going to throw the pieces in a pile there, and you can watch the monkeys eat the pieces. Meanwhile, the ants are eating you."

"You're crazy!"

"Assume I'm not."

"Money! Money! I can get you!"

"You said you know Benét."

"Yes, it's bad to be executed. But you have to see it was a badness of fate that put him there. It was a terrible position."

"Welcome to the position."

"But I have nothing to do with that!"

"Let's get back to your current position."

Johnny talked a little in Chinese, and then sounded as if he were answering himself. "Okay. I know. I know what you want."

"Then give it to me."

"This—please listen—this was not because of me, sir. Please understand."

"You're gonna talk to me."

"Let me shine my light."

"Keep that thing off me."

"Just to the side." Johnny shone his light on the wall. He raised his head and searched very carefully for some sign of a future in Storm's face. "Can I please say one thing to you? We are all one family."

"Johnny. Where's the colonel?"

"Oh, for the love of God, the colonel. Yes. Tell me what you want. He's not far. Only in Thailand, across the border. You can go straight there by the trails. Let's go back to the town, and I'll get you sorted out. Whoever takes the rubber trail to those villages in the Belum Valley, he can find the colonel easily. Anyone knows that."

Storm backed off two paces and sheathed his knife. "Get up."

"I can get up. I can do it easily!" He rose with a lightheartedness Storm recognized from having survived, himself, when he thought the Coast Guard would murder him. Johnny led the way another forty meters to a brilliant hole in the floor.

Storm dropped his flashlight through the opening and followed it, feet first, and dropped two meters down into the daytime. Johnny's feet dangled above him and he gripped the leg of the fat man's shorts as he lowered himself until his arms were stretched full length above his head, his hands gripping rock, and let himself fall. He smiled stupidly and shook his head.

Storm said, "Let's go."

He stayed close to Johnny while they made their way around the mountain and back to the place where they'd taken lunch.

"Here we are!" Johnny said. "You see?" he said as if in demonstration of an important truth.

"I need a map."

"Of course! Of course! I have maps at my hotel."

"What's in your pack?"

"Of course! I forgot I have a map in my pack!" He squatted and tore open the flap and hauled out his baggies of grub, a blue poncho, a three-meter swatch of colorful fabric which unrolled around him and which he explained was his blanket, and handed Storm a ragged map folded all wrong. "Unfortunately the writing is Malay. But you just want to take the rubber trail and speak to the headmen along the way. Someone will guide you."

Storm spread the map out on the ground. "Show me."

"We will go back to town. Tomorrow you can hire a car to this place. Then it's no more road. The motorcycle can take you."

"Is this the Thai border?"

"Yes, but here is the village you will go to."

"I don't see a village."

"It's there. I can't make a mark. There's no pen."

Storm did his best to get the map into compact dimensions and jammed it into his own pack. "Let's go."

They shouldered their packs and walked. Climbing the hill they didn't speak. It wasn't as far uphill this way as it had seemed coming out. Storm dogged him while they passed along the ridge, and preceded him going down the other side. Even on the downhill side Johnny breathed heavily and had nothing to say.

When they'd reached the trail along the river, he seemed more certain of his position. "You gave me a concern! But we're getting along now."

"Not if you fucked me."

"Of course I don't do that. We're friends."

"Bullshit."

"I believe it! We are friends!"

In a place where the muddy river ran level with its banks they stopped to wash the guano away.

"I won't run off," Johnny said, wading out. "So you can trust me. Anyway it's too far to the other side. And there—I see a crocodile."

Immediately he launched out. Storm watched him flounder the hundred feet across the water. He hit a deep spot and flailed at the current, taking buoyant leaps sideways downstream, finding his footing at last and grappling with the vegetation and hauling himself out to rest on all fours, drenched and shrunken, raising his head, gasping for breath, lowering it again. He didn't look back at Storm.

Storm watched for only a few seconds, then turned and hurried down the trail to meet the boatman before Johnny did.

All the while he hiked downriver he asked himself: Why did I mention the colonel before he did? I gave him his cue. He might have sent me chasing anything.

He sat on the straw tatami at Johnny's hotel taking off a sock stained brown with his own blood. He'd daubed the leech bites with river mud, but he'd missed one.

Johnny's old woman came around the corner of the hall stirring up the dust with a three-foot broom. "Ah! You back!"

"Ain't it the truth."

"Where is my husband?"

"Still with his friends in the jungle."

"Then Johnny he staying another longer maybe?"

"Yeah. Like that."

"You want tea?"

"No. I want a car to the border."

"You have money?"

"I'm the richest person you'll ever meet."

"I get you a car tomorrow morning. You got some friend in Thailand?"

"I sure do."

"Your friend is waiting."

"It's a definite possibility." He stared at her, searched her face. But he didn't feel it yet. So much closer, and he didn't feel it. "I think I'll change hotels," he said.

For a dozen miles by the blurred odometer he rode shotgun in a Morris Minor. At a bridge over a river he didn't know the name of, his driver asked for the fare and put him out, refusing further risk. The bridge's weather-eaten boards looked rotten. Storm offered more money but the man said, "Can you buy me one new car?"

"Coward. Fuck your mother," Storm said.

He hitched a ride atop a pile of kindling on a modified pedicab driven by an old man and pulled by an animal that might have been a donkey and might have been a stunted horse. Storm wore cutoff jeans, and the kindling chafed his underthighs. He carried nothing better in his pack, no change of clothes, only his flashlight, knife, and a plastic poncho; and his notebook and Johnny's map. They stopped at a village two or so miles along, where Storm tried to barter with the old woodman for further assistance, but without any luck. Sapling rubber trees had invaded the roadway ahead, and his woodcart couldn't pass. Locals came to the doorways of the hooches to stare. A man approached Storm, hesitated just out of reach, and stomped boldly forward one more step to touch the stranger's arm. People screamed. The man turned away laughing.

Storm didn't know how far he'd have to walk to reach the border. Less than twenty kilometers, if he read the map correctly.

The old woodman came from behind one of the hooches with a flat-faced, staring young man walking a motorbike. The boy kicked its pedal and straddled it and started off so quickly Storm doubted he expected a passenger, but he leapt on behind him anyway, shouting, "Where you go? Where you go?" It sounded as if the boy said, "The Road." As they made for the habitation's edge an old woman, face bursting, shouting and moaning, threw herself into the dirt in front of the bike—the brakes yelped, Storm

pitched forward, his lips touched the driver's hair. The boy stuck
his legs out and tried to get around her but she spun like a swimmer, kicking in the dirt, to block his way. Storm lurched from
side to side as they rolled over her with each tire in turn and she
said, "Hm! Hm!" People in doorways cried out at them—people
laughing—a child came out and spit at them. Storm felt the wind
string the saliva out along his bare thigh as they accelerated. He
clutched at leaves on a tea plant and scoured the spit away as they
rounded the bend out of town. The road was red gouged mud.
Sometimes a great puddle slowed them as the boy skirted it, sticking out his feet for balance.

Ahead grew mostly rubber trees. A carpet of leaves covered the
track there. Light washed down among the trees. The bike
thumped twice over a thick snake with brilliant bands. The road
narrowed to a trail and they bucked continually over roots, the
small engine buzzing like a horn, sounding that insignificant, that
drowned amid all this organic life. Three hours, four hours, but
they didn't stop for lunch, or even water. Storm kept low behind
the boy's shoulders as the trail narrowed and slender branches
whipped across the boy's face. The boy wiped continually at his
face and his arm came away each time bloodier. He pressed on
shouting, weeping. They scraped forward almost entirely in the
lowest gear. Storm smelled his rubber shoe sole burning on the
tailpipe and repositioned his heels on the struts, but in such a way
that they kept slipping off.

By one in the afternoon it was quite dusk in the tall woods and
the road was almost impossibly glutted, no more than a path, and
then they came into daylight, open spaces, gray elephant grass,
emerald rice paddies. Here the path crossed a dry streambed with
sheer six-foot walls. The motorbike couldn't pass.

They dismounted and the boy ran the machine some yards off
the path into the high grass and let it fall there on its side, and fell
with it himself. He jumped up quickly and came away wiping at
his face. Blood spiraled down his forearm where he'd gashed it
badly in the tumble. He noticed his injury and smiled at Storm

and then suddenly sobbed angrily. Storm took hold of his arm. "Unwrinkle your soul, man. You ain't dead. Fuck," he said, "it's deep." He untied the bandanna from his brow to bind the wound and had hardly finished knotting its ends when the kid turned to lead the way again. They clambered down one side of the creek and up the other. Storm tried him—"Kid. Kid. I want to give you money, money"—but the boy didn't answer or pause, and they continued along the dikes of paddies and into a village where everything stirred in the afternoon wind.

On the porch of a wooden home stood a man in brown slacks and a blue shirt, like anyone on the corner of any city. "Welcome to you! Come in for some teatime and I will show you my specimens."

"We need water."

"Come into my museum. Please. Come."

He ushered them into something on the order of a café without chairs, only several tables with big jars standing on them. He lifted a large one, in it a brown insect as long as his forearm, maybe, if it hadn't been curled like a bracelet and floating in what looked like old piss. "I have quite a collection of insects. This centipede killed a thirteen-year-old boy."

"What about some water."

"Do you want me to boil it first? Because you are American." His eyebrows pulled apart and crashed together as he talked. Bug eyes and fat lips. Big forehead. Except for the fat lips, he resembled one of his specimens.

"Just fill my jug. Please, I mean. I got the shit to fix it with."

The strange man took Storm's canteen through the doorway into his kitchen, in which a cot and stove were visible, and immersed it in a galvanized washtub and held it under. Storm followed him, twisted the dripping canteen from his grasp, and dosed it with two tabs. He screwed shut the lid and shook it. "Fuck, I'm thirsty."

"I believe it, yes," said the man.

They stood among the specimens, and Storm drank off half in

a series of violent swallows and handed the canteen to the kid,
who drank briefly, exhaled and inhaled deeply as it came away
from his mouth, and grimaced in surprise.

"That's iodine."

"Yes," the man said, and spoke in Malay with the kid.

"He will not tell me his name. That is his privilege. I am Dr.
Mahathir. And may I ask your name also?"

"Jimmy."

"Jimmy. Yes. You say a bad word a lot, Jimmy. You say 'shit.'
Isn't this a bad word?"

"I'm a fucking foulmouth. Where do you get these jars, man?"

"I am a scientist. An entomologist."

"So you shit big jars out your ass?"

"Oh!—these jars. I have twenty-six of them. People sell them
to me. They realize an entomologist requires jars for the specimens. Here is a scorpion."

"Yeah. How many thirteen-year-olds did he kill?"

"The bite isn't fatal. Only numbing you for a time. Swelling at
the site of the puncture. It's the largest scorpion to be found in this
region. Therefore, yes, I preserve it."

"Formaldehyde, right?"

"Yes. Formaldehyde."

"Is that shit antiseptic?"

"Of course."

"Have you got a jug of clean stuff? This guy ripped his arm
open."

"Yes, I saw that plainly." He spoke to the kid, who held out his
arm while gently the scientist unwound the bandanna from the
wound. "Nothing to it. We'll clean the damage, and put some
sutures. I can do it."

"Medical sutures? You have the stuff?"

"No. Needle and thread."

"What about Xylocaine?"

"No."

"You better explain that to him, Doc."

They spoke, and the kid continued to seem very upset.

"He says he must hide the wound. His body must have no blemish."

"No blemish? Look at his face. He scratched the shit out of it banging through the bush like he had a grenade up his ass."

"I don't know. It's his belief."

"He'll get you stitched up," Storm explained to the kid as the doctor found his materials in the kitchen. "It's gonna be unpleasant."

The doctor came back dragging a bench with one hand and carrying a Pepsi bottle in the other. Between his lips he gripped a needle, thread hanging down from it. "Sit here, please." He and the boy sat on the dirt floor and he rested the boy's arm across the bench and lowered his suturing materials down into the bottle's mouth. "I'm going to sterilize," he said, and fished out the needle by its thread and immediately pinched closed the wound and ran the needle through the flesh. The kid inhaled through his teeth with a hiss, nothing more. "He is a stoic," the scientist said.

"Can you talk to this guy? Translate for me, man."

"Of course."

"First off, who was that old woman he ran over with his motor-bike?"

The two spoke, and the scientist said, "It was his grand-mother."

"You're shitting me. Who *is* this guy?"

"He is not permitted to tell us his actual name. I know who he is. I have heard of him. He's traveling to a village up ahead."

In silence, except for the boy's hissing with each suture, the scientist finished his work. The wound was bloodless now, closed with five tight blue knots. Storm said, "That's some number one stuff. You're Elvis."

"Yes. It's good. Thank you."

The boy stood up and said a few words.

"He says that from here we must walk."

"No shit? We've been walking for an hour already."

"Tomorrow is an important ceremony. This man has made a very serious bargain to participate."

"Where does this happen? He said 'The Road.'"

"Yes. I will write it for you. You can spell it this way." With his finger he gouged at the hardened film of dust on his tabletop, among the floating monstrosities: *The Roo.* "I will go also."

"Can we get a car?"

"We can only walk. It's a few hours, but very easy. You see, we are on a plain. Then we go down to the valley."

"All right, fuck it, let's walk."

"You are going to accompany us?"

"No, man. *You* are the fucking new guy. I'm already on this ride."

The scientist rubbed his hands together and frowned. "All right! You can accompany us for a while, Jimmy, okay?"

The boy had already walked out the door. Storm followed, and Dr. Mahathir caught up to them on the path as it gave over again to paddies outside the village. "Do you have water in your canteen?"

"I'm half full."

"It's enough."

The boy did not look back at them. He pulled his shirt on over his head without pausing or even slowing down. The three clambered along at such a pace none of them had breath to speak until they'd regained the path after half a kilometer of successive dikes and ditches. Mahathir called after him in Malay with a plea in his voice.

"I have told him we must stop to rest at the next place. I think he will allow it."

"Señor, what is this kid up to? Ask him to tell me what he's doing."

"He cannot answer you. From this place until we reach that place, he must keep his silence."

"What for?"

"He has a function to perform. There will be a ceremony."

"What kind of ceremony would that be, Mr. Bugs?"

"It's very unusual. It is not often to happen. I will observe it."

At the next village they stopped outside a small wooden house and sat on two benches in the shade and drank iced tea without ice. The entomologist said, "It is a hot day."

"Damn right."

"Here is a good place. It's far enough for you. Can you rest?"

"No way I stay here. I'm going farther than you."

"Farther will be Thailand."

"If that's what it takes."

Mahathir hunched his shoulders and sipped tea from his plastic glass, looking as if it tasted bad. He knit his brow, cleared his throat, poured out the last drops on the ground, and wiped down the glass with the hem of his undershirt, making sure to keep his dress shirt clean.

They all three rose and began walking. When they reached the last house at the edge of the village Mahathir halted, wrapped his arms around himself, and said, "Excuse me, Jimmy. I think you should not go on from here. No, you must not come now. I'm very sorry to bring you here."

The boy was getting away. "Let's go, Doc. I gotta talk to some people."

"This is not the proper day for you to do it. Do it another day, okay?"

They'd left behind them the shade trees of the village, and they passed now among scrubby bushes streaked with rain-washed dust. "This is bad, it's even terrible. Yes, it's terrible," Mahathir said.

They began the descent into the Belum Valley.

"There he is," Storm said, "there he is."

"Who is there?"

Before them stretched the jungle canopy beneath which in a

substratum invisible to the eyes of Disneyland right now MIAs were getting the fuck tortured out of them.

"Who is there?"

"Let's go. This kid ain't waiting."

The path descended gradually, cutting along the side of the hill, or the mountain, Storm didn't know which it was, because even on the steep decline the trees grew tall enough to hide both the sky and the valley's bed. After another kilometer they came onto a grassy flat. The path took them toward a clearing and some dwellings, hooches of woven straw and batten, roofed with galvanize. He heard the river somewhere and some birds or perhaps people.

"The boy will stop here. I am stopping here also."

"Where are they?"

"We will go closer to the river."

A hundred meters on, beside the river, they found a couple of dozen villagers and a burn pile nearly five meters in height and twice as wide at its base. Its preparation was apparently complete. Three women wrapped in dirty sarongs circled the edifice with armloads of dry tree limbs, inserting kindling where they could. Beyond these women, men in G-strings stood in the river up to their knees, bathing, splashing water one-handed up into their armpits and dousing their heads and swaying from side to side, bent over, to shake away the drops from their long hair.

"They've made the pyre."

"They're gonna torch him."

"This boy? No."

"Then who?" — Storm wondered if it was himself.

"With this fire they are going to destroy his soul."

Four men also in G-strings stood to the side acknowledging no one, as if they waited to be photographed, as did the pyre itself, looming like a god assembled out of limbs and bones while the boy looked up at it out of his flat face.

Mahathir addressed the four. As if he'd broken a paralyzing spell, they approached, gesturing and speaking. "There is a problem," Mahathir said, "an infestation. They are burdened and tormented by the infestation of a curse. They say if we look we'll see the teeth marks on their possessions. What is the infestation? One says monkeys, some are saying rodents. They will not say. They are angry because of fear. They will lose everything. They will starve."

One man came close and spoke only to Mahathir. "He says the priest is waiting in a special place. We can go see him."

Storm and Mahathir and the boy passed through the collection of dwellings, the entomologist leading along a path to a small clearing where they found three very small hooches and one man in a G-string standing around by himself.

"Another fucker with no clothes."

"He is the priest, especially hired for this important ceremony. But don't worry. He is a false priest. He is a charlatan."

The boy stopped walking some yards from the little savage, who crouched as if about to leap violently into the air, and studied him.

Mahathir put his hand on Storm's arm. "Stay here. It's not for us."

After some seconds the priest relaxed and stood upright again and approached Storm and Mahathir, giving the boy a wide berth. To Storm he held out both his hands as if expecting Storm to take them, but they were filthy with mud.

"Tell him if he wants to shake, he'd better wash up first."

"They must dig for larvae. Don't be alarmed. It's good protein. Better than rice. Rice gives energy, not strength. But it's a good source of carbohydrate."

The men by the river had worn burlap over their groins, but the priest's G-string was woven in a complicated pattern of reds, greens, browns. Mahathir spoke to him at length, interrupting frequently. Plainly the scientist was excited.

"There is a kind of animal," he told Storm, "a monkey. These people call him sanan. I don't know what it means. It's their language. They believe he is a small man, a human being. This sanan is making war against them now. One month ago, I think two month ago at least, almost one thousand of sanan came to this place and they are eating any plants to eat, and the people cannot eat and they had only some rice. And he says also one months ago these one thousand of sanan attacked the village and stole the rice and destroyed their belongings. Also, he says, the sanan bited many people and tore some babies open." The man spoke. "I don't know if fatally. He says they came like a typhoon. From every side. Nothing to escape." The man pointed up the valley while speaking. "He says that a child is missing. The sanan took the child away. Another child was taken, but she was found the next morning alive. I think he is exaggerating. For a visitor they like to make it seem exciting. How could one thousand sanan live together? There's not enough for sustenance. I know these monkeys. They subsist in a size of two dozen creatures. That's their limit. This monkey has a white face with a lot of hair on it, white hair. He looks very intelligent, with a cruel expression at all times. He's not a person. They think sanan is a small human. Well, this man is required to say such things. It's how he makes a living. These people are superstitious. They will pay him. And even more to the young man."

Meanwhile the boy stood alone some ways off. The man spoke while regarding him. "He says we must not talk to this boy because he has made a very serious bargain. Also he wants to know about you," Mahathir told Storm. "He asks if you are a friend of the white man on the other side."

"What other side."

"Across the valley."

"I'm not anybody's friend."

"If you go there, you will be in Thailand."

"Is that a problem?"

"It is another place, that's all."

"I'll stay here tonight."

"The ceremony is tomorrow. It must come at sunset and finish in darkness."

"Where's the kid sleeping?"

"In one of these huts. We can stay too."

"I could use some food."

"They have nothing. But there is a store."

They returned to the village. The sun had passed below the hills opposite. The village vendor had raised his awning and lit a lantern and stood silhouetted in its glow, the president of a few canned goods and packages on two rough shelves. Storm bought a pack of 555s and a bottle of Tiger Beer probably years old, its flaking decal barely legible. It tasted no worse than a fresh one.

"They have gathered together all their ornaments and precious stones, and they put it together with all the rubber they collected for a year, and they came and sold everything in my village where I met you. I saw their headman when he came to sell. That's how I learned about this boy. He's going to be paid. This boy will make a lot of money. But he will destroy his soul."

"It's like that all over, man."

Storm drank his beer quickly and in the last light the three made their way back to the priest's domain and they retired to the hooches, Mahathir and the priest each alone, while Storm and the boy shared the third. They lay in hammocks while pungent embers smoked in a stone hibachi beneath them to fend off malaria. Storm soaked his bandanna in river water and covered his face to filter the fumes.

All night the boy's weeping ruined his rest. At dawn he left for the other side.

Three men showed him where to cross the river at a narrow place. One waded in up to his waist, laughing, arms raised, to demonstrate its depth. Storm believed the other two wanted to show him an alternate crossing as well, but as the path up the mountainside opposite was visible from here, he waved and bowed and showed his middle finger, bared his feet, and forged across through a slow current with shoes and socks held high in one hand and his pack in the other. At the opposite bank he tossed his gear onto land and followed it ashore and examined his legs for leeches and found none. The men hooted encouragement while he tied his laces and as he climbed the path and until he was out of sight watched him possessively, as if they'd fashioned him and sent him forth.

High cumulus clouds in a rare blue sky. He still had the morning shade from the mountain. He went quickly. After an hour the sun topped the ridge across the valley. The glare crept swiftly down over the terrain ahead and at last assaulted him, stunned him with its weight. The path went sidehill, the grade was easy, but the mountainside itself was too steep for trees. Wherever shade came from taller scrub he stopped in it to absorb the breeze coming steadily down the Belum Valley.

The path took him north until in the heights it rounded a point and turned south, the mountainside now on the east, shading him, and he stopped to sit and drink. He'd reached a vast crab's claw through which he could see the journey ahead, the path curving westerly and then northerly, keeping level until it headed straight north over the mountaintop. On the other side, Thailand.

In the absence of further hardship, he could conclude that the encounters and negotiations of these last few days had been enough, that he faced only physical terrain and had already come into the province of whatever god had him now. It occured to him all this might have been easier—a road, even public transit—from the Thailand side. But then he wouldn't have paid entrance.

In twenty minutes he'd rounded the rim and climbed over the northern ridge to overlook a two-acre saddle of ground between a pair of small hills. Higher mountains in the distance. Below him, a tin-roofed wooden house and a small barn or shed. A narrow creek descended the western rise and cut behind the house and down over the saddle's lip. Stunted chickens jerked along among the stilts of the house getting at food. Storm heard a goat bleating not far off.

He headed for the creek. Looking for a place he might fall and put his mouth in it, he followed the water around the clearing's edge. Twenty meters from the two buildings he stopped. Out front of the larger one, under its thatched awning, in such a breeze as to keep the mosquitoes down, a white man sat on a bench resting his back against the wooden wall.

Storm approached, and the man raised a limp hand in greeting. He wore a light blue sports shirt, gray pants freshly washed and pressed, and rope sandals. Thin, with a fringe of silver hair surrounding a sunburned baldness. One leg crossed over his knee.

"Yow, Bwana."

"Good afternoon. Such welcome as we can muster is yours."

"Are you British?"

"I am, in fact."

"You need one of those British bwana helmets."

"A pith helmet? I have two. Can I offer you one?"

"Why aren't you wearing one?"

"No need. I'm enjoying a bit of shade."

"What else are you doing?"

The man shrugged.

Storm said, "I hiked up from the village—The Roo."

"Ah, yes. A gentle people."

"Who."

"The Roo."

"Yeah. Right on."

"They don't eat their neighbors. Or shrink their heads."

"They don't. I dig that about them. Are you by yourself?"

"At the moment."

"Who else lives here?"

The man uncrossed his legs, placed his hands on either side of him, and sat up stiff-armed, his shoulders hunched. "I've had some lunch, but you must be hungry."

"I'm on a fast."

"Then I'm thinking you might like some tea."

"You got ice?"

"No. It's the temperature of the creek. Which is fairly cool. It comes from higher country to the northwest."

"Aren't you gonna ask me who I am?"

"Who are you?"

"Remains to be seen."

The man smiled. His eyes looked tired.

He rose, and Storm followed him over to the creek, where the man bent to grasp an end of rope and hauled out a large glass jar in a macramé sweater. "Our tea may taste a bit flat. I boil it thirty minutes. Come into the house and we'll put you right."

Storm went as far as the porch. He stood at the door and watched. The place had a wooden floor planed smooth. Big wing-shutters propped open by struts at either end of the room let in the breeze and light. He saw an open kitchen, where the man poured the tea into two large glasses, and the door to what might have been a bedroom. As soon as he heard the sound of the liquid Storm's feet took him inside. "Good glasses," the man said. "Not old jars." Storm drank it all rapidly. Without a word his host took the glass from him and refilled it. He sipped his own and put his hand on a small refrigerator by the sink. "No propane today. Somebody's got to bring it over from town on a horse."

"Where's town?"

"About ten kilometers north."

"We're in Thailand."

"Yes indeed. Slightly."

Storm had finished his tea.

"We'd better keep the jar handy for you."

"What's your function here? What's your role?"

He hefted the jug by its rope. "I keep out of the way of things." He stood with his glass and his jar beside the door. "Take a chair onto the porch, won't you?" He waited for Storm to precede him out again and then sat on the bench and crossed his leg over his knee while Storm positioned the chair so all its feet rested on boards rather than in cracks and removed his pack and sat down to dig in it for his smoking materials. Storm was determined to out-wait him. He smoked a mangled cigarette and observed the chickens as they foraged mechanically.

"I think I will ask for your name again, if you don't mind."

"Sergeant J. S. Storm. Staff sergeant. Used to be."

"Do you prefer to be called Sarge?"

"No. Do you prefer to be called a spook?"

"I'm not in the Intelligence service."

Storm waited.

"Perhaps once."

"What outfit are you working for?"

"Allied Chemical Solutions. I'm happily retired."

"Solutions like, We solve the problems? Or solutions like, We dissolve fuckers in acid?"

"Solutions to problems, yes. But the pun was appreciated amongst us, Sergeant, never fear."

"You worked for the Company?"

"The CIA? No. Allied's entirely private."

"When did you come here?"

"A couple of years ago at least. Let me see. In June maybe. Just at the beginning of the rains. Yes. About the first of June."

"How's Saigon?"

"I haven't traveled as much as some. I'd like to visit there one day."

"Bullshit, motherfucker."

"I hear they're opening a Coca-Cola plant up north. Hanoi."

Storm snapped the end of his cigarette into the yard. "Are you telling me you ran some kind of ops up in North Vietnam?"

The man squinted at him and sipped from his glass.

"What could've been going on up north? Some kind of listening post. Is that what you've got here too? The same operation x years down the line?"

"Hm," the man said.

"What's the situation, man?"

The man leaned forward with hunched shoulders. He seemed not so much uncomfortable as pensive.

"You know who I'm here for."

"I'm afraid I don't."

"The colonel."

The man sat back and cocked his head. "Which colonel?"

"Colonel F.X., old maestro. Colonel Sands."

His host took a drink. In his movements, the thinness of his fingers on the glass, the frailness of skin covering his jumping Adam's apple as he swallowed, he actually seemed quite elderly. "Sergeant, I can't remember when I've had a white visitor before. So you're quite unusual here. But I think your manner of approach would seem out of place anywhere. May I ask: Were you a friend of the colonel?"

"We were very tight."

"A friend, I mean to say, and not a foe."

"Roger. 'Who goes there.' 'Friend.'"

"Cheers, then."

"Where is he?"

"The colonel is unfortunately deceased."

"I don't think so."

"Yes, it's true. Long ago. Somebody should have told you before you made such an effort."

"I don't think so."

"I can't offer to change your thinking. But it's true the colonel has died."

"That's what they said years ago. His wife was getting widow's benefits in Boston, meanwhile he was known to be living here, operating around these parts."

"I didn't know about this."

"I knew about it. And I know the colonel didn't die."

"I see. He didn't die."

"Fuck no."

"Do you know that for a fact?"

"Fuck no. But I do know the colonel. He's doing Plan B."

"And what's Plan B?"

"He let himself get captured in '69, he allowed it, man, as part of a Psy Ops scenario, and whatever that shit led to lies behind the veil, but I can give you this much on stone-ass tablets: he's still making it just a little bit harder to be a Commie."

"And that's Plan B."

"Set to music."

"Did he share this plan with you?"

"Shit don't work if you share it. It's a one-man show."

"A one-man show." The man smiled. "There's the colonel in a nutshell."

"What's in your shed?"

The man said, "You know, he was a captain when I first knew him. Though not officially. Officially he was separated from the service."

Storm lit another cigarette and snapped his Zippo shut. "Yeah?"

"That's the way they worked it then. His outfit came as volunteer civilians. America hadn't actually joined the war against Japan. But the captain had. Some of you Yanks were bombing the Japs long before they struck you at Pearl Harbor."

"World War Two. The Deuce."

"For you Yanks that was the best of wars. For me the best of wars was right here in Malaya, '51 through '53. We fought the Commies, and we beat them. The colonel was in and out with us all the way along, including Operation Helsby here in the Belum Valley. He and I may have hiked down through this clearing together. May have traipsed through my parlor before it existed. May have done it more than once. I don't remember. He and I were on the Long Patrol out of Ipoh together—one hundred three days of slime and such. One hundred three days running. That's when you know a man. If he was alive, I'd be sure of it. Nor would he have to tell me. Not when you know a man."

Storm nearly believed. "Well, what happened to him?"

"Are you after the legend, or the fact?"

"I'm after the truth, man."

"I'd venture the truth is in the legend."

"What about the facts, then?"

"Unavailable. Obscured in legend."

"How many tunes do you know, motherfucker? Because I'm running out of nickels."

The man stood up. "Let me take you someplace. Please come along."

The man led him beside the creek and over the hill to a water hole among a copse of tall trees and much other growth, light coming down among the elephant-ears, cool, damp. In the hole a buffalo had sunk itself, only its nostrils protruding. Storm and his host watched a couple of small children filling four buckets and shouldering them on yokes. They looked terrified. The man spoke to them and they finished their work before departing.

"Over here."

Just beyond the copse, overlooking the long view of mountains, the man set his foot on a mound and his hand on a waist-high four-by-four-inch post staked before it.

"Here's the one-man show."

Storm closed his eyes and felt for the truth. Sensed none. "Never happen."

"It happens here."

"Do you know how many jive-ass graves I've seen?"

"I couldn't guess."

"Fuckers have shown me his bones. I've tasted his so-called ashes, man. I've cooked his grease in a spoon and run it in my arm. That shit don't fly. I'm the tester, man. Every beat of my blood tells me he's alive."

"I'm told he's buried in this hole."

"If this is his grave, then he didn't die back in 'Nam."

"Right enough. If this is his grave."

"Well—is it? When was he buried? Who buried him? Did you bury him?"

"Not I."

"Who buried him?"

"I don't know. I'm told he died suddenly without explanation.

I'm sorry to say that somebody could have given him poison. That's one possibility."

A monstrous falsehood. But who were its perpetrators?

"I met you once in Saigon. In '67 or '68."

"Let's see. In '67 or '68. It's entirely possible."

"You're Pitchfork."

"I go by many names."

"Don't play like that. I met you in Saigon. You're the colonel's old buddy. You gave him an egg."

"An egg?"

"In the prison camp, when he was hungry. You gave him an egg."

"Did I?"

"He said you did."

"Well then, I must have done."

"You look the same. Are you always the same? You don't get any older? Are you Satan?"

"Now you're the one playing a game."

"Don't show me graves."

"Then what can I show you?"

Only the living colonel would suffice. The colonel smoking Cubans and up to his old shit.

"Here lies the colonel."

"Then what are you doing here?"

Pitchfork said, "I tend the grave."

Whether this served as the colonel's grave or someone else's, whether he lived or rotted, his zone remained. And Storm had walked into it.

"I want to see inside that shed."

They turned from the grave and went back up the hill. The sun hit their faces, but to the east, behind them, clouds formed. Storm said, "Looks like rain."

"Not this month. Never in the month of April."

"Show me inside that shed."

A board laid across wooden stays held shut the outbuilding's door. Pitchfork tossed down the bolt and stepped backward, drawing the door wide. Storm stepped forward. In the banded light something long and substantial lay across the ground. He couldn't imagine what. He swallowed involuntarily and audibly. A monster without limbs. He watched its face develop like a photograph and run rapidly through the colonel's innumerable dissemblances.

Pitchfork swung the door wider.

"What is it?"

"A mahogany log."

"A log?"

"A mahogany log. I kept a pile of timber here. That's the last of it. Till I get more."

Another fake and phony prophet. Another fucked-up revelator.

Storm drew his knife and grabbed the old man in a choke-hold from behind and put the point to the man's side, between the ribs, over the liver.

"Where's the colonel?"

"KIA."

"MIA."

"No. Deceased."

He tightened his choke-hold. "Fucker, you will tell me, or I will fuck you up. Who dug that grave?"

"I don't know." His voice came out like a frog's.

"Tell me who, or I will pull your tab."

"I don't know who buried him. And when you pull my tab, as you say, I still won't know."

"What are you doing here?"

"I got tired of the world."

"Who are you?"

"Anders Pitchfork."

"There was a point a long time ago where none of you fuckers could lie to me anymore, because I was the one distributing the lies. Half your shit came out of my ass."

"He's dead."

"Look," Storm said, his heart breaking, "I've gotta get out of this machine."

Storm released him. Pitchfork sat down heavily in the dirt, clenching and unclenching his hands and not touching his neck.

Storm said, "I suspect you of doing away with him."

"I'd suspect the same if I were in your position."

"And what is my position?"

"Unknown."

After a minute he tried to stand and Storm put his knife away and helped him rise.

"Do you have any idea how deep down that person burned us, man? How very deep down the burn went?"

"No."

"As deep as hell is hot and dark, brother."

"Don't call me brother."

"Don't deny me, brother."

Pitchfork headed for the house and Storm watched him go. He came out carrying a rifle with a short magazine and a skeletal metal stock which he unfolded from under the foregrip as he walked. Ten paces away he stopped.

"I think that's one of those World War Two machines."

"I think an M1 Garand. The paratrooper issue. A lot of people died by it."

"I heard you jumped out of planes."

"You know?—in the war itself, I only jumped out of one. Captain Sands was flying the thing. My first and last jump in that war. Although I made a few with the Scouts around here in the fifties." He raised the rifle and engaged the bolt and sighted carefully at Storm from ten feet away. His finger firm on the trigger. "You'll be going now."

Storm turned and marched south toward the trail, back the way he'd come.

He'd thought of continuing into Thailand, but fate had turned him around. Somewhere along the odyssey of years he'd negotiated

a crossing without acknowledging its keeper or paying its necessary
tribute. You don't recognize these entities for what they are until
after the crossing. Until after the dissemblances dissolve.

What could be left, what left undone?

From the trailhead he surveyed the distances he'd ascended
this day and witnessed how far he'd come. As it dipped below the
clouds the afternoon sun exploded down the valley.

He felt no fatigue. Only strength and heat. He believed he
might make it back down before sunset. He hurried. As quickly as
he descended, just as quickly the daylight withdrew up the mountain, and he saw his destiny entangled with the sun's.

He passed into the shadow. The valley rested in a moment neither light nor dark. With the change the animals hushed. They'd
begun again, the first chorus of night insects and sunset birdcalls,
by the time he reached level earth. Still he saw no column of
smoke, no fires ascending from the Roo.

He reached the spot at the river where the False Guides had
sent him over in their happy knowledge he'd missed this most
important thing. Without removing his shoes he raised his pack
high above his head and divided the waters.

Nothing irrevocable had begun. On the ground in the vicinity of
the tall pyre scores of candles flickered in the upturned halves of
coconut husks. The villagers wore colorful, clean apparel and
seemed busy with nonessential tasks, in and out of the hooches,
keeping the moments cool, clapping in a slow rhythm, but only
some of them, handing the rhythm from this pair to that pair of
hands, no one committed yet, the thing only beginning to build.
Maybe they saw him. Maybe they decided they didn't. The priest
stood next to the pyre wearing a headdress, his hair done in coils
and feathers, holding a soft-drink bottle in both hands and talking to Mahathir. The boy stood both with them and apart from
them.

Mahathir watched Storm come along the river's edge and

raised his hand. The priest seemed unperturbed, but Mahathir didn't like this. "The ceremony is quite soon," he said.

Storm said, "I can feel it."

"You did not go to Thailand. Why? Why didn't you stay with your friend?"

"If you don't know, I can't tell you."

"But, Jimmy, it's not a good idea for you. This man has something to do. I am a scientist, so of course I can observe. But for you it's not a good idea."

The boy stood rigid, face pulled tight, breathing hard. None of the Roo looked at him.

The females had begun to assemble, younger ones and tiny girls sheathed in sarongs, wearing lipstick and rouge, beads strung in their hair. Small boys stood behind them, feet stuck to their spots but shoulders working, vibrating all over with excitement and childhood. So happy to be alive in their bodies, jumping around in their slave suits. Sodomizers of the True Thing.

"Doesn't he have a special outfit? Where's his costume?"

"He will have no clothes. He will be naked."

"No, he won't."

Storm took up the rhythm, first inside himself, and then bringing his hands together loudly, and louder. They all watched him, neither approving nor disapproving. Mahathir gestured as if to silence him.

Storm stepped up beside the boy and raised his challenge.

"I AM THE TRUE COMPENSATOR!"

The clapping went on, but he had their attention.

"I AM THE TRUE COMPENSATOR!" He put his hands to his sides and bowed his head.

The priest spoke with Mahathir.

Storm raised his face. "Tell him I'm the one. This kid's an imposter."

"I will not tell him."

"Tell the kid, then."

"I cannot."

"Man, it's no good if he's doing it for money. You've gotta do it for the thing, man, the thing. You need a reason, you need to be sent by the signs and messages."

The priest spoke urgently to Mahathir, but Mahathir kept silent.

"You want to take this man's place?"

"It's not the kid's place. It's mine. I was sent." He spoke directly to the priest. "This motherfucker doesn't know what he's doing. I know what I'm doing. I know where it fits, I know what's real."

"I cannot say this to him. I don't know what will happen. We might get killed."

"They're a gentle people, man. Gentle, right?"

"Do you understand what you're doing? No."

"I'm getting this poor kid off the hook."

"No. You don't understand this."

"I thought you were a Muslim. Do you believe this jive?"

"Here in this area, where the trees are so tall, where the vehicles cannot come, where no one comes, this area is quite different. God is dealing with them differently in this area."

"Yeah—I get that, man. I just wondered if you did."

The priest spoke most emphatically. Now Mahathir replied at length, and the priest listened with his head bowed, nodding his head, interrupting at intervals.

The priest spoke briefly to the boy, who listened without protest, and Storm understood the sham would be revealed.

"Kid, you came into this business without settling certain things inside yourself."

"He is doing this to save his family."

"He gets the money. Tell him that. He gets the money. Hey, man, the money's yours. I'm not trying to step on anybody's game."

Mahathir spoke with the boy. The boy stepped backward several paces, turned, and pushed through the circle of females and the circle of young boys and stood beyond.

Mahathir said, "I knew this. I'm not superstitious. But it's not unusual to see the future. Many people see it. It happens. I saw your future. I tried to tell you."

The priest stood beside him and cried out in a strangled language and placed his hand on Storm's head.

The clapping ceased. An old woman moaned. Storm raised his arms high and shouted, "I AM THE COMPENSATOR, MOTHERFUCKERS. I AM THE COMPENSATOR."

The priest slapped his hands together once. Twice. Again, and he resumed the rhythm. The others took it up.

Men gathered in a third circle around them. The priest beckoned, and the headman came forth into the circle with Storm, the priest, and Mahathir. He carried an axe.

It takes what it takes, Storm promised the Powers.

The priest spoke loudly to the headman.

"He tells him to assemble the gods of the village."

The headman raised a hand and the circles parted for a quartet of women, each clutching the corner of a blanket. They laid it before the priest—a pile of hacked wooden carvings, most no bigger than a hand, several others up to half the size of any of their Roo worshippers. The four women threw back their heads and bawled like children as the headman attacked the figures with his axe. As he worked at it, getting them all, and as the women knelt to collect the pieces and add them to the pyre, Mahathir said, "They break their household gods and throw them on the fire because the gods haven't helped them. These gods must die. The world may end with the death of these gods. The sacrifice of the soul of the stranger may prevent the world's end. Then new gods will rise."

Storm observed the observers. Their faces barely showed in the light of the many candles strewn randomly at their feet. They looked not joyful, not solemn either—mouths hanging open, heads nodding as they clapped, clapped, clapped—looked ready in their souls.

Then the priest stood beside the headman and spoke loudly.

"Go there," Mahathir told Storm. "They will undress you now." Storm walked to the priest as Mahathir said, "God help you!"

The priest held the shards of the icons. The headman bowed and pointed at Storm's soggy shoes. Storm kicked them off. The headman bowed lower and touched Storm's foot and pinched the fabric of his sock. Placing his hand on the headman's shoulder, Storm peeled off his socks and stood up straight. Two young women came forward and tugged at his buttons and his fly. He thought of making a joke, but he was speechless. They pulled his pack from his back and then his shirt and helped him step out of his shorts and his underpants and then retreated into the circle. The rhythmic clapping continued. Every pair of hands now. Storm stood naked.

Facing Storm, the priest reached into the flap of his G-string for a folded sheet of paper which he straightened and held up close to Storm's face—Storm saw nothing on it—and spoke loudly to the Roo, and showed the page again to Storm. He spoke to the headman.

The headman called out. A man brought him a spear.

The priest spoke. The headman handed over the spear. The priest skewered the page on its point, marched to the pyre, and, extending the spear as high as he could, rising on tiptoe, he jammed the paper among the logs and scraped it from the spear-point.

"Wait," Storm said.

He squatted at his pack and found his notebook in its plastic bag. He tore out the last page and replaced the notebook and stood holding out the page.

"It's a little poem, man."

The priest came to Storm with spearpoint extended and accepted the offering and took it to the pyre and made it part of the sacred fuel.

Storm let it be known: "COMPENSATION, BABY. COMPENSATION TONIGHT."

The priest spoke loudly and threw down his weapon. Storm bowed his head.

The blanket, only rags now, lay almost bare of the remnants of the gods. The priest scooped up the last few scraps in his hands. The headman dragged the blanket a few meters from the pyre, the Roo widening their circles as he did so. He made a careful business of straightening its edges and pausing to look up at the heavens as if navigating by invisible stars.

Against his chest the priest held the shards of the icons. He came to stand facing Storm.

He spoke again, and Storm heard Mahathir's voice from beyond the rings of the Roo: "Kneel down." He did so. The priest knelt too and spoke softly, and the headman assisted Storm in lying out flat on his back on the mutilated blanket. Onto Storm's belly the priest let fall the few shards and made of them a small heap there.

He spoke, and Storm heard Mahathir: "He wants you to know this is only a symbol. It's a fire on your flesh, but they will not light it. You will not be burned physically."

Chosen to suffer penance because no one else is left. Traversing inordinate zones, the light beyond brighter or dimmer, never enough light, nothing to tell him, no direction home. One figure yet to be revealed in his truth.

Everyone had unmasked himself, every false face had dissolved, every dissemblance but one, his own.

Storm turned his head to follow as the priest returned to the pyre, where he stooped to pick up his soft-drink bottle and slosh liquid fromit around the base. In the air an odor of diesel arose. The headman brought two glowing coconut halves and they each used a candle to set the fire.

The blaze began slowly. As it climbed the pyre, the clapping accelerated in rhythm. Damp wood cracked and shot in the flames. The conflagration devoured the peak. A cry went up. As the fire began to roar, Storm felt a breeze rushing over his bare chest and heard a woman screaming like a cyclone. The priest went back and forth through the intense heat tossing liquid into the orange flames. It hissed and steamed, and he moved from side to side casting a blue shadow on the vapors.

From the trees all around came the waterfall sound of scrabbling claws and the curses of demons driven into the void.

More women screamed. The men howled; The jungle itself screamed like a mosque. Storm lay naked on his back and watched the upward-rushing mist and smoke in the colossal firelight and waited for the clear light, for the peaceful deities, the face of the father-mother, the light from the six worlds, the dawning of hell's smoky light and the white light of the second god, the hungry ghosts wandering in ravenous desire, the gods of knowledge and the wrathful gods, the judgment of the lord of death before the mirror of karma, the punishments of the demons, and the flight to refuge in the cave of the womb that would bear him back into this world.

His poem whirled upward as an ash. It said:

VIETNAM

I bought a pair of Ray-Bans from the Devil
And a lighter said Tu Do Bar 69
Cold Beer Hot Girl Sorry About That Chief
Man that Zippo got it all across

Man when I'm in my grave don't wanna go to Heaven
Just wanna lie there looking up at Heaven
All I gotta do is see the motherfucker
You don't need to put me in it

Turn the gas on in my cage
I drink the poison
Send me an assassin
I drink the poison

Dead demons in my guts
I drink the poison

I drink the poison
I drink the poison
And I'm still laughin

The wind was sharp, the afternoon sun quite warm, at least for late April, at least for Minneapolis. On a good dry day she could walk a quarter mile without discomfort, sit and rest for only a minute, and walk just as far before resting again. She left her car in a parking lot and her cane in the car and strolled three blocks to the Mississippi and crossed by the footbridge. Its action as vehicles passed below shuddered along her shins. Both knees hurt. She was walking too fast.

With the Radisson Hotel in sight she stepped into Kellogg Street to cross, and a truck, one of those small rented moving vans, came close to knocking her down, braking hard, failing to stop, whipping around her so closely the red lettering on its side was, for one-half second, all that existed. She leapt back, the blood sparkled in her veins—nearly dead that time.

She'd dropped her purse in the gutter. Going gently down on one knee in her polyester pantsuit, she suddenly remembered a time when the question of her own survival hadn't interested her even marginally. That glorious time.

Ginger waited just inside the door of the coffee shop among potted ferns. One of those women everybody calls Mom, though she wasn't any older than the rest. How long since then? Fifteen years, sixteen. Since Timothy had marched off to the Philippines, and Kathy had followed. Ginger had probably lived around Minneapolis for half a decade—both of them had, but had never made the effort.

"Can I still call you Mom?"

"Kathy!"

"I've got to sit down."

"Are you all right?"

"A truck almost hit me. I spilled my purse."

"Just now?—But you're okay."

"Just out of breath."

Ginger looked around, waiting to be told where to sit. She'd gained thirty pounds.

Kathy said, "I'd have recognized you anywhere."

"Oh—" Ginger said.

"But you can't say the same."

"Well, nobody's getting any younger. What am I saying! It's just that it's so good to see you, and . . ." The work of lying twisted her features. She gave it up.

"I'm a little worse for wear."

"It's not crowded at all. Sunday."

"What about over there?"

"By the window! No view, but at least—"

"I've got about thirty minutes."

"At least there's light. I mean there's a *view*," Ginger said, "but all we're seeing is traffic."

"I'm supposed to make a speech."

"A speech? Where?"

"Or some remarks. There's a recital of some kind next door."

"Where next door?"

"At the Radisson. In one of the convention rooms."

"A recital. You mean pianos and things?"

"I hope they have decaf."

"Everybody's got decaf now."

They ordered decaf coffee, and Ginger asked for a cinnamon roll and immediately called the waitress back to cancel it. The waitress drew the coffee from an urn and brought over two cups. "If you don't mind very much," Kathy said, "can I have a little real milk?"

"Coming up," the waitress said, and went away, and they didn't see her again.

"What kind of recital is it?"

"I don't know. It's a benefit for MacMillan Houses. For Vietnamese orphans. So I'm on the chopping block."

"Oh, right. Did you write a speech?"

"Not really. I just figured—I mean it's only a sort of, 'Thanks for the money, now give us more.'"

"The Eternal Speech."

"So I'm sorry we can't have a proper lunch."

"No problem. I'm seeing a play across the river with John. A musical. *The Sound of Music*."

"Oh, that's a good one."

"It is, it is."

"I've seen the movie."

"But I always thought it was a silly title," Ginger said. "Because music is already a sound, isn't it? They should just call it *Music*."

"I hadn't thought of that!"

Ginger's purse, a small one of soft gray leather, rested beside her coffee cup on the table. She opened it and handed Kathy the letter. "I'm very sorry about this, Kathy."

"Well, no. Why? I don't see why."

"It went to the Ottawa office and sat there a week. Colin Rappaport found it—"

"So you're still with WCS."

"Still? Forever."

"How's Colin?"

"I guess he's fine, but we don't have any contact, not really. He remembered you'd gone back to Minneapolis, and without calling or anything he just mailed it on to our office. I guess he tried finding your phone number, no luck. Plenty of Kathy Joneses, but he didn't know your married name. Are you still married?"

"Still married. He's a physician."

"Private practice?"

"No. The ER at St. Luke's."

"I guess it beats Canada."

"Why?"

"I don't know. Socialized medicine, I mean, but I don't know. I don't know what I'm talking about! . . . What's your name?"

"Benvenuto. What about you? Are you still with John?"

"Yep. No changing that, I guess."

"It's terrible! Asking after someone's husband and saying, 'Are you still together.'"

"Your husband isn't Seventh-Day."

"Carlos? No. He's all science."

"Oh, Carlos. Benvenuto."

"He's Argentinian."

"How does he lean? I mean religiously."

"He's all science. Not spiritual in any way."

"I've never seen you in church. Where do you go? I mean . . ."

"I don't go anymore."

Tortured silence. Kathy noticed the large number of paintings on the walls. Nonrepresentational art. This was an art café.

"Have you fallen away?"

"I guess I have."

Ginger still had that perpetually arch expression on her face, shaded by fear—she'd always looked worried and defensive, on the brink of guilty tears, always looked about to confess she hated herself—a false impression, as she'd always been a friend to everyone. "Maybe you haven't fallen away, Kathy. Maybe not exactly. Our pastor says the healthiest spirit is one who's been through the dry places. But even in the dry places, the church can help. In the dry places most of all, don't you think? Why don't we go next Saturday? Come with me." She actually had a wonderful face, ascending and plunging, taking you with it.

"It's been years, Ginger. I just don't feel the pull."

"Come anyway."

"I think I never felt it. I think I only went for Timothy's sake."

"Timothy certainly felt it! It glowed right out of him. It engulfed everyone around him and lifted us right up like a tide."

"I know," Kathy said. "Anyway . . ."

At the next table sat an old woman and another of middle age, mother and daughter, Kathy guessed, the old woman talking in a monotone, the daughter listening in a hate-filled silence. Kathy made out the words "and . . . but . . . so . . ."

"Well," Ginger said, "anyway"—indicating the letter by Kathy's plate—"So Colin sent it on to St. Paul. And I'm still in St. Paul."

"And I'm in Minneapolis."

"How long have you been teaching at the nursing college?"

"Four, no five . . . Since '77. Five years last October."

"Was he a friend of yours?"

"Who?"

"Benét?"

"Oh!"

The white envelope, thickly packed with what must be several pages, its right corner covered with stamps in many colors, had come from Wm Benét, Pudu Prison, Kuala Lumpur, Malaysia. Carefully she opened it. A newspaper clipping: a photo of a man in handcuffs. Wasn't this the Canadian, William French Benét, who'd been sentenced recently by the Malaysian courts? Sentenced to be hanged for dealing in firearms? Canada had protested the sentence. Then he'd been hanged. The prisoner had written to her, the man condemned, here was his letter. Prisoners got all kinds of addresses, any kind of charitable organization, any strand for a man going down, but how had he come by the name Kathy Jones? The letter comprised several—many—handwritten notebook pages folded around a four-by-six snapshot: dozens of people and their wild miscellaneous luggage surrounding a Filipino jeepney with one of its rear wheels removed. Every face smiling, every chest expanded with pride, as if they'd brought down the vehicle with spears.

"Once upon a time," the letter began—

Dear Kathy Jones,

Dear Kathy.

Dearest Kathy,

The blood rushed into her extremities and her face as if she'd plunged them into hot water: the same feeling she'd had twenty minutes ago when the van had nearly mashed her.

Once upon a time there was a war.

She set down the letter. Looked out over the restaurant.
"Are you okay?"
She picked up the pages and folded them around the snapshot.
"Is it something bad?"
"Mom."
"Yes."
"Do you remember Timothy?"
"What?"
"Do you remember Timothy? I mean very well?"
"Of course, yes," Ginger said. "I think about him often. It changed me that I knew him. He made a difference. That's what I was saying before. He really made a difference."
"I don't run into anybody who knew him. Not anymore."
"I wanted to say I'm sorry about Timothy. I wrote you just afterward, but here we are in person, and—it's been a while, I know, all these years, but . . ."
"Thank you."
"He was a remarkable guy."
"I have no memory of him."
"Oh."
"Memories used to come like beestings, ouch, out of nowhere, but now they don't come. But sometimes I get such an urgent, this urgent—feeling."

"I see . . . Or no, I don't."

"This fist just grabs me by the heart and yanks at me like a dog telling me, 'Come on, come on'—"

"Well, I guess that's, that's—well—understandable, in a way. And—"

"I don't know you well enough to talk like this, do I?"

"Kathy, no! I mean, *yes*—"

"Excuse me," Kathy said.

"Sure. Sure. Sure."

Making her way to the ladies' room, she set her purse by one of the sinks and splashed water on her face—thanked God she didn't use makeup. Looked in the mirror. A bit of graffiti on the tiles beside it in Magic Marker:

electric child
on
bad fun

The bathroom stank. In Vietnam the blood and offal had spilled everywhere, but it had all belonged to God, God's impersonal filth. Here in the public bathroom she smelled the proceedings from other women, and it was foreign.

She locked herself in a stall and sat with the letter on her lap. To read it was the least she could do. With a sickness in her throat, she unfolded the pages.

April 1, 1983

Dear Kathy Jones,

Dear Kathy.

Dearest Kathy,

Once upon a time there was a war.

There was once a war in Asia that had among its tragedies the fact that it followed World War II, a modern war that had somehow managed to retain or revive some of the glories and romances of earlier wars. This Asian war however failed to give any romances outside of hellish myths.

Among the denizens to be twisted beyond recognition— even, or especially, beyond recognition by themselves, were a young Canadian widow and a young American man who alternately thought of himself as the Quiet American and the Ugly American, and who wished to be neither, who wanted instead to be the Wise American, or the Good American, but who eventually came to witness himself as the Real American and finally as simply the Fucking American.

That's me. My name is William Benét. You knew me as Skip. We last met in Cao Quyen, South Vietnam. I still have the mustache.

After I left Vietnam I quit working for the giant-size criminals ~~I worked for in t~~ I served when I knew you and started working for the medium size. Lousy hours and no fringe benefits, but the ethics are clearer. And the stakes are plain. You prosper until you're caught. Then you lose everything.

So, what's my line? This and that. Smuggling. Running guns and such. Once I stole an entire freighter ~~once~~ and sold it in China. A freighter. (Can't tell you which city I sold it in, because ~~somebody~~ Our dearly beloved illustrious Warden Shaffee probably reads my mail before it goes out.) Mostly running guns.

That's what's got me in the calaboose here in Kuala Lumpur. It's a capital crime in Malaysia, designated such by the same government that buys arms from America. We're all the same bunch but, like I say, from my end of the telescope the ethics are clearer. Or as x said to x, I have one ship and they call me a pirate. You have a fleet and they call you an Emperor. I can't remember who said it.

To make a long story short, since the days when you knew me as Benét I've lived under a dozen aliases, not one of them government-issued. I've led a life of fun and frolic, a real life of adventure, and I never expected it to last very long. When I go, which will be soon, I won't be sorry, I won't have regrets. Anyway, as my uncle used to say, an adventure isn't actually any fun till it's over. Or was it you who told me that? Anyway, this one's over. Some of this that I'm saying is a bit of a false front, a bit of bravado, but it's true for the most part. In fact, if this note ever reaches you, I'm sorry to inform you they've already ~~hung hanged~~ hung me—hanged me? Somebody should decide once and for all, was he hung, or was he hanged?

I have a ~~wife~~ common-law wIfe and three kids in Cebu City in the P.I. It's just something that happened. I think she'd say the same thing. But I think I like the kids. They're teenagers, sweet kids. Haven't seen them for a while. Cebu City got a little too hot for me, in the law-enforcement sense of the word, and she wouldn't move to Manila. Loves her extended family and all that, couldn't leave them. Her name's Cora Ng.

If you have any sense, your traveling days are long over, but if you happen to get down that way, stop in at the Ng Fine Store near the docks and ask for Cora and say hi.

The Warden tells me the Canadian Consul's coming around today and I can pass along any letters for mailing. The Consul and I hate each other and I don't actually let him visit me, but he has to stop around anyway, especially in "The Last Days" here, just to keep up appearances for the press. So I guess this letter goes out tomorrow, and this is hello and goodbye from (I hope I hope) an old friend.

They've had me here since August 12. Today is April 1, April Fool's Day, an appropriate day to ~~put an~~ end the long fiasco, but I'm scheduled actually for April 6. I waited this long to write so I wouldn't have a lot of time to sit around wondering if I'd reached you, wondering if you'd answer.

Just had my supper. Now I'll start a six-day fast and go to the gallows nourished only in my soul. So what was ~~my~~ the condemned's last meal? Same as always, rice in some kind of fishy broth, and two breadrolls. Bon appet't!

Kathy, I believe I loved you. It never quite happened with anyone else. I take your memory with me. And I give you my thanks in return.

> Love,
> Skip

> April 2

The Warden came by last night to convert me to Jesus and pick up my mail but I didn't give him this letter. I guess I'll wait a few days. I guess I hate

—Someone came into the bathroom. She recognized the voice of the old woman who'd sat at the next table.

"Did Eugene say what his son died of?"

"Eugene never had a son."

"Heart attack?"

The stall two doors down banged open and closed.

Kathy looked at her watch. She was late. She put the pages in her purse and got up to go out past the old woman, who stood by the mirror with her head cocked and stared at the floor.

She went back and found Ginger and made her apologies and left.

She made for the Radisson Riverfront Hotel, the first door around the corner, and in the lobby looked around for the MacMillan Houses event. She gathered the function involved something for, or about, or by young women, for there were many present in the lobby—very young, twelve, thirteen, all of them pretty girls, explosive and giddy, heavily made-up as if for the stage, their imperfections made brazen by this accentuation of their beauty—knock-knees, low waists, blotchy thighs in short skirts, probably because they felt chilly.

Following the directions of a brass-plated sign by the elevators, she passed through the lobby and down a long hallway at whose ending, at a table, sat a woman with two shoe boxes. From the auditorium's open double doors came the kindly, amplified drone of someone reading a speech from a page.

"Are you here for the MacMillan fashion show?"

"Good. I'm in the right place."

"A to L, or M to Z?"

"I think I'm looking for Mrs. Rand. I'm supposed to speak."

"Well—Mrs. Keogh is downstairs."

"I don't think I know Mrs. Keogh. I think I dealt with Mrs. Rand."

"Mrs. Rand is at the podium."

"Do you suppose I can go in and sit?"

The woman said, "Oh." The idea seemed to strike her at the wrong angle. "There'll be an intermission."

"Or I can catch her at the intermission. I'll just sit over here." Except for the woman's chair and table, the area was bare of furniture. "Or I'll be in the lobby. I'll try back in a few minutes."

"If that's all right. If you don't mind. I'm sorry—"

"No," she said, mortified, her face flaming, "I'm late. I'm very sorry."

In the lobby she sat in a chair upholstered with brown leather and brass rivets and opened her purse.

April 2

The Warden came by last night to convert me to Jesus and pick up my mail, but I didn't give him this letter. I guess I'll wait a few days. I guess I hate to say goodbye. I didn't convert to Jesus, either.

Once I thought I was Judas. But that's not me at all. I'm the youth at Gethsemane, the one on the night they arrested Jesus, the sleazy guy who slipped out of his garment when the throng had hold of him, and "he fled from them naked."

I think you're interested in the concept of Hell. I remember you as something of an expert. Dante's 9th circle of Hell Is reserved for the treacherous—

To kindred
To country and cause
To guests
To lords & benefactors
I betrayed
My kindred out of allegiance to my lords
My lords out of allegiance to my country
My country out of allegiance to kindred

My crime was in thinking about these things. In convincing myself I could arbitrate among my own loyalties.

In the end out of shifting allegiances ~~I managed to~~ I betrayed everything I believed.

I have to restrain myself from writing down every little thing. I feel I could take note of every little thought and describe every molecule of this cell and every moment of my life. And I have plenty of time. I have all day. ~~But a limited amount of paper, and maybe your~~ But only so much paper, and only so much faith in your patience, so I'll rein in my thoughts.

April 3
This morning they hanged, hung, or in other words strung up a guy, some leader of a Chinese gang. They do it right out in the courtyard here at the prison, Pudu Prison, ~~not~~

far from downtown Kuala Lumpur, about a hundred yards from where I'm sitting, but I can't see the rig from this cell. Cells across the gangway get the whole view. But condemned guys, no. They keep us on the other side of the building. If I chin myself I can on the bars of my window I can see the roofs of houses across the street. The first time I get a look at the scaffold will be the last time.

There's some whacking with a cane, that's the preliminary punishment, but we don't hear any hollering. Anyway I haven't. The guy this morning was the fourth to be stretched since I got here last August. I suppose he had it coming, even the caning. These Chinese gangs are nasty, nasty and mean.

Maybe I'm covering up my fear. I don't mean to sound flip. Or I do mean to, just out of nervousness, but I don't want you to think I'm going to the noose with a flippant attitude. Three days from today, that's it. I die. With an empty stomach. No last meal but an unbeliever's prayer. If you still believe, Kathy, pray for me. Pray for me if you still believe.

April 4

In South Vietnam I thought I'd been sidelined. Removed to a place where I could think about the war. But you can't be sidelined in a war, and in a war you mustn't think, you mustn't ever think. War is action or death. War is action or cowardice. War is action or treachery. War is action or desertion. Do you get the idea here? War is action. Thought leads to treason.

My uncle told me once of seeing a soldier throw himself on a hand-grenade. Do you think that guy thought about it first? No. Courage is action. Thought is cowardice.

The soldier lived. The thing grenade was a dud. I bet he thought about it afterward, though, and plenty. Among the people he meant to save, would have saved if the grenade had blown him up, was my uncle. Uncle Francis survived that night, but the war took him eventually. Through the years I've heard rumors to the contrary, but he was the kind of guy to generate rumors, old Uncle Francis. A guy with at least three graves that I've heard about, and probably more, if I'd bothered to ask around. But I know he's dead and buried in Massachusetts.

I am my uncle's legacy. After he died, his spirit entered me. He died not long after I last saw you, Kathy. Just a few months after, I think.

I think you met him once. You called him a rogue. He was one of these guys who look like they're put together out of small boulders, with the biggest one in the middle. He had a gray flat-top haircut. Do you remember flat-tops? Do you remember my uncle? He was kind of unforgettable. He used to say, It's easier to get forgiveness than permission, Don't interrogate your opportunities, It's not what you do that you regret, its what you don't do, things like that. He died, and his spirit entered me. There was some question about whether he actually died, but not on my part. If by any chance he was alive, his spirit couldn't have entered me.

Please don't think I'm getting mystical here. When somebody close to you dies I think it's a pretty general experience, pretty run-of-the-mill, to start noticing how they've influenced you and maybe to start ~~cultivating those~~ encouraging those influences to flourish. So ~~they live on~~ our mentors live on inside us. That's all I'm talking about. Not possession by ancestral spirits or anything.

                                                April 5

That leaves God.

I'm dangerously close to refusing forgiveness. Dying impenitent, because of anger at myself. Dying without a prayer. I've lived for fourteen years without a prayer. Fourteen years heading for the other side of the street whenever I thought my shadow was in danger of falling on a church's wall.

> I know if you pray for me
> Your prayers will touch God
> And God will touch my heart
> And I will repent

I think I was drawn to you because you were a widow, like my mom. Child of one widow, lover to another. You scared me. Your passion and your belief. Your grief and tragedy. My mom had that too, but veiled and polite. So I ran away from both you gals. And then I didn't answer your letters. And here you go, one from me you'll never be able to answer.

OK . . .

OK, Kathy Jones. Our funny little warden's standing here waiting for this letter. Last chance for the mail train. Tomorrow morning I'm off.

Warden, if you're reading this, au revoir.

You too. Au revoir, Kathy Jones.

If I had it to do again, I wouldn't run.

Much love
Skip

Yes, she remembered the uncle. He was impressive at a glance. Prowess, a word she'd never used, came immediately to mind. Dangerous, but not to women and children. That type.

Skip she didn't remember nearly as well. More boy than man. He joked, he evaded, he dissembled, he lied, he gave you nothing to remember. This current representation of himself—even as it tore at her, she wasn't sure she believed it.

She looked again at the photograph, dozens of Filipinos surrounding a stalled jeepney, and felt very moved—more so than by the news photo of Skip, the smeary fading face and its crippled arrogance and self-pity, more so than if he'd sent from that Damulog era a photo of himself, or of her, or of both of them together.

She put it all back in her purse and sat with her eyes closed. She hardly remembered saying goodbye to Ginger. Had she been unkind?

"Are you Mrs. Benvenuto?"

It was the woman handling the tickets, no taller standing up than she'd been sitting down.

"Yes."

"I'm sorry—I didn't realize."

"That's all right."

"It's intermission now. Mrs. Rand's probably in the basement. The dressing rooms."

"I'll be right along."

Kathy followed down the slate-tiled, echoing hallway, thinking of gangster films and the Last Mile, and the woman led her to a door not far from the big ones to the auditorium and down a flight of steps. The walls twittered, and young models raced everywhere in their glad bodies, deaf to their matron, who stalked them calling, "Girls?—Girls?—Girls?—Girls?" as Kathy entered a large, low-ceilinged chamber. Lovely models posed. Flashbulbs popped. The girls themselves popped in and out of cubicles made of dividers on casters.

"Mrs. Keogh," her escort called, and the girls' matron waved and came over. "This is Mrs. Benvenuto."

"I'm sorry I'm late."

"We're all late! I'm just glad you made it. I'll tell Mrs. Rand. If you want to sit in the audience—is that all right?—if you just wait in a seat, she'll call you up and introduce you after she talks about the Orphan Flight. We've got a couple of girls here from the same flight—from the same—*your* flight. Three girls."

She referred to the evacuation flight out of Saigon, the plane crash that had broken Kathy's legs. Forty of the survivors had gone out on a later flight. Only a few had been adopted in the U.S. and a couple, apparently, here in Minneapolis.

"Three of the orphans?"

"Yes! A kind of reunion. Li—where's Li? She's not dressed! Girls!" cried Mrs. Keogh.

Kathy left her without saying goodbye, because a young Eurasian girl had just passed them to go out the "Exit" door across the large chamber, and Kathy felt compelled to get a look at her. She followed the girl out and up the concrete steps, at the top of which the girl leaned against the wall in an alley, alone. She moved aside slightly to let Kathy pass. Kathy went two steps beyond her, bringing into view the river at the alley's one end, the street at the other. Kathy thought she recognized this Eurasion child, or Amerasian, who would have been four or five years old the morning of the crash, thought she recalled her standing up on her seat on the plane, remembered her uncharacteristically long legs and round eyes and the brown tint to her hair. Kathy had seated one of her own exactly next to her in the plane's upper compartment, the lucky compartment. Many of her own had been in the upper deck and had survived. She'd put her children aboard, helped with the loading of others, had left the plane to head back to Saigon and at the last minute was offered a seat by an acquaintance from the embassy who'd decided not to go, not just yet—she couldn't remember his name, they'd never met again—to this day, he probably thought her dead in his place—and she'd leapt at the chance, not to escape the downfall, but to help, to be of use, to ease the terrors of tiny pilgrims. She hadn't even known the destination. Australia, probably. They hadn't made it. And eventually this child's journey had ended in St. Paul. In two-inch heels and a blue skirt and yellow T-shirt tight across her training bra, with lipstick and mascara, she looked like a little whore, arrogant and sullen, her auburn hair twisting in a wind that blew from the street through the alley and down the Mississippi. She opened her purse and found a pack of cigarettes and a lighter. Her cheeks pouched as she shielded the flame with her hand and lit a filter-tip cigarette. She exhaled and the breeze snatched the cloud from her mouth.

Kathy again slipped past the girl, down the stairs. She negotiated the basement's bedlam and went to the auditorium above, a decent space for public events, with firm, cushioned seats and a steep rise, though the walls gave back the PA in a slight echo, and the mike made piercing sibilants and popping p's. The event's second half had begun. The house had been darkened, but lights brightened the stage, and she saw her way. Many seats remained empty. So as not to make a disturbance she took the first vacant place on the aisle. At the podium a large-jawed, stately woman with a tight gray hairdo, presumably Mrs. Rand, in a pink ensemble, spoke of orphans. Apparently Mrs. Rand dealt with a small delay, going past her text, extemporizing valiantly. She talked about the "orphan runs" that had flown so many children to new lives in the very last hours of the terrible, terrible war, of Flight 75, which Kathy had ridden and which fate had brought down like a dragon; and Kathy reflected, certainly not for the first time, that the war hadn't been only and exclusively terrible. It had delivered a sense, at first dreadful, eventually intoxicating, that something wild, magical, stunning might come from the next moment, death itself might erupt from the fabric of this very breath, unmasked as a friend; and she mourned the passing of a time when, sitting in a C-5A Galaxy airplane as it bounced into paddies suddenly as solid as rock, hearing the aluminum fuselage tear itself into jags and swords, she'd pitied only the children around her and regretted only the failure to get them out of the war, when the breaking of her own legs had meant not shock or pain, but only bitterness

that she couldn't help the others. Mrs. Rand now introduced the
three girls from Flight 75, including Li, the Amerasian, all wearing the ao dai, the flared shift over satin trousers, pacing one by
one to stage left and again to stage right, compellingly self-
conscious and poised, spirits quivering in flesh, and seating themselves on folding chairs so that their shoes were visible, black
pumps with two-inch stiletto heels. Mrs. Rand described the crash,
eight years ago almost to the day, she said—although she was off by
a month—one of the worst aircraft disasters in history, she was sad
to say, with more than half of the three hundred children and
adults aboard, almost everyone in the bottom cargo compartment,
the majority of them children under two years of age, taken away
to Heaven. A mechanical failure. For some years afterward Kathy
believed a missile had shot them down. Mrs. Rand knew more
about the mishap than Kathy herself and described the final few
seconds, the plane breaking into burning parts that boiled in the
wet paddies, the clouds from ignited oil. On impact Kathy must
have shut her eyes. She remembered only sounds, predominantly
rending metal—a very vocal idiom of many vowels and grinding
consonants, ragged gutturals, magnificent vowels, all the vowels,
A, E, I, O, U, urgent, bewildered, gigantic. Then a general black
silence lacerated by pleas and outcries and weeping, including
her own. And one or two children laughing.

The girls left the stage to small applause. Mrs. Rand spoke of
MacMillan Houses and its good, good work, its excellent relationship with the government of Vietnam. Rather than listening,
Kathy prepared her own remarks, it's wonderful to see so many,
this kind of effort requires more than private donors alone, therefore government grants and legislation, therefore your congress-
men, your senators, above all your hearts, new lives given hope,
tremendous gratitude, no, stress private donors, the annual
expense for postage for just one office can amount to, food for a
single mouth for a year can exceed, no, not a mouth, a single
child, good food for a single one of these wonderful children can
cost about, the buildings and facilities, education, your generosity,

or rather education out of poverty, your heartfelt generosity, or
rather shelter, food, and warmth for young bodies, education out
of poverty, true hope for lives just beginning, all depend on your
unflinching, heartfelt generosity, or just unflinching. Or just
heartfelt. And, no, sacrifice. Dig at them. On more than just the
kind generosity of people like you and me, ladies and gentlemen,
but on, yes, our unflinching sacrifice. Dig away. To her right in
the dimness the ring glinted on the finger of a gentleman propping his cheek on his hand. He'd shut his eyes. Some of the men,
in order to endure this, may have given up the season's first afternoon of golf. On the women near her she saw the bright, interested faces of people trying to stay awake. A little lad with his
finger firmly in a nostril, doing nothing with it, just parking it
there. The scene before her flattened, lost one of its dimensions,
and the noise dribbled irrelevantly down its face. Something was
coming. This moment, this very experience of it, seemed only the
thinnest gauze. She sat in the audience thinking—someone here
has cancer, someone has a broken heart, someone's soul is lost,
someone feels naked and foreign, thinks they once knew the way
but can't remember the way, feels stripped of armor and alone,
there are people in this audience with broken bones, others whose
bones will break sooner or later, people who've ruined their
health, worshipped their own lies, spat on their dreams, turned
their backs on their true beliefs, yes, yes, and all will be saved. All
will be saved. All will be saved.